FLAMES
OF
PROMISE

SECOND BOOK IN THE HONEST SCROLLS SERIES

JACK WHITNEY

For all those treading in the water.
We keep fighting.

For my family.
Thank you for teaching me strength and resilience.
For teaching me that the struggles don't have to define you.
For teaching me how to breathe in the smoke.

For my dad.
I'll never need anyone to give me the world because of everything you taught me.
Thank you for being the most amazing Dad anyone could ask for.

Warnings

The Honest Scrolls series
is classified as an adult, dark, high fantasy series.

It is therefore not intended for persons under the age of eighteen.

Flames of Promise contains the following
triggers and subjects:
Graphic sex with one or more persons, graphic public sex, explicit
language, grief, death, graphic battle scenes, violence, abuse, drug
abuse, torture, mental manipulation, and mentions of sexual assault,
eating disorders, and suicide.

This is a work of fiction.

Please keep these triggers in mind as you proceed.

1

Smoke rose in the wake of each step Dorian took.

His fire form threatened to surface with every shortened breath.

Entire body trembling with the reality around him.

His sister was dead. His kingdom was about to be pulled into flames. And his mentor, his King, was about to...

Dorian shook away the thoughts and continued up the winding staircase.

He couldn't stop seeing the flames that had engulfed Aydra against their own mother's tree. He couldn't stop hearing Nyssa's screams and feeling her writhing against him in anguish as they were forced to watch. Nor could he stop the pounding in his head and his heart as he ascended the steps to the great tower.

He half expected to be met with a legion of Belwarks as he and his Second, Corbin Ashember, moved through the castle as Ash, the Dreamer Captain, had seen Dorian take Draven's horn from the lockup.

Reaching the top, Corbin stood outside as a precaution while Dorian entered. Dorian emerged into the tower and found the Venari King— his King, Draven Greenwood, sitting against the opposite wall, knees pulled into his chest.

"You're late," Draven grunted.

Dorian paused at the threshold and stared at Draven. "Would you like me to go back?" he snapped, unable to stop himself. "I can wait and show up another night."

A flicker of amusement danced in Draven's eyes, but he didn't comment. He pushed to his feet as Dorian crossed the room. "Thank you," he said upon Dorian's handing him the horn and a pail of water.

"Get your sister and get out of here," Draven told him. "Hide below the Belwark Temple and do not come out until sunrise. They will not know the difference between friend and foe."

Dorian nodded, unsure that if he spoke, it would be audible. "What will you do?" he forced himself to say.

Draven's gaze pushed past his shoulder to the open doorway to the Edge, as they called it, and his fist clenched around the horn. "Burn it to the ground."

But Dorian couldn't move. He knew what Draven intended to do. The entire plan, including what he would do once the kingdom was in ruins.

And he wasn't sure he was ready to give him up, too.

He watched Draven move the bucket to the center of the room and then stare at the horn in his hand. Draven's eyes poured over the object as though it held in it some cause for this predicament.

"You don't have to do this," Dorian managed, voice sticking in his throat. "I mean. You don't have to... Go."

Because he couldn't bring himself to say it.

"Burn the kingdom," Dorian continued. "But don't..." Dorian blinked back burning tears. "Don't go."

Draven rubbed his neck, face softening and eyes reddening. "You don't need me, Prince," he said softly.

"I do—"

"You don't," Draven argued.

"Who will teach me to be a King if not you?" Dorian practically begged. "Who will help me find my voice and speak up? To take care of people who don't even love me? How to be better than previous Promised Kings? Who will—" His chest heaved, and Dorian tried to take a breath, his hands pressed to his hips, eyes downcast and waiting on Draven to say something.

Anything.

Finally, he met the Venari King's eyes and managed, through a cracking voice, "How will I know if what I'm doing is the right thing?"

"You won't," Draven said simply. "And having me around to look over your shoulder as you make those decisions won't help you. You have to do this on your own. You have to fight for what you want your reign to stand for. No one can do it for you."

"What if I can't?"

"You will."

"How do you know?"

"Because you're a King. And I trust you."

Words that meant more to Dorian than any had before.

But even with Draven's confidence, Dorian couldn't stop himself from saying what he said next.

"Don't go," he whispered one last time. "Please."

Draven didn't speak. The deafening silence rang in Dorian's ears. A silence he wanted to run from and never hear again. One look at the tear trickling down Draven's cheek, and he knew there was no talking him out of his plan.

He wanted to be with Aydra too much. He would not run from this or bring another war to his people. A true King, but broken and raging. Vengeful and in need of fulfilling his promises. He would do anything for her, even in death.

So Dorian decided on his final plea.

"I could help." The words were so broken, he wasn't sure Draven had heard him. He cleared his throat as Draven's bold green eyes met his. "I could stay, and I could help. I have fire as every Promised King has had. I should be helping you. It was my brother that condemned her. I—"

"He is not your family," Draven snapped, and the way he said it stilled Dorian's chest. Rage burned in Draven's gaze. "Family doesn't do what that bastard did. Family doesn't condemn someone they claim to love because of jealousy and fear. That is not what love is."

A great, forceful exhale left the Venari King, apparent he was trying to calm himself. His hand unclenched from around the horn, color returning to his whitened knuckles as he collected himself, and he stepped up to Dorian.

A solitary tear fell down Dorian's cheek when Draven clapped his shoulder.

"Help me by making sure this treason ends with you," Draven said. "You're already a better King than the bastards before you. Their fate is not yours, Prince. Keep fighting. Keep doing the work. You can be— you are better. Your sister raised you to pull yourself out of their shadows. They're not meant for you."

Dorian choked on a sob he was desperately trying to stifle. Trying to stand firm before the greatest man and mentor he'd ever known. He forced his knees to lock and pulled his shoulders back.

Draven cupped his cheek and gave him a half-smile. "Don't let Hagen give you a hard time when you go to Dahrkenhill. Tell him the truth. What you have done for your family and what you will do.

7

Listen to every bit of knowledge he can give you. He will watch out for you."

"Why would he do that?" Dorian asked.

"Because you're family," Draven said. "You're my family."

Dorian barely reached the landing before collapsing into a heap, unable to control the screams and cries involuntarily escaping him. Alone and scared. Unsure of everything and what he was supposed to do next.

Or how he was supposed to do it.

Corbin grabbed him from the stairwell and helped him to his and Nyssa's rooms so he could pack before the kingdom fell into chaos.

But Dorian couldn't stop shaking, to the point that Corbin took his arms and held him a moment, allowing Dorian to break in his embrace before instructing him to sit while Corbin packed bags for both Dorian and Nyssa. By the time the pair arrived below the Belwark Temple, Dorian had no more tears left, and a numbing rage had settled into his core.

Nyssa raced to him upon their arrival. Lex stood at the door, fully dressed in her battle armor. Her gaze searched the skies, and Dorian knew she was looking for any sign of the dragons.

"We have to go," Dorian said, his voice stronger than it had been with Draven.

Lex straightened. "What's your plan?"

"This Temple could be barricaded beneath rubble when the dragons arrive. I do not wish to die alongside these traitors," he said as he glared around the space. "We go to the beach and wait it out."

People were praying at the altar inside. Dorian didn't bother telling them to leave or warning them to hide before grabbing Nyssa's hand and pulling her with him.

Wind whipped over their heads as they reached the bottom of the stairs. The four flinched and looked to the night sky.

Silence chilled the streets.

Eerie silence.

Silence so nauseating and oppressive, Dorian's heartbeat grew to a ringing in his ears.

The surrounding people whispered as they came out from their homes or straightened from the ground. Dorian couldn't see anything above them. The night was as black as death. Even so, the people searched the darkness, and the air tensed.

Fear gripped the kingdom.

A chill ran down Dorian's spine when he heard it.

Elongated wing flaps rippled in the soundlessness.

Much like paper thrashing in the wind, but larger. Grander. Belonging to beasts of the night. Beasts that had never been so far west from the caves and Forest of Darkness. Every hair on Dorian's arms raised when Nyssa squeezed his hand.

The dragons circled over the kingdom in silence, and smoke from the forges swirled beneath their wings.

"They're here," Nyssa said softly, and Dorian knew she'd heard the Wyverdraki beasts, the wild Noctuan dragons, speaking. Her eagle's cry cut the air as he passed overhead.

"How many?" Dorian asked.

Nyssa looked as though words had frozen in her throat. As though she were too petrified to speak. While her abilities were not as strong as Aydra's, she could still hear every creature.

And it rooted her to the spot.

"Nys? How many?"

A great beast larger than he'd ever seen—a dragon whose insides radiated purple fire with shining black scales on its spine. He recognized it from the drawings, though he wasn't sure he would ever see one in real life.

The Rhamocour.

The beast roared a violent curse that paralyzed the world. Dorian followed the purple light from the beast's throat and found Draven's figure illuminated in the tall window arch of the tower, the horn pressed to his lips. The Rhamocour grappled the building, stone crushing and falling beneath her talons, and she wrapped herself around its peak.

Purple fire splayed the air with Draven's horn bellow.

And every dragon followed, letting loose their flames.

Dorian's stomach flipped.

"We have to go." He tugged on Nyssa's hand. "We have to go *now!*"

Homes were already crumbling around them.

Dragon fire spread across the sky. People screamed—running, shoving, and pulling each other in every direction. Before they could get ten feet from where they were, a Dreamer rushed to them, grabbed the front of Nyssa's dress, and begged her for somewhere to go.

Nyssa couldn't speak.

Dorian pulled his sister from the woman's grasp, but the woman lunged after them and grabbed Nyssa's arm. The woman's desperate pleas echoed in Dorian's ears. He quickly lost patience with her. Nyssa was his sister. He would be damned if a Dreamer would be the reason they didn't get to the beach.

Dorian had to stifle his form down to keep from turning the woman to ash.

His knife met the woman's chin, and she stilled under the threat of the cold blade.

"Let her go," he demanded in a darkened voice unrecognizable to even himself.

Shaking, the woman released Nyssa. Her wild, terrified eyes stayed on him as she backed herself slowly for a few steps, and then she bolted away.

Dorian twirled the knife in his hand and pivoted on his heel. "Let's go."

Lex pushed in front while Corbin stayed to the back. They moved as a unit through the terror-stricken streets. Nyssa's eagle flew ahead to guide the way, and Lex followed him.

Children's wails sounded down side streets and from homes all around them. Nyssa almost stopped for one, but Dorian grabbed her before she could.

"But—"

"We cannot save them!" he snapped, voice coming out harsher than he meant. Nyssa's eyes widened as she backed away. He nearly broke at the sight of her. His shoulders slumped, and a cold sweat chilled him as his words replayed back in his mind.

"I'm sorry," he whispered, enveloping her in a hug.

While their kingdom fell to ruin around them, he held the only person he cared about at that moment. "I'm sorry," he repeated into her hair. "I know your instinct is to help them, but we can't." He pulled back and brushed her hair off her face. "We have to get to that beach. These dragons do not know us, and I'm not losing you too."

Nyssa nodded, the reality settling in her tear-filled eyes, but she still didn't speak. As though she had forgotten how to or couldn't manage it after all that had happened that day. He wasn't used to her silence and agreement, and it broke his heart more than it already was. Dorian knew the tears in her eyes were not just because of their people screaming around them. Not just because he was sure she was seeing flashes of their sister dying in front of them. But also because the creatures' voices were filling her ears at every turn.

Someone shoved them.

Lex—A roof collapsed to their left. Nyssa screeched. Lex shouted, "Let's go!" and they clung to one another once more.

It was all Dorian could do to not kill his own people as they continued to grab at them. It took all his willpower not to pull his sword and slice their throats instead of telling them where to go. But with every grasp on his arm, he pushed their betrayal to the back of his mind. He finally urged them to either the Highlands stronghold or beneath the Belwark Temple for safety. There were too many to stave off, as he had done the first woman.

He wished he'd thrown cloaks over their heads to hide.

The four dodged more falling structures as they bolted down the streets, sometimes jumping over debris. They couldn't stop. The Wyverdrakis' fire surged over the town, every scream and bellow as agonizing as the last. They were nearly at the beach wall when Nyssa suddenly dropped to her knees.

The Rhamocour's cry had cut the air, and whatever it cried had caused Nyssa's entire body to buckle. Nyssa wailed and held her hands to her ears. Dorian had never seen such terror and tears on her face, not even earlier in the day when they had watched Aydra burn.

This was different.

This was the voices and anger of every creature in the air pulsing through his sister's body. He crouched down, knowing they couldn't stop, irritated with himself that he hadn't thought to carry her earlier.

"Get on my back," he told her.

Nyssa forced her body to move, and Dorian lifted her from the ground. Her limbs wrapped around him, her head buried in his neck. Dorian held himself together as she shook against him.

They descended the last stretch away from the chaos.

The quiet beach swallowed them as they emerged onto the sand. Dorian's hearing numbed with the contrast of how loud the crumbling kingdom had been. The light from the burning castle cascaded all the way to the surf. They stopped when their feet hit the water, and Dorian released Nyssa.

She fell to her knees, her hands back over her ears. Dorian crouched down at her side as Lex and Corbin took watch around them.

"Are you okay?" Dorian asked Nyssa.

Nyssa's trembling hands slowly fell from her ears. She forced a silent nod and whispered, "Fine," to him.

A great roar swept through the air then, causing the four to look back to the castle.

Dorian's stomach sank. The Rhamocour had wrapped herself around the highest tower again. Purple fire filled the sky as the rocks crumbled beneath her claws.

"NO!"

Nyssa bolted forward. Dorian lunged to grab her. Her feet kicked into the air, but she continued to charge in the direction of the beast.

"Draven!" she screamed, nails digging into Dorian's arms. "*DRAVEN—NO!*"

Draven was back in the window.

And Dorian couldn't look away.

"Oh no," he heard Lex mutter. "No—don't—"

But she wasn't fast enough to turn them around.

"*No! DRAVEN!*"

The world stopped...

Everything stopped.

Noise.

Wind.

Breath.

His heart.

Sand hit his knees as a dense ringing filled his ears.

The Venari King was gone.

Dorian's body and core paralyzed. He stared at nothing and yet saw everything all at once. Nyssa's scream echoed as a distant sound—a shrill noise that made every hair on his body stand on end and his skin crawl.

He held her head to his chest on instinct, unable to tear his own widened eyes away from the horror.

Nausea.

His chest heaved with bile at the back of his throat, a reflex that he couldn't stop. He released Nyssa and scrambled away. Vomit spewed onto the ground.

The angst of what he'd just witnessed tore through him. The anxiety that had been that entire day. That entire month. His coming back from the mountains only to find one sister on lockdown, the other burned by his brother. The fight he'd had with Rhaif. How he'd been pulled back by his own stupid subconscious and his Second.

He should have killed Rhaif that night.

A hand came to rest on his shoulder. Lex, he realized. But he shrugged her off with more force than he intended.

"I need a minute," he said, body jolting with every lurch of his stomach as he stumbled out of her grasp.

"Dor—"

"No," Dorian said firmly. "No. Do not follow me. I just… I need a minute."

He knew if he didn't remove himself, he would pull them into his abyss.

So he held it in.

He held it in as his fingers stretched and curled at his sides. Held it in as every muscle in his body reached their edge. Held it in as he launched into that surf.

The smoke of the burning kingdom filled his nostrils.

He ran into the ocean until it crashed so violently against his thighs that his balance wavered.

He let his body go with a scream so long and painful, he could no longer feel his throat. His hands turned black. Lightning streaks of his form wrapped up his arms. The world vibrated in his blackening gaze, and his muscles overextended with rage.

Navy fire engulfed his body.

The Fire Prince's form surfaced.

Dorian released his fire as he'd never done before. Allowing his form and core to protect him, he let it consume and debilitate him to the point it actually burned his own skin.

The ocean and sand caught fire, but he didn't squash the flames. His shoulders ached with the weight of their reality atop them. He knew it would be a battle with himself. He would struggle with it every time he swore to protect his people from the strangers coming ashore—to protect those same people who had stoned his sister and condemned the true King and Queen to death. To protect his family and this land —even when it felt as though Haerland had betrayed them.

Dorian broke.

He fell to his knees in the water, hands pushing over his face as his fire continued to blaze. He stayed there for hours and didn't realize until the tide went out, and it left him sitting on the wet sand.

Continuing to shake, his fingers absentmindedly curled into the coarse grit. He watched as the fire and black streaks finally receded into his skin once more. Soaking wet and numb. Black tears from his crying while in his form smeared on his cheeks and hands.

A hand touched his shoulder, and he knew without looking back that it was Nyssa. She sank to her knees at his side and reached out for him.

"I told you not to follow me," he managed.

She squeezed his hand, and Dorian swallowed. "You and me against the world, brother," she whispered.

He almost choked on his breath as he squeezed her hand back. "From now until the end," he promised.

She sank into his arms as his lips pressed hard to the top of her head. Together they stayed on that beach until the sunrise.

2

Nyssa had to leave the Gallery quickly and run to her room after watching Aydra burn.

Every step was a chore down those halls. Belwarks tried to stop her. Dreamer servants whispered behind her back as she moved. But her ears rang, and her heart wouldn't stop throbbing.

She puked twice on the way there. Her eagle flew over her head the entire time. When she finally reached her room, she collapsed onto the cold floor, hearing the screams in her head but unsure if they were Aydra's or her own.

Until she thought her tears were nearly spent, and she glimpsed herself in the mirror.

Eyes swollen and bloodshot. Hair disheveled. Clinging onto the last bit of sanity she had left.

The broken Princess that had just watched her sister burn and had done nothing to stop it. The sister that had raised her and taught her to love herself no matter what their mother might call her. The sister that had been so proud of her.

And Nyssa had done *nothing*.

The failure.

You'll never be a queen.

You'll never live up to your sister.

You lack potential and a voice.

Weak and fat. You're just like Rhaifian.

Words from her mother as she walked around her on every dress fitting as a child. Sentences that had taken Nyssa a decade to move past with Aydra's help. She could still see Arbina standing behind her in the mirror. The white hair. The perfect face. Her chin always raised,

15

and gaze casting down at Nyssa as though she were vermin for being a few pounds overweight even before she had turned eight years old.

Nyssa didn't realize she had the fire poker in her hands until the great three-way mirror came shattering down before her. Her scream came so violently from her throat that it burned.

Glass cut through her skin as she didn't bother guarding herself against it.

She kept swinging.

She broke that mirror.

She broke that image.

She broke the *lies*.

And when it was in pieces around her, she didn't bother stepping over the shards before she turned to the trinkets on her dresser. Trinkets Nadir had picked up and poked fun with her about, knowing they were nothing she ever wanted. Trinkets Dreamers had given her over the years trying to woo her.

Trinkets symbolizing the prison she was in.

Nyssa raged.

Breaking everything she could. Taking her knife to every dress she'd ever been given. Ripping the pillows. The mattress. The lounger. Picking up and breaking her favorite chair across the post of her bed. Smashing glasses against the walls.

It didn't matter.

Because it all would be in flames in a few hours anyway.

The door opened, and she didn't look before whirling her knife in their direction.

It landed in the wood by Rhaif's head.

And she forgot how to breathe.

"Get out," was all she could manage.

Rage filled her insides. Her eagle landed on her arm as she trembled on the spot.

"I came to check on you," Rhaif said as he moved from the shadows, his one remaining eye wandering over her. "You're bleeding. Let me—"

Nyssa grabbed a piece of glass, the ridges cutting her palm. "Did you come to kill me too?" she asked, circling away as he stepped closer. "Did you come to secure your place as the last of our line? Knock Dorian and me out so she would give you immortality for finally living up to your potential?"

Rhaif stared at her for a long enough moment, she realized she was right.

"Maybe I should let you live," he said darkly.

"That *is* what you mean to do," she said. "How long have you been planning this? What charge were you going to kill her on had she not wound up with child?"

"She loved our enemy," he said. "It is his fault any of this had to happen so quickly. I loved her—"

"You just condemned her to death!" she cut in. "She was just burned alive before the entire Council and her own family! On your orders. *You* had the final say."

"It was only a matter of time before the Council decided she was not fit for duty and called for her removal or death. Especially after her attacking me."

"After *her* attacking *you*?" Nyssa seethed, lights flashing in her vision at the anger raging inside her. "*HER attacking you*? What about all the times you attacked her? All the times you raped her? Burned her? Are all those times excusable because you are the King?"

"She should have done as I asked," he snapped. "She should have learned to behave and followed orders given to her!"

"So she should have submitted to being the silent, beautiful trophy every other Queen has been."

"She should have learned her place."

Nyssa paused, letting his words sink in, never blinking away from his daring gaze. *Help,* she called out in her head through the windows to birds. *Help.*

"You were going to vote for her death no matter what charge they came up with for her," she said. "Secure your place as High King. That idiotic Council was always going to take your side. Even with her announcing to them how you've been abusing her, they didn't care."

Her eagle's talons sank into her arm, and it affirmed her raised chin and straight back. She forced herself not to break like her insides wanted her to.

"You've always been smart, little sister," Rhaif drawled. "We've always been close. You're just as eager for power as I am. I let you in that meeting room when you were just a child—"

"I walked myself into that meeting room," she argued.

"And I let you stay," he countered. "Your brother was never going to be the one to learn the politics. It had to be you. I watched and helped you crawl out from under our mother's thumb just as I did, to prove you were worthy of more than she thought you were. I stood by you and rescued you when those idiot boys tried to take you that first cycle when you turned sixteen. I have always been good to you—"

"*You make it sound like it was a chore,*" she heaved. "Like you should have been anything different. You were my brother. My family. And all this time—all this time you were raping and abusing her because why? Because you thought it was okay? Because you thought it was how to show love? That is not love—"

"You don't know love any more than Drae did—"

Nyssa whirled the glass at his face. "You do NOT get to call her that!" she shouted.

Rhaif ducked just in time to dodge the shard, and it landed in the bedpost. He stared at her as her breath shook, and she waited for the fire to rise on his flesh.

But it didn't.

And Rhaif straightened his shirt.

"I'm giving you a choice, Nysi. And you'll have two days to make it. Stay with me, by my side—"

"Why? So you can keep me under your thumb and subject me to your *needs*?" she spat. "I am not whatever meek Princess you think I am. I do not belong to anyone. I am not some possession for you to keep squashed down and quiet. My sister did not just sacrifice herself for me to sit back and become your slave."

"Let me finish." And the threatening way he said it made her eagle shift.

Kill him now? her eagle asked.

Call our friends.

Her eagle flew off her arm and into the night sky.

Rhaif watched the bird go, and then his eyes fixated on Nyssa. "Stay here. Help me command this kingdom. Once the Venari King is dead at sunrise, the rest of the world is ours to take."

Nyssa *laughed.*

She laughed at the fantasy her brother lived in.

"You want me to betray my brother—"

"I am your brother too!" he shouted.

"You are not my brother!" she yelled. "You are not my family. You are some... Some *vagrant and craven.* Unworthy of the crown on your head and the powers our mother gifted you."

Knowing those words might send him spiraling.

And she dared him to come at her.

Rhaif's eyes flashed fire.

"You were *never* worthy of that marking," she continued. "You do not deserve to sit on any throne or receive the love these people so blindly have for you. You had the chance to be better than Vasilis and those before. And you chose that... that *bitch* despite every torture and bad word she ever said to you. You were so desperate for her love when you could have had the love of your actual family. You *never* needed our mother. You had us. You had unconditional love right here in front of you. All of us wanted to love you. We wanted *you*. We didn't want a King. We wanted a brother. We just wanted *Rhaif*." She paused, sniffing back her tears, and she straightened. "And I am sorry you never saw it."

A tear trickled down his cheek.

"I will never betray Dorian," she continued, voice quivering and high-pitched as she started to break. "I am not you. I would never condemn someone I love for power. If you want Dorian, you'll have to take me too."

The words seem to bring him back out of the hole he'd nearly slipped into, and the hatred returned to his eye.

"Little sister... I know how much you want that crown. I know how much you want that power. You'll realize you'll do anything for it soon."

"Oh, don't worry. I will have your crown," she promised. "I'll come back, and I'll take it off your severed head after Dorian slices your throat. The last thing you will ever see in this life will be our faces."

"Why wait, Nysi?" he asked.

The windows slammed open.

Raptors and eagles filled the room. Ravens and owls. Snakes slithered in from having crawled the walls to come to her. Her eagle landed on her arm once more and screeched in Rhaif's direction.

Rhaif's eye widened as he looked at the plethora of dangerous beasts.

But Nyssa didn't flinch.

"I will wait because I want her screams and last words to haunt you as long as she promised they would. Because I want you on your knees begging for us to spare you—"

A black snake slithered up the lounger and wrapped itself around her arm.

"You will *crawl* before I take your life, brother," she swore. "Just as you always said my enemies would."

The words sent what was left of the color in his face to disappear.

19

"Now, get out of my room."

Lex found Nyssa back on her knees on the floor an hour later. The animals had not left her, but she was sobbing into her hands uncontrollably. Her voice stuck in her throat. She was unsure if she would ever speak again as she began to exhaust of the day.

But the night had only just begun.

And their kingdom would be in flames soon.

Nyssa could still hear the thudding of their crowns as they'd left them on their thrones.

Their giver, Arbina Promregis Amaris, had been nowhere to be found. Nyssa wondered if Draven had succeeded in punishing her into submission and, if so, how long it would last.

Nyssa had paused before the great tree the night they left, staring at the blackened limbs, feeling the ash still settling around the room. An emptiness filled her as she clenched her jaw at the sight of the tree's insides glowing orange and black in the dawning sky.

The pillars that lined the open walls were still standing, though the gallery had been destroyed. The steps leading up to the Throne Room still existed; however, Dorian had insisted he navigate them first, just in case one was loose. The castle walls behind the Throne Room were primarily intact. Some rooms caved in with rubble, including her own. A few of the halls were impassable. The black rug that twisted and wove through their grand hallways was now covered in white dust and ash.

The one thing completely intact was the high dungeon tower.

She swore, once, when she looked up, she saw Draven and Aydra standing in the window.

The village below their gates was the rubble that broke her heart.

But she tried to block it out.

What had been done to her kingdom was needed.

Magnice had been a prison, and the people deserved better than the lies they were being told. She kept telling herself that one day, she would bring them that freedom, along with the truth of their world, not the lies people in charge had pushed down into the streets to save face.

She persuaded Dorian to help her recover a few people the morning after it had happened. They pushed off boulders from homes and assisted some of the wounded to their feet. But it broke her heart every time someone would blame Draven or say Aydra had brought this upon their castle by consorting with the enemy.

She had to hold Lex back from taking a woman's head.

"They don't know any better," Nyssa argued with her.

"You would let them speak about your sister this way?" Lex hissed.

"What would you have me do? Hold a town meeting to tell them everything they've ever known is lies, and that Draven did this—"

"Draven did this because no one else had the spine to stand up to the tyranny and exhaust of this place," Lex interjected. "Draven did this because—"

"Lex, I don't disagree with you," Nyssa affirmed. "But we do not have time to try and fix a hundred years of lies in one day. These people do not know better. You want to be stoned and murdered in the street, be my guest. Tell them the truth. Watch as they strike you down just as they did her. The only way we win them is by taking our crowns, which we cannot do right now. We have more important things to do than worry about this place."

Lex had gawked at her a moment until finally, she released the grip she had on her sword and straightened. "What is your plan, Princess?"

"We're leaving. Soon. The Council has decided to stay to help move people into the cliffside strongholds and set up the beaches with supplies from the villages. Rhaif gave me a two day deadline to stay with him. I'm not staying. *We* are not staying. But the moment we leave, we will be considered traitors to the crown and kingdom. A bounty will be put on our heads, and I don't know how many people will come looking for us. The only reason they haven't thrown Dorian in chains for helping Draven is that we are helping and keeping quiet. We have to play the politics."

But their decision had been made for them the following morning upon the ships' arrivals. The strangers had apparently seen the fire and sailed around there instead of docking south.

The four left at nightfall.

3

Word of their departure spread between the Dreamer villages as the fire had spread over Magnice. By the time the group had traveled three days on their journey to the Forest, they'd already run into two companies of Dreamers and Belwarks from the villages looking for them.

It was Nyssa's eagle that woke her on the third morning. They'd slept at the Bedrani hill. Lex had a plan to steer off the roads from there to not attract more road thieves, but as the morning sun rose over the Hills of Bitratus, so did the mercenaries.

Nyssa bounded to her feet and shook her brother awake. When he grumbled and pushed her away, she huffed and screamed his name in his face.

"What— *the fuck*, Nyssa?!" he shouted as he bolted upright.

"What's wrong—where—" Lex was on her feet, as was Corbin, scythe and swords drawn in their hands. "Nyssa, what the Infi?!"

Nyssa gave an upwards nod to the east. "We have company."

Dorian rubbed his long face, a low groan emitting from his throat when he shook his fluffy black hair. "Fucking mindless soldiers following idiots' orders," he grumbled. "Can't get a bit of damn sleep— I'll be glad when we're in the Forest, and the only thing we have to worry about is Bala's snoring," he continued as he stood from the ground.

"If you think you'll be walking into a pleasant welcoming from the Venari, you're wrong," Lex said as she helped Nyssa unclasp her bow from the horse.

"What? Everyone loves me," Dorian replied.

Nyssa exchanged a glance with Lex, and the pair turned to Dorian, noticing the pure honesty in his features. A low whistle and raise of brows came from Lex, and she shook her head.

"Go in there with that attitude, and we will certainly be faced down with a canopy ambush," Nyssa muttered, giving her brother's shirtless self a perturbed once over. "Get your sword."

A great yawn escaped him. He stretched his long arms overhead, pulling at his elbows. "Are you really going to let them that close?" he asked as Nyssa tugged at the string on her bow, awakening her own muscles.

"I won't, but Corbin might. It wouldn't surprise me if he's tired of you already."

"Corbin will never get tired of me, will you, Bin?"

"I am here for my duty," Corbin replied as he pulled his own arrow through the great longbow he sported. "That duty is—"

"Keeping the Prince safe," Lex and Nyssa said at the same time.

"You keep saying that as if you wish it would change," Nyssa muttered.

"If you two are done trying to sabotage the relationship I share with my Second, I believe we have guests," Dorian interjected.

"No sabotage needed on our end," Lex said, lining up beside Nyssa. "You'll do that perfectly well on your own."

Dorian stepped around Nyssa, and she could see the smirk on his lips as he hovered over her shoulder.

Nyssa pursed her lips at his inappropriate smile. "What?"

"Want to make things a bit more interesting?"

She could see his fingertips darkening, and she fought the shake of her head. "Any chance for you to show off," she uttered.

"Says the one with three arrows pulled on her bow."

She resisted the urge to smile. "Fine. Make yourself useful, but don't catch my bow on fire this time."

"I would *never.*"

Dark blue flames pooled in his now black palm. Darker than Rhaif's bright blue ones. Dorian's looked almost of the night sky on fire, as though it were crushed navy velvet and royal blue embers on his flesh, dancing wickedly along the crevices of his long fingers.

"Ready?"

Nyssa inhaled a deep breath, straightened her arm, and stretched her every muscle as the string begged for its release. The arrows between her fingers were like daggers extending from her fingertips. She lifted her chin to line up the bolts with the men on horses coming towards them.

"Ready."

His fire engulfed the ends, and Nyssa released.

Lex and Corbin's arrows were released as well. The arrows thunked into the soldiers at the front. Two fell off their horses as the fire engulfed them. One slouched over on the horse, eventually falling off while the others shook their pain and rode towards them faster. Nyssa quickly pulled another arrow and sent it flying. The arrowhead chased into one man's throat.

The others bounded around her for their swords as what was left of the fifteen-person company continued forward, but Nyssa continued to pull her arrows, determined to take down as many as she could.

"Keep firing," Dorian said, grabbing his sword. "We'll take any who make it to the hill."

"No one is making the hill."

"What—don't take away my morning fun," Dorian whined.

Nyssa's gaze cut sideways at him. "Weren't you just complaining about us letting them get close enough for you to have to use your sword?"

"It's not my sword," he said. "I stole it from Rhaif the other night. His precious Amaris sword, gifted by our traitorous mother herself. The first of many punishments for his being such a dick to me all these years. And also, I underestimated my need to release anger this morning."

Nyssa let the bow dwindle in her hands and made a mocking gesture to the hills. "There are five left. Be my guest."

A sideways smile rose on Dorian's lips. He shoved his boots on without another word and bounded down the hill. The few guards left slowed their horses, apparently taken aback by seeing the Prince of Promise suddenly charging at them with no protection other than himself and a sword. But the smile stayed on Dorian's face, and he changed into his true form.

As many times as Nyssa had watched him morph, the sight of it still made her heartbeat slow.

The creature he wore so well. Daring and brave in such a form. The only emotion that settled into his bones was a great bloodlust. And the more he filled out in his growth, the scarier he became.

Shoulders rounding, fists tightening—the confident aura. Hesitation had no place in his core. He was hungry, and not for nourishment of body, but for nourishment of mind. For blood and for vengeance.

The true form of the Promised King.

Eyes blackening, the streaks of his form pulsed from his black hands up his arms and from his eyes down his cheeks as though ink were spreading over his skin in the pattern of nerves. Nyssa could see the faint cracks of royal blue glowing through the lines—

The sword caught fire.

The soldiers slowed. Dorian picked up his own pace, almost running. As he reached them, he slid on his knees to the ground. The tip of one guard's sword cut at Dorian's chest, but Dorian didn't flinch. Dorian's blade swiped the legs of the guard on his right. Dorian pivoted to a kneel mid-slide, and his sword slashed through the backs of the soldier's legs on his other side.

The guards fell, and Dorian paused for a moment on one knee, lashes lifting over his black eyes as he listened for his next victim.

A guard was coming up behind him. Chest heaving, Dorian grabbed a knife from his belt and thrust it upwards into the guard. The last two were now standing off to the side, exchanging terrified glances.

Dorian moved as though time did not exist. Slow and calculated between the attacks, but a whirl of black smoke and blue flames with every strike.

He rose deliberately from the ground and faced the remaining two. Dorian threw the knife into the dirt as he watched the guards circle him.

With a spin, he charged at the one before him. His blade cut the air in such a fiery rush that Nyssa hardly saw more than a whoosh of royal blue where her brother should have been.

The soldiers whose knees he had injured were attempting to grab their swords or spears.

Dorian sliced through the last standing soldier just in time to see one on the ground rising to his knees. Dorian's blade sliced through the guard's neck, and the Belwark's head rolled into a pile of fiery ash at Dorian's feet.

The last on the ground was moving. Dorian stalked him. His chest rose high, and his shoulders rounded further with every deep breath. Navy fire grew down Dorian's leg to his boot.

He stomped the soldier's hand just as the guard reached for his sword.

Dorian savored this kill.

Slowly, he shifted his weight. The guard let out a scream as his hand turned to ash. Dorian's head tilted with the guard's cry, and the noise of his begging filled the foggy air.

Dorian deliberately pressed his other foot onto the guard's neck. The movement of his boot touching the guard's skin was so much like a whisper, Nyssa wondered if perhaps her brother was enjoying his morning spill a little more than he should have.

Nyssa watched as the Belwark was slowly engulfed in flames, his scream loud over the landscape, and then his body turned to dust beneath Dorian's tilted gaze.

The final guard was running away.

Dorian turned. A spear laid on the ground beside him. He kicked it up into his hand.

It flew from his grasp, and the soldier's toes dragged the earth when the blade shot through his chest.

Dorian didn't move for a long moment. His fire slowly receded from his boots and hands with the black streaks. When he turned, Nyssa caught the moment his eyes changed from a total abyss of darkness back to their usual blue.

Wrath of the Promised Prince, indeed.

"That should keep him off the edge a few hours," Lex muttered to Nyssa.

"One would hope," Nyssa said back as Dorian rejoined them, ash and blood covering his leather pants and bare torso.

"Feel better?" she asked him.

"Much," he replied.

She held her hand up, and he gave it a facetious slap upon his passing, as though congratulating each other for a well-accomplished morning.

"You're bleeding," she noted, seeing the scratch across his pec and shoulder.

He looked down at himself, apparent he had not paid the injury any attention. "That explains the actual feeling in my bones this morning," he mumbled. "Wondered where that had been hiding."

"I'll stitch," Lex said. "Corbin, pack us up."

"No stitches," Dorian argued. "We need to get going. I hate this fucking hill."

4

They cut over the Preymoor the rest of the day, intending to stay off the road. Lex hoped they could evade any more companies of mercenaries. As the sun set, they set up camp and made sure to do so far enough from the Forest that if a Noctuan came wandering, they would know.

But it wasn't far enough away that Nyssa couldn't hear them crying out.

The Ulframs' howls sounded like a chorus, unmoving and bewildering. Nyssa was trying her hardest to keep calm and push out the nauseating grief they bellowed out, but it felt almost as though they were trying to get to her. As though they felt her presence and were reaching in her direction. Shudders that she'd never experienced before consumed her. It was all Nyssa could do to keep her composure and not shred right there.

"Alright, Nys?" Dorian asked as he turned the rabbits on the stick over their fire.

She zipped out of the space she'd nearly fallen into and gasped a breath, blinking back into reality. Dorian gave her knee a squeeze as she met his eyes.

"Yeah," she managed. "Yeah, I'm fine."

The howl sounded over the stillness, and Dorian glanced to the trees. "What's she saying?"

His voice was low enough the others couldn't hear, but it didn't stop Lex from staring at the pair across the fire.

Nyssa leaned her head on Dorian's shoulder and closed her eyes, hoping that she could perhaps block some of the cries out.

If anything, though, they grew louder.

"She's just... They're crying," she whispered. "I can't... I think I'll take a walk," she finally determined. "The smell is making me a bit nauseous."

"I'll come with—"

"No," Nyssa told Lex sharply. "No, I need a minute. Alone."

Lex looked like she would argue, but she didn't.

Dorian's eyes remained fixated on Nyssa as she stood and dusted off her pants.

"Will you take a torch?" he asked her.

She nodded, and he wrapped up the end of a stick with an old shirt from his bag before lighting it on fire in his palm. She reached down to take it from his hand, and Dorian pulled it back.

"Please be careful," he begged her.

"I'll be fine."

Her eagle landed on her bent forearm. His great talons dug into her arm but did not break the surface. He gave her a comforting peck before pushing his head against her temple.

Dorian eyed the great bird before letting go of the torch.

Her nausea did not wane as she stretched into the darkness. She just wanted a moment to breathe without anyone being around her. She'd hardly been left alone since their deaths, and she was beginning to feel suffocated.

The continued howls sent a chill down her spine. She may not have been able to connect with their cores as Aydra had been able to do, but she could still feel the grief in their wailing... the angst of their pain— as though they'd lost one of their own. Which she remembered, they had.

The noise became distant as she walked, and she wondered if perhaps they were moving on to a different part of the forest, intent on catching a meal.

She walked until the fire where the others sat was a mere blip in the distance. But even as she decided to stop, the wind encircled her, and she found herself standing at the edge of the Forest of Darkness.

A whisper filled her ears.

The enormous tree trunks stared back at her in the navy of the firelight. Wind breezed over her flesh. Trees swayed with it, and the limbs knocked and cracked against one another. Eerie and yet, inviting.

The whisper came again.

She couldn't tell what it was saying. As she looked into the abyss of the shadows before her, something tugged at her abdomen.

She knew she shouldn't.

She knew it wasn't safe. She knew it was more than likely a trick.

Possibly the Spy or shadow thieves preying on her vulnerability.

Her heartbeat picked up as she stood there, battling with her insides and the voices in her head.

Her golden eagle nudged her temple, and Nyssa's grip tightened around the torch.

Stay with me? she asked him.

Evermore.

The long howl of the Ulfram sounded so far off now that she could barely hear her.

Nyssa took a last deep breath and pushed it audibly out of her mouth before stepping into the Forest of Darkness.

The wood was silent except for the wind and the crunch of chilled dirt beneath her boots. The navy light was her only guide as she trudged carefully over the roots in the direction of the whisper.

A glow caught in the corner of her eye.

And she froze in her step when she saw it.

Noirdiem.

Her heart constricted at the sight of them. The glowing deer's skeleton bodies stood stark against the darkness. Their silver gleam bounced off the trees and lit up the forest floor around them. She wondered how they ate and drank or where it all went, as all she could see were the bones of the beasts glowing back to her.

But there they were. Eating off bushes between great trees in the middle of the Dead Moons cycle.

Nyssa could do no more than gawk at them as the herd of ten deer munched quietly on the bushes.

The one in the center lifted his head, and a great set of antlers rose with him. He looked at her with white-blue eyes, and when he shook, she swore she saw shadows move as fur along the bone-like structure.

Words she'd read about the beasts filled her mind. That they were the gentle Noctuans, Duarb's favorite of them behind the Rhamocour. He had loved how peaceful they were despite the appearance of their bodies. She remembered the passage Somniarb had written about them in the journal Nadir had shown her the night after the banquet. They had been Somniarb's favorite, and Duarb would spend hours waiting with them as Somniarb snuck out of her village to go see him.

But what Nyssa recalled most was how Aydra had spoken of them. Draven had called them when she was in the forest the night before taking her to the Berdijay.

She could still see the plastered smile on Aydra's face and hear the jaggedness in her sister's breath as she'd tried to tell Nyssa about them while she'd been hanging onto the stone wall and vomiting out of the window.

"Nys, I wish you could have seen them. You wouldn't believe how hauntingly beautiful they are," Aydra had told her as she sank against the ground. "The world seems so calm when they're standing before you. That singular soft glow in the void of complete darkness. Draven says they are more active in the winter, so this next cycle coming up should be a good time to see them. You can come with me next week. Sick or not, we'll go."

Nyssa nearly collapsed as the memory filled her. It had only been two weeks prior that Aydra had told her those words, and yet it felt like a lifetime.

Her sister had been right, though.

The world did seem a little calmer with the beasts standing in front of her.

A twig snapped beneath her boot, and they all looked up. The largest one started to move back, but Nyssa called out to them.

Wait!

The beasts paused. Nyssa lowered the torch onto the ground, squashed the flames with her boot, and held her hands up at her sides. Her eagle flew off her arm and into the canopy.

I mean you no harm. I am a daughter of Arbina.

You are not Aydra.

The smoothness of the male's voice in her head was almost like a purr. Nyssa stepped forward.

No. I am her sister. My name is Nyssari.

Hello, Nyssari, a female said as it joined the great stag. **Your sister told us of you.**

Nyssa clenched the muscles in her legs straight to keep from falling apart. *She did?*

The female gave her a long nod. **We feel your grief. You are very brave to be out here on your own.**

Or very stupid, Nyssa muttered without thinking.

The female seemed to find this amusing. A quiet huff of visible air emitted from her nostrils, and she stepped over the broken log towards Nyssa.

Something snapped at her back, and their heads all turned.

Dorian.

"You followed me?" Nyssa accused.

Dorian toyed with the flame on his blackened fingers. "Curiosity slayed the dragon," he said with a shrug. He started to edge closer, but the stag gave a huff, hoof digging into the dirt.

Wait, he's with me, Nyssa told them. *He's my brother.* She turned to Dorian. "Put out your flame."

Dorian did as she asked, and Nyssa motioned for him to slowly meet her. His eyes never left the Noirdiem as he stepped over the great roots.

"Are these one of the creatures Drae introduced you to?" he asked.

"Actually, she never got to introduce me to any of them," Nyssa replied. "She fell on the first night we were out here. Lex and I were forced to go to the Village instead."

She could feel Dorian staring down at her when he reached her side. "And yet you came out here by yourself… why?"

"I thought I heard something," she whispered. "I think I just wanted to see if it was actually real or if my own mind was the one screaming." Her jaw began to tremble then as the Ulfram's howl once more filled the air. Nyssa's balance wavered, and Dorian grabbed her arms.

"She was supposed to be here," she whispered, voice cracking. "She was supposed to be here with me when I met them. She was going to have us come here this week. She wanted to show me... Dorian, *she was supposed to be here.*"

The words had barely slipped from her lips before she broke into his arms. Sobs evacuated from her throat that she couldn't stop. Her head buried in his chest, and he gripped her tightly, lips pressing to the top of her head as he hugged her against him.

"I know," he whispered.

Her heart wept into the dirt as the two of them surrendered to their grief. Their knees hit the ground, and they held onto one another as though it would bring Aydra and Draven back. The tears emitting from Dorian, always so kept up and shielded, just as Aydra was, made Nyssa's own fall harder.

The Noirdiem did not leave them. A few settled on the ground. Their glow poured through the forest as they remained at the sibling's sides. As to why they were staying with them, Nyssa didn't know. But that comfort pulsed through the air, and she found she didn't fear the darkness as much.

Don't be alarmed, her eagle called from above a while later.

Nyssa's eyes finally opened, and she stilled.

The alpha Ulfram stood beside them.

"Don't. Move," Nyssa whispered.

"What—why—*holy fucking curses!*" Dorian started to jump, but Nyssa's grasp tightened, and her eagle landed on Dorian's shoulder. His talons dug into Dorian's flesh. Dorian let out a whispered cry before she shushed him.

"What—"

"Shut. Up," she said through clenched teeth.

The alpha merely stared at her, bright yellow eyes seeming to seep through her bones and dive into her core without her consent.

Daughter of Promise, the Ulfram acknowledged.

Hello, alpha, Nyssa managed to reply.

Although she'd never met the creature before, she knew it well from the stories. Its head rose slightly, bending at the neck so that it was looking directly down its elongated nose at her. Its silver fur reflected back to her in the pale blue glow of the Noirdiem still lingering close by, illuminating the beast in shadow and glisten.

She didn't know what to say. She pulled back from Dorian and shifted her weight onto her knees.

Soft padded steps brushing over the dirt told her they were not alone. Breath huffed on her left cheek. She didn't have to look to know there was another Ulfram by her side.

Pack hunters of stealth and shadow, as they'd been described.

But she knew better than to think they were there to kill them.

So she straightened and lifted her own chin, ignoring the fast beat of her heart.

I heard your song, Nyssa said.

My condolences to you as well, the alpha said. **Your sister was always welcome in our woods, and now as are you.**

We are heading to the forest kingdom.

Allow us to escort you through the dark tomorrow night. You can travel in peace. Take rest for a full day. I am sure your minds and bodies are both exhausted.

Her heart swelled in gratitude at the wolf's offer, but she knew she couldn't take it. *We are tired, but... It really isn't necessary. We will follow the edge and walk in daylight. I do not wish to disturb your hunts. We will make ourselves scarce at night. I do appreciate the offer.*

The Ulfram gave her a long nod. **Very well.** The beast paused and looked around them, apparently noticing the Noirdiem still grazing in the field. **The Noirdiem like you. We will not hunt them tonight. You are safe, Nyssari. Fear not of our dark.**

Nyssa bit back the quiver of her jaw. *Thank you.*

The beast did something then that made her heart stop.

The alpha leaned its forehead against Nyssa's.

Nyssa's body trembled as the emotion of such a salutation tore through her. For a moment, she couldn't breathe. Her closed eyes splintered with the tears threatening to drop. She hesitantly reached a hand up to the Ulfram's cheek and her fingers entwined in the long, soft fur. Every muscle in her body seemed to edge with the connection, and she realized what was happening to her.

She was connecting to its core.

She'd only ever been able to connect with her own eagle before, though she'd heard how Aydra could connect with any creature. She'd always been envious of such a power, and now—having it happen to her with a Noctuan of all animals—overwhelmed her to the point that she nearly started sobbing again.

But she held her composure and drew in the phenomena. It moved through her every muscle and down to the very marrow of her bones. She let go of her mind. Let go of every wall she'd ever built, all the blocks and restraints...

And there it was.

Pain... *such* pain. Sorrow and grief. And *hunger*. Such a hunger that she thought her stomach would rip to pieces. Her heart connected to its heart. She thought of Draven and her sister, pushing the image into the creature. An image of love and happiness and the two of them as one, those last few moments of the song they sang together.

A new warmth filled her. Chest swelling, heart burning... heat spread and tingled her extremities awake. She shuddered at the feeling. The alpha pushed back, and the image of Aydra on the forest floor pulsed back to her. Nyssa could practically feel her sister's hand stroking the Ulfram's head.

Something touched her arm—Dorian's hand. She grasped his fingers in her own.

Still shaking, Nyssa opened her eyes after a few moments to find the alpha staring at her.

Thank you, Nyssa whispered.

The Ulfram merely gave her a final nod—

And then it disappeared into the darkness.

A gleeful sorrow filled her, and Nyssa settled back on her legs. Her body felt of an exhaust she wasn't familiar with. As though she'd just used every single part of herself to connect with the beast.

Dorian was still holding onto her. She turned, tears rushing down her cheeks despite the smile on her face, and she had to pause to comprehend what she saw.

His eyes were widened to the point she could see the white around his bright blue irises. He sat tense, nearly frozen on the spot, and for a moment, Nyssa thought he was having some sort of anxiety attack.

A silent tear trickled down his cheek.

"Dorian?"

He blinked, inhaled a sharp breath, and met her gaze. "What did you just do?"

"What—"

"When you grabbed my hand," he interjected. "What was that?"

She stared at him, head tilting. "Dorian... I didn't do anything."

"But... I felt this warming in my chest—" his hands moved erratically, like he thought he could better explain what he'd felt by the movement "—this like pit in my stomach, a hunger in my core— I couldn't breathe, and then there was this almost fire around my heart, feelings of agony and grief and wild happiness swelling into my fingers and toes—"

It was Nyssa's turn to stare wide-eyed at him.

"You felt the Ulfram?!" she asked in a high pitch.

"I felt... something. When you grabbed my hand. It's like whatever it was moved from your body into mine."

"You felt the Ulfram," she affirmed. "How did you feel—"

"I don't know!" Dorian exclaimed, voice growing. "How should I know?"

"*Dorian, you felt the fucking Ulfram!*"

"Yes, I think we've established that!" His hands were in his hair, fingers tugging at the roots.

Nyssa got an idea. "Give me your hands."

"What?" his head shot up.

"Just give me your hands!" she nearly shouted. She glanced to her eagle. *Find me,* she told him.

Her eagle landed on her knee just as Dorian placed his hands in hers. Nyssa shut her eyes tight and felt out for her eagle's comfort. His core consumed her with a chill down her spine. She sank into the comfort of his embrace, the safety of his core's abyss. She allowed it to settle in her a moment before opening her eyes.

Dorian's eyes were closed, but she watched the visible shiver roll over his shoulders, the hairs on his arms stand, and then his lashes lifted to hers.

"Whoa."

Nyssa's eyes widened again. "Oh, this is *weird*. This is just *weird*—" She paused a moment upon seeing the corners of his lips slowly growing upwards. "*What are you smiling at?*"

"This is brilliant," he declared. "Do it again. Reach for the Noirdiem. I want to feel."

"I don't... This was the first I've ever been able to connect with a core. I don't know—"

"Try it," Dorian begged. "Come on, Nys. I want to feel something other than the agony of this last month. Please."

She sighed as she watched him, understanding where he was coming from and honestly wanting the same. "I think I have to be touching one of them," she admitted. "I've never done this before. I'm not... I'm not Drae. She could feel all of them. I... I can only hear them, process their grief through the sound of their voices. I..."

His smile faltered along with the brightness his eyes had held in them just seconds before. Despite his whispering, "It's okay," and squeezing her hand, she knew he was disappointed.

She would do anything to see that smile back on his face.

"No, wait," she said, standing. "Just..." The doe watched Nyssa as she moved, but Nyssa didn't let it deter her.

"Come on," Nyssa continued. "We'll get closer to one."

Still holding Dorian's hand, Nyssa crawled over the logs with him toward the creatures.

The doe stepped forward upon their approach.

Towering a foot above her, the Noirdiem finally bent its great head. Nyssa's palm flattened against the skeleton nose.

She had been right. It did feel like velvet beneath her fingertips.

For a moment, nothing happened. Nyssa realized she was holding back. So she did what she had done with the Ulfram, and she let go.

A blinding light flashed behind her closed eyes. Warmth akin to sunlight filled her. She held that joyous ache in her chest a second before pushing it out into her extremities.

Dorian squeezed her hand.

She looked over at him. His eyes were closed, but there was a singular tear stretching down his cheek. Nyssa's heart ached at the sight of it. When his gaze met hers, he watched her in wonderment, chest heaving jaggedly as hers was, and she knew he felt the same comforting vulnerability as she did at that moment.

"Amazing," he breathed. "Drae felt this with every creature?" he asked.

"Every creature is different, but yes. This is what she learned to do, only greater. And she could disconnect herself into one of them for brief periods too."

The words staled between them. Dorian slipped his arms around her and rested his chin atop her head for a long enough moment that she knew he was letting that information settle with him as it had with her the first time she heard it.

"Once we've fixed the broken relationships with the other races and bought some time in this war, I'll make sure he pays for all of it," Dorian whispered. "We will watch him choke and turn to ash just as she did."

"Except slower," Nyssa affirmed.

Dorian looked as though he might smile when he pulled back, but the darkness of his pupils reminded her of the anger in her own body. She knew it was a promise from him and not an exaggerated fantasy.

He kissed her forehead hard and agreed, "Slower."

5

Lex found the pair still curled up in the woods just before dawn.

The Noirdiem had stayed with Nyssa and Dorian the entire night. The two alpha deer that had connected with the siblings allowed them to sleep between their bodies. Even as restless as it had been with Dorian's fire flickering on and off all night, it was still a better night than those before. Nyssa wondered if the connection to their cores had helped calm her sleepy mind.

They were just disappearing when Lex roused the pair.

"Either of you want to tell me what happened?" she asked as they both rubbed their faces.

"Sort of hard to explain," Nyssa muttered, squinting at the sunlight coming through the trees.

"How far today?" Dorian asked Lex.

Lex glanced between them a moment like she didn't trust them. "As far as the kingdom line," she answered. "We'll camp outside the forest and go in at dawn. We need to be more careful tonight, though. I don't want you two going off on your own."

"Why not?" Nyssa asked as Dorian pulled her to her feet.

"Because we'll be entering dragon territory."

The trees loomed larger the further south they rode. Compared to where they'd camped the night before, this part of the forest made Nyssa feel like an ant. She had seen roots as tall as her sticking up out of the ground.

As night fell, all the confidence she'd gained the night before dwindled. The Wyverdraki's grief screamed through the air, and Nyssa was reminded of the night Magnice fell.

How the dragons had bellowed with rage and fire, intent on blazing every inch of that kingdom. How when Draven fell, the Rhamocour had screamed with such malice, she thought her eardrums would burst.

But this was different.

Since opening herself up to the Ulfram and Noirdiem the night before, feeling and talking to every animal had been easier. She'd felt everything her eagle and the horses had that day as they'd traveled. It was like some wall had been broken down inside her, and she could now sense all their emotions.

With that thought in mind, the first song she heard of the dragons made her nauseous.

She wasn't sure she was prepared to have their grief impart on and mingle with her own.

And she wasn't sure how to shut herself off.

She cursed herself for trying new things in the middle of the first Dead Moons cycle after the Noctuan King's death.

Every cry from the forest made her insides curl, her eyes shudder. Dorian insisted she eat something, but she couldn't bring herself to even smell it. She rocked back and forth beside him as she closed her eyes and tried to think of any way to shut it off.

"Nys?" Dorian whispered to her, ignoring his own food. "Talk to me. You're chattering like you're freezing. What's wrong?"

She placed her hand on his arm in response.

A moment passed, and then—

Dorian jumped up and ran. Vomit evacuated from his insides in response to the feeling that had passed into him. Nyssa didn't move. She held on to her spot, silent tears rotting down her cheeks.

"Can't you make it stop?" Dorian pleaded as he sat down beside her again. "Can you block them out?"

"I don't... I don't know how," she admitted. "Since I let them in, I can't make it stop. I felt everything on our ride today. The horse. My eagle. I don't know—"

"Nys, you can't do this all night—"

"*What do you propose I do?*" she almost shouted. "I don't..." Her hands gripped into her hair as she closed her eyes as the beasts started up a chorus again, and a nauseating chill ran over her skin.

"What's wrong?" Lex was on her feet and standing over the fire, watching them.

"It's nothing," Nyssa forced herself to say. "It's nothing. I need a minute. Alone," she glared at her brother.

As she trudged away, hugging her cloak around her shoulders, a wave of annoyed anger rushed through her.

Make it stop.

As if she had asked for them to invade her consciousness. She hadn't meant for this to happen when she allowed the Ulfram in the night before.

Her stomach turned with every bellow. She kept walking until she reached far enough away from their group that she was sure they couldn't see or hear her.

"*Make it stop,*" she grunted again, mocking her brother's words to herself. "Don't you think I want to? Don't you think I would if I could? You think I want to torture myself and hear this all night in addition to seeing *fucking flames?*"

The lonely darkness was the only thing that heard her words. She dropped to her knees in surrender when she heard the Noctuans again. Her head sank on her neck with the throbbing in her ears, and she pleaded with the sky, tears jerking down her face.

"Just stop," she begged aloud. "I can't help you. I don't know how. Please. Just tell me how to go back to the way it was yesterday. He is gone, and I am *sorry.*"

Exhaustion gripped her.

She'd gotten no sleep at Magnice. Had barely eaten since she and Drae had shared the snacks she'd brought up with her soup.

She was so tired she felt like a child on the edge of a temper tantrum. It was an annoying rage that she didn't know how to stop. Tears in the corners of her eyes. Sloppy words coming from her mouth that she didn't realize she was saying.

She didn't want to push them out, but she wasn't sure she had a choice.

She wanted it to end.

As she held her head between her hands, pressing on her ears to stop the voices from flowing in, she couldn't stop shaking. Rocking back and forth. It was a different kind of torture than her own grief. This was grief she couldn't ignore or push away.

"Please stop," she begged aloud.

She couldn't get the wails out of her head. She couldn't stop seeing the flames of her older brother. His words radiated through her insides on a loop, interjecting itself into the Wyverdraki cries.

Their songs turned to echoes in her ears.

And then the Ulfram began to howl along with it.

The great marsupial creatures, the Aberds, began their gibbering.

The Aviteth sang out in high-pitched calls.

And suddenly, there was a great chorus of mourning Noctuans singing through the trees that turned her insides to a fire she didn't know how to contain.

Hearing the dragons had been agonizing enough.

Hearing every Noctuan in the forest cry out for their King was something else entirely.

She purged nothingness onto the ground, unable to stop her stomach from flipping.

Stop, she begged. *Please stop.*

The grip her fingers had on her own hair was no reprieve from their pain. Tears and saliva collecting in her throat, she choked on her sobs. She tried to avert the pain to anything physical, tried pinching her skin and tearing at her roots. Digging her toes into the cold dirt.

Get out, she choked.

The sounds grew louder and louder in her ears as though the beasts had surrounded her on all sides.

"Please *stop*," she pleaded.

Back and forth.

Her core succumbed to the weight of their melodic void. Her fingers dug into her skull. Her muscles strained. She was pulled in all directions.

Burn her.

"Get out," she sobbed aloud.

Be brave for me.

I know how much you want that power.

"Just stop. Get out of my head."

She shuddered at the high-pitched howls of the Ulfram. The Noctuans had all come together as a family to grieve.

And Nyssa had been caught at the funeral.

She couldn't shake the anvil on her chest. They poured all their anxiety into her and the still night air. The grief of losing their leader and blood. The heartbreak of not telling him goodbye.

Back and forth.

"I cannot help you. Get out," Nyssa pleaded.

It had to end.

Somehow.

She would have to end this.

A new song— belonging to the Bygon, she realized— joined, and the rapture of the creature's sorrow finished shredding Nyssa's existence.

Blood trickled down her fingers from her scalp. She thought her heart would burst at any moment, and honestly, it would have been a welcome reprieve.

She just wanted them out.

Back and forth.

She wanted this over.

Done.

The creatures subdued.

Get out.

Back and forth.

Rage filled her insides. She was so exhausted, she didn't care how they left her. But she had to get them out.

Get out.

Out. Out. Out.

The song grew louder. The Ulfram appeared at the edge of the wood. It threw back its head with a great howl.

Go away! Go home! Get away from me! Stop—

But the Ulfram's howl grew louder. The Aviteth screech sounded the air—ear-splitting and vulgar.

Go away. Get out.

Get out.

Get out!

"GET OUT!"

—Silence.

A vibrating hum of nothingness paralyzed in Nyssa's ringing ears.

Her eyes opened, chest continuing to heave, and she stared through swollen lids into the darkness.

The wood shuddered in silence. Not even the chirp of a cricket sounded in its abyss.

The alpha Ulfram was standing at the edge of the tree line. Its silver fur danced back to her in the firelight. She expected the alpha to speak... to say anything. Ask her why she wanted them silenced or tell her some comforting words as it had the night before.

Nyssa's eagle landed on her knee and gave her a nip. He chirped, and Nyssa knew he had said something, but she didn't... she didn't understand him.

She didn't understand him.

Her eagle nipped at her again, this time extending his wings when he called out.

All blood drained from Nyssa's body.

She couldn't hear the Ulfram.

She couldn't hear her eagle.

Their songs were gone.

Their songs were gone.

She couldn't hear him.

—The realization of what she'd just done struck her. Her entire body curled and shriveled into a tremble she couldn't contain.

No.

No-no-no-no—

She couldn't feel her eagle.

No-no-no-no—

What had she done?

No-no-no-NO—

A scream so violent that her ears began to bleed emitted from her.

The Ulfram slipped back into the wood.

And Nyssa surrendered to the truth.

The creatures were gone.

She'd lost the only ability she'd been born with.

As to how she'd managed to get on her horse, Nyssa didn't know. But the next thing she knew, it was daylight, and she was sitting upright on her steed, hands gripping the reins.

She blinked at the sunlight piercing her eyes and looked around. They were in the Forest, treading slowly over the great roots. In front of her was her brother on his great chestnut steed. Her own grey-white horse gave a whinny—

The memory of what she'd done hit her. She grasped the reins as a lifeline, body constricting beneath the weight of her stupidity, and her horse began to buck erratically.

"Whoa—"

"Nyssa—"

Fear wrapped itself around her core as a tightening rope, threatening to hang her from the gallows of her mother's tree.

"No—No—" her eyes wouldn't fixate. Her body shook. All she could feel was the stress of her failure.

Back and forth.

"Nyssa—wait!"

Her horse gave a great whinny and rose up on its hind legs, but Nyssa didn't fall. She held onto its neck as she held onto her fear.

Her eagle.

Fire.

Ashes.

Evaporating in smoke.

A ringing filled her ears. Her vision blurred. She wavered in her saddle.

Back and forth.

She wasn't sure of the words emitting from her mouth. Her brother's voice was an echo in the distance. The world turned upside down, and the canopy of the trees began to spin. They swirled over her like water down a drain. Down. Down. Down—

"NYSSA!"

Reality jolted her.

She was on the ground, knees hugged into her chest. Dorian had knelt before her. A silver glisten tugged at the corners of his eyes. His hands trembled against her face—or perhaps it was her body that was shaking. She couldn't tell the difference.

"Breathe," he told her slowly.

Her hands clasped to his wrists as she forced a jagged breath into her lungs.

"One," he said as he inhaled with her. His audible exhale matched hers, and she watched his shoulders relax.

"One," she managed.

Dorian sighed heavily, and his forehead sank against her temple, hand coming around to clasp the back of her neck. "I thought I was losing you."

Embarrassment filled her as she sank into her brother's grasp. Corbin went back to the horses to try to get Nyssa's to calm down. Lex didn't move. She stood over Dorian's shoulder as he held and rocked her. As though letting her go was not an option. And after a few minutes, her heartbeat returned to normal.

"I need to tell you something," she whispered to Dorian.

Dorian pulled back, brows stern over his eyes. He nodded and looked up to Lex.

"Can you give us a minute?" he asked her.

Lex appeared pained, but she nodded nonetheless before turning and leaving their sides.

Nyssa sat back from him and wiped her face hard to rid herself of the drying wet on her cheeks. She could feel the heat creeping up her chest as the anxiety of admitting to him what she'd done coursed through her.

She didn't speak until she was sure Lex couldn't hear as Nyssa wasn't ready to see Lex's look of disappointment when she found out what Nyssa had done.

"You can't hear them, can you?"

Nyssa's eyes narrowed, heart sinking into her stomach as Dorian spoke the words aloud that she wasn't even sure she could say. "How —"

"You were screaming last night," he cut her off. "You kept saying 'come back' while I was holding you. And your eagle was having a fit. I thought he would skin me alive."

Her eagle.

"Where is he?" she asked as she sat up.

"Just above us," he promised, his hand stroking the side of her face. "He's here."

"I don't remember anything after telling them to get out," she admitted.

"I thought as much," he said. "You've never let me hold you to sleep... or help you onto a horse before... but it was like you weren't there. A body moving but void of its core."

Nyssa sank her head into her hands. "How could I be so stupid? I didn't... I didn't know what to do. It was so overwhelming. I panicked." She gripped her hair as the failure hit her. "I just wanted to breathe."

"It's okay, Nys," Dorian comforted her.

"But it's not," she argued. "I just meant to block *them*, and just for a few hours. Not block every creature all the time."

"Perhaps you can try reaching out to them again tonight."

The thought made the blood drain from her face. "I don't... I don't know that they'll let me in. They probably hate me. I told them to leave me alone. They won't want to see me. How could they possibly trust me with anything again? And... Oh, what if they *don't* trust me? What if they see me as a failure and a threat? What if—"

Dorian's hands pressed to her face again. "One," he repeated.

The word ceased her ramble, but it didn't stop every single drop of doubt from pouring through her head. She inhaled a deep breath with him, and Dorian sat back against the tree after.

"I don't understand how you're so well held together," she managed after a few minutes. "I'm a complete mess, and you're... well, you're *you*, as you always are."

Dorian looked as though he would laugh—and then he pulled something from his pocket. A slim leather-wrapped glass jar. He opened it and shot a long gulp back before handing it to her and reaching into his other pocket, where he pulled his pipe and a small baggie of dark green herb.

"Secrets, sister."

She could see the pain in his faux smiling eyes. It was the same pain he'd held in them when she went to him after Draven fell, that being the only other time he'd ever let it show. Even when Dorian had talked her down the night before Draven and Aydra's deaths, he'd appeared so stern and mature. It was the same the day after, when the pair had sat on the beach to discuss where they would go, what Draven's plan had been. Even then, it was an anger that filled him, not grief.

She remembered the hit of the ocean breeze on her face as she'd watched him skip rocks over the water. They'd hidden around the bend, the cliffside wall at their backs. They'd hardly spoken that day as the echoes of the lies Dreamers had been told sounded while they helped clear debris and rescued people from the rubble.

"I can't stop hearing her scream," Dorian had admitted as he skipped a rock over the water.

"Neither can I," Nyssa whispered.

She could see the taut of his stern jaw reflected back in the waning amber sunlight, his sun-kissed skin aglow with its warmth. With the sink of the last pebble, Dorian sighed and went to sit beside her, almost plopping onto the ground.

"You and me against the world, sister," he repeated of her words from the

night before. He pulled his knees into his chest, his arms hanging lazily over his knees.

"The moment we leave, we'll be condemned," she said. "Traitors to the crown."

"I don't think we have a choice," he said. "If we stay, we'll be charged with that fate anyway. They know it was I who took Draven his horn."

"What was Draven's plan?"

Dorian began to fumble with his fingers. She recognized the haze that washed over his eyes—almost like he was concealing his emotions with the matured facade he had picked up just over the last year. Something she was sure he'd learned from Draven on his travels with him.

"He always knew loving our sister would be the end of him, and he didn't care," he began. "He trusted Balandria to look after their people. He didn't care about his death, as long as he got to spend his last days with her. He told me the day of the banquet what he needed from me. Pulled me aside with Nadir, who had brought him more news that morning."

"What was it?"

"He told me ships had settled on the southwestern edge. That they had missed them in the last raid. But... Nadir didn't have the manpower or supplies to take them on his own. Apparently, they've already begun a small settlement, with supply ships coming in once a week. He said he'd hidden it from Drae, knowing that if she'd known, she would have marched there on her own. They've been there a full Dead Moons cycle now. Possibly longer."

Nyssa's stomach tightened at the new information. "What did he want us to do?"

"He wanted us to go help Nadir come up with a plan. Negotiate a peace treaty with them if possible. Stop the shed of blood so that we could hopefully stay safe through the winter. If we attack now, we'll be squandered. All we can do at this moment is hold them off. We're not ready for a fight."

Nyssa sighed her head onto his shoulder and stared at the setting sun. It was the last sunset she would see in her own kingdom for a while.

"We have a lot of work to do," she realized.

"Yeah, we do."

—"We're taking a smoke break?"

Lex's voice brought Nyssa back to the present. Dorian was packing his pipe at her side, leaning against the tree trunk. He slumped his arms into his lap upon Lex coming beside them and lifted his tired eyes to hers.

"My sister is in pain. We will rest until she is ready to get moving again," he declared sternly. "Besides, I am starving, and I've not seen her eat in at least two days."

"You speak as if I am supposed to know what exactly it is you want me to do, Prince," Lex snapped. "I am not your Second or your servant."

"I've no crown on my head, so I expect you to do nothing," he told her. "But as my friend, could you hand me our food bag?"

The corner of Lex's jaw tightened, but she reached around onto her own horse and took a bag from the saddle. She didn't toss it at them. Instead, she curled her feet under her and sat down at Nyssa's side. She took an apple from the inside and leaned back against the tree, pulling her knife from her side as she started cutting the fruit in her hand.

Dorian was staring at Nyssa with an expectant brow when Lex left the bag in front of them.

"Don't let this take you back there, Nys," he said softly. "Our mother isn't here anymore to put that in your head. You've worked too hard to sink back into those depths."

She knew what he meant, but it didn't stop her hand from shaking as she grabbed a bread roll. She opened the bottle Dorian had given her and shot a gulp of the burning liquid down her raw throat. Her nose furled at the sweet fire liquid, and she made a face at him.

"I thought it was just whiskey," she managed in a rasp. "You didn't tell me it was nyghtfire."

A crooked smirk rose on his lips as he finished packing his pipe. He didn't respond and instead simply lit the end of his pipe with his finger, then pressed it between his lips. His eyes fluttered with the inhale, head resting in the dip in the tree at his back, and then he held it out for her to take.

She eyed him. "You realize you've never actually allowed me to do that before, right?"

He chuckled under his breath. "Yeah, well, before all this, I was certain you would need to be the clearest minded of the pair of us—"

"In other words, you were overprotective," Lex uttered. "What kind is that at any rate?" she asked, leaning up to see around Nyssa. "That better not be—"

"The normal kind," Dorian cut in. He turned back to Nyssa. "It will calm your mind from all that overworking it's doing."

Nyssa hesitantly took it, feeling her anxiety creep up. She didn't want to do it wrong. She wasn't even sure there was a 'wrong' way to do it.

"Nys, you don't have to smoke it," he told her.

"No, I want to," she insisted. "If it will help calm my mind, I want to."

Dorian gave her a nod and leaned back against the tree. She fumbled with it again, allowing the sweet smell to pulse through her nostrils. After a moment, Dorian sat back up, apparently noticing her hesitation, and he leaned forward to hold it for her.

His explanation was brief. Nyssa frowned but did as he told her anyway.

She nearly fell over at the choke of the smoke leaving her body.

The noise of Lex's soft chuckle and the feeling of her hand on her back made Nyssa glare at her over her shoulder.

"Shut up."

"Give it, Prince," Lex said, gesturing him with her hand.

Dorian took the pipe from Nyssa and extended it to Lex, who pressed it to her lips without a skip. Dorian rubbed Nyssa's back. Abruptly, her head began to spin, but not the spin that had consumed her during her attack.

This was a numbing spin she held on to with a close of her eyes, her fingers digging into the cold dirt. She blinked a few times, unsure if this was what it was supposed to do. Dorian handed her the water, which she drowned down her burning throat.

"We're two hours from the Venari roost, and you three are taking a smoke break?" came Corbin's disapproving drawl.

Dorian leaned against the tree again. "Come now, Second. Loosen up. Join us."

"One of us should be sober and prepared for the ambush we're certain to find ourselves in if we sit here much longer," Corbin said.

A freedom Nyssa wasn't used to ran through her muscles. She suddenly felt like she could take on anything—but her mind told her she should just relax, enjoy the forest scents.

Speaking of scents… She'd never smelled dirt so fresh before.

Dying leaves. Dirt. Mist. It was the smell of winter in the southern Forest. A cold breeze rippled through the conjunction of roots all around them. She could smell its crispness before she saw it.

And then the rain began.

Soft droplets hit Nyssa's face. Her first instinct was to protest, but as the cold water soaked into her skin, the first smile in a week spread over her face.

Quiet laughter filled her ears, and she realized it was her own.

It was a melodic pitch of laughter she thought her insides had banished, and her face scrunched at the wonder of such a feeling against her skin. Her head tilted back, eyes closing... she stuck out her tongue and let the cold liquid dance in her mouth. She reached her hands out, relishing the sting of the droplets on her palms.

This was rain as she'd never felt before.

Raw. Succumbing. Free.

Her sideways bangs and long hair matted quickly to her head and her shoulders. Dorian's laughter mingled with hers. She turned, watching him with only one eye open, his mouth agape as he allowed the water to drop in his mouth and on his tongue.

Her brother. So haunted only minutes before, now smiling with her at her side. Black hair pressed flush to his forehead and over his ears. He grinned at her, nose crinkling as his laughter matched her own.

He held his hands up to the sky, gathered some of the water, and she squealed when he threw it in her face. She wavered off-balance, falling into Lex's arms. Lex's quiet chuckle joined them, and Nyssa watched Dorian eye the Second Sun over her shoulder.

"Don't you dare, Prince," Lex warned.

Dorian reached down into the dirt, delighting danger in his wicked gaze as he reared back to launch. But the noise of Corbin cursing at the sky made the three pause.

"There is seriously something wrong with you three," Corbin determined, hands sitting haughtily on his hips.

Dorian and Nyssa exchanged the same grin, and she knew he was thinking the same as she.

"What's wrong, Bin?" Dorian mocked over the sound of the pounding rain, hand curling in the dirt once more. "Getting a little wet?"

Dorian threw a flick of mud at his Second.

Nyssa snorted.

The mud landed straight across Corbin's face.

Nyssa fell into Lex's lap again upon seeing the anger stretch over Corbin's features. But Corbin took it in stride, and he bent down and gathered his own palm full of mud.

He was aiming for Dorian, but Dorian grabbed Nyssa and ducked behind her just in time. The mud splattered on the side of Nyssa's ear and hit the tree. Had she been sober, she would have gathered her wits and chased the Fire Second, who was now staring wide-eyed at her as he realized what he'd done. But Nyssa was spinning too much to stand, and it was all she could do to see straight when Dorian and Lex both rose from the ground.

Apparently, Dorian had struck Lex with mud as well. She chased him down over the roots, shouting his name and cursing his existence. Watching Lex chase her brother as she'd done so many times when they were younger brought life to Nyssa's numb heart.

"What the—*The fuck is going on here?!*"

Dorian nearly slipped on the mud as he skidded to a halt. As Nyssa leveled out, she realized they were no longer alone.

"Oh shit," she managed, her laughter fading.

But Dorian grinned as he turned around, pushing a muddied hand through his wet hair and moving it off his forehead.

"Venari King," came his mocking drawl. "I wondered how long it would take you to find us."

6

Venari soldiers surrounded them.

They stood in the trees and on the ground, poised to strike with arrows drawn and swords pulled. As to how they'd snuck up on the group so quietly, Nyssa wasn't sure.

But they were everywhere.

"Leave them," the familiar voice called out as the rain began to die.

Balandria Windwood, the newly crowned Venari King, was pushing through the throng of Venari in the group's direction.

A tenseness rested in Bala's jaw—settled as though it had been there for days. Her hair was braided back into a high ponytail. Her thick black tunic was matted onto her skin from the dwindling rain, revealing the swell of her breasts and taut of her muscled arms. Her boots splashed in the mud. She shoved her short sword into one of the criss-cross sheaths across her back, and Nyssa recognized the blades as Draven's phoenix blades.

"Promised Prince and Princess," Bala uttered. She reached down for Nyssa's hand and pulled her up to her feet. There was a bite back of a smile in her eyes, apparent that she was trying to hide it in the presence of the people around her.

"Go home," Bala called out to her people. "All of you."

"They should not be allowed here," someone shouted. "They are of the Promised—"

"They are not your enemies," Bala affirmed.

"They were part of those who condemned him!"

"They are the reason our King is dead—"

Bala's knife pulled against the person who'd shouted's throat in the time it took Nyssa to blink. The male nearly stumbled off his feet. But Bala grabbed him by his shirt and kept him upright as she seethed her words.

"*I* am your King now," she growled. "So when I tell you that these two are welcome in our home any time they please, I mean it. They are *not* the reason Draven is dead. They were *not* the ones who voted in that room. And if you think for a moment I will leave them exiled from every realm, you are wrong. These two are our allies. My *friends*. You will treat them as such."

She released him with a jolt. He stammered, but someone caught him before he could fall. A glower that would have rivaled the stare of the Rhamocour rested in Bala's face, and she turned slowly in a circle, eyes sweeping from the people on the ground to the ones in the trees.

"Put down your weapons and go home. That's an order from your King," she commanded.

The people exchanged wary glances, but they did as she asked and lowered their weapons. Bala continued to watch her people as each of them turned on their heels to head back home.

A low whistle emitted from Dorian's lips when the crowd thinned.

"Someone's taking their newfound title seriously," he muttered.

Bala took one more glance around, seeing to it that the last of her people had left. Once they were alone, the heaviest of sighs left her lips, and she threw her knife into the ground.

"I hope you don't mind," she started, pulling the belted straps that were across her chest over her head. "I've been itching to shed this face for days now." She threw the belt and swords to the muddied dirt and then simply looked between them. Nyssa recognized the stern face her friend was forcing upon herself as the same one Aydra had once worn.

"It would be nice to simply be with my friends again," Bala finally finished.

The side of Nyssa's mouth quirked upwards, and she stepped forward to engulf her friend into a tight hug, head lying at Bala's collar and covering the Venari King in mud. Bala hesitated at first, but then her arms sank around Nyssa.

"*She's high*," Dorian whispered, apparently at the surprised face Bala had given him. "You know… just… *just a bit*."

Bala smelled of pine and leather, of roses and dirt. Nyssa tightened her grasp around her friend and felt Bala's chest move with her chuckle as Bala dropped her head against Nyssa's temple. No words were spoken for a long moment until Nyssa heard Bala say, "Let's have it, Prince," in a mocking tone.

Dorian huffed under his breath and pushed his long muddy arms around them both. His great, squeezing hug consumed both of their bodies, and a laugh left Bala.

"I'm glad you're both safe," Bala said soon after. "I heard about the bounty on your heads. I was worried you might be picked up on the way here."

"You knew we were coming?" Nyssa asked.

Bala pulled back, her hands remaining on their shoulders. "I thought you might." Her gaze flickered behind them then, and a broad smile lit up to her eyes. "Second Sun."

Lex was smirking at Bala when Nyssa turned. "My King," she uttered.

Bala pushed past the siblings, and when she reached Lex, her hands pressed to Lex's cheeks, and Bala pressed her lips to hers.

Brows lifted on Nyssa's face. She wasn't sure if it was a thing or if perhaps this was simply something they did now. She'd seen Aydra kiss Lex on many occasions, knew they would share men or women together, but she knew it was simply... well, it was just them.

This, though... This was new. This was different. She'd seen looks from Lex to Bala during the week Bala had stayed at Magnice for the Gathering, but as it had been Lex, she'd dismissed it. She wished she'd paid a little more attention to them.

"I feel like we should talk about this," Dorian muttered to Nyssa.

Whispered words were spoken between Bala and Lex, and Lex hugged Bala tightly.

"We definitely missed something," Dorian added.

"We?" Nyssa repeated, holding onto his arm to steady herself as the forest wavered around her. "You're the gossip king. How did you not know about this?"

"I can't keep track of—"

"It's really none of your business," Bala said when she faced them again.

A crooked smirk lifted Dorian's lips. "You know what would be my business—*Ow!*"

Lex smacked the side of his head.

Bala and Nyssa exchanged a quiet laugh, and then Bala's gaze went to the silent Fire Second standing by the horses. Her gaze narrowed, and she hugged her arms over her chest.

"Who's this?" she asked Nyssa.

"This is Corbin," Nyssa told her. "Dorian's Second. You weren't introduced at the Gathering?"

Corbin stepped forward, holding out his hand to Bala. Bala eyed him as she hesitantly took it.

"Can't say that we officially met, no," she said. "You're a little quiet to be handling these three."

"We're trying to break him in," Dorian chimed in. "In more ways than one," he added with a wink at his Second.

Bala's expression faltered, and she looked back to Corbin. "Oh, you poor thing," she mocked. "You know there is room for another in my company if you'd like to join my ranks instead of trying to handle this little shit."

"S'not what you said last you were at the castle," Dorian muttered in a breath. "And where's my kiss? I believe I earned one after that night."

Her head tilted playfully in his direction. "Keep it up. I have a lot more violent things I can use to tie you up with here."

"The first promises from our Venari King," Dorian grinned, nudging Nyssa's side. "You know, Corbin might enjoy that."

And Nyssa didn't miss the lift of Corbin's chin at Dorian's suggestion.

She swore she even saw his lip twitch.

Bala turned to Corbin again. "I actually have a spot open for a new Second if you'd like that. I'm in need of one. Bael is trying to earn the position, but if you want it—"

"Don't try to take my guard," Dorian interjected.

"Scared he'll leave you, Prince?" Bala teased.

Dorian's weight shifted, and he hugged his arms over his chest, smile fading into a glare. "Yes, actually," he admitted.

The first genuine smile Nyssa had ever seen on Corbin spread across his face, stretching over his dark skin, full lips curling at the corners. The short twists of thick black hair on his head bounced when he let out a soft chuckle.

"Now we're having fun," he mused in a deep raspy voice she was sure he saved for later times.

Nyssa bit her lips together to stifle the bemusement of her brother's Second now with power over him.

Dorian shifted on his feet again, eyes cutting crudely at Corbin before looking to Bala once more. "Tell me, Bala, do you have somewhere we can all go to scream at the winds?"

"What—you don't like this clearing?"

Dorian raised a lazy brow at her, which she shook her head at and surrendered.

"Yeah. We'll go further in and upriver," Bala said with a wave of her finger. "Shortly, Prince. The Noctuans are more violent on this round with the slaying of their King. I'll not be caught out of the safety of my kingdom at nightfall. Not even with the speaker to creatures at my side."

Nyssa's stomach knotted at the words as everyone else began moving. But Dorian gave her elbow a squeeze, and she sighed out the lump stuck in her throat.

Dorian had to pause when they reached the Venari kingdom. People were walking on branches in the massive trees high above him. Some appeared to be scouting, some sharpening weapons, and some simply had their legs swung down and were eating.

Settled within the trees' trunks were various places like the armory and what looked to be an open mess hall. But the largest tree, and the one they seemed to be walking towards, was one fit only for a King.

"Why have you never built a castle?" Dorian had asked Draven on the road to the villages.

Draven looked as though he would laugh as he huffed out the smoke from his pipe. "What and cut down the trees that we're connected to to make way for it? The only ones on this land with a castle is your kind. Arbina being her extravagant self and wanting her children to appear greater than every other being. The open forest is freedom. Venari are not meant for cages."

"Do you live in the trees?"

Draven sighed back in the grass, arm coming up behind his head. "We do."

Dorian could see the pride in Draven's eyes. "You know, you talk about Arbina and her extravagance... I would bet your tree is the grandest, most audacious tree in all the Forest."

This time, Draven actually smiled. "King's tree. And she is. Nearly as tall as Duarb. Kings before me had it filled with trophies and furs... I got rid of most of it when I moved in. Had a great bonfire for some. Traded the rest with friends."

"Why?"

"I like the simple life."

Simple life, my ass, Dorian thought to himself.

He turned to say something clever to Nyssa and Lex about it, but when he did, he noticed the pair of them staring at that tree as though it had suddenly grasped onto their hearts and was slowly twisting its limbs inside their chests.

"Okay, Second Sun?" he called to Lex.

Lex gave him a hesitant smile and nodded before then wrapping an arm over Nyssa's shoulders.

Venari stopped and gathered around as Bala led them up the staircase. She paused a few steps up and looked out at her people, asking them, "Don't you all have work to do?" to try and stop them from staring at their guests as though they were meant for slaughter.

Dorian removed his boots and muddied tunic upon reaching the porch. He started to lay the shirt on the chair, but Lex grabbed his arm before he could toss it.

"That's theirs," Lex said firmly.

Dorian dumped the shirt on the floor instead.

A cot had been set up on the floor beside the oversized bed. Bala's cot, he realized. A blanket was mussed over the big mattress, a few shirts thrown on it as though someone had left in a rush—which Dorian was reminded was probably true.

Lex stilled in the doorway as Dorian passed her, and he saw Nyssa squeeze her arm. Lex forced a smile at Nyssa, but she could not hide the silver glisten forming at the bottom of her eyes.

Bala glanced back at Dorian. "Tub is behind that screen if you'd like to wash," she told him.

Dorian gave her a grateful nod and went to draw the water.

"You've moved in?" Lex managed to Bala.

Bala paused by Draven's desk, and her hand slowly stroked over a piece of parchment. "I didn't have a choice," she said softly. "When I got back, the rest of them were rioting, threatening to march to Magnice to take your heads." She turned to face them and leaned against the desk. "Bael was the only one who helped me settle things down. I had to take the King's Tree, or else someone would have put themselves in it, possibly tried to take his things or my crown."

"Have things calmed now?" Lex asked as she removed her boots.

"Somewhat," Bala shrugged. "You saw them today. They are on edge, and I don't blame them. Belwarks are just as likely to walk into our kingdom in retaliation for what Draven did, and I'll have a war coming at me on three sides."

Dorian sank himself beneath the water he'd drawn and leaned his head back against the lip of the greatest tub he'd ever been in. "Is there anything we can do?" he asked.

"Keep your heads down. Let me figure out our next moves," Bala said, rubbing her neck. Her eyes flickered to Nyssa, and she looked like she would laugh at the princess sitting cross-legged on the floor in her muddied dress.

"Dorian, what kind of herb did you give your sister?" she asked.

Dorian moved the screen from beside him so he could see them more clearly. "The normal kind," he affirmed, seeing Nyssa staring at her hands and turning her fingers over in slow motion.

Bala's brow elevated in Lex's direction, who huffed amusedly. "He's not lying. It was the normal kind," Lex replied. "She could use some food, maybe."

"Right—" Bala stood and went to the balcony. She called out for one of her men, and a minute later, a man with amber skin and loose shiny black curls appeared in the doorway. He shook his head, ear-length hair swooping out of his soft eyes as he looked at everyone in the room.

"Hey Lex," he said upon recognizing her.

"Bael," Lex smiled, giving him a once over.

Bael winked at her and then looked to Balandria. "You needed me?"

"Take our Princess down to the mess hall and find her some food. Her brother has corrupted her with herb," Bala explained, glaring playfully at Dorian.

Bael chuckled under his breath. "Not a problem." He moved in Nyssa's direction, who smiled up at him when he reached for her.

"Hey Princess," he leered softly.

"I remember you," Nyssa smiled as Bael took her outstretched hands.

Bael grinned a charming sideways Venari grin, his innocent eyes crinkling at the corners as she stood to her feet. "I remember you too," he said in a low voice.

"Overprotective brother with fire powers sitting right here," Dorian called out, eyes cutting at Bael from the tub. "Keep your leering to yourself if you don't want an ashen throat."

Nyssa swayed on Bael's arm as though she were coming out of a trance. "Remind me not to stand up that quickly again," she muttered. "And shut up, Dorian. I'm fine."

"You're *high*," Dorian argued.

"And who's fault is that?" she drawled.

Dorian settled back beneath the water. He cursed himself for getting his sister high when they were entering a kingdom where beings who all looked as beautiful as Bael and Bala were sure to swoon her off her feet with her being so out of sorts.

"Do you need me to carry you?" he heard Bael ask Nyssa.

"I can walk myself," Nyssa said firmly.

Bala snorted. "There she is." She gave Bael an upwards nod. "Keep her innocent, will you?"

"Of course," Bael said before following Nyssa down the steps.

As they disappeared, Dorian shifted again in the tub, this time moving to grab a cloth to dry with. "I don't like him," he said upon rising.

"Have you liked any person your sister has ever been consumed with?" Bala teased.

Dorian thought about it as he wiped his face. "Unworthy men have been throwing themselves at her for years. It's not her fault they're all idiots."

"It's that innocent facade she's perfected," Lex said.

"Certainly had me fooled my first time meeting her," Bala agreed.

"I remember that day," Lex sighed as she leaned back in the chair. "She was terrified. So uptight. Thought she would burst sitting at that table between you and Draven. She looked so small beside him."

"She did look pretty small at that table," Bala agreed. "Imagine what some of these males would have done if they'd found out how not so innocent she is?"

"Probably the same thing Nadir did," Lex said. She caught Bala's eyes, and together the pair burst into laughter.

Dorian wasn't sure he liked this conversation.

"If your man touches her while she's high, I'll burn him," he said over their laughter.

Bala straightened and pushed off the desk, going around to the bookshelf where Draven kept his stash of wine and whiskeys. "Bael is a perfect gentleman, Prince. He'll feed her and bring her back. Not to mention we don't exactly want a repeat of what just happened, do we?" she said as she poured four glasses of wine. "And if you threaten any of my men again, I'll knock you so hard out of this tree, you'll forget your name," she added with a smile.

Corbin snorted, and Dorian glared at his Second.

"Do you have any of the potion Draven gave Aydra when she was here?" Lex asked then, averting the conversation.

"I'm sure I can have the surgeon make some up," Bala replied. "Why?"

Lex met Dorian's gaze, and he knew she was thinking the same as he. "We need to get her under before the Noctuans wake," she said.

"Why? What's wrong?"

Dorian stared at the floorboards as he recalled the night before. How he'd found Nyssa in that field screaming. How he'd held and rocked her for what felt like forever until Corbin found them. Dorian's own tears had streamed down his face at the panic of not knowing how to help her.

He shook the memory from his mind as he slipped on clean pants.

"She's just having a hard time processing their grief," he said, unwilling to share his sister's secret.

"It would be better to give her a night off from having to worry about their cries," Lex added.

Bala nodded, and Dorian saw the hurt spreading over her features as he was sure she didn't realize the beasts had indeed been crying out for Draven since that first night.

"I'll go have the surgeon make some up," Bala said, setting her wine on the desk.

"I'll come with you," Lex said and stood. "Make sure our Princess isn't getting into trouble," she added with a glance at Dorian.

As they disappeared down the staircase, Dorian sank back into the chair he'd chosen. Corbin watched him from across the room.

"Don't give me that look," Dorian said.

"When are you going to tell them?" Corbin asked.

"Tell them what?"

"That your sister can't hear."

"It's not my secret to tell," Dorian argued.

"And when her life depends on it during this war?"

"I'll help her get it back," Dorian promised. "She'll be fine."

With one gulp, Dorian downed his own wine and then stood to drown the contents of the other two glasses sitting on the desk. His head shook at the bitterness, but he ignored it and grabbed a shirt out of his bag.

"Where are you going?" Corbin asked.

"Taking a piss," Dorian snapped. "Would you like to watch me do that too, or have you had enough of my cock this week?"

Dorian could hear his Second cursing him under his breath as Dorian made for the stairs, but he didn't care.

"You don't know where you're going," Corbin called.

Dorian paused in the door. He hated that Corbin was right. "Why don't you come with me, if nothing else but to watch my ass get kicked for flirting with the wrong person?"

This got Corbin out of his seat.

7

Bala made the potion herself per instruction from the surgeon. Nyssa took it with no hesitation once Lex told her it would help her sleep. After tucking her into the bed on the roof, Lex and Bala retired back downstairs to the porch.

Nyssa fell asleep before the first Ulfram howl.

Bala leaned over the railing as darkness settled and watched Dorian participate in the drinking game her people were playing around the fire. As to how much the Prince had already drunk, she wasn't sure. She didn't entirely trust that Corbin would keep Dorian from making a complete ass of himself even though the Fire Second was sitting just across from him.

"So," Bala started as Dorian began singing. "Nyssa is having blackout panic attacks, and Dorian has decided to drink himself to death."

Lex was quiet for a solid second before lifting her cup to her lips. "Yes," she finally replied.

"And how is the Second Sun taking her grief?"

There was another pause as Lex sat up, elbows leaning on her knees. "How is the newly crowned Venari King taking hers?" Lex asked softly.

Bala thought about it. How she'd screamed into the Hills on her way home. How she'd thrown all her possessions from her previous dwellings into a large pile and set it all aflame in the middle of the night. Spent the last four nights sitting at Draven's desk staring at maps and letters between him, Nadir, and Hagen discussing their nonsense as well as politics.

Bala raised her cup to Lex. "Duty first," she forced herself to say.

Lex mimicked her cheers, and together they downed their remaining bits of wine.

"You know, I never thanked you for getting me out of there that night," Bala said.

Lex waved her off. "I wasn't about to watch both my kings be murdered at the hands of the Bedrani."

Bala glanced again at Dorian, who had finally settled down on the log beside his Second. The pair looked to be discussing something more serious than who was the better singer.

"What is their plan?" Bala asked.

"I'm not sure they have one," Lex admitted. "Man arrived on the shores of Magnice the morning we left. Rhaif's reaction was to silence any rumors of their arrival and not tell anyone of them coming on our shores. It was only the two boats, almost as though they'd made a wrong turn or perhaps sailed around because they saw the fire blazing two nights before. We packed. Left under cover of night."

"What did you tell the rest of the kingdom?"

"They left their crowns on their thrones."

"So they are exiled?"

"I won't pretend to know what the Bedrani did upon finding out other than put a bounty on their heads," Lex replied. "I'm not sure what they told the people. Dorian was already being watched for taking Draven the horn. His days had been marked. The bounty on Nyssa's head is new." She looked out at the fire, a haze setting over her. "They're hiding something from me," she added.

"What do you mean?"

"I mean… today before you found us, Nyssa pulled Dorian aside to tell him something."

"They share everything," Bala said with a shrug. "What makes you think it's a secret?"

"Because I know my Princess well enough to know when she's hiding something that she believes will make me think less of her. I worry for her. I do not know how she is going to take this war even with all of us around her."

"You're not going to like my plan then," Bala muttered.

"Why?"

Bala tensed at the question as the worries of her own crown came to mind. "My crown may be stripped from me," she admitted.

"What?"

"My trouble with securing it when I arrived is not the only threat on my head. A year ago, when Draven brought Aydra back to our home, about a third of our people left us when she was injured. The older generation and followers of Parkyr. They wanted Draven to declare war on Magnice, either by killing Aydra or sending more Infi into Magnice's streets. Draven refused, and they left. Now that he is gone, they may come back and try to take over. Especially given the nature of Draven's death and his burning your kingdom. I'm sure they'll think it was him going through with the plan to take the crown, not as an act of vengeance for her."

"Why would they take your crown?" Lex asked.

"Because I won't want to march to Magnice to finish the job," Bala replied. "To be honest, I do not know how many people in my kingdom right now would agree and want to go with them. And if they do find Nyssa and Dorian, they will try to kill them." She paused and met Lex's gaze, the words she was about to speak stilling in her throat for a moment before she said them.

"They cannot stay here together."

Lex looked as though she would fight Bala right then—chest visibly caving, jaw tightening... The last she'd seen such a look on the Second Sun's face was when Bala had tried to refuse to leave Magnice.

"What are you saying?" Lex asked, voice tight.

"I'm saying they can stay for a few days, but not indefinitely. If rumor finds the rebel Hunters that they are both here, they will march in here for their heads, and not because of what happened to Draven, but because they will see it as finishing what they think Draven started."

"You told them they were welcome here."

"And they are, but... I cannot watch as either of them is murdered. They are my friends."

"What would you have them do?"

Bala looked back down at Dorian and Corbin sitting at the fire. "Nadir will be here tomorrow. You and Nyssa should go to the Umber. She is the only one capable of walking in that room with these strangers and reading them so as to not walk into an ambush. She has to help Nadir negotiate with the strangers to keep them at bay, at least for the winter. We need time. A ceasefire can give us that."

"You want to separate them?"

"It's not what I want—"

"Their sister just *died*," Lex argued as she stood. "I will not pretend to think how either of them will handle being separated. They've not been away from each other except a few weeks at a time their entire lives."

"I understand, but... It's the only way to keep them safe."

"What about Dorian?"

"He needs to go to the mountains," Bala said. "I would go, but I cannot leave my people with the threat of the rebels on our doors. He has to go to Dahrkenhill. He has to speak with Hagen and the rest of their Elders. He has to salvage the damage the Bedrani enthralled upon the relationship we just solidified."

"Do you truly think the Blackhands will welcome him into their towns when they could very well think he was part of the conspiracy to put the High Elder's best friend to death?" Lex spat.

"If he doesn't go, and we end up needing their aid because of these ships, we will not have it. He has to try to repair the relationship. If anyone can do it, he can. He's been there before. He knows them."

Lex stared at Bala a moment. A moment long enough that Bala straightened fully off the railing and lifted her chin. She waited on Lex to lash out, throw her empty cup on the ground and demand Bala come up with a better plan.

"You're telling them," Lex said, pointing in her face.

"As King, I would expect no one to do it for me."

Lex sighed her back against the railing and slumped on the ground again. Bala could feel her gaze on her when she stretched inside the home to change her clothes.

"You're welcome to share my cot tonight," she called to Lex. "It's not much, but it's more than the floor."

This time Lex laughed, but she laid her arms over her knees and glanced back down at the fire. "Should probably keep an eye on my Prince for a bit longer," she replied. "And I feel I can be honest with you... I'm not sure how much company I'll be tonight."

Bala changed into only her nightshirt and strode back out to the deck. Lex's stare poured through her as Bala moved, and Bala could see the dilation in Lex's gaze despite the words she'd just spoken. Bala ached for the comfort and familiarity of arms of someone who understood.

Lex had always made her feel wanted. With every smirk and sideways stare... the confidence of her entire being. Bala had shaken her head at her the first time she'd called her stunningly violent.

Seeing the Second Sun in pain there on that porch, Bala knew Lex could also use the comfort.

Lex watched as Bala sank straddle over her lap, hands hesitantly grazing Bala's bare thighs as Bala wrapped her arms around Lex's neck.

For a few moments, neither spoke. But Bala inhaled the ashen scent of the woman sitting before her, and she sank her forehead onto hers. The noise of her people echoed in her ears as distant as the Ulfram howl had earlier in the night.

Lex's arms wrapped around her, and the next thing Bala knew, Lex's cheek was lying on her breasts. A silent submission of herself that Bala was sure no other, say for perhaps Aydra, had ever witnessed. The tear that hit her skin made Bala's jaw clench, and she realized maybe Lex had not had a moment to allow herself to pull down that royal guard face and grieve for the loss of her best friend.

So Bala decided she would hold her there, her arms tucking around the Second Sun, and she would hold her for as long as they both needed.

8

Nyssa was standing in the Throne Room.

Her sister struggled against the bindings. Aydra called out, screaming Nyssa's name, but Nyssa couldn't move. Her feet were melted into the stone. Belwarks held her arms. She cried out, but nothing left her throat.

Alone.

—She jolted awake.

Dense sunlight warmed her chilled cheeks. Her eagle's cry sounded overhead, and she sighed at his comfort.

The smell of the dew on the forest floor filled her nostrils, her cheeks damp with the minuscule droplets of fog surrounding them. A cool breeze brushed through, and she closed her eyes to take it all in. The chirping birds. The crickets. The morning hum of Venari people down below.

Morning in the forest was a new sensation. She was so accustomed to the noise of crashing waves and the smell of salt that this all made her uncomfortable in her skin.

As if it would take much to do so.

Her back hit the mattress again, and she looked up at the cloud-streaked sky.

One.

All the way up to eleven.

She laid there and counted the numbers, forcing a deep breath into her lungs with each. One breath for every morning since it all happened. One breath for every morning she hoped to one day wake up and find it all to be a dream.

The bed shifted. Nyssa looked over and realized Dorian was lying atop the covers by her side, curled into a ball. His skin was streaked with his form, his body jerking as though he were having a nightmare. Blue light flared beneath those blackened lines, and Nyssa hesitantly pressed the back of her hand to his cheek.

Dorian flinched upright, back stiff.

His eyes were still black when he turned his head to her.

Nyssa swallowed, feeling her heartbeat pick up. "Dorian, it's just me," she managed. "It's Nyssa."

Dorian blinked.

The black receded, and he sighed as his form pushed back inside him. "Shit," he muttered, catching his breath. "Shit—are you—Did I hurt you?"

"No," she assured him.

His hands went to his hair, and he tugged the roots, knees pulling to his chest.

"I'm sorry," he breathed after a moment.

"I know," she said. "At least you didn't catch anything on fire this time," she added, trying to lighten his mood.

Dorian gave her a small smile over his shoulder. He didn't reply and instead fell backward onto the mattress again. He rubbed his forehead and his eyes with two fingers, wincing as though he were in pain.

"*Fucking Infi*, what did I do last night?" he asked.

"I'm sure Corbin will have the full story," Nyssa replied.

Dorian scoffed. "I'm sure he will. Probably add in a few things just to make me sweat."

"I knew I liked him," Nyssa bantered.

Dorian's brow lifted slyly at her from behind his hands. "Pretty sure his giving me a hard time is not the only reason you like him," he muttered. "Was it not you who I caught him taking in the stairwell after his being named Fire Second?"

"That was a one-time thing," Nyssa glared.

A quiet chuckle left Dorian as he continued to rub his face. "Was it, though?"

She shoved him, and Dorian openly laughed.

"Don't worry, sister. Your secrets are safe with me."

"You're one to talk. I do wonder how it is you ended up here without him."

"What—you think I would have taken him at the end of this bed with you sound asleep at the top of it?"

"Yes," she said without hesitation. "Wouldn't be the first time."

"Perhaps he wasn't keen on a drunk man fucking him and rather wanted to go sink his cock into one of these beautiful Venari women instead."

Nyssa almost laughed. "Sounds like you're jealous."

Dorian's nostrils flared, and she smirked at her brother when he mumbled, "Not hardly," and covered his face in his hands again.

Nyssa melted onto the mattress and stared at the sky again. It was the first morning since it had happened that she woke up without that initial feeling of dread in her bones—even despite the nightmare she'd jolted out of.

She'd not heard a single utter from the Noctuans the night before with the potion swimming through her, and she wasn't sure how she was supposed to thank Bala for such a luxury.

"What are we supposed to do, Nys?" Dorian asked softly.

"I'm sure whatever it is is not what you did last night," she joked.

He nudged her sideways again and shook his head. "I'm serious," he said. "What do we do?"

Nyssa exhaled audibly, deliberating their decision in her head as he was. "Probably go to the Umber," she said, though the notion made her stomach flutter. "Make sure Nadir doesn't hate us."

"The mountains after," Dorian suggested. "I can't imagine they're in a giving mood now that the High Elder's best friend has been murdered."

"Oh, good, you're smart enough to already know where you're going," came Bala's voice as she greeted them on the roof.

Nyssa and Dorian exchanged a frown, and together they sat up.

"Come again?" Dorian asked.

Bala paused at the end of the bed, arms crossed over her chest as her gaze washed between the pair. "I have something to tell you both."

Nyssa sat up on her knees, concerned with the look on Bala's face. "Is everything okay?" she asked.

"Not really. No," Bala admitted.

The way Bala avoided their eyes and sat sideways on the end of the bed made Nyssa's heart slow. She was hesitating, and Nyssa wasn't sure she liked it.

"Bala?"

"Both of you have to leave," Bala said.

"Kicking us out so soon?" Dorian mocked. "Here, I thought you enjoyed our company."

"I do, Prince," Bala said. "That's why this is so hard to say to you both."

"Where are you sending us?" Nyssa asked.

"Nadir will be here in a few hours. I want you—" she nodded at Nyssa "—to accompany him back to the Umber. Stay there. Help him deter the ships and possibly negotiate some sort of ceasefire with Man if it is possible."

Nyssa's heart skipped at what Bala wanted her to do, but she didn't have time to explore the feeling.

"Wait—" Dorian interjected, now fully alert with the conversation. "You're separating us?"

"You—" Bala affirmed to Dorian, blatantly ignoring the stretch of fear in his voice, "—are going to the mountains. To speak with Hagen and ensure they are still our allies should we need them."

"That's fine, but we go together," Dorian said firmly.

"You can't," Bala argued.

"Why not?"

"Because I do not want the Venari rebels to find you both and kill you together."

Nyssa and Dorian gawked at her.

"When you say Venari rebels..." Dorian began, "...You mean what exactly?"

"I mean a group of Venari that are followers of the old ways and who would see how Draven died as a sign that he wanted to take your castle. A group of followers that would heed little and not care that the two of you are in exile but would kill you on the spot if you were found."

The news stilled Nyssa. It was no wonder Bala was so on edge with her people. If the rebels came in, there was no telling how many Venari still under her reign would join them in retaliation. Some might see what they wanted to do as a sign of vengeance for Draven.

Dorian tensed at Nyssa's side, and she looked over to see his fist gripping around the back of his neck.

"You expect me to leave my sister alone... when there are men out there who would have our heads simply because of what we are?" he asked in a low voice.

A shadow clouded over Bala's features that hadn't been there a moment before. "Now you know how my kind have felt every time we've walked into your kingdom the last hundred years," she said darkly.

"Dorian, I'll be fine," Nyssa said.

His eyes blazed through her when he turned. "I won't allow it."

"*Excuse me?*"

"No, you are my sister, and I can't—" He rose from the bed and began to pace, hands tugging on the roots of his hair.

"If this is what she needs us to do, then we must trust her."

"It's the only option," Bala affirmed.

"I'm not going halfway around our land without you," Dorian said to Nyssa, his voice rising. "I will not leave you alone."

"She won't be alone," Bala interjected. "She will have Lex, Nadir, the Honest army. I am but a few hours ride away. She'll be fine."

Nyssa watched him pace, noticing a fear in his eyes. "Do you not trust me?" she asked.

He held up a finger in her direction, still pacing. "That's not fair."

"It's a valid question," Nyssa said as she rose to her feet.

Dorian stiffened, and she saw the black threatening his fingertips. Nyssa knew he would never hurt her, but the fear exuding from him reminded her of the night their kingdom had burned. How he'd shoved that knife in the woman's face and nearly killed the Dreamer for touching her.

Bala rose too, and she started to step between them, but Nyssa shot her a look.

"Wait for us downstairs," Nyssa told her.

Bala didn't argue.

Nyssa didn't blink away from Dorian as she waited for Bala's footsteps to disappear down the stairs.

And once they did, Nyssa nearly wrung his neck.

"*You're making me seem like some helpless child!*" she hissed at him. "I do not need you to constantly look after me."

"That is not what this is," he argued.

"So, what is it?"

"I just don't like us being separated, is all."

"Do you not trust me?" she asked again, a firmness in her voice that she rarely carried.

Dorian's hands threaded behind his head as he turned in a circle. "What I don't trust is the rest of this world," he admitted. "I don't trust Nadir. I don't trust his people to give you a chance when they're just as likely to blame you for Draven's death. And you know what? Yes, you're right. I'm not entirely sure I trust you not to throw yourself into something that will get you killed while you're trying to prove yourself."

"Do you not trust Lex either?"

"Do *you?*"

The question staggered between them. Nyssa shifted her feet and stared at the ground as she contemplated her answer.

"I trust her to fulfill her duty to our sister," she finally answered. "As much as I hate the notion that she is simply following orders, I cannot help but trust that she will look after me. Confronting her about whether I am simply a duty or if she actually trusts me is an argument for another day."

"And what happens when she finds out you can't use your powers? Do you think she'll trust you to do anything on your own after that?"

She hated how right his questions were, but she didn't understand where any of it was coming from.

"Make your point, brother," she sneered. "Why do you not want me on my own? What makes you think your being with me is—"

"Because at least with me, I can help you work through every stupidly brave idea that goes through that beautiful mind of yours."

"So now my ideas are stupid."

The huff of air that left him made the hair on her arms rise.

"That is not what I said."

"What is the real problem here?" Nyssa asked. "Why can you not simply take what is a good plan, what is essentially *Draven's* plan, and go with it? What is so hard about this? We'll be separated for a while. You should have known it would come to this."

"Draven's plan didn't include you going off on your own and playing hero."

"*What is the problem, Dorian?*" Nyssa nearly shouted.

"The problem is I do not want to lose you!"

His fingertips turned black, but he squashed it quickly. Nyssa's heart skipped at the final truth of it. He was visibly shaking as the energy tensed between them, and a lump rose in her throat.

"You're not going to lose me," she affirmed. "It is you and me, remember? Always us. Together or separated, we are connected, and you *know* it."

"I know... But I cannot lose you too, sis," he whispered, voice cracking. "I can't... I just... I *can't.*"

The tear that streaked down his cheek nearly sent her crashing into the floor. But she forced her legs to move in front of him, and she wiped it from his face.

"Letting me go is not the same as us having to walk away from them," she told him. "You did everything you were supposed to. Everything that she would let you. Everything that *he* would let you," she added.

Even with the words coming from her lips, she wasn't sure she believed them. That knot of her own guilt ate at her insides. But she would hold this facade for him and for every time he had comforted her back from her darkness.

"We have to do this," she affirmed. "For them. This is what they wanted."

Dorian's jaw visibly constricted before he exhaled heavily once more. She could see him surrendering to her statement, see the annoyance in his features and the clench of his hands at his sides as he stared at the ground. And then, finally, his eyes rolled up to meet hers.

"I hate you sometimes."

9

Nyssa pulled on a new dress when she rose from the tub— one of her warmer navy wool ones. She, somehow, still had some of the mud in her hair from the day before and had to scrub it out. The others had left her on her own in the treehouse. Bala had told them the Honest would be arriving soon, and she could use some help getting their goods together.

Nyssa's stomach was in knots. Not just at the notion that she would be separated from her brother by the afternoon, probably on a boat going downriver to a new realm she'd never been to before. But also at the notion of who she would be with by the afternoon and what exactly he expected of her.

Everything had moved so quickly.

She was still trying to grasp the reality of it all. She made a mental note to ask Bala for more of the potion to take with her as she wasn't sure how loud the Noctuans were at the Umber. She wanted to take precautions anyway. The last thing she wanted was to break down as she had two nights before and let on to Lex that she couldn't use her powers. She already had to hide the fact that she couldn't converse with her eagle, which in itself was hard enough.

Seeing the look on Lex's face when she found out was not at the top of Nyssa's priorities.

And then there was Nadir.

Her heart ached at the thought of seeing him again. She hoped he did not expect her to be the same bantering Princess she'd been those two nights. Two nights that had been freedom in a life she sometimes thought a dream. As much as she wanted to find herself in his arms again, that was not the reason she was here. That was not the reason she was in exile and fighting in a war that had abruptly been pushed on her less than two weeks prior. A task that made her knees weak whenever she thought about it.

She wasn't even sure she wanted to allow herself to feel happiness yet. Not when...

She shook the thought from her mind and forced herself into the present.

The noise of people chatting sounded in her ears below. Nyssa stepped onto the balcony, drying her hair in a cloth as she peered down at the throng of people now bustling in the clearing.

The Honest had arrived.

She continued squeezing the excess water from her hair and looked around for her brother or Bala. But what she saw by the edge of the trees made a lump grow in her throat, and she couldn't move.

Nadir.

Nadir *fucking* Storn.

Commander of the Honest army. Fastest blade in Haerland. Defender of the Honest.

The forbidden man she'd found herself wrapped up with at Magnice, falling over her own feet for every word on his tongue and his actual tongue.

Nadir was hugging Bala, his head buried in her neck. He pulled back a moment later, and his hands pressed to her cheeks. Bala reached up to wipe a tear from Nadir's face, and together they smiled at each other for a brief second before hugging once more.

The sight of him brought back the memory of their meeting at Magnice, how he'd been so adamant that he could not swoon her, and yet his being himself had done that on its own.

She remembered standing over by the buffet with Bala, attempting to sober herself up and stop the dizzying she'd felt after her brother had spun her on the dance floor.

"I hope that's water in your cup and not more wine," Bala had said to her.

Nyssa's lips twisted in an almost perturbed manner, glaring at her friend for calling her out. "It is. Unfortunately," she muttered.

Bala huffed amusedly and then handed Nyssa a piece of sweet bread pastry. "Eat the bread," Bala demanded.

"Someone's bossy," Nyssa mumbled, but she took the bread anyway. The moment the sweet honey and flaky crust met her tongue, she sighed into the taste of it, eyes closing. The audible moan that came from her throat, she didn't expect, and Bala was smirking at her when she opened her eyes.

"I'm not enjoying this," Nyssa said with a full mouth. "At all." She had to lean her hand against the table to steady herself from the pleasure of such bread in her mouth.

"Yeah, you are," Bala bantered back. "You love bread."

"I really do," Nyssa agreed as the room continued to spin around her.

Bala glanced past Nyssa's shoulder then, and Nyssa watched as the mockery on her features darkened. "Speaking of enjoyment..." Her voice trailed, and Nyssa turned just in time to see the one she'd been told to avoid coming up beside them.

They'd been staring at each other the entire night, and she'd wondered if he was ever going to converse with her or if he was a good enough man to heed her sister's warning.

Nadir's springing brown and blonde dreads were pulled back very loosely into a high bun at the back of his head. The long triangular set of his chin never wavered from her direction. The scruff he'd adorned on his face earlier in the day was now absent, leaving the stern of his jaw and acute of his sharp cheekbones exposed to the elements as he sauntered up to them.

One hand was wrapped around the hilt of his sword at his side lazily. His sleek muscles strained beneath the basic cream-colored tunic he wore, almost as though he'd not thought it necessary for him to dress up for such an event. His waist was strapped with a sword belt—three smaller belts making up the whole of it. A brown leather scalloped pad sat on his left shoulder, capping his strong muscles, and a small brown belt strapped across his chest. There was no cape attached to this shoulder pad as there was on her own brother's. This was simply an adornment of his status: the Commander of the only actual army Haerland had ever unleashed on her shores.

On his bowed lips, he carried a soft domineering smile that Nyssa wanted to slap off his perfectly gorgeous face. She allowed her gaze to wash over him the closer he approached, noticing the bare of his feet, the golden goblet in his hand. And when he finally reached them, he set his cup on the table, soft eyes looking down his nose at her, mouth slightly agape, and then he looked straight past her to Bala.

She didn't miss the teasing smile that rose in his eyes, replacing the smolder, and he relaxed sideways against the tabletop.

"Looking delectable, Bala," Nadir told her.

Bala looked as though she would burst into laughter. "Mmhmm... Don't come over here acting as though you've any interest in speaking with me," she mocked. "I'm aware of the circumstances."

"So then you'll be a good friend and stand here acting as though I'm talking to you while I speak with the Princess," he said, turning his attention *back to Nyssa.*

Bala chuckled behind her cup. "You've two minutes."

Nyssa's cheeks reddened beneath his stare, her heart constricting at the sight of his cerulean gaze penetrating through her own. He reached out for her hand then, and she cursed herself for the quirk of a smile on her lips.

"Hello, Princess," he purred, lips brushing her knuckles.

Her jaw tightened to keep herself from grinning. The wine was still very much relevant in her body, and she felt the swim of courage pulse through her just as much as she felt the heat radiating over her entire body.

"It's Nyssari, right?" he asked.

"Nyssa," she answered.

"I'm —"

"I know who you are, Commander," she said, hugging her cup tighter to her chest. "You're the one I've been told not to flirt with or become engulfed upon, although I've not really been told why. Which leads me to believe you've either done something very wrong or very right, and my sister simply doesn't want my heart to be broken by such a man."

Nadir paused, apparently considering her words. "That —"

"Sounds exactly correct," Bala cut in behind them. "Ninety seconds."

Nadir grunted under his breath. "Your sister is overprotective."

"She's my sister. She's supposed to be."

"Are you going to stand here speaking about the Queen, or are you actually going to compliment the beauty standing before you?" Bala cut in.

"I can't speak to her if you keep interrupting," he glared.

Bala pushed her cup to her smiling lips, and she turned her attention to the dancing again, catching Dorian swinging one of the Scindo twins around.

Nadir didn't say anything as his throat bobbed, and his gaze darted over Nyssa's face once more.

"Is something wrong?" she asked, tucking her hair behind her ear.

"Ah..." a quiet scoff left him, and he glanced down at the floor before meeting her eyes again, a small yet nervous smile on his face. "I'm sorry. This is... it's difficult to be here and not allow myself to try and swoon you."

"So why did you bother coming over?"

"Honestly, I was hoping you'd be this horrendous person and tell me to fuck off. Save me the pain of having to walk away from you without at least asking for a dance."

A soft laugh left her, and when she met his smirking, delight-filled gaze, she was reminded of the words her sister had said.

She sat her cup on the table before crossing her arms over her chest. "Perhaps you could describe the dance we would have had instead."

She watched his throat move with deliberation once more, and she knew he was trying to work out her game of whether she was serious or not. His eyes traveled over her, lingering on her dress only for a moment before he set his own cup down and turned directly to face her. "I—"

"That's time," Bala said as she pushed off the table.

Nadir snapped out of his daze, and his features faltered as Bala started to walk away. "What—No—Bala—wait— come on!—" Nadir's fist clenched in the air just as Bala left them, and he cursed under his breath.

"You're trying really hard, aren't you?" Nyssa teased.

He sighed heavily at her words, his hand reaching into his own hair as though he could push his fingers through it. "I respect your sister. So as much as I'd love to take you on to this dance floor and put the Blackhands to shame, I'll have to settle for the two minutes of conversation Bala was nice enough to allow us to have."

"I suppose that's it then?" Nyssa asked. "You'll be off to woo one of these Blackhand women? Charm one of them into your bed?"

The blue-green of his eyes was hardly apparent with the dilation he looked at her with. He grabbed his own cup, and the right corner of his lip quirked just so. "I doubt I'd enjoy it now."

"Why not?"

"None of them are you."

She had to bite her lips to conceal the outburst of laughter she so desperately needed to release. She wondered how many other women he'd used that same line on before.

"I can't believe you just said that," she mocked, eyes watering at trying to hold in the laughter. "Does that usually work?"

He hung his head as though she'd scolded him. "Occasionally," he admitted.

Nyssa snorted into her cup despite herself. "Those poor women," she bantered.

Nadir chuckled out loud this time, his head swinging back. "You know, you're really not helping our situation."

"And I really don't know what you mean."

"I think you know exactly what I mean," he said before taking another sip of his drink. "Do you know what else I think?"

She was grateful for the table behind her, knowing she would have been swaying with the wine otherwise. But she smiled crookedly up at him nonetheless, and she hugged her arm into her chest. "I don't, but I have a feeling you're going to tell me."

He leaned closer to her, his hand pressing into the table almost at her back.

"I think you're much more dangerous than anyone in this room gives you credit for," he uttered in such a low tone that the purr of it caused the hair on her arms to raise.

Nyssa cleared her throat and forced down the flutter in her chest, grabbing onto her sarcastic defense.

"That's a bit of an insult, Commander. How dare you," she bantered.

Nadir laughed under his breath. "I do dare, Princess," he winked.

She started to retort, but the appearance of Draven crossing the dance floor and joining her sister diverted her attention. She knew by the look on her sister's face that she would notice no others in the room.

So Nyssa pushed off the table and held out her arm to Nadir.

"Come. I'll show you who's available."

He eyed her, gaze narrowing with deliberate tension. "I'm not sure that's smart," he finally determined.

"Come now, Commander," she said. "We can't take each other back to our beds tonight, even if it is something we both want—"

His brows arched high, but she ignored his inherent surprise.

"—The least I can do is help find someone suitable to take my place," she finished.

"I'll need you to repeat the first part again."

Her head tilted at his banter, and finally, Nadir took her arm.

"Lead the way, Princess."—

"—Nys?"

The noise of Dorian's voice brought her back to her current reality.

Nyssa blinked, breath coming back to her.

"Nys?" Dorian called again. "You okay?"

Nyssa gripped the banister and turned to find her brother coming up the stairs. "Yeah," she managed. "Yeah. I'm fine. Something wrong?"

"Bala asked for you," he informed her. "You sure you're okay?"

"Yeah," she repeated as she pushed her boots on. She didn't know how to explain what had just happened to her, so she chose to keep it to herself.

Dorian walked her downstairs, but he did not join her to the armory where Bala was. He told her she was talking to Nadir, straightening out details, and that Bala had wanted Nyssa to help them with something. Bala had been vague, and Nyssa knew why.

Bala didn't want Dorian interjecting himself into whatever it was Nadir needed help with.

Raised voices sounded inside as she approached, and she paused on the other side of the door to listen.

"—want me to take her back with me?" Nadir was arguing. "I don't have time to look after her. I have my own people to look after, or did you forget I've strangers on my shores building themselves a village in the west?"

"No one is asking you to look after her," Bala countered. "And she can help you. She's versed in negotiations. Aydra was meant to bring her along the next time you all went to meet the strangers."

"Who's brilliant idea was that?" he muttered.

"Dorian's."

"Yeah, like he's much of a savior."

"Draven trusted him."

Her words stalemated the room, and Nadir stopped moving. His jaw tightened, nostrils flared. Bala crossed her arms over her chest.

"Draven trusted Dorian. So I trust Dorian," Bala continued. "If that means trusting Nyssari to try and negotiate with these people, then that's what we must do. You know she will see things that you have not, especially when you go to their camp. We do not have the men or power to continue to push at them. We have to find a middle ground. You know this, Nadir. You've known this for weeks now." Bala paused a moment to stare at Nadir's pacing figure. "I thought you liked her."

"I *do* like her—that's part of the problem," Nadir said, hands threaded behind his neck. "She'll be a distraction. I'll constantly be worrying whether she's okay or not. I don't have time for that—"

"If you think for a minute that she'll be flouncing around you in frilly dresses desperate for your attention, then you don't know her at all." Bala pushed off the table and rounded in front of him. "Her sister was just burned alive in front of her. The first thing on her mind is not how pretty you think you are or how charming your smile might be."

"I'm not worried about her being distracted," Nadir snapped. "Once she's settled, I'm sure she'll do the job fine. Probably tell me to go fuck myself in the process. That's not my concern. I'm worried about *me*," he admitted.

"Then handle your distraction," Bala snapped. "That is your problem, not hers. Do you think you can keep your dick in your pants long enough for us to take care of our realms? Or should I send a guard of Venari with her to make sure she stays focused?"

Nadir glared at her for a long enough moment that Nyssa had to force breath into her lungs from the still silence.

"Fuck you, Bala."

A quirk of a smile rose at the corner of Bala's lips. "You can come in, Nys," she called out.

Nyssa's heart skipped. She didn't realize Bala knew she was there.

Fucking Venari wind.

Bala had heard her footsteps on it.

Nyssa stepped inside. Her stomach knotted at the sight of Nadir's rapt stare, bewildered and obviously flustered that she had been outside. But his gaze traveled predatorily over her nonetheless, and her breath snagged in her throat.

"Hello, Commander," she said firmly, arms wrapping over her chest, back straightening and chin lifting as if she could make herself taller.

For a long moment, he didn't speak. And she knew why.

She knew hearing those two words come from her lips was making him question everything he was about to say.

"How long have you been standing there?" he finally asked her.

"Long enough."

Bala turned, picked up a few knives from the display, and then pushed past Nadir. "I'll leave you two to straighten out the details."

She exited from the room, and Nyssa continued to watch Nadir's unmoving eyes.

"I cannot look after you," he said once Bala was gone.

"Don't worry. I'll keep myself hidden so as not to be some great *distraction* to you," she snapped.

"Was this your idea? Coming to my realm?"

"You certainly think highly of yourself."

"You know—"

"I know *what*, Nadir?" she nearly shouted, the same anger from her fight with Dorian coming to the surface. "What, you think I asked if I could go to your realm because we shared a couple of sleepless nights together? That you were so amazing, *godly* in fact, in bed that you think I am here to fall over your feet and beg you to take me into your arms? Do you think I am some hopeless girl with no more wish than that to fuck you again? Do you think that's what I want?"

"What do you want, Princess?"

She stared at him, jaw quivering at the ludicrousness of his question. "I want my sister back. I want for this whole mess to never have happened—"

"What you want is ignorance," he seethed. "Comfort. To not be challenged or told you're wrong. You were given everything in that castle. Never knowing what it was like for someone to talk down to you because your sister ensured that no one ever did. She paved that way for you. She made life easier for you because no one ever did for her. You should be thanking her for throwing herself into those flames."

"Why would I—"

"Because if she hadn't, you would be defending yourself from your own guard instead of being able to be here focusing on defending this world and your people."

"I *am* battling against my own guard," she argued. "You think we didn't just have to dodge companies of Belwarks and Dreamers on our way here? Do you think they were happy about Dorian taking Draven that horn? Setting him free to do what he did to our castle? We are marked. There are bounties on our heads. We no longer have a kingdom to even defend."

Nadir ran his hands through his hair and then over his face, pausing a moment to consider her. She could see the bite back in his clenched teeth, the irritation in his gaze despite the dilation he watched her with. And then, finally, his hands came to rest on his hips.

"Do not come with me because you feel you have to or because you feel as though you owe my people something," he said lowly. "And not because Bala told you you would be safe there from the people trying to take her kingdom either. Come with me because you want to help us defend this world. This isn't a holiday. This is a war zone."

A fire blazed in her chest, and she glared up at him. "Then you'll show me to my station when we get there, Commander."

He paused over her, apparently debating her words.

"Grab your Second and get on my boat. We leave in an hour."

Telling her brother goodbye was tougher than Nyssa thought it would be. She didn't know when or even if she would see him again. They held onto each other for a long enough moment that she almost broke in his arms. He pulled back, his hands cupping her face, and they repeated the words that they'd promised each other on the beach.

Small smiles rose on both their faces at the words. Dorian brushed the tear from her cheek. "Stop crying," he choked teasingly. "If you cry, I cry. Can't let that happen. I've a reputation, you know."

"Oh, wouldn't that be a sight," she mocked, sniffing back the tears with a smile. "The great Dorian Eaglefyre crying. Someone call the scribe so we can write this moment down in the Chronicles."

"One of us has to be the strong, handsome one." His gaze flickered over her shoulder to Corbin. "Right, Bin?" he called out.

Corbin just stared at him, eyes narrowing, before turning back to helping Lex load up the boat. Dorian grinned at Nyssa, and Nyssa almost laughed.

"We'll be lucky if he doesn't leave you in the Mortis Lunar Pass," she muttered.

"I'm sure he'll try."

Nyssa huffed and hugged him one last time. Dorian always smelled like he was on fire. The sweetness of a flame being lit and the last embers of wood burning. Anytime she was away from him, she would always light a fire, whether it was the middle of a bright, hot summer day or if it was the dead of winter.

"Nyssari," Lex called out from the boat. "We're ready."

But Nyssa wasn't ready to give him up.

"Reach out for me every now and then so I know you're safe," Dorian said softly.

She finally pulled back and nodded. "I will. Try not to do anything stupid while you're there. I cannot imagine the Blackhands will be happy about what happened."

Dorian took a step back and gave her his best crooked smile, the one that made her head shake. "What would be the fun in not getting in trouble?" he grinned.

Nyssa looked at Corbin. "Try to take care of him?"

Corbin glanced between the two. "No promises."

Nyssa huffed, and Dorian stuffed his hands in his pockets, giving Corbin a leering smirk.

"I know you're joking, Corbin," Nyssa said, "but really. Try to keep him alive for me."

A small smile lifted his lips, and Corbin nodded in response.

Lex was relaxed at the front of the boat as Nadir showed her how to steer it when Nyssa finally joined them. Nyssa chose one of the boxes of traded goods he had piled in to sit on, and she pulled her knees into her chest just as they set off.

It wasn't long until she heard footsteps, and then a warm body sat next to her. She didn't need to look up to know it was Nadir.

"Are we going to talk about this?" Nadir practically whispered.

Nyssa wasn't sure what to say. She pressed her shoulders back and looked out at the river, attempting to pull her numbness to the forefront of her core and not think about the knot that made her want to vomit.

"Talk about what?" she breathed. "The fact that you think I'm some love-drunk girl who only gives a damn about romance and having your attention?"

"That's not—"

Her eyes cut to him, and she knew if she'd had her brother's fire that her gaze would be black. "You told me that night you'd hoped I would be some horrendous person and tell you to go fuck yourself," she spat. "So here's your wish: go fuck yourself, Nadir."

She glared and turned back to the river, allowing the noise to fill her ears again, and she hugged her trembling knees tighter in her chest. Nadir's energy was uncomfortable beside her, and after a few minutes, she felt him shift.

"I'm sorry," he whispered. "For earlier. What I said."

"You shouldn't be," she said. "I deserve everything you've said. I'm not some great warrior. I'm not my sister. I'm nothing more than a terrified girl who has no idea what she's doing. You have every right to not want me there."

"Nyssa—"

"I cannot do this, Nadir," she snapped, feeling her nose begin to burn.

The noise of her eagle screeching overhead made her eyes close. Even if she couldn't understand him, he was still there, and that helped her aching heart.

Nadir's hand hovered over her leg as though he would squeeze her thigh, but he hesitated, and she heard him sigh. "How are you?" Nadir finally asked, his voice barely audible.

She pondered the question a moment and debated her answer. She wanted to scream again, to let out the frustration and sorrow her body felt, the angst of her ripping heart, the swollen knot in her stomach...

but she settled for the answer she'd been spewing for a week.

"I'm fine," she whispered.

He must have heard the break in her voice, for the next thing she knew, he had wrapped an arm around her, and despite everything she'd said to him in the last few hours, she sank into his embrace.

"I'm glad you're okay," he said before pressing his lips to her head and pulling her entirely into his arms. "*Curses of Duarb*, I'm glad you're okay."

10

Dorian paused at Bala's side as the boats left. His arms crossed over his chest, and he stared sideways at her.

"Speak, Prince," Bala said without so much as a look at him.

"If anything should happen to my sister, it won't be Man burning this forest to the ground," he swore.

"If anything should happen to her, I'll help you destroy the reef myself," she replied. "Your sister will be fine. Nadir will let her become who she needs to be. He'll trust her. Draven trusted Nadir with his life, so I trust Nadir. Nyssari means a great deal to me, as do you. I wouldn't know where to begin without either of you."

"Is that the only reason we mean anything?" he asked.

A quirk of a smile rose on her lips. "No," she said. "I'm quite fond of you both, and as much as it pains me to admit it... I find you both adorable as well as great company."

Her arms continued to stay crossed over her chest as they began walking back to her kingdom. Dorian couldn't stop thinking about the look on Nyssa's face when she'd left—almost as though she were telling him a final goodbye. But he couldn't dwell on it, and he forced himself to acknowledge that this was the right thing to do.

"How will I know if what I'm doing is the right thing?"

"You won't."

"I admire the way you protect her," Bala said after a few moments, making Dorian blink back his tears.

Dorian broke off a small twig from a bush and began to toy with it. "Is there any other way to protect my sister?"

"No, I mean... I know the way previous Kings treated their sisters."

"How do you know about that?"

"I overheard Aydra telling Draven about it when we traveled back home after Rhaif killed her raven," she told him. "I'm glad to know that will die with him."

"I will protect my sister at any cost," he promised. "I will not allow what happened to Drae to happen to Nyssa."

"Your sister knew what she was doing."

Dorian shook his head as his own guilt poured through him. He started snapping the twig into small pieces. "I should have helped Draven burn it to the ground," he said. "I should have sliced my brother's throat before leaving."

"What and left your ignorant Council in charge?"

"Pretty sure they're plotting some sort of takeover anyway," Dorian argued. He ran a hand through his hair, fluffing it up nervously. "Unfortunately, all I can hear is Drae's last words. Promising him to be tortured the rest of his days." The memory of the day he'd come back from the mountains and found Rhaif had hurt Nyssa filled him with a rage so intense, the twig turned to ash in his hand.

Bala's brows raised as she stepped back, but Dorian shook his head as though it were an everyday thing.

"When I do finally take his life, I will make him repeat every poor word he ever said to her," he promised. "Watch him die slowly and deliberately, blood pooling in the back of his throat as though he is a deer strung up for slaughter. Mercilessly as he did her."

"Dark words for a Fire Prince."

"Promises from a brother who never knew what it was like to feel any sort of brotherly bond with someone that should have been a mentor and a best friend." He kicked the dirt, hands stuffing in his pockets. "He was never anything more than a King to me."

"What, you never shared any secrets? Inside jokes or laughter?"

"No..." Dorian sighed, recalling their past. "Nyssa and I were marked a full Dead Moons cycle before him when we were eight. It wasn't our fault our mother chose to mark us first, but somehow he always took that fact out on me. He never liked me, never allowed me to even share the same room with him on his own." He paused in his speech as they stepped over a fallen tree. "I don't remember ever hearing him laugh."

"You and Nyssa were marked together? Before Rhaif?"

"We were."

"She marked you at the same time? Like... gave you your fire at the same moment she marked Nyssa?"

"She did… Why do you ask?"

"No reason," Bala replied quickly.

A little too quickly.

"What about Rhaif's relationship with Nyssa?" Bala said then, changing the subject. "Was he so horrible to her?"

"Ah… No, actually. He was quite fond of her. Always told her she was quietly ambitious, which he liked as she never much spoke out of turn in front of him. But their relationship stayed mostly in that Council room. He grew to depend on her to notice any lies or exaggerations from the Council."

"Eyes of Haerland," Bala muttered.

Dorian's brow flinched in agreement, but he didn't reply to the comment. The anger started to swell in him again as he remembered how heartbroken Nyssa had been when Rhaif kicked her out of all meetings after the Gathering.

"I imagine you'd like Corbin and me to leave as soon as possible?" he asked.

"I would," she agreed. "I know it is the afternoon, but it has already been ten days since everything happened, and it will take you nearly five days to get to Dahrkenhill with the Dead Moons over us. I sent word to Hagen yesterday that you would be coming. You should be prepared for a company to find you at the Knotted Caves entrance."

"You knew we would accept?"

"I wasn't exactly asking, Prince," she informed him.

Dorian gave her a sideways smirk. "Venari King, indeed," he teased. "Is there anything you wish us to take along the way?"

"Just common sense," Bala answered.

Dorian almost laughed. "Thanks for the vote of confidence."

"You're welcome."

11

Nyssa laid in the bed for two days upon arriving at the Umber.

Two days of Lex coming in and checking on her, and Nyssa telling her nothing more than she was fine. Two days of her eagle staying by her side, knowing she could not hear him, but staying nonetheless.

Nadir had offered his home to her and Lex. It was a small shack, never meant for more than two people, but they made it work. Lex slept on the couch, insisting she wanted to be out in the open to keep an eye on things. Nadir had assured her nothing would come to harm them there, for he was the greatest threat, and no one would go against him.

The manner of his cockiness and the wink he'd given her after the statement had nearly brought a smile to Nyssa's face. She knew he was trying to make it all seem normal, and despite the hurt in her chest, she could not have been more grateful.

It was the afternoon of the second day when Nyssa finally tucked herself into a robe and went onto the porch. Salty air greeted her, and she closed her eyes to take it in. Her arms hugged across her chest. She sat down on the step and leaned her head against the railing.

Teal waves crashed onto each other. The sky was streaked purple and orange with the sunset. This was a different sunset than the one she was used to seeing at Magnice. Something about this one... perhaps it was the pale teal water with the slightly visible reef far out past the jetties. How the sunlight seemed to awaken the sea's very existence. As though the ocean itself were alive.

The Ghosts of the Sun and the Sea seemed to dance together—as perhaps they once had—to create the magnificence of such a sunset.

Whatever magic it was, it called to her.

The sight of Lex and Nadir making their way back to his shack made Nyssa hug her knees tighter. She'd barely spoken to them. Honestly, she wasn't sure what she was supposed to say. How she was supposed to act. She was trying her hardest to keep it together.

Lex caught her eyes first and gave her a small smile. But Nadir... When she found his gaze, his walk slowed, and he peered at her as though he was just seeing her for the first time.

Lex hit the steps before him. "The Princess rises," she teased.

"Trying," Nyssa replied, though her voice was barely audible.

Lex paused beside her and gave her hair a ruffle, much like Aydra used to give Dorian. Nyssa's jaw immediately quivered at the sensation of it, but she forced it away.

"I'll grab you some food," Lex said before going inside.

Nadir took each step deliberately and then sat beside her with a long sigh, gaze washing out to the ocean as the wind circled around them.

"Not exactly how I pictured your first time on my beach," he said softly.

"It's beautiful," she said. "It's no wonder you speak of it with such high esteem."

"It's home," Nadir replied simply. "Perhaps I can show you more of it tomorrow afternoon."

The first genuine smile she'd felt since arriving, as small as it may have been, rose on her lips when he locked eyes with her. "I'd like that," she managed.

Nadir reached over, took her hand in his, and brought it to his lips. Her stomach fluttered at the feeling of his mouth against her skin again. It sent her mind back to Magnice, reminding her of how they'd walked around the room together. He'd held firmly onto her arm so she did not waver with the remaining bit of wine in her.

They'd stopped walking when the music picked up, and Nyssa wrapped her arms around her chest as she leaned against the stone. She had watched the dancing, noticing Aydra's head thrown back at whatever it was Draven had just whispered in her ear, the unfamiliar blush on her sister's cheeks. Nyssa turned her attention to Dorian dancing with one of the Scindo twins, sure that he would take both of them back to his room, but the look Councilwoman Ebonrath was giving him across the room made her snort into her cup.

"What's so funny?" Nadir had asked.

Nyssa leaned over and pointed at her brother. "The girl my brother is dancing with is one of his favorites. He usually takes her and her sister back to bed with him, but if you look by the buffet, you'll see another one of his favorites looking as though she would give anything to be in his arms."

A low whistle emitted from his lips upon seeing the Councilwoman's stare. "If looks could kill," he muttered.

Nyssa continued and pointed back to Corbin. "You see Corbin standing in the shadows by the pillar? He's only just been named Dorian's Second, the Fire Second. I love watching the disapproval on his face when Dorian is doing something stupid or 'un-prince-like,' as Corbin calls it. He always gets a little twitch in his nose. His hands grip either the hilt of his sword or his cup. Look at him—" she almost laughed at the twinge in Corbin's gaze "—Dorian is trying to break Corbin's facade, but he's failing miserably. Oh, and there, Councilwoman Reid has been sleeping with Ash since he left my sister's bed. She thinks no one has noticed, but I caught them making eyes at the last meeting and then in the Chambers all this week during meetings with my older. You can always tell with Reid when she gets nervous. She starts fumbling with her bracelets. She—" Nyssa paused, having to look twice up at Nadir, who was staring at her with squinted eyes.

"What?" she asked.

"How do you know all of this?" he asked.

"I'm skilled at reading people," she admitted. "Perks of being the smallest and quietest in the room."

"Who lied and told you you were the quietest?" he teased.

She almost laughed but instead nudged him in his side. "Shut up," she muttered. She tucked her hair behind her ear and smiled down at the cup in her hands.

"I'm sorry," she managed. "I'm sure you don't want to hear any of this."

"Why would you think that?"

"We've only just met," she said. "You were probably looking for some woman to simply charm back into your bed... Quietly, at that. Not someone to talk to you about gossip and reading people's ticks."

"I actually love gossip," he informed her. "Tell me all their secrets, Princess."

"All of them?" she repeated. "That might take a while. We could get caught."

Nadir's gaze flickered to Aydra and Draven, and he gave an upwards nod in their direction. "Look at them and tell me if they notice anything else going on in this room."

Nyssa knew he was right. "Okay, Commander. I'll tell you all their secrets, but first, I want to know what this dance we didn't get to have would have been like."

Nadir chuckled at her under his breath. "Of course you do," he joked. He sighed and leaned back against the wall again, letting his head sink onto the stone. "All right, Princess. What do you want to know?"

"I want to know what it would have been like. As if I'd been any other woman you would have liked to take in your bed."

"What like if I'd been wooing one of the Dreamers or Blackhands?" he asked.

"Yes."

The smile on his lips made her heart flutter. "First, I would have introduced myself as the greatest Commander the Honest army has ever had —"

Nyssa snorted. "The greatest Comman— I'm sorry, you were speaking," she mocked. "Please continue," she said, tears rising from holding in the laughter.

His eyes narrowed playfully, but he continued anyway. "I would have boasted about the last battle we fought, knowing you knew little of the war but hoping you would be impressed by my bravery. Eventually, I'd have complimented your beauty, telling you how your eyes glowed in the fires, how it reminded me of the Eyes festivals we have back at the Umber where we have these huge bonfires on the beach, and we dance all night beneath the bright twin moons. You would have eaten another pastry after I insisted you needed something sweet to match the delicacy of your aura —"

Nyssa snorted again.

That brow elevated, and she muttered a quick "Sorry" to him as he shifted his weight.

Something changed in his energy then, and she felt it... The seriousness rising in his shoulders, his tongue darting out over his lips. He was hovering so close over her then that she had to swallow the dryness in her suddenly parched mouth.

"I would have wiped the powdered sugar from the corner of your lips," he continued, his voice softer, "felt the beat of your heart beneath my fingertips on your wrist." His touch whispered against her skin, and her breath heightened.

"The music would have picked up or slowed down, and I would have led you to the middle of the floor, where I would have held on to you until the pull of us became so much I would have had to stop only to stare at your laughing face. I would have brushed my thumb against your jaw, held your face a breath from mine, and told you I'd noticed no other since walking into this room. I would have told you how your spinning in this dress had me mesmerized the entire night—" He paused, his fingers curling around the *fabric of her sleeves, and his lashes lifted.*

Nyssa cleared her throat to snap herself out of her own daze. "And that would have secured my place in your bed?" she asked.

He huffed amusedly under his breath, the dominating facade breaking, and he hung his head briefly. "Probably not with you. But it would have left an impression."

"An impression is all you need, isn't it?"

"Always leave them wanting more," he said with a wink.

For a moment, she couldn't move. Couldn't blink. She didn't know if perhaps it was the story Nadir had just told, how she'd imagined every word he'd said, picturing herself in his arms as he danced with her around that room... Wiping icing from her mouth, his thumb stroking her jaw, his arms around her... But she wanted it.

She wanted it terribly.

The dilation in his eyes, the softening of his smile, the bob of his throat as his hand brushed her arm again... None of that was helping her stay away from him despite everything her sister had said.

"I think I need some air," she finally determined.

Nadir blinked, breath leaving him. "Yeah. Me too."

She pushed off the wall and strode out the double doors, making her way with him behind her to the terrace at the end of the hall that overlooked the whole of the kingdom. Nyssa didn't stop when the night air hit her face. She kept walking until she hit the railing. Her hands gripped the stone banister, and she closed her eyes, allowing the sea breeze to hit her cheeks. Moons' light cascaded down over her, and when she finally turned, she found Nadir standing in the middle of the open space.

"I was right," he said, stepping slowly towards her.

"About what?"

"You being the most dangerous person in that room."

He paused a breath away. She could see the battle he was having with himself in his features. Her cheeks flushed, heartbeat in her ears, fingers stretching at her sides as she itched to touch him. She allowed her hands to breeze his stomach, toying with his shirt, and then she felt his fingertips graze the back of her arm.

"This is a really bad idea," Nadir breathed.

Her eyes rose to his, head tilting back. His breath was sweet on her skin as his head bent, causing her heart to pound.

"Very bad," she agreed.

"I think you lured me out here just to be alone with me," he continued.

She almost laughed, the smile on his lips so close to hers that her chest caved. *"I didn't tell you to follow."*

Her heart did a somersault as his other hand touched her waist. Mouth opening and closing in front of him, battling with the decision to let herself have him or respect her sister's wishes. His forehead pressed to hers, and her chest fell with the jaggedness of her breath.

She was going to explode from the tension of having him so close to her.

"How could I have possibly resisted any moment alone with you?"

His words sent her spinning. Before she gave herself a moment to reconsider, she grasped his tunic in her hands, and she pressed her lips to his.

It was the most horribly beautiful idea she'd ever had.

A very bad—oh, but very good— idea.

She could feel the surprise in his features, but after a second, he groaned into her mouth, and his arms locked around her. His tongue slipped in her mouth, and she found herself in another realm. Arms wrapping around his neck, she pulled him closer. Heat pulsed from her chest down between her legs. Every sweep of his tongue sent her spiraling deeper. She was sure her heart would burst at the nerves threading through her.

Water over her head. Lungs tight. Muscles feigning.

She was drowning in his embrace.

And she didn't want to come up for air.

His arms bent behind her back and pulled her flush. So flush, he nearly pulled her off the ground. His hands threaded in her hair and in the tulle on the bottom of her dress. She'd never felt so wanted by anyone before. He consumed her—tasting of salt and wine and everything she ever wanted.

After a few moments, he pulled back, and his hand pressed to her cheek. Both were breathless and struggling to steady. She stared up at the darkness in his pupils.

"I am so dead," he whispered.—

—"Nyssa?"

She was back on his beach, Nadir still sitting in front of her, her hand in his. She inhaled a sharp breath as she returned back to the present.

"Sorry," she whispered. "I've just been... My mind keeps replaying things," she admitted. "I think it's trying to take me back to a simpler time."

How easily the words came from her lips surprised her. He squeezed her hand and whispered, "Tell me about it," against her skin just as Lex came back onto the porch.

"She's been awake an hour, Commander, and you're already swooning her?" Lex mocked.

Nyssa smiled as Nadir feigned surprise. "I really don't know what you mean," he said.

The grin on his face didn't waiver, and he winked quietly upon meeting her gaze.

Nyssa ate the pastries and stew that Lex had brought her while Lex and Nadir smoked and chatted about the day. Lex was asking him questions about his army and the different legions. Nyssa knew she should have been listening, but she couldn't stop staring at all the new sights around her. She'd hardly had a moment to take it all in when they'd arrived the first night.

After a while, Lex retired, and Nyssa insisted she take the bed and told her she wanted to sleep outside that night and get some fresh air. Honestly, Nyssa just wanted to feel the wind on her face and smell the familiar salt in the breeze.

"I nearly forgot," Nadir said once they were alone. "I had something I wanted to show you. Hang on. You'll love it."

She squinted at the smile on his face. He stood before she had a chance to question him. His pop inside was brief, and when he emerged back out, she chuckled at the sight of him holding up two books.

"Thought you might like these," he said as he sat down beside her.

She poured over the rich leather-bound book he gave her, even bringing it to her nose to smell, which he laughed at.

"What book do you have?" she asked.

"You'll not be able to read this one," he said, flipping through the pages.

"Why's that?"

"It's written in the old language."

"Really?" she asked as he opened it up for her to see.

The script practically jumped off the page. There was a beauty in the curves of each line. As though the words were alive and were meant to seep into her very core. She allowed her fingers to brush over the inscriptions. The lettering was unfamiliar, and yet... she swore she knew it.

Something about it comforted her.

"Is it like the one you showed me at Magnice?" she asked. "Written by a Lesser One?"

"This was written by one of our people," he said. "Short stories of fantasies and things that never happened."

"Could you teach me?" she asked.

"The language? Why do you want to learn?"

"It would be nice to know what your people are saying."

Nadir paused, eyeing her sideways. *"Iiyii,"* he uttered in a mocking tone.

"See!" she exclaimed. "What was that?"

His smirk widened. "I'm not sure you've earned it."

"Will you read it to me instead?"

Nadir sighed softly, considering her with that mesmerizing gaze. "All the things in the world you could ask for... And you just want me to read fantastical stories with you?" he mocked.

"The stories are always there," Nyssa said, tucking her hair back. "Beautiful and constant. Holding truth and pain and desire with every turn of the page. I can hear a story one day and know that that story will not have changed when I go back to it. If there is one thing in my life I will always be able to control, it is that. I do not know a greater comfort."

"Says the one that didn't believe words were supposed to be so beautiful," he mocked, referring to words she'd said the night they spent together.

"I have never heard words be as beautiful as those you read that night," she admitted. "And my statement still stands: I think you bring that book to help you swoon women into your arms."

"You're the one asking me to read more books just like it to you."

"A small comfort and escape from the current reality around us," she told him.

Nadir watched her a moment, his smile soft, and then he whispered, "Hello, Princess."

It was the first time he'd said it since her arrival, and the two words made her heart warm.

"Hello, Commander," she whispered back.

Their words.

He huffed, his smile widening. It was all she could do to keep her composure as he wrapped his arm around the back of the bench behind her. She turned sideways in the seat, pulled her knees into her chest, and Nadir cleared his throat in his usual comical way as he opened up the book to the first page.

He read her stories well into the night, first in the old language, followed by the translation of some if she asked for it. She sat beside him, moving her body to tuck into his when she started tiring, switching to him lying in her lap when his arms became heavy, to finally her lying between his legs, her back against his torso as she held the book and he read... Until her eyes drooped, and she fell asleep to the sound of his words and the crash of the waves.

12

Nadir was *fast*.

Nyssa couldn't pull her eyes away.

She didn't know how the bantering male she'd found herself consumed with at one time was also this person. This... *warrior*... His blades whipped quickly in his hands. He moved and pushed the person back he was fighting, whirling with each advance, and finally, he swept his opponent off their feet.

The water splashed around them where they parried. It was a whirlwind of silver and iron and waves. She couldn't help staring at every flex of his torso, every jolt and urge of his arms. His balance didn't falter even when a wave crashed into his shins, and his opponent stumbled.

The other male fell on his back, and the first smile of the day rose on Nadir's lips. He helped his friend up from the ground before the next wave could crash over him, clapping his shoulder and laughing about something. Nadir's head shook, and then he began moving his arms as though showing his friend what he'd done wrong. The male nodded in appreciation to Nadir, and Nadir gave him an encouraging handshake before calling out to someone else. The new person ran forward. Nadir clapped his person on the shoulder, explained something to them, and then he grinned between them before moving on and leaving the pair to parry together.

Nyssa hugged her arms around her chest, feeling herself biting the insides of her cheeks as she observed how gracious and doting the Commander was on his people.

But Nadir caught her stare, and he paused at the edge of the water, gaze wandering so predatorily through her that her weight shifted, and she couldn't help the feeling of her lips daring to rise at the corners. Nadir whirled his swords once before the right corner of his mouth quirked upwards just a flinch... And then he gave her a quick wink as he turned on his heel and went to help another couple.

For most of the afternoon, Nyssa walked up and down the dunes and watched the legions train. Lex chose to train with them, insisting that if Nyssa wasn't ready to join, she would practice in her place. Nyssa knew it was only to keep her mind occupied. Lex had hardly shown any emotion since everything happened, but Nyssa had seen the exhausted sadness behind her eyes.

Nyssa only left the beach mid-afternoon to stroll through the middle of the village where the Honest people were bustling with goods. But... there was an uncomfortableness that she couldn't put her finger on when she did.

Women huddled together with whispers upon her approach, and a few men paused to watch her. At first, she was too interested in the quality and plethora of their goods to truly notice, but once she did, she felt her very existence was being scrutinized. Hushed voices. Tightened jaws. Hollow stares.

Her feet led her back out to the jetty once she'd become so overwhelmed with the looks that she could not stand it any longer. She noticed Nadir training once more on logs out over the ocean. His quick feet moved in unison with the rolling timber, bamboo stick knocking with his opponent. Every now and then, the two would waiver, nearly lose their balance, but Nadir never did. And when his friend fell into the ocean, Nadir laughed heartily, pointing at the male as he rose to the surface. He tried to swat at him, but Nadir jumped into the sea on his own.

Nyssa couldn't help her quiet chuckle as she watched the two grown males fight in the water. She heard the pair laughing from where she stood. Nadir caught her eyes then, and she gave him a small smile before starting out onto the rocky jetty to meet him.

Nadir pulled himself up out of the water at the end of it, hardly bothering to do anything more to dry himself than squeeze the excess water out of his pulled-back hair.

"Come to join?" he asked as they reached each other.

"I've never seen someone move blades so quickly," she said. "Especially in water."

"Learn to balance in the surf or on those logs, and you can balance anywhere," he explained. "The ocean is relentless. Unyielding. Just as any good opponent should be."

"My sister did not think Man's soldiers to be so formidable."

Nadir rubbed his neck, a sign she'd learned about him that meant he was genuinely thinking over her words. "A different sort of formidable," he uttered in a low tone. He started unbuckling the pad attached to his shoulder and strapped around his bare torso.

"Why do I get the feeling you would kick every one of my soldier's asses if I let you onto this beach with a sword?" he asked.

Nyssa huffed under her breath. "I don't know what you mean."

Nadir smiled softly. "Most dangerous person in the room."

He was lifting the shoulder pad over his head then, his muscles stretching and twisting with his every movement. She didn't guard her stare and instead allowed her eyes to travel over his sculpted abs, the taut ripples on his sides over his ribs, her gaze even going as low as to notice the vein she'd licked once at the vee of his hip... Muscles that looked as though the sea itself had carved them out of its depths.

Which she was reminded, it had.

"That's two, Princess," he said.

Nyssa snapped herself out of her daze and forced her eyes back to his face. "What?"

He threw the shoulder pad lazily over his forearm. "I'm noting every time you leer at me. I've caught you staring twice now."

"You don't know what you're talking about," she lied.

"I could help you if you wanted."

Nyssa balked at the abruptness of the change in conversation. "Help with what?"

"Your training. Give you something new to learn. I know you have a foundation. But the water is a different animal than the stadium and sand you've trained in."

"Train with your people?"

"Not if you don't want to. I have some free time in the afternoons. We could go out by my shack. Practice away from everyone else."

She thought about it. She could use the practice now that she was away from her castle and couldn't train with her brother. She was at least comfortable with Nadir enough to train with him. But the thought of his people watching her made her skin squirm.

"I'd like to observe a few more days," she finally determined. "But soon. I would like that."

Nadir gave her a slow nod and said, "Okay."

Her eagle screeched overhead, and Nyssa smiled up at him.

Whatever mocking comment her eagle had made, she didn't hear, but she knew he was making fun of her for standing in front of Nadir just like she said she wouldn't.

She caught Nadir staring at her again, and the darkening of his gaze made her hug her arms around her chest. "What, Commander?" she asked.

"Ah... Nothing, it's just..." He paused, swallowing. "You're standing on my beach."

"You keep saying that," she smiled.

"My beach. My sunset. My home place..." His weight shifted, and he reached out, his knuckle sweeping her cheek. "My Princess... A perfect way to start the new year."

The words reminded her of what he had said to her the night after the meeting.

"You are my great prize, Princess," he had uttered in her ear as he took her from behind.

A jagged breath entered her lungs, and she cleared her throat. "You remember what happened the last time you claimed me," she mocked.

Nadir huffed, a sideways grin spreading on his lips. "Should I not want that again?"

Nyssa rolled her eyes and shoved him. He feigned off-balance, clutching his chest as though she'd actually hurt him.

"That's two for you as well now," she bantered. "Do you think you can keep it professional while you give me a tour of this beach you're so proud of?"

Nadir laughed. "No promises."

He held out his arm for her to take. The familiarity of such a gesture made her shake her head, and she knew he knew why.

But he kept his leering to himself, making good on the gentleman that he was, as he showed her more of his beach and introduced her to a few of his people. She didn't miss the bite of their pressed lips and the tenseness in their shoulders when they shook her hand.

Stares followed them as they walked, and after a while, Nyssa grew so uncomfortable that she dropped her arm from around his. The feeling she'd had earlier walking through the market was back and now worse with him at her side.

As to why his people watched her with such malice, she had a few ideas... Exiled princess forced on their shores. Perhaps they thought her part of the council that had condemned Draven. A danger to their great Commander and his ability to keep their people safe.

These were the stares and thoughts that made her stomach queasy and made her realize whatever she and Nadir had together could not be brought up in public again... Not until she'd proven herself worthy of his attention in their eyes.

Nadir told her he would show her the food forest the next day, that it was getting too dark to venture in there with the Dead Moons overhead. It was the Noctuans' last night, and Nyssa was grateful he did not press to show her much after night fell.

Lex met them back at the shack after dinner, already lighting her pipe as she relaxed on the porch. "Commander and the Princess," she drawled upon their approach. "The least you could do when escorting her around is put a shirt on, Nadir," she added.

Nadir huffed amusedly. "I'll make a note of that." He turned to Nyssa then, took her hand in his, and his lips brushed her knuckles as he backed up the steps. It physically hurt her heart to see the dilation in his eyes and know that she had to let him go.

He left them then and went inside to change. Nyssa sighed into the seat beside Lex, her head hitting the wall.

"Talk," Lex said without looking at her.

"What am I doing, Lex?" Nyssa breathed. "I mean... What are we doing? Should we not be marching to Man's camps and demanding peace right now? We've been here—"

"Three days," Lex finished for her. "I've never seen you urgent about anything. Why so urgent about this? You know it's the long game."

"Doesn't make it any easier."

The smoke from Lex's pipe entered Nyssa's nose, and Nyssa closed her eyes at the sweetness of it.

"Are you ever going to tell me whatever it was you and Dorian have been hiding from me?" Lex asked.

Nyssa sat up and pulled her knees into her chest, avoiding Lex's eyes. "I don't know—"

"Fuck off, Nyssari," Lex cut her off. "I've watched the two of you grow up. I know when you're hiding something. As your brother isn't here to keep that secret for you and help with whatever it is, I implore you to tell me."

Nyssa knew she was right, but she wasn't ready. She wasn't prepared for the look she knew Lex would give her, along with the stares of Nadir's people from the tour.

"Soon," Nyssa told her.

Lex leaned back, head lolling on her neck as she exhaled. "What's wrong? Thought you would be skipping after seeing you walk through the village with him."

"His people stared at me today as though I am a disease," Nyssa whispered. "As though my being on his arm somehow made them question his authority."

"They don't know you," Lex said. "Give them time."

A question burned through Nyssa then as the doubts in her head threatened to flood and drown her beneath their weight.

"Lex, would you be here if it wasn't your duty?"

A pause.

One long enough that it nearly confirmed Nyssa's suspicions and sank her further beneath that water.

"What do you mean?" Lex finally asked.

"I mean... If you had been given a choice between staying with Dorian or Bala or coming here with me... Would you have chosen me?"

"Doesn't matter," Lex said fast. "I swore to your sister—"

"What if—"

"Where is this coming from?" Lex asked, sitting up. "Have I given you any inclination that I do not want to be here with you?"

"That's not what I'm asking."

"So, what are you asking?"

"I am asking if you are following me because you trust and believe in what I can do and are not just here because you are fulfilling a promise to my dead sister."

Silence staggered between them, and Nyssa held Lex's gaze for longer than she knew it should have taken for her to answer.

"Why are you asking this?" Lex asked.

"Because I need to know if it is only to his people that I have to prove my worth to or if I need to prove it to you as well."

Lex considered her another moment, the pipe resting firmly between her lips. Nyssa could see the clench of her jaw, the tightness of her fingers around the end...

"Hey, Princess—" Nadir bounded back onto the porch then, and Nyssa and Lex both straightened in their seats, their conversation put on hold.

"I almost forgot," Nadir continued. "I have a task for you tonight. If you're up for it."

Nyssa exchanged a glance with Lex, who shrugged, obviously not knowing what Nadir had in mind. "Okay," Nyssa replied hesitantly.

"Your sister had promised to help me with the water serpent during the next Deads. I thought the beast had quieted down as I hadn't seen her, but she came on shore again last night and messed with some of the docks. Think you would be up for speaking with her?"

Nyssa's heart skipped. "You want me to speak with the sea serpent?"

"I would like to go with that option first, yes," he replied. "She's a century-old at least. I'd rather not kill her if I can help it. She usually keeps to herself. I'm not sure what's wrong with her."

A sweat had broken out in Nyssa's palms. "I... I can try, but she may not listen to me—"

"Perhaps the next round of Deads, Commander," Lex interjected.

"The serpent isn't a Noctuan," he informed them. "She just likes to use the darkness for hunting."

"Next week then," Lex argued.

"My men will want to kill her by then," he almost snapped. "I need to know what's going on."

"You will not—"

"Lex, it's fine," Nyssa cut in, her voice barely a whisper. "It's fine."

She knew it was a lie, but maybe... Maybe she could at least reach out to it. Try to let the creatures back in. For her sister. For Nadir and his people.

The voice in the back of her head kept telling her she would get eaten, but she pushed the thought away as she stood from the chair.

Nadir's gaze flickered over her, obviously seeing the hesitation in her features, but he didn't question it.

"Change clothes," he told her. "If she pulls you under, you should at least not be held hostage by a wool dress."

Nadir lit a torch and escorted her out to the end of the jetty once she'd changed, Lex following behind them. The further out they walked, the more Nyssa's heart began to stammer. Hands gripping and opening, sweat pooled not only in her palms but also in every crease of her body. Her skin felt more and more uncomfortable the closer they got to the end until finally, she had to push breath into her lungs.

Breathe, Nyssari, she heard her brother and sister saying.

All she had to do was reach out to the creature. Let it talk to her. Not think about the Noctuans crying in the woods.

The Noctuans crying in the woods.

The thought of hearing their wails again nearly made Nyssa forget how to walk. If she let the serpent in, she might let them in too. Their songs from nights before filled her memory, and she forced her feet to continue on, one after the other.

By the time they reached the end of the jetty, her teeth were chattering.

Face red and heart numb, she turned to both Lex and Nadir.

"Stand back in case she doesn't listen to me."

Nadir and Lex exchanged a glance, but they both nodded and waited back. Nyssa took the torch, continued to the edge, and stuffed the long stick between two rocks. The amber light bounced off the dark water.

Her eagle landed on her forearm and gave her hand a nip before tugging the end of her sleeve and urging her back.

"I know," she whispered. "But I have to do this."

A confused chirp left him, but he didn't tug on her arm again. Instead, he flew into the air, and she knew he would be circling above her.

She didn't even know where to start.

"Nyssa, what's wrong?" Lex called.

"It's nothing," she said quickly. "Give me a moment."

The Ulfram howl filled her ears, and that fear of hearing their cries again made her chest tighten. She dropped to her knees and closed her eyes in an attempt to just feel out into the ocean and keep the Noctuan cries as distant echoes.

Her hands hugged behind her neck, and she pushed her core out into the abyss of black.

For a moment, nothing happened. Nyssa could feel her own hesitation to let anything in. Body trembling at the thought of being back in that raging darkness she'd found herself in with the dragons.

She could still hear the Ulfram in the Forest.

Nyssa rose to her feet and shrugged her boots off.

"What are you doing?" Lex called out.

"Going in the ocean," Nyssa replied as she tossed the shoes behind her.

"Bad idea," Nadir cut in.

"Nyssa, it is dark. You cannot see," Lex argued.

"I can't hear anything," Nyssa snapped.

Lex's face paled, and Nyssa saw the realization of what was wrong rise on Lex's face.

"What do you mean you can't hear anything?" Lex asked slowly. "As in you cannot hear the creature because it is below the water or—"

"I cannot hear *any* of them."

Lex's chest visibly caved, and the color drained from her face. "What... *You pushed them out? Is this what you've been hiding from me?"

"What was I supposed to do?" Nyssa argued. "They were screaming in that Forest. Crying because of him—because of *her*. Pushing that pain into me and looking for answers. I couldn't..." Her voice trailed, and she stared at the ground. "I'm sorry."

The words had barely left her lips when she started forward and pushed between Nadir and Lex to head back to the beach. A tear fell down her face, but she wiped it away forcefully, determined to hide in the darkness for the rest of the night and possibly the whole of the next day.

Maybe the next month.

"She's worthless," someone said.

Nyssa almost tripped over her feet.

Her stomach dropped when she looked up.

A hundred people had lined the beach to watch them, torches in some of their hands.

"Never rely on any other than our own," another said.

What was left of her pride vanished until there was nothing left of her but a hollow shell of a Princess desperately trying to avoid reality.

One by one, she watched the people shake their heads, glaring through her, and then they turned away to go back to their homes.

Worthless.

The word echoed, and she nearly fell to her knees again.

—The water sloshed.

Violently.

Something reached out and latched on to her insides. Screams from the beach sounded behind her. She thought she heard her name, but the sight of what rose from the water startled her frozen.

Fangs.

Yellow slitted eyes.

It was the only thing she saw before the sea serpent's great slithering body wrapped her up.

She was pulled off the jetty and beneath the water.

13

The great snake's body only had to wrap her once, but the weight of it around her made her lungs struggle more than they already were. The circumference of the beast encapsulated her from her feet to her breasts. She'd hardly had a moment to take in a breath before it pulled her under.

Down into the darkness.

Nyssa struggled against its wrap. She pushed on the iridescent black scales and kicked her legs in the hopes she could break herself free. But it was no use, and she knew she would drown if she didn't do something fast.

She had to try and reach it.

Beneath the water. Away from the Noctuans and the eyes of the people. No noises except her own head and the weight of the water.

The ocean. One of her favorite places to be. This... This she could maybe do.

This she *had* to do.

She didn't really have a choice.

She remembered the way she had reached the Noirdiem and the Ulfram with Dorian the week before. She just needed to touch it. Push what she could into it and open up her heart.

Exhale the fire, sister.

Nyssa pressed her hands onto the beast.

And she let go.

She let go of the fear of hearing grief and rage. Let go of the tears inside her, of the hold on her insides and mind. She opened her core and pushed into the beast every blissful moment she could find in her head. Trying to make peace with the serpent and let her know she would not harm her. To show the creature love as it had not felt from a Lesser being before.

A hiss filled Nyssa's ears, but the serpent's grip loosened. Nyssa kicked her legs and freed herself from the beast's grasp before turning and opening her eyes.

The serpent stilled in front of her.

Her head was wider and as long as Nyssa's body, narrow and snake-like, yellow eyes staring back at her. She hissed slowly this time, showcasing her fangs.

Heart in her throat, Nyssa kept herself suspended before it. She couldn't hear the creature's voice, but she knew the serpent had felt her—short-lived as it may have been.

A low purring noise sounded in the deep.

Hello, beasty, Nyssa said, not knowing whether the creature would understand her.

For a moment, the serpent merely stared, her great, fifty-foot body slithering in the gravity of the water.

—The beast slowly blinked.

Lungs aching, Nyssa released the last of her breath as bubbles. The notion of what she'd just accomplished sat heavily on her shoulders.

And then she watched in slow motion as the great sea serpent turned to slither back into the depths of the ocean.

Nyssa's vision began to darken, lungs collapsing at the weight of her no longer having air. She made to move her legs and get herself back to the surface.

A hand grabbed her's, and she hardly saw Nadir in front of her before his lips pressed to her own.

Air filled her lungs.

Not a kiss. *No.* This was life pressing back into her body.

She was reminded that he could breathe underwater.

Her eyes opened again, and the stars that had begun to fill her vision waned. Nadir pressed a hand softly to her cheek and said, "Okay?" in a muffled voice.

Nyssa nodded, and Nadir pointed towards the sky. He kicked at the water, and she did the same.

Cold air brushed over her when they broke the surface. Lex was shouting. His people were all crowded together on the beach and calling out Nadir's name.

Nadir caught her eyes and gave her hand a squeeze.

"You didn't have to do that," she managed, pushing her hair back off her face. "I was fine."

"I know," he said. "I just needed an excuse to kiss you after seeing what you did."

The smile on his face nearly made her laugh, but as the mutters of his people filled her ears again, the notion of it faltered.

"Three, Commander," she said, splashing water at him.

Nadir chuckled under his breath as he moved closer to her. "Are you okay?" he asked when he was directly at her side.

What had just happened, coupled with the stares of his people, was quickly taking over Nyssa's mind. She wanted to tell him she was fine, but she couldn't.

A few of the Honest were coming out onto the jetty now that the serpent was gone. All of them spoke out in concern over their Commander's life having been in danger.

"Hey—" Nadir called her back. "Forget about them. Talk to me," he pleaded. "Are you okay?"

But she couldn't get their voices out of her head, and her heart constricted with every whisper of doubt.

"I can't do this, Nadir."

With one last look at his crestfallen face, she dove back beneath the water and swam to shore.

To all his people, the display had been nothing more than a show of how helpless they thought her to be. Her falling into the ocean with the serpent, unable to speak to it. Their great Commander having to rescue her. Stories circulated around the village that Nadir had combated the beast, as people were sure they saw him emerge from the depths with blood on his sword.

Lies that Nyssa knew she couldn't deny. That not even Nadir could argue about without his people thinking he was merely taking up for her.

But they knew what had happened.

"Why didn't you tell me?" Lex asked her later as they sat on the porch.

"I didn't want you to be disappointed," Nyssa admitted. "One more failure. One more thing I cannot do that my sister excelled so incredibly at—"

"You should have told me."

"And said what, Lex?" Nyssa cracked. "By the way, I shut out the Noctuans while we were traveling because I was terrified to hear their screams?" She paused and shook her head, holding back her breakage.

"How was I supposed to tell you that when everyone obviously wishes it were she here and not me? How was I supposed to allow you, someone who just lost their best friend and is being forced to look after someone like me, to look at me with such a failure?"

No words of argument came from Lex's lips. Nyssa shook her head again and turned back to the ocean.

"I could not stand to see that exact look of disappointment on your face."

"Nyssa, you're allowed to grieve," Lex argued.

"Am I?" Nyssa questioned, "Because the only time I've felt like I could was when I was with Dorian. I am a daughter of Arbina. A Princess of Promise. To grieve would be to show a weakness I should not carry."

"And to not be able to use the abilities you were born with would be a worse fate."

Nyssa held Lex's gaze for a solid moment, unsure of what to say next. She rubbed her neck with both hands, and the memory of the people talking about her on that beach swelled once more in her ears.

"Everyone is looking at me as nothing more than a burden, and I don't know how to change that. I don't know how to prove my worth to any of them," Nyssa admitted.

"We've been here three days," Lex said. "Tonight is the last night of the Deads. Your entire world was just flipped two weeks ago. Take a few more days to breathe and observe. It's okay to take time for yourself."

"Why are you so nice about this?"

"Would you rather I am mean to you?"

Nyssa considered it. "Yes, actually," Nyssa said. "I'm not used to you being considerate."

Lex looked as though she would laugh. "Okay. You can start showing your worth by training with me instead of standing on the beach and eye-fucking the Commander."

Nyssa's mouth nearly dropped, but she remembered she had asked for this treatment. "Fuck you, Lex."

Lex chuckled under her breath, shoulders seeming to relax slightly. "I—"

"I am fully aware that fucking the Commander is not how I prove anything," Nyssa affirmed. "Lust is not a cure for mental anguish or grief. Especially in his case. If his people find out about us, they—"

"You and I both know it is more than that," Lex cut in.

Nyssa groaned and wiped her face harshly beneath her hands. It certainly felt like more, though she couldn't explain it.

"I don't know what it is..." Nyssa whispered. "And that that scares me. Because if it *is* what I think it is—"

"Hey—" Nadir appeared from inside the house then, his gait slowing upon seeing them. He paused in front of her, and she couldn't figure out the expression on his face.

"Can we talk?" he softly asked Nyssa.

"I think she's had enough tonight, Commander," Lex said, protectively wrapping a hand around Nyssa's arm. "Save it for the morning."

"I don't recall asking your permission, Second Sun," Nadir said, the stern of his voice and glare making Lex tense beside her. "I am talking to Nyssari. If she wants to tell me I can save it for the morning, then she can. But you will not speak for her."

Nyssa had never heard anyone speak to Lex like that, and she half expected Lex to draw her sword or tell Nadir he could go fuck himself.

But all Lex did was give Nyssa's arm a squeeze, and then she stood.

"Very well, Commander," she said. "I'll see you on the beach for training at dawn, Nyssa."

Lex stepped inside, the door shut with a click behind her. Nyssa sank back into the chair and hugged her knees.

"Here to tell me everything is fine about what happened tonight?" she said, her voice barely audible.

"No," he said as he sat down at her side. "Just thought you could use a break from having to explain yourself to your sister's Second."

"It's fine," Nyssa said. "She's just looking out for me. Fulfilling her promise."

Nadir sank back onto the chair, picking a flower from the vase of those on the porch that he'd brought home earlier, and he began to toy with it between his fingers. "Fulfilling her promise..." His voice trailed, and he threw the flower stem on the ground. "Another person telling you you are their duty instead of standing by you because you're you."

Nyssa gawked at him.

Nadir caught her stare, and his eyes squinted at her. "What?" he asked.

"You... Did you hear us talking earlier?" she asked, remembering the conversation.

"When?"

There was genuine surprise in his features, and she realized he knew nothing about the conversation she was talking about.

"I... Never mind." Her hands pushed over her face again, and she leaned her head against the wall. "I'm sorry I couldn't reach the serpent."

"But you did reach it," he said. "Maybe not talking to it, but what you did under that water— whatever it was— that serpent was going to drag you into the depths and eat you. You stopped it. Why are you considering this a failure?"

"Because I couldn't do what you needed me to do. The only thing I accomplished was saving myself."

"Ensuring your own survival is not something you should be ashamed over."

"But I was supposed to be helping you and your people," she argued. "And I didn't."

Nadir sighed and picked the last petals off the flower. "You know, I am curious as to why you volunteered if you knew you couldn't speak to it."

"I thought I could at least try," Nyssa said softly. "Especially going under the water, away from the Noctuans. I hated the thought of seeing that disappointment on Lex's face... And yours... No one has ever depended on me to do something on my own. I thought it was the first step in proving my worth to your people." Her jaw tightened with the words, and she cursed herself. "All I did was embarrass myself and bring more doubt into your people's minds. How are they ever going to trust me to do what you need me to do if I cannot even do what should be easy?"

"I trust you."

The three words shouldn't have meant as much as they did, but they did.

Oh, they did.

She nearly kissed him right then.

But—

"But your people do not," she managed. "I do not want them to begin to question you because they disagree or because they see you trusting me as some blind affection towards me."

"That's not why I trust you," he argued.

"They don't know that."

Nadir considered her a moment. "Okay, get up," he said, rising to his own feet. "Come on." He held out his hands to her, and she eyed him.

"Where are we going?"

"You're going to kick my ass," he informed her.

She almost smiled at the assurance in his features. "Oh, am I?" she mocked, taking his hand.

He pulled her off the bench, grinning as he walked backward from her. "Definitely. It's going to be great. You can tell me all about what you're scared of while you're beating the shit out of me," he said with a wink.

Nadir grabbed two of the great bamboo sticks from beside the steps, and he had her grab a couple of torches before he led her out on the beach. Once the torches were stuck in the sand, he tossed her a stick.

Her feet set, and Nadir gave her an upwards nod as he did the same.

"One blow, one fear," he told her.

She huffed but nodded anyway.

Nadir charged at her. She blocked straight, pushing back as he whipped around, and she was reminded of the quick Commander she'd watched earlier in the day. So she held her ground and noted his movements. Every tense of muscle in his shoulders, every flinch of his thighs. He blocked the strike she jabbed at his legs, and he smirked triumphantly at her.

She glared but thought of a fear nonetheless. "Mirrors," she said.

Nadir paused. "What?"

"You asked for a fear. That's my first one. Mirrors."

She struck at him low, but he blocked. "Why mirrors?"

Nyssa's cheeks flushed. The warmth of it spread up to her ears as memories of her standing in front of the great mirror as a child with her mother behind her flickered in her mind. She wasn't sure she was ready to talk about it that night.

"Another night," she told him.

Nadir didn't push it. "Set up."

She did, and he lunged at her. She noticed where he was going this time and shifted just as he pushed. His stick caught the air instead of her, and she whipped around, cutting behind his shins.

Nadir landed flat on his back. Nyssa allowed her own smirk to rise on her lips as she stepped over him.

"Oh *shit*," he grinned. "My Princess came to play."

She bit the inside of her cheek to keep from smiling, and she offered him the stick. "What did we say about your claiming me?"

"Again, I wonder why you think I shouldn't want that again," he bantered.

Nyssa rolled her eyes at his flirtation. He grabbed the end and hauled himself to his feet.

He whirled the stick once, and then he jumped at her.

She flinched despite herself, bamboo coming up in front of her face, split shriek emitting from her lips, and Nadir's deep laughter bellowed out. He was mocking her, and she wanted to slap his stupidly gorgeous face.

So she swatted for his shins, and he blocked.

His laughter faded, and he set up again. "Another fear, Princess," he asked as the water brushed over their feet.

Nyssa gritted her teeth and kept forward, determined to take him to his knees again. They parried, and she blocked him again and again as she thought of her next one.

"Being alone," she admitted.

Nadir's brow flinched upwards. "That's fair," he said, the sticks clacking as they continued. "What—"

"I don't just mean being alone," she admitted, to which Nadir paused. "I mean... Being truly alone. Completely separated and cut off from everyone I know. I've always been surrounded by people, by my family, at least one of them, or even Willow. My eagle... Being truly alone terrifies me, and I think that's the scariest part about this war."

"You'll never be alone in this war," he told her.

It sounded like a promise, and she hated it.

"No one can promise me that," she said. "I'll have to face that fear eventually. With great retribution as I'm sure it will be presented to me in the grandest of fashions." She twirled the stick in her hands once. "What about you?" she asked. "What scares the great Commander of Haerland's oldest army?"

Nadir stared at the ground as though he were thinking over the question, and a silence rested between them as they started pushing at each other again.

"Ah... Failure," he admitted.

"Anything more specific or just general failure?" she asked as she blocked his overhead swipe.

"Everyone in Haerland depends on our reef and goods," he said. "It's not just our home. It's our entire way of life."

He avoided her gaze as he spoke, and she realized perhaps that no one had ever asked him such a question.

"If this reef falls, Haerland falls." He paused, finally meeting her eyes. "The Venari depend on us, and the Dreamer villages trade a great deal with us. If we were to lose this reef, the Venari would have to eventually pack up their kingdom and go somewhere new."

"I didn't realize so much sat on your shoulders."

"I wouldn't trade it," he said. "If anyone else was in charge of keeping my people safe, I would be a very poor soldier."

"Why's that?"

He shrugged as he pushed forward again. "I like knowing that I am in charge of my own fate, and if that means being in charge of the fate of our entire world, then so be it."

"A true hero," she mocked. "Funny, I've never met one before."

Nadir gave her a sideways grin. He caught her stick in his hands then and yanked her forward. She stumbled, catching herself in his arms. Her breaths shortened when he stretched over her, and his hand came to rest on the small of her back.

"Should I remind you what your great hero likes to do to Princesses?"

She had to ignore the chill running up her spine. "Princesses—*plural*," she mocked, the whisper of banter finally not feeling foreign on her tongue. "Do tell how many other princesses you've seduced into your bed during your immortal life."

"How many *I've* seduced?" He laughed, still hanging onto her. "Do we need to go over who seduced who that night?"

"No one forced you to my room," she grinned.

"You *kissed* me."

"And you're constantly saying things that warrant me wanting to kiss you."

Nadir scoffed, the smirk softening on his lips. She could have drowned in the dilated gaze he leered at her with or sank herself into the abyss that was his hand now on her cheek...

"I forgot how easy it was to talk to you," he almost whispered, eyes searching over her face. "I forgot how easy *all* of this was with you..."

Nyssa swallowed as she found herself agreeing with him. "So did I," she whispered.

As he leaned down, Nyssa's lips trembled. For a brief second, she considered giving in, and the thought made her heart flutter. His hand wrapped around her neck, only the stick between them... His lips brushed hers—

She struck his abdomen, and Nadir doubled over, head falling on her shoulder, his groan sounding loud against the crashing waves. His eyes rolled up to meet hers, and she grinned.

"You should run, Princess," he croaked out.

She barely made it thirty feet before he caught her up in his arms, her feet swinging out as he grabbed her from behind. He swung her in a circle. The laugh that emitted from her didn't sound like her own. As though it belonged to a Princess who knew nothing of the war and her own reality. Her feet met the ground again, and she struggled against his grasp, but he was too strong, and after a moment, she found herself surrendering. Sighing her back into his chest, settling in his embrace. Closing her eyes as he held her tighter, his forehead pressing to her temple as they steadied their balance.

And for just a moment, she allowed her heart to rest in the comfort of him.

Hidden away from all the stares of his people, the judgment and worries of what comes next.

Just them.

But the Ulfram howled from the woods, and Nyssa's heart sank. Nadir brushed from beside her, still holding gently on her arms as they stared at the Forest of Darkness.

The shriek of the Aviteth made her wince.

Fire.

She shut her eyes tight, trying to block it out and grab onto that wall in her mind she'd used before.

Again, the Ulfram howled, and Nyssa began to shut down at the agony of the wolf's cry… the memory of the Wyverdraki's screaming.

Nadir's arms wrapped back around her just as her knees gave out, and they both fell to the sand. He held her through it, arms so tight while she faltered that it reminded her of the serpent. But it helped her feel secure in a moment of chaotic drowning. A blanket of steady strength to quiet the anxiety of what she saw behind her eyes.

The Noctuans' cries quieted after a few minutes. Her heart returned to her chest, breath beginning to even, and Nadir's lips pressed to her shoulder.

"Do you want to go back?" he asked her.

Nyssa forced herself to look in the direction of the Forest again. "No," she finally determined. "I need to hear her."

Nadir stood and took her hands, bringing them both up to their feet again.

"When you hear them… What do you see?" he asked.

For a second, Nyssa looked past his arm into the darkness, contemplating whether to admit what he'd asked or to keep it quiet, go back to the shack, and close herself away once more. But Nadir squeezed her hands, and the words came from within before she could stop them.

"It's not so much *just* when I hear them as it is every time I close my eyes," she said softly. "Fire," she admitted. "Draven falling. Every time the Ulfram howls, I hear the Rhamocour when she was on the tower with him, watching him dive out of that window. She... She was *screaming*." She winced at the memory, staring into a trance as he stepped away and grabbed their sticks from the ground. He placed one in her hands then and gave her a nod.

"The alpha Ulfram was always his favorite," Nadir told her as he stepped back.

Nyssa set her feet just as Nadir did.

"She used to walk the edge of the river when he would boat with me to the mountains during the Deads—" Nadir pushed, and Nyssa blocked "—always watching him. Scared me senseless the first time she did it."

"I don't think I realized how close you two were," she said, pushing back.

Their sticks hit twice, and Nyssa ducked as he swung over her.

"He was my greatest friend."

The declaration of his words made her pause, and she realized then how much he had lost without ever getting to say goodbye.

"I'm so sorry, Nadir."

Nadir twirled the stick once and rubbed the back of his neck. "I knew who he was," he said, still staring at the ground. "Not that it made hearing what had happened any easier, but..."

He pushed forward again, swinging at her shins this time, and Nyssa had to jump to keep from having her legs wiped out.

"I'm glad he finally found her."

Nyssa paused again. "What do you mean?"

"Draven was sure love didn't exist for someone like him. He was certain he would be sentenced to nothing more than unrequited lovers his entire life, not that he had any problem with his... *Festivities—*"

His brow raised when he said it, and Nyssa almost smiled.

"Yeah," she uttered. "Heard about those. And heard them, actually."

Nadir scoffed and went at Nyssa again. "He was sure Duarb had stretched the curse of the Infinari to mean love would be as rare as his own kind—Infinari-marked Venari persons."

"I'm not sure I follow."

She blocked him over her head, coming down and pushing him into the water. Nadir stumbled and looked impressed.

"Not bad, Princess," he smirked.

She lunged again.

Nadir cut across her this time. "It's rare for Venari Kings to find true love. Only one past King ever married." He ducked as she swung over him. "He was so confused when he started feeling for her." Nadir paused another moment, and Nyssa watched as the happy memory cascaded over his face. "He went to the mountains after that Council meeting when she ignored him. Wanted to get his head straight, his hands dirty. Pound iron... I still remember how he paced in that armory when she came to the forest for the battle. Ready to lash out at the confusion he felt for her when he didn't know if she felt the same... I don't know that I've laughed so hard since that night."

Nadir pushed her back then, taking advantage of the wave in her concentration. Nyssa swatted. She went forward and blocked his next parry. The ocean wrapped around her feet, and she had to concentrate on holding her ground.

"Really not fair when you take advantage of my love of a good story," she said.

Nadir's smile broadened over his face. "Think fast."

She nearly skipped backward as he came at her, stick hitting hers with every step. Nearly as fast as he'd battled with his friend the day before. The ocean beat against her legs. She lost balance and wiped out to the ground. Another wave crashed over her head, and she was suddenly covered in sand.

Nadir was grinning at her when the ocean subsided. He held the stick out, but she shoved it away, to which he laughed.

"I told you the ocean was relentless."

"Funny how you think I've never trained in the ocean before," she said, helping herself to her feet. She took her knife from her thigh and ripped a piece of fabric off her shirt to tie her hair up with.

"Hair is going up... Must be serious," he winked, setting his feet again.

She glared poorly at him but grabbed her own stick from the ground nonetheless.

"Tell me about your travels with him," she begged, realizing perhaps he needed to talk about Draven as much as she needed to talk about

Aydra.

"Story for story?" he asked.

"Trading stories for wipeouts," she countered and took a step into the ocean.

His chest rose with deliberation as he took a breath to make the decision. But he whirled his stick once and then met her in the water.

"You're on, Princess."

For well into the night, they fought, and with each knock of the other on their back, they traded stories. Nyssa hadn't realized how much she needed to talk about her sister, about what happened to her. She wasn't stupid enough to think it would be a cure. But at least by the time they retired for the night—Nadir wrapping his arm around her shoulders, helping her towel dry her hair and wash off outside so she didn't drag sand into his house. Him simply kissing her hand upon telling her goodnight—The knot in her heart had loosened, if only a fraction more.

14

It would take Dorian and Corbin at least four days of traveling to reach Dahrkenhill, possibly longer since they would have to settle well before sunset due to the Dead Moons. The pair had no way to deter the Noctuans, and as the Deads were drawing to a close, they knew the beasts' hunger would grow for one final meal before the curse took them.

Bala had shown them the route they would need to take to avoid being found in the Hills. She urged them not to step foot north in the Forest past the Scindo Creek divide. It was in this area that the Mortis Lunar Pass began. Unless they were on the Impius River, the Forest and sharp mountains would devour them whole, and they would lose their minds before finding their way through it.

Dorian had never traveled through the Knotted Caves path to Dahrkenhill before. The last he'd traveled to the mountains, he'd pushed through the valleys from Magnice, coming up the backside of the mountains before climbing up the peaks.

They only had a few more hours ride to the cave's entrance, but the pair decided they were starving too much to continue without breaking for a few minutes. It was around mid-afternoon that they settled into the edge of the forest for the last time.

One look into the wood, and Dorian decided this part of the forest was far darker than the part where the Venari kingdom resided. The entire aura of it made his skin crawl.

A low fog hung around the ground, seeping and creeping over the root system and dead leaves like shadowed snakes. The air was cooler, damp with the moisture of that fog. Every sound seemed to linger for longer than it should have— like time hanging in the balance of the dense air. The tree trunks were almost black and diseased. Dorian's hair stood on end when he walked inside a short way.

Whatever it was, it made him uneasy.

He wondered if this was part of Berdijay territory.

A shadow passed by, or so he thought. He supposed it could have been a trick: shadow thieves following them as easy prey. Dorian focused a small flame on his shoulder as he relieved himself, hoping the fire would deter any such creature.

Then again, this was the Mortis Lunar Pass. No being ever went very far inside it and came back out alive unless they had a guide.

And there was Dorian. Taking a piss on a tree inside it.

Dorian straightened as he finished and buttoned his pants. But as he started to turn, that shadow passed by again. A tingle ran up the backs of his arms. He flushed the feathered flames from his shoulders and stilled, letting his body sink into the abyss of the wood as he listened out for anything.

A single cricket, but no birds. Just the press of silence and the lone insect in his ears.

Dorian allowed the ash to rise on his fingers when he saw the shadow again.

"Hey Bin," he called out, only his eyes moving around him in the hopes if he stayed still, he would catch it again.

"What—you need help holding your cock?"

Dorian ignored the comment. "You have your scythe handy?"

"Why?"

"Because I think we're going to need it."

A branch cracked overhead.

Dorian's gaze snapped up.

The last thing he saw before he was on his back was a hooded figure dropping atop him.

Dorian groaned as he hit a root. The person knelt over him, their knife thrusting beneath his chin.

"Don't make me take you back in pieces, Prince."

A woman.

Dorian started to snap back, but his words caught in his throat. Staring at him between the black covering over her mouth and nose and the darkened hood were blazing lavender eyes that caused his heart to still. "Who—"

Her head jerked up. Corbin swung down at her, but she caught his blade with the sword she pulled from her belt. She did it so quickly,

Dorian had barely saw. Or perhaps it was he had been too entranced by her eyes to notice.

This woman was fast. And agile. She began to battle with Corbin, blocking his every move. Dorian pushed to his seat as they fought in front of him. At one point, the woman kicked up the tree and came whirling over Corbin's head. She kicked him in the face, and Dorian's Second fumbled off his feet. Dorian backed up. She turned in one swift movement and a knife hurled from her hand in the Prince's direction.

Dorian caught it between flamed hands.

The woman straightened, and Dorian stared at the knife he'd caught. This was not of Blackhand make, but instead of raging cold silver. The smoothness of it felt like velvet beneath his fingertips. He knew the forges this blade had been made in.

This was a Dreamer blade.

His eyes lifted to hers. "Who the fuck are you?"

The woman straightened, pushed her hood off her head, and revealed her long silver-white hair tied in a braid over her breast, darker at her roots and yet an almost purple on the tips. She pulled the face-covering down to her neck, and Dorian gawked at the sight of the entrancing being standing before him.

She couldn't have been much older than himself, perhaps only a few years. Her light brown skin illuminated in the light of the sun as it bounced off her narrow jaw and high cheekbones, accentuating the apples of her cheeks. He could faintly see the dots of white freckles stretched across her brown skin. She'd painted a smokey black around her eyes, letting the lines fade into her hairline and slightly down her small nose. It was the mark of the warrior she intended herself to be. Her lavender eyes poured over him, tips of her bangs hitting at her long eyelashes.

He then noticed the tops of what looked to be four long scars beneath her jaw, stretching over her skin as though the Ulfram had tried to slice her throat open. And when she lifted her chin, some of her hair fell from over the point of her ears.

This warrior *was* a Dreamer.

"What's wrong?" she said as she unclasped her cloak and threw it to the ground. "Never seen a woman Dreamer warrior before?"

Dorian's mouth sagged as he gawked at her. "Ah no. No, I haven't. Since when do women Dreamers learn combat?"

Corbin grabbed her from behind. His knife thrust beneath her chin. His arm wrapped around her chest and the other around her shoulders, daring her to move. She appeared so small against Corbin's stature. His arms nearly swallowed her whole.

"Should I kill her?" Corbin asked.

She glared sideways. "Think I can't take you, Belwark?" she dared.

Dorian watched the woman from his knees, taking in the fight she stared at him with. The strong way she stood her ground in front of the Fire Second—muscles straining, a hand gripped on the end of her dagger—the other on a blade she was sure Corbin didn't know she had pointed back at his thigh.

Dorian saw the just noticeable smug twist at the corner of her lips, and he knew she'd seen him catch it.

"Corbin," he finally determined. "Put down your blade."

Corbin's gaze flickered twice at him. "You know her?" he asked.

"I don't, but—" he grunted as he made to his feet, and then he dusted off his pants "—I like to think she's my future wife."

She laughed openly. "Enjoy it in your dreams, Prince," she mocked. "I think you've more things to be concerned about than my taking your hand."

"So, you're accepting then?"

Corbin let the woman go with a jerk and shoved her forward. Dorian allowed himself the liberty of looking over the woman's petite yet delectably curvaceous and soft figure as she pushed her knives back into their sheaths around her thick thighs. Her eyes caught his stare, and she raised a leering brow.

"Take it in all you want," she toyed. "Touch, and it'll be the last thing you ever feel."

"You say that as though it wouldn't be worth it," he said.

She ignored the comment. "Tell me, Prince, why are you heading to the caves?"

"Wanted to visit a friend," he replied.

"And your sister? Where is she?"

"With other friends."

"You realize why I'm here, don't you?"

Dorian settled back against the tree behind him, arms crossing over his chest. "I certainly hope it's to take me hostage in some way. Forcefully with ropes would be preferred."

She paused, staring at him a moment with that squinted gaze that told him she was working out his game.

"They told me you wouldn't take me seriously. Why is that? Is it because I am a woman?"

"The fact that you're a woman makes me take you more seriously than I would have an army of Belwarks. As for why your friends told you I wouldn't take you seriously, I'm not sure. Sounds like *they* don't take you seriously."

She paused again, toying with her blade between her fingers. "I was sent up here to find you. Bring you back to Scindo and to Magnice to face trial for your crimes," she informed him.

Dorian exchanged a look with Corbin. "Who sent you?" he asked her.

"My father," she replied.

"So you've come to what? Hunt me down? Take me in for ransom? Break my heart when you push me into the fire?"

"I've come to take you to my village," she said.

"What were my crimes?" he asked, curious as to what the crown had deemed him worthy of.

"You don't know what you did?"

"I know the truth," he countered. "But I wonder what laughable lies my brother gave the rest of you to deem my sister and me worthy of parties of both Belwarks and Dreamer mercenaries to come after us."

"Treason to your kingdom. Conspiracy to take over the crown. Consorting with the enemy," she answered.

Dorian considered the charges. Corbin cleared his throat.

"Seems fair," Corbin said as his flexing arms strapped around his chest.

"Actually does, doesn't it?" Dorian replied. He turned his attention back to the woman. "Why are you out here hunting us? Alone, might I add. And in the northern part of the Forest of Darkness. What are you? Soldier? Bounty hunter? Mercenary?"

"I am no one to most," she replied. "But bringing you back means securing my rank as the leader of our militia. I'll not have you take that away from me."

Dorian caught Corbin's gaze again. "Ambitious," Corbin uttered.

"I think I'm in love," Dorian returned.

She didn't respond except with a stare that told him he was doing a great job of annoying her.

Dorian huffed, feeling his lips twist upwards at the corner. "Did you expect me to go quietly?"

"It would be nice."

"You know... As much as I would *love* to feel your hands hauling me over the Hills back to Scindo, I'm afraid I'll have to pass," he said with a shrug. "Mountains are calling. You understand."

She looked lazily up at him, her full bowed lips twisting with an almost bored expression. "Don't try me, Prince."

He grinned. "Or what?"

Corbin threw a rope around her throat.

She didn't hesitate. Her knife jammed into Corbin's leg, and she whipped him over her shoulder. Corbin landed with a thud on his back, his groan echoing.

"Getting your ass kicked, Second," Dorian muttered. "Tiny bit embarrassing."

"Fuck off," Corbin grunted from the ground.

"Is that it then?" she cut in, stepping over Corbin. "Promised Prince depending on his Second to try and strangle me instead of taking me on himself?"

"I could take you myself, but I don't know that that would be a fair fight," Dorian replied.

She laughed aloud. "Perhaps we should find out."

Dorian felt his core warm, his fingertips tingling as the fire grew in his eyes. The warmth settled in his palm.

He could see it.

Him taking her long, beautiful neck in his hand, pouring fire over her skin, blistering her in navy embers... But the thought of watching that brightness leave her eyes made him stay on his spot.

He pulled his sword from his belt instead and allowed flames to only grow from that one hand down the blade. Eyes black, streaks of ash steady on his right arm...

It should have widened her gaze. It should have made her weight shift.

But she stood firm, the only flinch being when her hand tightened around the hilt of her dagger in readiness.

"Oh look," she uttered, head tilting. "It's the *fire Prince*."

Not exactly the words of character he was looking for. The term *Prince* seethed from her lips as an insult, as though she saw him as weak, of little power and consequence... An opponent unworthy of her taking him down.

She was mocking him.

Dorian let his fire recede as he pushed the tip of his sword into the ground, hands resting on the pommel. He couldn't work out the tug in his stomach as his gaze poured over her figure again. The way the leather pants she wore fit snug around her curves, the leather corset cinched in her waist. He dared to think what her thick thighs would feel like wrapped around his head, how his hands would dig into her soft flesh as though it were saving him from the darkness consuming his thoughts. The knives strapped to her thigh and the sword around her waist made his heart thud. He'd never seen such a Dreamer woman strapped to the guild with leather and iron. And she certainly *was* a Dreamer. He could see the feathered wing markings etched into her shoulders at her neck, the point of her ears through her silver and black hair. See the luminescent glow bouncing off her vibrant tawny skin despite the fog of the wood around them.

"What's your name?" he asked finally.

"Reverie," she answered shortly. "Reverie Asherdoe."

He frowned at the surname. "Asherdoe? You're related to the Scindo twins?"

Reverie's jaw clenched, and her movements ceased, if only for a moment. She began to wipe her knife a little more violently than before. "My youngers," she muttered. "Pretty little things, Father's precious favorites." The words seethed from her lips like poison. "I'm sure you've met them," she added, eyes rising to his.

Dorian wasn't sure what his face was doing. He was sure there was either a look of surprise or guilt, as to which he couldn't be sure. Perhaps both. He'd spent far more nights with the Scindo twins after meetings than he could remember.

In more compromising positions than he cared to admit.

A quirk of a smile rose on her lips, and she shook her head as she started cleaning her knife again. "Figures. I'm sure they've wrapped their legs around you a few times just as they do every other man Daddy likes to bring home."

Dorian's eyes narrowed at the sneer in her tone. "You don't approve?"

"It isn't that," she said quickly. "Really, it isn't. Father knows little of their explorations, thinking they're the innocent ones and I am the whore—"

"Your father should pay more attention," Dorian interjected, staring at a singular spot on the ground as the vision of his own explorations with them played back in his head.

Violent and non-violent. Together and separate. Sometimes with guests of their suggestion.

"My thoughts exactly," she agreed, the words snapping Dorian out of his daze.

He could hear the drip of frustration in her voice, and he wondered what people had said to her over the years that had her so angry and desperate to prove herself different from the other Dreamer women.

"What if I gave you a rank instead?" Dorian said then.

"Excuse me?"

"Rank," he repeated with a shrug. "In my army."

"You don't have an army."

"I don't, yet," he agreed. "I also don't plan on hiding out in the woods while strangers take over our world," he continued. "I'll get my sister and I's crowns back. And when I do, I'll need a commander for the Dreamer army to take Man."

The dark lavender of her eyes stretched through him from beneath her shaggy bangs. Her light brown lips tightened into a pucker, sharp jaw twitching, and he watched as her chest rose and fell as she thought it through.

"What do you want in return?" she finally asked.

"Tell them I am dead," he answered with a shrug.

She laughed. "No one will believe me."

"They might," he argued.

"Really? How? They would expect your head in a bag."

Dorian's hand clenched around the knife at his waist, the knife he'd made himself with the help of his sister... the knife that he carried with him everywhere as though it were an extension of his own arm. He pulled it from its sheath and looked it over. The rough swirled carvings in the blade. The dark red leather wrapped around the handle. The curvature of the flame and sun crest on the hilt...

He handed it to her hilt-first.

"What—a knife? That should mean something?" she mocked.

"That knife is the last possession I truly care about," he admitted. "People who know me well know that I would never part with it unless it was pried from my dead fingers. Your father will know this."

"That won't work," she argued, handing him back the knife. "If you are supposedly dead, they would have wanted me to go after your sister instead."

Dorian sighed and ran a hand through his fluffy hair. "Then you can come with us to Dahrkenhill," he said with a surrendered clap of his hands. "Make sure I stay alive long enough to stand trial for treason in your realm and keep me out of trouble in the mountains because you can bet they will hold me accountable for Draven's death. If you can keep me alive through their trials, you can take me back to Scindo after. But—"

She had opened her mouth to speak, but he held up a finger.

"—my offer still stands," he said. "I will make you my High Commander. This war with Man has hardly begun… it is far from over. You will have a legion of Dreamers and Belwarks at your fingertips. I need all the strength and ferocity I can get to defeat them. And you…" He paused, giving her another once over, "You're certainly one of the most ferocious things I've ever met."

"You know nothing about me," she countered.

"You just put the Fire Second on his back and looked at me in my true form as though I were a child," he said. "Males have been given high rankings like the one I'm offering for less. Tell me why you shouldn't deserve this? Is it because ignorant beings like your father have told you a woman would never work her way to such a position?" Dorian paused, scoffing at the backward way of his people.

"My kingdom is the only one of this world who deem women as less than males. Every other race in this damned world sees no difference. I intend to change that. My sisters have not fought their entire lives to see that progress squashed down because there is suddenly no Queen on the throne."

A singular brow had lifted on Reverie's face. She eyed him in a scrutinizing manner, lips twisted and puckered, mimicking the deep thought she seemed to be in.

"Let me get this straight…" her arms crossed, and she started to walk towards him. "You trust me to protect you— a woman who just threatened your life— all the way through the mountain trials just so that I can bring you back to my home to face more trials and certain death?"

"Isn't that what you were going to do anyway?" he asked. "This is just a bit of a detour. A favor for me."

"Why I shouldn't just kill your Belwark and knock you out? Put you in a bag over my steed and haul you to Scindo now?"

A crooked smile rose on Dorian's lips, and he straightened over her. "Because you want only what I can give you. High Commander. The first Dreamer woman to ever lead an army—fuck, the first Dreamer woman ever allowed *in* the army, and you're going to lead the charge. A great 'fuck you' to all those who treated you as though you would never be any better than second place."

She considered him again for a long moment, her fingers tapping on her crossed arms. "Are you truly so terrified of the Blackhands that you think you need two guards?" she asked.

"Yes," he admitted. "I've spent time in the mountains, vanquished Infi at the Bryn... dined in Dahrkenhill. The High Elder's best friend was just forced out of our window to the Edge because he fell in love with my sister. Do you really think they'll be happy to see me?"

"If you're so terrified, why are you going? Why not stay in the woods, hide out until things calm down?"

"Because there are ships on our shores that we cannot defeat on our own," he said fast. "Not without aid and supplies. The Umber does not have enough weapons, and if the reef realm falls, the Venari will not have enough food or supplies to keep them alive. We will have to depend on the Blackhands for aid, especially when the Dreamer towns are more likely not going to help now. And I'm also following my Kings' orders, so there's that."

"Your King? Rhafian? I thought he was—"

"Kings, plural, and Rhaif is *not* my king," Dorian hissed, feeling his features darken. "That coward is nothing more than a stain on our race. The only kings I recognize are the last two of the Venari. The true Kings."

Reverie didn't speak. He could see her mind working behind her eyes, the purple in her irises dancing with thought.

"Very well, Prince," she finally determined. "I'll help you keep your head. And after we leave the mountains, if you haven't frustrated and irked me to my core, we'll talk about the High Commander barter."

He'd just thought it was safe enough to relax and move when her next word ripped the air.

"However—"

Always a 'however,' he thought to himself.

"—if you try anything or piss me off for any reason, I will bind your wrists and ankles, kill your Belwark, and then drag you behind my horse all the way back to Scindo."

Dorian was starting to really like this woman. "Keep talking dirty like that, and we won't need the barter," he winked.

Her eyes squinted as though she were trying to figure out if he had actually said such words to her. "Do you've any idea how annoying you are?" she finally asked.

"I do, actually," he admitted. "It's one of the two favored family traits."

"What's the other?"

Dorian grinned. "That's for you to find out, Lady Fyre."

"Fyre?" she balked.

"The surname I was given is Eaglefyre. I assume you'll take it after we're wed."

Her gaze flickered to Corbin. "How have you not murdered him yet?"

The sneer Corbin gave her told Dorian he did not like the new member of their company, and Dorian knew it was because she'd completely embarrassed him. Dorian smirked at his Second and then replied to Reverie's question before Corbin could try and redeem himself.

"Don't worry, he'll warm up to you," Dorian said with a wink at the Fire Second. "And as far as the murder question, my sisters should certainly get credit for trying. As should their Second."

"We should get moving to make it to the inside of the caves by sundown," Corbin said.

Dorian's eyes landed on Reverie again. "Do you have a horse?"

Reverie grabbed her cloak from the ground. "Of course."

Dorian glanced around for any sign of a steed. "Where?"

"With yours."

Dorian and Corbin exchanged a look as she pushed past them towards the hills. Corbin paused and waited for Dorian to catch up.

"You're sure about this?" Corbin asked.

"Seems better than getting hauled into Scindo right now, doesn't it?" Dorian replied quietly.

Corbin gave him a sideways stare as they started walking, but Dorian only felt his gaze on him as his own eyes were fixated on the determined and confident stride of the Dreamer, whom he was sure was going to be the death of him.

"Something tells me you're enjoying this a little too much," Corbin accused.

"What— a dangerously trained Dreamer assassin kicking your ass and mine? A being more stunning than I've ever seen threatening to end my life by tying me up and hauling me in front of the people that betrayed us? *No.* Why would I be enjoying that?"

15

"You know, I've never had a stalker before," Dorian said as they settled in for the night at the entrance of the caves. His eyes flittered to Reverie sitting across from him. Her annoyed gaze lifted to his as she sharpened her longsword.

"Now I've my own bounty hunter, an exiled band of rebels after my head, companies of Belwarks wanting to take me in, possible beheading by mountaineers, boats onshore, a kingdom in ruin..." Dorian glanced to Corbin, who was shaking his head. "Corbin, I do believe it might be my birth moons day."

"You should thank your older sister for the late present," Corbin said as he turned the rabbits over the fire.

Dorian gaped at him, his heart breaking. Corbin must have sensed it, for he paused and looked at Dorian.

"Too soon?" Corbin asked.

"A bit, yeah," Dorian replied.

Corbin turned back to the fire, not saying another word as he tended the meat. Reverie continued sharpening her blade. Only the noise of her striking the whetstone against the iron was louder than the crackling embers.

"What other news from my home, lady?" Dorian asked as he pulled his pipe from his bag. "What madness has my brother brought upon our people?"

"Your brother is the only reason an army hasn't marched into your beloved Venari's home," Reverie informed them.

Dorian went rigid. His eyes cut in Corbin's direction, who had the same confused look upon his face.

"Sorry, what?" Dorian asked.

"Your brother, Rhaif... He demanded the Council not send an army to the south. Insisted on us finding you and your sister instead to bring you to stand trial. The Council tried to push him, but he had Bard behead Councilman Engle as an example."

Dorian didn't know what to say.

He didn't know what to think.

But his fists curled, and he had to stifle the flames threatening his body. "He would rather send soldiers out to find us, to hurt his... His *family*... Than—" He had to pause his words at the thought of him, sitting on that throne. Weak and mutilated. Spewing demands and barking orders to a world he created.

"Sounds like he's making sure to take you two out first," Corbin uttered.

The words made Dorian cringe. "That is what he told Nys," he said, shaking as he continued to try and stifle his fire. "Secure his place on the throne without the threat of another coming to take it. Send an army out to the rest of the world after." His gaze lifted to Corbin. "You should have let me take his head that night," he said, referring to the night he'd come home and learned Rhaif had hurt Nyssa. "You should have let me end it."

"And you'd have died with Aydra," Corbin argued.

"He's right," Reverie interjected. "If you think the Council would have allowed her to have that child or for you to take the throne, you're wrong."

Dorian contemplated her. "You seem to know a lot about our politics."

"I grew up as my father's firstborn," Reverie said nonchalantly. "The only woman in our village to learn combat and read the stories of old."

"You mean the lies of old," Dorian corrected her.

"Lies?" Reverie balked.

"Yes," Dorian affirmed. "Lies."

Reverie sat down her blade. "The only lies I know are those told by the traitorous king you seem to follow," she argued. "Second only to the one who burned down your own kingdom and murdered some of my friends. I do not understand how you are not furious with the Venari. Their king killed your people. He is the reason your sister is dead. He seduced and brainwashed her into submission just like Duarb did to Arbina."

Dorian had expected this. He had expected every lie told by his predecessors and the Council to be burning on the surface of her mind.

Once more, he stifled his true self down, and he rubbed his hands together. He exchanged another look with Corbin, who huffed under his breath and shook his head.

"You'll be at it all night with this if you start," Corbin said to him. "Save it for another. We need to be alert when we meet our friends tomorrow."

"What and let her walk around believing those lies?" Dorian said.

"Rather her believe them one more night than you starting a fire inside this cave with little chance of us escaping."

Dorian glared at Corbin, but he knew he was right.

"Excuse me?" Reverie cut in.

"He's exaggerating," Dorian muttered.

"Am I?" Corbin said.

Dorian told them he would take first watch after they'd eaten. Corbin had been grateful, but in truth, Dorian didn't know if he could sleep. Reverie's accusations rang through his mind. Her words of Draven seducing Aydra—lies he knew were circulating in every village. He wasn't sure how he was supposed to counter them and prove them differently.

He took to sharpening his own blades during his watch, counting every stroke of the whetstone as days since it had all happened. Counting calmed his mind, as did tedious work of something so simple. A constant truth he could depend on to still be the truth the next day and the next.

It was something he and Nyssa had learned to do together when her anxiety would get the better of her.

He held onto those numbers and continued to count until his brother's blade was so sharp, touching the edge cut through his finger as though it were butter.

And he didn't wake up.

The slight pain jetted through his flesh and reminded him that this nightmare was his reality.

A rumbling sounded around him. Swords were being drawn. There was shouting. The sound of punches throwing. Horses stamping and whinnying wildly.

Dorian cursed as he forced himself awake.

The scene before him was exactly as he'd pictured it in his mind.

Reverie was trying to take on two of the Blackhands that had come to retrieve them.

Dorian sat up and rubbed his forehead. He noticed Corbin sitting on the rock beside him, lazily cutting an apple and eating it off his knife.

"How long's she been at it?" Dorian grumbled.

Corbin shrugged. "Couple minutes," he replied. "Pretty entertaining. She was on Dag's shoulders a second ago."

"Impressive," Dorian yawned. "Where's Hagen?"

Corbin gave an upwards nod, and Dorian followed his gaze, finding the High Elder of the Blackhand Mountains and his friend, Hagen Vairgrey, standing off to the side in the shadows.

His arms were crossed over his thick chest, veins popping out over his skin. His long dark mahogany hair was pulled back in a messy ponytail instead of his usual braid, the sides of his head still shaved. He seemed to be both amused and confused with watching his strongest men getting their asses handed to them by a Dreamer bouncing off the walls and over their heads, dodging past their every blow.

Dorian lifted a hand and waved to his friend when he caught his eye. Hagen gave him a crooked grin and then pointed to Reverie.

"Yours?" he mouthed.

"Long story," Dorian mouthed back.

Hagen looked as though he would grin, but he pushed off the wall instead. He strode into the light, sidestepping his men as they stumbled, obviously intent on dodging Reverie's wrath as he made his way over.

But Reverie was fast.

And she'd seen him.

Before Dorian could tell her not to, Reverie's foot swept through to kick Hagen's chest. He stumbled as she bolted off the wall and jumped clean over his head.

She forced him to his knees, and her arm pushed around his neck within a blink, knife threatening at his throat.

"Make a move, and I'll take you down like I did your friends," she dared in his ear.

She appeared so small behind him that Dorian wasn't sure how she'd gotten him to the ground.

Hagen scowled at Dorian. "A little help?" he asked through clenched teeth.

Dorian smirked. "I kind of like it this way," he bantered.

The tip of her knife creased at Hagen's jawline.

Hagen stretched his neck slightly, eyes darting back to Reverie over his shoulder. "If your point is to threaten me, lady, I am afraid you've lost. You'd be more likely to piss me off by standing there quiet rather than threatening my life. I think you would find you're very much turning me on with your knife at my throat."

Dorian snorted, and a soft grin appeared on Corbin's lips as he chomped on his apple.

"Reverie, he's with us," Dorian finally said. "Doubt you want to be responsible for murdering the High Elder of the Blackhand Mountains.

Reverie released him with a shove and straightened as her darkened gaze cut between the three males. "You're all disgusting," she hissed.

Dorian finally stood, and he helped Hagen up from the ground.

"Nice to know you came with protection," Hagen said upon rising. He dusted his pants off and turned around the room, noting his groaning men on the ground. "Dag, Falke, get up. You're embarrassing our kind in front of the Prince," he told them.

Dorian's attention remained fixated on Hagen's first statement. "Why do you say it's good I came with protection?" he asked, arms hugging his chest.

"Because you're going to need it." Hagen eyed him with an elevated brow before turning on his heel. His boot kicked both his men on the way over to his horse. "You've been marked by every race on this land, Prince," Hagen called back. "Did you think you would be walking freely into my realm and greeted with smiles?"

"I honestly thought you'd by chaining me to my horse the moment you spotted me," Dorian replied. "This bit of conversation feels privileged."

"You know, maybe I should be," Hagen said as he reached his horse. "Maybe I should be roping your wrists and binding you across that steed for the crimes of your kingdom. Maybe you should be the one answering for the murder of Haerland's first true High King and Queen."

Hagen reached inside his bag—

Reverie and Corbin both pulled their blades in anticipation of whatever it was Hagen was retrieving.

But Hagen merely pulled a rolled-up piece of parchment from the inside, and he frowned between them when he turned.

"Well, that's empowering," Dorian uttered upon seeing the beautiful pair standing in front of him. "Never had two people defending my stupidity before."

"Stupidity indeed," Hagen muttered in agreement. "You know what this is, Prince?" he asked him.

"Map of the caves? Deed to a home in the mountains for me to hide in?" Dorian mocked.

"This is orders from your kingdom," Hagen said as he stepped forward.

Dorian stiffened.

"It states if you or your sister are found to be in the mountain realm, war will be declared between us. Your King Rhafian will send an army of Belwarks into my home, and they say they will throw our children into the valleys from our Temple."

Corbin exchanged a look with Dorian over his shoulder, and Dorian's fists tightened at the revelation.

"Normally, I would laugh this off," Hagen continued. "Your king threatening my people seems like a fuck of a joke. I doubt he's that stupid, or if he is, I would love nothing more than to watch him try and take our towns. There is also the option of my sending you home, letting your brother deal with you for betraying your crown so that my people stay safe and do not have to worry of such a threat... But—"

Hagen stepped between Corbin and Reverie, and he paused in front of Dorian.

"I've my own reasons for wanting you in my realm. And as angry as I am about the events of this past month, I am, fortunately for you, inclined to trust the greatest man I ever knew."

Dorian could see the clench in Hagen's jaw.

Hagen pressed the papers into Dorian's chest. "Be glad the Venari King liked you as much as he did, little King."

The knot in Dorian's stomach twisted as though someone was wrenching it from his insides. His nose threatened to burn, but he pushed it away. He swallowed that feeling as Hagen watched him another moment, and then he started backward again.

"Pack up," Hagen said, gaze flickering between Corbin and Reverie. "We've a long way to go before we reach our valleys."

16

Nyssa spent her next morning watching Lex fight with some of the younger recruits, keen to observe her again. Nyssa had always enjoyed watching practices first before joining in. She liked to be prepared, to know what she was walking into and not look like a fool when she didn't know what she was doing.

Nadir had thanked Lex for the addition of her skills with a great hug and handshake, to which Lex had given him a face at that Nyssa knew all too well—a concealment of amusement while also scowling. Nadir had seen through the facade and promised her a smoke on the porch after dinner if she would continue to help him.

Lex, never one to turn down such a prize and chance to show off, agreed and returned the handshake.

"You should join soon," Lex said later as she joined Nyssa on the porch. She leaned back in the wicker chair and kicked her feet up on the railing. "Bit of training might help clear your head."

Nyssa gave her a small smile from the outdoor couch she'd curled up in, the memory of her fighting with Nadir the night before coming to mind. She wondered if Lex had seen them.

"Tomorrow," Nyssa said. "With you. You know me well enough to know I like observing first."

Lex chuckled. "Little Nyssari, eyes of Haerland," she mocked. "I'll be ecstatic when that Promised bloodlust finally kicks in."

"You'll be the first to know when it does."

She met Lex's grin then, and the sight of it made her chest constrict. She knew most of their relationship had been forced due to Aydra's persistence that Lex keep her safe. But she had come to love Lex, realized why Aydra kept her so close. In the days Lex had been forced to keep her safe at the Dreamer village when Aydra was injured, they'd come to understand each other a little more than before, even coming to share jokes.

Nyssa still held in the back of her mind that the only reason Lex was with her was because of duty, and Nyssa hated it. She didn't want to be the burden on anyone, and every time she saw the hurt in Lex's gaze—the hollowness she knew came from her missing her best friend —she was reminded of that promise Lex had made.

"Speaking of lust..."

Lex's words muttered from her lips, and Nyssa looked up to see Nadir coming towards them. Sweat on his brow and sand covering his bare torso, he looked as though someone had rolled him in the surf. He was wearing those same dark grey pants he usually wore for training —made of a fabric that felt of silk and water, stretching and molding over the skin, but thick with iridescent U-shaped scales that reminded her of fish scales. He'd told her the fabric was made specifically as their armor, repelled water, and would help keep the blood flowing through the muscles. He'd mockingly informed her no sword had ever penetrated the fabric, but she was sure he was exaggerating.

"I do love those pants," Lex said.

Nyssa snorted, glancing over to Lex, who was absentmindedly packing her pipe. "Surprised they haven't given you any," she said.

"Met a woman earlier who told me she'd fit me for a pair later tonight." Lex's gaze rose, and she winked at Nyssa.

"Oh, I'm sure," Nyssa bantered. "Should I think I'll not see you again until sunrise?"

"Well—" Lex stuck her match to the flame already going in the lantern, and she lit her pipe, inhaling the breath of the herb. "I was also feeling a bit crowded in there... All that *tension*. Kept waiting on it to break the last few nights, but the pair of you seem to be determined to eventually shatter."

"I don't know what you mean."

Lex grinned. "Yeah, you do." She exhaled the next breath of smoke in an elongated, mocking manner in Nyssa's direction. "You think I didn't see the pair of you last night?"

"We were talking," Nyssa said.

"I know," Lex said. "I'm not sure I understand what the problem is or why you two are dancing around this. I thought for sure he'd have taken you on that beach last night."

"I don't want people thinking he is favoring me," Nyssa admitted.

"You should have seen the stares they gave me yesterday... Even before he asked me to speak with the serpent. If his people think there is something between us, they will undermine him. Commander is the only thing he's ever wanted to be. I don't want to be what comes between him and that honor. Nor do I want to be what makes them question him."

"Noble, Princess," Lex uttered, considering Nyssa. "I'm not sure I like it."

"And I don't want to be another burden on someone," Nyssa said. "I am already enough of one on you."

Silence rested between them, and the fact that Lex didn't argue made Nyssa's heart break. Even if she had already known the truth of it. She glanced back up at Nadir heading towards them and her gaze traveled over every flex of him as he walked.

"He does look good in those pants, though," Nyssa agreed, her head tilting as she took in his body.

Lex huffed amusedly under her breath. "An image for you to take to bed instead then." Lex stood then and gave Nyssa's hair a ruffle before heading down the steps once more. Nadir caught her on his way and gave her a firm handshake. Whatever Lex said, Nadir feigned hurt, and then he grinned before continuing the stretch to his home.

Nyssa pushed the book in front of her face, curled up, and leaned sideways against the back of the couch as she pretended not to see him. But she couldn't help her eyes from dancing over the top of the book when he reached the porch.

"That's two, Princess," he called without so much as a look at her. His hands tapped on the top of the doorframe, and she had to let the book sag in her hands as she chuckled at his comment.

She was quickly consumed in the book of short stories he'd lent her not long after. There was one she had concluded was her favorite. A short story of a woman who combated the sea serpent at the end of the jetty. She knew it was a fairytale, a story of a warrior from the past or possibly one that had never existed, but it sparked something in her, and she found herself comforted by such a story.

Perhaps she would share it with Lex later.

She was so lost in the written words, she didn't hear Nadir come back outside—not until he'd sat down beside her and pulled her leg into his lap, gently massaging her calf. "Let me guess," he said, noting the book in her hands. "You found the one about Soli."

Nyssa ignored the goosebumps rising on her flesh. "She sounds so heroic and fearless," she replied as she looked up from the book. "Combating the serpent with nothing more than her strength."

"She is," Nadir agreed. "She knows it too."

"What?"

"Soli Amberglass. One of my greatest warriors and General of the Flights legion. The author of this book has a special place for her. A bit exaggerated as far as what happened that day, but when are stories not?"

"Wait... You're saying she's real and she lives here? And you were there when she did this?"

Nadir stretched his arm against the back of the chair behind her, his other hand still delicately swirling her ankle. "Do you want to meet her?"

"That sounds like a terrible idea," Nyssa said, anxiety swelling.

"Why?"

"Because she... *She's a warrior.*"

"She's a normal person with flaws just like everyone else. Believe me."

And the way he spoke made her stomach knot.

She tucked her hair behind her ear, shrinking into that space she'd found herself hiding in for half her life. "Maybe another day," she decided.

Nadir nodded. His hand clapped her shin before he leaned forward to kiss her kneecap. "Come to dinner with me?" he asked, looking as though he was going to stand.

Nyssa flipped the page in her book, her heart suddenly aching for a reason she wasn't sure of. "I don't think so."

Nadir settled back into the chair slowly. "What were your plans?" he asked, and she noted the drop in his voice.

"Reading," she drawled, eyeing him over the cover.

The corner of his lip quirked, and before she could find her place again, his mouth pressed to the inside of her knee.

And he didn't stop there.

He kissed her thigh next, lips dragging over her flesh as he moved. His lips met her skin over and over in a manner that completely distracted her. He shifted, his other hand curling behind her calf as he leaned closer. Nyssa's heart skipped. The words she'd literally just said to Lex rang in her ears. But she caught the leer on his face, and she closed her book shut with an audible clap.

"What are you doing?" she asked.

"Taking advantage of your sister's Second being occupied," he said as he bent her leg up. His open mouth kissed the bend at her knee again, tongue dragging over her skin and making her breath catch.

There was a tug in her abdomen, a voice telling her it was a bad idea, that she had a job to do and being with him was not part of it.

But damn if she didn't want him.

She couldn't help but bite her lip as he continued his deliberate torture. Her dress fell between her shaking thighs when he pulled her leg again to rest it atop his shoulder. Her toes pointed despite herself as he continued to kiss and lick her, going higher and higher. She blushed when he paused at the apex of her thighs and steadied there, breath tickling her through the dress, hands curling around her hips.

For a moment, she thought he would continue, devour her as he'd done so many times just in those two nights at Magnice.

But he seemed intent on teasing her.

The slight smirk he gave her made her own eyes dance. He lifted her hand off her thigh and kissed her palm. Her ears reddened as she heard the noise of other people on the beach, and she realized they were on the porch in broad daylight, his face between her legs.

"Your people will see us," she whispered, unable to suppress her smile.

He pushed up then, and her leg fell to the side of him as he came to hover over her. "They'll certainly hear *you*," he replied. He bent down, and her head tilted back as he dipped to the crook of her neck, his tongue raking over her throat. She cursed her body for its response and could practically feel herself dripping already.

"Whether they see us is a different story."

He was still holding her hand when he hovered over her again, and he guided her fingers between her legs. He bent again, his lips dragging across the fabric covering her abdomen. Mouth sagging, she watched as they both discovered how wet she was. She was soaking through the lace of her undergarments already. His chest visibly heaved, and he groaned, eyes shutting as though he hadn't expected it.

"*Infi*, are you wearing that tiny thing from the second night?" he asked in a rasp upon discovering which undergarments she had on.

Lingerie had always made her feel more powerful than she was, a confidence booster she enjoyed. Unlike her sister, who had always thought such things unnecessary.

The moan that left her was full of delighted amusement, and she removed her hand from his, wanting to touch him. She allowed her hands to graze up his chest to his cheeks, memorizing the stubble along his jaw.

"These are my favorites," she said innocently.

His nose brushed low on her abdomen. "I think you know they're my favorites as well," he uttered, lips pressing to her hip through dress.

His gaze landed back on her, and she nearly lost herself right then. But he watched her. Watched her as he pushed to a hover over her and deliberately stroked down her clit before moving the fabric and dipping inside her. Her breath caught when he pressed two fingers fully in, palm lying flat. The delicious friction made her hips buck into his hand.

Fuck, he'd barely touched her, and she was sure she would come apart if he moved any faster.

"Did you miss me, Princess?" he breathed, his long fingers hooking inside her. His hips moved against his arm, increasing that pressure. She could see him hardening through those damn pants. She wanted to touch him, but she also knew their game. *Loved* their game. So she lifted her chin, arched her back, and looked directly up at him, unable to suppress the breathy moan that emitted from her lips when she whispered, "Yes."

She thought he would continue, but he moved and pulled from inside her. She could see the stick and glisten of her juices on those long fingers, stringing when he separated them in front of her, almost triumphant in nature.

Watching him slip one of those fingers in his mouth and taste her shouldn't have turned her on as much as it did, but she'd seen that mouth do things she didn't know mouths were supposed to do—

And she had never ached for someone as she did for him.

She wanted that mouth on every part of her.

A low, satisfied groan left him when he pulled the finger from his mouth. "I missed you too," he uttered, the tone teasing from his lips and making her hips arch to his.

He settled against her, his hardened length pressing between her legs through the fabric. She groaned and pushed her pelvis against him as he brought his hand down to her lips. His other finger, still glistening with her wetness, brushed her bottom lip, and she opened her mouth for him to push his fingertip inside her. Tasting herself on his warm, salty skin. Tonguing his finger as she liked to tongue his cock. She grasped his wrist between her hands and held his hand there as she sucked on him. Up and down. Her mouth puckered with each sweep and soft moan. The corner of his lips flinched upwards as he watched. He pulled his hand away after a few moments and brushed his knuckles against her cheek.

"Is that what you want to do with my cock?" His hips pushed against her when he spoke, and he dropped his head low to the crook of her neck.

"Yes," she groaned.

He straightened, a quiet chuckle sounding from deep in his chest. His hand trailed down her front, and he found her wetness again.

"You'll let me play first, Princess," he said as he stroked her. "I want that tight pussy raining before I take you. Can you do that for me?"

Eyes fluttering, she tried to calm her shaking breaths. "Yes," she managed as she squirmed against his tease. With every slow press of his fingers, his cock pushed against her. She rocked her hips into his hand. Until he pulled out of her, and those digits tickled up and down her throbbing clit again.

"Filthy girl," he whispered playfully, and she dared to smile at the salutation, chest arching off the bench. Dared to enjoy when he called her that and more.

She met his darkened yet delighted eyes as his free hand slipped beneath her dress to grasp her breast. The second his thumb grazed her taut nipple, she heard someone shout from the beach, and she remembered where they were.

"Nadir, this..." The words caught in her throat, "...this is probably a bad idea," she finally managed.

"I quite enjoy our bad ideas," he purred before kissing her throat again. His teeth nipped at her skin, and then he moved to rest his forehead against hers.

"Look at me," he said in a breathless, raspy voice. "No one else."

He was intoxicating, *consuming*, and he made her want to forget reality.

He pinched her clit between his forefinger and thumb, and she decided she didn't care who was watching.

The entire village could watch as he fucked her into submission and sent her over the edge. She would deal with the consequences and glares later. But for now, she was his, and damn did he feel like home.

"Perhaps we should call them horribly beautiful ideas instead," she uttered.

His chest moved with the deep chuckle, and his nose nudged against hers. "Do you want me to stop?" he asked.

It was all she could do to shake her head. "I want you deeper," she breathed. "Harder."

"There's my Princess," he beamed over her. His fingers pressed deep inside, palm nearly slapping against her and making her gasp. Hooking and almost pulling her off the bench with every thrust. He groaned in her throat, whispering, "Fuck, you're so wet for me," on her skin. "Do you get this wet for anyone else?"

"You," she groaned as she ran her hands behind his neck, her own head throwing back. "Yours, Commander."

His forehead rolled against her arched chest with another moan, his shoulders caved as though he'd not thought she would say it. He kissed her jaw, bit her throat, and breathed, "Mine," against her lips before moving lower.

His thumb dragged along her clit as he moved those digits in and out, each time with increasing pressure and depth. Her back arched off the bench again, and his lips clamped on her nipple through the dress. He was beginning to pick up his pace. Making her body squirm and reach and rock with him. She cursed his name out loud, eyes rolling as she grasped his hair and held him on her chest. His tongue swirled over that hardened peak before pulling it into his mouth and sucking on her breast. She was already feeling her end near, her insides tightening around his fingers.

But his hand moved from inside her, and he swirled her wetness around her clit, pressing hard and making her groan again. He kissed up her chest to her throat, licked her neck, and nibbled her skin before stilling over her.

"Do you know what horribly beautiful idea I'm going to finish you with?" he asked, breath tickling her lips.

Open mouths nearly sweeping together, Nyssa leaned up, desperate to kiss him, and she uttered, "Surprise me," as her hands pressed to his cheeks.

A final smile spread over him, and his teeth tugged on her bottom lip. She knew the moment he kissed her that this teasing would be over, and they would both surrender to the other.

"Yes, Princess," were the last words he uttered before his mouth pressed against hers—

Someone cleared their throat.

Nyssa's heart skipped. Nadir groaned, his head coming to rest on her breast. "I will murder her," he muttered into her skin. He pushed up on his arms, "Fucking Infi, Second, I thought—"

But it wasn't Lex.

Lovi Piathos was standing on the porch.

Nadir stumbled at the rate he stood off her. Nyssa snatched her dress down fast and hoped the Lesser One had not been standing there for too long. Her entire body heated beet red under the old man's amused gaze.

"Grand," Nadir said, clearing his throat. "I—" He grabbed the blanket from the wicker chair and shoved it around his waist to conceal his indecency. "We were about to head down for dinner."

Lovi laughed a high-pitched chortle. "Came here not for you, m'boy," he said, his broken speech making Nyssa's head tilt. "Came for her."

Nyssa's color drained. "What... What did I do?"

"Not what you did," Lovi said, his thick accent coming through. "What she here for." He turned and pointed his staff towards the ocean. Nyssa followed his point, and she was suddenly glad for the couch she was sitting on.

The black phoenix was sitting at the end of the jetty.

"What..." Nyssa stood and brushed past Nadir to lean out over the banister. "What's she doing here?"

Lovi laughed again and held out his arm. "We find out together."

Nadir was staring wide-eyed at the beast when Nyssa turned, and when she caught his gaze, his weight shifted.

"How is she here?" Nadir asked.

"Venari King think he smart," Lovi said. "We find out what she want with her freedom."

Nadir came to stand by her side as Lovi caught her arm. But Nadir grabbed her hand before they could leave and gave it a squeeze. Nyssa looked back at Nadir when Lovi began leading her down the steps, hoping Nadir saw her silent plea for him to go with her, their fingers still hanging on to the other.

He nodded and started to follow behind, but Lovi slapped his cane across Nadir's chest. Nadir grunted at the abruptness of it, the wind knocking out of him.

"Stay," Lovi said. "Princess handle this."

"I can't hear her," Nyssa said fast.

"You no need hear creatures to speak with Mother Sun." Lovi's hand clapped on top of hers, and Nyssa had no choice but to follow beside him down the steps.

People had begun to gather around, obviously all confused as to why the black phoenix was not only free but also sitting at the end of one of their jetties as though it were perfectly normal.

Nyssa tried to push the people's voices out and focus on her feet as she and Lovi made down the rocky walk.

The shadows of the phoenix's fire pulled back into her great body upon their approach. Lovi, for whatever reason, was still grinning as he clapped his hand on top of Nyssa's. Nyssa was sure the man was utterly mental, and that was something she was also confident that everyone in that village would at least agree with.

A shudder ran down Nyssa's spine when she locked eyes with the beast. The Sun's great amber eyes stared back, a color so like her own.

But Lovi's chortle sounded beside her, and they paused a few rocks away.

"You free to your tricks, I see," Lovi laughed. He stepped up to her and gave the bird a pet on the beak as though he were greeting an old friend. "My father will look for his way out next," he said.

The Sun looked past Lovi, and her gaze landed once more on Nyssa.

Little Nyssari, the Sun said, her neck bowing again.

Nyssa wasn't sure what to do. Bow? Curtsy? Fall to her knees?

She chose a short bow, though it didn't seem like enough in the presence of the Sun herself. She swore the beast smiled at her.

Except now, she wasn't sure what to call her.

A laugh echoed in her mind, and Nyssa realized perhaps the Sun could hear her thoughts, for she said, *Sun will do*, to her.

Nyssa nodded. "Hello, Sun," she said aloud.

You wonder why I am here.

"Have I done something wrong?"

The Sun laughed. *No. I wanted to see you. I have a small job for you.*

Nyssa tried not to think about how reluctant she was to take on another job besides fulfilling her promises and saving Haerland from Man.

"Anything," she chose to respond.

I need you to be my eyes in this time as I look over the others.

She wasn't sure what she meant, but Nyssa replied, "Okay," anyway.

They are safe.

"Who?"

Your King and Queen.

Nyssa's heart fell to her knees. "What?"

But the phoenix didn't answer her directly. *Through every doorway, I will watch*, the Sun said. *There will always be one open for you should you call. I will come.*

The phoenix bowed her head then for a long enough moment that Lovi shoved Nyssa's back. Nyssa stepped forward, hand reaching out. And when her palm pressed to the great bird's beak, the familiar shiver pulsed through her.

It was the same shiver she'd felt upon first seeing it in her room when Aydra had come back for her. Nyssa sank into what felt like a warm hug wrapping her insides and quelling the ache in her chest.

Aydra's hug.

Nyssa nearly lost her balance as the abrupt comfort of it swelled inside her. She could feel Aydra's arms holding her head into her chest like she was standing just in front of her. Hear her heartbeat against her ear. Aydra's arms cradled around her, hands stroking the back of her head. Nyssa could smell her sister's hair. Ocean. Citrus. Sunlight. Nyssa held onto the feeling as she held on to her life. She dug her fingers into her sister's back. Held her with every fiber of her being.

Exhale the fire, sister, Aydra said, and Nyssa could feel her sister's breath on her skin with the words.

The sensation of it brought not sad tears but comforting ones. Comfort and belonging. Reassurance that she was where she was supposed to be.

Through every doorway, she remembered the Sun saying.

Had she just opened up a doorway to a memory of Aydra?

Nyssa pushed the thought from her mind, not wanting to get her hopes up for anything that might have meant seeing her again. She would settle for the few seconds the Sun had allowed her to relive.

Thank you, Nyssa said to the Sun as she wiped her face.

The Sun gave her another bow before letting out a great shriek that vibrated the entire reef. Lovi's hand was on Nyssa's arm, and Nyssa stood stunned with him as the wind from the Sun's great wings whipped the air.

She disappeared into shadow and clouds, and the bright orb that was the setting sun showed itself once more.

Nyssa stood steady in its embrace, letting her skin soak in the brightness. The warmth covered her cheeks. Until she heard Lovi laughing once more.

"You Sun children and your Sun," he said. "Always trickster. She be back."

Lovi left her there and started his walk back to the village.

She could still feel Aydra's arms wrapped around her.

It was Lex who reached her first.

Nyssa hardly realized the Second Sun was in front of her until she felt Lex's hands grasp onto her cheeks, wildly shouting before her.

Reality swooped over Nyssa as a cold splash to the face.

"—talk to me! *Nyssari!*"

Nyssa grabbed onto Lex's wrists. "Lex, I felt her."

"What?"

"I felt her, I felt my sister, I felt Drae—"

But it was a soft smile that spread over her lips—a smile in recognition of her sister, feeling the comfort of her instead of her absence.

"I felt her," Nyssa finally said.

She could see the tears in Lex's gaze, and Nyssa wrapped her arms around her. She would have given anything to let Lex feel what she'd just felt. A tear dropped on her cheek from Lex, and Nyssa hugged her tighter.

17

Lex tried to get Nyssa to go back to the house, but Nyssa wasn't ready. She wanted to sit in the quiet a little longer, relish the night air for the first time in two weeks without fearing the Noctuans' cries. Lex asked if she wanted company while she thought, but Nyssa told her no, even though she was sure Nadir would not let her stay on her own for long without his curiosity getting the best of him. Lex retired and gave Nyssa's hair a ruffle before leaving her out on the rocks.

Nyssa wasn't sure how long she sat there on her own—cross-legged on the last rock on that jetty, watching the moons rise over the calm water. But after a while, she surrendered back to the beach.

A noise caught her ears to the East, and she noticed Nadir alone by the river, loading boxes onto one of his boats as though getting ready to trek upriver. He cursed under his breath when a splinter caught his thumb, and she watched him suck out the wood and spit it on the ground.

"Great Commander being taken down by a splinter," she mocked, hugging her arms around her chest when she reached him. "Do you need some help?"

Nadir huffed amusedly and gave a nod towards the crates to her left. "I can always use help," he said. "Can you pass me those?"

Nyssa picked up a crate and passed it to him. "Big trip tomorrow?"

"Upriver to see Bala. She's forest meats to trade for fish my men caught," Nadir said. "Don't worry," he winked, "I'll be back to tell you goodnight."

She almost laughed. "Will you be tucking me in as well?" she bantered.

"Depends on if you're asleep," he answered as she handed him another crate.

"Really? Here I thought sleeping wouldn't be what deterred you from taking what you wanted."

That low chuckle emitted from his lips, and he circled slowly back to her.

—He gripped her arms and hauled her up. She was tossed in the air once she was level with him, making her yelp, and she had to wrap her legs around his waist upon falling back into his grasp. His hands strapped beneath her bottom, and her breath caught from him holding her like that again.

"Would you rather I take you right now on this boat? Finish what we started earlier..." His lips dragged across her throat, and Nyssa limped. She felt his hand moving closer between her thighs, and her mouth sagged when he grasped her ass hard enough to bruise.

"Should I make you scream my name for every person in this village to find out who exactly the Princess gets on her knees for?" he nearly purred.

Nyssa's hips bucked into his, inner thighs tightening around him. "Should you like them to also find out who their Commander gets on his knees for?"

Nadir scoffed at her banter but didn't press. "I know you didn't come here to flirt, Princess," he said before kissing her jaw. "I know you want to talk about that phoenix—" her eyes fluttered as he mouthed her throat, hands still massaging her backside "—And I am also rather curious to know what she wanted."

It took everything in her to pull him off her neck. "How do you expect me to tell you anything when you're doing that?"

"Multitasking," he shrugged.

Her lips pressed together thinly, and he chuckled as he gave her ass a smack and then put her back on the ground. Her neck remained heated, heart thumping rapidly in her chest from his holding her, but she hopped down from the boat and brushed herself off.

"The Sun said something—"

"So that was the actual Sun?" Nadir interjected.

Nyssa nodded, just realizing perhaps Nadir had not heard that Draven had released the phoenix. "It was. She bonded with Drae after Draven released her."

Nadir shook his head, almost looking as though he would laugh at any moment. "That bastard performed part of the Red Moons ritual."

"What's that?" Nyssa asked.

"You don't know what the Red Moons are?"

"It is not written in our Chronicles."

"The Red Moons free Haerland," he said simply.

There was a pause where Nyssa thought he would go on, but he didn't.

"That really didn't help," she said.

He chuckled under his breath. "Perhaps I'm hesitant to give you any ideas."

The words made her arms cross over her chest. "How crazy is the idea?"

"Completely mental," he told her. "Each of the rituals requires sacrifice. Aydra's raven, sacrificing itself for her safety, it's what that particular ritual required."

"How barbaric."

"Safety precautions," Nadir said with another shrug. "Making sure no one stumbled upon it and completed the entire thing. That is another level of security."

"So... how did Draven know the phoenix would bind with us?"

"Probably didn't. I'm sure he didn't know if it would work."

"Drae told me he wasn't surprised," she said. "That he looked at that phoenix as though he'd been expecting her."

"Don't think his releasing the Sun had anything to do with him truly wanting her free," he said, rubbing his neck. "I think he released her for Aydra. To have her feel such a bond with a creature and a mother that truly appreciated her. The Sun is healing and serenity for the children born of her trees. She is also a trickster. Now that she's at least partially free, I imagine you might see or hear some things you may not understand."

"Like what?"

"Images of future Sun children, memories you may not recall because they aren't your own. Perhaps images of the past, depending on what she feels you need to see."

Aydra.

The hug.

But it wasn't just that.

Nyssa thought to the images from the banquet that her mind had been filling with. The vividness of the memories and how they took her out of her own reality. Not like a daydream, but as though she were back in the middle and reliving it.

"Might explain what was happening to you the other day," he said, the same thought apparently going through his head.

"Why did Haerland curse her?" she wondered.

"Actually, all the Architects have been imprisoned by her—each for different issues. The Sun, specifically, tried to break the bond with Arbina," Nadir said. "She didn't like the person her eldest had become, what with how brutal and manipulative she was after Duarb gave his Hunter. The Sun wanted to put her daughter in her place and show her consequences for what she was doing. But Haerland didn't want that, took Arbina's side. So, she cursed the Sun and forced her into a prison deep within the depths of this land. The black phoenix is the form the Sun chose to roam the land in."

"Can she not form into her womanly self?"

"Not until the full ritual is performed. How exactly Draven got his hands on that scroll, I'm not sure. Probably on one of his journeys to the mountains. All of our most sacred scrolls are in a cave beneath the Mortis Lunar Pass at Lake Oriens." He paused and eyed her again. "It's not to be played with."

"But what exactly does the Red Moons ritual do? What do you mean by the 'curses'? Which curses?"

Nadir sat the crate he was holding on the boat. The playful expression that had filled his features just moments before had vanished. "No," he told her.

"Nadir—"

"I don't want you to get any ideas," he snapped.

She was taken aback by his harsh tone, and how he spoke made her weight shift. "I think I should have a working knowledge of this. This is our history. Would you rather I continue being blind?" she argued.

His jaw clenched. A low grunt emitted from his throat, and he glowered at her. "That's really not fair, Princess."

"If you would just tell me, I wouldn't have to use sentences like that."

"Fine..." he huffed reluctantly. "The Red Moons ritual removes every curse. It frees the Architects. Frees the Noctuans from the dark. Allows Duarb out of his tree, the removal of the Infi. Arbina would no longer be caged in her waters. And..."

The silence that followed made her stomach knot. He was hiding something, and she needed to know what.

"And what, Commander?" she demanded.

His eyes rolled up to meet hers. "It frees those trapped at the Edge."

"What do you mean trapped at the Edge?" she asked, insides

vacating. "I thought the void there was a myth, and it was simply a normal realm just like every other place in our land."

"The Edge is a normal realm. Quite beautiful too if you go during the Deads," he said. "It's the only time the lunaren flowers bloom. I've men who frequent there—"

"Don't change the subject," she interjected. "If the void is a myth, then how are—what do you mean trapped?"

"The void isn't a myth," he said. "It's very real. If you get caught too far into it, you'll be lost."

None of his explanations were helping, and the frustration began to swell in her.

He apparently caught her confusion and sighed as he took a seat on the edge of the boat. "The void you've read about that you think is a myth— it's real. It's like a pocket area within the Edge realm where the dead sometimes gets trapped."

"Okay... So, how does the Red Moons ritual free these people from that void?"

"Depends on what they want. Whether to go on into death or come back to avenge the land."

Nyssa stilled... How nonchalantly he'd explained it, as though if he shrugged it off as something minuscule, she wouldn't catch it.

Come back to avenge the land.

"And how exactly does one get trapped at the Edge?" she made herself say.

"Nyssa—" He stood and started to reach out for her, but she swatted his hands away.

"No, Nadir. Tell me."

A new fear had filled his constricted gaze. A fear she didn't know he possessed. For a moment, she thought he might turn on his heel, leave her without an answer.

But—

"They sacrifice themselves for Haerland," he finally answered.

Her entire body drained, and she had to grab hold of the boat to keep herself from limping to the ground.

Sacrificed themselves for Haerland.

Sacrificed.

Trapped.

Aydra.

"Nyssa—"

"How is it done?" she snapped. "How is the ritual performed?"

"You can't—"

"Why the fuck not? If it will free them—"

"It is not the time," he growled, suddenly standing over her.

"If you think—"

"This isn't something you do on a whim," he argued. "And it's not something you can do on your own."

Your king and queen are safe, the Sun had said.

"But I could save them—"

"Save them?" he repeated incredulously. "All right. Fine, Princess. Tell me you would sacrifice your brother to bring them back."

She froze.

"What?"

"You would have to sacrifice someone you truly love in this world to complete the ritual," he continued. "Not yourself. So tell me you could send him into oblivion to bring them back."

Her world stopped.

She wanted to say she could.

She wanted to tell him she would give anything to bring them back.

She wanted to demand him take her to see the scrolls.

But her heart wrenched at the thought of being alive without Dorian, the idea of her sacrificing him, and she nearly choked.

"That's really not fair," she breathed.

"Like I said," Nadir sighed. "Safety precautions."

"Who placed this part of the curse?" she demanded to know. "What sort of—"

"Your Sun," Nadir interjected. "The Sun made a deal with Haerland. That she would go quietly into imprisonment so long as Haerland would allow her children to rise again with her and the Red Moons. But not all of them. Only those who proved their worth, who sacrificed themselves for the land. Only those would be worthy of the phoenix fate."

A heavy huff left her, and she cursed everything in her life. "I hate this place sometimes."

18

Nyssa had awoken before the sunrise, hardly able to sleep after all she'd learned, and she'd gone out to the end of the jetty to simply sit. She couldn't stop thinking about what it would mean for her sister to be alive, for Draven to be back...

But every time she thought about sacrificing anyone she loved, she had to force breath into her lungs to keep herself steady.

Lex had pushed her that morning on her horse, insistent that Nyssa practice with her bow. Nyssa couldn't concentrate. She missed three targets and finally pressed her bow into Lex's hands after the sun rose high in the sky, feeling completely defeated. Lex hadn't said anything in response to her failure, but then again, Nyssa hadn't exactly given her a chance to. She'd curled herself up on the porch the afternoon with one of the books in the hopes she could escape her mind.

She wondered what Dorian was doing, whether he was having more success than her with whatever it was he'd been tasked with.

By the time the sun went down, Nyssa had taken another walk down the beach and then cradled herself on the end of the jetty again. She was trying to calm her mind with the beach waves and feel normal.

In all honesty, she missed her family.

The comfort of the castle walls. Nyssa certainly appreciated everything that was being done for her there, how Nadir was making her feel, how patient Lex was being... But she couldn't help missing that familiar reality. She wanted to see her sister's smile, hear Dorian bantering and poking fun at her...

Her eagle had sat on her knee as she stayed there. She was trying to reach back out to the creatures now that the Noctuans were once more asleep. But there was nothing in response, and her eagle simply gave her a comforting nip and purr when she would stroke his neck.

Nadir didn't make it back before she retired to the bedroom. Her body was pent up with all the anxiety and knowledge she'd forced into the depths of her core the last few days.

She just wanted to go to sleep.

So she tried to think of things that would relax her.

Lex's suggestion thundered through her mind. Not to mention what had happened the day before on that porch and on the boat. She could still feel his lips against her knee, trailing up her arm... His hands wrapped around her backside, tongue sliding on her throat. Perhaps if he had been back, she would have gone and crawled in his bed, gave in to their dance, and took him like she so desperately wanted to—tug on her heart be damned.

But as he wasn't home, the memory of the night at the banquet would have to do.

She sat up in the bed and pushed herself against the headboard, allowing the pillows to cradle her open legs, and she closed her eyes, stretched the muscles of her neck, and gripped the sheet over her chest.

She could still see that night in her head as clear as it had been while living it. More clear than any memory of every day after. Possibly her most explicit memory. It was a night she held on to as she held on to sunlight as a healing source. The freedom she'd felt those nights, not just with him but with everything going on in that castle. No judgments. No titles. Not him attempting to swoon her or impress her in any form.

It was all completely effortless.

She remembered how he'd come to her room with food, insisting he was only there to talk and help her sober up. He'd proceeded to go through every single one of the trinkets around her room, tossing some of them aside and making fun of her for having so many suitors knock on her door in the last few years. They'd laid together on the lounge chair, legs entwined, while he read from her poetry books. It was that memory that made her smile as well as squirm in her seat.

"Princess, these poems are filthy," he had mocked her.

She reached up and snatched the book from his hands. "Don't ruin my poems with your mockery," she argued.

He grinned. "You're a romantic, aren't you?"

"Oh, I'm a romantic?" she mocked. She fought the twist of her lips and the blush on her cheeks as her head tilted in his direction. "Says the one reading

such filthy poems aloud to the woman he's not even supposed to be in the same room with."

Her brow raised slyly at the softened smile that spread over his features then, and she stood from the chair, intent on placing some of the books back. She'd just reached to put the one on the top shelf in the opposite corner when she turned, only to find Nadir sitting on the edge of the chair, elbows pressed into his knees, fingers steepled beneath his chin. He was staring at her, heel tapping the ground, and she knew he was battling with himself again.

"I really shouldn't be here," she heard him breathe. "I—"

Whatever his words were, she didn't hear. He stood. Fast. Muttering words she didn't understand under his breath and looking around for his shoulder pad, she realized that he was finally deciding to leave before things went too far. Nyssa's heart fell at the embarrassment of thinking someone like him would ever truly be interested in her.

She went over to the bottle of nyghtfire she'd stashed in her dresser and pulled it out. She poured two glasses and then crossed the space back to him. Nadir's throat bobbed when she pushed the cup in his hands.

"To wanting what we can't have," she cheers'd him.

He let his shoulder pad slowly fall back onto the mattress as he watched her take a small sip. She couldn't help biting her lip when she pulled back, embarrassment flooding her.

Just as she looked down and started to turn away, she saw him snap back the nyghtfire and heard the glass shatter on the floor when he threw it over his shoulder.

"Fuck it."

He grasped her arm and hauled her back to him, lips slamming against hers, and she had to grip his waist to stay upright. The cinnamon taste of nyghtfire on his tongue and the salt of his skin made her knees weak. His lips were frantic against hers, arms hugging and hands grasping her back and the bottom of her tulle dress.

She'd never felt so wanted in her life.

Her heart fled at the desperate way he kissed her, as though if he let her go that she would disappear from before him. Every sweep of his tongue against hers had her nearly moaning in his mouth. He bent low, getting a better grip on her, almost picking her up off the ground as he stretched and clenched that tulle. She pushed her hands beneath his shirt, separating from him a moment to pull it off.

Fuck, he was perfect.

He went to kiss her again, but she pushed slightly on his chest.

"What?" he asked breathlessly.

She allowed her gaze to wander over him, memorizing every flex and ripple of his sculpted body. The broad shoulders and narrow waist. His muted olive-colored skin against her own pale hand. The way his body would have held around her perfectly. She reached out and traced the lines between his heaving abs, and he flinched with her touch, visible goosebumps rising on his flesh. She wanted to memorize him. Know every scar and line of his perfect body.

"I... Did the ocean carve you from a rock?" she heard herself mocking as she ran her fingers over the veins in his forearm and eyed the one at the vee of his hips. "How are you this... how—"

Nadir scoffed and bent again, his lips pressing to her throat and making her ramble cease with a soft gasp. That mouth... He was sucking on her skin, and with every brush of his tongue, she limped further into his abyss. She felt his hands traveling down her sides, and then the tightness of the strings on the back of her dress loosened. It fell to the floor, leaving only the corset and tiny creme lace undergarments covering her torso.

Nadir paused and gawked down at her, mouth agape. "You've been wearing that all night and I've been telling you jokes?" he managed, voice cracking.

"I literally threw myself at you earlier," she reminded him.

He grinned briefly before his gaze darkened so leeringly that her thighs clenched. His tongue darted out over his lips, and he bent, hands wrapping beneath her bottom and squeezing. She groaned as his fingers grabbed her ass, and the next thing she knew, her feet were off the ground, and her legs were wrapped around his waist.

He leaned forward, their lips brushing. "I'm such an idiot."

—The door creaked.

Nyssa jumped, stowing the sheet fully around her bent legs. Heat beat on her skin, splotching up and down her as if direct sunlight were radiating on her flesh. She glared at the door.

Nadir was watching her from the shadows.

She swallowed at the sight of him reflecting back at her from the firelight and then stiffened out a, "Don't you know how to knock?" hiss.

"I thought you were sleeping," he said simply. "I just came to check in on you."

Nyssa groaned under her breath, hating him for disrupting her when she was nearing her end. She shook her head and snapped out of her daze again, letting her hair fall over her shoulder as she replied, "I'm fine," in a barely audible breath.

But he was still standing there a moment later.

"What?" she snapped, avoiding his gaze, waiting on the mockery from him. "Let it out, Commander. Let's hear it."

"You could have waited."

"And exactly how long was I supposed to wait?" she managed, feeling her breath shorten under the beat of her blood pressure rising.

He didn't reply at first, and the quiet of the room lasted long enough that she finally forced her lashes up to see him still standing there. She ran her hand through her hair, growing tired of his silence.

"Are you going to stand there staring, or are you going to lock the door and get over here?" she finally forced from her lips.

He stiffened in the door for a split and then closed it behind him. The snap of the lock made her heart flee, and when he pushed his shirt over his head, slowly striding across the room, she had to swallow the dry spit in her mouth.

Architects, he was gorgeous.

The moons' light coming in cascaded over his every muscle crease and vein. She couldn't stop the travel of her eyes over him, the bite of her lip. If she hadn't been aroused already from the mere memory of him taking her, she certainly was now.

She could see the strain of him through the linen of his flowing pants, and she wondered how long he'd been standing in the doorway. She knew he didn't miss the rise of her brows at the sight of him wanting, but she tried to remind herself to breathe when he crawled on the bed. Up the mattress, all the way to her, a predatory glint in his eyes. Finally, his hands pressed into the mattress on either side of her bent legs, her knees spreading as he came to hover over her.

For a moment, he lingered a mere breath from her face, teasing her with the anticipation of his mouth on her body. Her chest heaved with every brush of his nose against her skin, every tickle of his mouth near her flesh...

And then she saw the smirk on his lips.

"What *exactly* were you thinking about, Princess?" he asked in a mocking tone she knew all too well, and she knew he'd smelled her arousal from nearly finishing herself before.

She shoved him backward. "Oh, fuck off, Commander," she uttered, failing at her attempt to keep a straight voice.

He fell onto his side, laughter emitting, and she smacked his knee. Nadir grabbed at her legs and pinched her skin. She couldn't stop her laugh. Couldn't stop herself from smiling wider as she pushed to her knees and swatted his tickling hands. The pulse of his laugh bounced off the walls and echoed over the noise of the ocean outside.

"Were you thinking about me?" he mocked again as she grabbed his hands and wrestled their arms back and forth.

It was laughter she'd only heard glimpses of in weeks coming from deep inside her as she shrieked out his name, unable to suppress it. He pulled her off her knees and sat her straddle over his waist. She was no match for his strength, and he had her thighs locked in his hands when he gave her ass a smack, chuckling into the crook of her neck.

"Were you thinking about the bath?"

She stabilizing herself by grasping the tops of his shoulders. His fingers pinched and tickled her, making her fight and buck against his grasp.

"Or was it when I held you against that door?"

A chill brushed her skin at the memory. She sank into the abyss of him when his lips pressed to the soft spot beneath her ear. Hands threading in his hair, her laughter dwindled to a smiling moan, and she pressed her breasts into his chest, arms wrapping around his neck. His hands tightened into her hips, her laughter fading, but smile not, as he continued to kiss her throat, up her jaw, and finally—

He cupped her cheek in his palm, pausing only to smile at her for a flinch, and then he pressed his lips to hers.

Her heart melted at the taste of him again. As if his absence had been years and not just months. She'd missed the softness of his lips, the whisper of his tongue.

"*Curses*, I missed you," he whispered against her lips.

Her hands pressed to his face, and she whispered, "I missed you," in a breath before kissing him desperately once more.

He held her firmly against him as though kissing her was the last thing he ever wanted to do with his life. She didn't know where to touch him first and ended up cradling her hands to his face while he grasped and dug into her waist and backside. Her shirt bunched in his hands. She pulled back only enough to hold her arms up as he pulled the nightdress over her head. Her chest rose high with the jagged inhale of watching him leer at her bare body. That same smile was on his lips from when he'd discovered the laced lingerie she was wearing after the banquet.

"It's not fair what you do to me," he uttered, his long fingers sweeping over her ribs, thumbs brushing her taut nipples. "*Architects*, you're stunning." His mouth clamped to her nipple with the last word, and she couldn't help but hold onto him as he leaned her back.

Rocking her hips against his, feeling his hardened length against her entrance through his pants. He slapped her ass again when her head dropped back, eyes rolling at the way he bit her breast and sucked on her skin.

"You think you don't do the same to me?" she whispered.

Nadir slowed and pulled away to move her hair from her face. "Show me," he said softly.

She grabbed his hand and guided his touch down her side to her hip and then between her legs. He bent his head into the crook of her neck, kissing her skin. His fingertips brushed her folds, and she sucked in a sharp breath at the tickle. He groaned against her—a groan she recognized all too well by then.

"Fuck, Princess," he breathed. "You're drenching—*Nyssa*—"

She wrapped both her hands around his neck, moving to hold him on her throat as he deliberately touched her clit. Mouth sagging and face scrunching as he stroked her. But the hug of him didn't last long. He reached up, causing her to whimper in the absence of his hand, and he took her arm from around his neck, kissing down her forearm all the way to her fingers— the same fingers she'd been using to pleasure herself not long before. His eyes met hers, and she allowed him to guide her hand between her legs, his fingers covering hers. She felt herself, how much wetter she was just in the presence of him and not having to use her imagination. He led her motions, his head forehead leaning against hers.

"Were you this wet when you were thinking of me earlier?" he whispered, kissing her between some of the words.

She couldn't catch her breath when his middle finger continued to lay on hers, and then he pushed their fingers inside her. Her own tightness surprised her, but she was throbbing for his touch, drenched in her own wetness. Nyssa moved her hand, letting him dip inside her while she slowly stroked her own clit. Her response to his question only came in the form of a nod, even if it was an exaggeration.

She felt the curl of his lips against her throat, and his other hand smacked her backside again, making her jump and smile softly at his play. But it was the dance in his daring gaze when he pulled back that made her swallow.

"Oh, Princess," he drawled teasingly. She moaned as his hand laid on her cheek, and she felt him sinking his other between her legs. Two fingers curling fully inside her, she limped at his deliberation but eyed the smirk rising on his lips. Whatever he was plotting, she couldn't help but smile at the anticipation of it.

His palm slapped against her clit. He jolted inside her so hard she nearly lifted off the bed. The noise echoed in the silent room, and she gasped as he chuckled.

"You're a filthy little liar."

The moment she started to laugh, his lips crashed into hers. She had to grab his shoulders to stay upright. He continued to thrust those fingers in and out. Harder. Faster. Until she thought she would come apart on him and scream. Her nails dug into his skin. She couldn't stop herself. White lights flashed behind her closed eyes. Breath ceased. A strangled cry released from her lungs. Nadir's lips were still on hers, and her scream muffled into his mouth.

Her end found her with a shake of her entire body. But Nadir didn't stop.

He shifted from under her, making her fall back onto the mattress as he kissed down her front. Her body was so sensitive from the release that every kiss made her jerk. He nipped at her peaked nipples, but he didn't remain. When he reached her stomach, and she realized where he was going, her thighs tightened in response. But she couldn't stifle the drip of herself down onto the bed.

She watched him settle himself between her legs, kiss down her thigh from her knee, and then his mouth pressed to her still throbbing clit. She whimpered and bucked at the sensitivity of him licking her orgasm. Mouthing and bringing those nerves into his mouth, taking his time in claiming her. Kissing her pussy as though it were her mouth.

Dammit, she'd missed that mouth.

"Princess…" he breathed against her. "I forgot how psychedelic you taste."

Her hips bucked, hands grabbing for the sheet as he tortured her. Her body jerked with every suck of his mouth, every flinch of his tongue. She was once more writhing as he devoured her. Body reaching again, muscles feigning. He grabbed her up by her hips, lying her ass against his firm chest, and his hands wrapped around her thighs as he sat up on his knees. She was on her shoulders and wholly at his mercy. His tongue continued to sweep her into oblivion. Her back arched. She stuffed the pillow in her mouth as she fought the cry of ecstasy. Unable to keep herself from straining against the grip he had on her waist and legs. Unable to stifle the clench in her thighs around his cheeks. She reached and cried out a strangled noise she didn't recognize.

She came apart in a fashion that should have embarrassed her, but she was shaking so that her mind forgot what embarrassment was. He lapped up her juices deliberately this time, making her whimper and flinch with every brush of his tongue.

When she was laid on the mattress, he slowly kissed up her body and paused to lay on his side beside her to watch her come down from the high. Touch delicate on her skin, she finally looked up, catching the slight smile on his face.

"You know what I want?" he said, thumb dragging over her bottom lip.

"What's that?" she managed to get out.

"I want to watch you come apart like that every day until there is nothing left of our world except you and me, and then all the days after."

It was when he said things like that that made her realize how right her sister had been.

She couldn't formulate a response, but the words made both her heart and thighs ache. And she wanted him to take her as his, to claim her and fill her. She curled her hand behind his neck and pulled him down to her, hungrily taking his lips. He pulled her thigh over his hip, fingers digging into her backside.

"Nadir…" she called out as he began to suck on her throat. "I want you inside me."

He paused against her neck, a low groan vibrating on her skin, and then pulled her tighter into him.

"Tell me again," he groaned.

Her chest caved when he nipped at her, the anxiety of the words she wanted to say playing on her tongue. "I said…" She tugged his head, urging him over her so she could see his face when she repeated it.

"I want you," she whispered, memorizing the dilation in his eyes, "and I want you inside me, in every way I can have you, every day and all the days after."

She watched as his lips rose just at the right corner. "That's a dangerous desire, Princess," he uttered.

She leaned forward, nose nudging his. "You are my dangerous desire."

He captured her lips in a hungry kiss that lingered on her lips even after he stood to remove his pants. His great length was stiff, making her salivate, and as he knelt back on the bed, he stroked himself.

Nyssa sat up to her knees. He watched her crawl to the end of the bed until she reached him. Lips parted, she kissed him once, her tongue licking over his as she moved his hand from his length. He allowed her to pull his hands up, and she set them around her neck. Her own eyes fluttered as his thumbs brushed her trachea, but she turned her attention to his wanting cock.

"Let me," she whispered against his mouth, stilling a breath from him as she pushed that bead of liquid up his length. "Let me pleasure my Commander."

His hands tightened around her neck, and she kissed him quickly before pulling away and moving to her elbows. She left her knees spread wide, her hips arched high, knowing how much he liked watching her ass. Her lips wrapped around the tip of his length. He cursed her name aloud as he pushed her hair off her neck and grasped the roots. He tasted like the ocean, and she groaned at the familiarity of him.

Deeper and deeper, she teased. Until finally, she took his length nearly all the way in, relaxing her throat and choking on his thickness. His hand tightened in her hair. She stilled at the deepest she could take him, but Nadir didn't. He held her head and moved his cock further down her throat, making saliva drip from her lips as she sucked.

"Nyssa—" he cursed again as he moved in and out of her mouth. She couldn't breathe, and she didn't care. And when he pulled her back, she wrapped her lips tight, tongue dragging on the underside of him. He was rock hard in her mouth, and she wanted him to send her over the Edge.

His finger reached beneath her chin after a few more passes of her taking him deep. "Are you ready for me?"

She wrapped her lips back around his length in response, and she watched as his eyes rolled back. She withdrew her mouth from his cock and made her way flush to him. He kissed her hard, causing her mind to spin. His arm clasped around her waist and hauled her up off her knees. For a moment, she forgot everything that had just happened, what he'd asked her. There were just his lips against hers.

Until he moved his lips to her ear, biting her earlobe, and he whispered, "I want to see that beautiful ass in the air when I take you," in a demand so wanting that the hair on her neck stood. "Touch yourself. Tell me if you're ready for me."

"No," she dared. "I want you to touch me."

His dangerous gaze blazed through her, a soft smirk on his lips that made her heart skip. "There you are."

His fingers latched the backs of her thighs, spreading her cheeks in the squeeze of his hands. He yanked her legs off the bed and whipped her around to her stomach in one move. Barely giving her time to yip before he pulled up at her hips and smacked her backside hard. She let her forearms sink onto the bed, arching her back as she settled on her knees and groaned at the sting of the slap on her skin. His hands found the bend of her hips, and he moved her legs wider with his knee, pulling her hips up. A finger trailed her spread folds, and he inhaled a sharp breath.

"You're so fucking wet," she heard him breathe, his lips pressing to her ass. He delved lower, making her whimper when his mouth brushed between her cheeks, and then his tongue sank inside her.

She grasped the sheets and moved her hips towards him, desperate to feel him any way she could have him. He licked the entirety of her, parting her folds and her ass, tongue swirling her.

"Tell me you're always this wet when you think of me, Princess," he breathed against her entrance.

She groaned in response as he straightened, middle finger dipping inside her, thumb inserting between her cheeks. And he pushed against her. Holding her in that spot and curling his fingers, the pressure of it causing her to cry out. She couldn't help the high-pitched noise from her throat, saliva dropping on the sheets in anticipation of his tease.

"Yes—Yes— *Commander*," she managed as his fingers squeezed inside her.

He pulled out and yanked her hips up again, nearly lifting her off the bed. The sting of his slapping her ass harder rippled through her muscles and sent another chill down her spine. She moved her hips against him in response, arched her back, and touched her entrance to his throbbing cock. He groaned as she moved, his hands stiffening into her hips.

She felt how wet she was by the soaking of his finger on her skin. Again, she pushed her ass towards him, this time slipping herself onto his tip. Her body caved at the feeling of him finally inside her again, even if it was only a little. She wanted him buried there, thrusting inside her hard enough to make her forget her name.

His hands splayed over her backside, massaging her ass in his hands as she ground barely against him. He moved out of her. His hand slapped against her ass again, making her jump, but the tingle brought a moan to her lips.

"You're going to end me again before I get to fuck you properly," he uttered as his fingers dug into the back of her neck.

She shuddered at the press of it, her thighs quaking. "Nadir..." she practically begged.

His fingers traveled down her spine to the bend at her hips as he straightened, and then he wrapped the other hand into her hair. Every inch of her skin rose in goosebumps.

"Press your hands against the headboard, Princess," he told her. She moved, pressing her palms against the wood. "Just like that. That's my good girl," he cooed, the vibration of his voice causing her wetness to nearly trickle down her thigh. His fingers spread out against the back of her head, digits pressing as a massage into her scalp, and this time she did feel herself dripping.

Maybe she would just ask him to play in her hair and call her 'good girl' the rest of the night.

Between that and his length brushing her entrance, she was ready to come apart.

"There's my *prize*," and she noted his playful tone. He slapped her ass again, and she flinched with another moan she couldn't suppress.

She almost laughed at the word he'd called her but instead glanced at him over her shoulder and shook her head. "I will end you on the arm of that chair later," she warned.

His grip yanked in her hair, making her gasp and whimper delightedly all at once. "I'll take that as a promise." His breath was on her shoulder, and he whispered, "Don't move," into her ear as a final instruction.

The Commander's first thrust was deep enough to make her cry into the sheets. He cursed, pausing for a split, and then he did what he'd told her he would.

Every slap of their bodies echoed in the quiet room. His balls hit her clit and made her groan with every stroke, every pulse. He was buried in her, fitting her and filling her completely. She bit at the sheet as she tried to resist her own end, knowing if she did that, he might too, and she wasn't ready yet. She clenched around him with stolen breaths. She wanted him to stay inside her for hours, needing his touch and his own need for her.

His hand slipped from her hair to her shoulder, making her whimper in the absence of that grip. She reached around and moved his fingers back to her roots, to which he slowed his thrusts.

"You like when I hold you there?" he asked, the now deliberate yet stern movement of his hips making her push back against him.

She groaned at the chill once more rising over her skin. "Yes," she begged.

He stilled behind her. "Don't move, Princess," he repeated.

"Then you'd better, Commander," she said impatiently.

There was a huff of amusement, a hard smack on her backside, and then his hand once more tightened in her hair. Yanking her head back and causing an elated gasp to escape her. She nearly came apart right then.

"Your ass looks so good red," she heard him say as that free hand brushed over where he'd just slapped her. She flinched at the sensitive touch, and his fingertips dug slightly into her skin.

"So beautiful—*Nyssa*—"

His pace picked up. She could hear him cursing again, feel him straining. The pain of his pulling her hair made her insides convulse. His heavy thrusts quickly became erratic, and she knew he was nearly there, knew she was already there but holding it until she couldn't any longer. Her fingers dug into the wood. Her body shook, shuddering at her skin starting to stretch, her muscles to reach, her breaths to cease. High-pitched noises from her own throat echoed in the room. She was there. She couldn't stop it. His fingertips dug in her hips, head throwing back with the tug of his grasp. His cock twitched inside her, and he slammed into her three more times. The third sent her whirling, sent her soaring over that edge and into darkness. And she came apart just before him.

He held her firmly against his hips as they both shook with their releases, the elongation of his groan reaching her ears. She told herself to breathe and come down, but she couldn't help her own high-pitched moans as his fingers sank in her hair and her muscles limped.

Nadir finally slipped out of her, and she surrendered to her stomach. Stretching her arms above her head and allowing her cheek to lay on her bicep as he settled on his back.

She watched him in fascination, noticing the move of his throat, the run of his hand over his brow. A pleased groan emitted from him, and he smacked her ass once more.

"Dammit, I missed you," he uttered in a breath, and she couldn't help but chuckle under her breath.

He turned his head in her direction, lifting his arm up over his head onto the pillow. "What?" he asked.

She sat her head on her palm, bending her elbow beneath her. "Sometimes I forget you're also the Commander," she admitted.

Nadir frowned. "What do you mean?"

A flash of a smile quirked on her lips. "Nothing," she whispered.

His gaze narrowed, but he didn't push it and instead simply stared up at the ceiling again as his breath evened.

"Tell me why you made me wait a week for that," he said after a few moments.

"Where was the fun in giving in to you right away when you didn't even want me on your beach?" she asked.

Nadir smirked crookedly, and he grabbed her backside hard, making Nyssa jump as his fingers clenched between her cheeks and hooked in her, fingers spreading their releases over her ass.

"I hope you're hydrated, Princess."

"And why is that, Commander?" she dared as she sat her head on her hand.

His gaze traveled predatorily over her. He turned onto his side, his body nearly hovering over hers again. Hand still on her ass, he gripped her flesh tightly, and then he pressed his lips to her shoulder.

"Because I plan on ravaging you until the sun rises. You're going to rain on my tongue and my cock until you can't stop coming."

She couldn't stifle the grin as she turned on her side. "Ooo... *Commander*." Her hands wrapped around his cheeks, and she surrendered to his kiss again.

19

"You should know, when we arrive today, you'll be feeling the wrath of a thousand men and women torn apart by what your kingdom did," Hagen told Dorian as they prepped the horses.

"You say that as though it should have me quivering in my boots," Dorian replied.

Hagen paused, and Dorian saw him lean around to catch Corbin's gaze. Hagen's brow lifted, and Dorian turned just in time to see Corbin shake his head.

"If you're expecting him to be scared of anything, you'll have to do better than the wrath of beautiful people," Corbin informed Hagen. "He's too much like his sister to have such a threat send him running."

Dorian grinned at his Second. "That's the nicest thing you've ever said about me."

Corbin finished tightening the strap on his horse. "I'm not entirely sure it was a compliment," he replied.

They'd come out of the cave system into a valley where they'd rested the night before. But now started the climb past the Blackhand giver's mountain, Mons Magnus, and then the ascent into the high town of Darhkenhill.

The snows had begun when they'd crossed into the valleys.

Reverie had reacted to the snow as though she were battling a horde of bees. With swats of her hands and flinching when it hit her skin. The men had merely stared at her, and none had been able to finish eating their food as they watched the scene.

"What's happening?" Dag, one of Hagen's guards, asked in his gruff tone. "Why's she dancing like that?"

"Dreamer," Falke answered. "Never seen a bit of snow before, has she?"

Falke's accent was as thick and quick as Dag's tone was gruff. Dorian and Corbin had to listen closely to understand the pair.

Hagen noticed the confusion. "Falke is from Monsburne," he said low to Dorian. "They talk a fraction faster."

"A fraction seems modest," Dorian muttered back as he continued to watch Reverie.

"Should we tell her?" Corbin asked from the other side of him.

"What—that it's not going to kill her if she gets wet?" Dorian asked.

"This is the most entertainment I've had in weeks, mates," Hagen said. "Maybe we let her keep it up a bit longer."

"Poor thing," Falke chimed in.

"I've an idea," Dorian announced as he put his soup down.

"I stand corrected," Hagen said upon Dorian standing. "This will be the most entertaining thing I've seen in weeks."

Dorian sighed. He was sure Reverie was as confused with the weather as they were confused with watching her.

"Go get her, Prince," Hagen mocked him. "Maybe she'll let you keep her warm," he added with a wink.

Dorian kicked him but started his walk over to her anyway. She was still swatting and trying to blow the snow away when he reached her.

"Would you like a partner to dance with?"

"What?" she snapped.

"This new dance, I'd love to learn it. You could teach me."

"It's not a dance," she glared. "It's—*what the Infi is this?!*" she asked. "It's not rain. It's not ash. It's—"

"Snow," Dorian informed her.

Reverie stopped as if he'd slapped her. "Oh." She shifted, and he watched a blush rise on her cheeks, something he was sure was as rare as her. "Oh. *Oh*, were none of you going to tell me?" she said, having realized they were watching her.

"Who? Our friends? No. Definitely not," he teased. "They were quite enjoying the free entertainment."

Her lips twisted in annoyance. "I should murder you all in your sleep."

As she turned to grab her gloves from the saddlebag, her hood fell, and for a moment, Dorian simply stared at the stark silver of her hair against the landscape. The mountains behind her, snow dusting the valley. A fleck landed on her cheek, and he resisted the urge to wipe it away.

"I can feel you staring, Prince," she uttered as she turned back to him, her lavender eyes now appearing more prominent against her skin and hair.

He forgot how to talk.

"Speechless," she muttered as amusement rose in her gaze. "You know, with this lighting and your closed mouth, you're actually not so bad looking yourself."

A compliment he was going to hang on to as he hung onto the image of her against that morning sun.

With a smirk, she deliberately pushed past him to make her way to the others. The Blackhands all greeted her with mockery, asking her about her dancing and teasing her for not realizing what snow was. She gave it back to them without missing a beat and settled onto a rock.

Corbin caught Dorian's gaze. Dorian gave him a look of furrowed brows and scrunched face, mouthing *'fuck'* to his Second, hands curling up at his bent elbows— trying to bring a face to the embarrassment he felt at becoming speechless. Corbin chuckled in response, and Dorian knew he would be hearing it from his Second later.

It took them the rest of the morning and a few hours into the afternoon before they reached the outskirts of Dahrkenhill, and once they did arrive in the town, they were greeted with a throng of people on their own horses.

Dorian frowned at the people coming up on them as though they were some enemy company. Reverie and Corbin had both pulled their swords, but Hagen held up a hand.

"No need for that," he told them.

"I forget you all and your... *Sensitivities*," Dorian remembered, referring to how Blackhands could feel vibrations in the earth.

Hagen's lips flinched like he was fighting a smile. "Hang tight here while I speak with them." He clicked his tongue and picked up pace in front to greet his people.

"What is our plan?" Reverie asked as Hagen went ahead.

"What do you mean?" Dorian replied.

"I mean, he plans on putting you in chains, does he not?"

Dorian shrugged. "Probably."

"How are you so nonchalant about this?" she asked.

"You get used to it," Corbin muttered.

"We are to let you be taken as a prisoner?" Reverie continued.

A sly grin crooked on Dorian's lips. "Concerned for my safety already?" he bantered. "Does the way I looked in that snow yesterday morning have something to do with your suddenly being soft? If I recall correctly, you liked it."

"Do not mistake my wanting to secure you as my own prisoner and leverage as my being nice to you, Prince," she snapped.

"Looks like you'll have to learn to share for a while," Corbin interjected.

Hagen rejoined the group, calling out, "It seems we have a welcoming party," as the sneering men he'd conversed with turned back toward the town. He gave Corbin and Reverie upwards nods. "Seconds, you'll want to flank your Prince. Do not stop. Do not engage. Dag, Falke—" Hagen called back, "—keep them back. They've started the riots."

"Riots?" Reverie repeated.

Hagen considered her a long moment, and then his gaze flickered to Dorian. "Riots," he said firmly.

Riots didn't exactly cover what they walked into.

Throngs of people lined the streets. Children ran up and down, between their horses and around them. Snow and mud were thrown at the group. Dorian's steed bucked a few times, and Dorian had to keep his legs steady to calm her down. At one point, he pulled his hood up after the soil slammed into his face.

But that only edged them on more.

Dahrkenhill was built into the side of a sloping mountain. Streets entwined as winding courses and separated levels all along both sides of it. Homes were built into the mountain on the outskirts of town, and there was a small square located in the middle where two levels separated the shops. But Dorian knew they were going to the bright circular Temple situated on the ridge.

Dorian tried to concentrate solely on keeping his horse calm as they climbed. He tried to ignore the shouts of the people surrounding them. But with so many, his chest hardened into a numbness he hadn't been prepared for.

The Blackhands were *pissed*.

When they arrived at the Temple, Dorian threw his cloak into the fire pit going outside the doors. He was soaking with snow and mud down to his skin. Starting to shiver so much that he paused outside the temple and lit himself on fire.

Hagen stared at him, brow lifted, apparently surprised the Prince would light himself on fire without warning.

"He does that," Corbin muttered upon seeing the High Elder's confusion.

Hagen's eyes darted between the pair as he slacked off his own fur-lined cloak. Dorian didn't respond or look at them. His stomach was still knotted at the echoing taunts they'd just walked through. He shut his eyes tight as he returned to his usual form and pushed away the thoughts. Not thinking, he pulled the nyghtfire from his pocket.

"Not nervous there, are you, Prince?" Hagen asked.

"Is there a reason I shouldn't be?" Dorian asked after taking a gulp.

Hagen seemed to contemplate it, but he didn't respond directly. "Get inside. Snows will be coming down any minute now."

"Again?" Reverie asked, hugging her arms around her chest.

"Welcome to the mountains, little Dreamer," Hagen grinned.

Dorian glanced over at her shivering figure. The whiskey was still warm in his chest, and he felt the knot in his stomach loosening. "Perhaps you could use some of that *fire Prince* now," he mocked as he pushed near her.

Her eyes rolled tiredly up to his, and she snatched the flask from his hand. "I'd rather cuddle the Ulfram," she said before taking a swig.

"Ulframs actually do like cuddling," he informed her. "My sister could arrange that for you if you like."

Reverie pushed the flask back into his hands. "I knew I should have gone after her instead," she muttered before walking through the double doors Hagen was holding open.

Dorian didn't miss Hagen's gaze following her, forehead knitting as he took in her figure. Dorian paused in front of him, and Hagen gave a low whistle.

"That's dangerous, mate," he mocked, clapping Dorian on his shoulder. "You sure you're up for it?"

Dorian watched Reverie as she began to strip her cloak and talk to Dag. A slow smile spread on his lips, and he looked back to Hagen. "I've been training my entire life for her," he replied with a wink.

Hagen laughed. "She's going to maim you, and I hope I'm there to see it," he said. "Come on. I'll show you around before the fun starts."

"Which fun?"

"The fun where my people decide if you get to keep your head."

Hagen led him through the halls, all the while pointing to paintings on the walls showcasing creatures they'd fought and secured. One depicted them executing Infi outside that very Temple.

The painting that Hagen was most proud of, though, was one of a great cat creature with a mane of fire. This being, Dorian was told, was the creature form of the Blackhands' Architect, the Ghost of Fire.

Dorian hadn't gotten such a tour the last he was there, and he started to wonder why Hagen was presenting him with such a luxury. They'd asked Corbin and Reverie to stay downstairs. Dorian hoped Reverie didn't showcase her skills by further pissing anyone off while she was alone. But Dorian knew Corbin would keep watch on her while they waited.

Dorian realized why Hagen was pulling him away as they reached the fourth level over the circular hall.

The room below was being set up for trial.

Four chairs on the towered dais. A few smaller chairs were set up behind the pillars in the halls. People were beginning to file in.

Hagen paused and leaned over the balcony railing, and Dorian stopped to do the same. An audible sigh left the High Elder as he looked down at the room.

"The last time I saw my best friend was at your castle," Hagen said solemnly. "And now, I'll never see him again because of your Council... My people have been shouting for us to ride to Magnice since we received the letter." Hagen shifted to look at Dorian. "Tell me why I shouldn't."

Dorian's hands pressed together as he held the scene below in his gaze despite the fire dancing in his mind. The screams in his ears. The silhouette of Draven in the window. But he stifled that emotion and picked up his dropping chin.

"As much as I would love to see that—and I really would— I know my older sister and Draven died so that specifically wouldn't happen," Dorian replied. "And also because what's left of that kingdom is not yours to take. It's mine. Along with my brother's last breath."

"When did you and your sister leave?"

"Two nights after it happened," Dorian replied. "A ship arrived that morning. She and I fled after dark."

"The strangers?"

"We think maybe they saw the flames and followed them around the edge to see what they could take."

Hagen didn't turn to look at him, but another long sigh left his lips, and then he straightened up, arms crossing over his chest.

"Prince, I need you to tell me something," Hagen said, to which Dorian himself straightened.

"Okay."

"I need you to tell me why my best friend trusted you," Hagen said. "And I need you to tell me why it is not my first instinct to put you in chains and throw you into a dungeon."

Dorian stilled, his eyes flickering on the ground as he contemplated his answer. The memory of Draven entered his mind, traveling with him, his last words, and Dorian's chest began to ache.

"Each time someone says they were such great friends with him, I find myself envious," he admitted. "I only grew closer to him this last year, and in that little time I spent with him on the road and at my castle, he became more of a brother to me than my own ever was." Dorian settled against the pillar behind him, arms hugging his own chest. "I took him his horn—" Hagen's forehead wrinkled, and Dorian realized this was news to him "—that night."

"You were the last person to see him alive?"

"I think Rhaif was the last one to see him," Dorian replied. "But if you mean his friends, yes."

"How did he seem?"

"Pissed," Dorian said shortly. "Ready to take it all down with his bare hands if he had to. I should have helped him burn it."

"And you would be dead with him," Hagen said. "You've had many choices to make in the last few days, Prince. Yet, you're here. Even when I told you my people wanted your head, you still willingly walked into this town. Why?"

"Because I need your help," Dorian said. "I need peace with your people and an alliance if it is possible. Aydra secured that at that meeting. I'd only like to make sure it has not gone amiss because of what happened. I will do whatever you need to secure that. If things go wrong in the south with these strangers... If the reef falls or the forest is taken... Our people will need a place to go, food to eat—"

"When you say 'our,' who do you mean?"

"I no longer have a crown. Until I can reclaim my sister and I's thrones, we will do all we can to help our King and Commander. It is their people I speak of and their people I am worried about. My own people will have to wait. I cannot fight a battle on four sides. I'll follow Bala and the Commander's guidance and assist them however I can until we are ready."

"Humble step back from a Promised Prince," Hagen mocked.

"We are not stupid enough to think we are some sort of saviors just because of who we are," Dorian said. "The Promised crowns should not sit on any head that has not earned them. I plan on earning my place, as I'm sure my sister will. That crown has been given to too many who only sought it as a birthright."

Hagen considered him another moment, and then he pushed off the pillar. "You know," he started, clapping Dorian's shoulder again, "I can see now why Draven liked you."

The words almost made Dorian nauseous. "Why?"

"Because you're as crazy as he was," Hagen said. "I imagine he saw some of himself in you... And if that is the case..." He paused to glance back over the balcony, and then he looked again to Dorian. "This will be fun."

A slow smirk had spread over Hagen's lips that Dorian wasn't sure he liked.

"Not sure how much I like that look," Dorian muttered.

Hagen's smirk widened. "This might be more fun than watching your Dreamer dance in that snow. Let's go Prince. Your audience awaits."

Dorian followed behind Hagen all the way down, his gaze landing on the people who had begun to gather. Reverie and Corbin met him at the bottom of the steps.

"People are beginning to talk," Reverie muttered.

"Yeah? What are they saying?" Dorian asked.

"They're talking about putting you in stockades to starve and then beheading you."

Dorian forced a smile to disguise his nerves. "I think you'd miss me too much to let that happen."

"I think you underestimate my loyalty," she countered.

"Hey—" Corbin nudged Dorian's side, and he realized the four Elders were gathered talking by their chairs, and Hagen was summoning him.

Dorian removed his belt and handed his weapons to Corbin. "If they decide to take my head, you're to go back to the Forest."

"Stop," Corbin argued.

"Tell my sister I love her," Dorian continued. "You are to help Bala and the Commander with anything they need. Do not stay here or seek any sort of revenge—"

"Prince—"

"—And when my sister marches back to Magnice to take our home, you make sure you're with her."

Corbin clapped Dorian's face harshly, almost as a slap. "Your older didn't die for you to be killed by our allies."

"I'd like to have my affairs in order anyway," Dorian affirmed. His gaze moved back to Reverie, who was glaring around the room, arms strapped over her chest as though she wanted to murder them all.

"If they kill me, I expect *you* to go full ravenger on the town for taking me from you before we had a chance together," he said with a wink.

"If they kill you, I'll take your head back and say I did it myself," she replied.

"That's cold," Dorian said. "Bin, you would let her take my head?"

"What happens to your head is not in my instructions."

To this, Dorian finally felt a genuine smile. He glanced between the two once more before turning on his heel and heading up the steps to meet Hagen. Hagen had settled on the arm of his chair, arms crossed. His chin rose as Dorian approached.

"Did you say your goodbyes?" Hagen mocked.

"Thought it would be stupid not to," Dorian replied.

"No goodbye kiss for the dying Prince?" Hagen grinned.

Dorian almost laughed. "Haven't earned it yet."

The grand double doors opened wide, and in strode a woman whom Dorian had to pause to stare at.

Nearly as tall as Aydra had been, this woman commanded a room just as she had. She was wiping the blood off her hands and pulling the leather braces off her wrists as she crossed the room. Her long brown hair was pulled back off her face, small braids on the left side of her head above her ear. The rest of her hair was crimped and pulled back into a ponytail. She pulled the ribbon out of it and shook her head to fluff the waves as they cascaded down her back and over her shoulder.

"Here we go," Hagen muttered at Dorian's back.

The woman's dark eyes ran deliberately over Corbin when she passed him and made her way up the steps.

"Is there a reason we've a Belwark in this Temple still alive—" she was saying, not looking up yet to where the others stood "—or should I have one of my men behead him now?"

Her gaze finally lifted, and Dorian straightened as it landed on him. She gave him a full once over upon hitting the top step, obviously surveying him as she would have an enemy on the battlefield, and then she looked past him to Hagen.

"I'm not sure why you're all standing around," she spat. "Were you waiting on me before you took the Promised Prince's head?"

Hagen stood from his chair and grasped Dorian's shoulder. "I've had a long chat with our Prince. He came to barter peace."

A great sneer found its way on Katla's face, and her hand clenched around the hilt of the axe at her waist. "*Peace?*" she dared, voice rising. "Did he barter peace when his people condemned the great King of the south to death?—"

"Katla—"

"—Our ally and friend, murdered because of the lies of his own kingdom—"

"Katla," Hagen droned, his tone more of a warning than before.

"—Tell me why I shouldn't behead his pretty head right now and send it back in a bag—"

"Katharos!" Hagen finally shouted.

Katla's words ceased, but her scowl remained.

"I will speak with you in private," Hagen demanded.

The others dispersed to talk amongst themselves once more, though Dorian swore it was only pretend. He was sure they were all listening intently to whatever Hagen wanted to speak with this Katla about.

Katla pushed past Dorian to Hagen, knocking her shoulder and glaring through him when she did. Hagen took her arm lightly and led her back behind the chairs out of earshot. Dorian didn't bother trying to listen. He was too busy staring at the blood on Katla's shirt and across her chest. The axe strapped to her hip. Even moving so that he could see the dagger on her calf.

To any on-looker, he was sure he looked as though he were taking in and memorizing every inch of her curves. So much so that when they came back towards him, Dorian startled himself straight.

"I suppose I should introduce you properly," Hagen said, pointing to the woman. "Dorian, this is Katla Katharos. One of my finest Generals, my executioner, and three-time Forest trial champion."

The doors opened again, and more people strode through to gather around. But Dorian barely saw, entirely too focused on the woman before him to dare breathe away. His lips curled upwards at the name Hagen had called her.

Katla.

A smirk worked its way onto Dorian's lips. "Kat, huh?"

Her knife was on his throat the moment the words emitted from him. But Dorian didn't flinch, hands pressed behind his back, leering smile still on his face.

The tip of the blade brushed the lump in his throat, and she seethed from her lips, "It is Katla or Katharos. Not *Kat*. I am not some feline mongrel to woo into your bed, little King."

"Have you ever been with a King?" Dorian wondered.

"I have," she answered, a sly smile rising to her eyes. "One far more formidable and—" her gaze darted over him "—brawny than yourself. At least he knew how to handle a woman such as I."

"Sounds like a challenge."

She stared at him a moment, only the whisper of chuckles sounding from the other Blackhands who were listening to the exchange. She smiled at the ground and then back at him, head tilting, breasts brushing against his chest, the clench of her jaw apparent at his mocking shenanigans.

"I will ruin you," came her warning.

The right corner of Dorian's lips quirked higher, and he allowed his own head to tilt, his eyes to travel deliberately over her again, settling on her hips, over the curves to her waist, admiring the hug of the corset wrapped beneath her breasts.

And then his long lashes lifted to hers.

"Name a time and place, Kitty Kat."

Katla lunged.

Dorian nearly stumbled off the back of the dais at the rate he fumbled backward. Her knife was in his face. Rage billowed from her eyes.

"Shit—"

"Call me Kat again—"

Dag and Falke sprinted up the steps. Hagen moved between Katla and Dorian and pushed on Katla's chest. Dag and Falke grabbed her arms to pull her back, having to lift her off the ground to take her down. She kicked the air, still lunging at Dorian and shouting threats about his calling her by such a name.

Despite his running from her, Dorian had never been more pleased with himself.

And Katla knew it.

"You're *mine*, little King—" she continued. "If you ever call me that again, I'll cut off your cock!"

"Katharos!" Hagen shouted. "Enough." But Hagen's eyes cut back at Dorian. "Way to piss off the executioner, kid," he muttered to him.

"It's in my nature," Dorian shrugged.

Katla calmed and shrugged her arms away from the pair holding her. "I'm calm," she almost shouted to them. "I'm fine." She glared between Hagen and Dorian. "Should I think we'll be putting him on trial, or have you decided to let him walk free in our streets without consequence?" she snapped.

Dorian saw Reverie grasp at her knife. He shook his head, making sure she did not try to take down an entire room full of Blackhands— though he knew she would have tried. He glanced back to Hagen as Katla stepped back, and then he pushed his arms and wrists together in front of him.

"If you don't put me on trial, they will question you," Dorian muttered. "String me as your captive, High Elder."

Hagen considered him a moment, and then he gave Katla an upwards nod. A quiet chuckle emitted from Katla's lips, and Hagen looked as though he would laugh.

"Try not to enjoy it so much," he uttered under his breath.

"Oh, you know me," she uttered as she sauntered before Prince. A rope was tossed in her hands by a woman behind her. "I wouldn't *dare*," and the tone in which she said it made Dorian's neck hair stand on end.

"I honestly wasn't speaking to you, but I suppose it does go for you as well," Hagen said, gaze darting to Dorian.

Dorian's wrists were bound so tightly in front of him, the ropes nearly ripped his skin.

Hagen exchanged words with the other Elders. People shifted, and Katla shoved Dorian to the center of the dais. Fists clenching, Dorian tried not to let the uncomfortableness of his current predicament rest on his face.

He was ready for whatever verdict these people decided for him.

Because he knew the truth.

Katla gave him one more look before pulling her axe from her side and hoisting it up over her shoulder. "I wonder, Prince," she said in his ear. "Are your insides made of blood and bone, or is it of fire and cowardice treachery like the rest of your line?"

Were it any other moment, he would have smarted back at her, told her she could find out later with a bit of blood play, but the room had become silent, and Dorian found he couldn't speak.

A man stepped forward upon Hagen's call and pulled a scroll. He read the date, the time, and place, recorded the Elders and Generals in attendance, and finally read Dorian's charges.

"—Dorian Eaglefyre of the Magnice realm. Born to the mother,

Arbina Promregis Amaris. A child of the Promised line. The Fire Prince. Charged with conspiracy and treason to Haerland for the death of the Venari King." The man paused, and all eyes fell on Dorian.

"How do you plead?"

Dorian straightened as tall and broad as he could make himself. "I am not guilty."

Murmurs broke out around the room, but Hagen held up a finger, and the whispers stopped. Sitting lazily in his chair, legs spread, hiding his mouth with his hand, Dorian wondered if the High Elder was using it to hide his expression—to seem impartial to the verdict his people would decide for him. But Hagen glanced to his left and gave a nod to the Elder he'd introduced as Marius.

The gait Marius took to walk before him was deliberate and calculated. As though his every step meant a break in the room. A crack in the dais. He paused before Dorian, shocking hazel eyes staring through the fire Prince—

He spat in Dorian's face.

Dorian winced and cursed under his breath. "Bit uncalled for, don't you think?" he muttered, wiping away the saliva with his bound hands.

The handle of Katla's axe swung behind Dorian's knees. The break against his thighs sent his knees buckling, but he forced himself to stay upright.

"Silent unless spoken to," she warned.

Dorian grumbled and pressed the ash on his fingers back down, unwilling to let that form come to the surface.

Not yet.

Marius adjusted his shirt with force. "You are a Prince of Promise. A member of the Bedrani Council that condemned our King and ally—"

"I am *not* a member of that idiotic Council," Dorian seethed.

Katla's weapon came down on him again, and Dorian's grunt was audible this time. His jaw clenched, teeth trembling against one another with the weight of keeping his fire down. He stumbled to catch himself and once more forced his knees straight.

"You said *unless spoken to*," he cut back to her. "He spoke to me."

"Would you like another strike?" she asked.

"It's always been my favorite foreplay."

The strike hit the bend in his left knee, and his leg finally buckled. A groaning huff emitted from him as the searing pain debilitated his leg.

Dorian inhaled sharply and used that pain as fuel.

He pushed his good leg into the ground and straightened back to his feet, chin rising even higher than it had been before. The world vibrated before him, and he tightened his fists to stifle his form.

Marius began walking around him. "Regardless of your involvement with that Council, you were in the room when the sentence was given. And you stood by to watch—"

Dorian shut his eyes as he waited for the words he knew might send him spiraling.

"—You, the Fire Prince, self-proclaimed *friend* of the Venari, watched as your sister, whom you also claim to have loved, was burned alive. You watched silently as our King threw himself from a window of your beloved castle. And you did *nothing*." Marius stopped in front of him. "Tell me why we should not have Katharos slicing your throat."

The pain of his leg shot up through his body. Rage poured through his muscles with it. Shaking, Dorian opened his eyes, not even sure if his mouth was moving but hearing words from his lips nonetheless.

"Because I was the one who brought him the horn so he could take Magnice down with him," Dorian said slowly. "I was the last of his friends to see him alive."

The room began to murmur again.

"Should you think this changes our opinion of you?" Katla asked. "Last person to see him alive... Perhaps we should be charging you with murder instead of conspiracy and treason."

Dorian turned slowly, heart stilling in his chest. "Draven knew what he was doing," he glared. "He'd known it would come to that point for months. My only regret is that I did not help him burn it to the ground."

"Why would the *Venari King* sacrifice his life for—"

"That's enough, Katharos," Hagen cut in, standing.

But Dorian wanted to hear it.

"No," Dorian interjected, and Hagen paused in his step. The world vibrated once more in Dorian's gaze when he looked back to Katla. "Let her continue." He stepped forward, the noise of his boots sounding like an echo on the marble. He allowed the stretch of his form up his arms, the faint glow of darkness settling on his neck.

And the words seethed from his lips in a tone he didn't recognize.

"Why would the Venari King sacrifice his life for *what*?"

Weights shifted around the room.

The ropes on his wrists turned to ash as he stepped before her.

Swords drew. But Dorian didn't back down. The stretch of his stiffened back and rounded shoulders were as strong and affirmed as he'd ever felt. A reassurance of his form. And he let his body settle into it.

"*Say it,*" Dorian demanded.

The room flinched. All looked to Hagen for the order to strike.

But not Katla.

Her chin rose to meet his, and her crossed arms pushed on his chest.

"Why would the Venari Alpha... The greatest of them, our friend, our ally, our *King*... Why would he have sacrificed his life when she was already *dead*?"

Dorian's ears rang. Even though he knew the words were coming, they still crushed his heart.

"Because for the first time in his life, he'd found true happiness," Dorian affirmed. "He'd felt what it was like to see into the light and not wonder if it would consume him. Fall deeply into shadows with her at his side, with an equal queen. She was his match, his world... And he trusted the rest of us to keep our shit together long enough to save Haerland from destruction and slavery."

No one moved.

Dorian allowed his ash to dwindle on his body, pulsing back into his usual self. He turned again, his shoulders relaxing in front of Hagen and the rest of the Elders.

"I realize it may be hard for you to believe that someone as strong and formidable as he would have done this. And I question every day if this world was worth their dying for when it apparently wants to tear itself apart instead of uniting against a common enemy," Dorian continued as he settled into normalcy. "But I am doing what he and the newly crowned Venari King have asked of me. I am here asking for your aid. Not your soldiers. Not to give you marching orders. I only wish to confirm the alliance my sister and Draven secured at the Gathering. Or should I think the word of Blackhands is no longer a reliable currency?"

"Your war in the south is not our concern," another Elder said.

"If we lose, it will be," Dorian said.

More whispers filled the chamber. The other two Elders stood from their own chairs and circled around Hagen. Katla moved, giving Dorian a once over as she also joined the men.

"Put him in the ring!" someone shouted.

"Have him prove his trustworthiness!" came another.

More shouts like these echoed around him, the people now in an uproar about what should happen. Dorian turned and locked eyes with Corbin. Corbin looked concerned, his hand on the end of the dagger on his belt.

Within a few moments, the Elders dispersed, and Hagen held up a hand. Shouts quieted as Hagen stepped forward.

"Your trust will be earned, Prince," Hagen said. "You are hereby sentenced to the Ring Trials. If you are innocent of your crimes, you will survive. If not..." His voice drifted, brow raising, and Dorian shifted.

Ring trials. *Combat trials.*

This... This Dorian could do.

The corner of his lip quirked, and Dorian nodded.

A great horn blew. The conclusion of the spoken trial. People talking loudly entered Dorian's ears again, and the room began to disperse into groups. Bounding footsteps behind him caught his attention.

"What are the Ring Trials?" Corbin demanded to know.

"And why do they all look so happy about it?" Reverie asked.

But Dorian continued to hold Hagen's gaze.

"You realize what this means?" Hagen asked him.

"You're going to throw all your worst things at me?"

"It means my people want to determine your worth by our giver and Architect's eyes. It means they are basing your trustworthiness on whether Mons Magnus and the Ghost of Fire like you."

"Wasn't aware your people valued religion, Elder," Dorian said.

"It's the only word they'll care about," Hagen said. "Anything I say will not matter as much as what they think."

"Is this a warning?"

"This is my saying that what Draven told me of you had better be true, Prince," Hagen said in a low tone. "The Ring Trials are not a mockery. We take our fighting seriously and as a currency greater than gold. Not just whatever Belwark trials you've seen in your kingdom."

Corbin's hand tightened around the hilt of his dagger, and Dorian almost laughed. Hagen caught it as well, his lips lifting at the sight of it.

"No offense, Belwark," Hagen smirked, and he looked back to Dorian. "I'll allow you to train between trials. There are three."

"Sounds like a liberty," Dorian said. "Are you sure you're looking for me to lose these?"

"I would actually prefer you to win," Hagen said. "From what I hear, you're a great fighter. A king in the making... And like I told you, I have my own reasons for wanting you here. You will be secluded to this Temple and the Ring for training, of course. Dag will show you around. The first trial takes place in four days. Make sure you're ready."

"Will you tell me what I'll be up against?"

Hagen smiled back at him. "I don't think I will."

Dorian couldn't help but grin as Hagen left him there.

"You've just been told you'll be put through trials to determine whether you're a trustworthy being, trials that mean to kill you, and you're smiling?" Reverie asked.

"I told you he does that," Corbin muttered. "What will you have us do during your trials?"

"Help me train," Dorian replied. "Keep an ear out for anything from Magnice." He turned to Reverie. "Do you think your sisters would tell you if anything was amiss at home?"

"What—like write them?" Reverie scoffed. "They would think it out of the ordinary. That something was wrong. We've never been close."

"Right," he uttered, rubbing the back of his neck. "Stick close to Corbin then. Listen out for anything we might need to know. Nadir's traders should be coming through every other week or so as long as things are normal. If you could find out any information on my sister, that would be great."

"You don't trust the Commander?" Corbin asked.

"I know my sister well enough to know that the first mention of someone telling her it is their duty to protect her will send her into a spiral. I'd like to know what sort of stupidity she throws herself into when they do."

"And if you do find out she's over her head in some situation?"

"Then I'll know to start with the Umber when I set the southern coast on fire."

20

A nap had taken Nadir and Nyssa after their lengthy surrender the night before. Her backside was sore and pink, clit aching and satisfied, muscles weak. There were bites on her collar and breasts. She honestly didn't want the sun to come up over the horizon.

Waking early, Nadir had only given her a kiss on her cheek and a firm grasp on her ass that nearly picked her up off the mattress before leaving the bed. She'd smiled into the sheets and shoved him off after the obscene comment he made in her ear, only to have Lex come in an hour later and wake her by pulling her by her ankles onto the floor. Lex had also given Nyssa a slap on her ass but left her with a demanding, "We're losing sun, Nyssari," before leaving.

At least practice with Lex was more of a success than the day before. With some of her frustrations waned, Nyssa allowed herself to relax into her training, firm with the determination in her bones.

Until the people began to gather on the beach to watch her.

Lex had sensed it and pushed her harder. Nyssa didn't mind. She appreciated what Lex was doing. Helping her. Knowing the best way Nyssa responded to her was to challenge her. Noon rolled around, and after nearly vomiting from the ache in her body— from holding herself steady and straight on her horse and hitting the targets back to back with arrows, using every muscle to keep her body upright— Lex gave her a firm clap on her shoulder. One that Nyssa knew she had earned.

"Keep this up, and they'll be wondering why they ever questioned you," Lex said when she handed Nyssa the water canteen.

Nyssa poured the cool water over her face, letting it wash the sand off her and drip on her tongue. "Does that go for you as well?" Nyssa asked.

Lex eyed her, but she didn't respond directly and instead started wrapping her hands. Nyssa watched her curiously.

"What's that for?" she asked.

"I want to keep my hands from bleeding when I punch you and the trees later," Lex replied.

"Why are you punching me?"

"You'll find out after lunch," Lex said. "Go. Have a bath. Fuck the Commander—" Nyssa caught her wink "—Rest a few hours. I'll come get you when I'm ready."

The bath hadn't felt that good in weeks.

Or perhaps it was the company that joined her.

Nadir had spotted her from the beach where he was training others, and she hadn't waited to see if he would follow. She certainly hadn't expected him to.

But the door opened when she was pulling her shirt off, and Nadir paused just inside, hand still on the doorknob.

"Hello, Commander," Nyssa said as she finished unbuttoning her pants. She kicked them off, leaving only her undergarments.

Sweat continued to drip down her spasming muscles. Nadir hadn't stopped staring. He was watching her with as much, if not more, lust than he ever had.

Nyssa had worked a long time to be confident enough to stand naked in front of another being and be proud of her body. Especially to stand before someone who looked like him. Years of battling and pushing herself against her brother, growing muscles, and finally storing some fat on her petite frame in the place of the frailness she'd once thought was the only way someone would think her beautiful or worthy of their attention. She'd fought to push her mother's voice out and focus on her own.

Exhaling the fire. Breathing in the smoke.

Nadir closed the door.

"I'm going to take you as mine against this door, Princess," he said as his gaze lingered on her heaving breasts. "And then I'm going to devour you in that bath like I did at your castle."

The corner of her lips quirked when his eyes locked with hers, and she reached for the tie on the front of her leather corseted bra.

"All yours, Commander," she uttered as her supple breasts sprang free.

Before she could blink, he was on her. Lips crashing into hers, his hands on her wrists. He threw them above her head and shoved her back into the wall.

The want from him sent her head spinning and made her body come alive.

All the pain in her muscles seemed to wane with his grasp. His mouth was on her throat, hips pushing into hers. He moved to cup her face, and she reached for his pants. The criss-cross ties on the front quickly came undone. He reached between her legs as she began to stroke him, and he pushed her underwear off in a manner that had he not been hanging onto her, she might have stumbled.

Pressing his torso flush with hers again, he allowed a finger to rake between her folds. She couldn't control the sharp inhale of breath against her sensitive nerves, the tease from the night before making her ache already.

His lips curved against her throat as he felt her already soaking. "Good morning, Princess," he purred in her ear. He didn't wait for a response. His hands moved to her backside. She was hauled up onto his waist with a jump, and he filled her completely. He cursed in her neck as her head threw back into the wood.

The door rattled with every thrust. She didn't hold in her moans as he took her, claiming her as he'd said he would. Until she couldn't breathe and her nails raked into his flesh. She came apart with him in a manner that limped what was left of the feeling in her legs.

Despite his saying he would devour her in the bath, he quickly realized his tub was not the size hers had been in her castle. He had instead held her backward on his lap and hugged her from behind as she pleasured him slowly. His forehead had laid against her spine, fingers snaking around her waist and dipping between her thighs, causing her breath to hitch and for her to find her end before he.

She relaxed back against his chest after, and he drew circles on her arms as he told her about the legion he had been working with that morning and where he hoped they would be by the time the spring arrived.

Nyssa was enjoying learning more about his army and the way he cared for his people. The way he spoke about each person... She wondered if his people realized how much he cared for them both individually and as a unit.

"I was honestly surprised to find you do not have an underwater legion," she said as she toyed with the bubbles on her hands. "What with your water breathing abilities," she continued. "Or even a secluded village beneath the water."

"There are remains of such a village out by the home place," Nadir said. "Underwater. It was pretty spectacular back then. I'll show you one day."

"What happened?"

"Ah... We were once a divided people about sixty years ago. Back then, we were at each other's throats because of the way everyone thought we should be sharing our resources. Some of us knew it was the only way to secure our place in Haerland and become an essential part of the world. Others thought we should keep all of it to ourselves. Only worry for our own."

"How did you come to a settlement?"

Nadir didn't speak for a moment, and she felt him tense behind her. "There was a great battle fought between us, but the battle wasn't what destroyed the underwater village."

"What was it?"

"The sea dragon," he said, and she leaned up from against him.

"The one you fought to secure your place as Commander?" she remembered.

He nodded.

"What happened?"

"She didn't like our fighting," he said with a shrug. "She destroyed everything she could because of it. The people were forced to unite against her, but I ultimately took her."

"You're such a hero," she teased.

He gave her a small smile, fingers delicately touching her back. "Nearly died in the process. Gave a whole speech after about what we would be doing with our resources since we were forced to live above land from then on."

"Why did you not rebuild?"

"It's actually really annoying to build underwater," he admitted, to which she smiled at his comical expression. "Honestly, very annoying. The materials are ridiculous to acquire. You have to scour all over the cliffs for the right pieces to move. It takes twice as long as building on land— oh, and *then* there are the creatures. What with no way to communicate with them, they—" he paused in his rambling with a soft sigh, and she watched that stern brow of frustration soften. "You don't want to know about building materials," he considered.

"I want to know anything you tell me," she countered.

Nadir's hand brushed her back, and he brought her fingers to his lips with the other for the briefest of seconds, almost as though he'd never had someone interested in his ramblings. But he didn't continue to talk about rebuilding.

"It made more sense to simply stay on the beach where we could protect what we'd built and leave the ocean to the beasts."

"How did you nearly die?" she asked, her gaze traveling over the few scars on his skin, none of which she thought were large enough to have come from a sea dragon.

He took her hand and guided it up to his neck, where the barely visible slits were on each side that helped him breathe underwater. His eyes closed when he paused her fingers against the left side. She felt a sink beneath her finger, and her brows furrowed.

"It had me in a bind like the sea serpent had on you," he explained. "I finally got my knife into her, but she has these really sharp scales down the spine. I actually have one I can show you—when I cut her back, she jerked and sliced into my throat here." His neck moved, and just faintly, she saw the scar that ran from his collar, through the gills, to his jaw. "The hole there is where she got in the worst. Sort of snagged on my skin. For a while, I couldn't breathe out of that side."

Nyssa's eyes were wide as she imagined him bleeding out beneath the waves. "How did you survive that?"

"Drove my sword into her head the moment she circled back around to me."

He made it sound so casual, and yet she was sure there had been more to such a battle.

"I dragged the damned thing's heart to shore after. Lovi did a ritual that night to signify our uniting villages and my place as Commander. Her bones still lay in the middle of the old home."

"That I would like to see," she said with a smile.

He looked like he would laugh. "Dragon bones and a destroyed village," he mocked. "Yes, why *wouldn't* our innocent Princess like to see such things?"

She rolled her eyes as she settled her chest against his, propping her forearms on him as she continued to trace his scar with her finger. "This healed much better than it should have."

"The Nitesh likes me," he winked.

"Does she come here?"

"Not often," he admitted. "Usually only during the summer Eyes festival or if Lovi calls."

Nyssa had never been to an Eyes festival. The Eyes were when both moons were full. It happened every cycle, but the summer Eyes were always a special night. It was said Haerland herself came to be on such a night, so the people would celebrate their homeland's birth the entire night. Each race would party in their own unique way. The only race to not have such a tradition was the Promised.

"If I am looking forward to nothing else this year, I am looking forward to finally seeing the festival," she told him.

"It's a week-long celebration at the Village of Dreams," he said. "Maybe we can go there too."

"Sounds dangerous considering I'm an exiled Princess," she bantered.

"I'd like to see them try and take you from me."

The words shouldn't have made her heart skip, but they did, and she found herself drawing a jagged breath and stifling the warmth pooling between her legs. She reached up for his neck, her finger trailing down over the slits in his neck, and his eyes visibly fluttered.

"Do you like that?" she asked, only half teasing as she'd felt his cock twitch against her thigh.

"That's very dangerous," he managed.

The words intrigued her. "Really? And what if I do this?" She leaned forward, lips brushing over the indention he'd shown her. But she didn't linger and instead pressed her lips to the length of his scar. His hands wrapped around her hips, and he squeezed her ass when she reached his mouth.

"You really shouldn't do things like that in the middle of the day," he uttered.

She smirked, nose brushing his. "What are you going to do about it, Commander?"

His brow raised, and his fingers sank deeper into her flesh. "I'd like to do a lot of things, but unfortunately, I don't have time to take care of you like I want before I have to be back out on my beach."

Her grin widened, stilling for a moment as he wrapped a hand around her neck. His fingertips gently massaged in her hair, and an involuntary moan left her.

"And yet, you keep doing that," she said.

Nadir huffed amusedly. "I bet I could end you just with this, Princess."

Her neck nearly rolled as the tingles rose on her flesh. She couldn't help herself from reaching between them, her hand curling around his already firming length. "Should we find out?" she suggested, leaning forward, lips pressing to that soft place again. "Should we find out if you can end me just with that... And I can end you—" Her tongue dragged along his scar, and her thumb swirled along the tip of his cock, "—just with this?"

He cursed under his breath, and his hand tightened in her hair to the point he tugged on it. "I can't believe I'm about to do this," she heard him whisper. Her grip tightened around his cock, now fully hardened in her grasp, and he cursed again.

He pulled her hair this time, bringing her back in front of his face. "You have ninety seconds before I have to be back on my beach and ready for combat, Princess," he uttered.

She practically felt her eyes darken. "Count me down, Commander."

She reached behind her and pulled the plug on the water, noting the fascinated raised brow smirk on Nadir's face. But she only smiled and met his lips with her own while she waited on the water to go down more before she did herself. She toyed with the tip of his cock as he kissed her, and she could feel his smile against her lips, his hands curling in her hair and sending chills down her spine.

She never wanted to stop kissing him.

As the water receded, she moved her mouth to his throat, nipping on his scar and kissing his collar.

"Seventy-five," he whispered in her hair.

Nyssa sat up and moved between his bent knees, taking his length in both her hands, pressing her breasts together between her arms. "So greedy," she mocked as she watched him swallow. "Tell me when I have sixty."

She could already feel the bead of stick on his tip as she deliberately dragged her finger up him, her other hand massaging and pinching his balls. He cursed out loud, and his back arched against her grip. She bent low, knowing he would be telling her the seconds at any moment, and her tongue flicked over his length.

"Sixty, Princess," he strained.

Her lips wrapped around his head, and she reached for his hands to pushed them both in her hair again as she took in his entire length. Throat relaxing, she heard him utter her name, his fingers tightening. Her breasts hit his thighs. She left her lips just on his tip and pushed her breasts around his shaft. He grunted as she continued up and down his length.

"*Fuck*—Thirty," he managed, hips pushing up and moving his cock further down her throat.

She knew he was getting close. Making him count it down had him anticipating and reaching. She reached for his sack again and took his length as far in as she could, feeling him twitch at the back of her throat. She devoured him, faster and faster until he held her head steady, and he fucked her mouth for a few strokes.

"Ten," he breathed.

Her mouth pulled off him, she replaced it with her hand. Moving quickly up and down. Pressing her lips to his tip again and sucking hard. Her grip was tight, breasts pushing against his balls.

"Five..." she dared to say, lips teasing, hand working. "Four..." Her tongue swirled him. She pushed up, surprising him with a quick kiss on his lips. "Come for me, Commander."

She deep-throated him once more and hummed out a groan. Fingers massaging his balls. Nadir jerked. He spilled down her throat, and Nyssa couldn't help her pleased moan as she sucked him dry and devoured every bit of that salty stick. Making him twitch. Making him curse and writhe. Until finally, he had to pull her off, and she laughed. Laughed as he wrapped his hands beneath her jaw and kissed her hard. His tongue swept over hers, and when he pulled back, he pushed her sideways bangs back.

"I should have stolen you that night," he told her.

"You should have," she agreed. "We'd have started our own war."

"My reef would be on fire already."

She grinned and kissed him again. "But we would be far away."

"Running, Princess," he grinned.

When Lex had come for her, Nyssa was just putting on new clothes. Nadir had left her with another kiss and a wink that he had something to show her later.

"Shatter indeed," Lex teased her. "Knew it would be explosive. Tell me he's satisfying all your needs, Princess."

"Needs I didn't even know I had," Nyssa uttered in response as she put on her shirt. "Are you going to tell me why you're punching me now?"

Lex smirked and gestured for her to hold her hands out. Lex wrapped the same bandage around Nyssa's fists as Lex had around hers.

"You're going to pretend I'm Rhaif," Lex said, to which Nyssa's head snapped up. "And I'm going to pretend you're Rhaif—"

"Terrifying," Nyssa muttered.

"—And together, we're going to try to kill each other." Lex cupped Nyssa's cheek playfully. "Let's go, Princess."

Nyssa stared at her as she left out the door. "Wait— this is dangerous," Nyssa said as she ran to catch up with her. "You're joking, right?"

Fighting was something Lex did not joke about.

Within minutes, Lex had knocked Nyssa off her feet. Lex grinned at her when she helped her from the ground.

"Is there any chance we can work up to this?" Nyssa begged as she touched her hand to her bleeding lip.

"You and Dorian didn't fight hand-to-hand?" Lex asked.

"No, we certainly did, but... He's not... Well, he's not *you*," Nyssa argued. She could remember Aydra after sparring with Lex, how the pair would come back with bleeding lips and bruises, sharing each other in celebration of a well-accomplished day before Aydra would sink into their mother's waters for healing.

Lex's bare feet dug into the ground again. A smirk rested on her perfectly narrow and beautiful face, a wisp of her now shagging blonde hair falling into her eyes.

She'd been away from Magnice sixteen days, and already Lex was starting to look more of a feral feline than she did before. That Belwark illusion was loosening into one more dangerous, of savagery and determination. She'd acquired a pair of the scaled armor pants from Nadir, making her legs look longer and more muscular than they already did. The lightweight tunics she'd brought had been cut up— sleeves now missing, open down the sides, showcasing the muscles Lex had earned and the strapping she'd started wearing around the swell of her breasts, as though Lex had decided she no longer needed the keptness of her title.

The Second Sun: obsessively confident and yet fragile. Ready to explode on those that had betrayed them at any moment.

She jumped at Nyssa, and Nyssa jerked to her knees, flinching and not meaning to allow the screech that came from her lips.

And Lex wailed with laughter.

It was the first genuine laugh Nyssa had seen on Lex's face since it all had happened, and the sight of it softened Nyssa to the point that she too began to laugh.

"I hate you," Nyssa laughed.

"I haven't seen you flinch like that since the Village," Lex said, holding her stomach as she doubled over. "Oh, that was amazing," she continued, wiping her face. "Thank you, Princess."

Nyssa shoved the sand off her knees and shook her head. "You're welcome? I guess," she replied, still smiling despite herself.

"Get out of here. We're done for today. You did good," Lex told her.

Without another word, Lex pushed past her, gave Nyssa's hair a quick ruffle, and Nyssa watched as Lex ran off to join Nadir in the surf to help him with the younger recruits.

21

By late afternoon, Nyssa had taken up comparing translated books to the same ones in the old language, intent on learning it so that she could understand whatever Nadir's people were muttering about her under their breath.

"Do you ever break?" Nadir asked as he joined her on the porch.

She smiled up at him. "Not when I've a job to do," she admitted.

"What happened?" he asked, gesturing to his lip.

She remembered she had a cut on her own from fighting with Lex.

"Never mock the Second Sun," she said simply.

Nadir looked as though he would laugh, but he just shook his head. "Come on," he said, closing her book with his foot. "Your tour isn't complete. We've some time before dinner. I can help with the translations later. Besides, some people thought perhaps you should start pulling your weight around here," he added with a wink.

"Oh really?" she mocked, knowing it was a joke. "What task do your people have for me?"

"Thinking you'd be great at shaking fruit out of trees," he bantered.

She frowned. "Shaking fruit out of trees?"

"Yeah—" he reached for her arm and held it up as they walked down the steps "—You've strong arms. And these thighs—" his gaze traveled over her, and he let out a low whistle "—they're powerful enough to kick the tree over if you needed to."

"Sounds excessive," she replied.

"You might enjoy it," he said as they hit the beach.

His people were preparing the long tables and greeting each other after a day's hard work for dinner together as they always did. But Nadir was taking her in the opposite direction towards the river, and she knew he was heading for the food forest. He'd been so proud talking about it to her in the days before; she was surprised it took him this long to show her.

With the sunset at her back, Nyssa soaked in the remaining bit of its warmth while they walked, relishing that lilac and orange glow rippling off the clouds, the streaked cerulean of the calm ocean beside them.

Just like the eyes he stared at her with when he turned and began walking backward.

He lifted her hand to his lips, swallowing when he kissed her knuckles, and then he paused before her.

"What?" she asked.

"I'm trying to memorize this moment," he said. "This sunset. This setting light reflecting off your hair. My home behind you. The fifty-three freckles on your cheeks—"

She couldn't help her smile, remembering how he'd counted them after the banquet.

"They're really popping out today," he said, his tone changing as he squinted at her cheeks. "I think... There are new ones. I'll have to count again tonight."

A lone laugh escaped her. "Show me your food forest, Commander," she said before he could say anything else that would have her knees weakening.

His hand wrapped around her cheek, and he kissed her, sending her heart fleeing. Deep enough that she had to grab onto his sides to hold herself steady, and for a moment, she forgot they were exposed on the beach for all his people to see.

If his words didn't have her falling over her own feet, his mouth certainly would.

When he pulled back, he continued to hold her in place. "Dammit, you're beautiful," he cursed beneath his breath as he pushed her hair back. "I don't think I realized how much more breathtaking you would be standing here on my beach," he added.

She scoffed, cursing her own heart for its erratic pace. "*Every* word that comes out of your mouth," she mocked, to which he laughed and hung his head. "All of them. I'm starting to wonder if these women who glare at me truly hate me because of who I am or because they're all your ex's."

"Actually, I only have one ex," he admitted as they started walking again, his hand holding onto hers. "But I will not deny the string of unrequited lovers I have just as you do," he added. "Most of them are of other races, though. Being Commander... I've tried to keep that life separate from the people I protect."

"And the one ex? What happened? Did you love them?"

Nadir eyed her playfully. "That's a lot of questions, Princess."

"Curiosity slayed the dragon," she said of her and her brother's words. The recollection of such a phrase made her stomach knot, and she held onto Nadir a little tighter as they came upon the river.

Nadir squeezed her hand, apparently having felt the shift. "I thought I loved her," he admitted. "But, she only ever saw me as this image I couldn't live up to."

"What do you mean?" she asked when he helped her over the stepping stones.

"I mean, she didn't allow me to have flaws. At any sign of weakness, she would talk down to me. Tell me true Commanders shouldn't show such things."

"Not even just to her?"

"Especially not to her."

"But that..." Nyssa didn't understand how a person who claimed to love someone could force them to keep such a part of them hidden. "That's horrible. You're a person just like anyone else."

"She thought my position should have held me to a higher standard," he said as they finished crossing. "After her, I stopped seeing women here. Started thinking perhaps love wasn't something I would find because of my title."

It broke her heart to hear him think such things about himself when he was so... Well, *him*.

"Nadir, you deserve everything," she said, almost stopping. "More than others. You... I see you out there every day with your people. Making sure they are ready for the battle coming. Individually and as a unit. You're always the first person to wake up and the last one to leave after dinner. You always make sure everything is clean and tidy, and the village is back in order. You check in on every legion and every market in that village every day. You know everything there is to know about the goods you're trading. You fix all their problems. You... You are not just the Commander of your army. You are your people's savior and leader. You carry so much on your shoulders, and you do it without any complaints or ever carrying how tired you are on your face."

Nadir had stopped walking, and as he held her gaze, the thought of

Nyssa's own kingdom came to mind.

"Sometimes, I wonder if they truly know how lucky they are to have you," she finished.

He shifted, his throat bobbing. "I don't even know what to say to that."

The corner of her lip lifted at the sight of the wonderment on his face. "You don't have to say anything," she said. "I'm simply telling you what I see. I will never understand how it can be thought that just because you hold a title, you should be perfect," she added. She reached for his other hand then and cradled them both in front of her chest.

"I crave the day when you let me see you. Raw and free Nadir Storn. Walls broken around him."

A visible jagged breath left him. "I'd like that too."

This time she kissed his knuckles, and then she tugged on his hand for them to start moving again.

Nadir was silent a few moments. Nyssa soon realized she didn't know where she was going, so she paused to wait for him to lead.

"You spoke about perfection as though someone wanted you to be simply because you're the Princess," he said after a while.

Nyssa sighed, watching the ground. "Some of us never asked for these titles," she said, voice almost dripping with disdain. "We never asked to be placed on a pedestal to have to prove our worth day in and day out in every way possible."

Nadir smiled back at her. "Struck a nerve, have we?"

"Yes," she said faster than she meant to.

"One of your many suitors?" he asked, and she knew he meant it playfully.

"Ah..." Her heartbeat picked up so much she felt the heated throb of it in her ears. Nadir's hand tightened around hers.

"Nys?"

She tucked her hair behind her ear, staring at the ground, confused as to why she suddenly felt this need and want to talk about such a thing that she'd only ever shared with her family before.

"A few of the suitors, yes," she said. "But... When I was a child, when Zoria and Vasilis were still alive, it was still tradition for Arbina to have a strong role in raising us. That changed a lot once Drae began to distrust her— after Dorian and I were marked." She paused to swallow the emotion in her chest. "It was different with Dorian and I than with Drae and Rhaif. Arbina adored Dorian just as she doted on

Drae. But with me... I... Do you remember when I told you about the mirrors?"

Nadir nodded, but he didn't speak.

"Mirrors remind me of my mother. Because every time I look into one, all I can see is what's wrong with me," she finally admitted. "All I can see is Arbina walking around me when I was a child, telling me of every flaw I possessed. That I wasn't good enough of a person to ever be Queen. Poking and showing every pound I needed to lose. I think I starved myself to the point of nearly dying the cycle before Dorian and I's markings. She was so *proud* of me for that. Told me I had found proper discipline and marked the two of us together as though that were my prize."

Nadir nearly stopped walking. "That's fucked," he uttered. "How old were you?"

"I was eight."

This time he stopped. "What?"

She almost laughed, but she tugged his hand, and they started walking again. "It's okay. I've... *handled* it—whatever that means. Most days. I, at least, can see myself without completely flinching and picking it all apart. Drae helped me see a different love than the one our mother offered. One that didn't depend on my being an image of what someone else thought I should be. Drae always told me I was enough no matter the words in the back of my head."

"Do you still get those days?" he asked.

"More so now than before this all happened," she admitted, and she didn't know why she was telling him. "I think I've pushed my entire life because of those years. To be... Worth *everything*. Enough of someone to be proud of. Even with Drae always telling me how proud she was of me, I always wanted to be the very best before I let her see. I wanted her to be proud of me more than I've ever wanted anything else. Last year, I finally decided I liked the person I was becoming. I was finally finding my voice and standing up for myself. Taking what I wanted. Until two weeks ago when it all came crashing down."

"In great extravagance," he muttered.

"The pair would have sacrificed themselves in no other way," she said, glancing to him. "The grandest exit. Audacious and dangerous, just like the two of them together."

"Why do you call her Drae?" he asked.

She started to frown. The nickname came so naturally to her by then that she never thought anything of it. But the memory made her smile nonetheless. "I didn't speak very well as a child—one more reason my mother decided I would always make a poor Queen. I couldn't say Aydra or Zoria. So Aydra became Drae, and Zoria became Zozi. Drae just sort of stuck, and after a while, it was all Dorian called her as well. Sometimes Rhaif."

"Do you remember much about Zoria and Vasilis?"

"Not much," she answered, trying her hardest to pull for any memories. "I remember Drae sort of shielding us from them. She never let Dorian and I alone in the room with either. And Rhaif did the same. Neither of us realized why at the time, but now..." She paused to stifle the emotion in her chest, and Nadir squeezed her hand reassuringly. "You know, I'm just glad she found Draven. Even with what happened to them. It was nice seeing her truly smile."

"It still feels unreal," Nadir said. "Pulling aground the last two times at his home... I still expected him to be there. Talking shit to me about the goods I'd brought. Felt almost as though he was simply at Magnice for a meeting, or I'd missed him going off on a hunt."

"I feel the same," she said. "That she has dropped me off here and gone on an adventure with him."

"Maybe that's how we can think of them," he suggested. "Off on one of their adventures."

The thought hurt her heart, but it did make her feel a little better. "I'd like that."

A soft smile spread on his lips, and he leaned down to kiss her again. Delicately, almost as a silent promise that they were okay and together, they would help one another through this.

"Come on. We're almost there," Nadir said when they pulled apart.

They continued walking in silence then, and Nyssa hugged his arm as he led her through. How easy it was to talk to him continued to surprise her. She wanted to sit with him and learn it all. Every whisper of his past. Every story. Hear his words and his laugh. She ached to tell him everything too. To talk about her family and her castle and hear him make fun of her and every suitor to have ever graced her room.

She started to speak, feeling so much lighter with the feeling of that weight off her chest, but the forest opened up around them, and she forgot everything she was about to say.

Fruiting trees of all kinds, some of which grew blooms and greening leaves, others bare, but all of them reached up toward the dark lavender sky. Pale moons' light poured in around them.

It was the sight of the fireflies dancing around them that brought a smile to her lips.

Magnice had only ever had them in the summer. She delighted in seeing them as it brought back the memories of her and Dorian catching and letting them light up their rooms as they played.

Nyssa stepped away from Nadir to see beyond the yellow glow and touch some of the barked trees she'd never seen before. She'd honestly never seen how the food she ate was grown.

It was a connection to the land she wished she'd known about earlier. To be at one with the surroundings that gave her life. She reached out to one of the trees, its bark peeling back from the limb. Rough and jagged beneath her fingertips, she allowed her body to sink into its vibrance.

Traveling to the Forest with Aydra and Lex had been the first time she'd ever seen trees other than the few scattered along the cliff sides. She'd felt a small comfort there, but not as much of a comfort as she felt at Nadir's reef. Here in this forest, with the ocean still in her ears.

This felt like home.

"I lied earlier," Nadir said then, and the words brought her back to him.

She turned, finding him simply staring at her. "What do you mean?"

"When I said I wanted to memorize that moment back on the beach." The space between them closed, and her heart warmed at the look on his face and the light from the fireflies dancing on his skin. He took both her hands and lifted them up at their sides, elbows bent, and then he sank their palms and forearms together. His long fingers lined up against her petite ones and then curled to entwine their hands together. Such a slight movement shouldn't have sent a chill over her skin, but it did, and her chest caved at the stare in his eyes.

"I want to memorize every moment," he said softly. "I want every moment that we can just be... Us."

That warmth spread through her entire body as the tug in her stomach reached out for him.

"Just us," she whispered, the words once more coming so easily from her that she didn't know how to stop herself.

His lip quirked a fraction upwards, and it made her head tilt.

"What?" she asked.

"I like the way you say, 'us.'"

His hand pressed to her cheek, and the smile on her lips widened as he bent to kiss her.

Lingering and yet desperate, his tongue swept her own in a manner different from how he'd kissed her earlier that day. The fiery heat was absent, replaced with a longing she had never felt before. As if he needed her as much as he needed breath.

She was pressed and cradled against a fruit tree, the solid trunk at her spine, him lifting her up until she was sitting in the vee of two great branches. She reached for his shirt, and it pulled over his head just before he bunched her dress in his hands and pulled it over her. Her undergarments shuffled off; she reached for the ties on his pants and swiftly undid them. The bark on the tree scratched her skin, but she hardly noticed.

Because his lips were on hers again, and he was already pushing inside her.

The tingle ran over her arms when he filled her, and she moved her hips up to meet his, gasping and then pulling back so that she could see his face. See that flutter of his eyes, the rise of his chest, and the crinkle in his forehead when he stilled inside.

"What?" he whispered, kissing her palm that rested on his cheek.

"I..." She swallowed, not even trying to still her thumping heart. "I wanted to memorize you too."

He moved slowly out of her, and when he thrust back in, her mouth sagged at the deliberation and depth of him inside her, feeling his pelvis against her clit, his sack on her cheeks, and then she felt him press harder, as though he thought he could bury himself further inside and wanted to try.

A low groan left him when her heels pressed into the back of his thighs. His forehead leaned against hers as they settled, and she felt her breaths shaking with an emotion so strong that everything else around them seemed to mute.

"*You* are everything, Nyssari," he whispered, his hand wrapping around her cheek. "You are everything and enough and *so* much more. And I will be at your side no matter where this war takes us."

His lips pressed softly to hers, but he didn't linger. He reached up and grabbed the branch above them.

"Evermore."

She knew he meant it. And the confirmation of the look in his eyes sent her heart spiraling.

With his every deepened and slow stroke, the tree marred her back, the bark scratching at her bare skin and her butt. His need for her passed from his body into hers. Up and down, her movements matching his, that depth of them together making her feel whole. It hardly took a few strokes more for her to see stars. She could feel herself tightening around him as his pace picked up, and he buried his head in the crook of her neck. She heard the branch above them crack slightly with his grip. Her fingers dug into his back, her mouth agape, body moving quicker with his. Until he started coming further out of her and then slamming back in. Until she could resist her undoing no longer, and the noise of her high-pitched moan echoed out into the darkness. She felt him shudder when she came apart, and with only another two strokes, he came apart with her, stilling in that depth within as he came down.

The branch he was holding broke off in his hand when he pulled back. She nearly laughed at the 'oops' expression on his face.

"Florna won't be happy about that," he uttered as her feet hit the ground. She pushed off the tree, and he leaned the great branch against the trunk where she'd been. As though it was meant to be like that.

Nyssa snorted, quickly clapping her hand over her mouth when he raised a brow at her. But he grinned nonetheless and grabbed her dress from the ground. She pushed a hand through her hair to fluff it only to find bits of bark and flowers in the strands.

"I am going to have to bathe before dinner," she said as she picked the blossom out of her hair.

Nadir stepped forward and leaned around to look at her back. A low whistle emitted from him. "Why didn't you tell me the tree was eating you?" he asked as he brushed the bark off her skin.

"What and interrupted... Whatever that was?" she asked, taking the dress from him.

She pushed it over her head, and he was smiling down at her when her head popped through the neck.

"Whatever that was?" he mocked.

He squeezed her waist and kissed her again when she couldn't respond.

Because she genuinely didn't know what this was, and it scared her that it was happening so quickly.

"Come on," he said with a tug on her hand. "Let's go to dinner, and then we can talk about whatever this was while you're kicking my ass again."

"I'm starting to think you like my putting you on your back."

"Being on my back beneath you is quickly becoming my favorite thing."

The wink he gave her made her shake her head, but she followed him out of that food forest and back onto the beach without another word.

It was the sight of the stares when they reached the rest of his people that killed every moment of bliss they'd just shared together.

Every head seemed to turn in their direction, smiles dropping from laughing faces. Whispers fluttered between groups. Nadir didn't seem to notice. He greeted all of his friends with his usual words of charm and smiles, clapping them on their shoulders and giving a few of the older women kisses on their cheeks. They all smiled back at him, and then they looked at her in the same disgusted manner they'd looked at her in the days before.

Their glares made Nyssa feel smaller than she'd ever felt, and every time Nadir would smile at her or take her hand in front of them, their eyes would travel over her in such a manner that she once thought she might vomit. Hatred and distrust. Wondering why she was on his arm. She could see their itching to question him on their tongues.

Stares that reminded her of their reality.

They'd had a day of bliss together, and Nyssa knew it was the only day she could allow them to have.

They couldn't be. Not in front of these people. Not right now. She would have to earn their trust before she could be seen on his arm again.

The knot that wove itself around her heart confused her. There was an overwhelming buzz in her ears with the decision. So much so that she barely picked at her food.

She didn't understand why it hurt so much.

Lex had given her arm a squeeze when she sat beside her as if she could tell what was wrong. And by the time Nyssa excused herself early, she was shaking.

The slender moons' light cascaded over the darkened water when she sat in the surf to think. She was so confused. So upset with herself that she'd allowed the one thing she told herself couldn't happen to happen. She'd opened up that whisper of doubt in his people's ears, and she just hoped she could squash it before it became too much.

22

"You're too guarded there," Nadir pointed out later when he'd brought the bamboo sticks to the beach to meet her, long after dinner had subsided and he'd helped them clean up. She could use the practice to ease her mind, and honestly, she was hoping it would help her figure out how to tell him what she had to.

"Relax your shoulders." He came around behind her, placing his hands over hers as he explained the wipeout. And when he walked back around to set up, she tried it. Nadir didn't hold back. He came at her hard, forcing her to jump when he swiped at her legs. She landed on one knee and pulsed the stick out for his legs.

It caught his shin, and Nadir cursed to the sky.

"Oh fuck," she realized as she actually hurt him.

"Dammit, Princess," he cursed, limping it off.

"Shit—I'm sorry," she said as she darted for him.

But Nadir laughed, wincing when he met her gaze but smiling anyway. "Don't be. That was good." He wrapped an arm around her and kissed her forehead. "Just give me a minute to walk it off before you try to kill me again."

She almost laughed, but she settled against the bamboo instead, cheek lying on it as she watched him walk in a circle, his limp slowly disappearing.

Every time he looked at her, her heart dropped to her stomach.

"You going to tell me what was wrong at dinner?" he asked after a few moments.

"What do you mean?" she lied.

"Every time I looked at you... Your smile felt forced. You looked at me as though I were dying."

"I don't—"

"Nyssa, please," he begged as he picked up his stick. "Tell me what's wrong. Tell me why after all those things we've said to each other and shared the last few days, you suddenly could not stand to look at me in the presence of my people."

She bit the insides of her mouth, her eyes darting to the ground and then back to him.

She could do this. She could tell him.

But her heart felt like someone was twisting a knife in it.

"Your people hate me," she finally blurted. "They hate me, and they hate seeing me with you. They—"

"Why do you care what they think?" he asked.

"Because I do not want them to think less of *you*," she said, voice sticking in her throat. "Every time they see us together, I can see them beginning to doubt your judgment." Her mouth felt full of sap, and she had to force the words out. "What... What happens when they decide you're favoring me?"

Nadir paused, and she watched as it sank in. He shifted as he leaned against his own stick, mirroring her. Jaw clenching, eyes blinking as though biting back the look in the gaze he washed out to the ocean...

He already knew what she had seen and had perhaps chosen to ignore it. And the realization of it made the lump rise in her throat when he met her eyes once more.

"I don't care what they think," he finally said.

"Yes, you *do*," she argued. "Your people mean more to you than your own life."

"And what if you meant more?"

It pained her to see the confirmation in his eyes.

"Then I would say you've completely lost your mind," she affirmed. "We hardly know each other."

"I know how I feel," he argued. "I know how you make me feel. And I—"

"Nadir, what are you going to do when it comes time for negotiations? When I request to be in that room and they all speak out saying they do not want me there? Will you put your entire life and position on the line to keep me in there?"

"I trust you."

"They don't," she confirmed. "I have to prove myself worthy of their trust, and I will not have you risking your position for me."

"What does that mean?" he asked. "For us?"

That word again.

"It means... It means we cannot be as we were today and every other day in front of your people. You have to show just as much of an aversion towards me as they do. You have to let me earn their trust."

"Is that what you want?"

"What I want doesn't matter anymore."

"Yes, it does," he said, stepping towards her. "What you want always matters. I want to know what you want, Nyssari. Do you want me? Do you want us—*whatever this is*?"

"Of course I want you," she choked. "Nadir, I want you as I want to breathe. I want to know everything there is to know about you. I want to hear every secret you've ever had. I want to know all your own fears and doubts. I want to tell you everything about me while I lie in your arms. I want... I want to fight with you, get angry at you. I want to storm off, and you come rushing back in to call me out on my bullshit. I want to read fantastical stories and hear you tell them in this language and the old. I want to wake up beside you and see the sunlight on your face, to kiss away every darkened thought that comes in your head. I want *you*. I want the real you. I want to learn *you*."

He was standing before her, a glisten in his eyes. She was trembling, and a tear rolled down her cheek as she forced the rest of the words.

"And it's because of how much I want you that I know we have to make a choice."

"Nyssa, don't—"

"Commander of your people is the only thing you've ever wanted to be," she cut him off. "I will not be the reason they take that away from you. If they continue to think I am worthless in this war and you are favoring me, they will. I know your people love you, but this war is terrifying for all of us. They would remove you at the first sign of doubt. And me... I have to prove myself worthy of their trust. People think I am weak and submissive because of who I am. That because I am the Princess, I will sit back in fluffy dresses and have no contribution to this war. Spoiled and dependent on someone else to fight my battles. They think I don't understand the danger or logistics of this. You heard them the other night when we were on that jetty. No matter how much either of us wants to tell them the truth, you know as well as I that they will not believe it."

"So we make them listen."

"No," she said, her voice almost breaking. "No, I can't let you do that. I can't let you risk what you've worked for your entire life for this.

I won't have your people thinking just because we are together that you are allowing me in that room." She paused, closing her eyes and sighing as the frustration swelled in her chest.

"We have two choices," she finally said.

"Don't do this, Princess," he whispered, an audible tremor in his voice.

But she had to.

"We can either keep this a secret—"

"Nyssa, people have eyes," he interjected. "They're going to know."

"Then guard your face when you're around me. Pretend you hate me. I don't know how else we can keep each other if not to do this."

Nadir slumped onto the sand as though his knees had suddenly given way. A surrender to the conversation that made her nervous.

"You certainly know how to break a heart," he said in a tight voice.

"I don't mean to—"

"I understand, Nyssa. I really do." He sighed heavily as she knelt beside him. "I just... I don't think I realized it would hurt this much."

His broken expression nearly finished her. His hands were clenched around themselves. She could see the throb of the vein in his neck. She reached out for him, but he flinched from her touch, and the knot wrenched her heart. She didn't know what to say.

"Nad—"

"Nyssa, I want you too," he cut her off. "I want *all* of you. I want everything. And I have meant all the things I've said to you. But this..." He paused to rub both his hands behind his neck, heel tapping quickly in the sand.

The decision stretched over his features, and the knot around her heart twisted.

"I understand what you're saying," he continued. "I do. I know you're right. But, I don't know that I can handle looking at you every day, surrounded by sunlight and my beach, while you throw yourself into this war with my having to guard every look upon my face. It is hard enough having to guard the pain I am in since this whole thing started... To have to guard my eyes against looking at you and smiling when you are the only thing bringing me joy right now... I don't... I don't know how to do that too."

It was her breaths that stilled this time. What he'd said rang true for her as well. But there was nothing she could do about it.

The second option.

"I suppose that's it then," she managed, the tear rolling down her cheek.

"Yeah," he whispered.

She swallowed the choke in her throat, letting the tear dry on her face in the hopes he didn't see her breaking. "I'll make myself scarce," she forced herself to say. "No more leering at you across beaches. No more... No more of whatever this last week has been. I'll train with Lex. All I ask is that you let me in the war room when it is time."

He nodded and turned towards her. "Okay."

For a moment, they didn't look away from one another. The wash of what they'd just decided poured through them both. He leaned forward, pressed his lips to her forehead, and took her hand. What was left of her heart vanished, and she was left with an open fissure where it should have been, bleeding out as a restless heat along her extremities. She squeezed his fingers as he entwined them together.

The quiet promise of a simple touch.

"Tell me this isn't forever," he whispered.

"You make it sound like we're saying goodbye."

"It feels like we are," he admitted. "It feels like another part of me is dying. Like this war has already taken more from me than I ever anticipated losing. If this is the last I can be with you--"

"It's not forever," she promised. "It's only until they trust me enough that they do not think differently of you as well."

"Even still," he rolled his head against hers, and his forehead pressed to her temple. "*Curses*, why does this hurt so much?" he said, more to himself than to her.

Nyssa slowly stood, still holding onto his hands. "I assume you have a bottle of nyghtfire somewhere in your shack?"

Nadir nodded as he stood, and he led her to his home.

No words were spoken at first in the quiet of the house as he grabbed the glasses and poured them both large helpings of the spiced whiskey. Nyssa pushed herself atop the counter as he did. The drink was pressed into her hand, and for a moment, they simply stared at each other, his hand grazing her knee.

"To wanting what we can't have," she finally managed with a raise of her glass.

She could see the clench in Nadir's jaw, and he breathed, "That's really not funny, Princess," in a voice so low she hardly heard him. But it quirked a smile on her lips nonetheless, and she pushed her drink against his.

"I think it's perfect."

He watched her another moment, glistening gaze reflecting back to her in the moons' light. She sipped the nyghtfire, letting its burn wash down her throat, and she watched as he did the same.

"Why is this so hard?" he whispered.

Nyssa sat her cup down. "Because whatever this is isn't something either of us thought we would have to lose."

Nadir's weight shifted before her, he set down his own cup, and he reached up to push her hair out of her eyes. "What is this?"

She covered his hand with her own and kissed his palm. "Everything," she whispered.

The kiss he pressed to her lips was not one of heat-filled lust but rather of a good-bye, of a last promise to each other. To find whatever this was again.

Nadir's hands wrapped around her, bending over her and making her grasp to his neck. She could feel the tear on his cheek but wasn't sure if it was his or hers. Because this was the only thing either of them had to look forward to at that moment, and they were choosing to give it up. For the good of their people and the war they hadn't asked for.

She pressed her hands to his cheeks as their kiss deepened. Her heart continued to shatter with every sweep of his tongue against hers. She wanted to hold him until sunrise, pretend this was all a bad dream...

Just them.

The counter was the first of many surfaces he chose to bury himself in her for the remainder of the night.

The Commander did not surface. No. This was the Nadir she'd asked for. Raw and free. Able to tell her of all his secrets and brush them off with his jokes. The bantering, carefree man she'd met at that banquet, making her laugh into the darkness, blush at his whispers, and kiss every inch of her body. Holding her against him as he pushed deep inside her on the bed or over the chair, against the post, and on the table.

Wherever they could hold each other.

She didn't care that her body would be sore the next day or that her neck would be splayed with raised marks as it had been after the banquet. She didn't care that the next day she would have to push herself into the war or that she would have to fight the stares of the people who thought her weak.

What she cared about was him and the freedom they shared together. How when she was with him, she didn't remember the war or what had happened to her family, or even that she was a lost princess.

Here.

On his beach.

In his home.

Holding onto him not as though it were their last moments, but because it truly was. At least for now. The fact that they would have to give each other up with the sunrise made her cherish every moment.

It was the first time she'd ever begged the sun to be late rising.

23

Nadir was gone when she woke.

Nyssa groaned into the bedsheets as the memory of the night before rushed through her. Her face was swollen from the tears they'd both shed, not just for each other but also as they'd talked about the war, of how they would bring vengeance for the people they'd lost for it. She knew he would be there if ever she needed him, but until then... She would keep her promise. She would make herself scarce. Train with Lex. Avoid him when possible so that they did not show anything on their faces, as hard as that might be.

Her body ached with satisfaction. How easy it was to share herself with him made her question everything. She was never embarrassed in front of him and instead always felt supported and trusted. The conversations they shared and questions he would ask were different from every other man who usually only wanted to bring her gifts and offer her a place on their arm as though *that* were some grand prize and she was not.

Sometimes she thought perhaps she should have listened to her sister.

Because she was falling for him faster than she could catch herself.

Nyssa put clothes on before making her way to the beach.

Standing there, the water lapped around her toes. Her arms reached over her head, and she inhaled the scent of the ocean. She wondered what her brother was doing and if he had made it to Dahrkenhill.

The sun had hardly peeked over the horizon. She stretched her legs, pulling one ankle behind her, followed by the other. Her eagle circled her overhead, screeching out to tell her good morning as she cracked her neck and gazed at the long stretch of beach to the east.

No other thoughts wandered through her mind before she took off in a run.

Her toes hugged the sand with her every step. That morning felt like the first morning of a new beginning. Something about it... She wasn't sure what, but her insides felt numb to the tears that had been present in the weeks before. Replaced with anger, rage, and determination. A desire to actually prove her worth on her own, not whatever it was she had been doing. No more allowing her heart to get in the way of what she had to do.

The weight of it sat heavier on her shoulders. She'd been inside her own head for eighteen days now. She had a job to do. Questions to be answered.

A war to win.

Perhaps that was why she had decided to go on a run that morning without telling anyone.

Truthfully, she wanted to scream one more time at the wind just to be sure she had it all out of her system before she did something stupid.

By the time she arrived back at the Umber, the sun was nearly a third of the way in the sky. She hadn't screamed, but she did feel a little more at ease with the decisions running through her head.

It was once she reached the edge of the Umber, though, that she realized she probably should have told Lex where she was going.

Because Lex's knife was pointed beneath Nadir's chin, and she had his throat in her hand.

"Hey—*HEY!*" Nyssa bolted towards them, just in time to hear Lex shouting in his face that he was an idiot and asking if he'd run her off or broken her heart.

"LEX!" Nyssa shouted.

Lex finally saw her, and she released Nadir with a jolt. He barely wavered off-balance, hand coming up to rub his throat as he met Nyssa's gaze. Her heart broke at seeing him that morning. The once over he gave her was brief, as was his solemn nod before he turned on his heel.

Nyssa didn't have time to let her sorrow get to her, for Lex was marching across the sand with a scowl more fierce than Nyssa had ever seen of the Second Sun.

Lex's hand seared backward across Nyssa's face.

"Where the *Infi* have you been?" Lex shouted.

Nyssa nearly fell to the ground.

"I've been looking for over an hour!" Lex continued. "Do you realize something could have taken you? What happened? Did he do something to you?"

Shaking, Nyssa's hand pressed to her bleeding cheek. The sting of Aydra's ring cutting her flesh enraged her, and Nyssa rolled her eyes to meet Lex's.

"You think *he* did something to me?" Nyssa seethed. "No. You will leave him out of this. Nadir has been nothing short of perfect since we've arrived. Do not bring him into any of this. I went on a run to clear my head—"

"Don't you *ever* do that again!"

"I am not a prisoner here," Nyssa affirmed.

"No, you are not, but you are to tell me where you are going."

"I don't need a sitter."

"I am your Second," Lex growled. "It is my duty to protect you, and I will not lose you too, Nyssari."

The words made Nyssa's chin rise. Numbness took over her body. She watched Lex grab the same bamboo spears she and Nadir had used the night before, and then she tossed her one.

Nyssa caught it, gripping it tight in her fingers for a moment as Lex began to walk around her. Nyssa's insides trembled with rage. Words of anger and doubt dripped through her deteriorating mind.

The blood continued to trickle down her cheek.

And Nyssa didn't tell herself to breathe.

"Defend yourself."

Lex lunged.

Nyssa pushed her feet deeper into the sand to set herself and struck back at the blow Lex had taken. Lex's stick whirled and met her again, nearly hitting her thigh, but Nyssa blocked. The rod whipped over Lex's head, and Nyssa jumped as it swept towards her calves and then under her feet.

Nyssa met the ground in a kneel and dragged the stick behind Lex's legs— the move Nadir had taught her. Lex landed on her back, and Nyssa stood to glare over her.

"Are you actually concerned about me, or is this just you not wanting to fail in the task my sister so *desperately* gave you?"

The tone came darker than she'd intended it to. Lex stiffened on the ground, hair falling into her eyes.

"I strongly encourage you to think through what you're about to say, Princess," Lex warned as she brought herself to her feet.

Nyssa set up again. How her rage had gotten stronger, she didn't know. But she couldn't breathe, and her teeth felt like someone was compressing them together.

A group of Honest had stopped at the edge of the beach to watch the exchange.

It was Nyssa's turn to lunge. Lex caught her quickness. Again and again, their sticks struck, the clack of the bamboo sounding over the ocean waves. Lex pulsed low and whacked Nyssa's calf. Nyssa landed flat on her back. The throb of it shuddered through Nyssa's muscle, and she cursed into the air.

Lex's chest heaved, her green eyes reflecting that same rage back to Nyssa, and she extended her stick down to Nyssa. Nyssa grabbed the end and pulled herself to her feet.

Nyssa crouched low and buried her feet in the sand again as Lex started towards her.

"You could have stayed with Bala," Nyssa said. "Stayed with a King already confident in her duties. Someone brave and fearless as Drae was."

She blocked Lex's next hit, and Lex swung around to the ground. Nyssa jumped and pushed forward. Lex caught her and pressed, her figure towering over Nyssa, the cross of their spears between their faces.

"Tell me you actually want to be here with me and not with she or Dorian," Nyssa seethed.

Lex stared at her, but she didn't respond.

Nyssa shoved her off and took three steps back. "That's what I thought."

The pair began to circle.

"Care to tell me why we are going through this again?" Lex dared.

"Because you just struck me when I came back from that run as though I'd done the worst thing I could possibly do," Nyssa said. "If it had been Drae coming back without telling you where she was going, you would have simply asked her if she was ready for breakfast."

Lex swung at her again. Nyssa blocked it this time, knocking her three times in defense. Lex caught her legs and wiped her out. Nyssa's back landed in the sand, but she sprang to her feet before Lex could come at her again. Nyssa swung towards Lex's stomach, and Lex jumped back. But Nyssa whirled this time, the swell of her adrenaline threaded through her, and she caught Lex's chest in a high kick.

Lex stumbled, and Nyssa started to circle again.

"Aydra was a Queen," Lex spat, dusting off the sand from her shirt. "Aydra had years of training over you, years of throwing herself into the fire and coming out on the other side a stronger woman. You—"

"Are what?" Nyssa interjected. "Incapable?"

"Inexperienced."

The word deadened between them.

Stilled between them for a long enough moment that Nyssa noticed more people stopping to stare.

"There is nothing wrong with being inexperienced, Nyssa," Lex said. "We want to help. We need you to do what you do and let us do what we do."

The words came calmly from Lex's lips, but Nyssa could see the tense bite back of attitude skimming the surface of her features, feel the drip of frustration with every breath.

"Which is what?"

"Protect you."

Nyssa paused in her circle, back firm and chin high, and she held that spear in front of her with such a grasp, she felt it crease beneath her fingers.

"Then tell me you're protecting me because you truly believe in me and not because it is your final duty to my sister."

Silence.

A ringing started in Nyssa's ears, and she scoffed under her breath. "Right," she muttered. She shook her head and whirled the stick in her hands once before stepping forward.

And then she shoved it in Lex's hands.

"You are relieved as my Second," Nyssa snapped. "I have no crown and therefore no need of one. We're finished."

She pushed past Lex to trudge through the sand back towards the shack.

"Where are you going, Princess?" Lex called.

"To make myself scarce as I promised I would," she called back. "You are free of me and your promise to my sister. You may do what you please."

"*Fucking*—Aydra, give me strength," she heard Lex mutter under her breath. "Don't be stupid, Nyssari," Lex shouted. *"Nyssa!"*

Nyssa ignored Lex's shouts as she pressed across the beach to Nadir's shack. That hollow numbness had spread to all her extremities. She filled her bag and grabbed her bow. She wasn't sure what she was doing. She didn't know where she would go.

But she couldn't stay there.

"*Nyssari!*" Lex shouted again.

Nyssa pushed her boots on her feet and made northeast into the Forest of Darkness.

Nyssa cursed herself the moment she stepped into the forest.

She walked in an almost trance-like state, re-living every word she'd spoken not just to Lex but also to Nadir the night before, memorizing the tone of her voice. She cursed the sky, muttering out loud as she stomped over great roots and stray broken limbs. Her only comfort was that her eagle was following overhead. Even if she couldn't hear him, at least she was not completely alone.

Truthfully, she didn't know what to do.

Where to start.

How to prove herself worthy of being in that room when Nadir's people clearly didn't trust her or how to prove herself worthy of Lex's protection and friendship without being simply a duty to her.

It was an uncomfortable situation Nyssa never thought she would find herself in. She was still grasping at the fact that her sister was gone, and now she was expected to fight a battle she didn't know how to win.

Nyssa pressed on.

Through the whispering forest for hours until the beach filled her ears once more. With the familiar smell of salt mixed with pine back, she paused at the edge of the surf and shredded herself of her bags and bow.

It was here that she finally allowed it all to consume her. Away from the judging gazes of her friends and the Honest people. Completely alone and numb.

Only she and the crashing waves.

She screamed into the nothingness.

Acknowledging every doubt in her head. Every whisper of her failures. Every fear. Every fire. Draven falling. Her sister burning. Rhaif burning and shouting at her that day. Her being separated from Dorian. The cries and songs of the Noctuans. Pushing Lex away. Telling Nadir goodbye.

She allowed every shred of it to flow through her muscles and agonize her existence.

Her screams shattered the air to the point she could not feel her throat and far after. Her pores ignited and twisting. The voices were so loud she thought her ears would bleed. As though the Aviteth were standing behind her and shrieking.

But she had to get it out.

She couldn't hold herself hostage with it all any longer. Snapping and shouting at her friends was not an option. She had lost and pushed away the last two people around her that gave her any sort of comfort. She knew if she didn't do something, she would lose more than what she already had. She had a job to do, and she couldn't keep pushing people away to do it.

Her muscles became so on edge from the memories and fears while she screamed that she felt like they were peeling her skin off. But she didn't shake it. She sank herself fully beneath its weight and succumbed to its depths.

Her knees hit the ground, and she grabbed her hair, pushing her hands through the strands at the nape of her neck. Muscles stretching and writhing, her bones almost vibrating. The physical pain matched the turmoil inside her.

A warmth pooled in her stomach and moved outwards to her limbs.

Her core twisted and came alive. There was a snap. A break inside her. A release of something unexpected. What felt like knives piercing her skin raked up her forearms, and a cold wind wrapped her skin. She screamed again as the pain twisted her heart and stomach.

Blood trickled from her ears.

Something was wrong.

This was new.

A different sort of fear caught her.

This was fear she hadn't expected.

Shaking, Nyssa opened her eyes, and she nearly jumped out of her body at what she saw.

Black smoke surrounded her knees.

She pulled her hands back—

And a petrified scream left her lungs.

Her hands were *black*.

Black lightning streaks like Dorian's pulsed up her arms. But it was not blue flames beneath the lines. It was amber and obsidian.

She couldn't breathe. Couldn't move.

She was on *fire*.

Terror gripped her to her spine.

She couldn't have fire. Dorian had fire.

Her lungs nearly collapsed. She buried her head beneath her hands, pressing her eyes together in the hopes it would all be a nightmare.

Back and forth.

But her body continued to shred and burn.

She knew she would vomit at any moment. Her limbs felt as though they didn't exist. This was fear unlike anything she'd ever experienced.

What was happening to her?

The ocean crashed a few feet ahead. She forced herself to focus on getting to it, to put herself out of whatever this was before it grew out of control. But she couldn't find her limbs to move.

As though another was moving her, she felt wet sand beneath her nails. She was on her stomach, and she didn't know how she'd gotten there. The water curled over her hands, and her entire body shuddered violently, almost like it was hurting her. Nyssa screamed again, vision going in and out.

This can't be real, she told herself. *This isn't real.*

—She was back in the Throne Room.

It was the day of her and Dorian's markings.

They'd gone into that pool together. Arbina had stood at the edge of it, Rhaif and Aydra to the side, Vasilis and Zoria on their thrones.

Only eight at the time, together, she and Dorian had been terrified. She could still see him writhing beside her under the water as it cut through her skin for her eagle mark. But Dorian... Dorian had screamed as though his insides were being ripped out of him. Nyssa had taken his hand while they were under...

—Reality jolted her back with a great heave.

The ocean sloshed around her, and she coughed, hands pressing into the ground. Water spewed from her lungs as though she'd just been drowning. The sea rushed and crashed over her body again. Nyssa forced herself up to her knees and then crawled backward out of the surf.

She noted then that she was completely naked.

Her heart continued to throb in her ears as she replayed the moment of her and Dorian's markings. She had felt his agony when she took his hand. She had felt the pulse of his form in her own core.

Her eagle screeched overhead. He was having a fit. He shrieked over her almost in a scream. Nyssa pushed every thought to the back of her mind. The ringing in her ears faded slowly as she willed her breaths to calm.

She couldn't get the image of her streaked hands out of her head, but as she looked down at her palms, she wondered if it had all been a trick of her exhausted mind.

Perhaps she'd passed out during her meltdown and had dreamt it all.

Her eagle continued to cry out over her. She hung her head in the failure of not being able to hear him and stood to go to her bag. She didn't see the clothes she'd been wearing anywhere, so she pulled on another set of pants and a shirt.

She'd just finished dressing when she noticed a ring of black in the sand. Nyssa stared at it a moment as the water rushed up and over, and she swore she saw shards of glass beneath what looked to be handprints. But as the sea swept over the ash, it all disappeared.

Maybe it hadn't been a dream.

Nyssa crouched back down to find the canteen of water in her bag. Maybe she was dehydrated and hallucinating. She couldn't really have fire, could she? And if she did... How the Infi was she supposed to control it? Or tell Lex about it?

She would have to talk to Nadir again. She knew he would have answers. Or Lovi.

Yes, she would take it to Lovi.

"Well, well—"

Nyssa's heart stopped. She wrapped her hand around her bow.

"—If it isn't the Princess."

An arrow pulled, she whipped around to face the stranger, only to be met with fifteen Lesser beings standing in a line before her, their own arrows pulled.

It dawned on her then why her eagle had been screaming.

Her eyes flickered over the smirking faces and finally landed on the male in the middle.

He was nearly as tall as Draven, a crown of long black braided hair laid over his broad shoulders, some of the small braids pulled back off his face into a high bun—much like Draven used to do. His thin, stark hazel-green eyes smirked at her from beneath hooded brows. Mischief danced in his gaze, but she could see the darkness resting behind it, the shadows resting in his partially sunken cheeks, sunlight glowering on the sleek razor of his cheekbones and dark brown skin.

It was then that she noticed the phoenix markings on the backs of these people's forearms.

Her eagle screeched again.

Arrows turned towards it.

"Stand down your bird, Princess," the man said.

"I'm not a Princess," she argued.

"You think just because you've run away from your kingdom, you're not who you are?" the man mocked. "It's Nyssari, isn't it?"

Nyssa focused on her dropping elbow while tightening her thighs and shoulders in her stance.

A quiet scoff left him, and his gaze wandered around the beach. "Where is your Second?" he asked.

"She went to get firewood," Nyssa said fast. "She'll be back soon."

Quiet laughter radiated through the crowd, but she didn't lose her stare with the leader. He held up a hand, two fingers moved, and the people all lowered their bows. The once-over he gave her made her insides twist. So different from the comfort she'd felt within the safety of Bala and Draven's people. She realized then why Bala was so desperate to keep her and Dorian a secret.

These were the Venari people she'd been warned about in the Chronicles.

The traitors and the power-hungry. The ones Draven had fought so hard against.

"She isn't here, is she?" he asked. His smirk widened, and then he tapped the woman beside him on the shoulder. The woman smiled and started forward.

The arrow released from Nyssa's bow and landed a step in front of the woman. The woman grinned fully at her. "Fiery," she mused, glancing at the leader behind her. "I like it."

Movement caught in the corner of Nyssa's eye, and she had to look twice towards the tree line. A hundred more Venari were coming out from the shadows, and Nyssa's heart caved in on itself.

She turned her attention back to the leader. "What do you want?" Nyssa managed.

He grinned outright, dark eyes dancing over her in delight. "You."

Nyssa's mind spun as she looked at the swarm of Venari rebels all around. Smirks on all their beautiful faces. There was something more about it than bloodlust. Their faces did not read murder. They hadn't killed her yet.

Which she knew meant one of two things: they were either going to take her to Bala to try and barter for Bala's crown... or...

They would take her to Man.

Nyssa let the bow sag in her hands.

Her eagle screeched again.

Do not interfere. Just stay overhead.

She wasn't sure if he could hear her. She didn't know if he'd be able to understand. But she kept repeating the instruction nonetheless.

She may not have heard her eagle's response, but she watched as the bird soared upwards into the blinding of the sunlight.

She was on her own.

24

They bound her hands in front of her, and Nyssa could tell by the look in the leader's eyes that he knew she was giving in for more than just their threat to kill her. But Nyssa kept her mouth shut and allowed the knowing glare to rest on her face as they led her into the woods and away from the comfort of the beach.

She noted their every weapon, every flex, and every look they gave her. She noted the differences in some of the people, how some looked like Balandria, others like Bael, Dunthorne, and Draven, and some... a small few... had the most brutal scars on their faces she'd ever seen. As though they'd been marked by lightning and vines, mutilated and pieced back together again. Any time they went near her, an uneasiness settled in her core, as though her bones were foreign inside her body.

And yet, they all shared that primal Venari confidence about them that comforted as well as terrified her.

She lost track of the time that they walked, but she knew they were trailing the eastern edge of the forest, back past where the Venari kingdom would have been west of the Impius River. She was sure they were having to travel so far to avoid being seen by any of Bala's sentries. They walked slower than she would have liked, but with so many of them, their leader, whom she learned was named Gail, was keeping track of every one of them.

It was nearing sundown when he finally announced their stopping. They were just inside the edge of the Forest, but she could still hear the ocean waves and smell the comforting salt of its depths in the air.

The Venari at least gave her food and water when they shoved her onto the dirt by a tree. Her bound hands were tied to another rope, which was looped around the tree at her back. She watched them scuffle around, preparing fires to stow away the chill in the air from the winter surrounding them.

But the main person she watched was Gail. Observing how he spoke to his people, noting the way he moved, the way his people looked at him… He was the last person to settle in front of a fire, the last person to start eating. He kept a careful eye not just on her but on his people as well. She could see just within those few hours why they had chosen him as their de facto leader, and why they had chosen him to follow when they'd decided they disagreed with Draven's not wanting to take over Magnice.

She wondered if Gail and Draven had ever been friends. If perhaps he had been Draven's Third at one time instead of Dunthorne. She could tell Gail knew the in's and out's of leadership. He had the same aura about him that Draven had had… The dangerous energy, the determined power swagger that rested in his broad shoulders, the gait of his walk, the firmness in his voice, the stilled force of his domineering gaze. Every flex of his body language told her he would just as soon slice every one of his own people's throats rather than let the power he desired slip through his hands.

It was the same intense energy Draven had had when it came to Aydra and his people.

It should have scared her.

It should have had her quivering in her bones.

And yet, there she was. Sitting numb on the ground, hands tied, back stiff, chin high. Surrounded by traitors to the true King.

Her heartbeat even.

Too entranced by the task her sister had left for her. She may have failed her sister by standing by and not fighting when she was burning on that tree, but she would be damned if she would fail in the one thing she'd asked her to do.

So she watched Gail. Noted every word he spoke, every gesture of his head and hands. Knew he knew she was watching him. But she didn't dare tear her eyes away, insistent on making him uncomfortable if possible, and if not… at least he would know she was not afraid of him.

"Speak, little Sun," Gail uttered after nearly finishing his meal of rabbit. He chose to sit alone with her at the fire once his people had started to part off in groups for drinking games. The noise of his sucking on the bone echoed in her ears, making her cringe at the slurp, and she felt her jaw tighten.

"You've been watching me all day," he continued. "Do you like what you see?"

There was a flicker of amusement in his eyes when he glanced fleetingly in her direction, but she ignored it.

"What do you want with me?" Nyssa finally asked.

Gail surveyed her thoroughly for a beat, and she didn't dare blink. "My guess is you've heard of our new friends on the western shore," he said.

Nyssa went rigid.

So he was planning on taking her to Man.

"I have," she answered.

He picked his teeth with the bone in his hand. "There is a Noble there," he continued. "His people were the first to arrive and settle on our shores without a fight from the Honest. Across the seas, they are calling him the conqueror of ghosts."

Draven's plan rang in her mind, the memory of Dorian telling her about it. What he'd said about a settlement they'd missed. She pushed it to the back of her thoughts, not allowing the knowledge of anything to rest on her face.

"What does that have to do with me?" Nyssa dared to ask.

"You will be my bartering chip," he informed her. "A princess of what will soon be a forgotten race will be very rare to him, so rare he'll likely present you to the King as a gift. He'll give me anything I want."

"And what do you want?"

A coy smile rose on his lips as he threw the bone he'd been sucking on into the fire. "You and your people bowing at my feet," he answered, hanging his arms over his knees. "Allies across the seas. A place in the new King of Haerland's court."

"My life cannot buy you all that."

"No," he agreed. "But it can buy me a place at the table. One step closer to the crown."

Nyssa considered his words, the stillness of the cold air sweeping her muscles. "My brother's crown is practically in ruins," she finally said. "Why not take it instead of bowing at another's feet?"

He paused as his eyes moved over her in a manner that should have made her uncomfortable. She wondered if he were determining whether she would be of more value to him in Man's hands or in his own.

"Because the races of Haerland will soon be under the rule of Man,"

Gail answered. "Why would I take a crown that would mean my fighting against them? Why would I not leash myself to the ones who will inevitably take over this world?"

"And what? You'll take his crown when it's the right time?"

Another pause.

Another pause long enough to let her know he was genuinely debating telling her his plan or if he should keep her in the dark. But Nyssa knew the game. Males hungry for power liked to talk. To boast. To have confirmation from a beautiful woman that they are smart and mighty and all-knowing. That their plans were brilliantly thought out, and the reward for such bravery should be a wrap of the woman's lips around his cock.

So she would let him talk.

"You're smart," he noted. "Tell me, *Nyssari*. Have you never wanted the power of the High crown?"

"Never."

"Liar," he accused. "I can see it in your face. You want power just as I do."

But the truth was, he was right.

Of course, she had thought about it.

Standing at the back of the Council Chambers during meetings. Listening and watching Rhaif's every move. Calculating just as he did. Watching the members and noting the tell-tell signs of their lies and exaggerations. She knew Councilwoman Reid was lying when she scratched behind her ear. She knew something made her uneasy when she would touch the bracelets on her wrist. Councilman Asherdoe always exaggerated about the splendor of his water culture crops; she knew he blinked two times before assuring Rhaif of the seasonal bounty. And Rhaif... Rhaif's left eye would twitch when he knew something was out of turn.

She knew every flinch of every person on that Council, and she could read them as well as she could read a book.

Nyssa had dreamt about hauling over the entire Council, tiring of their games and lies... Slicing Rhaif's throat in the knowledge that although he seemed to know how to keep a kingdom prosperous, she was always in the negotiations with him. He'd grown to count on her tapping twice on any surface or giving him a slight move right of her head when someone was lying.

Until the Gathering.

That was the last time he'd allowed her into negotiations and meetings. Something had changed that day. Whether it was his knowing she had consorted with the Commander of the Honest or if he'd been jealous of her and Aydra, she wasn't sure.

But he didn't trust her after that day, and the end of their relationship had been explosive.

She wished she'd allowed her eagle to end his life the night he burned her or allowed Dorian to finish strangling Rhaif when he found out about it, even after Aydra had spared Rhaif's life. She wished they'd overthrown the Council. Secured Aydra's place as High Queen, her brother's place as King, and Draven's place as High King. She'd have placed herself in charge the new Council they would have surely had to put in place.

But she hadn't.

She hadn't allowed any of that to happen. Thinking she was doing the right thing at the time. Doing what her sister wanted. It was her biggest regret, and the one she would always go back to for blaming herself for Aydra's death.

"The only power I want is the power to take my home back," Nyssa finally affirmed. "To fulfill the promise I made to the true King and Queen before their deaths."

Gail's left brow quirked a minuscule fraction, and a knowing smile spread over his features. "That's right... Greenwood finally living up to his full potential. I didn't realize he had it in him until the end. Shame he couldn't go all the way through with it. Take the crown. Take our world back—"

"Draven was *nothing* like you," Nyssa interjected. "Draven did not care for those things. He wanted peace for his people. If he'd officially taken the High crown, it would have been to rule beside my sister, not take over our kingdom and put her in chains."

"He was weak," Gail spat.

"Draven was the *greatest* King to ever walk this land."

The words seared through her strangled chest with a seethe she rarely recognized. She didn't realize she was straining against the bindings until they jerked her wrists. Gail's sharp eyes met her over the fire, his glare tearing through her with what she was sure would have been his deadliest stare. But she held her ground, feeling her nostrils flaring as she dared herself to blink. Dared herself to give in to the game. Dared herself to let him see her flinch...

It was Gail who shifted first.

"The greatest King..." He scoffed and shook his head. "That man murdered your people. Set your castle aflame with creatures of the night. And you think he was the greatest King to ever walk this land?"

"Perhaps if they hadn't condemned her, he wouldn't have had to. If they'd only allowed them to love one another, he could have been everything we needed. A great, passionate king loving of all his people and fiercely loyal to them. They could have united everyone— They *did* unite everyone. Those people repaid them with treachery."

"What if I told you you were wrong?" he asked. "What if I told you he did it all on purpose? That he truly did seduce her with intentions of taking her kingdom?"

"Then you would be grasping at straws to get me to turn against them."

"How are you so sure?"

"Because I knew my sister. I saw them together. They were *real*— " Nyssa paused to stifle the breakage tugging in her chest. "He poured vengeance onto a kingdom undeserving of its title," she said, more calmly this time. "That place was a prison. Those crowns were a sentence to slavery beneath Arbina's thumb—"

"Is that why you gave yours up?" he cut in before she could continue.

Nyssa straightened herself, forced a long breath into her lungs, and lifted her chin. "My brother and I left so that we could finish what they started."

Gail considered her a long moment. Again, Nyssa dared herself to blink. The fire cracked and bent in her peripherals. Finally, he stood and picked up a canteen. It was only two steps for him to cross the space to her, and he held it out for her to take.

"Drink," he urged her.

She eyed the canteen, her mouth dry still from only getting a whisper of drink when they'd first settled. Her hands reached—but he pulled it back a smidge, and the crooked smirk flowed over his features.

"Say the magic word, *Nyssari*," he mocked in a glowering tone that should have made her hair stand on end.

She felt her teeth grinding as she glared up at him. "I'd rather die than say anything that would bring you even a flinch of satisfaction," she said. "You need *me*. Not the other way around."

Gail seemed to contemplate her words.

He didn't hand her the water. Instead, he unstuck the cap and proceeded to pour it over her head. Nyssa allowed herself the flinch this time as the cold liquid drenched over her face and matted her sideways bangs to her skin.

The canteen was thrown at her feet, and he crossed back to his seat, flopping onto the ground.

Nyssa dropped her head and wiped the water out of her eyes. She ran her tongue over her mouth, savoring the liquid but still firm in the satisfaction of not begging for his kindness.

Gail had pulled his pipe and herb from his pocket and was leaned against the tree, beginning to pack the end, when she looked up. Nyssa pushed her hair out of her eyes and brought her knees to her chest as she continued to stare at him, making sure he knew she had not been affected by his antics.

"You're making me blush, girl," he said not long after. "All this staring."

"What will you do when you lose?" she asked, determined to keep him talking. "When my people strike Man down and send them back over the ocean?"

Gail openly laughed this time. The profound radiance of his chuckle vibrated between the trees. "Are you sure you're not a Dreamer with such words?"

"My brother—"

"Which one?" he interjected. "The blind one or the drunk?"

The words made her pause.

And Gail knew it. He shifted his attention back to packing his pipe.

"I hear he's making quite the ass of himself in the mountains," he added.

Breath hadn't returned to her lungs. From what she'd noted of Gail so far, eye contact while explaining his greed had been a sign of his honesty. But Gail had blatantly not looked at her when he said it, which made her wonder if he was actually telling the truth.

"You're lying," she finally managed. "My brother wouldn't squander his time there with mindlessness such as what you're accusing him of."

"Really?"

This time his eyes did meet hers.

"Are you quite sure about that?" he asked.

"NYSSA!"

The noise of someone shouting her name made her heart skip, eyes widen.

Nadir.

"NAD—"

A knife found her throat, and a hand threw around her mouth.

She hadn't even seen Gail move.

But he was behind her, firm arm wrapped around and pushing her shoulders back into his chest as his elbows clamped her arms down. She struggled against his grasp, but he was too strong.

Water doused the fires.

"Make a sound, and your eagle will fall from the sky," he hissed in her ear.

The edge of his knife scratched her skin. It pierced her flesh just at the surface when she wriggled against his grasp.

She could hear Nadir's voice bouncing off the trees from the beach, hear Lex's shout in the soft breeze.

Nadir and Lex. They were looking for her. Her muscles strained against Gail's grasp, heart breaking, stomach knotting. She wanted to scream. She wanted the echo of her cries to bounce off the trees and get engulfed by the darkness.

But the voices of her friends became echoes, and her heart once more numbed.

Gail's grip on her weakened. The hand he had around her mouth moved to clamp her shoulder.

"Pack up," Gail sounded to his people. "We're moving west."

Nyssa was hoisted as dead weight to her feet, and Gail pushed her forward. "Quietly, little Sun," he growled. "Unless you'd like me to take you for a ride before the Noble does."

It was the first time one of his threats actually caused a chill to run down her spine. She cringed at the feeling of his breath over the top of her wet head and the touch of his hand still on her shoulder.

And when he stepped around her, a torch was shoved into his grasp, and the firelight reflected back the mocking stare in his shadowed features. A dangerous stare that told her he was serious, that he'd already plotted such a conquest in his mind.

"Careful, Venari," she drawled, lips pursing at his confidence. "You remember what happened to the last one of your kind to fuck a daughter of Promise."

Gail's eyes traveled deliberately over her, and Nyssa swallowed at the sweeping intensity of it.

"As much as I disliked the pair, I will admit, it was a tragedy what happened to them," he uttered. "Such a child, it would have been the greatest weapon to ever have walked these lands. I wonder—" he reached out and twirled her hair between his fingers, the touch making her hair feel as though it weren't attached to her own body "—do you think your mother gave this same ability to you as well?"

His rasp made her flare, but she didn't flinch. "If you touch me—"

"You'll what? Call your eagle?" A smug grin fluttered over his features, and his head bent towards her. "Go ahead. I'll strike it down as I'm fucking you."

Her spine pressed into the tree behind her.

She didn't even know he'd been pushing her backward.

"Draven had the right idea," he continued, towering over her. "To bring a weapon into this world that would have finally put your people in their place. It would have brought the monarchy down to its knees. Every race would have bowed to its grace. Except he was too weak to go through with it."

"That's not what Draven wanted—"

He grabbed her wrists and shoved them over her head. The raw tree bark scratched her skin. Her body's response was to push back, to wriggle beneath him—

But his free hand found her face, and he pinched her cheeks in his hand, holding her jaw between his thumb and pointer finger. She could feel his breath on her skin, and it made her shudder. Her feet moved, but his chest was flush against her, pinning her and shoving her into the tree. The stern of his broad body over hers nearly made her disappear beneath his shadow.

"You know, Man wouldn't know our kind can't normally have children," he breathed. "I could fuck you and then sell you. A place at the table while my child grows in your belly beneath their watch. My own personal spy in their grasp. You would teach him to use his powers. Man's kingdom would grow around him, with me sitting at their table. And when he's grown, I could take everything. Your kingdom and theirs. Dreamers enslaved at my feet. The Honest and the Martyrs vanished. Your precious giver torn apart. This world could truly be mine… I might even let you rule beside me. Mother to the greatest child in our history. You could be *my Queen*."

Nyssa's heart pounded at his words, his greed… Her sister's face flashed before her eyes, and she pulled for the small part of herself she'd learned from her.

"Tell me, Venari… What would stop me from killing you and taking over?" she asked.

"You'll like fucking me too much to kill me," he promised.

Nyssa found herself impressed by the quickness of his banter. She lifted her chin to meet his. "And exactly how far on your knees before me does that declaration take you?"

She could see the surprise rise in his gaze. But being the true Venari he was, she knew he wouldn't back down. The right corner of his lip quirked just so, and he growled, "Don't tempt me, *Nyssari*," in a warning tone that told her the firmness she felt against her abdomen wasn't his hip.

Nyssa almost smiled at the feeling of it there, the power in her hands that he didn't know she was squeezing out... drip by drip... enjoying the toy of wringing him in her hands.

"You're an idiot," she finally snapped.

He tensed. "Come again?"

"I said you're an idiot," she repeated, this time more firmly than before. "You think my mother gave a damn about simple Venari persons?"

She could see the confidence draining from his eyes.

"You think my mother would allow any being not holding a true throne to put a child in our bellies?"

Gail let go of her face.

"Those were not the beings whom she knew would bring Duarb to his knees," Nyssa continued to spit. "She *knew* the only children Duarb ever truly loved and gave a damn about after that fucking curse were his Infinari-marked Venari children. His *Kings*."

Gail released her wholly, stepping back from her as if she'd suddenly cursed him. But Nyssa didn't stop. She had him. Had him exactly where she wanted him. Confident and dangerously on edge. Hard and needing. Core depleting.

Nyssa stepped forward as far as the rope would allow her.

"Go ahead, Venari," she seethed. "Fuck me until I cannot walk. Fuck me until you break me. Make me cry your name in the darkness of these trees. But you'll never sire a child in my belly. You will never know the power of the High crown, of seeing your blood and flesh walking these grounds with a name you were able to provide. The last being to have ever had that ability was Draven. And every inkling of that power died with him."

Gail paused, staring at her as though working out the words she'd just dared to speak to him. She didn't know if the words were actually true, but she knew he was considering that they were. She thought for sure he would have had a knife at her throat again by the end of it.

That he would be seething with angst, not of his planning.

But his lips flinched upwards, and she found herself staring at the volatile smirk on his face.

"It is a *shame* your giver has such hatred for us," he finally determined. "I feel as though our people were made for one another."

Her nostrils flared, back straightening stiff, and she lifted her chin again. "Now, who's the Dreamer?"

25

Nyssa couldn't see where they were walking.

Even with the fire torches lit around her, she was still having a hard time moving over the roots. Gail had decided he and four of his people would escort her across the Preymoor to the Noble's estate instead of his entire company. The air was getting colder by the day, and she once more found herself wishing she'd worn heavier clothing when she'd run away.

Then again, she hadn't exactly planned on being gone more than a day at the most.

Being kidnapped by people she'd only just learned about a week prior was not at the top of her list.

Gail had hardly spoken to her while they traveled, only commenting on her keeping herself hydrated so that she did not die before meeting the Noble.

Nyssa hadn't stopped watching him interact with the small company he'd brought along. There were two women in the company, both of which hadn't said a single word to her. Part of their job, she realized, as the sentries and support guard. To stay quiet and alert. To not get distracted. It seemed the pair of them were the only ones Gail trusted to keep a watchful eye out for any intruders. They moved in shadow as he did… of stealth and grace. They reminded her greatly of Balandria.

The other two men he'd brought along could not have been more different from one another. One reminded her more of a Blackhand. So much so that she'd actually asked Gail if he was. But Gail only chuckled, telling the man about her question, and the man had chortled so loudly birds had risen upwards from the trees.

She wasn't sure what was so funny about her question.

The fourth man... Nyssa learned was an Infinari-marked Infi... One of the mutilated beings she'd noticed in his company on her first day. She hurt for this man. He was taller than Gail, white hair strangled its way down his back, some of it in braids she was sure hadn't been touched or redone in weeks. His skin was pink and white, as though it had forgotten its actual color before the scarring had occurred. He never wore a regular shirt over his lean body, just the long black cloak-like coat with an oversized hood that hid his mutilated skin from the sun. He looked like the sun was hurting him, and he would hug that coat tighter, pouring his body in shadows instead of sunlight. But it was the dark yellow of his eyes that would startle her every time he looked her way. Not yellow like the Infi had been at Magnice. She remembered those eyes. She remembered the way they glowered at her. Even when their heads had been in the stockade with her sister's axe on its way down towards them.

This man's eyes were different. Kinder. Sadder. She could see the pain of his even being alive reflected back in every part of his body. His face looked as though it had once been handsome, reminding her of her brother's own long features. This man was one of the original marked-Infis. Possibly as old as the Age itself. Before the mutation of the marked-Infis turned them more like the true Infis. Those at her castle had been marked-Infis from before Draven was crowned king, but they differed from this man. More manipulative and volatile.

Her heart broke for him. It was not his fault that he'd been marked Infi.

This was Duarb's curse.

She wondered how he'd survived this long.

It was on their second night that she'd nearly fallen asleep, tucked into a ball by a rock, when she felt herself being wrapped up in something soft. Her first reaction was to balk, jump at the suddenness of someone touching her.

Gail had placed a fur over her shivering body.

Nyssa forced a deep breath as she met his dark hazel green eyes, the weight of the blanket wrapping around her as a comfort she didn't know she needed.

"Thank you," she managed.

His hair fell over his shoulder when he nodded, and then he sat back on the ground, his slow movements still puzzling her like he was trying to conserve energy.

"Can't have our Princess freezing, can we?" he muttered, holding his palms out to warm them by the fire.

It bothered her that she hadn't figured him out yet. Everything she'd learned and watched of him puzzled her. *Everything.* From the way he'd spoken to her the first night, telling her of his plans, but not pounced to slice her throat when she'd provoked him. The kind way he treated the Infi, how he spoke to his soldiers, laughed with his men...

Nyssa sat up, and she watched him again as he pulled his pipe from his pocket. The wind billowed over the grass, the rake of it shimmering over the sharp blades of the meadow's soft green. She hugged the blanket tighter, pulled her knees into her chest, and held her own hands out to warm them.

"Say what you mean, little Sun," Gail rasped, having apparently felt her gaze on him again. "Else, you'll have me pushing you against that boulder tonight and showing you what it really means to be taken to the Edge... maybe then you'll stop eye-fucking me across the fire."

"You have Infi in your ranks," she stated, ignoring his banter.

"She sees something other than me," he mocked. "I wondered if you were paying attention to anything else after all that stumbling you did earlier."

"Draven would never have allowed them in his kingdom," she continued. "Why have you?"

Gail lit his pipe from the fire and puffed on it before exhaling the smoke in her direction. The wind brushed the smoke in her face, and she couldn't help herself from breathing it in, the sweetness of it reminding her of her brother's herb.

She had to tighten her jaw at the memory, but it didn't stop her heart from constricting in her chest.

"These Infi were once Infinari," Gail said. "What our father marked them as was not always true. He chooses favorites, only marking Venari with those he wants as kings. It's why we challenged Draven when Parkyr died."

"Were you once close with him?"

The vein in Gail's neck seemed to twitch, and she knew just from the sight of it that she'd struck a nerve. "I was Draven's Third," he said, confirming what Nyssa had guessed. "Leader of the pure Venari born. But I don't know that I would call us close," he went on further. "Draven had his favorites just as Duarb does. He took who he wanted with him on his trips, not those of us who had earned such titles."

"You mean he took his friends," Nyssa said plainly.

"Venari rankings should not be delved out based on friendship," Gail spat.

Nyssa caught the clench of his fist, the tightness in his gaze towards the fire. She wasn't ready to get him riled up. Have him shut down. So she changed the subject.

"What about the ones that were born Infi?" she chose to detour. "Do you trust them?"

Gail seemed to relax slightly at the question, and he took a long draw on the pipe. "I will not lie," he uttered, blowing smoke her way again. "I do not trust anyone in my own ranks. Any one of them would give up everything for the title of Commander or king. Take North for example—" he pointed silently at the Infi man shying away from the firelight. "—he would just as soon slice my throat than to have to walk across this fucking meadow out in the sunlight."

"So why is he here?"

"Because I'm paying him to help me deliver you."

The answer was simple enough, but she couldn't help but notice the twitch in his neck, the tightness of his fingers around the pipe.

"Liar," she accused.

Gail almost choked on the inhale he'd just taken, a quiet smirk playing on his lips. He gave her a sideways once over that made her pause, and she waited on his snarky response. But his brow simply raised, and his throat bobbed when he released the smoke from his lungs.

"You know, if I didn't need Man's crown so badly, I would keep you," he said, a dilation in his pupils. "Perhaps once I've taken the world for myself, I'll find you again. Make you my Queen. Dazzle you in jewels and velvet. Remind you of the elegant dresses you once wore as the Promised Princess. I might even let you take control of Council and delve out punishments and duties as you were born to do. I think you would enjoy watching as men cowered and fell to their knees—"

"I am perfectly capable of making my own way in this world," she interjected. "My sister did not die for me to depend on a man to do it for me."

The wonderment remained in Gail's darkened eyes. "So you do want it."

"I want nothing more than to see my people remain free," Nyssa argued.

"What if that means taking the High crown?" he asked. "What if keeping your people safe meant taking all the power of this world? What if it meant rising the Red Moons and breaking every curse? Would you do it then?"

"I'm not a hero."

"No," he agreed. "You're much better suited for the life of villainy. Much more so than one of heroism on a silly Commander's arm."

The accusation made her heart stop.

She didn't realize she wasn't monitoring the look that possessed her face. And by the time she did realize it, it was too late.

Gail *laughed*.

The deep-seated chortle dissipated into the stark darkness around them and made her teeth clench.

"How—"

"Did you forget the Infi can shift?"

There was no calming the chill that settled in her bones. A thousand thoughts echoed in her mind. She questioned every single encounter she'd had with a new person the last few months.

But it was the people Nadir and Hagen had brought with them to the Gathering that made her mind frantic.

She met Gail's delighted face.

"How many?" she demanded to know.

"Don't worry, little Sun," he winked. "They've all left your court."

She hated the smirk on his face. She wanted to pulverize him, to call her eagle to take out his eyes and strike his throat.

"Tell me how many people you've sent to infiltrate my streets," she snapped.

She could feel her facade breaking. The smell of the herb wrapped into her lungs. Her mind began to swim, and she had to blink back the fear threatening to surface.

Her fingertips vibrated.

Her core warmed.

A violent swirling began in her abdomen. Angry and volatile. Itching to shed itself and take over.

Fire threatened to take over.

The fire she had no idea how to contain or control.

She knew without looking down that she was on the verge of ash rising on her fingertips. She let her eyes flutter and tried to push her frustrations down. She tried to count, but she forgot the numbers.

She didn't know what would happen if she let that fire out again. She might consume them all. Burn their entire world. There was no ocean to stop her this time. She had come no closer to figuring out what was happening to her, and she didn't want to find out in the middle of the night, stark in the middle of Haerland.

A shudder passed through her insides. The hair rose on her flesh. The smell of the herb filled her nostrils again. Her own smoke dissipated, and she opened her eyes to meet his again.

"How. Many?" she seethed, voice rising and cracking with every syllable.

The smirk on his face had vanished, and he was staring at her with more of an interest this time rather than mockery.

"Interesting," he said in such a rasp that Draven's face flickered in front of her. But she shut him out too, unsure of what was happening to her. Why she was breaking her well-trained facade simply at the infliction of the Commander's name.

The herb smoke filled her nose again, and her heart sank when her lashes lifted.

The herb.

"What kind of herb is that?"

The smugness was back, and Gail chuckled deviously. "Didn't realize you would be a lightweight," he accused. "Especially knowing how much of this your brother and sister consumed."

Nyssa blinked back the stir in her mind. Her vision was starting to blur and spin—a different sort of spin than she'd felt with Dorian's smoke. This was... This scared her. She couldn't keep her eyes focused. Fear and rage entwined inside her. Her chest heaved at the anxiety of it going over her head, of her losing control.

The fire cracked, and suddenly she was back at Magnice, screaming in the gallery. Her brother's arms around her as she lurched forward, watching the flames consume her sister.

Wind whipped.

Back in the clearing.

She pushed her hands over her face and pressed the heel of her palms into her eyes.

Back and forth.

"Nyssari—"

A tremble settled in her knees. Slipping quickly.

Back and forth.

A hand touched her shoulder—

She was on her feet. Ropes snapped.

And Gail's throat was in her hand.

The world vibrated.

Black wrapped up her arm. Her mind blanked. Her body emptied. Darkness pooled her vision. Her skin cracked and an amber hue emitted from beneath the blackened streaks. All she could feel was the beat of his deteriorating pulse beneath her fingertips, the cold wind on her numb skin, cool fire licking her flesh.

She was no longer in control.

Footsteps pricked her ears.

Her other hand shot out behind her.

Another throat caught beneath her fingers. The struggle of their bodies made her own heartbeat slow. Steady. Holding them with this new power consuming her…

The second person's neck was smaller. Her vision vibrated around her again. Her shaking fingers tightened around the person's throat, and then she turned her head to watch life leave the woman's eyes.

Light stilled. Fear and panic faded into nothingness.

Nyssa's arm jolted, flamed fingers striking. A crack pulsed beneath her fingertips.

And something struck the back of her head.

26

"If you weren't a Princess, what would you want to be?" Nadir asked, fingers delicately swirling over the inside of Nyssa's thigh as they laid together on the chaise lounge.

Nyssa wasn't sure how to answer. "What do you mean?"

"I mean what I said," he replied with a shrug as he pressed his hand behind his head. "What would you want to be? If you could do anything."

"No one's ever asked me that."

"I figured as much." His gaze traveled over her deliberately, fingers squeezing on her thigh. "What do you want, Princess?"

Her head sighed back on the lounger arm, staring at the ceiling as she contemplated his question. "I don't... I don't know," she admitted. "I've never thought about it."

"I think your sister would travel or go live in the Forest. Be with the creatures she loves so much," he said, obviously trying to spark ideas. "Would you want that?"

"I would love to see more of our world. See the traditions and celebrations of our people that I've read so many stories about. Watch the Eyes rise over your reef. Dance beneath the Deads in the mountains. I've heard grand tales of the Eyes festival in the Village of Dreams. That I would love to see. They say Somniarb's tree is lit up as fireflies against the night sky."

"And how exactly would you be financing such a journey? If you weren't a Princess, I mean. What would you do?"

"What possible occupation needs the skill of reading people besides being in the King's court?"

Nadir smiled. "Perhaps a spy, then," he suggested.

"Are spies needed in Haerland?"

"Of course," he affirmed. "Never know when you need to foil some plot to

243

take the throne," he added with a wink.

"Planning on taking my kingdom, Commander?"

"Maybe not tonight," he bantered. "I'm having far too much fun being seduced by the Princess to worry about working."

She laughed, shaking her head as her chest swelled at his mockery. "What about you? If you weren't the Commander. What would you do?"

His eyes dazed, hands massaging the muscles behind her knee a moment. "Commander is actually all I've ever wanted," he told her. "Ever since I was a boy, I wanted to take care of my people and be the one to lead them to safety if ever they needed it."

"How did you earn the title?" she asked.

"Ah..." He paused, even his hands, and she felt her brows narrow.

"What?"

"I'm not sure I should tell you this story."

"Why? Did you slay some great creature?"

Another pause.

Her smile drifted from her face.

"Oh no."

"Okay, first, it was a nasty creature—"

"What kind of creature is so bad you needed to kill it?"

"It was a water dragon," he argued. "A great beast, as large as the Rhamocour, but lives beneath the ocean."

Nyssa bit her lips together, hiding the amusement her insides begged to let loose. "You slayed a dragon?" she teased.

He glared at her, lips twisting in an annoyed manner as if he knew where she was going with her words. "I did," he finally uttered.

"How very fairytale of you, Commander," she mocked. "Tell me, was there a damsel in distress waiting just on the island past it?"

Nadir grabbed her just as she started to laugh. The giggle grew, her head thrown back as he grasped at her knees.

"Did you have to sweep her off her feet—" he grabbed her up, tickling her sides and wrestling her, tugging her onto his lap "—I bet she swooned right into your arms, didn't she?—" her legs straddled over him, and he grabbed her arms, making her laugh harder "—A great prize for the great Comman—"

His lips pressed to hers, and her body exhaled into his embrace. She couldn't help sinking into him. His hands wrapped around her, stroking her sides, making the hair on her flesh rise. She grinned against his lips and pulled back just long enough to meet his eyes, her hand pressed to his cheek.

Her heart fluttered as his hands splayed flat against her back, his strong *arms hugging her closer. He leaned forward, nudging her nose with his. A wide smile was on his lips, amusement dancing in his eyes.*

The kiss he placed on her lips was soft, like a whisper on her skin. Her eyes rolled when his mouth moved, those same kisses trailing down her jaw to her throat. She bucked her hips into his, holding him closer as he tugged on her skin, her heart beating faster. One of his hands trailed down to her hips, and he grasped her backside tight, pushing her harder into his own hips. A groan emitted from them both, her mouth sagging as he bit her skin. And when his finger dipped into her, he moaned into her throat.

"I want to fuck you over this chair, Princess," he breathed in her ear. "I want to hold that beautiful ass in my hands as I bury myself in you."

"Yes," she almost begged.

He didn't allow her to move. Instead, he stood, her legs wrapped around him, and he placed her bottom on the arm of the lounge chair. His lips bit at hers, her thighs squeezing his waist.

"Turn around," he told her.

Her feet hit the ground, and she gave him one final kiss before turning. His hand splayed on her back, and he bent her over the arm of the chair with a force she wasn't used to men using on her.

But she liked it.

She liked it a lot more than she dared to admit.

His hand stilled on her neck, fingers digging into her skin a moment. "Spread your legs," he said softly. She did, and he rewarded her with his hand wrapping around her breast, his mouth pressing to her spine.

"That's my good girl," he whispered.

She nearly whimpered and came apart at the praise.

His grasp moved to her hips, where he dug those fingers into her skin to hold her steady. She was practically dripping, and she held her breath when she felt his length brush her entrance.

"There was a damsel," he said as he sank his cock inside her. She cursed into the cushion, relishing that feeling of him filling her and the goosebumps on her skin. "Not on an island, but in a castle," he continued, deliberately thrusting inside her. His hand threaded around her ass, and she pushed against him as he continued. "And not one in distress... A forbidden Princess... Every creature I took... Every swipe of my blade... Every move that got me to the position of Commander... All of it was leading me here... To you..."

He leaned over her, both of his hands coming to rest at the bend of her hips, and she gripped tight to the chair's edge.

"You are my great prize, Princess."

The words made her skin tingle, and she was sure he had full intentions of railing her into the next life with the breath that left him... However...

She wanted to show him his prize.

She straightened, back arching so that she kept him inside her. She took his hands in hers, led one to her breast, the other to her clit, and then she pressed her hand behind his neck. His mouth wrapped around her throat as his fingers squeezed her breast to the point her mouth sagged.

"What kind of damsel would I be if I didn't take care of my savior?" she teased, moving her hips against his length. A smile spread over her lips, and she shook her head. "Oh, that's right..." She turned around, finding him staring.

She shoved him back onto the bed.

Pausing, she savored the surprised smile on his lips, and then she crawled over him, her entrance hovering over his tip. "The kind that doesn't need one."

Her hips sank onto him, causing Nadir to groan, his back to arch, and he grabbed her hips in his hands. She grabbed the back of her own neck, hips moving up and down him and burying him deeper with every move.

Nadir pinched her skin, nails digging into her flesh. "Fucking Infi, Princess," he breathed. "Keep talking to me like that, and I'll have to steal you tomorrow."

A smile spread over her. "I might not stop you."

Another low groan emitted from his lips, and then he held her hips firm. "Turn around," he told her.

She bit her lip but did as he asked nonetheless. He scooted up onto the bed until his shoulders were against the headboard. The fire danced in her eyes when she turned, and she hovered herself over him just long enough for him to grasp her hips. Her back arched as he maneuvered her. His hand creased in her waist, the other in her hair. A low curse and the sound of her name emitted from his lips when he filled her. She had to settle a moment to take in his depth.

She rocked, slowly, up and down his shaft, his hands holding her sometimes when she was fully wrapped around him. His length buried inside her made her entire body alert, restless, as though he had some power over her she wasn't prepared for.

Her eyes had just closed, mouth agape, when she felt him shift, and suddenly his face was a breath from her neck. He wrapped a hand around her own and guided her fingers to her clit. Teeth pressed to her skin when he moved their hands together. His other hand threaded the front of her neck. One finger crept up to her jaw, to her mouth, and she took that finger in her mouth, sucking on it as she would have his cock. Nadir's lips curled against her shoulder, and he whispered, "Relax," in her ear.

The breath of it made her eyes roll. Nadir sighed back onto the bed.

"Keep touching yourself, Princess," he told her.

She didn't argue. Her body was quickly reaching, and she began to rock on his length with more speed, squeezing her own thighs when she would push onto him. His finger trailed her bottom, between her cheeks, and she heard him tell her to relax again before the digit slipped inside her ass.

"Oh—fuck—Nadir," she cried out.

The sensation that matched inside her against his length made her weak, but Nadir caught her and moved her hips as he wanted her to move. She wasn't complaining. His hands guiding her were the only thing keeping her head straight. A new feeling she knew she would crave from then on, Nyssa pressed her fingers harder against her clit, grasping her thigh in her other hand as she groaned loudly, saying his name and cursing the air. Despite the hand on her hip, she felt her movements become erratic. She didn't know how long she would be able to keep her composure with him inside her in two places.

But he sat up again, his finger going deeper. "Do you like when I play with you?" he breathed on her shoulder.

His words sent her spiraling. He wrapped his hand around hers again and pressed onto her clit, side to side. Her mouth sagged, lungs desperate for a breath to answer his question, but as her body reached, she found she couldn't. She didn't want to. She wanted to crash. She was sure her heart would burst when she did come. She pleaded with her body, on edge—

The explosion of it jerked her, set her wetness spilling and quivering onto him and the sheets. She was hardly aware of him moving his finger from inside her, both hands on her hips as he guided her up and down him a few more times. She couldn't stop herself from nearly screaming as he continued. He groaned into her neck, and she felt him stiffen inside her and then release. His hands grasped her arms, body trembling as his own orgasm rippled through him.

The breath that returned to her lungs was short. She slipped off of him and sank into his arms as he held her from behind. His lips pressed softly to her throat, then to the nape of her neck. Until he had nearly traced the wings of the eagle mark on her back.

"You're a filthy girl, Princess," he purred against her skin.

She smiled at the chill over her flesh just from his simple touch. He rocked her in his arms a moment, and she could feel the curl of his lips against her neck.

"Try not to divulge my secrets, Commander," she said. *"I've a reputation, you know."*

—A fire crackled at her feet.

Nyssa blinked rapidly at the warmth of it so close. She hated that she was waking when her mind had traveled to a memory she was hanging on to as she was hanging on to her life.

The smell of grass and the meadow filled her nose, and she was reminded of where she was.

In the grasp of the Venari traitors. Being taken to Man.

She wanted to close her eyes again and forget about it. Put herself back in the Commander's arms and hang on to that moment of happiness and the flutter of heart that she could still feel in her chest.

"My Queen rises."

Unfortunately, reality called her.

Nyssa started to move her feet, but she found herself unable. She realized there were not only ropes around her wrists but around her ankles as well.

"I suppose I should call you *fire* Queen now," Gail corrected, popping a piece of dried meat back into his mouth.

"I am not a Queen," Nyssa grunted through her haze. "My sister was the Queen. Not me."

But as she said the words, the kind of Queen he called her rang in her ears.

Fire Queen...

The memory of her losing control entered her mind, and she winced as her temple began to throb. Nyssa shoved the memory back as she forced herself up into a sitting position. Her muscles were stiff, hair matted to her face. Her reality had barely set in when she found Gail staring at her.

"What?" she snapped.

A slow smile spread on his wide mouth. "You choked me last night."

"And you're smiling about it."

Gail scoffed. "Be glad I'm getting rid of you tomorrow," he said as his eyes danced back to her. "I'd marry you otherwise. Law or no law."

Nyssa glared again at his declaration. She allowed her gaze to look over him, landing on the handprint darkened on his throat. Gail chuckled under his breath and reached for something at his side. Food, she realized. And water.

She took the canteen hesitantly from his hands and unscrewed the cap.

"How long was I out?" she dared to ask.

"Only the day," he replied, settling back against the grass.

"Did I hurt anyone else?"

"Just me... and Noda."

Her stomach soured as she remembered the crack she'd felt in her palm. "Her name was Noda?"

"It was," he sighed. "She was one of my finer sentries. A great warrior... And you snapped her neck like a twig. Burned her body to nothing more than a skeleton in your blackened hands. My father barely had anything to sweep back to his roots."

Nyssa began to pick at the dried meat he'd given her. "What did it look like?" she asked.

The pause that passed between them was long enough that she knew he was surprised she did not know. Her jaw tightened at the silence, and she cursed herself for ever bringing it up.

"You don't know?" he asked.

"It's new," she sneered, stretching her chin high as she once more began to eat the dried deer jerky. The irritation inside her came out with every forced chew and tug of her teeth on the meat.

For a few moments, it was only the crackle of the flames that filled her ears until Gail sat up, and his arms rested over his knees.

"Is that the first person you've ever killed?"

The jerky tasted like ash and dirt. She spat it out. "With my hands, yes," she finally answered. "I didn't mean to kill her."

"Nevertheless, you did," he said. "I'm glad I was here to see it."

Nyssa couldn't stop staring at him now, and not for the reasons she'd been watching him the last three days. She'd killed one of his men, and he was watching at her like he would jump her bones at any minute.

His gaze dropped, and he pulled his feet in closer.

"It started with the shadows around you," he began, voice soft. "They rose from your seat and your shoulder blades. I thought I just saw smoke from the fire. But then I saw your hands, your shaking... the build-up of ash beneath your fingertips. You lunged at me quicker than I could blink. Your eyes turned gold. Not just the amber they are normally. This was the color of the Sun, of molten fire in a forge. The black streaks ran up your arms and on your neck, spreading as rivers over your skin, stretching under your neck and then up your cheeks. Black around your eyes like battle makeup and nerves. But when you caught Noda's throat, the flames rose on your arm. They never rose on the hand that had me, just heat. *Searing* heat. And then you snapped her neck."

Sweat pooled in her palms as she hunched over her bent knees. She couldn't remember it. Couldn't remember what had snapped in her to make her go off. Couldn't remember what they'd been talking about to make her flee.

"Makes me wonder if you've a soft spot for me," he finalized.

"Do not mistake my not burning you as a kindness," she growled. "I'm right-handed. Probably funneled into my dominant hand before stretching to the left."

It was the first whisper of banter that had left her lips in days.

Gail chuckled and grabbed another piece of jerky from the bag. "Eat up," he told her. "We'll reach the Noble's estate tomorrow. I can honestly say I don't know when you'll have another full meal."

"You're still handing me over to them?"

His head tilted. "Is there a reason why you think I wouldn't?" he asked.

There was a sincerity in his question, a look in his eyes that told her he was truly asking her to make him reconsider.

"Are you genuinely asking me?"

A heavy sigh escaped him, an audible one that rattled the fire. Gail pushed his hands over his face, something she hadn't seen him do, and the action of it made her heart still.

"I am," he finally said, his voice softer.

Nyssa allowed the question to live in her bones, to settle in her ears. She could have pleaded with him, told him she would make a bargain for her life... begged for him not to take her.

But the truth was, Nyssa needed to know what Man was thinking. She needed to see them for herself. She wanted to meet them. She wanted to infiltrate them.

"What possible occupation needs the skill of reading people besides being in the King's court?"

Nadir smiled. "Perhaps a spy, then."

Nyssa straightened her back.

"You will take me to the Noble's estate tomorrow," she said firmly.

Gail's forehead wrinkled with the raise of his surprised brows.

But Nyssa ignored him.

"You'll take me to the estate," she continued. "You'll barter your place at the table and confirm your position in his court.

Gail contemplated her a moment. "Why?"

"Because I believe in keeping my enemies close, Venari," she said. "I know nothing about these people, and neither do the people I am trying to keep safe. The only way I learn anything is from the inside. So the inside is where I will go."

Gail's lips quirked, apparently both amused and impressed by her decision. "You're more dangerous than anyone realizes," he decided.

"Funny," Nyssa said. "That's what my silly Commander keeps saying about me."

27

They woke before the sunrise.

Gail was sure it would only take a few hours to finish walking to the camp, and he wanted to arrive before the sun rose too high in the sky —intent on thinking he would be a welcome guest at their dinner table for bringing such a prize.

Something didn't feel right every time Gail would look at her. It was not the same leering and confident gaze he'd watched her with that entire week. Not once did he call her Queen or refer to her fire again. Not once did he make any snide remarks.

She wondered if he was also becoming wary of the plan.

The closer the camp became, the more Nyssa's entire body started to shut down with the reality of what she was doing.

Volunteering herself into slavery.

Because at this point, it was voluntary.

Her ears began to ring, and for a long while, she couldn't stop it.

At one point, her legs stopped moving. But the woman, Antha, had given her a stern look, and Nyssa forced herself forward.

Her eagle flying above her was the only comfort Nyssa had and the only comfort she knew she could hang on to.

"You'll be on your own," Gail said after a while. "I will not pretend to know what they will do to you."

"Whatever it is is nothing worse than what my imagination can come up with," she replied.

The camp's outline entered her vision ahead, and this time, Nyssa wasn't the only one that stopped.

This was much larger than she'd expected.

There were fences and shacks built from the Preymoor's rolling grasses all the way to the dunes. A few tents were scattered around the beach as well, some connected to others. She could see small herds of livestock moving around in the fences. Sentries lined the gates.

"There was once a small wood there around that watering hole," Antha muttered. "They've taken all of it."

"Looks like they're bringing in rocks from the cliffs on the west as well," Gail added. "How many ships do you count?"

"Seven. And that's just here," Antha replied. "This is a lot more than we bargained for, Gail," she said, tone hesitant. "This is not the small camp I was expecting."

"We'll be fine," he affirmed. "We have something they want."

"Something they don't know they want," Antha mumbled.

Antha gave Nyssa enough of a glare that Nyssa questioned whether Gail's people agreed with what they were doing.

They had worked out the plan the night before. Gail had laid out everything he needed them to do. After he'd given her a tonic and she passed out, he'd sent their fourth companion back to the Forest to report on where they were. He was sure they would be asked to leave their weapons at the Noble's entrance if they weren't stopped by guards first.

Gail gave the others nods, and then he pulled something from his bag. A long black cloak. Nyssa didn't move as he placed the oversized garment over her shoulders and pulled the hood up. It went so far over her head that she almost couldn't see.

"If you see something wrong, signal North," he muttered as he tied the cloak.

"Using me to your advantage, Venari?"

"I'm betting on you watching these people as closely as you've been watching me. And I'm also betting you won't want to be alone in their hands if they kill us." He paused as he finished, and she watched a small smirk rise on his lips. "Keep that glare on your face, Princess," he mocked her. "You'll have every man in there turned on with those puckered lips."

As the rage curled inside her, she reminded herself that this was only the first day of what she was sure would be many more taunts just like it. She didn't know how Man treated their women, but judging by the memory of what the one had said at Magnice, she didn't expect it to be very well.

Wait—*Princess?*

Her eyes narrowed as he turned. Something really wasn't right. Gail had only called her Princess the day he captured her. The rest of the time, he'd called her Queen, little Sun, or Nyssari.

Not Princess.

Nyssa continued to watch Gail as they walked in silence, thoughts pouring through her head at the uneasy feeling in her bones.

She wondered if perhaps she was simply paranoid.

Nyssa couldn't see Antha and North beside her, but she felt Antha's hand on her back every now and then. They were a mile out when her eagle screeched overhead. The wind whipped past them, and she knew it was Duarb's wind telling them of the company of Men riding towards them.

"Fifteen," Gail said.

"Sounds like they've spotted us," Antha said.

Nyssa looked up, and she saw a cloud of dust on the horizon. Men on horses galloped in their direction, arrows already threaded through their bows.

"Put your swords on the ground," Nyssa snapped. "Belts too."

"I am not releasing my weapon," Antha affirmed. "Gail—"

"Listen to her," he said as he began to unbuckle his belt.

Antha grunted a curse, but Nyssa heard her and North taking off their weapons.

The horses slowed, and Nyssa's insides began to squirm. She didn't know what to expect from them. Having met and dealt with every other race on their land was different. These people were new. Born of each other, as the Nitesh had said. Savages that could not be trusted.

Her heartbeat throbbed in her ears.

"Hold your ground," Gail told them.

The three Venari backed up in a circle around Nyssa, their hands up. Fifteen horses surrounded them on all sides. Incoherent shouts filled the air. Gail and Antha were both shouting back, Antha arguing with Gail, Gail trying to speak clearly to the one with the sword drawn.

The one whom she assumed was their captain jumped down from his horse, and he leveled against Gail.

"Small company for an invasion, Haerlandian scum," the man seethed.

"It is no invasion, Captain," Gail said. "We have come to barter with your Noble."

"Why would His Grace barter with you?"

"I have something his King will want."

"What's that?"

"Princess of Haerland," Gail said.

Nyssa froze.

If she hadn't been in ropes, she might have murdered him right then.

"Princess?" the man repeated.

"The last daughter of a now-forgotten race. A rare specimen for your King. Imagine the bartering power he would have over Haerland with their Princess as his slave."

Nyssa couldn't breathe.

He was not supposed to tell them who she was. He had said he wouldn't the night before. She was simply supposed to be the last child of the Promised. There had been no mention of him selling her as the actual Princess.

"Let's see her," the captain said.

Nyssa didn't move as Gail nodded to North. The hood whipped back off her head. Nyssa's chin rose, and she locked eyes with the armored captain.

Gasps sounded. Horses shifted. The captain took a step back, and for a moment, he didn't look away.

"She has fire for hair," he said softly. "What sorcery is she?"

"As I said, Captain," Gail said, and Nyssa forced herself not to flinch when he touched her hair. "A rare specimen."

The man looked as though she had cast a curse over the whole of his men. He swallowed as he looked at the others. "Gather their weapons. We will take them to His Grace."

As a couple of the men moved from their horses and began to gather their weapons, Nyssa caught Gail's eye. Gail paused before her and reached for her hood. But the moment she started to speak, her words were taken away from her.

Gail's darkened gaze flashed yellow.

Nyssa launched.

"YOU—"

Infi.

He was an *Infi.*

A hand wrapped around her mouth, and North grabbed her arms. Her feet nearly kicked off the ground as she struggled against him.

"Quiet," Gail warned, his hand covering her face.

The soldiers had started to stare, but Gail gave them a nod.

"Prisoners," he said with a shrug.

Her body was shaking so violently she felt ash on her fingertips.

Infi.

Infi-Infi-Infi.

Gail slowly removed his hand from her mouth, looking as though he dared her to speak.

"Where is Gail?" she forced herself to ask quietly.

He leaned closer and pulled her hood back over her head. "The long game, Princess," he uttered in her ear.

Nyssa was given no more time to discuss it. The men pushed them, and Gail—if it ever even was Gail— wrapped his hand around Nyssa's arm and pulled her forward.

Nyssa didn't remember how to walk.

Had she ever met the real Gailnor Fairwind? Had he been an Infi all along? He wouldn't have been. He couldn't have been. Were the rest of them Infi?

No, she decided.

She had met Gail.

She had been Gail's prisoner.

He had given her a tonic to sleep the night before so she didn't turn into a flaming heap. He may have been taking her to Man, but he had at least treated her with decency.

Had they been ambushed?

Was this indeed Antha?

And North? Had he been behind all of it?

Where was Gail?

She remembered what Gail had said about North, how he didn't trust him or any of his own company.

Had Infi infiltrated his ranks and taken over?

Nyssa couldn't see straight. At one point, the Infi's grip tightened on her and shoved her forward. But her feet didn't want to move. The men asked around her why she wasn't moving, but their voices were echoes. Until finally, she felt her feet leave the ground, and she realized she had been tossed over North's shoulder.

Thoughts paralyzed, Nyssa hung as a ragdoll.

"You're embarrassing yourself," Gail—or who she had thought was Gail—said as he slowed to walk by North.

"Where is Gail?" Nyssa asked the Infi.

Because as of that moment, Infi was all he was to her.

"Dead," he said simply.

Her heart shouldn't have broke, but it sat in pieces in her chest.

Although she wasn't entirely convinced he was telling the truth.

"Where did you come from? Do they know?" she asked, referring to North and Antha.

The Infi turned, and she watched as his face shifted from Gail's handsomeness to the face of the companion she'd been told they'd sent back to the forest.

He'd been with them all along. And Gail had thought him a friend.

He shifted again, and Nyssa recognized the face as one of the men from the Gathering—a guard from the Bryn.

Her stomach sank.

Dorian.

Nyssa nearly hurled herself off North's shoulder. "You *bastard!*"

Horses bucked and stalled. She could feel the ash on her fingertips. The Infi shifted back to the form of Gail, and he gave North an upwards nod. Nyssa didn't know what it meant. All she wanted to know right then was how many people in her life had been replaced by Infi shifters. She felt North moving as though he were retrieving something from his bag, but she couldn't focus.

"*How many?!* How many towns have you taken? How—"

North handed something to Gail. In a flash, a cloth threw over her mouth, and the smell of a potent opiate made her eyes heavy. She fought against it: legs kicking, bound arms beating on North, but it was no use.

Darkness surrounded her.

There was wood beneath her body. Echoes of voices surrounded her. Her head ached, and she reached for her temple to steady herself. The smell of manure and sand filled her nose. She groaned despite herself as she pushed to her knees.

Iron sheathed. Cups clanked together. A man laughed.

Her eyes snapped open, and she realized where she was.

In a grand tent on Man's beach.

It was only the one guard that had seen her move. An arm grabbed her and hauled her up to her feet. Nyssa wavered as she blinked into reality.

The Infi disguised as Gail was smirking at her.

The knowledge of where she was put a stop to her movements. Guards lined the tapestry-covered walls of the decorated tent. Plush chairs were scattered about the room. Ornate rugs covered the makeshift wooden floor.

She noted the men Infi-Gail spoke with. The one, whom she assumed was the Noble, was a middle-aged man. He had very much taken care of himself throughout the years. He continued to have a stern build, not as tall as Infi-Gail, but tall nonetheless. His hair, a mix of salt and pepper, swept back high off his forehead. His beard mirrored the color of his hair. And when the man turned, Nyssa noted the dark blue of his wide eyes. The jacket he wore looked like a thick material, high on the collar and scarlet in color. The shoulders were adorned with buttons.

"Well," the man said, his gaze dancing over her, "You were right, Fairwind. She is something."

"Something worth my place in your court, Noble Bechman," Infi-Gail said, and the Noble raised his glass to him.

Nyssa settled into her spot.

But she didn't miss the subtle wave of the Noble's fingers in the direction of the guard behind her.

The Noble turned back to Infi-Gail. "She is a Princess, you say?"

"Princess of Haerland. With her, your King will be able to take this entire land without spilling any of your own blood. You'll have legions of slaves to do your bidding and keep your people happy. Your choice of homes in any corner of our land."

"And all you want in return is a place in my King's court?" Bechman asked as he sat his cup down on the table.

"Unless you'd like to thank me for such a prize with gifts of gold and wives," Infi-Gail replied.

This broke the silence of the room with quiet, restrained laughter.

Bechman's hands in front of him, two fingers curling.

Nyssa tensed as she recognized the gesture.

The guards behind her altered just noticeably.

"Run," Nyssa hissed to Antha beside her, eyes never leaving the Noble as Infi-Gail continued to speak.

Antha's weight shifted. Her hand reached slightly for the blade Nyssa knew she had strapped to her middle beneath her cloak.

"Gail—" Antha called out.

Nyssa realized Antha did not know this Gail was not the real one.

Infi-Gail turned and gave her a sideways stare.

"We should wrap up," she said, and her voice shook. "Perhaps the Noble has somewhere we could rest for the night."

Infi-Gail turned back to Bechman. "She is right, Your Grace. Perhaps you could be kind enough to show us a place to rest."

A low chuckle emitted from Bechman's lips, and he wrapped an arm around Gail's shoulders. "Of course," he said. "Perhaps a few women to entertain you as well for bringing me such a trophy of your kind."

Nyssa's heart picked up. Staggered breath blew forcefully from her nostrils as she waited for the final command.

"Run, Antha," Nyssa hissed out of the corner of her mouth.

She watched Bechman's hand.

"Go," Nyssa breathed.

"Guards..." Bechmen said, a coy smile on his lips.

"Get out—" Nyssa kept whispering. *"You have to—"*

"—Let us make our new friends more *comfortable*."

Two fingers waved on Bechmen's hand.

Iron sheathing sounded. There was a gasp, a flinch at Nyssa's left. And she turned just in time to see blood rush from Antha's throat.

Antha's body dropped to the floor with a thud.

It was instantaneous. Man's guard locked North and Gail in grips by throngs of three. The pair shouted. Gail lunged at the Noble, but a sword caught his chest.

A tremble chattered Nyssa's jaw as she watched Infi-Gail's chest slide over the blade. A knife sliced across his throat. Nyssa winced as his near-black blood spattered on her face.

But the Infi caught her eye, and he winked.

His body hit the floor, followed by North's dropping hard beside him.

Life stilled in the balance of the stuffy room.

She wondered if Duarb's roots would reach into this territory since it was no longer their own.

There was no rumble of dirt as there should have been. No breakage of ground. Only the whisper of a breeze wrapped around her.

The world went silent.

And for the first time in her life, she was officially alone.

The realization should have sent her shredding her existence, hands blackening, and muscles shaking.

But her trembling body and screaming heart slowed with the full inhale she took. A silent tear found its way down her cheek, and she refused to acknowledge it.

Exhale the fire, sister.

Nyssa straightened herself stiff as the Noble looked around the room.

"Clean up the mess," Bechman declared, his foot rolling Gail over to his back. He paused over him a moment, head tilting as he looked the Venari over. His gaze lifted to Nyssa's.

"Are all of your people so stupid to think they can walk in here and demand a place in our court simply with the lure of a rare woman?" he asked her.

Nyssa didn't blink.

Didn't flinch.

Didn't breathe.

The Noble stared at her a long moment, and then he looked to the guard at her left and gave him an upwards nod. "Have my trophy bathed and brought to me for inspection."

She was taken to another part of the grand tent through a covered hallway to what looked to be servant's quarters. The dress she'd been wearing was cut off her. The women who bathed her scrubbed roughly. Nyssa tried to ignore them as they spoke in loud tones about her. Calling her people savages. Calling her freckles ugly. Pointing and staring at the eagle marking on her back. She swore she heard one say how they would have to cut it off her skin before being presented to the King.

She'd love to see them try.

Nyssa kept her mouth shut. Staring straight ahead of her and limp as dead weight as they bathed her. She noted every feature on the women's faces. Every scar, every shadow beneath their eyes, their scarred hands... Their bodies were frail and lifeless. Servants of Man, beaten and oppressed beneath someone's grasp.

She'd never seen such frailty and withered sadness in anyone before, and she was suddenly grateful for her own land. Even more thankful for the path her sister had made for her over the years: teaching her to push herself into a room and place herself at the table no matter what looks any person gave her. Her sister had struggled so that she would not have to as a woman in a room with Dreamers and within her own kingdom—the only realm of Haerland whose past was littered with treating women as though they were beneath the rest of them. The thought of any other race of Haerland thinking women were lesser was laughable.

One more lie the Chronicles had pressed upon her people to keep them in submission.

—"Leave it," came a new woman's voice.

Nyssa's eyes snapped up from the floor.

The cold of this woman's dark stare poured through her. She emerged from the shadows wearing a light blue dress that scooped at the neck, showing a great deal of skin, golden dangled necklace lying between her small breasts. The adornment signified her higher place in the court, perhaps a remnant of her life from across the seas where she'd once been bathed in jewels and gold.

Nearly as tall as Aydra but much thinner, this woman's firm features commanded attention. Curly pale blonde hair poured out around her shoulders. Her fair skin was of moons light against the wake of the fires lit around the small room.

A light brow raised on her face, and she gave Nyssa a deliberate once over.

The other women bent at the waist and bowed before her.

"Your Grace," one of them addressed her. "We were just bringing her to you."

The woman raised a finger. "Leave us."

"But your husband—"

"Leave," she affirmed.

The servants gave her another bow and shuffled from the room.

For a moment, this new lady didn't move, and neither did Nyssa. Nyssa noted every swollen scar on her face. A scratch across her cheekbone, split brow on the left, nose slightly bent at the end as though it had been broken... On her chest was a long pink scar between her breasts. Her cheeks sank into her mouth, making her features more gaunt-skeleton-like.

The woman crossed her arms over her chest, and Nyssa caught the sight of jeweled rings on her fingers glinting at the light.

"So you are the woman whom my husband thinks will be a good enough present for our Prince upon his arrival?" she asked, more to herself.

Nyssa didn't move. She held her chin high, back straight, pushing her arms firmly in front as the woman started walking around her, eyes scrutinizing her every feature.

She pulled Nyssa's hair off her shoulder and moved it between her fingers. "Beautiful hair, I will give you that," she muttered. "But this body..." Her hand was on Nyssa's waist, pinching her skin "—we will have to do something about it. You are built of sturdiness and grasp, girl. Such will not be tolerated by our King. We'll need to take fifteen pounds from you at least. Perhaps more. Especially with this... *Hardness*," she said as she grasped Nyssa's arm. Her eyes shifted down to Nyssa's hip, and the woman grasped her flesh between her fingers, pulling it away and tsk'ing her tongue at the small amount of fat Nyssa had finally been able to put on her body.

Nyssa's jaw clenched at the words, her mind flashing to her own mother walking around her just as this woman was doing when she was a child, scrutinizing her weight and calling her 'girl.' The memory of it made Nyssa's eyes flutter, but she held herself together. Board straight with defiance and rigor.

She wanted to punch this woman in the throat.

The woman circled back around and paused just in front. Nyssa could feel her eyes on her, knew the woman was watching her every flinch. But Nyssa kept her eyes looking past the woman's shoulder into the shadows, and she focused on her breathing.

One.

—The woman's hand seared across her face.

It caught her off guard, but Nyssa gripped in her toes and allowed the sting of the woman's rings to flinch in her cheek. Her hair landed over her skin, and the frailty of the strands burned against her stinging flesh. Nyssa couldn't help her eyes from rolling up to the woman's as she slowly moved her head, her hair falling back over her shoulder.

The woman's lips curled wickedly. "At last," she declared triumphantly. "A glimpse of your truth."

Nyssa jerked the hair off her face and straightened. She pulled her chin higher as though the act of it would tell this woman she would not be broken. But she didn't say anything.

The woman chuckled under her breath. "It will be fun breaking you."

Nyssa met her eyes. "Looking forward to it," was the only words she allowed herself to give.

The woman's brow lifted a fraction. She glanced over her shoulder and said, "Porter Quinn," just loudly enough for the man outside to hear.

The door opened, and the guard that had brought her down the hall appeared. He gave the woman a short bow.

"Quinn, I want you to shackle our guest and bring her up with me to my husband," she instructed him.

"Yes, ma'am."

Nyssa didn't stop staring at the woman as the guard, or Porter as she realized they were being called, shackled her wrists in irons.

The Noble was leaning against the table when they appeared back in the room. He swirled his drink in his cup as he pushed off, and then he gave the woman a kiss on her cheek.

"What do you think, my wife?" he asked as Nyssa was taken to the center of the room.

The woman's arms crossed, and she leaned into his hand that had settled around her waist. "I think you're an idiot," she muttered.

He seemed to find this amusing. "Tell me why?"

"Because for her to be a Princess worthy of us presenting to our King or Prince, we'll have to take at least fifteen pounds off her. Possibly more with all her sturdiness," the woman declared. "She needs a lemon washing of this hair. It should glow more against her skin. We'll have to save that therapy closer to his arrival. She should stay out of the sun until then. These spots on her skin are no good. The Prince will think her diseased." The woman stepped around to her back. "I saw she has a marking on her shoulder. A great big thing of black scarring that resembles an eagle. He will not be happy about it."

"Perhaps he will see it as his true triumph over this land," the Noble argued. "To have an Haerlandian with such a marking would show his true power and victory."

"Perhaps," she considered, though it didn't sound like she believed him. She stepped around Nyssa and finally came to a rest against the table again with her husband. "Tell me why you bought a woman with so many things wrong with her to present our Prince?"

"She was free in the end. Idiotic natives thinking they could barter a way into our court," Bechmen informed her. "I thought you would enjoy a project, my dear."

The woman gave Nyssa another once over. "Project indeed," she muttered. "She'll be up to standard in six weeks. Time after that will be spent grooming her for his servitude. I imagine he would like her unbothered? New?"

The Noble contemplated it. "No. I imagine our Prince would like one who knows her way around his cock," he argued. "A rare foreign girl with new tricks to pleasure him with."

Nyssa nearly hurled.

The woman considered her again. She stepped forward and reached out for Nyssa's chin, to which Nyssa resisted moving. The woman grabbed her face in her large hand, squeezed her cheeks, and forced Nyssa's head up.

"I would say she knows her way around someone's cock due to the faint markings on her throat," the woman declared. The abrupt way she shoved Nyssa's face then nearly made her fall off balance. But the woman turned to her husband, and she said, "Permission to break her how I see fit, my dear."

The right corner of the Noble's lip quirked, and his arm slithered around his wife's waist once more. "Permission granted."

The display of their jointed affection made Nyssa stare at the Porters standing by the door. She noted the armored shoulder pads on them as the Noble and his wife apparently forgot about everyone else in the room, and he pulled her leg up around his waist, hand very noticeably diving into her and making her moan against his throat.

Nyssa swallowed the vomit in her throat and started counting her breaths.

Forcing her attention to the walls. To the doors. To the size of the guards' swords and every weak point in their armor. She forced herself into her own head as the wife dropped to her knees and took the Noble's cock in her mouth.

She would have given her left hand to have her sister's ability to disconnect her core and press herself into another creature to escape. But she knew she couldn't if even she did. She needed to be present. She needed to stay alert of the dangers around her. She needed to learn everything she could.

The knowledge that she didn't have this ability didn't stop her from reaching and pushing herself outside. Begging for the connection to anything that wasn't her own reality. She had to start somewhere. She had to get her abilities back, starting with her own eagle.

There was a crest on a red flag on the wall. Two moons with a sword pointed across them. Nyssa focused her eyes on the moons.

The world blurred around her as her gaze fluttered, and she let her mind dissociate from her body to reach for her eagle. She would not close her eyes. She would not forget where she was. She would not block it out. But she needed her eagle.

A flicker.

A flicker of that energy.

A flicker of the comfort she'd been accustomed to her entire life.

She called out to it, willing her chest not to heave with the jubilation she felt.

But the energy faltered as a fire going out. And all she heard was the screech of him in the air as he called back to her.

At least he was there. As small as it was, that was the comfort that kept her chin high and her back straight. And so she counted the breaths in her head. In for four, out for six, and when she got to twenty-four, she started all over again.

Twenty-four days since her sister was burned.

Twenty-four nights since Haerland's true King gave his life.

Twenty-four sunsets she'd blundered through without knowing what to do next.

One.

One day in the hands of Man.

The first day of her new beginning that she would not fail.

28

Dorian tossed his short blade up and out of his hand, over and over, as he looked over the crowd that had gathered in the stadium for his first Ring Trial. It was a nervous tick he'd not realized he did until Draven had pointed it out to him during their travels.

"Nerves getting the best of you?" Draven asked.

"How do you know I'm nervous?" Dorian said.

Draven gave an upwards nod to the blade in his hand. "You're fidgeting."

"I'm not," Dorian argued.

Draven's brow lifted, and he shook his head as he stood from the ground. "Your sister does the same damned thing at every meeting. Constantly tapping on the fucking table."

A grin curled on Dorian's lips. "You notice my sister's ticks?" he mocked.

Draven straightened, his back to Dorian. But Dorian could see the tenseness in the Venari King's shoulders, the twinge in his jaw when he turned.

And Dorian grinned in delight at seeing him squirm.

"Careful what you insinuate, Prince," Draven drawled. "I've sat across from her at that table for near thirteen years now. It'd be hard not to notice something so irritating."

"I'm sure that's not all you've noticed," Dorian uttered.

Draven stared at him a long moment. "Pack up," he finally said. "We'll be at Scindo by nightfall."

Dorian smiled at the memory and chuckled under his breath at how irritated Draven had been with him for suggesting what he had.

"You're right," Reverie said to Corbin, arms crossed over her chest. "He does smile at inappropriate times."

Dorian's smile didn't fade as he turned to look around at all the people that had decided to come out to Dahrkenhill's stadium. The ground beneath them was muddied where light snow had fallen the night before. Sunlight bounced off Dorian's blade as he held it up to inspect it.

"Any clues what it might be?" Dorian asked Corbin.

"Heard a rumor about a great creature," Corbin replied.

Dorian cursed. "Of course it is."

Dorian had trained during the days between the Temple trial and that day with Corbin, trying to keep himself busy and preparing for anything the Blackhands might throw his way. A few people gathered every day in the stadium to watch him, and every time, a mix of nervousness and pride swelled through him.

Despite his being familiar with being put on display his entire life, this was a new sort of display. He'd never had to prove his worth before. One look at him in his form would back any Dreamer or Belwark down.

Here, though... Here, he wasn't sure.

Corbin had pushed him as hard as Lex ever had. Neither knew what Dorian would be up against, and that fueled the pair. There was an obstacle course of jumps and swings in the Ring, all of which Reverie took to challenge herself on while Dorian and Corbin trained in the mud from the snows.

But it was the nights that Dorian did not look forward to. On the road, he'd been able to watch the stars when he could not sleep and keep his mind occupied with counting them. Here, they'd not had a single clear night since his arrival. He was not stupid enough to think he could go into town to their tavern to find another way to kill the thoughts in his head. He had instead surrendered to pacing in the small room. Hands on his hips or threaded through his hair. Doing push-ups until his arms were so tired that he couldn't lift himself off the ground.

Because all he could see was Draven falling when he shut his eyes. And all he could hear was his sister screaming.

So he would drink the nyghtfire until his flask was dry, and he would smoke the herb until he couldn't feel his lungs. He asked Corbin to bring him more nyghtfire every morning, and each time the look Corbin gave him made his heart hurt, but he got it. Corbin had said he would only do it until the trials were over or he embarrassed himself.

Dorian never slept in the bed, too scared if he did that he would catch the mattress on fire. His powers had become erratic in his sleep.

He was managing to keep it under control when he was awake... But unconscious... It was as though his core was trying to protect him, pushing that form to the surface when it felt Dorian being threatened.

He slept naked on the floor to combat this. Every morning, Corbin would wake him with a poke of his scythe as Dorian was always aflame. Dorian knew Corbin could see the pain he was in, but Dorian pushed it aside as he always did.

That morning had been no different. Dorian had risen and stared at the ring of black on the floor along with Corbin. The look in his Second's eyes was one he'd come to hate. Dorian had snatched the flask from Corbin's hands and doused the entirety of it back down his throat, allowing it to burn his insides.

Dag and Damien were the two who came to escort them to the stadium.

"I think you're enjoying this too much," Reverie had said when Dorian's wrists were shackled instead of roped.

"I'd much rather you be placing me in such bindings, but I suppose Dag will do just fine," Dorian teased.

Dag had been completely taken aback by the Prince's flirtation and had turned Dorian towards the doors with such a jolt, Dorian nearly fell to his knees.

Dorian had caught the near smile on Reverie's face when it happened.

The streets were quiet when they strode through. Dorian had held his head high, his back straight as they walked, allowing his eyes to haze over with the weight of the herb he'd also smoked that morning.

When they reached the stadium, Dorian had wasted no time in moving from beneath the shadows of the fabric canopy and out into the brightness of the sun. He'd not felt direct sunlight in a few days as it had been cloudy, and the warmth of it on his skin filled his insides with a familiar comfort.

After inspecting his blade in it and having the conversation of his inappropriateness with Reverie and Corbin, he curled back under the canopy to see whatever Corbin had for him to prep with. But the sight of Reverie in her leathers and corset against the sun made him pause. She'd braided her hair up into a high ponytail. The wisps of her bangs curled at her long eyelashes. Dorian ignored whatever Corbin was about to say and instead stepped up to her.

"You know, I might die," he said as he leaned against the stockade. "I believe a kiss for good luck would save me from such a fate."

Reverie glanced to Corbin, and then she smiled at the ground for a split. Dorian tensed as she came to rest flush against him.

"Come out with your life, and perhaps you'll get more than this kiss you're so desperate for."

He recognized the mockery in her lavender orbs. "You're fucking with me, aren't you?"

"Yes," she affirmed with a roll of her eyes. "Although I do, unfortunately, have money on you, so try to win."

"You made a bet on me?" Dorian asked as he straightened off the stockade.

"I did."

"Were you planning on splitting it with us?" Dorian asked. "I believe it's my head on the line. I should get a portion."

She crossed her arms over her chest, gaze moving to Corbin who had rejoined them. "I suppose you think you deserve a portion as well?" she asked Corbin.

"You can't be our friend if you don't know how to share," Corbin said.

Dorian grinned at his Second. "We're friends?" he asked delightedly.

Corbin gave him a poor sideways glare, and Dorian felt a swell of something unfamiliar in his chest. Corbin's attention turned back to Reverie. "How much?" he asked with an upwards nod.

Reverie was silent a moment, swaying with the hug of her arms around her chest. "Hundgld," she muttered.

"What?" Dorian asked.

"I think she said a hundred golds," Corbin said.

Brows raised. "Did you—" Dorian balked at the number. "You get a hundred golds if I win?"

"Depends on how you win, really," Reverie replied. "If you lose a limb, I don't get as much."

"Why? What did you bet?"

"I bet you would walk out of here with only scratches and bruises," she admitted.

This widened Dorian's eyes and made him shift, pride rising from his stomach. "Sounds like you're wearing down, Rev," he said, winking. "You sure about that kiss?"

"The odds against you are ridiculous," she said instead of giving his charms a comment. "I'd be an idiot not to take such a bet when you're... *you*. I'm sure you could easily flame yourself and have this whole thing over within a matter of minutes."

"I don't need my fire to win," Dorian countered. "Just makes things easier."

"So I've noticed," she said.

And Dorian knew she'd been watching him train. The knowledge of it made his smirk widen.

He leaned to Corbin. "I'm taking that as a compliment."

"I think you're right to," Corbin agreed.

Dorian clapped Corbin on his shoulder. "Bin, we're going to be rich. You should tail it to the Temple while we have a minute and grab my gold."

"You're already rich, and you're on soon," Corbin said. "I don't have time."

"I don't think the Prince betting on himself is part of the rules," Reverie said.

"And my guard betting on me is?" Dorian said.

Her lips pursed. "Fair," she mumbled. "I'll go check on the timing. Make sure they're announcing you before letting loose their beast," she said as she excused herself.

Dorian turned around in the yard again, his eyes bouncing off every shouting Blackhand in their seat, most drinking mead or wine. It was a great turnout. He noted Hagen and the other Elders in a box by the edge of the wall. Hagen relaxed in his chair, a cup of ale in his hand. Dorian's gaze narrowed at Katla sitting on the arm of the chair beside him, and he wondered if perhaps she was a partner of the High Elder's.

The glint of a blade turned his attention back to his Belwark. Corbin was holding Rhaif's sword, Amaris, up to the sun, and pouring over the rough silver for any miscreants.

"I just sharpened it," Dorian told him. "Should be ready."

"I don't want you using this one," Corbin countered.

"Why not?"

"Because it wasn't made for you," Corbin affirmed. "It's as likely to cut you as it is to cut what you're up against."

"Sounds like you're concerned," Dorian mocked. "You'll let me use your scythe instead."

To this, Corbin laughed. Such a cackle that Dorian shifted.

"What's so funny?"

"Your thinking this blade is something you can use like your swords," Corbin said. "Stick to your short swords instead. You're faster with them. With any luck, the beast you're fighting will be slow."

Dorian nodded in agreement, and he pushed the wrist braces on, gaze continuing to flicker in his Second's direction. He had noticed the worry in Corbin's dark eyes earlier, noted the stretch of concern over his stern features. He didn't like his Second in such a state, especially for himself. It created a hole in the pit of his stomach when he saw it.

"If I live, you can congratulate me later," Dorian said in a low tone as he attempted to make him smile. And he noted the wash of amusement over Corbin's features, watched it rise in his eyes as he sheathed Amaris.

"Kind of hoping you die now," Corbin said.

The smirk rose on Dorian's lips at Corbin's bantering tone. "What—no kiss for good luck from you either?"

A quiet chuckle escaped the Belwark, and he clapped Dorian's cheek harshly, making Dorian wince. "You got nothing from the woman, and you'll get nothing from me," he informed him. "But try not to die. I'd rather not have to explain that to your sister."

Dorian backed out of his grasp and snatched Amaris from him. "Oh, right. Because *that's* the reason. I'm sure you'd explain it to her *very* thoroughly. Make sure she was consoled in every way possible."

Corbin smiled as he pushed past him. "I might." He took Amaris back as he moved. "And you're not using this."

A great bellow sounded behind him.

A deep roar that chilled him to his spine.

Dorian froze.

Corbin turned, and Dorian watched his Second's eyes widen as he looked past Dorian's shoulder.

"Tell me that was a Blackhand belch," Dorian asked as his heart began to throb.

Corbin gulped. "I wish I could," he said without moving his gaze.

Dorian heard Hagen announcing the battle and reading Dorian's charges. He heard cheers and Blackhand shouts coming from the stands. The beast roared again, and a loud stomp shook the ground as though it had come down off its hind legs to all fours.

Reverie was halted to her own spot, having come down to meet them again. "You're battling *that?*"

The remaining color drained from Dorian's face. "Describe it to me," he asked them.

"Bear," Corbin said.

"The size of three horses," Reverie added.

"Antlers."

"Red eyes."

"Teeth. Lots of teeth."

Dorian had never heard of such a beast.

Corbin stepped forward and pulled Dorian's short swords. "You'll need these—" he grabbed his own knives from his side and shoved them into Dorian's belt. "And these—" the last knife was in his boot, and Corbin strapped the buckle to Dorian's calf. "This one too."

The clap Corbin gave him on his shoulder didn't help Dorian's nerves.

"You got this, Prince," Corbin said, though he didn't meet Dorian's gaze.

"Lies," Dorian accused.

"Felt like the right thing to say."

The beast bellowed again, and Dorian finally turned.

His friends hadn't been wrong. It was a great brown bear, twice as tall as he, and that didn't include the set of white antlers growing out from its forehead. It shook the snow off its backside, and the brown fur shimmered in the sunlight. Faint scars and patches of missing hair were easily spotted, as though this beast had been through battle after battle and had always come out on top. The beast turned to him, and Dorian saw the scar stretching across its right eye.

The beast let out a shout, and Dorian's heart began to thud.

"Hey Bin," he said.

"Yes, Prince?"

"Don't tell my sister about this."

"Definitely the first thing I'm telling her when we meet again."

"I thought we were friends," Dorian argued.

"That's why I'm telling her."

The beast gave another great roar, and Dorian's mind spun. The last thing he wanted was to spill this magnificent creature's blood all over the mud and ice. A beast which he was sure meant more to the Blackhands than his life.

But he wasn't sure he had a choice.

Dorian's fists enclosed around his swords, and he stretched out into the stadium.

He noted his surroundings. The obstacle course had been moved. There were only the three great poles around the empty circle. Poles he knew were where people had been chained to them for executions.

The beasts' scarlet gaze met his. A great huff emitted, the show of his exhale hitting the cold air. Teeth bared, its head dipped.

Dorian wondered when it had last been fed.

A whistle sounded from the box.

The beast charged.

And so did Dorian.

He dove onto his side beneath it, skidding through the frigid mud. His swords caught its back ankles, but they didn't seem to have much effect. The bear cried out in pain, a cry that made Dorian wince. Dorian made to his feet and crouched ready as it circled around. The bear's head dipped again, and Dorian's ears began to ring.

He blocked out the crowd.

Just he and the beast.

It circled him just as Dorian did it. Feet jumping forward, the beast mocked Dorian and made him flinch. His head jerked, and the bear took advantage of the stumble. The next thing he saw were antlers. Dorian scrambled backward and fell to his back.

The antlers came down on the ground on either side of his body. The tip of one scratched his throat.

Too close.

Dorian kicked. His foot hit its nose, and the beast reared back with a shout. Dorian jumped to his feet, but the beast was already swinging. Its paw caught Dorian in the side.

The weight of it sent Dorian flying into the air. Pain grabbed him. He landed in a pile of snowy mud by the wall. His breath knocked out of him, Dorian gasped for air and held to his side. He pushed up and leaned against the wall a moment to try and collect himself. Something wet touched his fingers, and he realized the bear had slashed his side. But the cut wasn't what had his breath struggling. It was the ache of the hit he'd been clamored with.

The beast found him, and it once more bellowed in his direction, saliva spewing from its great mouth.

Dorian realized then he didn't have his swords.

It charged for him again. Dorian slumped flat against the ground at the last minute. Its antlers jammed into the wall where he had just been. Dorian frantically crawled beneath it, pushing his pain away and focusing on any glint of silver he could find. The beast jerked its antlers just as Dorian forced himself to his feet.

He couldn't find his swords.

"LEFT!"

He followed Corbin's voice and saw them.

Wood caught his chest. He was swept off his feet once more. He landed in a pile of snow this time, head thrown back. He shook as his eyes re-focused. Wood broke, and he saw the beast breaking the pieces that had stuck to his antlers across the wall. Dorian remembered the knives Corbin had given him. He pulled the two from his belt and forced himself to his feet.

A jagged breath entered his tight lungs, and he stood his ground.

The beast found him again. Blazing eyes poured through him. It came at him and reared back on its hind legs. Dorian swiped twice but caught only air. The bear boxed towards his face. Dorian managed to block one paw, but the other came swinging by his head.

He arched backward just in time.

A single claw whispered across his throat.

Dorian stumbled. He'd just escaped death, twice, and his mind seemed to paralyze at the reality of his situation.

The bear roared back and swiped again. Dorian pulsed back again and swung low. The knife caught in the bear's side. It roared in pain and threw its arms. Dorian fell. His entire body groaned. The agony of his bones radiated through him. He could feel his form threatening the surface. But he didn't want to use it if he didn't have to.

The bear wailed and shook. Dorian forced himself up again, clutching his side. He saw his swords on a pile of snow on the other side of the beast. Unable to suppress the grunt sounding from his lungs, he lunged forward, almost stumbling as he made his way to them. A cough choked his throat just as his hand touched the hilt.

The ground trembled. Dorian stayed low, fingers wrapping around the leather, the other hand stilling around his bleeding side.

One...

His ears perked, and he closed his eyes.

Two...

Shouts echoed around him, but he focused only on the noise of the beast.

It bellowed again. Closer.

Three.

Dorian straightened and whirled. The beast was on him, and his sword caught its shoulder. It boxed at him. Dorian set his feet and pushed it back. It bent its head and threw its antlers at Dorian's arms. The jagged point caught one, and Dorian cried out as his skin ripped. The sword fell to the ground again. The beast reared back, and both paws shoved at Dorian's chest.

Dorian fell. He couldn't breathe. Both paws had knocked the wind out of him again. Blood collected in his throat. He rolled over to cough up scarlet stick onto the white snow.

The beast had him, and it knew it.

It hovered over him as though taunting Dorian's final moments.

But Dorian saw his sword a few feet away. He crawled. He forced his muscles to move.

Saliva dribbled from the beast onto his pants. A low growl vibrated in Dorian's ears as the blood continued to cough up his throat.

Dorian wasn't sure he would make it to the blade. He could see it, but it seemed so far away.

He kept moving. He kept gasping for breath.

The bear shoved the sword away.

A tremble took over Dorian's body as he stilled on his stomach.

This was it.

The beast's breath was warm on his chilled neck. Dorian closed his eyes as tears jerked down his frozen face.

"I'm sorry, Nyssa," he whispered to himself.

A roar sounded above him. Its paw pressed to his back, and Dorian cried out as its weight settled on his shoulder.

Something sharp brushed his ankle.

Corbin's dagger.

Using the last bit of fight he had in him, Dorian reached for the blade he'd forgotten about. The beast's weight shifted as it moved to devour him.

Dorian whirled to his back.

The blade sliced clean through the beast's neck.

Blood spilled, and darkness swelled over him.

Silence rang in his ears.

The beast collapsed atop him.

Dorian wasn't sure he was still alive.

The taste of blood stilled on his open mouth.

The beast's weight crushed Dorian's body into the mud. Using the little strength he had left, he allowed his body to shudder and swell. He pushed his form to the surface with a great shout, his arms moving and shoving at the beast.

It rolled off him, body aflame. Chest heaving, Dorian forced himself to his stomach, every movement making him grunt. His form entirely consumed him as he pressed to his knees.

And with his last bit of strength, he stood to his feet. Hand wrapped around the hilt of the dagger, he screamed. Shoulders rounding, muscles reaching, and fire bellowing—

The Fire Prince exhaled all that was left in him.

His fire pulsed the yard and caught the walls. He should have cared that he was demolishing their stadium, but he didn't. He'd nearly died. He'd nearly *failed*.

He wanted them to remember it.

As his voice vanished, so did his balance.

He fell into a heap of fiery muscle and blood.

29

Dorian settled into the great pool within the Temple that Hagen had been nice enough to let him use. Bruises cascaded up and down his body, with scratches and scrapes from the ground and beast. Despite his own flame, he continued to be chilled to his bones. So much so that when he sank beneath the water, he morphed into his form just to keep from freezing.

Every strike he'd swung played back in his head. How overly confident he'd been. How stupid he felt for thinking this would be easy. That beast had nearly taken his head. Twice. Of course, he had prevailed, but he wondered how it had made him look in the eyes of the rest of the Blackhands. Probably as a child, one they would seek to mock from now on and remind him of his slights.

Thoughts consuming him, Dorian screamed beneath the surface until he no longer felt his throat.

Fire bellowed and bubbled the entire pool. Smoke rose. He pulled at his hair, and only when he thought he would pass out did he rise above it again.

"When I said to use the bath, I hadn't meant for you to set it aflame," came Hagen's voice.

Dorian hardly moved, his head sank back against the edge of the marble, and he glanced to Hagen crossing the room.

"Come to gloat?" Dorian asked.

"Came to see a friend," Hagen countered. He started rolling up his pant legs then and gave an upwards nod. "You mind dwindling that a bit? My feet could use a soak in hot water that I haven't had to work for."

The fire doused with a hiss, leaving only the smoke settled on top.

Hagen sat at the edge and sank his calves beneath the water.

"Oi, that's nice," Hagen uttered in a grunt. "Maybe I'll keep you as a servant to heat my waters through the winter instead of putting you through the remainder of the trials," he winked.

The huff of amusement that Dorian tried to let out choked in his chest, and he coughed so harshly, he almost fell off his seat. Hagen's brows were raised upon his straightening, and Dorian settled with a heavy breath.

"You look like death, mate," Hagen mocked him. "But you fought like a King today."

Dorian scoffed. "I fought like an overly confident child," he muttered. "Certain he would be invincible no matter what was thrown at him."

"You say that as though nearly failing was a bad thing."

"Considering I almost died, I think the statement stands true."

"Failure teaches you more about yourself than success ever will," Hagen said.

Dorian looked down at the red swellings on his chest and the scratch on his arm, and he shook his head. "Tell that to my insides."

Hagen laughed softly and clapped Dorian's shoulder for a shake, to which Dorian grunted at the pain. He knew Hagen was doing it on purpose--a gruff show of affection that Dorian actually appreciated despite the agony of it.

"How old do you think that creature was?"

"Decade, perhaps?"

"And you noted the scars and burns?"

Dorian nodded, unsure of where the conversation was going.

"That creature has lived beneath our mountain since Haerland walked these hills," Hagen said. "Our giver, Mons Magnus, trapped it in our caves back then, saying it would be his executioner. The only creature capable of determining worth and innocence by Mons's standards. He was the only being to ever go up against it and survive. Until you."

Dorian stilled in the revelation. "Can't imagine Mons is happy about my killing his executioner."

"I imagine you were too exhausted from blood loss to truly see what happened in those stands when you emerged from beneath the beast."

"You would be right," Dorian mumbled. "Why? What happened?"

"I don't think I'll tell you." And the crooked smile on Hagen's face made Dorian fall back beneath the water. He stayed for a moment, pressing the heels of his palms into his eyes and letting the water wrap his lungs.

"How are you feeling?" Hagen asked once Dorian broke the surface again.

"Like someone has ripped my insides out," Dorian admitted. "If this was Mons's trial, should I think your Architect's trial will be next?"

Hagen nodded.

"And last?"

"Live through our Architect's trial, and we'll talk about the last one."

Dorian lifted a brow but decided not to push it further. He rubbed his face again and allowed the shudder over his bruised muscles.

"I'll have my surgeon come check on you before you head up to your room. You'll be allowed out of that room now for dinners if you'd like to join the rest of society."

"One trial, and you're setting me free?"

"One trial and your victory brought my people speechless and some to their knees today," Hagen informed him. "I don't think you realize what you did."

Dorian felt like he'd battled the entire horde of Noctuans.

"What did I do?" Dorian asked.

"You proved to me and many others why our Venari King trusted you so much."

"And to the rest of them?"

"They'll wait to see how our Ghost likes you."

Hagen clapped his shoulder one last time before rising from the edge of the pool. Dorian watched him leave and replayed the last words Hagen had said over and over in his head. Surely, his near-death that day had not meant as much as the Elder said it did. Surely, Hagen would not have put him into such a trial that he knew he would not come out of it.

And what did it mean if he really had?

No wonder the bets on his head had been with those numbers.

The surgeon came to see him not long after. Dorian was inspected and a paste placed on the bruises. His body was wrapped in a soft linen to keep it in place. Corbin had come to retrieve him as Dorian could hardly walk. Dorian hated that he needed the help, but he took it nonetheless. The moment Corbin had put him on the bed, Dorian shook his head and pressed himself to the floor.

"Prince, you need the bed—"

"What and burn it too?" Dorian argued. "No. Everyone is suddenly nice to me because apparently, they think I had some triumph today. I hate to take that back by burning their Temple." He paused and gave Corbin a look over, noting the clench in his fist. "Did you bring it?" he asked.

"I don't think you need it tonight," Corbin argued.

"I think I need it tonight more than I have any other," Dorian affirmed. "I can see it in your pocket. Give it."

Corbin considered him a long moment before pulling out the flask. Dorian snatched and tipped it back, ignoring the pain shooting through his muscles when he moved so quickly. The fire whiskey rushed down his throat, and he leaned his head against the edge of the bed.

"What?" Dorian glared upon seeing Corbin's face.

"You cannot keep thinking that will take this all away."

"Why can't I?" Dorian breathed up at him. "Why can I not continue doing this if it helps me get a moment of rest? What is the difference between this and however anyone else thinks I should process what is happening around me? Do you have any suggestion otherwise?"

Corbin didn't speak, but he did sit on the floor beside him, knees pulling into his chest. Dorian couldn't stop staring at the flask. The crutch of its weight took him into a slow haze. His insides grew numb, and the only reason he felt a tear on his cheek was that it hit his lips.

"I nearly died today," Dorian whispered. "I walked onto that field as though I owned it, and I nearly died."

"You survived," Corbin countered. "Just like you will do every day, regardless of what is going on in your head."

"How would you know what is going on in my head?"

"I know you feel—"

"You have no idea how I feel," Dorian argued. "You didn't lose your entire world in a matter of days. I have always been nothing more than a duty to you. As a Prince no longer with a crown, I wonder why you are even still here. Especially after that display today."

"Because I am your friend," Corbin said. "And because I believe in what you can do."

"Why?" Dorian asked as he began to doubt everything he'd ever stood for.

"Because why shouldn't I? Yes, you did walk onto that field as a fool today, but why had you any reason to think otherwise? You work tirelessly to better yourself and not so you can boast about what you could accomplish, but because you are so desperate to be the person

Draven and Aydra knew you could be. Today, just before you walked out, you were more concerned with putting me at ease than you were with thinking about your own fate. I follow you because of moments like that. I would not have wanted the position as your Second if I did not believe in what you could bring to your kingdom."

"Yeah? And what's that?"

"True freedom from the lies and safety from the past. You and your sister are the first of your line to truly support and love one another instead of trying to take the other out."

"I will do anything to protect her," Dorian promised.

"I know."

Dorian rubbed his hands over his face, hair still damp from the bath. Corbin's affirmation stilled in him, but the emptiness of failure continued to ring in his ears.

"You have to fight, Dorian."

It was rare for Corbin to call him by his name, and the sound of it made Dorian's ears perk. He narrowed his gaze at his Second. "I am fighting," Dorian managed. "Did you not see me today?"

"Not that kind of fight," Corbin countered.

A heavy sigh passed through Dorian's lungs. He knew Corbin was right, and he hated it. Dorian ached for the feeling of anything that would keep his mind off the war and what he'd lost. He ached for his home and the sense of genuine laughter. He ached for pleasure and for endorphins through his blood.

"I know it's only been a few weeks," Corbin continued. "And I know you'll be struggling through this for years. With good days and with bad. But I need you to fight. You have to fight for yourself first."

Dorian's hands ran behind his neck. Corbin's words reminded him of the ones Draven had said to him the night of the fire.

We keep fighting.

"How do I do that?"

Corbin sighed. "We'll figure it out together," he promised. He reached out and clapped Dorian's shoulder then, to which Dorian winced, but said nothing.

"If you weren't in such a state, I might even congratulate you," Corbin said, his tone one of slight playfulness.

And Dorian knew it was an attempt to make him feel better. He gave his Belwark a half-smile, to which Corbin winked at him— the first time he'd ever played a part in Dorian's games. If Dorian had felt more like himself, he might have kissed Corbin and pushed him against the wall. But all he wanted at that moment was the darkness of sleep. His body was so exhausted from the day, and yet his mind was not.

He wasn't looking forward to the night.

"Do you want me to stay?" Corbin offered as he rose from the ground.

Dorian thought about it. He considered it for a long enough moment that Corbin started to sit down again. But finally, he shook his head. "I'm as likely to kill you in the middle of the night, Bin," he said softly. "You just decided you are my friend. I'd rather not ruin that relationship with death."

"Might impress the woman," Corbin bantered.

"Perhaps." He sighed heavily. "Get out of here. I'll see you in the morning."

"Hagen left a tonic for you," Corin said as he handed a large cup to Dorian from the table by the door. Dorian sniffed it, and it made his nose wrinkle.

"I told him you wouldn't like it."

"What does it do?"

"Supposed to help with the pain and let your mind rest."

Dorian clenched his nose and gulped it back. Corbin was at the door, hand on the handle when Dorian called him back.

"Hey, Bin?"

"Yeah, Prince?"

"Thank you," Dorian managed, and he hoped Corbin knew how much it took him to say the two words.

Corbin stared at him as though Dorian had just admitted his greatest secret. "Are you *sure* you don't want me to stay?" he asked again.

"No, I'm... I'm good," Dorian replied.

The door closed behind Corbin with a final nod, and Dorian slumped forward onto his stomach on the floor. The cold stone wrapped around his bare skin as it had in the nights before, and he felt the mix of the tonic and nyghtfire drown his thoughts.

30

"Wow, you are a *child*," Reverie argued to Dorian. "Have you never been injured before?"

She was helping Dorian the afternoon after his trial to redress his bandages, having told the surgeon she knew her way around healing and could manage. Dorian was sure she just wanted the chance to torture him.

"Many times," Dorian replied as he squirmed beneath her touch. "Broken ribs, my sister cut my side open once, I broke my foot trying to show off on the cliffs, multiple canonstinger injuries. Nyssa actually broke my nose a couple of times—"

"At this point, I think you're exaggerating," she drawled.

"I'm not."

"Are all your injuries from your sister?"

Dorian thought about it. "Most of them—*ow!*" he flinched when she touched his bruised rib. "Don't they teach bedside manners at Scindo?"

Her eyes widened, and she looked like she would laugh. "You are *such* a spoiled Prince," she mocked him. "How is it you've had so many injuries, and you're this poor with healing?"

"Usually, all I have to do is go sit in my mother's pool," he answered. "Takes a few times for larger wounds, but for the most part, I'm healed in a day or so."

"You're telling me you've never had to deal with lengthy injuries because your mother healed all of them?"

"Her waters, but yes."

"Fucking Infi, you're spoiled," she muttered for the third time. "How exactly do you think you're surviving this war without knowing how to deal with injuries?"

"By taking their heads first," he said almost as though it were obvious.

To this, she laughed. "You're going to die quicker than I thought."

"That's why I have you," he argued. "To protect me, so I don't have to deal with this." He winced with the words when she cleaned the gash at his hip. It stung his skin, and he gritted his teeth. For a flash, he saw his fingertips blacken, but he kept it under control.

Reverie saw it too. It didn't seem to bother her, for she continued wiping him, only slower from then on. "I thought you were dying yesterday," she admitted.

Dorian sighed and surrendered against the wall. "So did I," he said.

"Did Hagen tell you what happened? In the stands? I know he's been to see you."

"He didn't—or he wouldn't rather," he replied. "Why? Were people rioting because I killed their beast?"

"Prince, I saw people kneeling."

"Why would they do that?"

She shrugged and started dripping a potion onto the wound, making him squirm, but he tried to keep the shudder to himself.

"I wondered the same thing until Katla told me who that beast was. That the only other person to go up against and survive was Mons himself."

"Doesn't mean anything," Dorian managed. "It nearly took my head. Twice. I got lucky."

"I think it was more than that," she told him.

He eyed her. "Don't tell me you buy into that 'Lesser One favoring' talk," he grunted.

"You don't?"

"I've met my mother," he argued. "I've met Lovi Piathos. The two couldn't be more different. But neither of which would 'favor' anyone — Well, except the Commander."

"Who is this Commander?"

Dorian tensed, Nadir's face and charms coming to mind. How he'd swept Nyssa off her feet. Bala's notion of what his 'type' was.

"Doesn't matter," Dorian said fast.

Reverie didn't push it, and instead, she continued dabbing his wound. "It is no fault of mine that Dreamers as a people have never met our mother," she said softly. "So perhaps I do buy into some of it because what else have I to hang on to when it comes to something greater than me?"

"You know why you don't see her, don't you?" he asked, wondering if she knew the truth. "You know why your mother secluded herself into her own tree and decided to stay away."

"It was her choice to let us grow without her," Reverie said, and Dorian knew she only knew the story from the Chronicles. He shook his head at her as he recalled Draven telling him the story of the Dreamer giver, Somniarb Crelib, when they'd visited the Village of Dreams together, and Draven had shown him her great tree. A large lavender and white willow as grand as his own mother's, at the edge of the creek that flowed through the town.

"That's not why," Dorian said.

She paused and sighed heavily. "Don't tell me this another of your Venari King's stories," she said, and her tone made his jaw clench.

"Why do you think Somniarb, as free-spirited and happy as she is told to have been in the Chronicles, would have suddenly locked herself away without Haerland doing it to her?"

"I just told you—"

"Somniarb was scared," Dorian said as he sat up. "Somniarb threw herself into her tree because her sister terrified her to the point she thought her life was in danger. All because she actually enjoyed Duarb's company. Arbina wanted Somniarb to never speak to him again when they had their spat."

Reverie's lips pursed. "One day, I hope you can show me proof of such stories from your Venari," she uttered. "And are you telling me you also do not believe in the Architects?" she asked.

This one, Dorian thought about. "I won't pretend to know any of it. What I do know is that these are actual beings. Omnipotent or not, I do not know."

Reverie didn't respond and instead simply started wrapping the gash on his forearm. The conversation made him think of Aydra and how Aydra had always told him not to trust beings claiming to be of greater importance than himself to save him. That the only being he should ever pray to was himself.

"What's funny?" Reverie asked, and Dorian hadn't realized he was smiling.

"I was just thinking what my older sister would have said if she heard you talking about the Lesser Ones like this," he replied.

"You were close with her, weren't you?"

Dorian realized then that he'd not talked about his sister any more than just talking with Hagen about her death. He ran a hand through his hair, and it reminded him of her always giving it a shake.

"Yeah," he said softly.

"Why don't you tell me about her?"

Dorian stared, unsure of why Reverie was being so nice and offering to listen. "Why?"

"The only thing I ever knew about our Queen was that my friends at Magnice thought her gracious. They said they did not worry for their safety because she would protect them from anything."

"If they thought such, they shouldn't have stoned her in the streets for falling in love with another King," Dorian said out loud before he could stop himself. "They should have trusted her."

"The enemy King," she corrected. "How did you think our people would react at seeing such a display? Their Queen, seduced by the ancient enemy King."

"She wasn't seduced," Dorian said, getting tired of hearing it already. "If you think such things about her, why ask me to tell you?"

"Because you claim it all to be lies," she admitted.

"You know nothing about my family, and yet you simply follow the word of people sitting in their chairs and barking orders. Not people out here doing the work. My sister did the work. Draven did the work. Everyone I trust is *doing the work*. Can you say the same thing about the people you follow? The ones that condemned them in that room or pushed you so hard you felt the need to go after the exiled Prince on your own?"

She watched him, and he could see the words settling in her mind. "No," she finally said. "So tell me about her."

Before Dorian could stop himself, he was talking about his sister with a voice that didn't seem to want to stop. He didn't go into detail about any of the last year. What he told her were stories of his childhood. How Aydra had always taken care of them and shown them the love that their mother hadn't. How he and Nyssa looked to Aydra for everything and idolized her. He told her about the fights they had as all siblings did. He spoke so much about her that by the time he stopped rambling, he realized his cheeks were starting to hurt from smiling.

"She sounds amazing," Reverie concluded after a while.

Dorian toyed with the blanket over him. "Yeah. She was," he said simply.

A knock sounded on the door, and Corbin stuck his head inside without bothering to wait for an invitation. His brows elevated playfully, and Dorian threw his shirt at the door, knowing what the Belwark was about to say.

Corbin grinned. "Rev, Katla was looking for you," he told her.

"Oh, shit—" Reverie bounded off the bed and pushed her boots on her feet. "She will murder me—Sorry, Prince—"

"Whoa, what has she got you doing?" Dorian asked upon seeing the franticness in her eyes.

"I've been training with her company. If I'm late, she'll have my head. *Fuck*, I'll have to do laps again—"

Her voice trailed, and she bounded out the door, leaving both Corbin and Dorian to stare after her. The pair exchanged a concerned gaze.

"Glad to know she's making friends," Dorian said.

"I don't know that I would call Katla torturing her, her being her friend," Corbin countered.

"Actually," Hagen's voice sounded as he stepped inside the room. "Torturing is exactly what Katla does to her friends."

He smirked between the pair and leaned against the door. "How are you feeling?" he asked Dorian.

"Like a bear tried to kill me," Dorian mocked.

Hagen scoffed. "Can you walk?"

Dorian started to move, but Corbin pushed him back down. "He's not going anywhere, Elder," Corbin insisted. "If you all expect him to be ready in a week for another round, he'll be in this bed until that day."

"Came to talk to you about that," Hagen said. "I've convinced them to give you two weeks to recover and train before the next one. Your bruising should heal in a few days with the tonic and paste. The rest of the time, you'll have to prep yourself. Maybe once you can walk, you'll join us at the tavern."

Hagen moved then and settled in the other chair. Dorian saw the tap of his heel on the ground, and his eyes squinted.

"Something on your mind?" he asked.

"I have a job for you after the trials," Hagen said.

Dorian exchanged a look with Corbin. "What kind of job?" Dorian asked.

"The dangerous kind," Hagen said.

To this, Dorian forced himself upright. "More dangerous than these trials?"

The answer came in the form of a slow nod.

"What's wrong?" Corbin asked.

"When you two went to the Bryn weeks back, did everything seem... Normal?" Hagen asked, gaze darting between them.

Dorian tried to remember it. "We didn't exactly have anything to compare it to. The place is harsh. People aren't very friendly. I'm not sure if that's what you mean."

Hagen fumbled with his fingers. "I think the Infi have infiltrated the whole of their people."

Dorian froze. "What?"

"You vanquished Infi in their streets, correct? Took them to the caves?"

Dorian nodded.

"I think it was a ploy," Hagen added. "Something hasn't felt right about that place or the people there for some time. Back to before the Gathering."

"But that would mean there were Infi at our meeting," Corbin said.

"I know."

"Did you tell Draven about this?" Dorian asked.

Hagen nodded. "He had told me he would come up himself after they went to the ships. But things... Happened."

If Dorian hadn't been in so much pain, he would have bolted out of bed and demanded his horse be ready for them to travel immediately.

"Damn this next trial, Hagen," Dorian grunted. "I need to go as soon as I'm healed."

"I can't back you out of that trial," Hagen argued. "As much as I want to, I can't. The Bryn will have to wait. You get through this next trial, and then I'll put together the details of this trip. Infi are not going to take over our world in just three weeks. We have time. You'll need to take your Second and this girl you favor with you. You might know your way around a sword, but you'll need backup."

"I was taught by the best in my kingdom," Dorian replied.

"The tall blonde one, right?"

Dorian almost smiled. "Lex, yes."

A slow grin spread on Hagen's lips. "She was fun," he bantered. "You should have brought her with you."

"Left her protecting my sister at the Umber," Dorian explained.

Hagen paused, brows knitting at the revelation. "You left your sister... At the Umber... With Naddi and your sister's Second? I thought this whole time she was with Bala."

"More of Bala's idea than mine," Dorian replied. "Why?"

"Interesting move. How did Nadir take that instruction?"

"He didn't seem very excited to have my sister going to his home," Dorian recalled.

"Yeah, I imagine not," Hagen agreed. "Something happened between them while he was at Magnice, and not just the sex. I'm not sure what it was, but I've never seen my friend with such a face on him. That's saying a lot considering it's Nadir..." His voice trailed for a second, but he pressed his hands together and met Dorian's gaze. "He'll be more worried for her safety than the safety of his own people."

"You say that as though it should make me worry," Dorian said, seeing the sudden anxiety in Hagen's features.

"You should be worried. If you want to win this war."

"If you're trying to tell me I should put this land before another sister, you may as well stop talking," Dorian affirmed. "I will not lose her to this world. If it comes down to my choosing Haerland or Nyssa, I will choose her. Every time."

"Do you think your Princess would do the same for you?"

"My sister would take herself out of the equation before giving me a choice, and she would take as many with her as she could on her way out."

The darkness of his declaration radiated in the room.

Hagen's lips quirked upwards just so. "Two sides of a river, the pair of you. It's no wonder Bala had you separated."

"What do you mean?"

"Bala's smart. Much smarter than people credit her for. She'll make a great King once she grows into the title," Hagen declared. "If she'd left the two of you together, the world would already be on fire. Your sister would never find her own place in this war. And you would be so focused on making sure she was safe, you would have forgotten the task your older set out for you."

Dorian stilled.

But Hagen didn't seem to care. "Tell me you would have sat back with a level head while those strangers called her a whore or worse."

The thought made Dorian's fist clench.

Hagen apparently found this amusing. "That's what I thought." He turned on his heel and started towards the door. "Do not worry for your sister's safety, little King," he called back. "Nadir will give her the space she needs to find her place, but rest assured, he'll not let anything happen to her under his watch."

31

By the time Dorian could limp out of his room without the aid of Corbin, seven days had passed. Hagen had allowed him to soak in the bath every day, given him the tonic every night.

The sun met him on the seventh afternoon when he pushed himself up the grand staircase to the high balcony of the Temple.

Sitting at the peak of that mountain, the balcony was the highest point in Dahrkenhill. It overlooked the northeastern ridge. That afternoon, there were no clouds in the sky. He could see far beyond the stretch of the mountains, all the way to where hills began to slope instead peaking jaggedly. West, the mountains grew larger. The Bryn was northwest. He could see the great mountain in the distance, snows covering the whole of its cap instead of spotted in places like the rest of the mountains. A great bird called out overhead. He only had to see it disappear into the waning light of the sun to know it was the Aenean Orel.

The sight of it swelled his chest, and he rested his arms against the banister. Images of Aydra jumping onto the beast and soaring off filled his mind. He almost laughed at the memories. How fearless and confident she'd been in her abilities to simply jump out of windows or off cliffs because she knew the flying beast would catch her.

Dorian ached for the safety of her arms again or for any familiarity for that matter. He was glad Nyssa had been going somewhere with familiar people. At least he knew she would feel comfortable enough to be herself and to feel like she could grieve.

But Dorian felt more alone than ever.

He decided he wouldn't have traded it. If one of them was to be forced into solidarity, he wanted it to be him. He wondered how she was doing and if she'd been able to communicate with her eagle again.

"You're walking."

Dorian glanced back over his shoulder at the noise of Reverie's voice. She was wearing a dark fur shawl around her shoulders. The tight brown leather pants hugged her hips, but the length of the wrap made it hard for him to admire her as much as he wanted. As she met beside him, he swallowed at the sight of her against the mountains and setting sun. The apples of her cheeks were an amber pinkish hue that seemed to glisten, her eyes settled with a softness he hadn't seen her wear. And when her long lashes lifted with her piercing gaze, he steadied himself against the banister.

He realized then that she was speaking, and he'd heard nothing she said.

"Sorry, what?" he said, cursing himself for faltering before her again.

"I said I'm surprised you're walking after all that complaining you've been doing," she mocked him.

His gaze rewashed over her before he leaned back on the railing. "What are you doing up here?"

"I've been coming here every day the last week," she said, mirroring him. "Honestly, I never thought I would see the mountains. I come up here to remind myself this is a reality." She glanced at him. "What about you?"

"Fresh air," he shrugged. "Finally able to straighten and walk without the pain of the bruises. Healing like a normal person is horrible. I'm not sure how you all do this."

She leaned up. "Do you feel like walking a little further? Everyone has gathered in the square and tavern for a celebration. Apparently, it's a popular birthing moons night for the Blackhands. A few people have asked about you."

"Wanting to know whether I'm dead?"

She almost smiled. "Come on. Corbin is waiting downstairs. He'll be happy to know you're out of that room. I'm tired of watching him stand guard outside the Temple at all hours of the day."

Reverie stood by his side the entire way down the stairs as an aid only if he needed it. Corbin met them at the door, his grin widening at seeing Dorian come out into fresh air. The three walked together down to the square where people were bustling with an apparent celebration, and Dorian's chest swelled at the sight of it.

There was a band playing over by the tavern entrance. Lit lanterns hung from wires overhead, with torches placed on the stone ledge barrier around the upper and lower squares. The dancing had already begun. A sort of constructed jig was being danced in the middle of the lower level square. Each couple interchanged numerous times throughout the dance to taking new partners, all the while laughing and talking.

People ran around the whole of the square like it was an obstacle course. They chased each other up and down the steps connecting the two levels, through the arched walkways of the market, around the tables, and by the edge of the stone wall; the whole time jumping, dancing, smiling, laughing, talking, and of course, drinking. Children skipped up and down between the couples, causing havoc and making the adults chase after them.

Heads turned in their direction as they entered the throng, and not because of who Dorian was, but because the three of them stood out against the crowd.

While the Dreamers had their specific characteristics, like the pointed ears, flawless skin, and dream-like appearance, the Blackhands could not have been more different.

Most of the men had a rugged quality about them, probably due to the fact that many spent much of their time in the farrier shops. Their builds were all different, though as so many were so skilled in working with their hands and pounding iron, most were all brawn and strength.

They cared not for shaving daily or keeping their hair tamed. It wasn't that they were dirty or did not bathe regularly. They simply had more things on their mind than paying so much attention to the upkeep of their facial hair. Some's hair was long as Hagen's was, kept braided back off their faces, and some of those who spent hours in the forges had their hair short after burning so much of it off over the years.

The women had a sort of restrained yet pure beauty about them. Their hair was neither perfect nor silky, and their skin was neither flawless nor lustrous. They were an imperfectly perfect race of women, one who had intrigued Dorian since the day he stepped foot in the mountains.

The unabashed and confident quality each of them displayed without reservation was more intoxicating than even the superior beauty of a Dreamer. Dorian had fallen in love with the race on his first visit.

This celebration felt like a home he'd never known.

He wished Aydra had been able to experience it.

He could see how she would have danced and laughed, changing partners with the organized jig they were doing on the dance floor. How she would have propped her feet on the tables or sat on the stone banister and smoked with each of them while she listened to their stories. He imagined Draven would have been with her and showed her around to his friends and laughed at her mingling in the dance until she pointed to him and urged him to join her.

His chest knotted as he thought of how these people would have bowed to her without thinking twice about it. How she could have walked into that Temple with nothing more than her confidence and a smile, and they'd have given her anything she wanted. The respect she commanded without ever asking or forcing it on someone was something he had always been envious of.

Dorian didn't realize he'd stopped walking until Corbin touched his shoulder and asked if he was okay. Dorian inhaled sharply and nodded.

Corbin led them through the crowd towards the tavern. Reverie was stopped on the way by a Blackhand asking her to dance. Dorian thought for sure she would have turned him down, told him she didn't do such things, but Reverie smiled at the man and took his hand.

Dorian wanted to punch a wall.

Corbin laughed at his side, having apparently seen the reaction, and Dorian scowled at him.

The tavern was filled with a ruckus that made him forget about his jealousy. Amber light filing around the great bar, Blackhands were settled at all manner of tables, clanking their drinks together and pouring them back. Their drinking games were well underway.

Dorian couldn't help the smile on his face.

Corbin clapped his shoulder firmly, to which Dorian winced, but pushed away. "Looks like you're being summoned," he said in his ear.

Dorian followed his upwards nod to the back corner of the room where a round table of Blackhands sat, laughter and high clanks of mead mugs sounding. The haze of herb filled Dorian's nostrils, and he saw then why Corbin had signaled him to that table.

Hagen was sitting there, his hand thrown in the air and motioning the two to sit.

"I'll grab the drinks," Corbin told him.

"Here—" Dorian pulled in his pocket for a few golds and gave them to his Second. "Have him keep them coming."

Corbin nodded, and Dorian left him to filter through the crowd to Hagen and his friends. Hagen stood upon his reaching them and gave him a great hug.

"About time you rose from the dead," Hagen said gruffly, clapping him on his back and making Dorian stifle his wince. "I was beginning to think that woman of yours had poisoned and chopped you into pieces, mate."

Dorian forced a smirk. "Not yet." His gaze flickered around the table then, and Hagen shook his shoulders.

"You remember everyone?—" Hagen threw his hand out as though he were showing off the table and then began to point "—Falke, Damien, Dag—" but the noise of booming laughter drowned out Hagen's voice, and Dorian strained to hear the rest of the names.

"OI!" Dag shouted as he rose from the table. "Your High Elder's trying to introduce you, idiots," he said to the ones who hadn't shut up.

The others muffled their laughter behind their hands and turned in Hagen and Dorian's direction. Hagen gave Dag an upwards nod. "Thanks," he said, a noticeable crack in his amused voice. Dorian resisted the urge to laugh as Dag sat back down. One of the others said something under their breath, and Dag jumped mockingly at them, to which the man flinched and spilled his drink on his partner.

Hagen chuckled under his breath and squeezed Dorian's shoulder. He continued with the names, none of which Dorian would remember until finally, he returned to Katla sitting at Hagen's side. She had pressed up to the table as Hagen spoke.

"You're still alive," Katla said to him.

Hagen pulled out the chair for Dorian, and Dorian sat. "For now," he replied.

Corbin joined them then, along with the bartender who had brought another round for the entire table. Dorian settled back and merely listened to the Blackhands talk, hearing them contradict one another with tales and stories of the week's training battles. Katla was apparently very proud of the recruits she had been working with. So much so that when Damien tried to interject his own version of the story, Katla sat up and cut him off.

"I am much better suited to tell that story," Katla countered, an obvious swim of the drink in her. She sat up in her chair.

"Here we go," Hagen muttered playfully.

"Oi! Smythies—" Dag called out, raising and snapping his fingers. "Another round. Kat's got a story for us."

A razor blade whipped from Katla's side and cut the air in Dag's direction. It landed in the wood of his cup just as Dag had pressed it to his lips. Mead spewed over Dag's clothing, making him bolt out of his seat. But a glare did not spread on his face, and instead, a smirk rose.

No one seemed to think this out of the ordinary.

The man whom Dag had called Smythies grinned. "A double then?"

Echoes of laughter filled the tavern. The one closest to Smyths gave him a slap on his arm. Katla glared but pushed her elbows atop the table anyway.

"I didn't think you liked being called Kat," Dorian said to her as he leaned back in his chair.

A quietness settled. A few of the group stifled laughter beneath their hands. But Katla's head tilted in Dorian's direction. Her knife twirled, tip digging into the table beneath her finger.

Hagen cleared his throat. "I think I'll go help Smyths--"

"Sit," Katla said as he rose from the chair. Her hand had caught the back of his knee, and she didn't even look away from Dorian as she squeezed Hagen's leg.

Hagen cursed under his breath with a flutter of his eyes. "Dammit, woman," he uttered as he sat back in his seat. He leaned back in the chair, jaw tensing, and his predatory eyes danced over Katla's smug figure.

"You're certainly asking for it tonight," he grunted.

Her eyes flickered to his. "You enjoy it," she muttered before turning her attention back to Dorian. "Hagen, tell our little King what will happen if he dares call me that again."

"You might be favored by Mons, but you'll have a struggle with this one," Falke said to him in his usual fast speech.

Hagen adjusted himself and met Dorian's gaze. "She won't be aiming for your drink, that's for certain," he said. "She likes Dag. It's the only reason he's still alive. He only does it to get a reaction out of her."

"Bit of rough-housing with her usually does the trick," Dag winked.

"Drinks for Katla's adventure," Smyths announced as he reached them. The drinks were passed around, and the subject of Katla's unwanted nickname went arie. She told her story, with great detail and at least three side stories if he was counting correctly, before finally determining that the one line she wanted to tell them was actually just that someone had sent an arrow flying and cut the shear above Damien's ear.

Not having laughed so much in weeks, Dorian couldn't help himself from cackling at the story, and it hurt his chest. Corbin had doubled over, clasping Dorian on his shoulder. In the midst of it all, Reverie had appeared and sat on the arm of Dorian's chair. She stared around them as though they had all lost their minds.

"You know, my older sister would have liked you," Dorian said to Katla when he'd recovered himself.

A soft silence murmured over the table, and Hagen grabbed Dorian's shoulder as he sat up, but he didn't speak.

Katla's head tilted at him. "Was she anything like you?" she asked.

Dorian huffed under his breath. "I will not claim to be as strong and amazing as she was, but if you're referring to the getting herself into danger and laughing at it, then yes."

Katla's smile softened. "I think I would have liked her too," she said. "Besides, any woman enough to hold the Venari King's attention like that and be the one to unite all our kingdoms for a singular cause deserves to be put in the stars."

Her chair scratched the floor when she stood, and she raised her cup high in the air.

"To the High King and Queen," she roared.

An incredible rumble of both jeers and feet pedaling the floor filled the tavern, glasses raising in the air as Katla stood.

Dorian swallowed upon seeing the affirmation on all their faces. His heel began to tap on the floor, and he stifled the emotion of such a salutation. Reverie squeezed his knee, and Corbin grasped his shoulder.

Katla's smile widened when she caught his gaze. "May we keep our promises to both."

Roars and bellows of the words came back, and every person in the tavern drank. A sharp breath took Dorian's lungs, and he quickly brushed the tear off his face before anyone saw it.

The room settled down then, and Katla returned to her seat, still smiling at Dorian.

"Does this mean I'm out of the last two trials?" Dorian dared to ask, knowing the response but asking anyway.

Katla twirled her knife, deviance dancing in her dark eyes. "Oh my dear, little King... These are purely for our entertainment now. Perhaps we'll raise the bets on the next one so your girl doesn't take all our money again."

"Something tells me the odds won't be as much in my pocket's favor this next time," Reverie grunted.

32

Dorian pushed himself into training the next day.

And the next.

And by the time the week was over, Hagen had joined them in the training ring. Hagen, being the beast he was, made pushing the massive boulders they had in the stadium look easy. When Dorian tried it, he fell flat into the mud.

Hagen grinned and offered him a hand. "You should see Nadir trying to push it," he said as Dorian got to his feet.

Dorian brushed off the excess dirt from his pants. "I wasn't aware the Commander came to visit."

"He and Draven would travel upriver with supplies— we'll work up to that one—" he gave Dorian a nod to the smaller boulders instead "—try those. You're moving them across to a pile," he told him. Dorian nodded and did as Hagen instructed. He struggled with the rocks but gritted his teeth and didn't complain.

"Nadir is made for the water," Hagen said, continuing the conversation as he stood back and watched Dorian. "He's strong, but speed is more his style. You should see he and I battling."

"Did the three of you do a lot together?" Corbin asked as he, too, stood back and watched the Prince.

"We did," Hagen replied. "Draven and I used to race with those boulders," he said, pointing to the two largest boulders in the stadium. "Crowds would come to watch when he was here. Naddi was such an ass. He'd stand atop them and jump back and forth, showing off his balance and shouting taunts for us to move faster. Clapped in our faces. Bastard."

Dorian threw down the third boulder and straightened, his abs already spasming as he rested his hands on his narrow hips. He could see the fond smile threatening Hagen's lips. "Why do I get the feeling Draven was the mediator between you and Nadir," Dorian teased.

Hagen looked like he might grin. "Keep tossing, Prince," he ordered.

Dorian nodded shortly and started working again.

"You're right— other shoulder—" Hagen said once Dorian had picked up another. Dorian shifted it as he said, the left side a little weaker than the right.

"Draven was usually the best at everything. It left Naddi and I to constantly battle for second."

"Sounds like a grand time," Corbin said.

Hagen pressed his hand to the back of his neck, and Dorian saw a sadness stretch over his features. "It certainly was," he said in a soft tone.

Dorian tuned the pair out as he fought the cave of his muscles. The boulders got heavier with every walk, and with the last one, he threw it to the top of the pile and fell to his knees. Hagen helped him from the ground, asking if he wanted a break, but Dorian shook his head and started moving the boulders back.

For the next three days, Hagen met them in the stadium and helped Dorian get stronger. He still wouldn't tell Dorian what he would be up against in the trial.

The day before the trial, Hagen insisted that Dorian let his muscles relax.

But Dorian, being him, refused and instead went to the stadium on his own while Corbin and Reverie chatted with the traders that came through. He was honestly starting to worry about his sister. He'd heard nothing from the Umber nor anything from Bala. He took out his frustrations on tossing the boulders that day instead of walking them.

Despite the snow falling, Dorian didn't bother pushing on the fur cloak to walk back to the Temple when he finally retired himself late in the afternoon. He passed a few women along the way, and as the Blackhands seemed to be warming up to him, he felt no awkwardness in returning the leer they smiled at him with.

Perhaps after the next day's trial, he would be accepted enough to walk his way into their beds.

Reverie was waiting for him outside the Temple, arms crossed over her chest as the wind blew her bangs off her face.

"I see you're making friends," she said, her eyes darting to the women who had walked by. "Should I think they're noting you because they watched you practice or because they think their giver favors you?"

A smirk flashed on his lips, but he didn't stop walking upon pushing past her. "Jealousy suits you, Rev," he uttered, pressing the door open.

"Keep dreaming," she mumbled as she followed him.

Dorian almost laughed. "Says the Dreamer," he leered with a wink over his shoulder. "Tell me, woman. What did you find out?"

They reached the steps, and she followed him upstairs. "Nothing," she said shortly. "Nothing at all. And they were very suspicious about it. I don't trust them."

"Is there anyone you trust?" he asked.

"I trust you. And Corbin," she admitted.

They reached his room a few steps later, and he pressed inside. The moment he stepped in, he pushed his shirt off. Reverie paused to lean on the frame.

"What did they tell you exactly?" he asked her.

"They said, and I quote: she is fine, stop asking."

Dorian paused as he grabbed his pipe off the table and started packing it. "That's not bothersome at *all*," he grunted, mind wandering as to why the Honest would have responded in such a short sentence. "Is that what they told Corbin as well?"

"I believe their response to the Belwark was to go fuck himself," she replied.

"Fantastic," he mumbled. He tried not to let the Honest's words about his sister get to him. He trusted that if she needed him, her eagle would find him, or Bala and Nadir would have sent word. He decided he would ask Hagen about how trustworthy the traders were after the trial the next day.

With the thoughts pushed to the back of his mind, he turned his attention back to the Dreamer before him, noting the raise of her brow as her gaze danced over him, lingering on his shoulders and then at the vee of his hips. He fought the smirk on his face and settled against the table.

"And what does my wife have planned for her afternoon?" he bantered, finger lighting the end of the packed pipe. He puffed the stem between his lips and allowed it to swim in his lungs a moment before exhaling. The spice of the smoke hit Reverie and made her eyes flutter.

"Have you come to make sure I'm well rested before tomorrow's trial?"

Reverie rolled her eyes. "I'm not your wife."

"I didn't hear a denial about the making sure I'm well rested bit," he suggested.

"Again… You're dreaming, Prince."

Though he didn't miss the amusement in her eyes.

"You never call me by my name," he said abruptly. "Why is that? Are you afraid you'll like the sound of it too much on your tongue?"

"You would like that, wouldn't you?" She pushed off the door, slowly stepping his way. "My calling you the name your mother gave you."

"You could call me your King."

"Please tell me why I would ever do that."

"Because as your future King, if you don't, there are those who might want you in chains."

"And does your sister expect me to call her my Queen?"

Dorian grinned. "No, this is just for me. Pure selfishness, actually."

"Imagine that," she mocked.

She paused a moment, and he shifted under her gaze.

with. "What?" he asked.

"You realize I can see through you, right?"

He took another inhale of the pipe, smug brow raising. "If you wanted to see what's beneath these trousers, all you had to do was ask."

"That right there. This whole… *charade* you're putting on." Her eyes darted over him once, and his smile fell. "Hiding your true pain behind this mask."

Every muscle in his body went rigid. He wasn't sure he liked where this was going.

"You don't know what you're talking about," he said, voice dropping.

She paused before him, arms still crossed over her chest. "I know this war scares you. That you're terrified of failing your sisters. That you would do anything to make sure your Princess was safe, even if it meant tearing a hole through our world and bringing everything down with you."

He sat the pipe back on the table and settled his arms over his chest, feeling a numbness rise inside him. "Anything else?"

"I know you cannot wait to get back to Magnice..." she continued. "That you would have marched yourself back with me the day I found you had you not been instructed by both your Venari Kings to go to these mountains. I know you would have gone willingly to Scindo, with a skip in your step even, if it meant getting back there and slicing your brother's throat—"

"Careful, Reverie," he warned.

She was but a few inches away, her defiant figure staring up at him as though she were daring him to use his powers. He didn't know where this was coming from or why she was saying this to him all of a sudden.

But there she was. Standing before him as though she dared him to go off.

"You think I haven't heard and seen you at night?" she said, head tilting. "Screaming your older's name. Flames pouring over your naked body. Your body flinching as you run through the fires of your nightmares to try and get to her. So *desperate* to pull the only one of your olders that ever loved you out of danger—"

"Reverie, I mean it—"

His core turned to stone. He could feel the vibration of his ash pulsing up his heating fingers.

"I know the only reason you smoke and drink all hours of the day and night is to try and numb yourself of the pain—"

"Reverie, stop," he cut in, eyes closed.

"—from the voices and screams clouding you. I heard the stories of how she wailed when the fire struck her—"

His fists curled in on themselves. His heart pounded in his ears.

"I wonder how it is you can live with yourself after *letting her die.*"

—His hand jumped around her throat.

His vision vibrated. Heat struck his fingertips.

The edge of a knife met his chin.

Reverie stretched her neck beneath his grasp, and her lavender eyes blazed.

"There you are," she seethed. "There's the *Fire King* I was promised."

He didn't realize he had picked her up and slammed her against the wall until he noted her as tall as him—something she certainly was not. The black streaks ran up his ashen hand to his chest, and he knew his eyes were as black as his markings.

Her words reverberated in his mind. He knew she was right. And he wouldn't deny it.

But it still hurt.

For a moment, neither spoke. He could feel her steady pulse beneath his fingertips. As though the fire he threatened her with had not startled her. Her knife creased his skin. His muscles strained beneath the weight of trying not to evaporate her right there.

Aydra and Nyssa's faces flashed before his eyes.

He released Reverie and took a step back, forcing his flames back inside with a shudder of his body. The crack his neck took chilled him, and his eyes flashed to her figure once more.

"Get out."

"Why?"

"Are you trying to send me over the Edge?" he snapped. "Do you want me to burn you in my fingers without realizing what I am doing?"

"You do not scare me."

His heart chilled. "I really should," he breathed. "Get out."

"Do your other friends not call you out on your bullshit—"

"No, they certainly do," he growled in such a dark tone, he swore clouds covered the moons. "But as someone who knows nothing of the decision we had to make that day, you are not allowed to speak of it. You have no idea what we all were put through the day our world came crumbling down around us. You have no idea what that day was like. You have no idea the pain and the agony of the silence we were forced into."

He paused, swallowing hard, knowing if he continued to speak that he would break into the floor. His hands pushed on his hips, and he shook his head with an audible breath.

"People are allowed to process their grief however they see fit," he finally continued. "I care not of a fuck how you think I should be processing this, or if you approve or disapprove. You do not have to be here. *You* can go back to your home and tell them you did not find me. *You* can go sit comfortably in your little village while you wait for slaughter or slavery. But I will be out here, trying to fix the wrongs of people I do not follow. And I will do it however I should like."

She shifted on her feet.

"Get the fuck out of this room."

33

A recklessness filled Dorian as he paced, so angry with all she'd just said and hating her for it. He wanted out of that room. His second trial was the next day, and he couldn't even get his head straight now. He hated to think how she affected him and how if he didn't get his head numb, he wouldn't be awake enough to pay attention in his trial.

He would die in that stadium.

So Dorian ran down the steps to the cellar he'd discovered the day before. His palm flamed upon his entering, and he went to the back where he'd seen the tapped barrels.

Washes of whiskey filled his throat and made him wince. He filled his flask up twice before also grabbing a handful of the herb from its own barrel, and then he ran back up the steps and out into the night air.

Snow fell on his cheeks. It was late, but there were still people coming down from the tavern and the square. But as he started walking towards them, a hand caught his arm.

"You're supposed to be asleep," Corbin said, and Dorian realized he was standing watch by the Temple doors.

"Can't sleep when I've just been accosted by that bitch." He paused, hands on his hips, and he looked around him.

"Yeah, she looked a bit upset when she came running out," Corbin said. "I wondered what had happened."

"She riled me up until I threw her against the wall and nearly burned her," Dorian said bluntly. "I genuinely think she only did it to get a rise out of me."

"Sounds right," Corbin muttered. He straightened and squeezed Dorian's shoulder. "Come on. You need to get some sleep. Big day tomorrow."

Dorian snapped his arm away from his Second. "I'm not entirely sure how you suggest I go to sleep after—"

"You're not going down to that tavern, Prince," Corbin drawled, and Dorian could hear the tension rising in his voice.

"You are my Second, not my sitter, Corbin—"

Corbin grabbed his face, and before Dorian could blink, his back slammed into the Temple door.

"I don't care if I have to tie you to the legs of that fucking bed. You're not going down to that tavern to get drunk and waste everything we've accomplished," Corbin demanded through clenched teeth. "She is not going to be the reason you lose their aid. We keep fighting with or without her."

Dorian shifted his neck beneath Corbin's firm hand, and he noted the darkened hunger in his Second's gaze. He knew that look, and the sight of it made him forget about Reverie.

"If you needed a fuck, all you had to do was ask," he said.

"I'd rather make you beg."

A daring smile raised on the Prince's face. In one move, he turned them, pinning Corbin between him and the door—thigh coming between Corbin's legs and his hands shoving Corbin's wrists into the wood. Corbin's cock twitched, and adrenaline surged through the Prince.

Dorian's nose brushed against Corbin's cheek. "You know I don't beg for what I want, Second," he uttered in his ear.

"What exactly is that, Prince?"

"Right now?" Dorian leaned into Corbin, teeth grazing Corbin's lip. "Right now, you have me curious about your wanting to tie me to the bed."

"Thought that might get your attention."

Dorian scoffed triumphantly. "So you do want my cock."

Corbin captured his mouth before Dorian could utter another word. The familiar limp in his knees seized him, and Dorian found himself consumed by the kiss, the power, and the lust pouring through them. His grasp on the Belwark's wrists loosened, and he pushed his hands to Corbin's face, their lips crashing together with a desperation Dorian hadn't felt in a long time. He could already feel himself beginning to harden when Corbin grabbed his hips and pulled him flush.

It had been weeks since Dorian had found pleasure in another being, and he wasn't surprised that with every grind of Corbin against him, he thought he might lose himself.

Corbin finally pulled back to catch his breath. "We're outside."

"Bit obvious with the snow," Dorian mocked before leaning in and kissing Corbin's jaw. "What's your point?"

"We should go upstairs," Corbin insisted.

Dorian pressed Corbin back flush against the door, mouth enclosing on the bob of Corbin's throat, and he said, "Your cock is throbbing, Second. You sure you don't want this right here?"

Corbin groaned as Dorian pushed against him, tasting the Belwark's fiery flesh. Corbin pulled Dorian back, hands grasping around Dorian's own that had found their way to his pants. "Not entirely sure these Blackhands would approve of this display."

"Perhaps they should find out what they're missing," Dorian said before kissing the Belwark again.

Corbin kissed him fiercely back, hands pressing to Dorian's cheeks —until he tugged on Dorian's hair and pulled him off.

"Don't make me carry you up those stairs," Corbin warned.

Dorian almost laughed. "That I would like to see, actually."

Corbin's brow elevated, and Dorian's grin faltered.

"Wait—you're serious—"

"I am."

Dorian took a step back and held a finger in the Belwark's face. "No."

"Then get your firm ass upstairs, Prince."

A chill ran over Dorian's arms, and not because of the snow. "So *demanding*, Second," he toyed. "You should speak to me like this more often." His hand smacked on Corbin's cheek with a wink, and he made his way back through the doorway with Corbin on his heels.

The moment they were both in the room, Dorian started to say something clever to his Second about escorting him upstairs because he was horny, but Corbin had other plans.

Because the door shut and Corbin shoved Dorian's back into it before he could speak. He tugged Dorian's shirt off and threw it behind him, Dorian doing the same with Corbin's. Corbin's mouth was on Dorian's throat, and Dorian let his head fall back against the door.

He was straining in his pants already, and all he wanted was the Belwark's mouth wrapped around him.

Corbin freed Dorian's length from his pants with barely a snap on the strings. Dorian hugged Corbin's body against his, feeling the strength of his muscles against his own, seeing the stark of Corbin's dark skin on his in the moons light. His eyes rolled as Corbin fell to his knees, and when his lips pressed to the tip of his cock, Dorian cursed to the sky.

His fist tightened around the lip of the dresser by the door, and he realized he was quaking when that same dresser shook against the wall. He wanted to stretch his toes and legs with the restlessness that took over his body as Corbin teased his head, tongue swirling and two fingers pulsing up and down his cock.

Dorian's entire body strained as Corbin took in his full length.

Strained to the point that his fist hit the door, knees quivering. He grabbed Corbin's coarse hair and stilled his head so that his cock was all the way down the Belwark's throat. Corbin's tongue dragged the underside of him, and when Dorian felt him pinch his sack, he pulled Corbin back. The Belwark's mouth tightened.

Fuck, Dorian was already close.

Dorian's head fell back against the door, and he uttered, "Stay there," before sternly thrusting himself down Corbin's throat. Corbin's hands moved to hold Dorian's hips. The dig of his fingers made Dorian curse. There was no pattern to his movements, his mind was in such an animalistic state that all he felt was the strain of his muscles and the tightness of Corbin's lips around him. Dorian was ready to shatter completely. He cursed out loud again, fist hitting the door once more as his legs started to give. And then Corbin held him firmly, Dorian's cock all the way down his throat, as the Prince came apart.

Dorian gave out with the completion, breath heaving, muscles flinching. He poured himself down the Belwark's throat, and Corbin devoured every bit of him. Dorian's hand pushed over his sweating face as he started to slump down the wall as he was unable to keep himself on his feet any longer. Corbin pulled back and sank himself against the wall at his side.

Dorian gave Corbin's thigh a squeeze. "Good job," he managed, eyes closing as he tried to catch his breath.

Corbin huffed amusedly beside him. "I wonder if you tell your women such words after," he bantered.

"I do, actually," Dorian said, head moving sideways to see the laugh on Corbin's handsome face. Dorian squeezed the Belwark's thigh again. One glance down, and he saw Corbin's own strain.

"Give me a minute," Dorian said.

"You should get some sleep," Corbin countered. "I can handle myself. You've a trial tomorrow."

"What—I thought you wanted my cock?"

Corbin shook his head, Dorian's words apparently both irritating and intriguing   to him. "I'll settle with the image of you slumping against that wall in surrender to get me through," he decided.

"I can't leave my Belwark in need. That's just bad manners," Dorian mocked.

"You've done worse."

Dorian couldn't help his raised brow as he remembered the times he'd teased the Belwark beside him and left him cold.

Not tonight, though.

Dorian reached over between Corbin's legs and began to move his hand along Corbin's length. Corbin's eyes closed, and a low groan emitted from him. Slowly, Dorian unbuttoned the pants, and he teased the tip of Corbin's thickness, thumb swirling on the tip.

"Tell me you want me to stop," Dorian dared, his finger trailing down the underside of Corbin's length. Corbin twitched in his hand, and Dorian smiled.

He could see the annoyance on Corbin's face that he was enjoying it. The irritation that the Prince had once more brought him to surrender.

But the looks only fascinated Dorian.

Seeing Corbin in such a state with barely a few strokes of his hand had Dorian hardening again. He usually had his way with him and sent him out, or on occasion, had teased him until Corbin shoved him off and handled himself. But that night was different. That night, he wanted to make sure his friend was taken care of.

He moved his knees and yanked Corbin down to his back. Hand still threaded around his Second's length, Dorian bent low, and he could see Corbin lifting his head to watch him.

To be honest, he'd never wrapped his mouth around another man's cock. Only ever having used men for his own pleasure before. But watching Corbin writhe had him interested in knowing what it would be like to watch him be teased as he liked watching his women.

Perhaps he would take it slowly, he decided.

He could see Corbin's confusion, and Dorian locked eyes with him as his mouth brushed Corbin's length.

"What are you—" Dorian's tongue ran over the slit, and a low groan emitted from the Belwark. "Fuck, Prince," he cursed, eyes closing.

Dorian hovered there. "Would you like that?" he asked. "For my mouth to be wrapped around your cock—" he kissed the base "—taking you all the way to here." Dorian dragged his lips up the underside and then wrapped his mouth around Corbin's tip. Corbin's legs jerked, hands clenching. Delight danced in Dorian's stomach, and he watched the Belwark look up to see him tongue his cock. His lips wrapped around the tip again, and Dorian heard Corbin curse as he tasted the saltiness of the moisture on his head.

But Dorian didn't stay there. Instead, he replaced his mouth with his hand and straightened over the Belwark, as far as he was willing to go that night.

"You're going to make me beg for it, aren't you?" Corbin asked as Dorian paused.

Dorian wrapped his hand around Corbin's length, and he leered at his Belwark. "You know me too well," he winked. Before Corbin could respond, Dorian started working up and down Corbin's cock.

He hovered so he could watch him grab to nothing on the ground. Corbin's hips moved with him, Dorian teasing and then moving faster. He watched Corbin's face scrunch, felt his own chin lift as he stared. And then he kissed him. Kissed him as Corbin began to squirm on the ground. Kissed him as he moved his own hips against Corbin, the friction of their lengths and weight of their bodies mirroring each other. Until Dorian pulled back and grasped him tightly as he would have his own cock, quickening and pulsing with every stroke. The muscles in Corbin's neck strained, and he came apart with a long groan.

Dorian sat back against the bed and finished himself again as Corbin recovered, that final stroke making his body finally surrender with satisfaction.

Corbin was watching him from against the door again when Dorian opened his eyes. The proud smirk rose on Dorian's lips, and Corbin flipped him off.

"Good job, Prince," he mocked.

To this, Dorian laughed, and Corbin stood to put back on his clothes.

"Get some rest," Corbin said as he started for the door. "I'll come at dawn. Who knows what they'll put you through tomorrow."

"What—no cuddles on my last night?" Dorian teased.

Corbin shot him a glare. "Goodnight, Prince," he drawled.

Dorian continued to chuckle and lean his head back against the bed as Corbin left the room. Even as the satisfaction of that night calmed his muscles, one look at the pipe sitting on his table reminded him of his fight with Reverie. He wondered if she would even show for the match in the morning. He wasn't sure he even wanted her there.

The cold of the floor wrapped around his muscles as he curled himself up, and this time he settled into a soft dwindle of his form as a way to keep himself warm instead of trying to keep it hidden. He only hoped with the settle of his mind for once that he could control it throughout the night.

34

Dorian woke to Corbin poking him with the end of his scythe as he'd done in the days before. But when he rose and pushed his hands over his eyes, he noted the confusing look on his Second's face.

"What's wrong?"

Corbin was squinting at his stomach. "Why are those still there?"

Dorian looked down, and he realized he still had black streaks stretched over his ribs, reminding him of tree roots or lightning as they stilled on his skin. "Core deciding I need protecting without the full form?" Dorian suggested, even though he had no idea.

Corbin seemed to consider it as Dorian rose to his feet.

"At least it isn't my eyes," Dorian said, grabbing pants from his bag.

"That is terrifying enough just when you're in your form," Corbin muttered.

"Taking that as a compliment," Dorian said upon pulling his shirt over his head.

Corbin was holding out the full flask when Dorian came back up, and Dorian eyed it a moment, pausing mid-movement. He swallowed at the temptation of numbing his insides and pushing away all his confusion.

But Reverie's words from the night before rang in his mind, and he turned his back.

"Not today, Bin," he said softly.

He sat back on the bed and began to pull his boots on. Corbin sat the flask on the table by the door. Dorian noted the shift in Corbin's weight, his scratching the back of his head.

"Spit it out, Second," Dorian said.

"Someone is waiting for you," Corbin replied.

Dorian stilled a moment from tying his boot. "Is it her?"

Corbin nodded.

A low grunt emitted from him. "I don't want to see her."

"She's pretty insistent."

"And I really don't give a fuck."

"Prince, let me in," came Reverie's voice from the other side of the door.

An expectant brow lifted on Corbin's face, and Dorian finally surrendered. "Fine."

The door opened, and Reverie pushed her way inside. Dorian had to pause upon seeing her that morning, in her usual leathers, but black today instead of brown. He wondered if these were what she'd spent her gold on after his last match.

"I'll be outside," Corbin said once Dorian had given him an approving nod.

The door closed, and Dorian allowed his gaze to wash over her again.

"I see you bought yourself new leathers with my winnings," Dorian accosted.

Reverie's arms crossed over her chest. "I did," she said simply. "Blackhand leathers are a lot more formidable than Dreamer—"

"What do you want?" he cut in. "Shouldn't you be halfway through the valleys back to your comfortable home by now?"

"I came to apologize," she said.

"Why? Did you come to apologize because you are truly sorry or because you just want your ranking?"

"I wasn't aware that you cared."

"I do," he growled, towering over her. "I care a lot more than I obviously should."

For a second, he didn't move, only considering all the possibilities of her being in that room. "Tell me why you provoked me last night," he asked of her. "Why push me like that? That's the second time. Why are you so keen on making me lose control?"

"Perhaps I wanted to see if the stories of the Fire King were true," she replied.

"Which ones? The ones of their bravery and promises the Chronicles seem to only tell? Or do you mean the ones of them losing control on their sisters with fire and rape?"

The words came quickly from his lips, and the memory made him nauseous.

Her tensing before him confirmed the latter.

"Where did you hear it?" he asked.

"People here like to talk," she said. "And because they are not clouded by prejudice and have nothing to gain by spreading lies, I am inclined to listen. Especially to the traders who told the stories." She paused, and Dorian saw the pain stretching over her face as it had once stretched over his when he'd learned the truth of his kingdom.

"Is it true?" she finally asked.

Dorian turned in a circle, his hands threading through his hair. "Yeah," he admitted. "Yeah, it's true."

"But not you."

"Never me," he swore.

She didn't speak, her eyes wandered to the ground, and then she moved to settle on the bed behind him. As though the truth had suddenly shocked her to her bones and sitting down would help her process the information.

Dorian sat beside her. "I know it's a lot—"

"A lot?" her eyes snapped to his. "A *lot?* That's the only word you can find to describe it?" She pushed her hands over her face and shook her head. "What else?"

Dorian huffed. "That could take a while—and not what we have time for now." A deep sigh left him as he saw the reality sink in her mind. Her eyes were fixated on the ground, a blank expression on her face. He resisted the urge to touch and comfort her.

"There are many wrong things about our past written in the Chronicles," he said softly. "Much that your people have believed for a century now that is untrue. I cannot right the wrongs of past kings, but I can try to save us. My being here in the mountains and securing this allegiance is the first step. When we go to the Dreamer villages, and I have to try to correct those lies, I'll need your help." He paused to meet her gaze. "Do you think you can stick around without pissing me off long enough to do that?"

The darkness in her eyes lifted a fraction, skin wrinkling at the corners as though she wanted to smile. "You're worried about *my* pissing you off?"

"Out of the two of us, that is the most likely scenario," he argued playfully.

This time, a soft smile did spread over her face, and he sighed at the sight of it. But he ignored the warmth in his abdomen and continued.

"If you want to know which rumors of my kingdom are true, all you have to do is ask," he told her. "Never think you have to provoke me into doing something I'll regret."

"Dorian, you had the chance to burn me alive last night, and you didn't. You should have. But you didn't. Do not think I will ever shy away from arguing with you just because of that form. If you didn't take me out last night, I daresay there is little I could do to provoke you more."

"I am not saying you shouldn't challenge me. Fuck, I like when you challenge me," he admitted. "But don't do it for the purpose of a show."

"Okay," she said simply.

Dorian pushed his hands through his hair, elbows sinking onto his knees.

And then he realized what she'd called him.

His head lifted, confusion on his face, but the moment he opened his mouth to speak, she said something else he didn't expect.

"I am sorry."

Words turned to ash in his mouth at the sincerity of her tone. He wasn't sure what to say.

"Thank you," he finally managed.

"Are you ready for today?" she asked.

"Not sure what to be ready for," he admitted as he ran his hand through his hair again. "Ghost of Fire. Makes me wonder if it's some trial of flames. What would that mean for my form? Do I need weapons? Do I—"

He heard her huff at his side and turned to find her smirking at him. "What?" he asked.

"I wasn't aware you knew how to worry."

"There's a lot you don't know about me," he said. "A lot you should learn considering you'll be taking my hand," he added.

"Why don't we start with these lies you say about your kingdom before you start picking out gambeson colors," she suggested.

"No need to search for colors." With a move of his hands, he motioned up and down her body as though presenting her. "Black."

"Was that supposed to be obvious?" she bantered. "I would have thought you to choose navy."

"Navy blends with my fire. I enjoy a bit of black."

"Dangerous Prince, indeed." Her sly brow lifted, and he knew she was messing with him on purpose.

He straightened and turned, hand pressing into the mattress behind her. Her sideways gaze stayed on him, and he saw the whisper of a smile on her lips. She didn't move as he leaned in towards her, his head settling beside hers, nose brushing her cheek.

"Should you like to know how dangerous?" he asked in her ear.

"Highly doubt you have the time to prove yourself before this trial," she dared.

"If you think it would take me longer than two minutes to bring you *screaming* with your end, you're wrong."

She pulled back, bottom lip dropping in disbelief. "That's the most preposterous thing to ever come out of your mouth."

"Wit and promises are not all my mouth is capable of."

For a moment, she didn't move, and it made him curious as to whether she was actually considering his proposal. It was such a long moment that he leaned forward again. His lips brushed against her jaw, and he swore he saw her eye roll.

Reverie cleared her throat and moved back just as he opened his mouth—his intentions to suck on her throat until she stopped him.

So close.

She pushed to her feet, hands fumbling in front of her. "I think your Second is waiting on you," she told him.

Just as she turned, Dorian stood, and he grasped her wrist to pull her back. He heard her breath catch as she came flush against him. The moment he blinked, her knife was once more at his throat. Dorian almost smiled, but he didn't take it any further.

She'd done exactly what he had expected her to.

He had meant to mock her and lean in to the knife, but the sunlight hit her hair. It bounced off the flecks of brown in her lavender eyes and the white freckles on her light brown cheeks, and his intentions went out the door.

"Sometimes, I wonder if you know how mesmerizing you are," he said.

She scoffed and pushed on his chest. "How many women have you told that to, Prince? I'm sure my sisters have heard it a few times."

"Your sisters have nothing on you," he said firmly. "I hope you know I mean that."

Her eyes flickered over him once, and then she backed out of the room. "I'll see you downstairs."

Dorian sat back on the bed and rubbed his hands over his face. His own words repeated back to him in his head, and he wondered if he sounded as stupid as he felt.

Corbin was leaning in the doorway when he looked up.

"Don't," Dorian warned.

Corbin chuckled lightly. "I wasn't," he said as he pushed off the frame. "Let's go. Your audience awaits."

The sun was blinding.

It bounced off the white snow on the roofs and windows.

Dorian was not escorted by Blackhands that morning to his trial but rather just by his own guard. He rubbed his wrists some of the walk. His stomach knotted in places he didn't know stomachs could knot. He'd never been so nervous in his life.

People passed by on their own way up to the stadium, but Dorian hardly noticed them. He was too focused on his own determination to let himself get further distracted than what the night before had done to him.

In the walk over, he almost felt like jumping and psyching himself up for whatever it was they deemed a trial of their Architect. Shoulders rounding with his determined stride, he forced the dangerous aura out from his insides. And when they entered the stadium, he decided he had never heard so many cheers.

Dorian twirled the short blades in his hands. His heart pounded in his eardrums as he looked at the people. His muscles were restless and uncomfortable beneath his skin. As though he were sitting on the edge of a cliff and gravity was pulling him down.

Ghost of Fire.

He wondered what the Blackhands had deemed worthy of their Architect's admiration.

"What's the number on my head today, Rev?" he asked without turning around.

"Half of last time," she replied.

A twinge in his bones, Dorian knew today was different from the last. Today, there was no grinning with arrogance or asking for good luck kisses.

Today would decide his place in Haerland.

Today decided his fate.

Whether he would become the person his sister wanted him to be and secure the aid of the Blackhands. Or if he would die without ever stepping foot into the war.

The mocking purr of a raven sounded to his left. He glanced over his shoulder. Black as night. Shiny feathers glistening. It chortled out again, and Dorian smiled.

"Fuck you, Drae," he bantered under his breath.

The raven few upwards.

Corbin's arm brushed his as he came to stand at his side. "Ready?"

"I don't know what that means anymore," Dorian said, still staring at the crowd. "Have you heard anything this morning?"

"About?"

"Anything from my sister?"

"No news is good news, right?"

"Unless they're too scared to tell me," he mumbled. Dorian glanced to Corbin at his side, noting the stern clench in Corbin's jaw, the sweep of the wind through his twisted hair. Sunlight bounced off his dark brown skin and handsome features. With a great sigh, Dorian looked back to the crowd.

"I have some things to say to you," Dorian said. "I feel it could be my last words."

Corbin sighed in an annoying twinge. "Since you'll probably not shut up until you've said these things, let's hear them, Prince," Corbin drawled.

"Thank you for not throwing me on my ass the moment I was exiled," Dorian said. "Thank you for staying with me despite your duty to Magnice. And thank you for not giving me a worse time these past few weeks." He paused, and he knew Corbin was staring at him. "I'm not sure I would have kept my sanity had you not been with me."

Corbin clapped him hard on his shoulder and gave it a tight squeeze. "Fighting, Prince," he said, the words making Dorian turn. "We keep fighting."

Dorian nodded as Corbin left him.

Fighting.

Dorian took another glance around the crowd and caught Hagen's eye. Hagen raised his cup, and Dorian raised a sword.

The entire stadium erupted. The ground vibrated beneath the jeers and the excited stamping of their feet on the floors.

Entertainment, he remembered Katla saying.

He wondered what kind of *entertainment* he would be in store for that day.

As Hagen stood and began announcing the fight, Dorian closed his eyes and relished the sun's warmth as it beat his skin. He blocked out the noise of the people and the sound of Hagen's voice in an attempt to calm his nerves.

Sword twirling in his hand. Neck cracking. Cheers echoing.

He could do this.

Hagen hadn't finished talking, but Dorian made his way out into the middle of the Ring anyway.

The gate opened where his opponent should have come from. Dorian set his feet. He was ready. Ready for whatever the Blackhands had for him.

The crowd quieted. The iron gate groaned and creaked as it lifted. Dorian squinted at the darkened tunnel as a small creature emerged from the shadows.

A goat.

Dorian straightened. The noise of people muttering filled his ears, and he realized they were just as confused as he.

A wisping shadow caught the corner of his eye. But as he turned, it vanished.

Silence fell over the stadium. Dorian's eyes narrowed as he looked around him, chin still dipped down. His stomach emptied of feeling, and his heart stilled. The silence thickened, and his palms began to sweat.

An elongated purr reverberated through the air.

One so deep and bone-chilling that every hair on Dorian's body stood.

Dorian froze.

He fixated on a singular spot on the ground, focusing on movement in his peripherals. His every muscle paralyzed in anticipation.

A growl sounded behind him.

Low, deliberate, menacing.

Dorian's fist clenched around his blade. He could feel the beast behind him. Feel its breath on his neck. Its growl soaking his skin.

Dorian whirled.

But his blade only caught smoke.

"BEHIND!" Corbin shouted.

Dorian turned. Fanged teeth bared at his face.

The beast lunged, mouth open, growl echoing. Dorian stumbled and fell to his back. All he saw was fire. He swiped at the beast, but it evaporated in smoke.

Dorian jumped to his feet and set up again, heart pounding in his ears. He listened for movement and that purr again. He was only granted sight of it in vapors.

Gasps sounded from the crowd.

The creature had appeared again, this time staying in one spot.

Dorian held his breath as he turned.

And then his insides caved.

This was no ordinary creature.

Dorian recognized it from the great painting in the Temple—the painting Hagen had droned on about for longer than the others.

The Ghost of Fire in his creature form stood just feet from him.

A great smokey brown cat larger than the Ulfram. Mane of fire that shook like dreads of hair. Flares of shadow settled around it. Its nose was flat, blackened eyes that stared through Dorian. Every time it stepped, smoke rested in the paw print. Its long tail twitched.

"Dorian, get out of there!" Reverie shouted.

The beast jumped at him with its front feet. Its bellowing roar cut the still air.

Dorian ducked to cover his ears. He didn't see its tail moving until it was too late. The tail wrapped around his torso and sent him flying backward.

Corbin and Reverie ran.

Dorian slammed into the dirt. The tail had wrapped his chest and blistered his torso.

They grabbed his arms and dragged him out of the ring.

"You cannot compete with this!" Reverie said as they reached the tent. "You have to forfeit. You cannot go against an Architect! *He will kill you!*"

But Dorian pushed to his feet and ignored her. He cringed at the blisters on his skin as the pain shuddered over him. He met Corbin's eyes, and he knew Corbin understood. Corbin gave him a nod and darted back to the table. The beast continued to blaze around the stadium. Disappearing and reappearing in clouds of dark amber fire and smoke. Blackhands once more stood to their feet.

"You cannot seriously be going back out there," Reverie said at his side.

Dorian didn't lose his gaze from the beast. A fit of anger pulsed through him. That an Architect had walked into the affairs of Lesser beings. Toying and manipulating with their fates once more rather than allowing them to be as they were and simply use a creature deemed worthy of it to decide.

Judge, jury, and executioner.

"*How the fuck is he here?*" he cursed under his breath. He snatched the wrist braces off the table and pushed them on. "Corbin!" Dorian snapped through clenched teeth.

"That's the Ghost of Fire," Corbin repeated.

"No shit," Dorian grumbled. "How is he here?"

"I don't—"

"Reverie, find out," Dorian demanded.

"You want me to leave you?"

He rounded on her, every muscle in his body fuming with anger. "I want you to go to Hagen and find out how the fuck an Architect is roaming these grounds when he and the Ghost of the Sea should still be caged by Haerland," he said in a firm growl.

Reverie swallowed, eyes darting nervously over his face. "Yes, Prince," she surrendered in a breath.

"The only way you match this is in your form and maybe with this," Corbin said as he stepped between them. He shoved a whip in Dorian's chest. "You have to tame him and put him in a bind. No blade will penetrate his form. He's too fast."

"That one might," Dorian said with a nod to Amaris.

"Do you really want to kill an Architect?"

"I thought that's what I was doing."

"No," Corbin said fast. "You're showing him who he's dealing with. You're showing him a Lesser being will not cower before him simply because he is an Architect. And you're showing these people what a real King of Promise will do to secure aid for his allies and friends despite the treachery of his family's kingdom." His hand clapped around Dorian's neck. "You're Dorian fucking Eaglefyre. Make them remember your name."

Adrenaline surged through the Prince.

Dorian's heart was beating so fast he didn't realize he was kissing his Second until he felt the sweep of Corbin's tongue against his. His chest caved with the confirmation of the heated exchange. And as he pulled back, he clenched a hand around Corbin's face. "We keep fighting," he affirmed.

His gaze caught Reverie's then, and Dorian snatched her up beneath her bottom with one arm before she could speak.

If he was going to die, he would make her remember him too.

His lips pressed to hers, and his heart dropped. She tasted of vanilla spice and pine, and for a brief moment, he forgot about the trial. Her legs wrapped around his waist, hands securing on his cheeks. He nearly limped at the clench of her around him and the desperation of her kiss matching his.

Fuck, he hadn't thought this through.

He forced himself from her, and her feet hit the ground again. She grabbed his hand when he went to turn and pulled him back.

"Show me my King."

The words sent a chill down his spine. The world vibrated in his gaze. He allowed the form that had been sitting on edge to trickle up his body.

The Fire Prince stepped back into the stadium.

Flames did not settle on his skin. *No.* He let the black streaks snake their way from his hands up his arms, from his now black eyes to his cheeks, and down his neck. Meeting across his chest and back. One flame on his hand, and his shirt turned to ash.

The crowd quieted, and the Ghost of Fire turned toward him.

Dorian let the whip dangle in his hand. His arm jerked, and a navy flame moved from the inside of his wrist to wrap around the leather. The great flaming cat moved, its roar echoing around the stadium. But Dorian didn't flinch. He wound the whip with a flick of his wrist.

"Here, kitty, kitty," he said as he crouched and set his feet.

Knowing the Ghost of Fire wouldn't like being called 'kitty' any more than Katla liked being called such a name.

The beast lunged. Dorian wound up, but he knew the beast would move in smoke. In a split, the beast disappeared. He anticipated it, and when he struck the whip to the air, he turned to his left.

An excruciating cry sounded. Navy and amber flames crashed together. The crack of it shook the ground. Dorian dodged back out of the swing of its claws. He set his feet as it shook its great mane: fire and flicks of amber ash flittering in the air. Fangs bared, the beast dipped its head, claws imprinting in the mud.

Dorian counted and watched the tail.

One flick left. One twitch right.

Claws retracting.

Shoulders setting.

Two.

Dorian slashed the whip at the beast. The end caught its shoulder with another crack. The beast roared out. Dorian pulled the leather back in and wound up. He didn't give it time to recover. He slashed up and over, hitting it twice and backing it into the wall.

With each clash of their fire, the stadium trembled. The ground broke. Smoke settled behind the imprints of both their feet.

A visible shudder passed over the beast, and it whipped its head when Dorian paused. Ash landed on Dorian's cheek, but he wiped it off with the back of his hand. It crouched, claws digging, apparently having had enough of Dorian's taunts.

It launched into the air. He didn't know where it would disappear to. Black smoke appeared in its wake. Dorian whipped the air above him.

Claws caught his stomach and ripped his skin all the way to his ribs. Dorian screamed.

His eyes closed, his body nearly limping to his knees. Until he felt the tug on the whip.

He'd caught its front leg.

The beast landed on its side and bellowed out. It kicked and blazed fire down its limb. Dorian pulled his strength. He ignored the pain. He knew his form would protect him as long as he could control it.

His own fire pulsed down the whip. The beast flinched in smoke as it tried to get away. It tugged and pulled at its caught leg, faltering to its side as it struggled. Dorian didn't know how long the bind would last since he'd only trapped the paw.

Hands wrapping around the leather, Dorian dragged the beast towards him. Every inch of his body wailed. The flamed whip tight around his hands, and he screamed out with each tug. Until the beast was mere feet away. The pain clouded him, and his form flickered, but he forced his feet before the Ghost of Fire.

Slowly, it bared its fangs, lips curling up in an attempt to intimidate him. The world vibrated in Dorian's gaze, and he heard his own deafening growl emit from his throat.

The true form of the Fire Prince stood over the fallen Ghost of Fire, its paw caught in a wrap of a navy flamed leather whip.

A fly caught in a spider's web.

The beast was so giant, even with Dorian standing at his full stature and the beast on its side, it still came up past his chest. Every muscle in Dorian's body edged.

"How are you here?" Dorian seethed.

Your Venari is not the only one knowing of the ancient Scrolls' location, it replied.

Another growl came from his own throat at the news, teeth bared. He wrapped the whip again around his hand and yanked at it, navy flames searing up the beast's leg and making it flinch and roar in his face.

But Dorian stood his ground.

"Stay out of our affairs," Dorian warned it. "This is *not* your Age."

Until you call, Prince, the Ghost of Fire answered, blackened eyes blinking at him. *Now set me free.*

Dorian straightened, chest heaving, torso spasming with pain, and he unwound the whip from its paw. The moment it was free, the Ghost of Fire shot to its feet and towered over Dorian once more.

"*Leave,*" Dorian warned.

The beast slowly closed its growling mouth. It took one step backward.

And then it disappeared into a cloud of black smoke.

Breath finally left Dorian's lungs. His form flickered. His knees buckled.

He collapsed in the mud.

Shouts and gasps echoed all around. With his form dwindling, the pain of the gashes and burns on his side slammed into him. A pain so great that he couldn't feel anything else. Dorian nearly vomited. He could do nothing more than squirm on the ground, hands holding to the wounds. The stick of blood pooled beneath his fingertips.

A lot of blood.

With the sun blinding him, he coughed and cringed his knees up as his body shuddered beneath the pain. Blood collected in his throat. But a shadow pressed between him and the glare, and Dorian forgot how to move.

The male was more of a beast than Dorian had ever seen. Shags of dark hair fell over his eyes. A thick stubbled beard wrapping his chin. He was middle-aged, older than most of the other Blackhands he'd met who most had been Aydra's age. Small bags wrapped beneath his darkened gaze, wrinkles at the creases. His creme tunic strained against his muscles. He looked like he was covered in soot, and in fact, was wiping his hands with a small cloth as though he'd just come from the forges. There was a smirk on his lips, and he hovered over Dorian.

"Son of Arbina. Wasn't expecting that" was all he said before extending his large hand down to Dorian.

Dorian's gaze flickered around the stadium as he forced himself to reach for his hand. Blackhands were on their knees—including every Elder and General. The male wrapped an arm around Dorian when he pushed to his knees, and he helped him to his feet. Dorian still hadn't found his voice.

Blood vomited from his insides.

Though it wasn't just blood. It was blood and fire.

Corbin and Reverie rushed out into the field. Corbin pushed his arm beneath Dorian's other side just as dizziness took his balance.

"We need the surgeon," Reverie said.

"No surgeons," the man said.

"Who are you and why—"

Whatever she said, Dorian didn't hear. His ears began to ring, his vision clouding. He coughed hard, and if it hadn't been for the two on either side of him, he would have fallen to his knees. His legs gave way beneath him, and his toes dragged the rest of the way to the shelter.

They laid him on the table. He'd never felt such agony in his bones before, not after using his form. His form usually protected him from pain like this. He rolled over to his side as the blood began to pool again at the back of his throat, and he couldn't help it as it evacuated on Reverie's shoes.

"Prop him up," the stranger instructed her.

Through his haze, Dorian saw the widened fear in her eyes, but she nodded and moved behind him. She pushed herself onto the table and sat his back against her when he faltered, her hand moving his hair off his face. Every muscle in his body spasmed, and it was then he saw how bad the cut was on his side.

Four slashes stretched from the bottom of his left ribs over his strong abs to his hip. One was much deeper than the others, and Dorian swore he saw his insides. Deep scarlet blood oozed out, and Dorian closed his eyes.

Sweat was already on his forehead. Chills ran down his spine.

"Corbin—" he forced out, a fear stretching in him that this was it.

This wasn't like the last time.

The last time, he had come out with bruising and scrapes. The last time, he could breathe and wasn't losing blood. The last time, he had nearly lost his head, but the fact remained, he hadn't.

This was how he would die.

In a fucking Blackhand trial surrounded by people who told him this was now purely for their entertainment.

"Don't start," Corbin said on the other side of him.

Dorian realized where his Second was, and he clasped his forearm as hard as he could. "You have to go to the Forest—"

"No," Corbin argued.

"Tell Bala—" but he could hardly speak over the sap of blood "—Follow her. Tell my sister—" another cough caught in his throat, and Reverie's arms tightened around him.

"Can't you do something?!" Reverie pleaded to the stranger, her voice breaking.

"Tell my sister I love her—"

"You can tell her yourself," Corbin said as he gripped Dorian's forearm back, and Dorian swore he saw a tear on his cheek. Corbin looked to the stranger on the other side of Dorian. "Help him!" he almost yelled. "Aren't you a Lesser One?"

A hand pressed to Dorian's side, and he squirmed beneath the touch. "Stop moving, kid," the stranger told him.

But Dorian couldn't help himself. He could feel his form fighting with the loss of blood, threatening to surface in an attempt to try to save him. His body shuddered with a scream as he squashed the ash, hands tightening around both Corbin and Reverie's to the point he thought he might break their fingers.

"Stop moving," the stranger repeated.

"Fuck off," was all Dorian could scramble.

More shadows appeared around them.

"Do something," he heard Hagen shout. "Stop fucking around and *do something*."

His tone was dark, almost as a warning. Dorian should have been listening, but a tear had dropped from Reverie's cheek onto his. The chill spread, his hands sweating. Pain rippled through his chest, and he jerked upwards.

"You think he's suffered enough?" the stranger asked.

"Are you fucking— *Heal him!*" Hagen shouted.

"Please," Reverie pleaded again, her hands continuing to wipe Dorian's now sopping hair off his forehead.

It was all Dorian could do to keep his eyes open. The streaks of his form pulsed over him again and yanked his chest high. A sharp gasp took his breath.

Reverie trembled behind him, but she held tight. "Shh... We've got you," she said in his ear, though as he started to choke again, he wasn't sure he believed her. "We've got you, Dorian. Stay with us." Her lips pressed to his clammy temple.

Dorian started choking on the blood again. He couldn't breathe.

"*Now, Mons!*" Hagen bellowed.

"Right, right," the stranger said. "Hold him down."

The hand moved over Dorian's skin again, and Dorian nearly bolted off the table.

Searing heat stretched over the cuts. Not of his form, but a fire of a different kind. This felt of molten iron dripping on his flesh. A pain pulsed through his body hotter than he could stand. He thought he would vomit at the excruciation of it. As though his skin and insides were being melted together. Reverie held tight to his head and shoulders as Dorian's entire body jerked. Corbin's arm tightened around his to its limit. He couldn't breathe. His chest was off the table, muscles seizing—

All the pain stopped.

His muscles edged one last time, and he surrendered into Reverie's chest. A bucket was passed from Hagen to the strange male. It was thrown under the side of the table just as Dorian's stomach lurched. Blood and amber fire emptied into it, and the stranger gave him a clap on his shoulder.

"Get it out, kid," he said gruffly. "Your form will want to evacuate the unfamiliar fire. You'll be puking like this a few days."

Trying to catch his breath, Dorian slumped back against Reverie's chest and closed his eyes. The stranger moved closer to his head, and Dorian once more found him grinning over him. He clapped Dorian's cheek harshly.

"Breathe," he said. "You'll live to fight another day."

Reverie rested her head against the top of Dorian's, her hand continuing to stroke the hair on his neck. He heard her curse, and she kissed his forehead again. He ignored the chill running down his flesh and pulled all his strength to speak.

"Who are you?" he managed. His gaze caught the place where his gashes had been, and his eyes widened. The gashes were completely closed, four significant scars across his left side and abs now looking as though his skin had been melted together along the lines.

Hagen was glaring at the stranger, arms crossed over his thick chest. Dorian's lungs started to heave again as no one was speaking.

"Hagen, who is he?" Dorian forced.

Corbin exchanged a look with Hagen, and then Hagen stepped forward to the edge of the table. "Dorian Eaglefyre, this is our father. Mons Magnus." Hagen's dark eyes cut to the male again. "Fuck of a time for you to show up, mate," Hagen sneered.

Mons shrugged. "Heard my beast had been killed. Wanted to see which bastard survived it." His darkened gaze danced over Dorian, and a slow smirk spread on his lips. "Never expected a son of Arbina."

Dorian was still grasping onto it being the Blackhand giver and Lesser One, Mons Magnus, standing in front of him. Mons Magnus, who had saved his life.

Mons held out a hand, to which Dorian forced himself to take. "It's good to see a son of hers not swallowed by her fury. Perhaps that's why my father likes you too," he said, referring to the Ghost of Fire.

"It feels like your father tried to kill him," Reverie snapped. Her arm wrapped around Dorian's shoulders and the front of his chest, hugging him against her, the other hand still entwined in his hair. Dorian could feel the tenseness in her hands, almost as though she were trying to protect him.

Between her grasp on his shoulders and Corbin's still clutching his arm, Dorian was sure he'd never felt safer.

Mons's stared at her as though he'd just actually noticed her. "A Dreamer? Now that's a story I want to hear more of." He clapped Dorian's shoulder again. "Welcome to the *real* fire family, kid," he said with a wink.

35

The wife, whose name Nyssa learned was Shae, was good on her word.

For three weeks, Nyssa's body was inspected and poured over. Not only by the wife but also by surgeons and men who looked at her as she'd never been looked at before. Men who told her her face was stunning but that it was a shame she had such muscles and fat on her.

The same muscles Nyssa had worked for her entire life. Desperate to be stronger than people thought she was. Muscles that she'd earned in the sand, fighting and climbing cliffs with her brother, the pair pushing one another to their limits.

She wondered if anyone had told him she was missing.

The world wasn't on fire, so she assumed not. She was sure Lex was keeping that bit of knowledge quiet.

On the fifth day, every hair on her body was stripped using wax and ribbon. She'd gritted the inside of her mouth so harshly she'd drawn blood. Some of her skin had burned beneath the heat of the wax, and some had torn off with the ribbons. She was thankful for the creme that was put on the burns, as Shae insisted to the men she did not want her dead.

They thought they could burn off the dark freckles on her shoulders. That if the skin was grown new, it would not carry such spots. She wanted to tell them the scars from their burning her would be worse than any so-called defects the freckles made already.

The notion of taking those freckles made her think of Nadir and how he'd counted them the night of the banquet as he hugged her from behind.

Everything they pointed out 'wrong' with her was marks of a proud past that once was— a Princess training to be a Queen. To be as fierce and fearless as her sister. To live without restraint and laugh until her face hurt.

To love herself as she was and not what anyone else wanted her to be.

Memories of such a time were one of the things that helped her close her tired and swollen eyes at night.

Her mark, the surgeons had determined unable to remove. Her stomach had knotted the entire time they'd poured over it. Finally, it was decided to leave such a mark untouched—that the Prince would want a reminder of how he'd conquered their world while he was taking her from behind.

She'd hardly been able to keep her composure during that conversation. But she promised herself she would set the entire camp aflame, take herself down with it, before such a thing happened to her.

The air was thick with the stench of manure from an animal she'd only ever seen at the villages. Pigs, she remembered. She'd never smelled such a stench, and the heaviness of it burned her nostrils at night as the place they were keeping her in was just beside the stalls. It was a small room, cold wooden slats on the ground that did not always meet at the seams. Every morning, a Porter came to fetch her, and every morning she did not move, forcing them to pick her up as dead weight and take her to her next inspection.

Every night, for a few moments when she was thrown back into the cell, she would try to remove herself from her consciousness, and every day she was able to connect a fraction of a second longer to her eagle again.

This was what she looked forward to at the end of every day. And it was this connection that kept her head on straight.

Endure.

Her shoulders ached that morning with the burns, the wool on the wrapped wounds felt so uncomfortable she could hardly move her arms.

—Water was thrown on her face.

This was not the regular wake-up call. She hadn't even been asleep. She'd just been staring at the ceiling, counting the slats in the roof and her breaths.

She wondered what they would want to take from her now.

She was picked up again, not given a towel to dry herself with but rather taken wet into the bathing room where the three women were waiting on her. Her burns were nearly healed on her shoulders, the skin pink and discolored from the rest of her. She was placed in the tub as usual, and the women began to scrub. She listened to them talk, apparent by now that they thought she was dumb or perhaps couldn't speak.

Nyssa sat limp and heavy, staring at the filthy water. Her stomach grumbled as she wavered on her seat. What she would have given for actual food and water and not just scraps. She'd tried not to pay much attention to her changing body, knowing if she did, she would send herself into more of a spiral than she already was.

The women were talking about the ocean, how that day seemed more active than others. They spoke of a great storm on the horizon, and Nyssa immediately wondered if she would be put in better quarters. She was sure if she was left in the room they had her in that she might drown.

She decided to bring it up to the Noble.

There was a stark difference in the way the wife treated her and the Noble. She'd noted the soft looks the Noble gave her in comparison to Shae.

The wife seemed wary of her. The Noble seemed to think her stupid. So stupid that he didn't guard what he talked about when she was around.

He had shown her off to the captains and generals of their army. Shae had gone out to market with her maidens to oversee the goods being produced and quality—whether they were in line with what they were accustomed to across the seas.

More and more ships seemed to be sailing in. Nyssa could see the ocean from the slats in the walls, and she'd counted two arriving every other day. Though sometimes, they did not bring their rowboats to this settlement. Sometimes they would go further east.

She didn't have to wonder why the boats were heading east, though. Because the Noble liked to talk.

The day he showed her off in their meeting, he'd had her stand on the table and strung her arms up in chains above her head to the board at the top of the tent that kept it from collapsing.

Nyssa had kicked one of them when he tried to touch her, and she'd received one lashing in response. For the remainder of that meeting, she stayed steady. Keeping herself firmly planted and staring at their flag on the wall while they talked.

They had talked about the settlement and castle they were building for their King on the western shore. Savigndor, they were calling it. They were excavating parts of the cliffs for such a place. The captains and generals spoke of their legions across the seas and when they expected them to arrive. It seemed their plan was to use the entire peninsula coast as their base. The Noble's settlement would be the home ground and their livestock feed. One of the generals told Bechmen he would need to quadruple his farms to feed the number of soldiers coming in within the next two cycles.

Things were moving a lot faster than Nyssa had anticipated.

There were two other estates lining the coast east between this one and Savigndor. Each place they were starting for specific goods. One thing they hadn't been able to do well was grow fresh vegetables or foods. One man had been dispatched to try and trade with an Haerland settlement. But they didn't say what had come of it, and Nyssa's heart was left broken.

One captain brought up a fire they had seen further up the western coast a few weeks back. The mention of it made Nyssa's ears perk. She knew he meant Magnice.

But the Noble had said the information he'd been given was that it was an Haerlandian squabble that resulted in the destruction of one of their monarchies and that that was one less race for them to have to worry with.

This settled the turmoil in her stomach. At least if they thought her home was in ruins, they would stay to the south a while longer.

Being back in the game, even with her chained to the ceiling and being presented as a trophy, kept her alive.

She ached for information on her own home as well as theirs. She craved the words and ignorant ramblings these men went on with. And even through the haze of her pain and rumbling stomach, it was one more thing keeping her from curling up and allowing her flames to consume her.

Exhale the fire, sister.

During the next meeting, Nyssa was given a job. To walk the room in a scantly clad dress and serve wine. She'd had to use all her restraint that day as the men grabbed at her or slapped her ass when she would bend to pour the wine.

That night, she'd shaken and cried so severely, she nearly set the entire place on fire.

The Noble only brought her into the meetings while the wife was away, and that day was no different. She was given another sheer dress. This one was a blue color that hung over her breasts and tied at the waist. It, at least, looked as though it hadn't been worn.

She wondered if there were new guests at the meeting.

Once she was dressed, the wife's favored Porter, Quinn, came for her. He'd been halfway decent to her, and even though he still grabbed her relentlessly, at least he never spat in her face or made crude remarks to her as the others did. They seemed to pick on him as well, calling him a uniq and shouting at him for being soft.

That morning, though, he brought her bread and a small drink of water.

Nyssa stared at Quinn. "What—"

"It was all I could do," he cut in.

Despite how hungry she was, she broke off a small piece and then stashed the remainder beneath the scratchy dress she'd been using as a blanket. The staleness tasted like the greatest delicacy she'd ever put in her mouth. And the water... The water was life itself. As dirty as it may have been, the wash of it down her dry throat made her chest cave.

"Thank you," she said to him.

But Quinn only gave her a nod. He removed the shackle from her ankle and placed the familiar ones around her wrists.

The new man that the Noble had been so proud to present her to the day before was back.

The man was a Commander of what she was told was their finest legion— he had smelled her hair the day before in their meeting. The Noble had asked what the Commander thought of her and if she would please the Prince. Nyssa had stood her ground firm, ignored the man walking around her. He'd said her hair needed to be brightened but that the rest of her seemed to be coming along.

A great burly man, he continuously pushed out his chest as though trying to make himself look more prominent. His tawny hair was cut short, a kept beard and mustache wrapping neatly on his face. Bechmen was speaking with him when she and Quinn entered the room. Together, the pair turned in her direction, and brows lifted on the man's face.

"Very good, Commander Luka," Bechmen said in a drawl, smile quirking on his lips. "This dress was a grand choice. Maid—" he snapped his fingers, and another servant came to his side, bowing before him "—You'll tell my wife to find more fabrics in this color from the traders and send word for more on the ships from home. We'll need to wrap our Princess in such a color to present to the Prince." He turned and clapped Luka on his shoulder. "One of your late mistress's dresses, I presume?"

"It was," Luka answered, his gaze shifting so predatorily over Nyssa that she couldn't help the squirm in her knees.

Bechmen snapped his fingers at Quinn. "Porter, remove her shackles today," he insisted. "She'll not be escaping anywhere under our watch."

Moving her wrists as she wanted felt of a luxury she didn't know she would ever crave. She rubbed her wrists and stood in the corner while the men settled, and then she started pouring their wine as the minutes were brought forth.

With the shackles off and the freedom to move about the room, she started to feel more comfortable. Unlike other times, the men were not ogling at her as possessively. Apparently, they were getting used to the Noble parading his little spoil around, no matter how sheer and revealing her dress might be.

The familiarity of her eyes darting from each person who spoke to the next... Watching the brushes of their fingers across the glasses... The cut of their eyes and raise of their brows when another would speak...

This.

This she could do.

This she knew.

She poured each of them the wine and then held at the back of the room opposite Bechmen. She had a good vantage point and was able to see both he and Luka. She watched from over the shoulder of the one that had pinched her breast the day before as she wished not to allow him to watch her the entire time.

Luka seemed to pay more attention to her than the rest of the room, presumably because he was the newest of the group, and she assumed because she was wearing a dress given by him. She wasn't sure what game he was playing at or if the Noble had bartered something with him, but she intended to find out.

They spoke of the usual. So much of the same that it was easier for her to pick up the noted movements of each person, remembering what they'd done at the meeting before and using it to her advantage.

She went around the room twice more with wine, and by the time they wrapped up, there were two of the men whose voices had gotten louder due to the alcohol.

She made a note of which ones.

Quinn shackled her hands in front of her again once the meeting was over, and he started to lead her back to her room when Bechmen called for them.

The pair stopped, and Nyssa noted the curious stare on Bechmen's face. She wasn't sure what to make of it, if whether he was up to something or perhaps wanted her to stay to show her off more.

"Take her to my bedroom."

Nyssa's feet wouldn't move.

She stood frozen and confused to the spot, her heart thumping loudly in her ears.

What did he want?

The sun had gone down by the time the Noble joined her. He threw back the door, and she pushed herself against the dresser upon seeing his taut jaw. She didn't know if he had decided he would have his way with her or if he had some other reason to call her in that room. Whatever it was, she told herself she would be ready.

This place would not break her.

Bechmen didn't say anything as he went to the table and poured a cup of water. His hips settled against the top, and he sighed, eyes traveling deliberately over her. "You can read them, can't you?" the Noble asked.

Nyssa stared, chin high, but she didn't answer.

He offered her the cup of water, and she knew it was a bribe.

"Come now, girl," he said. "I know you're thirsty. When's the last time my wife gave you more than bathwater to drink?"

Play the game, little sister, she could hear Rhaif telling her.

Nyssa hesitantly reached for the water, but the Noble held it back. She swallowed her dry spit as she sneered at him.

"It's all in your strategy," Rhaif said as he chatted with her in his study. *"Every move should be calculated. Three steps ahead at all times."* He paused to move a battle figurine on his large table map of Haerland, positioning it at the edge of the mountains. *"This world is yours to take, little sister. It's your own personal battlefield and chessboard."* His eyes lifted, and he held out a soldier figurine to her. *"Make your move."*

Nyssa set her teeth as she recalled the memory.

She made her move.

"Your Commander is lying about his troops being prepared for battle," Nyssa said firmly. "He scratches the table with two fingers when he's exaggerating."

The Noble looked impressed, and he gave her the cup of water.

Nyssa sipped the cool liquid. Her insides caved at the sensation of it.

She held the cup firm in her hands as she felt her stomach grumble with the drink.

"Tell me more," he requested.

She considered him, took another sip of the water, and resisted the urge to throw it all back down her throat. "Why should I?"

"You've been in my meetings for... Two weeks now?" he calculated. "Twice a week, sometimes three. Luka has only been in two of those meetings. And it took you just that long to figure out his tell-tale sign." He swirled the wine in his cup. "Princess of Haerland, your guard called you... Something tells me you were involved in the meetings of your kingdom more than you wanted to be."

"Perhaps I like the politics."

This time a low chuckle came from his lips. "That I believe." He pushed off the desk again and went to the tent door, where he said something to Quinn. Quinn nodded and left.

"Luka has taken a liking to you," Bechmen said upon facing her again.

Nyssa resisted the urge to shift with news she already knew. The Noble smiled.

"He's never exaggerated before in my company," he continued. "The fact you think he is exaggerating about his soldiers tells me he is attempting to impress you."

"Why should he not be impressing you or the rest of the Generals?"

"Luka is the most powerful man at that table," he replied. "He's no reason to lie or spin words when he could easily report back to our King anything, and the King would blindly listen to him."

"Your King sounds like an idiot."

He looked like he might laugh, but he didn't comment on her statement. "We've new traders coming in five days. Another meeting in seven. You'll attend both of these gatherings and report back to me what you see."

"Why would I do that?"

Quinn came back in the room then, carrying a towering tray of foods. Her mouth began to salivate at the sight of actual food and not just the scraps she'd been given. Quinn sat the tray on the bed, and Nyssa looked at the Noble, meeting his smug smile.

"Food is your barter?"

"You're starving," he noted. "I can hear the grumble of your insides every time you walk by in that room."

"I doubt your wife would like you feeding me, considering how much she is working on getting me ready for your Prince," Nyssa seethed.

Bechmen considered it. "Then tell me what else I can give you."

"You cannot buy me."

"Do not think that because you are a prize for my Prince, I will not use other methods to persuade you," he warned.

"I didn't know your Prince liked damaged goods."

"Once he learns why you're damaged, he'll agree with me."

The smell of the food made her eyes flutter. But she would not be bought with that. She would not cave for pastries or meat.

But she would play the game.

"No more burning me," she requested. "If you think the spots on my skin were horrendous, you must agree the burns are worse."

"What my wife does with you is not my territory," he told her. "Name something else."

"A walk in the market," she countered. "Daily."

"Weekly," he argued. "One walk per week. With guards."

"Not in chains," she added. "And not surrounded by one of your legions."

"Two guards, and you'll wear a scarf, so my people do not get ideas about your hair."

The Noble held out his hand, and when she frowned at the gesture, his lip faintly twitched at the corner.

"You shake my hand, and the deal is done," he explained.

Nyssa hesitated. "Repeat the terms aloud."

This time, he did smile.

"You *do* like politics, don't you?" he knew.

When she didn't respond, he turned back to the table and poured two glasses of wine.

"You'll watch my meetings with me and report back what you see," he said. "Anything out of the ordinary. Lies. Exaggerations. Treachery. In exchange for your help, I'll allow you to the market for a walk once a week. Escorted by two guards, without chains, and with a scarf to hide your hair and keep your skin from getting more of these spots—"

"They're called freckles," she practically snapped.

The Noble huffed under his breath as he extended the goblet to her. Nyssa eyed him but reached for the goblet anyway. The moment it was in her grasp, he stretched his free hand to her once more.

"Do we have a deal?"

She let her breath settle, gaze darting from his outstretched hand to his face—

And then she shook his hand.

The corner of the Noble's mouth quirked upwards as he moved their hands up and down in the air. When it was released, she grasped the cup with both hands and waited for him to drink first.

"You know, I never got your name," he said, and she could see the red wine at the corner of his lips.

She smelled the liquid and hesitantly let it touch her lips, but she did not let is fall down her throat. "Ari," she responded, fake swallowing.

"Just Ari?" he repeated. "Do people of your land not have surnames?"

"Ari Storn," she blurted, and the name that rolled so quickly off her tongue made her heart break.

The Noble raised his cup to hers and pressed it against it. "You'll make a grand addition to our court, Miss Storn," he cooed.

The wink he gave her made her cringe.

But the deal brought a restlessness to her extremities.

Make them crawl, Nysi.

36

For three days, Dorian couldn't move out of the bed.

And for three days, Dorian puked so much ash that he wondered if his insides had been replaced with it.

His form had stayed inside while he was under with the tonic Mons had made for him every day. He hardly remembered the days. And he certainly didn't remember the nights. What he did remember were the touches of someone changing his bandages. He remembered words being spoken about him, mumbles of conversation, but nothing more.

As for how many days he had actually been out, he wasn't sure. After he got rid of the unfamiliar fire inside him, his body had surrendered to the pain, and he lost track of everything around him. The next thing he remembered was waking to Reverie and Corbin sitting on either side of him in the bed. Their voices were quiet. Reverie held his hand while Corbin apparently checked his injury on his side.

The bandage pulling off made him inhale sharply, and he opened his eyes. "Fuck—you're worse than her," he grumbled, head lifting off the pillow.

Corbin's smirk met him, and he gave Reverie an upwards nod. "Knock him back out, would you?"

But Reverie only laughed softly and squeezed Dorian's hand. Another sear of pain rippled through him, and he pressed his head back down. "How long have I been out?" he managed.

"Not long enough," Corbin grunted.

"Five days," Reverie answered.

Dorian groaned into the bed. *Five days.* Five days longer than he should have been.

"Tell me you've heard something since I've been out," he asked them.

The silence that rang in the room made his head lift. "Nothing?" he asked, looking between them.

Reverie and Corbin exchanged another glance, and Dorian started to move.

"We need to go—"

Corbin's thumb jammed in Dorian's bruise.

Dorian limped back against the mattress, cursing and whimpering at the searing pain. He nearly puked as it quaked down into his bones.

"You're not going anywhere," Corbin said firmly. "And besides, you can't forget about the job Hagen has for us."

Dorian glared at his Second. "This is my sister," he argued. "I need to know that she is okay."

"What you need to do is trust her," Corbin affirmed. "She's smart—"

"Annoyingly reckless—"

"More than you?" Reverie cut in.

"—She's got Lex—" Corbin continued.

"She's likely run her off by now," Dorian grunted.

Corbin paused, but he didn't say another word about Nyssa. "You know this job Hagen has for us is important," he said instead. "Your sister can manage the south for now. If the Infi take over the mountains, we'll have no backup plan."

"Wait, Infi?" Reverie asked, and fear rose in her gaze unlike he had ever seen. Her hands pushed to either side of her neck. "Why are we talking about Infi?"

Dorian closed his eyes and surrendered to the pillow again. "Corbin, tell her."

As Corbin explained what Hagen had come to them with, Dorian tuned them out. He pressed his hands over his eyes and tried to reach inside himself for any sign of his sister.

They'd always shared a connection deeper than kings before them. Ever since they'd been marked in their mother's pool together, they knew when the other was in pain and could share words without speaking. Of course, it could have been because they knew each other so well that they could finish one another's thoughts, but Dorian wasn't sure.

He'd been in so much pain lately, he wondered if perhaps it had all run together—her agony and his. If she had been killed, he would have known. Her eagle would be with him. He knew she was alive, but he needed to know she was okay.

When he felt nothing, he wrapped his hands around both Corbin and Reverie's legs and pulled himself to a sitting position, slumping over his knees, still burying his head in his hands.

"I need both of you to quiet a moment," he asked them.

Just as he started counting his breaths to numb his surroundings, someone knocked on the door.

Dorian cursed the sky.

Corbin yelled for the person to come in, and Hagen popped his head in the door.

"Oh good, he's awake," he said upon coming inside. "Wondered if I needed to wrap your ass in the snow outside to get the rest of that fire out of you," he continued. "You're lucky the woman didn't want your cock to shrink."

Hagen winked at Reverie with the last words, and Reverie threw her boot at him.

Hagen laughed and dodged it as he turned to Dorian. "How you feeling, mate?"

"Like I nearly died," Dorian grumbled.

"So better then?"

Dorian's eyes cut at him over his hands. "What's on your mind, Elder?"

"Think you're up for standing?"

"Doubtful," Dorian admitted. "Why?"

"I've spoken with the people and the rest of our Elders. They've decided to forego the final trial."

Dorian frowned and his hands moved entirely away from his face. "What?"

Hagen gave him a half-smile. "Get some clothes on. Your guard can help you up the steps. I want you to have this presentation before Mons leaves." He stepped forward and squeezed Dorian's knee. "Draven would be proud of the way you handled our Architect," he said. "I daresay he'd have done the same thing had it shown up to meddle in our affairs without our asking it to."

Emotion grew in Dorian's chest. He knew Hagen was right, and he knew it was exactly how his sister would have reacted as well.

"How was your Architect here?" he forced himself to ask.

"One more reason I need you healed and on the road," Hagen said as he backed out of the room. "We need to know how many Scrolls the Infi have gotten their hands on."

Dorian hated that he had to rely on both Corbin and Reverie to help him dress. Every time he moved, the cuts on his side would stretch, and despite their being closed, he was told his muscles still needed healing.

Were it any other day, he would have made sly remarks to them both, but his mind was spinning with all the possibilities of what the meeting was about, the thoughts of him not being able to connect with this sister, and lastly—what the fuck Hagen had meant about the Infi getting their hands on the Scrolls.

By the time they got down to the dais, a great crowd had gathered on all the upper levels to look down on it. Reverie had to walk in front of them to part the people so they could get down the steps. Every move was torture, and they had to stop twice for him to catch his breath.

It was the sight of some of them giving him low nods that made his eyes narrow as they reached the bottom level.

"Corbin," he managed, swallowing his pain. "Why are they nodding?"

"They're bowing," Corbin replied.

"Why would they do that?"

They reached the bottom of the dais steps, and before Corbin could answer, Hagen met them.

"Can you make it, or should I need to carry you?" Hagen said upon reaching him.

Dorian slipped himself out of Corbin's grasp and flipped Hagen off. "I can make it."

He had to hold up a hand to Corbin as the Belwark started to reach for him again. Determination poured through Dorian, and he forced his feet to move. He fought the vomit in the back of his throat with every lift of his knees. Pain tore through his abdomen, but he held his head high. The only thing he couldn't stifle were the tears rising in his eyes.

By the time he reached the chairs at the top of the thirty steps, he felt as if he'd climbed a mountain.

It wasn't just the Elders there.

Mons Magnus was sitting in Hagen's chair, grinning at him.

Every muscle in Dorian's body continued to flinch as he stood there, forcing his back straight and pulling his chin high.

"Relax, kid," Mons told him. "You're no longer on trial. Take a seat."

Dorian looked to Hagen, and Hagen smiled.

"Whether you stand or sit, the outcome of his meeting will be the same," Hagen said.

"I'll stand," Dorian forced himself to say. "What's this about?" He pushed breath into his lungs, ignoring his abs spasming at holding himself upright, as one of the Elders began to speak—Marius, he realized.

"You came into our realm a prisoner and a traitor to our friend and King." Marius stood from his chair and started deliberately towards him. "You dared to stand before us and claim your innocence and friendship to that King. You claimed you had nothing to do with his and the Queen's death. You stood before us with a boyish confidence in your eyes and demanded a worthy trial. And then you dared to ask for the same aid our High Elder had promised the High King and Queen." He paused just in front of Dorian, arms pushed behind his back.

"I do not know how you are alive. But you are. And I daresay you've earned every ash of respect our people have for you."

Dorian tensed.

And then Marius held out his hand to him. "You've got your aid, Prince Dorian," he said, and a smile rose on Marius's face. "You're free."

Dorian nearly puked.

His eyes closed as he exhaled the weight of everything, his head finally hanging. He exhaled the weight of his failures. He exhaled the weight of his promises.

He exhaled the fire.

Claps and shouts sounded. Emotion bubbled in his chest. He could feel the movement of feet all around as though the people were celebrating with one another. He let his head limp back onto his neck.

Sunlight coming through the glass dome overhead poured on his face. His body began to tremble, and he once more pushed back the tears.

Because all he could see behind his closed eyes was *them*. Aydra giving his hair a ruffle and grinning at him. Draven pushing him on the road together to do the work. To get his hands dirty as kings before him hadn't done.

To prove he was more than just another of the Promised line.

Over the last year, he'd wondered if he would be doomed to the same fate of Kings before him and he would inevitably fall into manipulation and one day burn or torture his sister. If it was something that would one day snap in him and he would not be able to stop it. And every day, he fought against those stories, desperate to be a greater person than all of them.

He wanted to earn the crown that was his birthright.

And his stomach knotted at accomplishing one step.

Someone clapped his shoulder, and for a moment, Dorian forgot he wasn't back at Magnice with Draven and Aydra standing in front of him.

He didn't realize he'd been unable to hold in his tears until he opened his eyes and the glisten shrouded his vision. Hagen stood in front of him, and one look at the High Elder's face told him he understood why Dorian was crying.

"Don't," he forced with a knowing smile, knowing whatever was about to come out of Hagen's mouth would send him over the edge.

Hagen smiled and clapped his cheek. "They would be proud of you," he told him.

Dorian groaned with the shake of his head, and his tears fell on the floor. "Fuck you, Hagen," he bantered, not even trying to keep the sobs away now.

But Hagen merely gave him another smile and then wrapped his arms around him as a brother would have.

Dorian almost collapsed, and not just because of his pain, but because between Hagen and Draven, he'd found the mentors he'd been searching for his entire life. A bond with another male to teach him and push him and show him what it meant to be a true leader of the people.

To teach him what it meant to be a leader who doesn't cower behind fire and a Council and sit back on a comfy throne.

To teach him how to be a King.

He knew he had a long way to go, but he was willing to put in the work if Hagen would show him how.

When Hagen pulled back, he patted Dorian's cheek, and Dorian nearly stumbled with the weight of how much pain he was in.

"Do you mind if I sit now?" Dorian managed.

Hagen's laugh bellowed over the talk of the temple. "How about the bath instead?" he asked him.

Dorian eyed him and sniffed back his tears. "You just want me to heat it for you."

"What? *No.* Why—Yeah, mate," Hagen admitted gruffly. "Yeah, that's definitely it."

37

Corbin and Hagen both helped Dorian down the dais and into the Temple bath. He wasn't the only one to sink into the great pool, though. Mons and Marius joined them, along with Corbin himself stripping down to settle in the water. Dorian used the little strength he had to bring the water to a nearing boil, then he sank against the bath wall.

The Blackhands had taunted Reverie in an attempt to get her to strip and join them, but she'd rolled her eyes and instead posted up between Dorian and Corbin on the edge to let her feet dangle in the pool instead of getting all the way in.

Dorian nearly fell asleep as he tuned the rest of them out. His eyes closed as he laid his head back and took in all that had just happened.

Despite the supposed victory, he knew it was only the first step in the long battle for the continued safety of his home and his crown. He knew they would be packing up in a week or so to travel to the Bryn— a three-day ride on horseback over rough and jagged terrain. To a place where it snowed half of the year and rained the other half.

Dorian shuddered at the thought of going back there. The last time he and Corbin had gone, he'd felt like his hair was standing on end the entire time. And now, with the thought that everyone in that town might be Infi, he dared to think what they would be walking into.

His thoughts were interrupted by the feeling of Reverie's hand in his hair, pushing his shaggy locks back and making goosebumps rise over his flesh. He didn't say anything to her, too fearful he might spook her. But what he did do was shift so that he could lean his head against her thigh, and she continued to toy in his soft locks.

He settled into the newfound feeling for a few blissful moments before opening his gaze and looking over to his Second, finding Corbin snickering at him. Hagen, Mons, and Marius were in their own conversation on the other side, not paying any attention to the three. Dorian splashed water at Corbin for mocking him.

Reverie flinched, a rare laugh emitting from her as she swatted at the pair. "You two are children," she mocked.

"Unfortunately, you're stuck with us," Corbin said as he settled his head back against the side.

Dorian glanced up at Reverie then, and the sight of her glistening gaze confused him. "What's wrong?" he asked. "Does the thought of you being jointed at our hips upset you that much?"

"Nothing... Just thinking about the other day on that field." Her lashes flickered up and down as though she were avoiding his eyes. "Prince, you scared me," she finally admitted. "You were dying."

Dorian's eyes narrowed at the comment. "I wasn't aware you cared that much."

She stared sideways at him, a soft smile daring to form on her lips. "I can't believe I'm saying this, but... You're *really* hard not to like."

Dorian fought a grin, his stomach fluttering along with his heart. "Corbin, next time she tells me she hates me, remind her of this moment."

Corbin huffed amusedly, but he didn't move. "I'll remind her of her cradling you and crying on that field."

Reverie's mouth dropped, and she kicked Corbin's shoulder. "I thought you were on my side," she exclaimed.

"Whoa—what did I miss?" Dorian asked, staring between them.

Reverie glared at Corbin, to which the Second grinned, but together they didn't speak anymore about it. Reverie suggested helping Dorian redress his wounds a few minutes later. Corbin helped him out of the pool and wrapped him in a towel to sit on one of the benches by the wall before going back and relaxing in the water once more.

Dorian tried closing his eyes as Reverie made the healing paste and gathered the bandages from another room in the Temple. And when she returned, Dorian immediately started grumbling about having to go through healing again. He hated it more than anything else.

Perhaps he was a bit spoiled after never having to actually endure elongated pain before.

"I am requesting another person to dress me next time I have a near-death experience," he said when she started blotting the paste over the burn from the beast's tail grabbing him.

"The next time you have a near-death experience, I'm putting you out of your misery myself," she said. "Or somehow acquiring waters from your mother so that we do not have to do this."

"Hey, kid—" Mons called out, having heard the conversation. "Was that your brother's sword I saw the other day?"

Dorian frowned. "It was. Why?"

"The one your mother made?"

Dorian exchanged a glance with Corbin.

"Why?" Corbin asked, and Dorian could see the worry on his features.

Mons rose from the bath, stark naked, and Dorian watched Reverie's eyes widen at the sight of his display before quickly averting her head back to mending him.

Dorian watched Mons as he crossed the space and sat on the bench beside them. Reverie's cheeks were red, and honestly, Dorian could also feel a twinge of heat on his own face.

"Could you put on anything?" Dorian asked, forcing his eyes to Mon's face and not the graciously endowed length Mons apparently had no intentions of covering up. "Anything at all. Perhaps a bandage even."

Mons grinned. "Modesty is not exactly a Blackhand's strong suit," he said. "Why? Do I make you uncomfortable?"

"Not me, but I'm sure Corbin might need to excuse himself soon. And Reverie's face might explode—*ow!*" She'd punched his side, and he nearly limped into the wall. "Fuck—I'm injured, woman."

"And you'll be a lot more injured if you speak for me again," she snapped.

Dorian grunted but settled himself again while she continued working. Mons was smirking delightedly between them when he looked back, as was Hagen and Corbin.

"Why did you want to know about my brother's sword?" Dorian asked, ignoring the others.

"You can turn any water into your mother's waters with it," Mons responded as though it were obvious.

Reverie tensed on his arm, and Dorian locked eyes with Corbin. Corbin shook his head, but Dorian needed to know.

"How do I do that?" Dorian asked.

"No," Corbin said firmly.

"I'm not saying we have to use it," Dorian argued. "But it would be nice to know how."

"Nothing good—"

Dorian held a hand up, and Corbin grunted before pushing himself underwater. Dorian locked eyes with Mons again. "Tell me how."

Mons shifted, legs spreading and hand pressing into his thick knee. Reverie's head dipped low as she continued blotting Dorian, but Dorian saw her gaze flickering. So amusing that he hardly heard Mons speaking.

"Cut your hand with the blade and let the blood wash over the iron as it is in the water you want to change."

Dorian balked at the giver's instructions. It sounded too simple. "And that will turn the water to her healing water?" Dorian asked.

"Or poison for anyone else," Mons replied with a shrug. He stood then and clapped Dorian's shoulder upon passing. "See you all at dinner."

Reverie's eyes were still wide and staring at Dorian's arm, almost fixated on a point. But Mons's finger flicked her ponytail, and she flinched.

"Dreamer," he teased with a wink.

Dorian watched Mons exit the room, and once he was gone, an audible exhale left Reverie.

"Is he gone?" she asked.

"Yeah," Dorian answered. "He's gone."

"Thank the Architects," she muttered. "It felt like that thing was staring at me. What—is he part fucking horse?" she said, voice going high-pitched at the end.

Dorian snorted at her fluster. "Lesser One," he winked.

"There is nothing lesser about him," she argued. "*Fucking Somniarb,*" she cursed under her breath. "It is burned in my retinas now."

Movement sounded in the bath, and Hagen also pushed himself out. He was decent enough to wrap himself in his robe. "Dag's for dinner," he told them. "His wife decided to make our Prince a victory meal."

"I wasn't aware Dag was married," Dorian replied.

"Wait until you see her," Hagen muttered. "You'll be asking how he landed such a beauty." A sly brow elevated on Hagen's face that reminded Dorian of Draven, and Hagen gave them an upwards nod. "An hour. She doesn't like tardiness," Hagen said.

As Hagen left the Temple and the quietness settled between the three, Dorian met Corbin's stare.

"No," Corbin said firmly.

"You don't even know what I was going to say."

Corbin rose from the pool, and he also didn't bother to put on clothes. "I know you're thinking of using that sword to bring your mother's waters."

"What if I was?"

"*Architects*, Corbin, put on clothes," Reverie glared. "I swear I've seen more cocks here in these mountains in just a few weeks than I have my entire life," she grunted.

"You say that as though you haven't enjoyed the displays," Dorian bantered.

"The male appendage isn't exactly a work of beauty when it is simply... *limp*," she argued.

"So you'd rather they all be erect around you?"

She huffed, mouth opening and closing as she chose her words. "I— You know what?" she finally said, hands surrendering into her lap.

"Yes. I said it. If you're all going to walk around showing them off, you may as well show them off in their full glory. Except for Mons—" she added fast. "I don't... If he walked around with it erect, he'd poke someone's eye out."

Dorian snorted, and Reverie sank her finger into one of his bruises until he whimpered.

"Anyway—" Corbin said as he reached them, still naked but using a towel to dry himself. "You don't know what could happen if you turned those waters to your mother's," he said, getting back to their conversation. "We don't know if she's actually confined to that tree. You bring her waters somewhere else, and you could free her."

"I'm not saying turn an entire river or pool into her waters. Just maybe—what about one pail? A bucket. She can't pop out from a bucket, can she?" Dorian asked.

"Do you truly want to find out?" Corbin asked.

Silence rested between them.

Dorian's heel began to tap on the floor as Reverie put the paste on the scratch by his collar. "If it meant not having to endure any more of Reverie's terrible caregiving, I might consider it more," he finally said, smirking sideways at her.

"I thought she was entrapped? Or dead?" Reverie asked. "Whatever the Venari did to her."

"No one's ever killed a Lesser One before," Corbin said.

"Is it even possible?" Dorian wondered.

But Corbin and Dorian both seemed to have the same thought at once.

Rhaif's sword.

"You think?"

Corbin wrapped his arms over his chest, giving the notion apparent thought. "Maybe you should have sliced through that Architect. We'd have found out."

"But would that mean any weapon made by a Lesser One could kill them?" Dorian wondered aloud. "And you wouldn't let me use it against him."

"I stand by that decision," Corbin affirmed. "How many other weapons have been made by Lesser Ones?"

Dorian shrugged. "Draven's horn. Not exactly like he could have stabbed her with that, though. I don't believe the phoenix blades were made by Duarb. I think that was Draven's design."

For a moment, the pair settled into their thoughts, stillness ringing between them. Until—

"Too bad we can't," Dorian said, realizing it would be a mistake to kill her.

Corbin's head tilted. "After all she's put your family through, you don't want to end her?"

"I definitely do," Dorian said. "But if we do, there won't be a backup plan for if we screw something up in this Age."

Corbin cursed. "The fucking Signs."

"Yeah," Dorian grumbled. "The fucking Signs."

"What signs?" Reverie asked. "What are you two on about? Why would you want your mother dead? If she did come when you changed the waters, wouldn't that be beneficial to you? Perhaps she could help."

Dorian kept forgetting how much she didn't know. He sighed, and Corbin gave him a half-smile.

"I'll let you handle that," Corbin muttered as he slipped on his clothes.

"What's wrong with your mother?" Reverie asked.

"Remind me to tell you of her crimes one day," Dorian mumbled. "It's too long of a story for tonight."

Corbin huffed at them and slipped his shirt on. "I'll meet you both up at Dag's for dinner."

The Belwark gave the door two slaps as he exited. Reverie continued smearing the paste on his wounds, face squinted in concentration. Her finger pressed deep against one of the bruises, and she rolled her eyes when he grunted.

"Spoiled," she repeated.

He eyed the smugness on her features. "You know, I've not seen anyone blush like that in years," he said, referring to when Mons had walked naked around the room.

"Oh, I'm *sorry*," she drawled. "Did you not see that thing?"

"Oh, I did," Dorian chuckled.

"That thing could make the Sun blush," she said. "What do you even do with it? That cannot possibly fit anywhere."

Dorian laughed aloud, her banter bringing a swelling to his chest that he'd not felt in a long time. "Maybe he can change the size of it."

"Fuck, I hope so," Reverie said. "Those poor people who have ended up in bed with him."

"Maybe that's why he and Arbina never got on."

"Yeah, he probably whipped it out; she took one look and said, 'You're joking. You want that where?'" she laughed, shaking her head. "I wonder: are all Lesser Ones so graciously endowed?"

He eyed her. "Making me feel a bit inadequate, Rev," he said, faking hurt.

"You're certainly not inadequate," he heard her mutter under her breath, to which he couldn't help his smile from broadening.

Reverie paused in wiping his arm and finally looked at him, lips twitching at the corners as though she were trying to fight a grin. "Tell me the Prince of Promise isn't intimidated by the great body of Mons Magnus," she mocked.

"I'm not intimidated," he said fast.

Reverie snorted, and Dorian's cheeks began to heat beneath her stare.

"Keep training with them, Prince," she cooed. "Perhaps you'll get to his stature one day. Although—" her fingers trailed up his stern bicep. "I will say you have gotten stronger since being here."

He didn't miss the playful dilation in her eyes. "Nice to know you've been keeping track of my shoulder breadth," he mocked.

"The only reason I noted it was when your shirt was tugging around your back and shoulders this morning. And—" her voice trailed, and she started spinning up the bandage.

"And what?"

"And when you were dying in my arms, I noted how much broader you felt," she said. "I don't remember feeling so small against you when I cornered you in the Forest."

Dorian huffed amusedly. "We should fight again."

"We should," she agreed, and he could see the pride in her eyes. "Though I'm inclined to believe your wanting to fight me has more to do with your wanting my legs around you however you can have them rather than you actually wanting to fight."

"You don't have to sound so repulsed by it."

Reverie stood to gather the bandages and paste she'd made a mess of while cleaning him. "You would love that, wouldn't you?" she teased. "My giving in to your charms."

"It'd be nice to finally bed my wife," he bantered, sure she would hit him again at his words.

She shook her head, but the smirk didn't fade. "Is that what you would rather a handmaiden have done when tending to her poor, wounded soldier? Bed you?"

He wasn't sure what was happening, but the intensity in the air had changed, and he found himself leaning his back against the stone, watching every flex of her enticing body, every flinch of her long lashes.

Dorian stiffened as she pressed before him and her finger brushed over the cut on his cheek. He couldn't stop himself from leaning into her touch.

"Would you rather I have—" she straddled over his waist, and Dorian couldn't look away as she sat facing him on his knees. He forced a swallow, his heart beginning to skip.

"—tended you like this?" she asked, eyes darting over his wounds. "With my legs wrapped around you?"

Dorian didn't know what to do with his hands.

"Perhaps kissed your skin—" her lips brushed over the healed scratch from the last match on his collar, and the sensation sent chills down his spine, an involuntary groan sounding from his throat "—taken care of my Prince the way you've always been taken care of?"

Her hand traveled down his taut chest, all the way to the gash wound, and his abs flinched at her touch.

"Careful, Reverie," he made himself utter. He dared to move his hands to her thighs, hesitant to do anything that might spook whatever toying she was doing with him right then.

"Would you like me to worship your scars as a symbol of your great triumph?"

Her mouth dipped to the crook of his neck, and Dorian's hands tightened around her legs. His breath shortened as she scooted further onto his lap until he felt the dig of her hips into him, and he realized he had not guarded himself.

Because the moment her mouth opened on the front of his throat and her tongue dragged across the lump, he felt himself hardening against her.

He wanted to plow that beautifully smirking face. But her hand wrapped the hair at the base of his neck, and he shuddered at the chill down his spine when she once more moved on his lap.

"There he is," she teased, coy brow lifting. Shoulders rising, her hand curling in his hair, she began to move her hips deliberately against him, each stroke firmer, and all Dorian could do was curse under his breath. He didn't know why he wasn't moving. Why he was sat frozen on that seat and letting her take him without doing all he wanted to do to her.

Perhaps because it had been too long since he allowed a dangerous woman to take control of him. He hadn't had that since the week before the banquet with Bala—and even she had merely strung him up in ropes to play. It wasn't what Reverie was doing.

Reverie was torturing him in a way that made him want to surrender.

His eyes opened, and he met the sweep of her darkened lavender gaze. Her hand moved between them as he let his head lean back against the wall again. One touch of her on his cock made him groan into the quiet air. He could feel his muscles starting to reach with every movement of her against him. Her fingers on his tip through the towel. Her thick thighs around his waist, pelvis grinding into his. Her breasts pushing against his chest.

It was the moment she moved the towel down that his heart dropped into his stomach. A sharp breath took her when she touched him. He cursed, head falling against her shoulder. Her touch was delicate on his tip, moving that bead of liquid over his length.

"Do you like this, Prince?" she uttered in his ear. "Is this what you wanted?"

"Yes," he breathed.

He needed her. He needed her around him. He needed her lips against his and her naked body flush. He dared to move his hand to her cheek, intent on kissing her—

But she grasped his throat and shoved him back against the wall. A brow elevated on her commanding face as she lifted her chin.

Fuck, he nearly came apart right then.

A slow smirk spread on her lips, and her hand tightened around his length. His chest caved with every shortened breath. The harshness of her fingers loosened around his throat, and she began to massage the soft indentions on either side of the lump in his neck just as her other hand moved on his cock.

"Handmaidens don't usually treat me with such *violence*," he mocked.

"Seems to me you've not had the right sort of handmaiden then."

She had moved so that his length was against her clothed folds, and he wondered if she was intent on enjoying herself as much as she was intent on draining him dry. Dorian's gaze fluttered with a groan, and then she released his neck to grab onto the wall behind him. His head sank onto her shoulder again, hands grasping at her hips now as he held her tighter against him.

He had lost control, and he was spiraling into her grasp faster than he could stop himself. A low groan emitted from him as she continued to toy with his hair, her hips grinding up and down against the shaft with her hand. Faster and harder. His forehead rolled against her shoulder as he fought the release.

"Fuck, *Reverie*," he uttered pleadingly.

She smelled of vanilla and snow, and he wanted to sink himself within her the rest of the day. Dinner with the Blackhands, be damned. He wanted this. Every torture of her. He began to flinch, and she knew it too.

"Let go, Dorian," she whispered against his ear.

The sound of his name sent him over the edge. He came apart beneath her grasp. The tremble raked over his body. He settled onto her as he came down, and she held him against her shoulder, one hand moving in his hair and pulsing down his neck, the other spreading his release over his length and milking him dry. He groaned at the pleasure sweeping through him.

His arms tightened around her and the soft trim of her nails scratched his scalp, making every hair rise on his body.

"Keep grasping my ass, Prince, and you won't have hands," she uttered in his ear.

Dorian huffed against her and his hands moved to her waist. "Yes, my love."

The smile he'd been intent on teasing her with faltered when he pulled back. She had brought the hand she'd been using to pleasure him with to her lips, and she was sucking on the skin between her thumb and forefinger.

Licking his cum off her hand.

Dorian forgot his own name.

She made a pleased groan as she licked her thumb, a wicked delight in her eyes upon obviously seeing him stammer before her. "That tastes like fire, too," she teased him.

Dorian couldn't help himself.

He kissed her before she could move.

She balked at first, almost pulling away, but he grabbed her behind her head and pulled her forward, his teeth dragging against and biting her bottom lip, and he felt her almost collapse into his grasp. She pushed her hips against his again and wrapped her arms around him. Desperate and fighting, he kissed her like she would kill him at any moment. Their lips crashed together again and again. His head spun. She bit his tongue, and he groaned into her mouth. Both his hands pushed behind her neck to bring her closer—

Her hand flew back around his throat. They parted fast, and Dorian's head slammed into the wall again.

Chest heaving, he swallowed as her lavender gaze blazed through him. But despite the flare of her nostrils and the shortness of her breath, he swore he saw her lips twitching upwards at the corners.

"Do not think this was anything more than my taking care of your *poor* injured self," she warned him, and he could detect the play in her tone. "And I'm not your love."

Dorian huffed, daring to smile as he felt his cheeks flushing. "Yes, ma'am," he bantered, arms bending at his elbows in surrender.

She shoved his chest as she stood, and he winced at the jolt.

"I think you owe me another round for that," he choked.

Reverie bent down to the pool and stuck her hand in the water to wash away whatever was left of Dorian's release. Her bangs fell over her eyes as she dried her hand with a towel, and she met his eyes again.

"You should clean yourself up," she told him. "I would hate for the rest of the town to see you in such a disheveled state," she teased.

"This is Dahrkenhill. I'm sure they've seen worse." He leaned back on the bench and wiped himself with the towel.

When he looked back up, he noted the squeeze of her thighs, the blush on her cheeks, and the avoidance of her gaze as she pushed her fur shawl over her shoulders.

"I could help with that," he uttered.

The corner of her lip quirked, and the smoldering jest on her features made him shift. "I'm sure you could," she said. "But you'll have to earn that just as you've earned these people's trust."

She pushed the things back into the bag again, and as she shoved it on her shoulder, intentions of leaving him, Dorian realized something.

"Hey, Rev?"

"Yes, Prince?" she sighed, slight annoyance in her tone.

He rubbed the back of his neck. "Could you help me to Dag's? Can't exactly move very much on my own," he admitted.

A small smile spread on her face, and she pushed the bag further up her shoulder. "Corbin left on purpose, didn't he?"

"Definitely," Dorian replied, meeting her eyes.

She shook her head, chuckling under her breath. "Fine. I'll grab new clothes for you. Just don't do anything stupid until I return."

38

Dinner at Dag's had been exactly what Dorian needed. The camaraderie and songs. The laughter and smoke. He may have sat in the corner most of the night, hardly able to move, but he was glad to have had Corbin and Reverie seated on the floor by his side. He heard them tell them stories of Reverie's training with Katla and how Katla was pushing her until she puked.

Watching the pair laugh together made his stomach knot. It was weird not being at the center of the room and telling jokes or come-ons to every woman there. He was able to see everything going on in the room from where he sat, and he silently wondered if this was how Nyssa felt when she would stand or sit over to the side in every crowd to watch. The thought of her made his heart hurt, but he shook it from his mind and pushed his attention back to his present.

Hagen had been right. Dag's wife was much prettier than Dorian would have ever guessed, and he had a sneaking suspicion Dag was much more of a romantic than anyone realized.

It wasn't a great crowd at Dag's. Only about ten people. It was cozy enough that by the end of the night, they had all crowded around Dag's sitting room and were passing pipes and smoking herb. With his injured condition, the herb had gone quickly to Dorian's head, and he hardly remembered how he got back to the Temple.

For seven days after the decision, Dorian was forced to stay in his bed. Hagen told them he would give them another two weeks for Dorian to heal before they set off for the Bryn. He thought that would give them time to get there and get things sorted before the next rise of the Dead Moons.

For once, Dorian did as he was told. He rested, knowing he would need all his strength for traveling. Reverie and Corbin tended to him at all hours of the day, and Dorian started to wonder if they were sleeping in the room with him, as every time he would wake up, at least one was in there.

Dorian had taken his time with Reverie as an opportunity to tell her of some of the stories he'd learned had been lies through the last year. He was grateful she actually listened to him and asked questions. Every time he told her of one, he saw the same break in her face that had been in his own.

On the seventh night, Dorian decided he'd had enough of the Temple and had walked with Corbin down to the tavern. He was greeted with claps on his shoulder that made him wince, but the smiles on their faces swelled his chest. The women that leered at him and brushed his arms when they passed had his mind once more wandering.

Corbin shook his shoulders as Dorian propped up by the bar. He told him that he had to settle a game of dice with Damien, and then he left him. His warning to Dorian not to get himself into trouble only made Dorian smirk.

As he settled alone and asked for a whiskey from the bartender, Dorian took in the familiar scene: the drinking and the terrible dancing, the haze of the smoke in the amber-lit room, the boasting and laughing, the drunken brawls over games of dice or darts.

Fucking Mons, he loved this place.

It was a closeness and freedom he'd discovered he craved from his first visit. To not have to project such a royal face here. Somewhere he could just... *Be*. Without the worry of a kingdom in ruin. Without fear of the war on their shores and the treachery of his brother and his people.

There were moments when he contemplated giving up every thought of the war and simply living out his days there in peace. When he considered going to the Umber, kidnapping his sister, and bringing her back there, desperate to keep her safe while the rest of their world fell into servitude and squander.

At least they would be okay. At least they would live.

But every time such a thought entered his mind, he remembered what all he'd accomplished in his time there, and he knew he couldn't give all that up when he'd come so far.

His gaze continued to wander around the room to the groups of men and women, all laughing, some dancing. Giggles and slaps from the women when men they knew would grab their asses playfully and whisper sexual banter in their ears. The women would do the same, each as aggressive as the person they were bringing back to bed with them.

Dorian caught a glimpse of Hagen on the stool at the opposite end of the bar with Katla pushed between his legs, her head dipped in front of him. Hagen squeezed the backs of her thighs. His mouth brushed Katla's jaw, and Dorian didn't miss the whirl of her dagger suddenly pointed at Hagen's jaw for whatever it was Hagen had just said. But Hagen didn't seem to care, not then, not with the smokey haze and drinks in them. He grinned at Katla, dare in his gaze, and then he kissed her hard.

Dorian took a long drink upon the bartender setting his whiskey down in front of him.

"Congratulations on your victory, Prince," Smyths said, wiping out a cup with his rag. "That last trial was quite a feat. I think I speak for most of us when I say we are glad to see you back on your feet."

Dorian raised his cup. "I appreciate that," he said sincerely.

"What will you do now?"

"I think I'll stay for a bit," Dorian replied as his eyes washed around the room once more.

"Not eager to get back to the war, are you?"

"Is there a reason I should be?" Dorian asked.

Smyths smiled at him. "I'll keep your drinks coming."

Dorian thanked him again with a raise of his cup, and then he knocked back the familiar nyghtfire. A couple of women came up to him after a few minutes, and Dorian pulled his usual flirtatious banter up, making them giggle and swoon. Until the pair gave him directions to their home, and Dorian told them he would find them later in the night.

After a while, he made his way back outside to still in the night air, allowing the chill over his bones. He'd just sat down at one of the tables by the edge of the square and pulled his pipe from his pocket when he heard the noise of Reverie's laugh.

He recognized it because it was so rare that he'd committed it to memory.

She was laughing at a Blackhand's joke over by the tavern door. He had his arm pressed over her against the wall. She swirled the drink in her cup and shook her head when he whispered something in her ear.

Dorian felt his jaw stiffen, and he started packing his pipe a little more ravenously than before.

He didn't bother looking away, not even when she looked over and caught his gaze. A knowing smirk spread over her lips, and he continued to watch her. She pressed on the Blackhand's chest after a few more laughs and then turned to join Dorian.

"You should guard your gaze," she said as she approached. "Or at least your form."

"I wasn't aware you were seeing a Blackhand," he said, voice a little more snappy than he meant it to be.

"Neither was I," she countered. "You have a problem with my flirtation?"

"Nope," he assured her, lips popping the 'p.'

But even as the conversation seemed to be over, Reverie smiled and sat on the tabletop.

"I'm curious, Prince," she said. "If we weren't going to the Bryn, would you have decided it was time to go to my village?"

"Are you really so desperate to get back to whatever life it was you had before this?" he asked, head tilting.

Reverie considered it, an evident surprise stretching over her features. But she didn't ponder it long. Her hand tightened around her cup. "No," she decided. "But I wonder if you are."

His eyes met hers for a long time, long enough that he almost forgot he was packing his pipe. "Have you given more consideration to our deal?"

"Why is it you thought you ever had to offer that deal?" she asked. "Do you not think people will follow you of your own accord? That you need to strike such deals to make people do what you need?"

"Are you saying you would follow me without one?"

Reverie set her cup down. "You fought in those trials, not as a Prince of Promise, not even as a son of Arbina, and certainly not for your own life. You fought for *them*. You came to this town looking for acceptance and an alliance. And you found it."

Dorian tossed away the stem of the herb he'd just plucked from. His feet kicked up, landing on the tabletop, and he leaned against the stone wall at his back. "You didn't answer my question."

"What question?"

"If you would follow me without the deal."

The gaze she stared at him with made his movements pause.

"I think I would follow you into my village," she finally said. "I would watch as you commanded respect from every person... Faced

362

down the lies and the shouts of treachery, all to prove yourself a worthy King and savior of our realm. And I think I would find myself between you and them, your Second at my side, protecting you from the rope they would try to place around your neck."

If he'd been standing, he'd have grabbed her and kissed her.

But all he could do was gawk and try to process the progression of her feelings towards him.

"So you'll take the position?" he asked.

She looked like she might smile. "I'll not be calling you my King. Not yet. Perhaps not any time soon. But I would like to keep you alive long enough to see you earn the title and crown."

"That's fair," he agreed.

Silence rested between them as he finished, and he lit the herb with his finger before drawing in a deep inhale and holding it. His gaze flashed over Reverie sitting opposite him on the top of the table, allowing his eyes to rest on her hips and hands wrapping around the cup. For a moment, he remembered the feeling of those hands wrapped around his cock, and his mind wandered to how it would feel to taste her, her thighs squeezing his face as he devoured her...

The exhale of herb left him, and he met her lilac eyes. A faint smirk rose on his lips as he cleared his throat.

"You should get some sleep," he said, knowing he would take that image with him to whomever's bed it was he would be in later.

"Pushing me away for once?"

He took another long inhale of the smoke, eyes fluttering as he began to feel the swim of it. "Unless you've finally decided to give in to this little dance and allow me to bring you to your end here on this table, I suggest you walk away."

She swung around, legs falling over the edge of the table at his side. "Tell me what would happen if I didn't."

Fire flashed in his eyes.

The bench crashed on its side at the rate he rushed to his feet. She didn't have time to protest before he'd pushed her legs apart and pressed himself between them.

Her knife met his throat the moment his hands met the wood on either side of her. The press of the cold iron against his skin made him smile and his heart thud. He could smell the fire of the forges in her hair as he leaned his head towards her, his nose brushing her cheek.

"Do you still want to know?" he asked, both aroused and wary by the knife at his throat.

Her feet tucked behind his knees just so, chin tilting as her gaze fell upon his. "Yes."

He moved deliberately. His nose brushed her cheek, his hair entwining with her bangs when he shifted across her face, their lips grazing but not consuming. He felt her suck in a breath when his lips dragged across her jaw to her collar. He paused at the spot beneath her ear, only to flick his tongue on her earlobe.

Lower, he went. He stilled again upon reaching her supple breasts, his lips whispering over her shirted nipple.

"If you stayed, I would edge you from here," he breathed against her breast. "Watch you grip this table and my hair, hear my name beg from your lips as I took you and held you at your end for so long this table would begin to shake."

He watched as the goosebumps rose on her arms, and he didn't stop. His lips brushed her stomach. He kissed down her front, feeling her chest and belly rise and fall with every jagged breath.

Slowly, his knees met the ground, and he chanced a touch of his hands behind her calves, noticing how her feet had pointed, knees almost lifting as though she were tensing every fiber of her being. She didn't protest at his touch, though the knife was still there, reminding him of her power over him.

Dorian looked up at her as he pressed his lips to her calf and then trailed up to the bend at her knee, closer and closer to the apex between her thighs. He paused at a hover there, and his gaze fluttered as he restrained himself. He wanted to rip her pants off, take her in his mouth right there, make her scream his name for every person in Dahrkenhill to hear.

His lips brushed the seam, and her thighs jerked.

"Tell me you don't want this, Reverie," he uttered, looking up at her.

The blade didn't move from beneath his chin. But the dilation in her eyes and heave in her chest made his muscles sing. He turned his head to kiss the inside of her thigh, still holding her eyes. He saw her swallow, watched her tongue dart out over her dry lips. He nudged between her thighs again and then dragged his tongue along the seam.

"Tell me you don't want me to devour you here."

Her hand was in his hair, and he thought she would jerk him off her. But she merely ran her hand through the now shagginess of his black locks, and he looked up at her again. His teeth tugged on the fabric, and her mouth visibly sagged.

"Tell me you want this," he whispered again, pressing his lips between her thighs. "Tell me you want me to kiss you here—" he kissed the seam "—To have my tongue send you over the Edge—" his tongue dragged up that fabric ridge again, his hands tightening around her thigh and calf. "—To take you right here on this table for everyone to hear."

There was a quiet pause, and then—

"Yes."

A low groan emitted from him, and his heart skipped.

Fuck, he hadn't expected that.

He had to pause a moment to let that word register. Her hips pushed forward, and he tugged that seam between his teeth again. All he had to do was burn that fabric, and she was his. He could have her. Take her. *Claim* her. Make her scream his name loud enough for every other person in that damned town to hear.

It took every bit of restraint he had to do what he did next.

He stood.

She ogled at him, mouth sagging, and he pressed his palms back into the table on either side of her hips.

"Here I thought you wanted to make good on your claims," she managed, her free hand grasping at his shirt as he towered over her.

The corner of his lip quirked, and he leaned forward, close enough that he was sure she thought he would kiss her, but he paused.

"I want you to beg for me as you're making me beg for you, Reverie," he growled. "I want you to feel on edge and unable to restrain yourself as you make me feel. Completely surrendered and fighting your instincts. When that happens, I'll taste every inch of you and keep you on that edge until every muscle in your beautiful body *shakes*." His nose dragged along her cheek, breath tickling at her ear when he spoke his next words.

"You will *shatter* before me."

Her lashes lifted to his, and she grasped his shirt tighter. "Big words from a fire Prince."

Dorian reached for his pipe. He pressed it between his lips and inhaled a long draw as he continued to hover. The herb swam in his body, and he placed a finger beneath her chin to tilt her head back.

"Promises from your King."

The silky smoke dragged out from his mouth as he spoke, and he watched Reverie's mouth open. His lips brushed hers as she inhaled it.

The sensation of her lips so close and watching her inhale that smoke nearly sent him back to his knees. But Dorian pushed off the table, pausing only to watch her catch herself from falling over in his absence, and he forced his feet to walk away.

Had he stayed any longer, he would have ignored his own words. He would have thrown her back on that table and done exactly what he'd promised.

The herb filled his lungs, and the remainder of the night became a haze.

A haze of mouths and naked bodies. Of an unfamiliar room and unfamiliar women. He was consumed by the whiskey and smoke that numbed his pain and deterred his wandering mind.

A haze he only remembered glimpses of the next morning when he woke outside in the snow. Body blue and begging for warmth. Someone, not Corbin, helped him to his feet and wrapped a fur around his shoulders. He hardly got his legs to move, but the person helped him to the Temple and up to his room where he fell into his bed.

The only glimpse of the person he got was an axe on their side.

39

The morning was bustling when sunlight peeked through the roof and onto Nyssa's body.

She was stiff with the terror of the day before, of the whip the wife liked to use. She'd been punished after being put back in her room after the latest meeting. The meeting had gone well. She'd stayed after to inform the Noble of the exaggerations of his guests. But it wasn't Quinn who had escorted her back to her room.

Shae had discovered her husband using Nyssa to do his bidding and taken it upon herself to take Nyssa back to the room and interrogate her herself. Nyssa had taken Shae's verbal abuses with a clench of her jaw. She'd stood stiff as the wife accosted her about how much of a whore she was for being the only woman in a room full of men and reporting lies back to her husband. She'd told her her husband was only using her for a show.

And then she'd brought in the whip.

A strike for every time Nyssa didn't respond to her question.

A lashing for every time the wife thought her husband wanted to bed her.

And finally, when the wife had stripped her to look over the scars on her shoulders and told her they were worse than the spots, Nyssa lost it.

She'd lunged at the wife in her chains and called her a fool for not realizing burns would scar.

Nyssa had been so exhausted and enraged by the wife's idiocy that she couldn't help herself.

The whip had come down across her back five more times for the comment. And she'd not been reclothed or cleaned after.

Nyssa begged herself to move, even if it was only an inch. Her body felt heavier than it had the day before, as though the slats on her back had broken her somehow. But she forced movement into her bones, wanting to at least push some blood through her veins and frigid muscles.

The shackle on her ankle clanked, and she reached down to rub the rawness beneath it. The scarlet rash was welted on her flesh. Her heart numbed, and she laid back down on the hard wood.

Breathe, Nyssa, she could hear her sister and brother saying.

One.

Two.

Three.

All the way up to fifty-six.

One inhale for every day since her sister's death.

One exhale for every day she knew she might one day try to shudder out—even though she knew she couldn't.

Her lungs were tight with the smoke she'd breathed in.

But she would keep inhaling it.

And she would exhale the fire of her reality.

For her family.

For her friends.

For the freedom she hoped to one day secure for her people.

For Haerland.

The shriek of her eagle sounded overhead as she laid on her stomach, her arms forked out at her sides. Her eagle, whom she had only just been able to speak with again the night before.

At least with him there, she was not completely alone.

Tears ran down her numb face as the wood cradled her striped muscles.

Thirty days until the Dead Moons rose.

Forty-four days until spring.

She could do this.

It had been two weeks since the deal with the Noble. She'd only seen sunlight once. The meetings had been more of a repeat of information as the previous ones, and she'd spent most of the time simply choosing one person to memorize at a time.

Luka continued to watch her the longest, and she was starting to wonder if he knew what the Noble was using her for. He had left the day before to go to Savigndor. His men were arriving within a week, and he wished to make sure their quarters were in line before they came.

During the trading meeting, there had been more talk of an Haerlandian trader coming to bring exotic goods and furs that they could use to send across the ocean as currency to trade with and bring more items over. The Noble was skeptical about the goods, but he asked the messenger to inform the trader he would be welcome at their estate nonetheless.

Nyssa wondered if the trader was Nadir, but she wouldn't get her hopes up. She didn't think he was stupid enough to come to the settlement himself when he had more important things to worry about.

She certainly hoped he wasn't stupid enough to be letting a messenger go all the way to the Umber.

It was an hour more before Porter Quinn came to bring her a bucket of water to wash the grime off herself with. The maidens had stopped bathing her a few days before. The wife had them doing other things, and now that her 'reconstruction' was over with, the wife said Nyssa would not need tending to again until closer to their Prince's arrival.

Even picking up the washcloth was more of a chore that morning than it had been the days before. It felt bulky in her hand, though she knew it wasn't. She knew it was only as heavy as her mind made it, but that morning... *Something* about that morning... whether it was the chill of the winter air, the streaks of the lashing she'd received the day before, or the starve of her stomach, she didn't know. But she hardly felt like bending her muscles or opening her eyes. She half thought her lungs would give out on her at any moment, that she would crumble beneath gravity and fall into a heap on the floor.

A coreless shell of what once was a beautiful Princess, primed for the battle she was now losing.

This place will not take me today.

The Porter brought her a new dress that hung off of her deteriorating body. It would have been pretty under normal circumstances. A simple light blue, flowing and wool, with fitted sleeves and a square neck, a rope belt to cinch in the waist attached to it. She clenched it in her fists as she sat on her knees. The thread of the wool scratched her skin and bled beneath her raw fingertips.

She cherished every touch of reality that wasn't a punishment.

She lifted the dress to her cheek and closed her eyes, fantasizing that it was another person's touch—a callused hand telling her it was okay. That she had survived nearly six weeks of this.

That she would survive the next few.

Endure.

The knot she had to tie in the belt made her curse. Muscles and fat that she'd worked so hard for over the years... squandered with starvation. The feel of her rib bones made her shudder and her jaw tremor as she repressed the waking memory of it.

She braided her hair over her shoulder and left her side-swept bangs to hang down over the sides of her face—a small comfort to hide the lessened spark in her eyes.

The Noble had continued doting on her. She wondered if he were making it more of a show now that he had her tasking for him. Trying to make her appear less suspicious by calling her a beautiful prize and saying she was mindless. It was all a show, and she hated herself being on display.

As her mouth clenched at the memory, she noticed the black ash suddenly rising on her fingertips, and she shut her eyes tight to quell the frustration inside her that threatened combustion at every waking moment.

No longer could she feel her heart ricocheting in her chest. She wondered if perhaps the wife had somehow ripped it from her the day she was handed over. She wondered how Shae could have replaced it with the nothingness Nyssa was doomed to feel for the rest of her days —as numbered as they were.

The noise of horses and carts filled her ears as she crouched down to the floor again, hugging her thighs against her chest but not sitting. Her forehead met her knees, and she closed her eyes. Another tear trickled down her cheek.

One.

Only for a moment. Only for a breath.

She knew the only reason she'd been given a new dress and bathing water was that the Noble wanted to show her off to those coming in from the other two estates with tradable goods. The High Noble, first crusader, and conqueror of the southwestern Haerland shore. And he had the rare Haerlandian slave to prove it.

There had been more talk of the Haerlandian tribe trader coming to bring goods, but Nyssa had heard no more details, and the Noble hadn't been forthcoming when she'd asked about it.

The shackle was taken off her ankle when the Porter came to fetch her.

He didn't bother binding her hands in front of her on that day.

The sun barreled in through the slats in the poorly made home as they walked down the hall. The Noble was keen on moving into his larger house within the next few weeks as he'd had slaves building it and the rest of their small village at every hour of the day and night—a constant stream of whipping and hammering filled the beach air.

Nyssa's eyes closed at the feeling of the sun beaming on her figure through the slats, as brief as it was. She craved the sunlight and the healing of her body that she knew it would give her. She craved it as she craved oxygen. The beat of its warmth on her flesh, the energy felt in her muscles as water riding over her bones... She could feel her lips quivering as she was shoved too quickly past the first glare of it that she'd felt in over a week.

Her broken lungs depleted in her chest. But she pushed the pain away as they rounded the last corner, and the audience she would be entertaining that day entered her blurry vision.

The smell of roasted chicken in the air, wafting with the stench of pig manure outside and the salt of the beach waves. The noise of men slopping at their food, the saliva, and gnashing of teeth as they chomped on the bones or swished their broth was cringe-worthy and demeaning to her ears.

Yet despite the grotesqueness of it, her stomach rumbled in yearning for any nutrients.

The Porter's hand tightened around her arm as they reached the table the Noble and his wife sat. The wife glared at her over her fork.

As her stomach grumbled again, she saw the Noble's mouth quirk out the corner of her eye, and he offered her a chicken leg as though offering a dog a bone.

Nyssa jerked her head high in response, making sure he remembered she would not be tempted. A low chuckle emitted from him, and the sound of it made her fist clench. Nyssa didn't speak, but she felt the saliva in her mouth as she craved the food, and she swallowed the spit, pretending perhaps it was soup.

She missed the taste of the honey bread she and Dorian had once attempted to make together as children.

Her body caved at the warm memory. She could see his lopsided grin as they threw flour at each other, his chasing her through the halls of the castle with the stuff—Willow shouting at them for being childish, Aydra laughing and then joining in on their fun. Dorian had accidentally thrown the white power at Lex's face that day, and she'd chased him all the way up to the tower dungeons before picking him up over her shoulder and hauling his eleven-year-old self back to the kitchens.

The tear streaked down Nyssa's cheek, nostrils exhausting as she pushed the distant memory to the back of her mind. Magnice seemed like a dream. As though she'd been suffering in the nightmare of the last few weeks her entire life, and her true home had only been a fantasy of the spy she was currently consumed by.

She wondered how Dorian was doing in Dahrkenhill and how Lex was holding up at the Umber... whether she'd left and gone back to the Venari kingdom to help Balandria or if she'd stayed to help Nadir.

What was left of Nyssa's heart broke at that moment, and she had to press her toes together and lock her knees to keep herself upright.

"What of the trades today?" the Noble asked one of the men who had just arrived.

The man gave a short nod and then opened his mouth to speak. Nyssa's mind blanked as she allowed her eyes to wander out the door, trying desperately to squint and see any shimmer of life other than those of Man. She could only see people herding chickens into a corral and a few women passing by with baskets.

"—A trader of the local Haerland tribe," she heard the man say. "He says he has furs and fruits from their forest."

Her ears perked at the conversation.

Nadir.

A lump leaped into her throat at the fantasy. Her chest began to heave, suddenly anxious with flashes of what could happen if Nadir did grace the estate. Her mind spun. She didn't think Nadir would be crazy enough to come trade with them himself. Not the actual Commander of the Honest army. Perhaps he'd simply sent one of his men to exchange or try and get information about their settlement.

The Noble gave the man a nod. "Bring him in."

The man disappeared through the door. She heard a shout, a familiar coy of words, an annoying twinge in the returning yell. She thought her chest would burst at any moment at the anticipation of whether it was him, and her feet shifted, sweaty hands suddenly clenching and unclenching around the fabric of her dress.

The moment the sun hit the caramel brown and sun-bleached curls and dreads, tied up in a high bun, and he straightened under the flap of the door— she had to remind herself to stay steady and not fall apart at the sight of him.

Nadir Storn stood in the doorway.

Her breaths edged. She tried to conceal it, but she wasn't sure she knew how. She didn't want him to see her like that— beaten, broken, and deteriorating. She was terrified of the reaction on his face she knew he would hardly be able to conceal.

But he looked up, a stern expression on his features as his gaze traveled over the people in the room. And when he found her, she watched as the anger slipped, and his chest visibly caved in on itself.

A tear cascaded down her cheek. She shook her head as much as she could without drawing attention to herself in the hopes he would understand her pleas for him not to identify her.

The color drained from his cheeks. His brows knitted together, and for a moment, he looked like he would move, but she pleaded with her body for him not to: head tilting, eyes furrowed, lips gritted firmly together. She tried to hold in her deteriorating core, and keep it from bursting to the surface and revealing everything.

Nyssa nearly stepped forward but thought better of it. Nadir's hand tightened around itself, the vein in his arm puckered. She could see the strain in his neck, the taut of his jaw, and she knew it was taking every muscle in his body to keep him from pulling his sword and wiping the whole of the room with blood.

The Noble spoke, but Nyssa didn't hear what was said. Nadir's eyes only flickered away from her own when the man asked him a question. The voices were echoes.

All she saw was him.

A ringing stretched through her eardrums. She looked down, seeing her nail beds turning black. Her hands she shoved behind her back, and she closed her eyes, willing her breath to calm.

"I wonder if I might be able to make an exchange, Your Grace," she heard Nadir say after a moment.

Their gazes met. She could hear the strain in his voice as though he were holding himself back from doing something that would cost him everything.

"Oh? What kind of exchange?" the Noble asked.

"My finest furs, in exchange for a night alone with this beautifully striking creature at your side."

Her heart swelled.

Her heart.

Her heart that had been numb an hour earlier, was suddenly back alive in her chest. Or perhaps it was the muscle memory of it—of the memory of what a heart should do, the beating and pumping and aching for a person so familiar and comforting—

For the safety of a simple touch.

The Noble reached for Nyssa's arm. She flinched at the abruptness of it. Her skin crawled with his possessive graze, the pinch of squander on her elbow. His eyes were on her, she knew, and she averted her own to the ground, determined not to look at Nadir. She knew if she did, he would go full Commander on the tent, and there would be no plan for her to go through with.

"You like her, trader?" Bechmen asked.

There was a pause, one long enough that Nyssa chanced a glance up at him. His nostrils moved with the shift of his weight, and a blank expression filled his eyes as he obviously pushed his true self to the very depths of his being.

"I wonder where you found such a creature," Nadir replied. "Or why anyone would give her up."

"Paid a high price for this one. We are having to break her in, of course."

"I'm sure," Nadir said. "Every cinnamon-haired woman I know from our land is much too ferocious to tame."

Her chest expanded at his words, stomach fluttering, and with it came the tremble of her jaw. His adornment echoed in her mind, and she missed the sentence he said next. But the Noble rose from his chair, and he clapped his hands together.

"Let's see these furs you speak of first."

Quinn pushed her arm, and she walked behind the wife outside the tent.

—*Sunlight.*

She nearly melted at the feeling of it wrapping her skin. Quinn led her to the side of the cart as the Noble and his wife began inspecting the goods, and Nyssa had to force herself to put one foot in front of the other, too entranced by the weight of warmth on her skin that she almost forgot how to walk.

Her sighing muscles sank into the abyss of it. She allowed her head to loll back, her eyes to close. Body weeping, jaw quivering, as she vibrated in its radiance. The heat of it seeped into her flesh, curling into her waning and exhausted muscles, down into the marrow of her bones. The winter sun's warmth mixed with the shrill wind shuddered her body—for once, she didn't mind the whirl of it around her. It whipped over the wet the tear had just made on her cheek, sending an icy shiver down her spine.

A reminder she was still alive.

Perhaps Duarb and the Sun were reminding her of her promises.

So she counted the breaths in her head as she soaked in the glow.

But it was the heated feeling of a body coming to stand beside her that made her entire being shake with the angst of such an overload. She dared not open her eyes, terrified if she did that, it would all be a dream.

Nadir.

Here.

Standing beside her as she soaked in the first sunlight she'd felt for more than a glimpse in over a week. She wept at the overwhelming anxiety of it. She wasn't sure she cared then if the wife caught her looking so disheveled. She was broken and free all at once.

And then her eagle cried out overhead.

"Hello, Princess."

She hardly heard him utter the words, but they shattered her existence nonetheless. She wasn't even sure he'd said them, or if perhaps it had just been her imagining them in her head, wishing for him to have said them to solidify his being at her side. But the silent tears seeped down her cheeks, her eyes pressed firmly together as though pressuring her brain to grasp hold of the reality.

Their words.

And when his fingers grazed her own, her entire body resigned into the reality of his being at her side. The hurt of her heart felt as though someone was tying a knot around it, binding and constricting it into the prison of her chest. She forced her knees straight so they didn't buckle beneath her. His pinky finger wrapped around her own, and she nearly vomited outright as the feelings overpowered her.

The warmth of his skin. The clench of his finger.

No touch had ever meant so much. It was a promise. A hello. An *'I've got you.'* Just his finger curled around hers. Even if they didn't get to speak, she knew everything she needed to know simply from that moment.

Sunlight blinded her when she finally opened her eyes. But it wasn't the light that made her grieve. It was the look in Nadir's own as he stared down at her. If she'd thought she was broken before, it was nothing compared to the cry of her body upon seeing the weeping dread in his swollen eyes and the tear settled in the corner creases.

She wanted to break the necks of every man there just to embrace him.

"I think these will work beautifully," the Noble declared.

Nadir and Nyssa both stiffened out of their dazes. Their heads turned quickly in the direction of the Noble—hands separating. She nearly lurched at the abruptness of it, but she straightened and pushed her shoulders back, careful to conceal any dried tears on her cheeks and hoping the Noble was stupid enough to think the swollen redness of her eyes was simply from her being tired.

"Very well, trader," Bechmen said. "One night with my slave for all of these furs plus the entire supply of foods you've brought."

"All of it?" Nadir repeated.

"Is that a problem?"

She could feel him gazing down at her, and as much as she wanted to meet his eyes, she knew if she did, she would collapse into a puddle and reveal it all.

"You can have everything."

As Nyssa was taken back inside, she saw the Noble nod to Quinn. She wasn't sure what was going on, but when Quinn took her to the Noble's room instead of back to her own, she wondered if perhaps Bechmen had seen something and was suspicious.

It was an hour before Bechmen joined her, and when he did, Nyssa straightened out of the chair she'd sat in.

Bechmen eyed her from the door. "Do you know him?" he asked.

"Know who?"

"The trader who just bartered everything in his carts for one night with you," he said, stepping into the room and going to pour himself a drink.

Nyssa knotted her hands in front of her. "I have never been to the Honest realm," she lied. "As Princess, I did not leave my castle much."

"That castle being the one that was destroyed," he asked.

"Yes."

"Does he know who you are?" he asked, leaning back against the table.

"I wouldn't think so," she affirmed. "As I said, I did not travel much."

Bechmen's gaze narrowed, swirling his cup. "As you can imagine, I am skeptical."

"Honest beings are a race of disgusting traders who think of nothing more than their next fuck," she snapped. "I imagine he saw something you held tight to and wanted to say he was the first to have a taste of a foreign woman. They are savages and imbeciles. My own kingdom would not even let them near our home."

"You think he does not know you are of his kind?"

"How could he?"

The Noble seemed to contemplate this a moment. "Why would I trust you alone with this man?"

"Do you think I want to be left alone with a male who apparently only saw me as his next great conquest?" she sneered. "To be forced to suck some cretin's cock and endure his pleasures? You sold me for *fruit and bread*. Today was only the second I have seen sunlight since our deal. Were you ever planning on letting me walk again?"

"My people are starving," he argued. "If getting them food means I have to let an Haerlandian fuck you before my Prince, then so be it. You overestimate what your life means to me."

"And you overestimate my continued will to be your servant and spy."

For a moment, neither moved. She wondered what he was thinking. If he could see through her lies about Nadir and knew it was an act.

But he poured her a cup of wine, and as she took it, a pass of mutual understanding settled between them.

"I will have men stationed around every inch of that tent," he told her. "If you or he tries anything, I will not hesitate to kill both of you."

Nyssa almost laughed. "If you think any of your idiotic Porters will be paying attention to anything other than jerking themselves off at the sound of my screams, you're just as much of an idiot as they are," she said darkly.

"Someone thinks well of herself," Bechmen amused.

"You saw the marks on my neck when I first arrived," she said, chin rising. "What do you think?"

The Noble contemplated her another moment. "I think my Prince will like you."

He pushed off the table then and took her cup, pausing to stare down his long nose over her. "Quinn will stand guard," he decided. "And tomorrow, you'll serve my men in nothing more than that fur scarf the trader sold for your fuck. Luka will like that."

40

Nyssa paced inside the tent. An anxiety she couldn't get rid of swept through her bones. She was repeating in her head her instructions for later—to put on a show so that Quinn reported it back to the Noble that Nyssa had pleased the trader well.

Nyssa knew the moment she saw Nadir, her mind would blank.

When the door opened and Nadir walked in, her heart caved in on itself, and she forced her knees to stay upright.

He started to bolt to her, but Nyssa forced her feet firm. "Wait!" All she could see were yellow eyes. "I need you to tell me something only the real Nadir knows about me. Something... Something you and I have shared together."

"What?" Nadir managed, shoulders sinking.

"Just do it," she begged. "Please."

Nadir swallowed, and she could see his mind searching for anything. "Ah... *Fuck*... Okay... To wanting what we can't have," he finally managed.

Her jaw began to quiver, and the tears dripped down her cheeks. "Nadir..."

She bounded to him.

He caught her, swung her up off the ground and into his arms. Clenching her as though he feared she would disappear if he let her go. The pain of him squeezing her wounds made her wince, but she didn't care. She buried her head into his neck. Her entire body trembled, and it was hardly a moment before he sank to his knees, still holding her, his hand stroking the back of her head, other clenching her waist. She sobbed into his embrace, unable and unwilling to keep up her composure in front of him—not giving a damn about the facade she was supposed to be wearing.

Because this was Nadir.

And he'd found her.

"Hello, Princess," he whispered into her hair.

"Hello, Commander."

For a short while, they simply held each other. Nyssa was desperate for him to be real and for her not to be dreaming. She let her tears fall down her cheeks and soak his shirt, his tears doing the same to her.

"Is this real?" she managed.

He squeezed her waist, and finally, he pulled back. It was the first time they'd truly seen each other since the night they'd given one another up. His eyes were as swollen as hers, and she pressed her hands to his cheeks.

"Are you real?" she said again, her voice cracking with every syllable.

He reached up, pushed her hair from her eyes, and he breathed, "I'm not sure," in a voice so rasp-filled and choked, she broke in his arms again.

For however long they sat and cried in one another's arms, Nyssa wasn't sure. Because for the first time in weeks, she wasn't alone. She was back in her own world once more and not drowning in the nightmare of her surroundings.

Back *home*.

Nyssa let go of every emotion she'd kept pent up in her these last few weeks. Of having to lie and endure the taunts of man. The wife's abuse. Keeping up her face in front of the Noble to ensure her staying alive and finding out information for her people. To keep her world safe.

"Are you okay?" he asked after a while.

He hadn't stopped touching her. She assumed he was as desperate to make sure she was as real as she was him.

She sank her head against his chest as he held on. Her knuckles were brought to his lips, and he kissed each of them deliberately. Her heart turned to warmth in her chest, and she closed her eyes for a moment.

"I'm trying to be," she whispered.

She clenched to his shirt, memorizing the thread of it beneath her fingertips—the jagged edges and thin lines of the white linen. A tear stretched down her chilled cheek, and she tucked her legs behind her.

"I thought you were dead," he said against her skin. "I thought... I wasn't sure I'd ever see you again."

"Me too."

She pulled back, and he reached up to her cheek, thumb tracing the scar along her jaw. But he didn't speak, almost as though neither of them knew the words to say. He simply hugged her against him, softly kissing her head or squeezing her hand and waist every once in a while. Her wet tears dried on her skin, making her flesh stiff and chilled. Nadir reached up on the bed for a blanket and wrapped it around her after apparently having felt the chill on her skin.

His eyes closed as he pressed his forehead against her temple and his fingers gripped the blanket around her.

"I need you to punch me."

Her brows knitted, and she pulled back to see his face. "Why?"

"Because I still cannot believe this real," he admitted. "I'm hoping I'll wake up back at the Umber, and these last few weeks will never have happened. That you'll be in my arms sleeping peacefully back in my bed just as you were the morning you left."

She almost smiled, and the quirk of it made her heart constrict. She hadn't smiled in weeks. But the muscle memory of such a feeling brought tears back into her eyes.

"You found me," she breathed.

He buried his head into her neck, chest flinching, and she realized he was sobbing in her arms. His hands moved on her back as he held on. Unwilling to let her go even for a breath.

"Of course I found you," he whispered. "I haven't stopped looking. I —" He paused and pulled back, forehead resting against hers as he held her face. "I'm sorry I couldn't get here sooner. I had to barter and plea my way in. And I didn't know if you were even here or if you'd been taken back to Magnice. I... I thought I failed you. I *did* fail you."

And she knew admitting that word meant more than anything else he could have told her.

"I'm okay," she managed, hating seeing him broken so. She wanted to assure him it wasn't his fault. That she had been there to get information for them. To put him and their people in a stronger position in this war.

"No, you're—"

But she wiped the tear from his cheek, and his words ceased in his throat. "You could never fail me," she promised.

Eyes swollen and tears glistening in that cerulean gaze, he cupped her face and kissed her forehead, but he didn't speak as he pulled her back into him.

Her stomach growled as she held on, and she realized she hadn't had anything except the bread that morning and the wine. It was about the time Quinn would bring in scraps for the night.

"You didn't... You didn't happen to bring any water or anything, did you?" she asked.

He brought her hand to his lips, and they brushed her knuckles just briefly before he stood from the floor. "Hang on. My cart is just outside. Still think I have a bit saved even though he took most."

She grabbed his arm as he turned. "Make sure you say something obscene to the Porter. Something about wanting to seduce me with your wine or delicacies. I told them you were an idiot just wanting to say you got a foreign lay."

"Do they not know who you are?"

"They do," she said. "But I told them I was secluded and did not travel from my castle. I told them you do not know who I am."

Nadir's eyes narrowed, but he nodded anyway.

He brought in a bag a few minutes later, and she almost started crying again when he dumped it onto the bed. Apples and breads rolled in every direction. She stood to stare at the plethora of foods. Her hand reached out for his arm as she constantly wanted his touch against her to keep her grounded in that space and not miss a single moment. He moved and took her hand, fingers squeezing around her own, and he pulled her into him to kiss her temple once more.

It took her a minute, but finally, she settled onto the bed and he sat across from her. The first thing she went for was the water.

He chuckled under his breath as he watched her gulp it down. "Wait—slow down—" his hands wrapped around hers on the canteen, and he pulled it away before she could choke on it. "Slow down. You're going to make yourself sick."

The wash of the cool liquid pouring down her throat and into her stomach caused every muscle in her to awaken. She leaned back against the headboard and closed her eyes, allowing herself to drown in the nourishing abyss. A cool sweat beaded on her forehead, and when she finally opened her gaze again, she was met with Nadir's softened one upon her.

She willed her breath to even, still recovering from taking the liquid so quickly. He hesitantly handed her back the canteen.

"Slow."

Her head moved in a nod that she didn't feel. But she took the canteen back into her hands, this time just sipping. She let the liquid settle in her mouth a moment, memorizing the familiar swish of it around her teeth and on her tongue. The cool crystal of the Umber water—brought down by the barrel from the mountain traders sometimes or simply distilled from the pebbled stream. She relished the difference in it and the rotten water Man had been giving her.

"Are they not feeding you?" he asked.

She swallowed the bread that she'd decided upon as her first food. "Hardly," she replied. "Usually, it is leftovers from their dinners, if there are any. The Noble has tried bartering scraps of food for information on his generals, but..." She paused, shaking her head at the thought. "I keep feeling as though my body will simply exhaust one afternoon."

She had to pause at the look he gazed at her with then—the sorrow and break in his eyes... She sighed into the bread she was chewing and shook her head.

"Don't look at me like that, Nadir," she whispered.

"Has he touched you?"

The words caught her off guard. Her chewing stopped, but she pushed it from her mind as she looked back down and pulled off another piece of roll. "No. No, he hasn't touched me."

"How long have you been here?"

"Five weeks," she said. "The Noble's wife... she... I think she thinks if she beats me enough that he'll decide just to kill me instead of presenting me to the Prince. The Noble doesn't know she's hurting me. He seems to like showing me off as some sort of forbidden foreign slave girl. An exotic fruit he wants to parade around—"

"Wait," he cut in. "You said he's trying to give you food for information on his own men?"

Nyssa nodded.

A small smile spread on his lips. "You've been here five weeks, and you've already infiltrated their meetings and become a spy for their leader."

"And for us."

"Eyes of Haerland," he teased under his breath, smile widening. He reached for a piece of bread and tore it aggressively in his teeth.

"You're coming back with me," he determined, mouth full. "This is too dangerous. If they find out—"

"No, Nadir," she cut him off.

"Nyssa, I'm not leaving you here."

"I have a plan."

His jaw clenched, head tilting slightly as he let the words pour through him. "No, Nys—"

"I'm more use to you here," she argued. "Finding out information from the inside, I mean."

"I don't want you to do that."

"I can do this," she insisted. "We need to learn all we can about them. What better way than my being on the inside?"

"Nyssa, they're torturing you."

"I'm fine. Besides, it was your suggestion."

His face faltered, and he looked as though he would glare at her. "That's really not funny, Princess."

She almost smiled at the way he eyed her, but she shook her head. "I can do this. I am already in the meeting room," she said again. "You have to trust me."

A heavy breath evacuated his lungs as he watched her. For a moment, they didn't blink, and she saw as his eyes darted over her, obviously contemplating and trying to think of anything that would change her mind.

But he surrendered with a throw of the bread onto the bed, and his head shook.

"What do you need from me?" he asked.

"More ships will be here by the time the Deads rise."

"Did you hear them say that?"

"Along with a great deal more. Their ships are carrying more and more supplies. They're preparing a castle for their King, a settlement around it, nearly all the way on the western edge. These ships coming after the cycle aren't supply ships. They'll be bringing more civilians this time to start the village around what will be their home. Promising these people a new life, grander than their old one. Apparently, they'd nearly squandered all their resources at the last. They're calling the settlement Savigndor. Their King will be here in two Dead Moons cycles." She paused and met his gaze. "We need to be in a good enough position to negotiate peace with him or kill him."

"What's your plan, Princess?"

"I'm going to use the Dead Moons as a cover and destroy this place."

His brows lifted. "Not what I was expecting, but go on."

She stared at the food in front of her again, picking at it now that she had something in her stomach. "This camp... They're using it to build up their livestock supplies for when they start bringing in civilians in two cycles. If I can hit this place, it might deter their plans and hold them off a little longer."

"They also might see that as an act of war," Nadir said.

"There will be no one alive to tell the King who did it. They have no idea what I can do," she promised. "I need more time to learn what I can about them before we take this place. We cannot simply go about this blind any longer. We have to know more about their people."

"You know, when your sister gave you the occupation of diplomacy, I don't think this is what she had in mind."

"Yes, well, my sister isn't exactly here to make that decision, is she?"

Nadir balked, and Nyssa sighed heavily with a shake of her head. "I have to do this, Nadir," she breathed. "I need you to trust me."

"I do trust you... But how do you plan on doing this on your own?" he asked. "Can you hear your creatures?"

"I... I can hear my eagle again. Most days. But I haven't tried for any others." She paused, unable to look at him, her heart thudding at the thought of bringing her fire when she wasn't sure how to control it. But she had to show him.

"There's something else..."

She thought of the beating she'd received the night before—the whip coming down on her back. Her fingertips began to blacken on her right hand, and before she could stop it, it had traveled up her arm.

Nadir flinched backward. "What the—"

Smoke billowed from the amber-glowed fissures in her palm. A shudder swept over her. He grabbed her normal hand, and Nyssa blinked herself back into reality.

She expected Nadir to be on his feet running away from her. But he crawled his way to her side and took the hand that had just been black into his.

"When did this start?" he asked, inspecting her skin.

"That day on the beach when I ran away. I remember screaming at the ocean, so mad with myself for what I had done. I just wanted to get it out, go back and apologize to Lex. But fire grew around me... black and orange fire. It was terrifying. I didn't know what was happening. There was no one there to help. I couldn't hear the creatures to even ask for it. When I woke up, the sand was black around me. I don't know what happened—"

"Your mother marked you with Dorian," Nadir interjected.

"We were marked at the same time, yes."

He contemplated her for a long moment. "Your mother isn't very smart sometimes," he finally determined.

"What do you mean?"

"I mean, if you're exhibiting this, she may have accidentally given you fire as well."

Nyssa frowned. "That doesn't... I haven't been able to do this until now. Dorian has been dealing with his fire since we were children."

"You've also never really exerted yourself into situations where you've been as scared as this in just these last weeks," he said. "And with you pushing the creatures away, your core probably latched onto the last thing it could use to protect itself."

Her first thought was to argue with the accusation. But she knew he was right, and so she simply fumbled with her fingers a moment and allowed his words to sink in.

"Perhaps you unlocked something," he continued.

"Yes, well, whatever it is, it needs to go back in," she snapped. "It's quite terrifying not knowing how to control it or when it's going to unleash itself."

Nadir chuckled under his breath. "And yet, you're planning to use it to get yourself out of here," he noted.

Red crept on her cheeks as she chewed on the piece of bread again, and she met his smirking eyes, feeling her own smile at the mock on his face. Nadir leaned forward, the stubble on his chin scratching against her cheek when he kissed her temple.

"I cannot wait to tell Lex I found you," he whispered.

Her stomach knotted at the thought of how she'd treated the Second Sun before she left, and she hung her head. "How is she?" she asked.

Nadir paused, a long enough pause that color began to drain from Nyssa's cheeks.

"Pushing herself harder than she should be," he informed her. "She's training with the Flights, with Soli. Honestly, she's hardly spoken. She didn't like my coming here. She insisted you were being held by the Venari deserters somewhere in the Forest—"

"I *was* being held by the Venari," Nyssa said. "I was. They brought me here. And then the Noble cut their throats."

Nadir met her eyes, and he sighed as he sank against her. "Will you tell me everything?"

Before she could stop herself, she was.

From the moment she and Lex got in the fight, all the way to her being lashed the night before by the wife. Nadir didn't cut in except for his eyes widening about the Infi—a fear stretching across his face that she knew meant there was more to this story than what she knew. And when she finished, he simply held her tighter.

"I wish you would come back with me," he whispered.

"This is something I must follow through. Something I have to do on my own. I got myself into this mess. You have to let me get myself out of it."

"What can I do?" he asked.

Her heart bled at his agreement. "Come back in a week," she forced herself to continue. "But don't barter for me. He'll be suspicious. I can meet you in the market. I'll tell them I'm looking for things for his wife."

"I don't like it," he argued. "What if they catch you?"

"They won't," she insisted. "I'll have more information for you. Whatever you do, do not allow Lex to come with you."

"She's not going to like that. She's been completely beside herself."

"Which is why you are to leave her at the Umber."

Nadir sighed again and rubbed his neck. "Right. That will be fun to explain."

She almost felt her lip quirk. "Have you heard any news from my brother?"

"Ah... Not much," he replied. "I hear he was put through the Blackhand trials, and he beat both." He shrugged, a half-smile forming on his lips. "Seems to be okay. He has been asking a lot about you, though."

The way Nadir avoided her gaze when he'd said the last sentence almost made her smile. "No one has told him I ran away?"

His entire face furrowed up at her. "I actually like my body intact and not on fire," he muttered. "Can you imagine? I wouldn't have a home."

The laugh that left her made her choke. I was so foreign in her body that she wasn't sure what to do with it. She knew he was right, even if it did annoy her. But her chest swelled at the thought of her brother actually succeeding in the mountains, and she exhaled out the worry for him.

For a small while after, she finished most of the food, eating it in small pieces as much as she could, pacing herself so that she did not puke it all up. It pained her to have to break her food into such small pieces again. But she pushed through it, knowing how to help herself this time, unlike the last when she'd been just a child. Once she decided she was finished, Nadir simply threw the rest onto the ground.

The bed was almost uncomfortable to her after having laid on the wooden floor for the last month. Nadir laid down crossways in front of her, taking her legs in his lap and massaging her now limp muscles, the soft words between them a safety and comfort she didn't know she needed. She waited for him to make a comment about her legs, to say something about how skinny and depleted she was. She waited for it so much that she nearly didn't hear anything he said for a while.

"Nys?" he called, bringing her back. "Hey—What's wrong?"

She fidgeted with her fingers. "Ah... Nothing, it's just... I thought you would have said something about—about what I look like."

He paused, brows creasing. "Should I have?"

She sighed out the thoughts in her head with a close of her eyes. Of course, he didn't have anything to say about it. This was Nadir. Nadir fucking Storn. The most genuine person she'd ever known, constantly making her fall more and more in love with him with every sweep of his long lashes and flick of his tongue. Both Commander and charmer in one. Of course, he didn't comment on her starving figure.

Because he didn't see her as the helpless, starved Princess. He saw her for her. Terrified and running into the fire anyway. Supporting her and standing by her side should she ever need him.

Allowing her to prove herself and conquer the world without ever offering it to her on a silver platter.

"No," she finally said.

She sat up and turned so that she could lay beside him. His hand came to rest on her hip, and for a moment, she simply searched his face. He kissed her palm when she touched his cheek.

"I'm sorry I wasn't by your side," he whispered.

She sank against his forehead and scooted closer so that her legs entwined with his.

"You weren't supposed to be," she told him. "You were protecting your people and letting me do what I needed to do."

He pulled back then, his hand on her cheek. "You will never feel alone again," he promised. "Even when this place rips us apart again in the morning. I know where you are now. You are not alone."

"I told you this world would bring my fears to the surface in grand fashion," she said, almost smiling.

His lip quirked and his grip on her tightened. "You realize the only thing holding me back from picking you up over my shoulder and hauling your ass back to the Umber is that I trust you, right?"

She smiled up at him. "Thank you."

His lips pressed to her cheek and then her jaw, and she sank her head into the crook of his neck.

For the first time in weeks, she felt safe, as though the reality of what she would have to face the following day didn't exist. And, for the second time in her life, and once more with him, she begged the sun to be late rising.

The Porter did not wait for the sunrise before he came for her.

Nadir's bargain for an entire night was well brought to attention when Quinn had come. Quinn, at least, had the decency to knock, but even that had only given them time to prepare.

They knew the Porter would expect her disheveled and naked, especially after the mockery of a show they'd ended up sounding off in the middle of the night. It had been ridiculous. She'd almost started laughing at one point, to which Nadir had stared at her for a long enough moment that her heart began to ache, and he'd hugged her in his arms.

What had hurt the most, though, was the look on his face when she'd asked him to mark her throat for show. To bite her skin and make it look as though he'd thoroughly had his way with her and enjoyed it. She could see the break in his eyes, that the action would not be sexual in any way, but rather as something to ensure both their survivals. But he'd done it, and she had held his trembling hand, closing her eyes as the tears washed down both their faces.

Until Nadir broke in her arms and pleaded again for her to let him take her home. Seeing him in such a state sent what was left of her heart into shambles, and they'd held each other tighter.

Nadir threw her clothes into a heap on the floor along with his when the Porter knocked that morning, and he tousled her hair in the thirty seconds they had between the knock and the Porter bursting in.

Quinn paused upon going inside. Nyssa yanked the blanket up to cover her breasts.

"I bartered for the entire night, Porter," Nadir seethed, his hand placing on her leg through the blanket. "The sun has not yet risen. Get out."

"Your time with the slave is done with, by order of our Noble," Quinn affirmed.

"My time with this enchanting creature is still running," Nadir argued. "Get out. I did not give over all of my furs so that I could be cheated. If your Noble wishes to remain part of our trading route and enjoy the hospitality of my people on a land not of his own, I suggest you walk out of here and wait for the sun to rise."

Nyssa had only heard Nadir speak with such confirmation a few times before, and suddenly it was the Commander in the bed beside her.

Quinn looked like he would argue, but only for a flash. His eyes trickled to Nyssa, and then he backed himself out of the room.

Nadir's eyes closed as though bringing himself back to it just being them in the room once more. His back muscles flexed in the shadows of the fire-lit lamp by the bed as he strained his hands over his face.

"For a moment, I forgot where we were," he whispered. "For a moment... this weight on my chest had been lifted. You were back in my arms. That we were at my home in the Umber..."

His thoughts trailed, and he reached over to the floor, pulling her dress up from the ground. She fumbled with it before pushing it over her head. The stiffness of her lashing wounds made her wince.

"Wait—"

He'd caught a glimpse of the wound that wrapped her rib, and his eyes widened. She pushed her arms through the dress but left her back open as he moved, and then his hands trailed over her skin.

"Your mark—"

She flinched when he barely touched the ripped skin, and it made her cringe to realize the whip had cut through it.

"I will murder them with my bare hands," he promised. "That woman will feel what it is like to be tortured before she dies."

She didn't say anything as the dress fell the rest of the way around her and bunched at her bent legs. His forehead came to a rest on her temple.

"How long do we have?" she whispered.

"An hour, probably," he managed.

Her shoulders caved as the hurt of it pressed her chest, and he laid back on the bed. She went with him, lying her chest and arm over his torso. But he turned so that he was facing her, his arms still wrapped around her, and she closed her eyes as his forehead leaned against hers.

"Tell me about the Umber," she whispered. "Tell me how preparations are coming. If Lex has driven herself mad."

A small smile slipped on his lips. "Okay, Princess."

For the next hour, he spoke softly about what was happening at home: the food that would be ripening in his forest soon, the water serpent still coming near the shore but no longer threatening them. With every joke and witty comment, she found her mouth recognizing the feeling of a smile again. She memorized the crinkle of his eyes, the soft dimple in his cheek, his stubble beneath her fingers...

And when the Porter came back the second time, Nadir bartered with gold for two minutes to say goodbye to her.

"Do you want me to bring anything?" he asked in a low enough voice that the Porter couldn't hear.

"You're not bartering for me next time," she breathed. "I doubt it would be wise."

"An entire batch of flaky pastries then."

The banter made her heart melt, and she clenched her jaw to stifle the tear from dripping down her cheek. He apparently felt it, for he wrapped his arms around her one last time, whispering, "I don't want to let you go," in her ear.

"You have to."

He trembled in her arms. A last desperate ploy. She knew he would have taken her if she'd asked it. One word would have had him slicing every person's throat, had her bringing her fire and calling on her eagle. Him throwing her a dagger to help him as they pushed their way out of the camp. And they would have succeeded with grand effect.

But she had a job to do.

So she pulled back, pressed her hand to his cheek, and then she forced herself out of his embrace.

"Porter Quinn," she made herself call out.

The door swung back, and the Porter entered once more.

"The sun has risen. I believe you'll be taking me back to His Grace now," she uttered, knowing to avoid Nadir's eyes.

Nadir's arms dropped from her, and Nyssa forced her legs to move.

41

During the day, she would wear her mask and do her duty... For Haerland.

The wife had not been happy about Nyssa spending the night with the trader. Even with Quinn reporting back with the noises the two had made overnight, Shae continued to be wary of her. The Noble had shrugged it off after seeing the marks on her throat and the bites on her collar. He'd asked her for information on the trader and whether he'd realized who she was. Nyssa had told him no, that the male had boasted the entire night about his being the first of Haerland to bed one of the strangers.

The Noble had given her a cup of water from his own stash in return.

But the wife had set her in a chair and made Quinn pour ocean water over her face until Nyssa nearly drowned.

She had slept naked and sobbing that night. The only thing that kept her from breaking completely was that Nadir knew where she was now.

During the middle of the night, she heard a quiet knocking beneath the floor. Nyssa hardly had the strength to move, but she did. And when she lifted the loose floorboard, she found her eagle on the ground beneath it.

Her eagle had hopped up into her room and wrapped his great wings around her without hesitation. It was her first time actually seeing the creature up close in six weeks, and she couldn't help herself from falling into his embrace.

She'd only been able to communicate a few words to him, but the fact that he'd walked beneath floorboards to get to her made her heart swell. He stayed with her the remainder of the night, standing guard at her side until the sun rose, and he nipped at her finger before heading back out.

There was only one meeting during the following week. A new man had joined them, and he'd poured over her like the others had done. He, too, came with more news of the King's arrival, to which the Noble had become visibly nervous over. Bechmen had hardly spoken to Nyssa that afternoon when he'd pulled her into his room for her to report on the movements of his men. To the point that Nyssa had blatantly fibbed about something she knew he would catch, and he didn't.

She learned what was wrong with him later that night.

The new man had requested he travel to Savigndor.

With the gift for the Prince.

With *her*.

The man had told Bechmen a few of the Prince's maidens had arrived to oversee that things were in order and to his liking before he arrived. The man wanted these women to inspect his gift to ensure she was in line with what the Prince would want.

Bechmen had told her they would leave in two days as requested. Once the maidens determined what else needed to be 'fixed' on her, they would return for the wife to finish.

Nyssa decided she would not be telling Nadir about this.

On the day of Nadir's arrival, Nyssa begged Quinn to ask Bechmen if she could take her walk, especially since she would be carted off to their castle the next day. Quinn had taken her to the Noble before their breakfast, and she'd walked in on him getting dressed.

"Your Grace," Nyssa said with a curtsy and bow, avoiding looking directly at him. "I wonder if you would allow me my stroll this morning," she asked. "It has been a week."

He contemplated her a moment as he pushed his shirt over his head. "Very well, Ari. I'll have Porters escort you. Wear your hood. I do not want any more of these spots to appear before the maidens have a look at you."

Her chest tightened with his agreement. "Thank you, sir," she said with another bow. "Is there anything his Grace would like me to look for? Perhaps the exotic fruits from last time."

The Noble bent over his dresser, pulling something from the drawer. A bag was tossed into her hands, and he gave her a nod. "My wife was looking for more dress fabrics. Perhaps you can find a few she would like."

"Yes, sir," Nyssa nodded. "Should I think your Commander has left more dresses for myself to be presented in for our Prince?"

She was still getting used to calling Luka such.

"He did," he informed her. "You'll be trying them on later tonight."

Quinn and another Porter she didn't know escorted her outside. It was odd for her to be walking amongst people again. She didn't realize the number of people he had in his estate until that morning. The noise of chickens and pigs entered her ears when she rounded the corner. She bought eggs and dried meats, offering the Porters a ration even though she knew she shouldn't have. But they took it with a nod of their heads and devoured the food as though it were a royal treat.

It was when they were on the last turn that she finally saw Nadir.

Her heart began to thump louder at the sight of him. She had to stifle the smile on her face, and she could tell by his eyes that he was doing the same.

—*The smile.*

It was foreign on her lips, and emotion bubbled to the surface at the feeling of it.

Nadir turned his back to her the closer she approached and began pulling a few crates from the stacks on his wagon and placing them on the ground. His muscles strained beneath the black wool shirt he had on, his hair pulled back into his usual thick bun. And when he finally turned around upon her reaching him, it took everything in her to keep from bounding into his arms.

She pulled her facade to the surface, and she raised a stern brow as she picked up one of the browning apples from a crate.

"Here I was told the Honest trader would have the best fruits," she muttered before tossing the apple over her shoulder with a roll of her eyes. "I suppose I should have known better than to trust such words."

Nadir's shoulders rounded before her. "That's not what you said the last I was here," he mocked. "I'm pretty sure you enjoyed those fruits more than anything your Noble could offer you."

She had to clench her jaw to keep from smiling.

"Don't be daft, trader," Nyssa argued, glaring at Nadir as the Porters watched her. "These apples are as useless as your tongue. What would you propose his Grace do with such rotten things?"

"Perhaps you could shove them up his rectum," Nadir suggested. "I hear Nobles of Man like a bit of ass play."

The Porter at Nyssa's side pulled his sword, but Nyssa pushed against his chest. "Don't worry, Porter," she said. "I'm sure he meant no disrespect. Just the coy of these reef savages. They've always been a bit hard to tame."

The Porter put his sword back in its sheath, and Nyssa gave Nadir a subtle wink beneath her hood. She stepped past him then, her shoulder brushing his, and she looked to the fabrics he had rolled up at the end of his wagon. Her fingers trailed over the soft satin, and for a moment, she was reminded of the elegant dresses she once wore at banquets. The grand tulle and satin forms, making her feel like she could take on anything.

She blinked hard at the memory and cleared her throat.

"Porters," Nyssa said as they stiffened. "Please find her Grace and have her come meet me. I think she would appreciate the satins our trader has brought."

As the Porters left, Nadir settled back onto the side of the cart, a small smirk on his lips as he looked her up and down.

"Eating out of your hands," he mused under his breath. "One day, you'll have to tell me how you managed it."

"I'm not sure you want to know," she told him.

He considered her a moment, gaze darting around them as she continued to run her hands over the fabrics. Nadir pushed off the cart and came to stand beside her, pretending as though he were helping her decide which material would be best.

"He's arriving in two cycles," she uttered without moving her lips. "The other Noble estates won't know me. Once we've taken care of this place, I can come back to help you negotiate with their King... when the time comes."

Nadir took a roll of fabric out of the cart, holding it up as though for her to admire it.

"What about these guards?" he asked quietly.

"The Porters?" she scoffed and shook her head, rubbing the fabric between her fingers. "Fools. Quiet. They don't question orders, especially when I've been feeding them foods the Noble refuses to give them."

"What do you need from me?"

"I need to talk to Bala."

His brows elevated, eyes widening. "Bala?" he balked. "She'll murder everyone once she finds out you're here."

"Bala trusts me. She needs to know about Gail and the Infi," Nyssa said. "Bring her here next week. Have her wear a dress and pretend she is your assistant. No weapons."

Nadir looked as though he would laugh. "Venari King disguised as an Honest seamstress. Can't wait to tell her that," he muttered.

His fingers brushed hers then, and her heart skipped at the warmth of his touch. She met his eyes, and for a moment, forgot where they were as the weight of his fingers enclosed around hers, pretending as though he were helping her fold up the fabric. The callus of his fingertips rubbed over the back of her hand, tickling her flesh. The swell of her chest spread down into her stomach and settled between her legs. Her mouth dried, and suddenly she found herself back in her room after the banquet as the pair poured over the book he'd brought up to show her—one written by the Dreamer giver, Somniarb Crelib herself.

—*"Tell me why you carry this with you," she'd asked, fingers tracing the mark on his chest.*

"It's the only copy," he told her. "Lovi gave it to me a long time ago and asked me to keep it safe. I like reading the passages in here that no one else knows."

She snuggled into him and pointed to one at the bottom of the page, written in the old language.

"This one. Will you read it?" she asked of him.

Nadir cleared his throat comically, and she almost rolled her eyes. But he settled his arm around her, holding the book in one hand as he read, the other hand caressing her side. The words flowed lyrically from his lips. The noise of the old language came off his tongue as smooth as wine pouring into a glass. She didn't know what he'd just said, but it made her blush nonetheless, even if it wasn't supposed to.

"I think I need a minute," she said with a deep breath once he'd finished.

"Why?"

"Because words are not supposed to sound that beautiful."

"I think that's exactly what words are supposed to do," he countered.

She sat her chin on his chest and gazed up at him. "What does it say?"

"Flowers beneath our feet. A wind on the sea. You are the night. And I am the trees," he breathed.

The words, as vague as they were, brought a smile to her lips. "Do you know what I think, Commander?" she asked.

He huffed under his breath. "What's that, Princess?"

"I think you bring this book with you just to make women swoon," she replied. "How many others have you cuddled with and spoke such words to?"

He hung his head, laughing quietly. "Actually, only you."

"Lies," she accused playfully.

"Truth," he argued. "I'm an honest being. You'll find few lies from me."

"Says the one born of the Honest," she mocked. "Are all of you so truthful as you say?"

Nadir chuckled. "Not at all. I'm impressed you actually believe me when I say it."

"I still don't understand why Lovi chose to call you all the Honest."

"He thought the word represented the purity and innocence he thought necessary for an immortal life."

Nyssa sat up on her forearm, face scrunched in bewilderment. "That ship has clearly sailed."

He feigned hurt, laying the book over his chest as though covering up a wound. "What do you mean? I'm the epitome of those words."

"You are the furthest thing from innocent I have ever met," she countered.

A slow grin spread on his lips, and he grasped her bottom in his hand. His nose brushed hers as he grinned against her lips. "Says the Promised Princess who has every person in this kingdom fooled into thinking she is the epitome of those words."

She almost laughed but instead shrugged her shoulders. "It's a gift." —

—The feeling of Nadir's hand tightening around hers again brought her back to reality. She blinked, sunlight swallowing her eyes as she met his gaze.

"It's still happening?" he asked softly.

She nodded, sucking in a jagged breath. "A little more wanted now than before."

The slight smile he gave her made her heartbeat quicken. "I should have danced with you that night," he whispered.

Her lips quirked as the fantasy of what that would have been like filled her mind. "Flowers beneath our feet," she whispered.

For a moment, he simply stared at her, jaw clenching as he visibly bit back the emotion from his insides. "A wind on the sea," he finally breathed.

"You are the night."

"And I am the trees."

Nyssa's eyes fluttered at his touch. "I still don't know what it means."

He looked as though he would laugh, but her heart warmed at his smile, small as it may have been, and his thumb dragged over her own.

"I'll tell you when you're home," he whispered.

Home.

"Ari, girl—"

The noise of the Noble's wife startled her. A deep gasp entered her lungs, and she shook herself out of the daze she'd been in. She let go of him, turning around, and she gave the woman a short bow.

"Your Grace," she said, not meeting the woman's glare. "I thought these fabrics the trader has brought would interest you. Some are of the finest cottons and linens, perfect for the warmer weather we're due for in a few weeks."

Shae's eyes darted between them. "I see…" Her gaze narrowed, and Nyssa fixated her eyes on the ground, waiting for the woman to speak. "Well. Let's see them, trader," she demanded. "I don't have all day."

As Nadir showed Shae the fabrics, Nyssa could see the bite back of his grimace, his forearm tightening with his fist. She knew one look over this woman, and all Nadir could see was the lashing on her back, and it was taking everything in him not to cut off her head.

Nyssa didn't get to tell him goodbye this time.

Shae ordered Quinn to take her back to her room before Nadir had wrapped up with her. Nyssa hadn't met Nadir's gaze as she was carted off, knowing if she did that, he might do something neither of them could come back from. She gave Quinn the bag of goods she'd bought for him as he left her in her room.

Nyssa sank onto the floor and pulled her knees into her chest as she waited on the wife to come for her. But as she sat there, the weight of sleep took over her exhausted body.

A bucket of water to the face startled her out of the dreamless nap.

It was dark outside.

And the wife was standing over her.

"Get her off the floor," she demanded the two Porters.

Nyssa limped as dead weight. The Porters pulled her up, and she was strapped to the familiar chair, hands tied behind the back of it.

Shae stepped over her, the sneer shadowed in her features. "You think I didn't see the way you looked at that trader?" she asked.

Nyssa didn't speak.

Shae nodded to the guard. Nyssa's seat was tilted back, and she held her breath. Water poured onto her, deliberately, to the point that her lungs fought back, and her entire body trembled beneath the weight of it.

Her chair slammed back onto the ground. Nyssa coughed and gasped, chest heaving.

"My husband may be an idiot, but I am not," Shae seethed. "Again."

Nyssa had hardly caught her breath, and she was forced to hold it once more.

Her chair hit the ground.

"Tell me who he is," Shae demanded.

Coughing, Nyssa remained firm and refused to speak a word.

Shae's fingers snapped.

Chair back, water over her head. Her muscles fought. She could feel that ash threatening her body, her core trying to keep her safe. But she fought against it just as she fought for breath.

"Speak, girl," the woman demanded.

Nyssa blew the water from her mouth and glowered at Shae through her matted hair. "I cannot speak if you *drown* me," she finally snapped.

Shae grabbed the hair on the top of her head. Nyssa was yanked back, front chair legs lifting off the ground again, and the wife held her there and pulled her head so she was looking up at her.

Nyssa refused to wince.

"I know the deal you've made with my husband," Shae said. "If you so much as look in the direction of that man the next you're allowed at the market, I'll—"

"You'll what?" Nyssa cut in, having had enough of the woman. "Tie me to this chair? Drown me? Whip me? Burn my skin?" Saliva collected in her mouth, and she spat it at Shae's face.

The back of Shae's hand whipped across her face.

Nyssa fell, still strapped to the chair.

Shae's rings cut through her cheek. Her head whipped with the weight of her landing so hard on the floor. And her arm snapped as the back of the chair landed on it.

The gasp of agony that involuntarily took her ricocheted through her body. Nyssa cursed the sky and bit back the taste of ash in her mouth. The world vibrated in her eyes, but she shook the tremble of her new form and pushed it back down. The room dizzied around her. Pain grasped her entire body, making her slowly writhe against the ground. Her head throbbed, and a tear fell down her cheek at the pang running up her entire arm.

The woman's eyes were wide when Nyssa met them again, and she knew black lightning streaks had flashed on her skin.

"Pick her up," Shae told the men.

Nyssa's arm ached with restlessness when she was lifted back up.

She fought any more tears threatening to rise and inhaled a deep breath as she was steadied again.

But she couldn't stop herself from shaking.

"Your husband asked me to look for fabrics for you today!" Nyssa managed through the spasms. "*That* is the reason I was at that disgusting man's cart. You think I wanted to be near him after the things he did to me last week?"

Shae's weight shifted, and then she gave an upwards nod to Quinn. "Quinn, call the surgeon. I believe she's broken her arm."

Quinn left the room, and Shae crouched down before Nyssa.

"I am watching you, girl."

Aydra's face flashed behind Nyssa's eyes.

"Look at me, Nys," Aydra had said, taking Nyssa's twelve-year-old face in her hands. Nyssa had struggled against her, too upset at what their mother had just taunted her with to want to listen. She pushed her away, hitting at Aydra's arms to try and wrench herself free, violent tears and unrelenting sobs evacuating from her.

But Aydra held her tight.

"Hey—Nyssa!—Look at me!"

Nyssa straightened, seeing a glisten in Aydra's eyes as she went rigid in her sister's grasp. "You are not a filly," Aydra told her as a silent tear spilled over onto her cheek, her voice almost cracking. "You are not a ladder. You are not a toy. You will not be tamed, climbed, or silenced."

Aydra swallowed hard and brushed away Nyssa's tear with her thumb, and Nyssa saw the tremble in her sister's jaw. "You, little sister, will not be broken." Aydra's voice went in a higher pitch at the end, her own sobs threatening, and Nyssa had fallen into her embrace.

The memory surged through Nyssa and grabbed her depleting heart. An enraged numbness swelled through her aching bones.

You will not be broken.

Nyssa's lashes rolled up, and she met Shae's smug smile through her wet bangs.

"Watch me, then," Nyssa hissed.

42

Once the surgeon had looked at her forearm and determined it was broken, Nyssa was given a bandage and a sling to wrap herself in.

The Noble had not been happy about her state, and he'd dragged his wife outside to accost her for harming Nyssa the day before she was to be presented to the Prince's maidens. Nyssa had heard Bechmen's fists slam into Shae, and when Shae had come back into the room to help her try on the dresses Luka had provided, the wife had not spoken a single word.

For a moment, she nearly felt sorry for her.

Until Shae wrenched her arm around to maneuver her out of her clothes as though she hadn't just broken it. But even with the stinging agony pulsing through her, the sight of the dresses that were brought in made her still.

Her heart shouldn't have skipped at seeing them...

But it did.

Oh, it did.

Three of the dresses were simple. With the long sleeves and a-line bodies, scooping off the neck and in different colors. But the other two...

Tulle.

So much tulle.

So much tulle that Nyssa nearly wept. With bodices of boning and corset backs. A navy one that fell off the shoulders, its bottom shimmering with tiny jewels in the fabric. The Noble had liked it but decided it showed off too much of her skin that was still healing.

But the second one.

A pale blue loose ballgown with the sheer corset fabric over visible boning and long sleeves, a high neck that sat on her protruding collarbones. Nyssa had to hold in her emotion when she felt the fabric against her skin and held the skirt's layers upon layers in her hands. This was the one the Noble decided he wanted her brought to the maidens in.

A carriage was sent for them the next morning.

Nyssa was put in the dress and given a black cloak much larger than herself to wear, presumably to keep her hidden. She'd been brought out of her room a while before dawn to be scrubbed clean, her hair actually brushed. They took her arm out of the sling but left it wrapped, and Nyssa was forced to hold it against her stomach on her own. The pain of the broken bone made her tremble, but she tried not to let it take over.

It was just she and Bechmen who went in the carriage. It was a great, audacious thing with the crest of Man on the doors. The Porters who accompanied this carriage wore different gambesons than the ones the Noble had. Like the carriage, they were clearly part of the King's personal collection.

They spoke very little throughout the ride. Nyssa tried not to fumble much with the tulle of her dress, but as it was something she never thought she'd feel again, she couldn't help it.

"It will take us half of the day or more to get there," Bechmen said as they got a few miles down the road. "We will only stay tonight."

Nyssa didn't reply.

The beach to her left, she looked out of the windows as they rode. The path they were on was still being worn in, and the carriage bumped over rocks and into holes. The small patches of forest that had once settled sporadically down the coast were now absent. They passed by the two smaller estates, both of which resembled the one she was at herself, though not as large. The noise of seagulls filled her ears the closer they came to the settlement, and as it rose in her sightline, blood drained from Nyssa's face.

It was a castle.

Not an estate of tents and men working to build around it, rummaging with stone and building materials... Thinking it would be a stage of a castle being built, perhaps a few rooms including their Throne Room and Great Hall.

No.

There was still a long way to go with the towers. She could see stone being hoisted on pulleys to continue building up. Rocks and men lined the beginnings of a great wall around it. But the first level was done, parts of the second and beyond going up faster than she thought possible. She began to wonder how many slaves they'd brought with them.

And then there were the ships.

More than she could count. They sat in the ocean, some moving, some anchored. A few were pulled near the shore. Small boats moved from the ones further out, bringing men ashore.

With the sight of this castle and the ships, Nyssa's heart knotted.

A different fear gripped her than before, and she realized there would be no vanquishing these people.

The only thing she could do was keep her people from falling into slavery. She would have to negotiate peace, tradings... Whatever she had to do to keep the people of Haerland free and safe.

Nyssa blinked back the panic threatening her insides, and she sat back in the seat again.

"Does the sight of such a castle being built make you miss your own?" the Noble asked her.

Nyssa didn't respond. She continued to watch outside as they entered the settlement, staring at the people who paused to watch the carriage go by. Starved men with lashings on their backs. Porters walked between them, whips winding in their hands. Nyssa's chest hardened as she watched one strike down a man who had fallen to his knees.

"What's in this for you?" Nyssa finally asked the Noble. "Why go through all this to bring the Prince a gift of Haerland when he has not asked for one?"

Bechmen shifted, apparent that he had not expected her to ask such a question.

"Earned respect and riches," he answered simply. His head tilted as he looked her over. "And you?" he asked upon meeting her gaze.

"I wasn't aware I had a choice," she countered.

"You cannot tell me you are still here because you feel yourself imprisoned," he said. "If you truly wished yourself free, you'd have fled with that trader."

Nyssa didn't blink.

And she didn't answer.

A slow smirk pressed on Bechmen's lips. "I imagine this all comes easy for you, doesn't it?" he asked.

"What?"

"The castle and the dresses," he noted. "People staring. Addressing you as Your Highness. Lavish quarters and all the riches that come with being royal."

"You say all those things as if they should entice me to submit easily to being entrapped here," she said. "As if I should welcome such things selfishly for myself while the people in my world become your slaves."

The carriage stopped.

Bechmen stood as the door opened, but he met her gaze before stepping out. "I'll say it again: You'll make a grand addition to our court, Miss Storn." He paused just outside of the carriage and held out a hand for her to take.

As she stepped out of the carriage, the breeze blew the hood off her head. Sunlight hit her cheeks, and she inhaled a deep breath of the ocean air.

She didn't realize every person within looking distance had paused to stare at her until she noted the silence of the yard.

Bechmen moved and reached for her hood, pulling it up over her head. "Fire for hair and heart," he muttered so only she could hear. "Hang on to that, Princess."

Nyssa ogled at the grand wooden doors that opened before them. The rounded courtyard was so much like her own that she had to force her feet to move when he tugged on her. The stone beneath her feet broke her heart, and all she could see in her mind was Aydra teaching her to dance in the yard while all their Belwarks watched.

She could see Aydra coming out the doors, dressed in one of her usual black linen day dresses, arms over her chest as she watched Dorian spin Nyssa in the grass. Only sixteen at the time, Dorian had run past her, pushing his way back into the castle and saying he would bring them a picnic to share. Aydra had laughed and reached for Nyssa's hands to pull her off the ground.

"I need you to do something about your brother's growth," Aydra said as Nyssa rose to her feet. *"Perhaps break his legs or find a potion to stunt him. If he gets any taller this year, I won't know what to do with him."*

Nyssa almost laughed, beaming at her sister as the sun hit her perfect ginger curls. *"He was showing me a dance he'd made up."*

"That was not dancing," she laughed. *"Here—"* she held up her hands and reached for Nyssa. *"I will show you dancing."*

Nyssa eyed her sister. *"You? But—"*

"I can lead," Aydra assured her, and Nyssa smiled at the assurance in her features.

Nyssa met her hands and followed her lead. She stepped on her feet, but Aydra only laughed and instructed her in counting, telling her back or forward, and Nyssa hung onto her every word.

"You'll be attending banquets this year as an adult," Aydra said as they danced. "Are you ready for that?"

"No," Nyssa admitted.

Aydra smiled. "Neither was I," she said. "The Dreamers that will come to call on you—" her eyes rolled, and Nyssa laughed. "It's exhausting, but you get used to it. Thankfully, it only lasts a few years with their throngs and then dwindles to a few favorites you have chosen. The first rule is to not fall for the first one. Believe me, they'll all want to put you in lavish jewels and give you audacious gifts, and they'll all say they'll bed you softly and with love as you so deserve." She spun Nyssa around and pulled her back in. "They're all liars."

"I thought you liked men?" Nyssa asked.

A coy laugh came from Aydra's mouth. "I love men," she bantered. "I love to watch them crawl on their knees as they offer me the world and work to make me scream."

Nyssa's cheeks heated at Aydra's words, knowing she had heard such noises coming from her sister's room. Aydra's hands squeezed hers, and she looked back up to her, only to find Aydra staring into nothing past her head.

"I wonder if there is anyone out there willing to sacrifice the world for love instead of offering it up for their own personal gain." Sadness flashed in Aydra's eyes, but it was gone in a blink, and Nyssa was left wondering if she'd imagined it.

Aydra slowed in the dancing as she met her gaze again.

"Remember, sister," Aydra said. "All of these men will want to give you the world. They'll tell you you deserve it. That on their arm, you could be the greatest Queen to ever take our kingdom. But do you want to know the secret they're hiding from you?"

Nyssa nodded.

"They need you, and they're terrified of you learning it. Every man in our kingdom wants you to think you need them. Because the reality is, they need you to think it so they can use you to climb their own way to the top. They are scared that if you learn you don't need them, you'll only use them as toys, and they'll never get any further than a source of pleasure for you."

"Like all the men in your bed?" Nyssa asked.

Aydra's smirk widened. "Exactly like the ones in my bed," she toyed. "You're not someone's ladder, Nyssa. You are the prize at the top. Any man deserving of you will take their place at your side as your equal, with respect and trust. They'll stand by you as you rise to take your own crown. Not try to squash you beneath them." She spun Nyssa around and pulled her back, chin rising high as she spoke her next words.

"You'll never need a man to gift you the world, sister. You'll take it on your own."

The confident smile Aydra gave her made her chest swell. "Play the game?" Nyssa asked.

Aydra laughed. "As dear Rhaifian says: make them crawl," she winked.

—The Noble tugged on Nyssa's arm.

A dimly lit hall greeted them. There were no paintings on the walls or rugs along the corridors. Just the stark quiet and chill hanging in the still air. A Porter walked in front of them and led them down to the next set of great doors, and Nyssa knew without them being open that this was the Throne Room.

Her stomach knotted as the doors opened.

Great stone pillars lined the room. The large arched windows on either side were still missing their windows. There were steps at the back of the room, a grand white throne in the middle, surrounded by two smaller ones behind.

The noise of boots clapping quickly on the floor caught her ears, and she looked past the chairs to see three women coming down from the stairs in the corner behind. The taller woman in front reminded her of Shae, yet older. This woman held her chin high, and her back as stiff as Nyssa always made hers.

Bechmen released Nyssa's arm and gave the woman a bow upon their approach.

"Lady Etta," the Noble addressed her, to which the woman gave him her own short nod. "I did not realize you were here personally."

Pale brows lifted on Etta's face, lips pursed as Bechmen straightened. "And trusted these girls to make sure things are in order for my Prince? You know better, Bech. I am told you secured the coast first, even found the Princess of this land to bring my boy..." Etta stilled, stretching over Nyssa.

Nyssa kept her head down, staring at the woman only through the light black fabric of the oversized cloak shielded down to her nose.

"Yes, my Lady," Bechmen said.

Etta stared at him expectantly. "Well? Let's see her."

Bechmen stepped between Nyssa and Etta, and Nyssa noted the deep breath he took as he pushed her hood back.

Nyssa pushed her breath out as she lifted her eyes. The two other women gasped, and Etta stepped back, her eyes wide.

"Her hair—"

"I thought it would entice Prince Ryne," the Noble declared. "Lady Etta, this is Ari Storn," he introduced. "Princess of Haerland."

Etta took a hesitant step towards Nyssa, and she reached out, taking Nyssa's hair between her fingers. Nyssa hugged her pained arm at her waist, staring past Etta's shoulder as the woman began to circle her.

She was growing tired of being inspected like livestock.

Etta moved Nyssa's arms and her hair, noting every inch of her. When she came around to Nyssa's front again, Nyssa felt her eyes on her face, and her gaze squinted at Nyssa's cheeks.

"What are these spots?" Etta asked. "I am unsure the Prince will want his children to come out with such things on their faces."

Nyssa almost snorted. But she kept her composure.

"I am sure the Prince's heritage will surpass the girl's," Bechmen replied. "Their children will merge the lands. Come out strong with dark hair and olive skin as he has."

Nyssa couldn't help the confusion on her face.

Etta considered Nyssa another moment. "What happened here?" she asked, pointing to the scratch.

"She has a bit of an attitude at times," Bechmen admitted. "My wife is breaking such habits."

Etta smiled. "I've always liked your wife," she noted proudly. "Girls," Etta called to the other women. "Find our seamstress. We need to have her measured while she is here—" she turned back to the Noble. "You will be staying overnight, yes?"

"Yes, my Lady."

"Good," Etta said. "I need a full rundown of her measurements, and she'll need to be groomed."

"My wife has had her groomed once," Bechmen told her.

Etta's smile widened. "Perhaps we will hold off on it then until closer to his arrival."

"And when will our Prince be joining us, my Lady?"

This time Etta met Nyssa's eyes. "He is due the first day of the Black," she replied.

Nyssa squinted at the use of the word. *The Black...*

Bechmen stiffened. "That is just two weeks from now," he stammered.

Her stomach caved. The Black... *The Dead Moons.*

The Dead Moons of Spring would rise in two weeks.

Nyssa's knees nearly buckled.

"It is," Etta said. "Let us hope there is not much more needing correction on your gift," she said as she turned and motioned for them to follow.

Bechmen's hand on her back was the only thing that forced her feet to move.

Nyssa was separated from Bechmen and taken to a room that made her heart hurt. One of the finished bedrooms, grander than her own had been at Magnice. The washroom and closet areas were separated through a door from the bedroom. She was stripped in front of a beautiful three-way mirror, and it was the first Nyssa had seen of her body since the Umber.

She didn't recognize herself, and it hurt so much that she had to focus her eyes on a singular spot on the wall while Etta looked her over. She made comments to her maids, having them write down things she saw wrong, but the list was short, and soon the seamstress joined them. Her measurements were taken while a slew of servants brought in different fabrics to hold against her skin for color. Etta decided on her favorites and had the rest of them turned away.

Nyssa counted her breaths throughout the entire ordeal.

A ready-made dress was brought into the room towards the end, and Nyssa realized why Shae had been so adamant about her losing weight. The thing was tiny. A white linen dress, A-line with flared sleeves that reached the ground. Lace panels on the sides. High scoop neck. Nyssa was placed into the dress, and then her hair was pinned up in sections, apparent that they were attempting to curl it. Nyssa didn't have the strength to tell them it was no use.

As they left her hair to dry, Etta announced they needed to get to the kitchens to finish setting up for dinner since they were having guests. And as every person trickled out of the room, Nyssa felt herself breaking second by second.

The door clicked with a lock behind it.

She finally truly looked at herself in the mirror again. Back in a beautiful dress and surrounded by a kingdom. The familiarity of the gold and the posh decor. Servants around her once more. Clean water. A hairbrush. No shackle on her ankle.

And yet, as trapped as she was at Magnice.

Nyssa wailed with the sob that evacuated her, and she fell to her knees.

Everything about being back there brought memories of her home that seemed so far away, almost as a dream. Every day, the memory of her sister felt more like a past life instead of a memory of weeks before. As though it hadn't been just weeks since her death. As though it had been a lifetime ago. She half expected her to barge in the doors, stand behind her and tell her how beautiful she looked, or for Dorian to bounce in and tease her as he slouched in the chair, tossing his knife up and down. Telling her of his plans for the evening after the banquet.

Even standing in that room made her think of Nadir and the nights they'd shared at Magnice.

She wondered if she would ever feel such happiness again.

She still wanted to go through with her escape plan, but as she sat on her knees, she realized that eventually, she would be forced to succumb to all this. That when they did come back to negotiate, she would have to put herself back in this same place.

To join their lands together.

That the only way she could protect everyone she loved was to barter herself into a trading deal. To find a way for them all to work together to build a better land instead of waging war against one another. Their people needed food, and Haerland had it. They had things they could help each other with.

And she knew she was the only one capable of securing that deal.

This would be her home.

By every means necessary.

The thought sent her heart shredding to whispers of muscle and evaporating in her bloodstream. Sobbing until she couldn't feel her face or her body. Until she forced herself up off the floor, chest heaving, clutching her broken arm to her stomach, and she met her own eyes in the mirror.

The fire her sister always told her to exhale was now consuming her, and she wasn't sure she'd ever stop choking on the smoke.

Etta escorted her to dinner in the Great Hall a few hours later. Every person stood to greet Etta, and the new men who had joined them all stared at Nyssa. The ones that already knew her merely leered at her.

Etta told her she would be serving she and the Noble just as she would be tending to the Prince when he arrived until the Prince decided otherwise. Nyssa served the wine with her good arm and stood to the side while the rest of them ate, and she listened to the things Etta said still needed 'correcting' on her.

The list wasn't long, and by the time they wrapped up dinner, Etta and Bechmen were cheers'ing to a well-accomplished partnership.

Nyssa was taken back to that same room for the night and given a couple bread rolls and pieces of meat as her dinner. She waited until they left to scarf the food down.

Sitting back on a bed made her nauseous. It had been so long since she'd been in one, minus the scratch of a cot she'd been allowed in the room when Nadir had bartered for her. But this was a *bed*. One as plush as the one she'd had at Magnice.

She hated it.

She hated every scrap of luxury around her.

She hated the manipulation of it and how it made her feel. She hated the faux comforts of their trying to make her feel like she wanted this.

She hated it so much that she dismissed the bed and curled up in the great tub instead. Pretending its high sides were arms around her and the tuck of the blanket was body heat.

She was able to count the stars for the first time in six weeks that night.

43

Traders came through Bala's kingdom as scheduled, but Nadir was not with them this time. Bala inspected all the goods as she usually did, leaving her people to distribute and pack them away as she checked on the things they were sending back. One of Nadir's men gave her a letter from him. The letter burned her pocket the entire day, but she couldn't rest. Not when her people were on the verge of unrest still, and they'd had a group of the rebels come in the night before.

Stress gripped her. Bael could sense it, and he'd hung a little closer to her in the weeks that had passed. Most nights, she didn't sleep. She sat up at Draven's desk and poured over the letters and maps, memorizing his writings in the journal he kept.

She had been under his watch since her being marked Venari—the first woman in fifty years to be marked a King, and he had taken to her quickly. They were both so young when Parkyr died, she almost felt like she was learning it all with him.

But Draven had had a presence about him that she was still learning. The dangerous, all-knowing aura exuding from every pore of his confidence. Most days, she could fake it, and on the days she didn't know how to, she did it anyway.

It was after nightfall by the time the traders left, though some stayed overnight for rest and games. Bala welcomed them just as she always did. Bael brought her dinner up and stayed with her for some time. He spoke with her about the goods and the next day, and gave her an update on the rebels that had decided to come home. One of their own had been badly injured on the road, and they'd brought him back in the hopes of healing him.

"Are they talking of vengeance?" she asked him as she sat at the

412

desk.

Bael shook his head, leaning against the table. "Nothing. They seem only to want Gail healed."

Bala's mind went to the injured Venari male and the memories of how he'd challenged she and Draven over the years. The mere presence of him back in her kingdom made her fists curl.

"Is it bad that I'm hoping he'll just die?" Bael asked, and the first smile she'd felt all day rose on her lips.

"Don't let them hear you saying that," she muttered. "I didn't get a good look at his injuries. What were they?"

Bael ran a hand through his hair. "He looks as though he's been mauled by something large," he told her. "But the wounds are a few weeks old. Four, five weeks maybe. They should be readily healed now, but whatever they've been using in his wounds has festered and infected his entire body."

The rebels had said nothing more to her about where they had been or how Gail had received the injuries when she'd questioned them. She wasn't happy about their being back in her home, not when her people were just starting to respect her as a leader.

"What's that?" Bael asked with an upwards nod to the desk.

She'd nearly forgotten about Nadir's letter.

Bala sat up. "Letter from our Commander," she said, and she started to rip the paper. "Let's hope he's not done anything stupid," she mumbled.

The words on the page were simple:

Come in five days. We have business to talk.

"Important?" Bael asked.

"Something is," Bala answered. "I'll need you to cover me a day or so when I travel to him."

"We have new rebels in our midst, and you're leaving?" Bael asked.

"I don't think he'd be asking me to come if it weren't important," she countered. She tapped the letter on the table with a sigh. "Get some sleep, Bael. We need to do another weapons inventory tomorrow and possibly every day after. I want to know if these rebels have taken anything and what they're planning."

Bala left Bael in charge when she left on the fifth morning, and a nervousness rattled her heart as she left her kingdom on foot.

She passed by Duarb on the way, just wanting a quick drop in to say, "Hello Father," to him before pressing her hand to the trunk and sighing against the black wriggling tongues. To any other person, it probably looked odd, but she'd been coming and doing this same ritual to her father's tree for years. Even Draven had called her out on it one day, and the memory made her smile.

"Why do you do that?" *he asked, staring at her, arms crossed over his chest.*

Bala smiled back at him, noting the squint of his sage gaze. "It's our tree."

"It's tongues," Draven countered. "Tongues of the Infi, at that."

"I'm aware," she insisted. "But... It's like you can feel him breathe. It's comforting. You should try it."

Draven's left brow jetted upwards, and she almost laughed at the familiar look.

"Come on," she urged him. "Feel it."

Draven sighed, still eyeing her, but he stepped forward anyway. "Yeah, okay," he gave in. The grimace that spread over his features made her bite her lips to stifle the amusement. He reached out, and his hand was slowly consumed into the black tongues.

"This is..." Words seemed to stop in his throat, and he took a deep breath as he settled there, head hanging.

"Home," she said as though it were obvious.

"Disgusting," he countered.

Her mouth dropped at his choice of words, and Draven laughed. His deep bellow made her head shake.

"You don't feel it?" she asked, voice a higher pitch.

"No, I get it. I see what you mean," he said reassuringly. "It is slightly comforting to the core. Doesn't make it any less disgusting. I think... Yes. One did just tongue my palm as though my hand were a woman."

At this, Bala's smile faltered, and she shook her head at his banter. Draven laughed a great, "Ha!" and he jokingly pointed at her when he pushed off the tree.

"Come on," he said, dusting his hands on his pants. "Naddi will be beside himself if he thinks we've forgotten him."

Bala's heart hurt at the memory, and she closed her eyes a moment longer.

By the time she reached the Umber, the sun was high over her head. People were gathering off the shores to break from their duties for lunch. A few of them greeted her, including some of the children. They bounded to her with hugs. One of them asked her where the big guy was, and she knew he meant Draven.

"He's not with me this time," she said. "Maybe when you're older, you'll see him again."

It was an exaggeration of a hope she wasn't sure she knew how to hang on to.

As Bala worked her way through the market and homes, she finally reached the stretch of beach, and she sighed as she embraced the sun on her skin.

"Venari King," a familiar voice drawled. Bala knew that voice, and she turned to find Soli Amberglass approaching her. Bala's lips pressed together thinly at the sight of the great warrior, but she hugged her nonetheless.

"Hello, Soli," she said forcibly. "Do you have an eye on your Commander? I am supposed to meet him."

She liked reminding the warrior that Nadir was, in fact, her Commander, as it usually made Soli shift and sometimes glare.

Soli did as Bala wanted, and then she gave an upwards nod out to the logs at the end of the jetty. "Balancing with the Second Sun," she informed her.

Bala followed her point out to the jetty, and she saw the pair. She gave Soli a nod and then made her way out, dropping her bags on the sand before moving to the rocks.

The sight nearly made her laugh.

Nadir and Lex, rolling and balancing on the great log in the calm alcove, sticks in their hands as they crossed one another. Lex kept up with him, a determined look on her stern features. It was the sight of how disheveled she was that made Bala's head tilt.

The tight-fitting scaled armor pants, the oversized sage green tank with open sides, the leather strap across her breasts under the shirt. It was so long, Lex had it tucked into the front of her pants, revealing the belt on her hips, the great Belwark sword on her side. Wisps of her now shaggy blonde hair fell over her eyes as she gritted her teeth and blocked Nadir's blows. Seeing Lex relaxed in this garb as compared to the stuffy gambesons she'd first met her in was night and day.

She and Bael had been the ones to meet Lex and Nyssa when they'd rode into the Forest to check on Aydra that day. They had been on patrol in the trees just outside the kingdom. The wind had brought the noise of two riders, and the pair had drawn arrows in ready.

Lex dropped down from her horse. At the time, Bala hadn't known who she was, but when she shook her hair from her face and glanced up, Bala's bow had sagged in her hands at the sight of her. Because the woman was stunning and fierce, bright cheeks glowing against the darkness of the woods, short blonde hair swept back off her forehead, a single unruly piece that curled down over her eye. Her eyes were round and wide, taking in every detail of the forest around her. She spoke something to the girl still on her horse and reached a hand back to steady the reins.

"I know you're here," Lex had called out. "We mean to see the Queen. We are her Second and the Princess."

Bala exchanged a glance with Bael, who shrugged. Bala nodded, and she jumped down from the tree first. The wind caught her as she leaped down the forty-foot drop, and it slowed her so she could land safely on her feet. Lex pulled her great sword the moment the wind whipped. Bala landed with her own swords drawn, and for a moment, neither moved.

Lex's darkened green gaze wandered over Bala, and her sword limped in her hand. "Hi," she had said as she straightened.

Bala eyed this beautiful woman as well as the girl still on the horse. "Second Sun and Princess?" she repeated as she straightened. "What—no great army to retrieve Her Majesty?"

"I am the army," Lex countered. "Take us to our Queen."

A quiet chuckle emitted from Bala, and she glanced back to Bael, who shared her amusement. "Take you to your Queen?" she repeated. "Never walk into a kingdom not of your own and try to give out demands, Second Sun," she mocked. "You'll embarrass yourself. Especially in this one."

Lex was clearly taken aback by her words. "I'm willing to take that chance if you're unwilling to cooperate."

"Lex—" the Princess called out, "—taking her head is getting us no closer to seeing Drae," she said quietly.

Lex's gaze didn't leave Bala's, and the smugness rising on both their faces challenged the other.

"Lex?" Bala repeated, the name sounding familiar. "As in Hilexi Ashbourne?" She'd heard stories of her trials through the years, how she'd defended her Second Sun title multiple times over and was rumored to be the fiercest warrior in the west.

A crooked smirk lifted Lex's lips. "Glad to see my name trickles all the way across Haerland," she uttered arrogantly.

Bala scoffed, whirling her blade in her hand. "You should listen to your Princess, Belwark," Bala said in a low tone.

"And you are who to be giving out such orders?" Lex asked. "I was not aware the Venari allowed their beautiful women to hold positions of power. "

Bael openly laughed. "One more thing you do not know about the people you have deemed beneath you for a hundred years," she muttered. "My name is Balandria Windwood, and I am the Venari Second."

"You're the next Venari King?"

"I am," Bala replied. "You should remember it."

"Whoever you are," the Princess said then, her horse beginning to get restless, "we are wasting sunlight. Do you think you can stop leering at each other long enough to show us to your kingdom? I cannot imagine what sort of tortures you've put my sister through. We need to see her and get her back to the safety of her own people."

Bala considered the Princess a moment, nearly laughing at the words that had come from her mouth. She glanced back to Lex. "Quite the attitude," she muttered.

"You think I don't know?" Lex muttered back. "Do you want her? We can do an exchange."

To this, Bala grinned. She gave her a once over before sheathing her blade and glancing back to Bael. "Bael, take the leads from them. We need to get back before everyone wakes and there is an ambush." She turned back to Lex. "If your coming gets us any closer to being rid of your Queen, by all means. Please come along."

Lex chuckled under her breath. "Glad to know she's not lost her fight while being in her enemy's kingdom."

"Lost her fight?" Bala balked. "If anything, it's gotten worse."

Bael stepped forward then and took the reins of the two horses then, and Bala didn't miss the smile he gave the Princess.

"Hey, Princess," he drawled, to which Bala nearly laughed.

The Princess looked like she might smile, but it faltered into a glare, and she raised her chin. "You don't need to lead my horse," she snapped. "I'm perfectly capable of following."

Bala exchanged a grin with Bael. "Better luck next time," she winked.

Bala sighed out the memory, arms crossing over her chest, and she called out to Nadir and Lex on the ocean log.

"Do you two think you can break long enough to greet your King, or should I come back another time?" Bala called out.

Nadir lost his balance at her shout, and he launched himself into the water. But Lex caught her gaze, half-smile quirking on her face, and she jumped from the log to the rocks before Nadir could pull her under.

Bala's chest swelled at the sight of Lex's smile. Having not felt such a moment in weeks, it almost overwhelmed her. Bala skipped over the rocks towards her, and Lex threw the stick to the water at her back.

"Thank the Architects," Lex smiled. "I thought I was doomed to look at the Commander the rest of my days." Lex grabbed Bala around the waist and hauled her flush as she reached her. Lex leaned to kiss her, but Bala pressed a finger to her lips.

"I'm not sure you deserve that," Bala mocked. "I've not heard a word from either of you in weeks."

Lex hung her head, and instead, she simply kissed Bala's forehead and pulled her in for a hug. "Blame the Commander," she shrugged as she pulled back to nod towards Nadir, who was bringing himself up out of the water. "He's put a damper on communications."

Bala's brow raised playfully at him. "Something you're hiding, Nadir?" she asked.

Nadir scratched the back of his head but didn't respond directly. "It's good to see you too, Bala," he said before going to hug her. She returned his embrace, not caring that he was soaking wet and getting her wet as well. He paused and clasped her face when he pulled back, and she noted the sadness in his gaze. Compared to the smile he'd had on him the last time he'd gone to her to trade, which had been weeks before, this was concerning.

"What's wrong?" she asked.

"We can talk back at my home," he said. "Let us get out of these clothes."

Nadir urged them back up the jetty, and Bala couldn't help her smile as Lex wrapped her arm around her shoulders.

Lex hardly spoke as they walked, and every time Bala would look at her, she saw that same twinge of sadness in her gaze as had been in Nadir's.

"Has something happened I should know about?" Bala asked Lex.

"We'll talk when we're out of these clothes," Nadir called sternly back.

Bala met Lex's gaze, and Lex shrugged, to which Bala frowned.

"Since when do you listen to his orders?" Bala asked quietly.

The tired sigh that emitted from Lex made Bala tense. "It's new," Lex admitted.

The remainder of the walk was taken in silence, and Lex and Nadir left Bala on the porch while they washed off and changed out of the sandy clothes. Bala pressed her hands into the banister as she looked over the beach, still wondering where Nyssa was and why she had not come to greet her.

"I expected my Princess to welcome me," Balandria said when the pair reappeared on the porch. "Where is she? I thought surely she'd be barking orders to your people by now. Where—"

Nadir was drying his hair slowly with a towel, his eyes blank and fixated on the steps. Lex's head hung, and she slumped into the chair, leaning over with her elbows on her knees.

Bala's stomach tightened. She shifted on her feet as a coldness poured through her. She didn't like the looks on their faces, the aversion of their eyes...

"Nadir, what happened?" Bala demanded to know.

His eyes finally met hers, and he held his hands up. "Calm down."

Bala's fist tightened around her knife at her side. "I swear if you did something to her—"

"Bala, put the knife away," Lex interjected.

"Where. Is. She?"

"She's okay," Nadir said.

And she knew he was lying.

"I did not ask if she was okay," Bala corrected. "I asked where the *fuck* she is."

Shame burdened his features, Nadir pressed his hands to his hips. "She's at the outskirts of Savigndor."

"And where exactly is that?" Bala managed shakily.

"It's what Man has started calling their settlement."

—Her fist pummeled into Nadir's face.

He stumbled on his feet, grasping at his nose, but he didn't fight back. Anger surged in her veins. She lunged, her fists grabbing his shirt, and she yanked him forward.

"You let her be captured?!"

She released her right hand, only to send it flying into his face again.

Arms grabbed her from the side.

"Bala!"

Bala lunged again, but Lex's arms caught her. Her feet flew into the air, and Bala kicked his chest.

"You're a fucking *idiot*, Nadir!"

Nadir tumbled into the door, holding onto his side. Wild terror ran through Bala's veins.

"I trusted you!"

Bala shoved Lex off and jumped on Nadir again. She picked him up by his hair and slammed his head back into the door.

"Bala, *stop!"*

Lex wrapped her arms under Bala's shoulders and hauled her off him, but not before Bala railed her foot into Nadir's side once more.

Lex threw Bala into the railing. "Enough!"

Bala pushed off, but Lex stood her ground before her, pulling her back with her hands tight around Bala's arms.

"Listen—"

Bala's heart raced. She shoved against Lex's grasp. "You fucking coward," she spat at him.

Blood dripped from Nadir's broken lip and down his chin.

"I should have known you would let this happen," Bala cried. "You with your lax judgment, your everything-is-fine attitude—"

Nadir still hadn't looked at her. He grabbed onto his side where she'd kicked him and pushed himself to a sitting position.

"What happened—did you fuck her the first night and then leave her? Break her heart and have her run away? Did your people condemn her because of who she is too? Did you not stand up for her? —"

"It's not like that—"

"She's the fucking Princess—she's my *friend!*—You were supposed to look after her!"

"Bala!" Lex shouted in her face.

Tears were in Bala's eyes as her heart broke.

"You were supposed to look after her," she breathed.

Bala finally stopped struggling. Her insides continued to shatter and tremble as she watched Nadir groan and lean back against the wall.

"It's okay, Lex," he finally said, touching the bleed of his lip with his thumb. "I deserve it."

"No more than I do," Lex said, looking over her shoulder at him.

"What happened?" Bala demanded.

Nadir leaned his head back against the door and pulled his knees into his chest.

The pair told her everything.

Everything from Nyssa and Nadir giving each other up, to the fight with Lex, to losing her. Everything about him looking for and finding her.

By the time they were finished, tears had fallen down Bala's cheeks, and she couldn't help but wonder why Nyssa had pushed herself so far into this.

"I don't understand," Bala finally managed as she sat on the chair. "If you know where she is, why are you not storming the gates to get her back?" She met Nadir's eyes. "I thought you loved her?"

Lex's widened eyes snapped in his direction, and Nadir sighed heavily.

"Don't you think that's what's making this so hard?" he managed, pain strewn across his features. "She made me promise—"

"Damn your promises, Nadir," Balandria interjected. "Where is she? We'll go get her tonight."

"You can't."

"Why the fuck not?"

"Because she's gathering information for us," he almost shouted. "She's somehow managed to worm her way into negotiations and meetings between the Noble and his guards. She made me promise to allow her to do this. She has a plan."

Balandria's fist tightened around itself. "I'm going to kill her."

"Yes, well, you can get in line," Nadir muttered.

For a moment, Bala didn't speak. She merely stared at Nadir, her hands still on the phoenix dagger on her side.

"What's her plan?" she finally snapped.

"Their King is set to arrive in two Dead Moons. She plans to get herself out, possibly call the Noctuans to aid her."

"She wants to use my creatures?"

"Do you have a better idea?"

"Yes," she said fast. "Go get her tonight and take it all down with us."

"That will look like an attack from us. My home will be ambushed," Nadir argued.

"So I should be okay with using my creatures as bait?"

"This is the only time the Noctuans will actually go near their home. She's just using them to scare the strangers. If she can even call them. There is a chance she won't be able to."

"What do you mean?"

"She couldn't hear them when she left us," Lex said. "She'd shut them out."

Bala rubbed her face in her hands, sighing at all the new information. "Fucking curses," she uttered before slapping her hands to her knees. "Why am I here?"

"She wants to talk to you," Nadir answered.

"About what?"

"About the nature of her arriving in Man's hands," Nadir said.

Bala felt the warmth drain from her face as she thought of the group of rebels that had made their way to her home. "She met them, didn't she?"

"I don't know the details," Nadir sighed.

Bala cursed her luck under her breath. "How do we see her?"

"You'll come with me to market in the morning. Look as my assistant." He stood from the ground, wincing as he grabbed his side. "Nyssa asked that you wear a dress and cloak. To blend in."

"Excuse me?" Bala balked.

"I told her you wouldn't like it," he muttered. "There's something else too."

Lex and Bala both straightened. "Are you planning on keeping us in suspense a little longer?"

Nadir glared at Bala. "She has fire."

The statement staled between them.

"Sorry, what?" Lex asked.

Nadir rubbed his neck in his hands. "She has fire. Similar to her brother's but different. I asked Lovi about it. He thinks because Arbina marked them at the same time that she may have given that power to Nyssa as well."

"Nyssa has never shown any—"

"She's also never been pushed to her limits and felt as scared as she has these last few weeks," Nadir cut in. "I think her core latched onto the last source of power it could find to try and protect her once she pushed out the creatures. She said the day she ran away, she had another attack on the beach, and it manifested around her." His gaze flickered between them, and he hung his head. "She doesn't know how to control it. It rises like the Prince's does. As ash and black streaks on her skin. But her eyes are not black. Her eyes are molten fire. And the flames... They're black and amber."

Bala clutched the edge of the chair as she sat up, gaze staring at the ground, her chest stilling with the news. "Shadow fire," she uttered breathlessly.

"You've heard of it?" Nadir asked.

"I saw a story of one of the past kings to have a fire like that. The first Promised King, when they weren't even kings yet. When Arbina used to mark her children with the Sun in the room with her to show off."

"How is it I do not know this?" Nadir asked.

"Probably because I only saw it when Draven and I went to the scroll cave beneath Lake Oriens a couple years ago," Bala answered.

"I knew it," Nadir declared. "That's where he found that damn scroll."

"That's neither here nor there," Bala said as she stood. "But what it did to that King... He could walk in shadows. Burn things with a flinch of his finger. And he was well practiced with it."

"Nyssa met the phoenix two days before she left," Lex interjected then.

Nadir and Bala both turned. Lex's gaze met theirs, her arms hugging her chest.

"Lovi took her," Nadir remembered.

"She said she felt Aydra hugging her," Lex said.

"You think the Sun did this?" Bala asked.

"I think it's no coincidence that the Sun appeared and Nyssa unlocked her fire powers two days later with a panic attack."

"What if Arbina did accidentally give her fire—"

"And the Sun made it stronger," Nadir finished. "Like the first King's. What if she sensed it in Nyssa and remembered what it had been when she used to be in the room with Arbina?"

"And her panic set it off? Her core grabbing onto it like you said," Bala said with a nod to Nadir. "One more thing to get back at her daughter for," she muttered. "I am so tired of her children being pawns."

"Wait—" Lex interjected, face furling with confusion. "When you say her core grabbed onto it... What does that mean? You make it sound like she has some different entity inside her."

"The Kings of this land have always had powers greater than the rest of us. Arbina and Duarb constantly showing up the other," Nadir said. "Their cores have always been the source of that power."

Bala rubbed her hands together, eyes fixating on a spot on the floor. "It feels like a constant knot in your gut," she said softly. "It feels like a connection to something that constantly wants to overpower or protect you. When I was learning how to manipulate wind, Draven would always tell me I had to keep a lock on it. That if I allowed my core to take over, it would protect me in any way it saw fit."

"I think that's why Aydra could connect so strongly with the creatures," Nadir said. "I spoke with Lovi about it. It wanted to protect her. It's what the Promised King's true forms are connected to. And I'm thinking when Nyssa let go to feel the Ulfram that night, she allowed it some leverage over herself."

"Until it broke, and she shut the creatures out," Lex cut in.

Nadir nodded. "And it pulled for the next strongest thing." He pushed his hands behind his head, a great sigh emitting from him. "We could ask about it," he suggested, looking at Bala.

"Ask who?" Lex asked.

Bala didn't need to ask who he meant. "How do you plan on calling the Sun?" she asked.

"I can't," Nadir said. "But you could. You're a child of the Sun too."

Bala shifted on her feet as she considered it. "I don't think finding out how she acquired those powers is our first priority right now," she said. "I would rather focus on—" A realization hit her then, and her heart stopped. "She's going to use it, isn't she? To get out of there. She'll call the Noctuans if she can and use her fire. She'll use all her powers."

Nadir didn't respond immediately, but then he nodded his head, and she knew he was thinking the same as her.

"Nadir, we have to get her out of there before she does that," Bala affirmed.

"She won't allow it."

"*I don't care*," Bala argued. "She doesn't know what it will do. Her core being stretched in too many places, it might... She might..."

The chair hit her again, and she stared off, thoughts of what might happen to their Princess clouding her vision. Her becoming nothing more than a shell, as though the Berdijay had taken her. Exhausting herself and dying.

"That's why I'm going to be there when it happens," Nadir said.

The confirmation in his tone made Bala look up, and she saw a glisten in Nadir's eyes.

"I will not lose her again," he promised.

Bala almost laughed. "You know damn well you can't make that promise. This is Nyssari. Running into situations with fear coursing through her bones. Putting herself on the line in a far different way than Aydra would have."

It was Lex that scoffed this time. "Aydra would have rather died than become a silent prisoner," she muttered.

"You haven't sent word to her brother, have you?" Bala asked then.

Nadir looked at her like she'd grown another head. "You still have a forest, don't you? No, I didn't tell him. I'm not ready to die. With any luck, she'll do what she needs and get out of there before he ever finds out."

"Which is another reason why we need to get her out now," Bala affirmed. "If Dorian even gets a feeling she is in danger, he will take down everything on his way to her."

Lex snorted.

Bala and Nadir stared at her.

"What?" Bala asked.

Lex laughed. "Nothing, I only wish he were here to hear this conversation," she said.

"You can't actually let him know we're terrified of him," Bala said. "He'd never shut up about it."

Nadir crossed his arms over his chest. "As I said, I'm not ready to die. I've a lot of things left on my list to do."

"Like what, Commander?" Bala asked.

"Like getting my Princess back."

Bala exchanged a smile with Lex, who seemed to share her amusement. "You really need to tell her," she said.

A long sigh left him, and he shook his head. "She will do what she needs to do to prove to herself that she is worthy of her crown, and when she's ready, she'll let me love her. Until then, I will stand by her side as I promised her I would."

"You're adorable," Bala mocked.

"There's something else I need your help with," Nadir said.

"More than what you've already asked of me?" Bala countered.

Nadir stared at her, and the weight of whatever was on his mind became visible in his eyes.

"Fine," she surrendered. "What is it?"

"It's meeting night," he said. "I haven't told them about Nyssa."

"Not even Lovi?"

He shook his head.

"Why not? They should know she's risking her life for them."

"Because the last she was here, they called her worthless to her face and more. They didn't trust her."

"What do you expect me to do?"

"Stand by my side and tell them who she is."

Bala's weight shifted. "Why haven't you done that?"

"Because they're all smart enough to see how I feel about her. They think I'm simply favoring her because of that. We gave each other up to counter it, but they know."

Bala glanced outside to the setting sun. "When is the meeting?"

"Now."

44

A significant number of his people had already gathered in their main tent, all sitting at tables set up, settling from eating the meal that had been served. Lovi stayed out of these meetings, saying it was not his Age or affairs to intervene with.

Nadir sat at the front of the room, with Bala and Lex on either side. Nadir quieted the room after Bala had acknowledged a few friends.

Explaining why the meeting had been called seemed to be more difficult for the Commander than she'd ever witnessed. Every word seemed forced, as though saying it aloud made it a reality he didn't want to come to terms with.

"Surprised you didn't storm the castle to bring her home," Soli muttered as she sank back in her chair once Nadir had finished talking.

"I trust her to do that herself," Nadir affirmed.

"Why should we trust her?" someone called out.

"Because she is risking her life right now for you," Nadir nearly shouted. "For *all of you*. Being beaten and starved just to find out information that will help us keep our home."

Nadir's chest was heaving, hands visibly shaking.

"No one asked her to do that," Soli said.

"No, but you all made it perfectly clear when she was here that you did not like or trust her," he seethed. "Even when you should have trusted me to make that decision, you all took it upon yourselves to make her feel inferior as though she had to prove herself to you when you should have—"

Nadir had to stop talking, his hands threading behind his head as he pushed a deep breath into his lungs and stared out at the crowd.

"You should have trusted your Commander," he finished.

427

"You were blinded by her beauty," Soli called out.

"Give me one instance while she was here that my being with her made you question my decisions," he asked. "Tell me when I ever put her over any of you."

"Can you swear never to put her first?" called out another.

"I'll never have to make that decision."

"Why?"

"Because she will always make sure you all come before her," he affirmed. "Because that's the kind of Queen she will be."

His people began to exchange glances, a few muttering around the room. Bala took the opportunity to stand.

"Your Commander is right," she said, placing a hand on Nadir's arm. She gave him a nod, and Nadir finally took a seat. Every person's attention moved to her, and Bala straightened.

"If there is one thing I learned about her during my time at Magnice, it is this: Nyssa is methodical, patient, and observant. She memorizes everything and will know your weaknesses before you know them yourself. It's why Dorian trusts her as he does. It's why I trust her, and I'm sure it's one more reason your Commander trusts her—" She glanced down to Nadir, who gave her a silent nod.

"Dorian is impulsive, much like Aydra," she continued. "But Nyssa... Nyssa will sit back and watch you for hours, calculating her every breath and counting yours. Nyssa craves information just as Aydra craved blood. Her need to prove herself goes beyond selfish greed. If she sees an opportunity for power, she will take it. And not for herself, but so that she can keep all of you safe, whether you see that or not. I know all you people see is that innocent facade. I'm sure you all thought her a weak girl when she arrived, but that entire act is her greatest ploy. She is a shadow. She will know how to kill you just by watching you walk. And when she works out how best to do that, her brother will take you out like the mercenary he is. Together they are more lethal than anything else in our world. They were *made* for this war."

Bala paused, letting the words settle in the Honest people's minds and watching as they each shifted in their chairs.

"What do you want from us?" Soli finally asked. "Would you like us to throw her a parade when she gets back?"

"What I want from you, Soli," Nadir said slowly, his eyes rolling up to her, "is for you to get your head out of your ass and stop pretending like you would have done what she is doing."

Bala sat down at the dare of Nadir's words. His hands settled between his legs as he leaned back in his chair.

"We need to double our food production. Synchronize and strengthen our legion fighting. Soot—" he looked to the seamstress in the corner "—I need more armor."

The woman, Sutor, answered, "I'll need more material."

"I'll get it," Nadir promised. "Florna, what do you need?" he asked the arborist.

"More hands," she replied.

Nadir nodded, and then he stood, his hands pressing into the table. "Everyone in this room is now working more than one job. I don't care if you think you don't have time. Make it. Food is now being rationed. A third of what we were giving ourselves now goes into storage. Smoke it. Cure it. Jar it. I don't care. If you're trading in the villages or the mountains, double the price. Everything is more precarious now, and it will only get worse."

"What about trading with the Forest?" someone asked.

"Bala and her people are just as much in danger as we are. We provide her with anything she needs, and she will do the same for us. Just as it has always been."

"Should we be concerned that you sound as though our home is in jeopardy?" Soli asked.

"If you think it isn't, you're blind," he affirmed. "Bala and I travel to the camp tomorrow to see the Princess. We'll hold another meeting in three days to go over what we've learned, and I want an update on what we've discussed here."

His eyes traveled over the room once more, and then he slapped the table twice. "We're finished."

No one spoke to Nadir as they filed out of the tent. Soli was one of the last to rise, and Bala knew she was repeating every demand Nadir had just said and possibly plotting to go against him somehow.

Lex pulled her pipe from her pocket and began to pack it as the last people left. Bala moved from her chair to sit on the table between them, curling her legs under her.

"What is Soli's problem?" Bala asked.

"You know her," Nadir said, kicking his feet on the table. "Anything other than duty is considered weak. Can't imagine she was very ecstatic about Nyssa and I. I'm sure she was the one leading the charge to take my title away."

"What—did she think she would be a better Commander?"

"Probably."

"That's laughable. You'd all be dead or starving."

"I know," Nadir agreed.

Lex kicked back in her own chair then, and she passed the smoking pipe to Nadir. Bala's thoughts wandered back to their task for the next day.

"When do we leave tomorrow?" she asked.

"Sunrise," he said as he blew out the inhale. "Most of the merchants do not have their goods ready until a couple hours after. It'll give us time to get there and make ourselves hidden."

"Don't they know you already?"

"They do," he answered. "But I'll not be parlaying with the Noble this time. Nyssa will come to us."

"And if she is caught?"

"She won't be," he affirmed.

"How can you be sure?"

"Because I trust her."

Bala paused, rubbing her hands together as she contemplated her next words. "How long has she been there?" Bala asked.

"Six weeks now," Nadir answered.

"The long game, Princess," she mumbled under her breath. "And you bartered for a night with her the first time?"

Nadir merely nodded with his smoking exhale.

"How did she seem?"

"Scared," he answered. "But determined. I could tell she'd been holding it in."

"Sounds like her," Bala muttered as he passed her the pipe. Bala slouched as she inhaled it. She'd not allowed her own guard down in weeks, and the sweetness of the herb was a welcome reprieve.

"So..." Lex began, now picking at her nails with her knife. "We're just going to brush over Bala's claim that you're in love with my Princess?"

Nadir looked as though he would laugh, but instead, he simply shook his head, a small smile rising on his face.

"I am," he breathed. "I once asked Aydra about her. Obviously, Aydra boasted about her siblings and told me how proud she was of them, how beautiful her sister was and how she worked so hard to become a better fighter. She also told me that Nyssari was scared of everything, shy yet fiery... that once I met her, she would more than likely not say but a few words to me... The person I met that night at the banquet couldn't have been more different."

Lex snorted, and Bala exchanged a knowing smirk with her.

"She was funny… smart… gorgeous… charming—"

"Ah, that's the best word for her," Bala mused. "*Charming*. Actually doesn't surprise me that she's been enslaved but a few weeks, and already she's basically the Noble's hand."

"Aydra didn't know her sister as well as she thought," Lex said. "It wasn't her fault. Nyssa was always scared of disappointing her. Sometimes she would shut her out, let Aydra believe she was a shy little teenager. But the reality is, Nyssa is—"

"Fucking wild," Bala interjected, taking a long inhale of her pipe.

Lex chuckled fondly under her breath, and Bala passed the pipe to her. "So, what are you going to do about it when she's back in your arms?" Lex asked Nadir.

"Give her time to find herself again."

Lex and Bala met each other's awed pout, and then Lex smacked him on the back of the head.

"*Ow!*"

"That's not the right answer."

"What do you want me to say?"

"Be bold, Nadir. Take your Queen with style and ferocity," Lex said with a wink.

He huffed under his breath at her remark, and he sighed into the darkness. "She's just been enslaved and on her own for weeks. You want me to push her to the ground and fuck her senseless her first day home?"

Lex and Bala looked at each other again.

"Yes," Bala said.

"Oh, please do," Lex begged.

Nadir chuckled at them. "You two are horrible influences."

"We're the best," Lex affirmed in a breath, leaning her chair back on two legs.

"Venari King and Second Sun," Bala mused. "Do you think there will be songs written of us one day?"

"Valiant and preposterous ones, for sure," Lex grinned.

Bala huffed amusedly with the exhale of her herb. Nadir caught her eye and shook his head.

"I expect you to sing them considering you'll be here much longer than the rest of us, Mr. Immortality," she mocked at him.

Nadir smiled between the pair. "I'll write them myself," he

promised. "Lex can help me sing them," he added.

"That's right," Bala said, glancing to Lex. "Sometimes I forget you're a Belwark. Ageless and made of fire."

Lex's gaze darkened and a crooked smile slipped onto her lips. "Do you need me to remind you?"

Bala met her gaze. Lex extended the pipe to her just as Nadir cleared his throat and stood.

"Yeah, I'll just—" he pointed behind him, clearing his throat again, "—I'll be going," he winked at Bala. "You two have fun."

Bala hardly lost her gaze with Lex, eyes pouring over the attire Lex wore once more. Lex ran her long fingers through her now shaggy blonde hair and wisps of it fell over her eyes.

"I think I like this look on you," Bala finally said.

"What look?"

"*Relaxed* Lex," Bala said. "As much as I loved that winged shoulder armor, this look is..." Her gaze traveled over Lex again, noting the way the pants hugged her muscular thighs and gripped at her backside.

"More casual?" Lex suggested.

"Fucking hot," Bala countered.

Lex grinned at the ground, then back to Bala, the haze of her green eyes piercing her behind those unruly wisps of hair. Lex reached over, her finger trailing Bala's calf, and Bala wondered how such a person could already have her thighs squeezing.

Bala's gaze fluttered at the danger that was Hilexi before her, her mind going back to their time in the Forest when Bala had shaken her head at all her advances. And then to Magnice, remembering how Lex had swooned her for the entire week of the Gathering since she had her alone, finally pulling her into her bed that last night, Hagen joining them later with his own guest.

"How are you?" Bala asked, happy to have a moment to themselves.

Lex avoided her gaze a moment, sitting up in the chair only to move it so that she was in front of Bala, and she laid her head sideways on Bala's thigh, hands massaging Bala's calf muscle.

"Failing," Lex admitted.

"Didn't look like you were failing today," Bala said. "I'm sure Nadir appreciates you."

"He's been in an almost spiral since she's been gone," Lex said, her lips pressing to the inside of Bala's thigh, making her breaths tighten. "But only at night. He's as skilled as Aydra was at keeping up appearances." She sat her chin on Bala's thigh and looked up at her, tips of her fingers trailing their way up her leg. "How is the Venari King holding up?" she asked as she kissed her thigh again.

Bala almost trembled at the deliberation of Lex's moves, how the toy of her movements had her heart ricocheting in her chest. "Holding," Bala admitted. "Just holding."

Lex lifted her head and pulled at Bala's calves, bringing her to the edge of the table. "Anything from my Prince?" Lex asked, both her hands squeezing Bala's legs.

Bala tried to keep her heart from fluttering. "Nothing yet, she managed.

Lex sighed, and Bala reached out. She pushed her hand through Lex's hair, down to her cheek, and Lex moved to kiss her palm.

"Do you know what I've missed?" Lex asked as she met her eyes.

"Danger?" Bala suggested in an attempt to make Lex smile.

Lex huffed under her breath, her hands moving to the sides of Bala's thighs. "Apart from that," she smiled. "It sounds odd, but I've missed having a duty. It's what I was made for."

"Does Nadir have nothing he can put you in charge of?"

"He's tasked me with helping the younger recruits," Lex said. "It's not the same. I miss walking into a room and commanding it. People's heads turning, nearly dropping to their knees with a raise of my brow."

Bala laughed. "The entire army in herself," she mocked, remembering what Lex had told her.

"Never needed one behind me," Lex challenged. "I've only ever needed a Queen to serve."

"Or a King," Bala suggested.

A crooked smile rose on Lex's lips. "A King would do grandly." Dilation grew in her eyes, and Bala felt her chin lifting as Lex's hands moved further up her legs. "Does the Venari King have need of a new warrior in her ranks?"

Breath shortened in Bala's lungs as Lex squeezed her backside and pulled her to the very edge of the table. "Possibly," she toyed. "Unfortunately, the Venari King does not simply give out positions. The warrior will have to audition first."

Lex leaned forward, lips brushing over Bala's breast, and Bala felt her eyes flutter. "I do like a challenge," Lex breathed, and her mouth clamped over her shirted nipple. Bala sucked in a breath, hand threading through Lex's hair.

But Lex stood slowly, and Bala found herself squeezing her thighs around Lex's slim hips as she towered over her. Her hair fell over her eyes, mouths a breath apart, and Lex reached for Bala's chin, taking it between two fingers.

"Show me to the audition ring, my King."

Lex pulled her chin up, and she captured Bala's mouth with hers.

Bala's chest caved with the taste of her again. Hunger swept between them. Lex straightened, her hands threading beneath Bala's jaw as Bala grasped at her waist and pulled her flush. Every whisper of their tongues against one another sent her heart fleeing. No others compared to the wanted feeling Bala felt with Lex. Bala grasped Lex's backside, rocking her spread legs against Lex's hips. Her hand found its way into the gap at the back of Lex's pants, and she squeezed her ass, causing a groan to emit from Lex's throat.

As Lex moved her mouth to Bala's throat, Bala circled back to the tie on the front of Lex's pants, and she began to undo them. Her finger found her way into her pants, and the moment the pad brushed Lex's clit, Lex cursed in her throat.

Lex grasped Bala's hands and pinned them into the tabletop.

"I thought this was my audition," she uttered, nose nudging Bala's.

"You're moving too slow," Bala dared.

The familiar crooked smirk rose on Lex's lips. She leaned forward and kissed her again, teeth tugging on her bottom lip when she pulled back. "You have no idea how slow I can move," she promised. "I will send you over the edge with one brush of my tongue between your thighs, and you'll moan so loudly Duarb will send wind to protect you."

Bala forgot how to breathe.

But she swallowed, and she arched her breasts against Lex's. "Prove it."

Lex smirked, and she kissed Bala once more.

"Do I need to restrain your hands, or are you capable of keeping them to yourself?" Lex asked when she pulled back.

The Second Sun offering to tie her to a table intrigued Bala.

But she had a better idea.

"No hands for you," Bala countered.

Lex balked. "Excuse me?"

"You want your audition, Second Sun... These are my terms," Bala dared. "We can save your slow claims for later. This is what I want."

"You think I'm incapable of playing both?"

Bala practically felt the delight dancing on her features as she spread her legs wide and pushed her hands behind her into the tabletop. "All yours, Hilexi."

Lex's eyes fluttered with a cave of her chest. "I love when you use my full name."

Her mouth slammed into Bala's, and Bala grabbed Lex's hands, placing them on her hips. "Your hands stay here," she breathed between kisses.

Lex's fingers dug into Bala's muscles, hunger exuding from the kiss she was wrapped in. Bala couldn't help but hug Lex's head into the crook of her neck as Lex sucked on her skin. She could tell it was taking all Lex's restraint not to move her hands. But the squeeze of her fingers into her made her hips lift against her pelvis. Lex moved, kissing the front of Bala's throat and going down until the fabric of her shirt got in the way, and Lex paused to look at her.

"Take off your shirt," she requested.

But Bala only smirked.

Lex chuckled and hung her head. "Please," she added.

"I'm deducting points," Bala said as she pulled her shirt over her head, leaving only the leather strap around her breasts, ties cinching it together on the front. The ties pulled her breasts taut together, leaving cleavage slightly spilling over the top. Lex met Bala's gaze again.

Her hand squeezed into Bala's hip, and she bent to suck on Bala's collar. Her hips moved against Bala's, the friction of her pelvis against hers making her squeeze her thighs around her again. Lex's lips trailed to Bala's breasts, but she didn't stop there. She kissed down her deliberately until she sat back down in the chair.

She began to undo Bala's pants with her teeth, and Bala inhaled sharply. Lex grabbed the top of Bala's pants, and she locked eyes with her. "You can take off points for this too," she uttered. "Shift your ass, my King."

Bala obliged, shifting so that her pants pulled off. And as her pants were removed, she heard Lex curse, and she wondered if the Belwark could see how wet she was. Her pants fell on the ground, and Lex hovered between Bala's thighs.

"Balandria Windwood," she drawled, and Bala almost laughed. "Who knew the Venari King dared to dress in no undergarments."

Her nose nudged her clit, and Bala had to stretch her toes with the sharp inhale. But Lex didn't devour her. True to her word, she kissed everywhere but there... Trailing down the inside of her thigh, to every inch of her pelvis, to the point that Bala bucked her hip up and cursed

Lex's name.

Lex sat up, her mouth going to the ties of Bala's bra, and she pulled them free in one tug. She wrapped her lips around Bala's peaked nipple, and Bala brushed her hands in Lex's shaggy hair, eyes rolling as her teeth bit and her tongue swirled. Lex rose back to her feet, hugging Bala's hips against her pelvis. She continued to suck on Bala as she started moving her own hips. The friction of her movements made Bala's eyes flutter. That brush of the fabric against her clit where Lex hadn't moved her mouth to yet. She hated that every sweep of Lex's tongue had her breaths shaking. Hated that this woman was already having her see stars. Bala couldn't help her hips moving faster, knees lifting off the table. Lex's fingers splayed on Bala's backside, holding her against her as though she could get her closer. Lex bit her nipple. Bala was ready to cave.

She wanted her hands everywhere. Wanted her mouth between her legs. She was losing control with the tease, and she needed her release. She heard herself whimper when Lex's tongue flickered quickly around her hardened peak. So far leaned back over the table that Lex was nearly on top of her.

Bala grabbed Lex's hand and moved it. Lex pulled back, arching a sultry brow.

"Show me what you want," Lex whispered, their mouths brushing.

She led Lex's hand between her legs, and Lex cursed, eyes fluttering when she felt her wetness. Lex groaned, but as Bala left Lex's hand there on her own, Lex didn't press the digit inside her. She kissed her hard, moving her hips again, and she merely grazed her finger down Bala's clit, barely touching but making Bala jerk nonetheless. Lex's mouth captured Bala's breast again, and she sat once more.

"You're going to scream for me, Venari," Lex uttered when she pulled back. Her finger hovered at the entrance of her. The heat of her thumb sitting there, the anticipation of the pleasure sitting on edge. Lex kissed down the front of Bala again and then to her thigh. And when her nose once more brushed her clit, Bala felt herself start to shake. She watched Lex lean forward, open mouth, the heat of her breath billowing over those nerves. But not touching. Her lips pressed to the inside of her thigh again, moving slowly to the edge of her folds, and every time Bala thought Lex would devour her, she paused.

Bala's muscles stretched with anticipation. Every breath was forced. Her knuckles pale against the edge of the table as she waited for Lex to make her move. *Begging* for her to make her move. Her thighs squeezed, and she whimpered when a whisper of her tongue brushed that hardened spot. And she knew as soon as Lex decided to take her that she would fall apart.

Lex's eyes met hers, and Bala couldn't breathe. Lex moved her hand back to Bala's backside, and she squeezed her flesh, making Bala's hips move.

Which was when Lex finally licked her, and Bala's knees jerked.

Her mouth enclosed on Bala's clit, and Bala fell apart.

Every tensioned muscle in her body broke. She lost her composure, hand moving to Lex's hair as Lex devoured her. Spilling and coming apart over her lips. Her high-pitched moans echoing the tent and not caring that they were in the middle of the village and she would be waking people up.

Because Lex moved Bala's thighs to her shoulders, and Bala fell backward onto the table. Her muscles continued to flinch as Lex finished taking her, and she stared at the ceiling in an attempt to catch her breath.

After a moment, she finally opened her eyes, finding Lex standing over her and holding up her pants. She reached for Bala's hand and pulled her up again. Lex kissed her softly, and Bala could hardly keep herself from falling back onto the table.

"I think you need a second audition," Bala managed.

Lex chuckled as she pushed the shirt back over Bala's head. "I agree. You tried to sabotage my performance."

45

Lex was not happy about being told to stay behind. Bala could see it in every pore of the Belwark's face. But after they loaded the last of the crates onto Nadir's wagons, Bala simply wrapped her arms around Lex and told her they would be back that night.

No words were spoken as Bala and Nadir trudged over the Preymoor to the Noble's village. Bala didn't know what to say. She wanted to whip her wind violently over the sand and bury the entire southern coast in it. But she trusted Nyssa enough to know if she did something like that, the Princess would never forgive her.

As they reached the village, Bala had to stop.

"You didn't tell me it was this big," she managed at the sight of it. "Did Draven know it was this big?"

Nadir's dead eyes never left the direction of the village as he replied. "It's doubled in size since we found out about it. So, no. He did not." With a great sigh, he started walking again. "Come on. We need time to set up before she's out."

Bala kept her hood over her head as Nadir spoke to the guards outside the fences, and then they strode inside. People bustled past them, most glaring in Nadir's direction, as they apparently knew he was not of their kind. Bala's chest tightened with every stare. These were the people she'd fought against on that beach once. The ones who had killed her friends and part of the reason she'd lost her King.

More than once, Nadir had stopped to glare at her over her shoulder when the wind picked up.

They were just finishing taking the lids off the crates when in the corner of her eye, she saw a flash of dark red, and when she looked up, she found herself unable to move.

The sight of Nyssa coming towards them made Bala's heart stop. This was not the Princess she'd grown to love. This was not the Princess she'd sent to the Umber to take control of the negotiations and find a way inside Man's circle.

She'd never meant for her to be here.

Yet here she was... Deteriorating in front of her. Her once lively amber eyes were now swollen with redness, her once full cheeks sunken into her face. There was a pink scratch crossing under her eye. Nyssa kept her arms folded in front of her when she walked, her gaze darting all around them, obviously trying not to look at them as she neared and pretending to notice more about the goods she walked by. Bala squinted at the sight of what looked to be a sling around Nyssa's arm and chest.

"You did not tell me she looked like this," Bala muttered to Nadir under her breath.

Nadir pretended to be adjusting some of the fruits from his cart, pulling brighter ones to the top of the crate. "Would you have agreed to come willingly if I had?"

"I would have brought more than wind, that is for certain," Bala uttered. "Is her arm broken?"

Nadir slowly turned to glance at Nyssa. She heard him curse under his breath. "That's fucking new," he grunted. "As is that scratch on her face. *Fuck*—" His fists curled around the fruit in his hand so tightly it burst in his hand, and he pressed his palms into the wood. "The fucking wife," he uttered.

Anger surged in Bala's muscles. She sent a whip of wind rippling through the street, her stern gaze not leaving Nyssa as she circled it around her. She saw the corner of Nyssa's lips quirk, but she didn't turn towards her. The gust wrapped up the woman herding chickens walking past her, and it flipped the woman's dress up over her head.

The woman shrieked and nearly fell over. Guards on either side of Nyssa stopped, helping the woman up off the ground. Nyssa's gaze finally met Bala's, and Bala gave her a quiet wink.

Discombobulated by the wind continuing around them, the guards didn't notice when Nyssa slipped away, pretending as though she were moving out of the way, but in reality moving to the cart beside Nadir and Bala.

"You know I could pick you up without touching you and send you flying back to the Umber, right?" Bala uttered low when Nyssa approached.

"And you realize I am following my King's instruction," Nyssa snapped.

"In no way did I say get yourself captured by Man and become some sort of *spy!*" Bala hissed under her breath.

"Hey—" Nadir cut in. "We don't have time to argue."

Bala sneered at the Princess standing before her, Nyssa's chin high and back stiff, as though trying to make herself look stern and more formidable. The sight of the fight in her eyes made Bala grunt defeatedly, and her hands fell to her sides. The corner of Nyssa's lips quirked a fraction, but only for a blink, and she said, "Hey Bala," in a breath.

"Hey Nys," Bala sighed back.

"Why didn't you ask her for something only she would know about you?" Nadir asked Nyssa.

"Because only a Venari King can manipulate wind," Nyssa replied.

Bala wasn't sure what the pair spoke of, but it made her shift nonetheless. Nyssa started looking over the fruits Nadir was pretending to be showing her. Bala didn't miss the sudden brightness in Nyssa's eyes up at him, didn't miss the bob of Nadir's throat as their fingers brushed against one another.

At one point, Nyssa started to reach for the bruise on his cheek, her gaze narrowing at the cut on his lip, but she hesitated. "What happened to your face?"

"Venari King wrath," he said, his smile softening but eyes not leaving from Nyssa's. "What happened to your arm?"

"Couldn't keep my mouth shut," she admitted.

A quiet chuckle emitted from Nadir, and he uttered, "There's my girl." And Nyssa's face lit up at the sound of it.

"Should I leave you two alone?" Bala mocked, crossing her arms over her chest.

Nyssa's lips pursed, and she brushed past Nadir to Bala's side. "There's something you should know," Nyssa said, holding up a fabric roll. Bala helped her take it out of the cart, noting that it was an actual sling around Nyssa's arm, but she didn't have a chance to ask about it.

"Gail was the one who brought me here."

Bala froze.

This was news.

"What?"

"Gail. The—"

"Yes, I know who he is," Bala snapped.

Nyssa paused, blinking at the sudden snap. Bala avoided her gaze and pulled out another roll of fabric.

"Why did he bring you here?"

"Why do you think?" Nyssa almost breathed. Bala's brow raised at the attitude Nyssa was giving her, and the Princess sighed heavily, looking around them.

"He was trying to barter a place in Man's court," Nyssa said. "Use me as a rare gift for the King upon his arrival. He's dead now," Nyssa said simply.

"Why do you think he's dead?"

"An Infi replaced him," Nyssa said, and Bala realized why Nadir had asked about Nyssa confirming who she was.

Bala could only blink, shifting uncomfortably. "Tell me what happened."

By the time Nyssa was done telling her, Bala was shaking. The news of Infi infiltrating as much as they had brought a stillness to her chest. Killing her friends. Taking over the Bryn.

But she chose not to tell Nyssa that Gail was alive.

"I need to know if my brother is okay," Nyssa said. "If the Infi have taken over all of the Bryn, I wonder if they have somehow pushed into other parts of the mountains. We will lose this entire world before Man has a chance. They will surrender to Man, and we'll have lost without a true battle."

Bala nodded. "I'll go to Dahrkenhill myself."

"No," Nadir cut in. "You can't do that. I'll send word with my traders to find out. I need you nearby, Bala."

"What about the people with Gail? Did they all march across? Are they alive?"

"No. It was just he, the Infi- North, Antha—"

"Antha was with him?" Bala interjected, knowing Antha had not been with Gail when he arrived with the group of his people.

The solemnness in Nyssa's gaze made Bala nauseous. "She's dead. All of them."

"Did my father's roots reach here?" Bala asked.

Nyssa shook her head.

"Then North and the Infi impersonating Gail are still here somewhere," she determined. "You cannot trust any of these guards. If they—" Bala's eyes widened towards where she'd sent the wind. "This is the last you can come here, Nadir. Princess, you need to let us get you out of here tonight. If the Infi figure out or see you talking to us, they'll tell your Noble. You will be dead, and they'll send a company to the Umber."

"They don't know where the Umber is," Nadir argued.

"Really? You think they won't sail their fucking ships around the reef and set fire to all of it while they're searching?"

"We have a bigger problem," Nyssa cut in.

"What could be larger than this?"

"The Prince is arriving in a week," Nyssa said. "And I'm being moved to Savigndor tomorrow to get ready for his arrival."

46

Color paled from both Bala and Nadir's faces.

"We have to get you out of here," Bala demanded.

"You can't," Nyssa argued, the knot in her chest twisting around her heart. "I can do this. We need more information. He is the best way to do that." She turned, finding Nadir's eyes hardened on her, and she shook her head at the look on his face.

"Don't look at me like that," she managed. "With any luck, he'll be an idiot."

"Nys, you don't have to do this," he whispered.

"Three weeks," she promised. "We push my plan back to the end of the Deads, not the beginning. They're taking me to Savigndor. I can find out the kinds of weapons they have, possibly destroy some on my way out. I know I won't be able to take the entire fleet and castle on my own, but maybe... Maybe I can find out enough that we are in a better standing to go back and negotiate."

She turned to face Nadir then as the noise of thunder cracked in the distance. "I need you to meet me on the beach later."

"In the rain?"

"This will be the last I see you until I can fight my way out."

His eyes shut tight, and she could see the clench in his jaw. "*I just found you,*" he whispered. "You want me to leave you to take this on your own?"

"Yes," she affirmed. "You have to."

Nadir exchanged a glance with Bala, whose fists were creasing the fabrics in his cart. "I—"

People came through then, and Bala was cornered as they asked her questions about the fabrics. She obviously didn't know anything about them, but with a nod from Nadir, she quickly took the people over to the side and started speaking with them. Nadir continued to be pretending to show other goods to Nyssa.

"How do you plan on getting out if you're at their castle?" he asked through clenched teeth. "You think you won't be put in the dungeon or shackled to the Prince's bedchambers?"

"I'll figure it out."

"Nyssa—"

"*Nadir,*" she confirmed in a tone that should have meant the discussion of it was over. "I will meet you on the beach tonight. We can talk about it then."

Nyssa's muscles were on edge from the anxiety of what she was about to do.

The guard at the door was the one that liked her. She hoped he would stand simply as the sentry he was and not bother checking in. She had to take the chance. She had to see Nadir and tell him everything.

She slipped beneath the loose floorboard her eagle had used, having to crouch to her stomach and shimmy her way on the sand to get out. Only able to use one arm, it was more difficult than she anticipated, but she gritted her teeth and pushed forward, using her legs to help move her as well. Sand crept in every place it shouldn't have. She ignored it. Once she was out, she pulled her hood up over her head and bolted into the shadows of the surf.

Darkness engulfed her. She wasn't sure where Nadir was or if she'd even be able to see him. Her eagle called out overhead.

A hand clapped over her mouth.

She threw her elbow back, about to stomp on his feet—

"It's me!"

Nadir.

Her struggles stopped, and for a moment, she simply sank into his arms. Her heart nearly exploded with the safety of him around her again.

Lightning cracked over the ocean when she turned. He reached for her cheek and whispered, "Evermore," apparently having known she would need confirmation that it was him.

Her shoulders caved at the words, and he squeezed her hand.

"Come on," he whispered.

He led her not far east down the beach where the elevation began to grow, creating steep drops down the side of the terrain. It was a short section of the land she'd never seen before, but the faint moons light reflected off it, and she noticed the great rocks in the ocean.

"Mouth of the Sea," Nadir explained. "The rocks look like teeth."

"Where are we go—"

Shadows fell on a cut in the cliffside, and she saw a faint orange light coming from inside it. A small crevice, not a whole cave, she realized. He already had a small fire going inside, and she noticed a blanket, bag of food, and canteen. The blanket was mussed as though someone had recently been using it.

"Is someone sleeping here?" she asked.

"I am," Nadir answered as he let go of her hand.

"What—why?"

"Just a few nights," he assured her. "Once I found you, I knew I wanted somewhere close in case you needed to run. I was going to tell you about it today... But then you said they're moving you, and..." His voice trailed, along with his gaze.

Rain began to pour outside.

"What was so important you couldn't tell me at the market?" he asked.

Nyssa shifted her weight, pulling for the steadiness she knew she needed to get the next words out. "I need you to do something for me."

"Anything."

"I need you... I need you to tell Lex I'm sorry. I'm sorry for not being who she needed me to be. I'm sorry for being the brat she was forced to look after. Tell her she's truly free. And tell my brother—"

"Why do you sound as though you're dying?" he cut in.

"Because I don't know that I'll make it out of here alive," she admitted. "They're moving me at sunrise to the new fortress. The Prince is supposed to be here in a week. I don't know when I'll be able to take my plan into motion. And I don't know if I'll make it out of that void alive when I do."

"Yes, you will."

"I'll send all the information I have by my eagle," she promised, ignoring him. "Everything I learn. Ships, weapons—"

"Nyssa, I can help you."

"I can't let you do that."

"Why not?"

"Because you're much too valuable to your people to run into this fire," she argued. "These are the flames of every promise my brother and I have ever made. Every promise we made to Drae. Every promise to Draven. All my promises to you and to Lex and to Bala. I have to stoke this on my own. Smoke must rise from these ashes when it all comes crumbling down."

"I can help you fan it."

"Why, Nadir?" she asked, tone of agony that she couldn't suppress. "Why can you not just let me do this?"

"Because I refuse to lose you," he said. "I have already lost so much to these people. I can't lose you too. You... Do you know how much it pains me to walk away from you each week? To watch as you're carted back inside that home, knowing what you're going back to, that you'll surely be punished for simply speaking with me. Nyssa, I—" He paused, sighing as the thunder boomed over them, and he looked down at the ground.

"Whether you want me here or not, I will be at your side when you escape," he affirmed, meeting her gaze again. "And it's not about any need for killing or blood lust. It's not even about my own people. It's about you. You... you ferocious little infuriating... *thing*. You are the only reason I am anywhere near this place without taking them all out under cover of night."

She fought back her tears. "You really want to help?"

"I do."

"Then you can help by pulling me out of the void when the smoke consumes my flesh," she told him. "I don't know what it will do to me once it starts, especially if I call some of the Noctuans—the voices, their cores connecting to mine, the black flames... I will let go of every wall inside me and surrender my entire being to both. I will be consumed by the darkness. I will lose all control. I will fall into a void. You want me to live? You'll have to pull me out of it because I don't know how to do it myself."

His eyes never left her as the words settled through him, and then finally, after a long moment, he whispered, "Okay," in a barely audible breath.

Her heart skipped, and she had to clench her jaw at the fact that she'd just admitted such words to him. She sucked in a jagged breath and wiped the fallen tear from her face. But he stepped forward in front of her, and his hands wrapped around hers.

"I will fall into the void at your side before I let it take you from me," he whispered.

She limped into his embrace. She could feel his heart throbbing beneath her ear. He squeezed his arms around her, his lips pressing to her head again. She looked up, and her eyes closed when he kissed her temple, followed by her cheek, and then he bent as though he would kiss her jaw. But she sighed open-mouthed into his embrace, and her lips caught his.

Heart bleeding, chest caving, knees wavering...

His broad hand pressed to her cheek, lips kissing her over and over as though he were suddenly desperate to never let her go. Her body craved him as she craved sunlight. She hugged her good arm around him to stay steady as he bent her backward and off-balance, his tongue raking hers as he kissed her deeper. The weeks of her being gone combined with the conclusion they'd come to before she ran away poured through them. She couldn't hold him fast enough, and his hands moved frantically over her, from her cheeks to her waist that he hugged in his hands.

A flash of lightning ricocheted off the cavern walls, followed quickly by the loud crack of thunder just outside. The jolt of it made her jump, her lips pry away from his. Her eyes closed once more as she sighed into his touch, holding his head in the crook of her neck as he held her.

She wanted to pause the world, hold herself there at that moment for as long as she could. Her heart felt as though it would burst at any moment.

His lips pressed hard to hers again, sucking the inhale that she'd just taken. They wavered, and he pulled back to lay his forehead against hers, his mouth agape. She gripped his shirt in her hand just as desperately he did her waist.

"I need you home, Princess," he uttered in such a tone that the hair on her neck raised.

"Why?"

"I'd like my heart returned to my chest, or at least near it," he whispered. "Trying to function without it has been tormenting enough."

She pressed her hand to his cheek and noticed the small smile on his lips. "Oh, you poor thing," she mocked, feeling her own smile light up her cheeks.

He huffed amusedly under his breath, and he kissed her again, not as desperately this time, but still enough that made her heart flutter.

Air brushed between them when he pulled back, and she met his gaze with a heave of her chest. She wasn't sure how she was supposed to deny this. The realization that this might be the last she held him in her arms made a tear fall. His arm tightened around her, and he brushed the tear away.

"Don't give me that look," he whispered. "This is not the last I will see you."

"How do you know?"

"Because you're Nyssari Eaglefyre. And I won't let this be the last time. This isn't how this ends. I have entirely too many plans for us for this to be it."

She almost smiled, and his thumb brushed away another tear.

"Tell me them," she begged, desperate for visions of a future to hang on to.

"Ah..." A jagged breath left his lungs, and she saw his jaw clench. "Watching the sunrise with you in my arms," he began. "Showing you the ruined village under the water—"

"And the water dragon remains?" she fantasized.

He smiled, hand hugging on her waist. "Of course, the water dragon remains," he assured her. His weight shifted over her, and he swallowed as his thumb stroked her cheek. "Really fighting with you," he continued. "To the point that you slap me and tell me off," and she almost laughed.

"Domestic fighting, that's what you're looking forward to?"

"Abso-*lutely*," he grinned. "I cannot wait for you to storm off and for Lex to ask me what I did to send you spiraling."

"What would the answer be?"

"My calling you spoiled after you leave clothes everywhere around the house," he said as though it were obvious. "They catered to your every whim at Magnice. That's obviously the first fight we're having."

Her chest hurt at the laugh, and she choked on a sob. "What else?" she begged to know.

"Ah... Teaching you the language," he added. "And then hearing you tell off my people with it... Fighting with you in the water again and knocking you off the rolling logs. Your knocking me off and embarrassing me in front of my entire village. Watching you try to cook and burning food we've worked an entire harvest on... Oh, this is a good one— harvesting fruits from the forest."

His eyes were lit up with that wonderment she craved, and her body began to shake at the domestic bliss he spoke of. But he settled in front of her, his hand threading behind her neck and into her hair, and she watched the smile soften.

"You know what I am most looking forward to, though?"

She knew whatever he was about to say would be her end, but she wanted to hear it.

"What's that, Commander?" she asked.

"Dancing with you at the Eyes festivals."

And once more, reality seemed to falter around her.

She was back in his arms at Magnice. Floating around that dance floor in a dream that never happened. Back in his arms on his beach, fighting in the sand, holding him in the ocean as the water lapped around them. Walking with him through the forest and riding in his boat upriver. Lying in his embrace as he kissed every inch of her. Walking with her through the villages.

All fantasies she wasn't sure she would ever see.

"I want that too," she heard herself whisper.

His eyes glistened with hers, and he bent his head to kiss her softly. She clung to their bubble of happiness as she savored him. And when they parted, she closed her eyes, their foreheads rested together, and a tear slipped down her cheek.

Thunder rumbled, and reality crashed into her. She gripped to his shirt as desperately as she could, not wanting this moment to end. Words sat on her tongue that she begged to tell him, but she didn't want it to feel like an end or a last.

"Nyssa, I—"

"No," she cut him off, terrified of the words she thought he might say and if they were the same ones she wanted to. "No," she said again, pulling back, her hand cupping his cheek. "Not here. Not like this. You say this is not the last I will see you, then do not say that to me."

He kissed her palm, and she wiped the tear off his face. "Okay,

Princess."

Thunder cracked again, and it physically hurt her to know she had to walk away from him.

But it was time.

Her heart dropped to her stomach at the thought.

Everything would change the next day.

"I have to go," she whispered.

"I know," he said, still holding onto her.

For one last time, he kissed her. That radiating promise of evermore and the next. She breathed in the heat of his skin, savoring the abyss of his touch.

And then she let him go without another look, trudging out of the cave and up the sandy banks back to her captors.

Ready for whatever Savigndor had in store for her the next day.

Only Nyssa never made it to Savigndor.

47

In the two weeks between the decision and their departure for the Bryn, Dorian trained.

He threw boulders and climbed obstacles until he puked. Hagen, and sometimes Katla, watched his progress and pushed him to the very limits of his body. Encouraging and also relentless. It was slow work, but Dorian was determined to get back to himself and build on his injured muscles.

Hagen told stories of his adventures with Draven while he watched. He seemed to have an endless bounty of them as the pair had been great friends since they were children. Nadir had begun hanging out with them when they reached their teen years. Hagen claimed that despite Nadir being the oldest of them with his immortality, he acted as the youngest with his constant jokes and mockery.

Dorian wondered if Nadir's constant jokes and mockery were keeping his sister occupied.

He'd still not heard or felt anything from her. He'd even had Hagen check-in and send word to Bala, but Bala only replied that everything was quiet as far as she knew. That Nyssa was training, and they were planning to strike a meeting with Man's settlement soon.

Something about the shortness of her message had him wary, but he didn't push it. He knew Nyssa wasn't dead. He would have felt that. And he trusted her to do what she needed.

So he trained, and he made himself think about his own tasks.

On the fourteenth morning, Dorian rose before sunrise and trudged through the snow up to the stadium. A few people were out, scraping paths on the stone before the rest of the people woke. He shrugged the fur from his shoulders upon reaching the stadium and made for the weighted wagon. He'd not been able to push it more than a few yards the day before, and he was intent on moving it across the full oval length that day. He stared at it, cracking his neck and telling himself to get his shit together, and then he pushed on the handles.

Every muscle in his body came alive. From his fingers up his arms, settling in his shoulders, pulsing through his chest and down to his abs, to his hamstrings, and into his calves... He strained with every step. The mud made the wheels resist his push. Grunts of agony left him, but he kept on. Determined to ignore the pain.

"You're going to re-injure yourself," came Katla's voice.

Dorian's hands fell to his knees, and he slumped over to catch his breath. "What do you suggest instead?" he managed.

Katla smiled softly, and she went over to the practice weapons. "How about a warm-up first?" she said as she tossed him a wooden sword. "One or two?" she asked.

He straightened with a deep breath to catch it. "Two," he requested. She tossed him another and grabbed for a long spear and a wooden shield for herself.

"You're moving on cold muscles," she continued. "Has Hagen not been warming you up before having you throw the rocks?"

"Usually, he makes me use my form."

Katla eyed him. "That's cheating, little King. I'll have none of that when you train with me. You train as yourself and nothing more."

He caught the smirk on her lips, faint as it may have been, and he set up in front of her.

And as he did, she openly laughed. "You're such a royal," she mocked.

Dorian frowned and looked down at his stance, noting his perfect form and set thighs. Swords poised at the ready. "What's wrong with my setup?"

She grinned. "Let's see how you play."

Katla ran. Dorian hardly had a moment to comprehend. Full throttle in his direction, he blocked her and couldn't help his backward movement. Her moves were swift and forceful, pushing him back with grunts and gritted teeth. Until she shoved and kicked him in the chest, and Dorian went flying onto his back.

He wasn't sure of the look on his bewildered face.

And she didn't stop.

Whirling the spear in her hand, she pushed off her back foot and started towards him again. Dorian somersaulted backward and snapped to one knee. He blocked the strike she came at him with the shield and struck out his foot. It whipped behind her calves, and Dorian shot to his own feet as she fell into the mud.

He turned his sword over in his hand, heart pounding as she glowered up at him, mud caked in her hair.

Dorian couldn't help himself.

"Here, I thought cats always landed on their feet."

Her spear whacked his knee. Leg buckling, he cursed the sky as the pain ricocheted through him. Her legs wrapped his foot, and before he realized what was happening, she had whipped him sideways. Dorian crashed into the mud on his side. Her shield hit his chest, and he fell on his back again.

Dorian groaned into the mud, coughing as he tried to regain his breath from the shield hitting him.

"Did you get that out of your system?" she asked.

Dorian coughed and pushed on her thigh. "Yes," he croaked.

She shoved off him and reached out. Dorian grunted as he took her hand, and she pulled him to a seated position.

"Two laps around the stadium, little King," she instructed.

"You just kicked my ass, and you want me to run?" he asked.

An expectant brow arched on her face, and he sighed.

But being bossed around by women was his favorite thing. And he rose to his feet with a smile that made her eyes narrow.

"Complaining, and now you're smiling," she mocked. "Something you'd like to tell me?"

Dorian threw the wooden swords on the ground and grinned at her. "Familiar territory is all." He started backward. "Just the two?" he asked.

"Keep questioning me, and you'll be running benches."

Dorian grinned at the sky, his pace picking up, and he watched as a raven circled overhead. "You'd have enjoyed this," he uttered to it.

With the exhilaration of seeing the familiar bird moving through his bones, Dorian ran. Katla shouted at him to pick up or slow down. On the second lap around, she went to the rock launcher in the middle, and she started slingshotting small rocks in his direction. It looked almost like a crossbow, and she wielded it like one. He dodged most. One hit his arm, and he practically fell into the wall, slumping to his knees and holding his arm. But a laugh emitted from his lips, and he pushed himself to his feet again.

"Is something amusing about your getting hit?" she shouted. "That could have been an arrow. You'd be dead."

Dorian didn't reply. He saw Corbin making his way into the stadium then, and Corbin paused beside Katla.

"Belwark, tell me why he's smiling at being hit with rocks?" she asked.

Corbin chuckled and wrapped his arms around his chest. "Probably reminds him of home."

Katla glanced sideways at the Belwark just as she shot another rock towards the Prince.

"You get used to it," Corbin said fondly.

Dorian finished his laps and came back around to Katla. Corbin excused himself after shaking his head at him and told him he would bring back breakfast. As he left, Katla nodded towards the wagon and told Dorian to try it again. She propped herself up inside it as he started pushing.

"I am glad to see you've had no more incidents," she said as she settled onto the weighted crates.

Dorian gave the wagon a push and cursed his injured side. "What do you mean?"

"I mean my finding you in the snow two weeks ago."

Dorian stopped moving. "That was you?"

"You certainly were out of it, weren't you?" she mocked.

He started pushing again. The memory, or lack thereof, that night raced through his mind. How he'd not been able to rise from the bed that next day and Corbin had had to force him to eat.

A bad day. A *sinking* day.

One that he had been consumed by and told himself he wasn't good enough to have received any sort of help from the Blackhands after the spoiled child he'd been parading around as.

A day that he knew he would have more of despite anything he did to try and numb himself of it.

"Thank you," Dorian managed, taking pushing the wagon one step at a time.

"You know, I was where you are a few years ago," she said softly. "Well... Not with the whole losing your kingdom and all the lies and—" she stopped herself from going off on a tangent, and she sighed. "What I mean is, I lost someone close to me. A mentor and friend." She pushed her hand behind her neck, staring at the ground. "I don't remember the first couple of months after it happened. I pretty much lived in that tavern."

"How did you get over it?"

"I didn't," she admitted. "I still fight every day. Friends help if you let them in."

"What was the hardest part for you?" he asked, hanging on to her every word.

"Accepting it."

He slowed in his steps, nearly stopping, and his heart knotted.

"I never wanted it to be real," she continued. "Thought if I numbed myself, it would eventually go away. Maybe I'd wake up one morning, and it all be a lie." She sighed and sat up, leaning over her knees. "I won't tell you that it gets any easier, Dorian."

And he looked up at the sound of his name.

"—Or that one day you'll wake up, and the memory of it will no longer consume you," she said. "What I will tell you is that you *can* fight. You have that option. You can fight, or you can drown. Fighting means treading in the water. It means taking that next breath even when you think the weight of it all is pulling you under. It doesn't mean thinking you'll ever be over it or forgetting what happened. It means moving forward instead of moving on. And if anyone ever tells you to move on, you should cut their throats. No questions asked. Moving on is a preposterous lie."

He scoffed. "Had a lot of people tell you to do that?" he asked.

"Far too many to count," she grunted.

He paused and glanced up at her. "How long have you been waiting to tell me this?" he asked.

"Since you arrived, and I recognized that pain."

He remembered how Reverie had called him out on such a front. "Is it that obvious?" he asked.

"Maybe not to all," she said. "No one knows the extent of the pain you're feeling. I cannot imagine it. Everything you've been through in just these last few cycles after years of peace and not knowing anything but sunlight."

Dorian pushed a few more feet on the wagon, allowing her words to sink in and pressing his shoulder against the wood. His thighs quivered with every step, burning emotion settling behind his sinuses. Muscles tightening, he paused a moment, and he looked up at her as he caught his breath.

"How long before it stops hurting?" he asked, his heart feeling as though it were bleeding warmth in his chest.

"It doesn't," she admitted. "But we keep fighting. A little at a time."

Dorian nodded solemnly, hands resting on his hips as the morning sun peeked from behind the clouds. He sighed his head back on his neck, eyes closing, and he soaked it in a moment, allowing her words to settle in his trembling heart.

We keep fighting.

"I don't feel this carriage moving, little King," she teased then. "Don't tell me these growing shoulders are exhausted already."

Dorian huffed amusedly, and he opened his gaze to meet her smiling softly at him. "Thank you," he managed.

She winked at him in response, and then she clapped her hands together. "Enough small talk for today. Let's see that hustle," she said. "I want your Belwark to have to walk all the way across the stadium to bring us breakfast."

Dorian chuckled. "Dammit, I love this place," he said under his breath.

He pushed and pushed on that wagon, not looking how far across he was, stopping a couple of times to catch his breath. Until finally, it hit the other side of the stadium, and Katla smirked down at him.

Corbin had to trudge across the stadium to bring them breakfast, Reverie, and Hagen with him. Katla and Reverie left them soon after, Katla insisting the pair needed to get a head start on training. Katla told Hagen he should prepare himself for what she had planned for them that evening.

Dorian raised a brow at Hagen as the two left. "Sounds dangerous," he mocked once the women were on the other side.

Hagen stared after them. "Usually is." He turned to Dorian, a sly grin on his face that reminded Dorian of Draven. "Honestly hoping she finds the chains we no longer need for the bear," he said.

Corbin snorted and clapped Dorian's shoulder as he laughed. Dorian just grinned at the High Elder. "Chains? That's new," he bantered.

"Ropes aren't usually enough to keep me contained," Hagen explained. "Bear chains... That might do it."

Dorian laughed at the wink Hagen gave him, and he shook his head. "I expect her screams to wake me up later."

"Don't worry, mate." Hagen clapped his shoulder. "They will. You might even hear mine."

Training continued through the morning. Hagen decided it was a good day to tell him of a few Blackhand tricks and some stories of his own exploits. Dorian, never one to turn down a chance at learning anything, asked more questions than he was sure Hagen had anticipated.

Dorian caught Corbin's eye as Hagen explained a few, and Dorian could see the fire rising in the Belwark's eyes. The anticipated escape he knew made Corbin clench his arms a little tighter around his chest as he watched. Eyes traveling deliberately over one another with a need and desire that made both adjust their pants at different times.

To the point that after lunch, Corbin began taunting and talking shit to Dorian out of spite, and Dorian knew the game. Knew that the moment Hagen was out of sight or they were back at the Temple, he would put Corbin on his knees and take him. Knew the anticipation of it was eating at Corbin and, in turn, eating at Dorian.

Hagen excused himself towards dark, congratulating the Prince on a well-accomplished day. And as he disappeared out the other side of the dark tunnel out of the stadium, Dorian turned to Corbin.

"You're fucking asking for it today," Dorian bantered, lust rising in his chest and making his muscles tingle at the look on Corbin's face.

Corbin smirked crookedly, using his shirt to wipe the sweat off his brow. "Now why would I ever do that?" and the tone he used make Dorian curse under his breath. He glanced down the tunnel, noting that no one was coming up, and he threw his shirt over his shoulder.

"Fuck it."

Dorian grabbed Corbin and slammed him against the wall. Their lips crashed together, paying no attention to the people who might have been walking by. They were hidden in the shadows, but quite honestly, Dorian didn't care.

Corbin quickly took Dorian's hardened cock in his mouth, making Dorian strain and curse to the sky. Eyes rolling, Dorian grabbed Corbin's head, pushing his length down the Belwark's throat and moving his hips. Feeling Corbin choke on him. Corbin grasped Dorian's arms and pinned them into the stone, devouring Dorian's cock. Dorian squirmed as he denied his release, muscles edging. Until Dorian wrenched his hand free, took Corbin's chin in his fingers, and he told him to bend and hold to the side of the bench beside them.

Corbin obeyed, and Dorian pushed inside his Second with a groan that echoed in the darkness. He cursed, his cock throbbing as he stilled a moment in the tightness, and then he grabbed Corbin's hip and shoulder as he took him mercilessly. Dorian lasted as long as Corbin, both their groans and straining muscles nearly collapsing with their finishes. Corbin came all over the stone ground, and as Dorian straightened himself up again, he smiled at the sight of it.

"Corbin, how naughty," he teased as he tied his pants. "Someone will slip on that once it freezes over."

A deep exhale left the Belwark, and he pressed his hands to his hips as he turned to Dorian. "You're lucky someone didn't come down this walk," he said breathlessly.

"How do you know I didn't want them to?" Dorian dared.

Corbin pushed back on his shirt and grabbed his belt from the ground. A fond smile, a real smile, one not of mockery and sarcasm, grew on the Belwark's lips, and the sight of it made Dorian's stomach knot— an unfamiliar sensation that he didn't know what to do with.

"Why do I forget publicity is your thrill?" Corbin mocked.

The crooked smirk on Dorian's face widened, and he stepped up to Corbin, taking the belt from the Belwark's hands. Corbin swallowed as Dorian hovered there, his face an inch from his, standing only a fraction taller than the Belwark. Dorian's chest swelled as his Second seemed to tense with him being so close and not out of just sexual frustration.

"You know it's my thrill," Dorian uttered in a low voice, his nose nudging at Corbin's, hands working the buckle on his belt. "And you knew it the moment you started taunting me today with that grin." Dorian's lips pressed to Corbin's jaw with the last of the words, and then he finished buckling the belt with a jolt. Corbin grunted with the snap of it, his eyes fluttering up to meet Dorian's as the Prince paused once more over him.

"Tell me I'm wrong."

Corbin's features softened, and he looked like he might laugh. But he shoved Dorian's face away from him instead.

"Fuck off, Prince," Corbin muttered.

As Corbin went to turn, Dorian grabbed for Corbin's arm without thinking and hauled him back, lips capturing his Belwark's in a kiss not made of lust and ferocity. But one that made his heart flutter.

This was new.

His hand wrapped delicately against Corbin's cheek. Dorian's shoulders softened with every elongated sweep of Corbin's tongue against his. Corbin seemed to relax with him, and he pulled Dorian's hips flush. Dorian wasn't sure what to do with himself, where this new passion had come from or why he'd even kissed Corbin again.

This was a heart drop akin to what he'd felt when he'd kissed Reverie.

Fuck, he could have drowned in this.

To the point that Dorian had to force himself away from the Belwark's lips.

But he didn't move, hands still resting on Corbin's cheeks, their noses brushing as they tried to catch their breaths. Dorian's fingers curled softly in Corbin's coarse hair, Corbin's grip tightening at Dorian's waist. Confusion settled in Corbin's gaze, but he hadn't pushed the Prince away yet.

"What—"

"Just shut up." The words barely escaped Dorian's lips before he kissed Corbin again. Hungrily, with that passion that made his heart sink. Corbin's hands moved to his neck, bringing him closer.

Until they heard the noise of Blackhand bellowing laughter sounding from the stadium, and Corbin stumbled at the rate that he released Dorian.

Dorian's eyes narrowed. The urgent way Corbin had let him go startled him. Both their chests heaved, confusion settled in Corbin's widened eyes, and a blush on his cheeks, Corbin looked down the tunnel to the men that had appeared. The two Blackhands passed by, giving Dorian a clap on his shoulder and a loud grunt about seeing him later at the tavern for drinking games. As the pair continued past, Dorian's hands sank to his hips, and he stared at his Second.

The fact that he'd pushed him away like poison made Dorian's heart knot.

But Dorian played it off. He shoved his own shirt over his head. Stomach knotting, heart still thumping in his chest, Dorian merely gave Corbin a pat on his cheek and a wink as he left him in the tunnel.

"Have a bath, Second," he called back. "You smell of sweat and sex. Not sure the women at dinner will appreciate the combination when they've had no part in it."

But even as his confident swagger stayed on the surface as he walked back to the Temple, inside, he was screaming in confusion as to what had just happened.

48

Dorian didn't bother heating the bath. He sank beneath the cold waters, his mind swimming with not only the kiss he'd just shared with Corbin but also the weight of his task the next day. They would be leaving at sunrise for the Bryn. He wasn't sure what to expect. Whether they would walk in to what Hagen feared or if perhaps the Elder was wrong.

Dorian packed his warmest clothing, including the pieces he'd bought from merchants during his stay. The Bryn sat at the highest peak of Haerland. Thick snows would cover the ground and the trail up. He made sure to pack all his daggers and leathers. If they walked into a fight, he wanted to be ready.

Hagen was downstairs chatting with Marius when Dorian emerged. The two joined Dorian and made their way through the square up to the tavern. The familiar noise greeted him, and Dorian made his way to the bar while Hagen said he would retrieve a table. Dorian hopped over a few games of dice as he walked around to the end of the bar on the other side of the room. A few Blackhands greeted him joyfully, most already well into their drinking for the night, and as they offered him a round, Dorian laughed and insisted he would get his own.

Smyths saw him approach and poured him a nyghtfire, pushing it to him when he leaned against the bar top. Dorian cheers'd him and sank it back in a single gulp, wincing as it burned his throat.

"I'll take one of those too, Smyths," came Reverie's voice as she slid to the bar beside Dorian, her hand grazing his hip. "You can put it on the Prince's tab," she smiled at the bartender. "If he's putting me in danger tomorrow, the least he can do is take care of my drinks tonight."

Dorian chuckled down at her. "Was there ever a time when I wasn't putting you in danger?" he asked.

Her brows lifted in agreement, and Smyths grinned as he poured the pair another round. "Keep them coming, Prince?" he asked.

Dorian shot back the drink and pushed the glass across the bar. "No more whiskey for me," he said. "I'll take the mead. But give her whatever she wants."

As Reverie leaned forward to tell Smyths exactly what she wanted, Dorian finally got a good look at her. Hair down and feathered over her breasts, bangs brushing her lashes and stray strands sweeping over her highlighted cheeks. The tips of her ears were just visible beneath the straight length. She turned to face him once Smyths had given her her drink, and Dorian had to swallow at the wash of her darkened lavender gaze over him.

"Something on your mind, Prince?" she asked, and he had a feeling she knew how mesmerized he was by her.

"I'm not sure I've ever seen you with your hair fully down," he noted.

"Finally washed it, actually," she admitted, to which he smiled.

"It looks nice," he said, and his voice squeaked. "I mean—not that you didn't look nice before, but this. This is—"

"Stammering, Prince," she mocked.

Heat rose on his cheeks. The crooked grin settled on his lips, and he couldn't help but stare at her another moment.

"Have you packed?" he asked.

"Mostly," she replied, swirling the drink. "And you? Where's Corbin? Do you have him packing your things?"

Dorian's stomach knotted, but he pushed it away. "If I know him, he's probably getting the horses ready and making sure we have everything. He's very thorough."

Her lip quirked, and she gave him a full once over. "Is that what you call it?" she teased, and he knew she wasn't talking about the packing.

He allowed his eyes to linger as he took in her figure again, practically feeling his eyes darken beneath her banter. And then he leaned closer into her, nose whispering against her ear.

"Play the game, Lady Fyre, and you may find out exactly how thorough the two of us can be," he uttered.

Her eyes fluttered up at him when he pulled back, and he nearly hauled her to the top of the bar and took her right then. "Is it all a game to you, or is anything ever real?" she asked.

"Games can't be real?" he wondered.

"Are they?"

He considered her. "Everything I do is real," he said, voice a little softer than before. "I've lived through too many lies for my life to be anything other than this reality I've found myself in."

"Is that why you'll not be having more whiskey tonight?" she asked.

He smiled at the floor, the memory of what Katla had talked to him about coming to mind. "Maybe it's about time I let myself feel something more than what I've told myself I deserve for that night," he admitted.

For a moment, her gaze didn't move from his.

"Dorian—"

Laughter and a loud greeting interrupted whatever it was she was about to say. The man she'd been flirting with two weeks before was making his way towards them, stopping only to greet his friend who happened to be behind Reverie. He clapped his friend on the shoulder, and then he turned his attention to them. His hand wrapped behind Reverie as he spoke.

"Hello, beautiful," the Blackhand, Beron, said to Reverie. His lips brushed her cheek, and Dorian wasn't sure what his face was doing.

He nearly threw the cup Smyths had just given him.

"Beron," she smiled, wrapping her arm around her chest and bringing her cup to her lips. "You remember Dorian?" she asked him.

Beron straightened, obviously flexing his ample chest, brown eyes flickering over Dorian. "Prince," he said shortly.

"Beron," Dorian clenched. "How nice of you to wash the soot off your face before tangling with the rest of us."

"Surprised you're standing upright on your own," Beron said. "Where's the Second? He's usually on your heels or his knees."

Dorian's brows elevated at the comment, and he almost laughed. "Yeah," Dorian scoffed. "He's good at it too. Perhaps you should give him a go. You might enjoy the pleasure of something more than your own hand."

Beron started to step forward, but Reverie pushed back on his chest, still staring at Dorian. He could see the bite back of amusement on her lips. The leer in her eyes. But Dorian didn't press it. He caught Hagen's gaze across the room, and he gave his friend a nod, holding up a singular finger to tell him he was coming.

Leveling up with Beron, shoulders rounding, chin rising, and Dorian's eyes flickered black. Beron took a step back, and Dorian grinned triumphantly. He glanced down to Reverie, and he gave her a wink beneath his unruly hair.

"Join the rest of us?" he asked her.

"I'll meet you over," she smiled.

And when she winked back at him, he had to force himself past Beron to his seat.

Hagen was watching and shaking his head when he made his way over. "Starting fights in my bar, mate?" he asked. "At least make sure Dag isn't drunk before you get into it with Beron. He's who you want on your side in the brawl."

Dorian grinned crookedly. "I think I'd rather have Katla."

Hagen clapped his shoulder, shaking him jovially. "Prince... You want them both."

Dorian laughed as he and Hagen crossed to the table where Katla, Dag, and the rest of their self-proclaimed 'gang' sat. Falke was still in town from Monsburne, insistent that the snows were too much for him to travel, but Dorian was sure it had something to do with the woman he'd been keeping on his arm for some time.

The drinking game was announced, and Dorian settled into the chair, leaning on one hand and laughing at the rest of them as they told their stories. He sipped his drink that night, not wishing to be hungover or careless before their big trip the next day. And every time Katla caught his gaze, she raised her own drink to him.

Dorian sat up once in a while, pretending to be stretching, but in reality, glancing to his left towards the bar to see if Reverie was still flirting with Beron. She met his eyes a few times, each time smirking his way. He couldn't decide if she was flirting with him or Beron more despite her standing beside the gruff man.

The wandering in her eyes had him squirming in his seat and fantasizing about taking her back to his room. Stripping her and devouring every inch of her voluptuous body. His fantasy getting so out of control as he thought about her straddling his cock that he had to tug at his pants.

Dag pulled his attention back as he shouted across the table, asking him why he hadn't drank, and Dorian quickly took a large gulp.

"Hey!" Katla called out a few minutes later, arms in the air. "There's my girl," she grinned.

Dorian looked over just in time to see Reverie come up beside his chair and lean against it.

"Finally get rid of him?" Katla mocked her.

Reverie shrugged, grinning smugly. "Fake promises and a grab to the cock usually keeps them away a few hours before they come begging for more," she teased.

Katla turned to Hagen. "Can I keep her?" she asked.

Hagen huffed amusedly and settled back in his seat. "You'll have to ask our Prince if he's willing to let her go," he said. "Though I think he'd rather keep her for himself."

Dorian's eyes narrowed playfully at Katla's smile. "Don't try to take my Commander," he said. "I like having a female guard to keep me alive."

"There's a full-time job," Katla muttered into her drink.

"Tell me about it," Reverie mocked.

Dorian glanced up at her. "I think you enjoy keeping me out of trouble."

She rolled her eyes, her hand sinking behind his neck, and he cursed himself when her nails scratched his head. "Is that what you think?" she said, fingers slightly tugging on his hair.

"I think she'd rather get you into more," Dag chimed in.

Bellows of laughter sounded around the table. But Reverie merely shook her head at the Blackhands and continued to toy in Dorian's hair. Damien stood after a moment once their attentions turned back to the drinking game and offered Reverie his chair, but she held up her hand and sank on the arm of Dorian's.

"I'm fine here," she insisted.

Dorian stiffened as she got comfortable, knee bent onto the arm. He eyed her as she sat there, joining in with the game and drinking with them. Until she stood to shift, pretending to be helping Smyths with passing around the drinks...

And then she sat on his knee.

Every muscle in his body tensed at her sitting in his lap, and he didn't know what to do with his hands. She didn't turn into him but instead simply leaned up, her elbows on the table, and she sat straddle over his knee.

Hagen caught Dorian's gaze across the table and raised his cup just noticeably.

Dorian shifted in his seat. Reverie pushed further back on his thigh. He noted the side-eye she gave him, as though she were checking to see how far back in his seat he was or if he was stammering.

Her hand slipped onto his other thigh, and she leaned back just slightly. Dorian's adrenaline surged, and he remembered the looks she'd been giving him all night. He shifted and sat up, pretending to be getting the fuller drink.

"Something on your mind, Lady Fyre?" he uttered against her ear.

"Thought I might give this game of yours a try," she said quietly enough that only he heard.

His cock twitched. "Would you like to know the rules?" he chose to ask, gaze darting from her eyes to her lips.

She squeezed his knee, and she whispered, "I play by my own," as her hand moved further up his thigh.

Had he not been intent on seeing where this tease was going, he'd have told her to follow him out of the room and into the alley. Devoured her as the snow fell around them.

But his curiosity got the better of him, and he sank back into the chair, propping his opposite elbow up on the arm of it, fingers slightly over his mouth to hide his faint smirk.

He noted the way the fur shawl fell heavily over her, so heavily that he wondered what he could get away with. He tried to continue listening to the conversation as he moved.

The moment his hand slipped beneath the shawl and touched her back, her fingers squeezed his knee, but she didn't dare look back at him.

He realized she wasn't wearing a shirt beneath the shawl. Only the tight leather wrap around her breasts.

Dorian cursed under his breath.

He let his short nails brush up and down her soft skin. Goosebumps rose beneath his fingertips, and he allowed his digits to dip just so beneath the band of her pants.

The Blackhands were arguing about the rules of the new drinking game proposed by Damien. No one had noticed his movement or their quietness. When laughter roared around the table, Dorian made sure to include his own, and so did Reverie.

He took the distraction to move his hand to her hip, and Reverie moved up his leg to where her backside was at the top of his thigh. Dorian sat up to reach his cup, and in doing so, slid his hand between her legs. Her chest rose sharply when he paused there a moment, his fingertips brushing the seam of her pants. He deliberately hid his smile with his cup as he took a long drink, and then he settled back once more in the chair. Hand moving to the inside of her thigh, he squeezed her soft flesh.

Which was when he felt her hand move between his legs.

Dorian sat up again and subtly moved her hand to her drink, his head coming up behind her neck.

"Keep your hands around your drink and laugh when they do," he breathed against her skin.

He leaned back, free arm settled against the arm of the chair as he pretended to be joining in the conversation. His other hand moved, and he let his finger tease over the seam of the pants again. Her thighs squeezed around his after a few seconds. His touch pressed harder against her, and he watched her hands tighten around the cup, leaning up to laugh with the others.

Her weight shifted against him, hips moving backward again. He knew it was taking everything in her not to move her hands or show anything on her face.

Dorian began to unlace her pants.

He saw her gulp as they loosened, and when he got them undone, he slowly trickled his fingers inside.

It was a good thing a commotion of shouts bellowed at the table right then because Dorian cursed out loud when he felt her wetness beneath his fingers.

But Hagen had heard him.

Dorian's fluttered gaze lifted and met the High Elder's. Dorian immediately knew Hagen had caught what he was doing. Amusement spread over Hagen's features, and he shook his head subtly as he drank another swig of his ale.

Of course, Dorian didn't care. Reverie on edge in his lap in the middle of a busy tavern had his heart thudding.

He flipped the High Elder off and winked as he reached for his cup, to which Hagen grinned.

Dorian turned his attention back to the woman on his lap, eyes dancing over her, watching her swallow and clench her hand. He sat his cup down as someone asked him a question, and he answered it without hesitating, his fingers moving slowly up and down her slickness, swirling at her clit and then grazing teasingly over it. She flinched a couple of times when he pressed harder against the nerves. And when he pinched her, the cup went to her lips where he knew she stifled a moan.

The conversation turned to the actual drinking game instead of just talks of the rules, and new drinks were passed around the table. Reverie picked hers up with astounding speed, and Dorian wondered if it was because he'd started the back and forth movement to bring her crumbling to her edge.

Her hips shifted against his knee, thighs squeezing as he leaned back in the chair once more. Laughter picked up around the table. Dorian slowed back to a tease, his finger only threading atop her hardened clit. He could feel her reaching when he picked up the pace again, see the strain in her tense back, in her stiff shoulders.

Dorian straightened and leaned up in the seat again, pretending to be cheers'ing Dag for the story he'd just told as part of the game, but in reality, only wanting a firmer hand against her folds as he slowed again. Keeping her at the edge he wanted her on. Straining and whimpering for that release. He snuck a glance at her, seeing her eyes flutter, and then he straightened against her back again.

"Should I leave you on this edge, Lady Fyre?" he breathed into her hair. "Or do you want your finish?"

Her lashes lifted over her shoulder with a glare that told him if he left her on edge, she would murder him in his sleep, and the sight of it made him smirk. He stayed leaned up behind her, his chest flush to her back, and he snaked his other hand between her thighs. Squeezing her flesh.

Keeping his gaze with her's, he moved his fingers faster atop her clit, intentions on ending her and making her fight the scream. Wanting to feel her wetness on his thigh. Her legs squeezed with his every move. Her legs began to lift. She was right where he wanted her. Body begging, breaths ceasing in her throat. She was holding in the shake with every grasp of her hands around that cup.

He wanted her to have to hide the scream so much that she choked on her wine.

"Take a drink," he said in her hair.

She did.

Dorian watched Dag and Katla stand, shouting at each other about the details of the story she'd begun telling. And he seized the opportunity. His finger pressed hard with the quick movement. She bucked against his hand. Her breaths visibly ceased. Dorian moved her hair so he could reach her ear, and his teeth tugged her earlobe.

"Shatter for me, Reverie," he whispered.

The table shook with Katla slamming Dag's head onto it.

And the noise of Reverie's moan drowned in the ruckus with her release. His fingers were soaked as she constricted and came apart. The cup slammed onto the top, and she began to choke on the liquid. She grasped the edge of the table, stilling herself as she trembled and came down. Dorian watched her every movement and heave of lungs, continuing to rub his fingers and spread those juices, wishing he could taste her. She finally took a deep breath and forced herself straight again, chest still moving deliberately. He could feel her thighs continuing to twitch as he tied her pants back. She slowly looked back at him over her shoulder, the dilation in her gaze making his heart skip.

"The next time you sit on my lap in the middle of a crowded room with intentions of teasing me, remember who you're dealing with," and he felt her skin raise. He leaned around her, his lips whispered the skin just beneath her ear, and her head bent just slightly towards him. "I will fuck you right here in this chair. You'll sit on my cock, and I'll toy with you until the rest of the room is watching. And when you come, these wandering eyes will know you're mine."

When she looked over her shoulder, he didn't lose her gaze. He brought his fingers up to his lips, and he sucked on the two he'd toyed her with as though he were savoring the last bit of his favorite meal. Her mouth visibly sagged as his orbs darted from her darkened lilac gaze to her lips, and then he kissed her throat, almost claim-like in manner. She looked back at him.

"Yours?" she questioned.

"I'll make sure Beron gets a front-row seat," he dared.

A small smile grew on her lips. "Jealousy suits you, Prince."

He almost laughed, his lips close enough to hers that he could have kissed her and sprawled her on that floor, made good on his promises. But he didn't, and he squeezed her ass as he whispered, "Mine."

His nose nudged hers, but he didn't dare go any closer. He knew the moment he kissed her, he would lose any leverage he had in their game, and he would surrender to her completely.

He'd been confused about Corbin earlier, and now adding her and whatever this was into the mix had his head spinning. He didn't know what to do with the swelling in his chest and the sweatiness in his palms. And feeling this way with two people? It was enough to send him totally shutting down instead of having to deal with figuring it out.

"Little King—"

Fuck.

"Yes, Katla," he nearly snapped as he met her amused gaze.

"Would you like to go next?" she asked. "I think we'd all love an embarrassing story of yours."

He knew she'd only called on him to fuck with him, and he couldn't help the knowing smile on his face. "Sure," he agreed.

The Blackhands settled loudly back down at the table, and another round of drinks was passed around. Hagen caught Dorian's gaze and shook his head again, a broad smile on his face. Dorian wondered if he had watched the entire exchange.

Dorian once more relaxed back in the chair, his fingers simply touching Reverie's back again as he started telling a story in line with the theme of their game— sexual embarrassment.

Reverie hardly moved the remainder of the night, allowing him to continue to caress the bare skin on her spine, occasionally squeezing her flesh between the top of her pants and the wrap around her breasts. They played the drinking games with the rest of the Blackhands, and every time she looked back at him over her shoulder, he would give her a quiet wink or grasp her flesh harder. Until she finally told the rest of them she would be retiring for the night and blamed their early rising on why she was leaving. She gave his hair a long comb through as she passed behind the chair to go.

Once she was gone, Hagen stood as though he were going to get another drink, but he rounded back by Dorian and paused to clap his shoulder.

"You're in so much trouble, mate," Hagen laughed. "Maybe I should be more worried about her taking your life on this trip instead of the Infi."

"You're probably right," Dorian agreed.

49

Dorian brought both Reverie and Corbin mugs of tea the following morning, as well as pastries he'd picked up from the bread woman on his way.

Corbin stared at him when he presented it.

"Since when do you do anything for others?" Corbin said.

Dorian frowned. "What do you mean? I am the epitome of generosity."

Corbin choked on the sip of tea he'd just taken.

And Reverie simply snatched it from his hands with a glare.

He wondered if she'd thought he would seek her out after their exchange. But he'd stayed up far longer than he should have, enjoying his time at the bar, and his body exhausted into his bed before he could bring himself to go find her.

She was up and with the horses long before them, as though she'd been there since way before the sunrise. She tacked her bags on with jolts that made Dorian and Corbin exchange a frown. But neither pushed it, and they instead went to their own horses to tack their bags.

Dorian had also noted a tenseness in Corbin on their way over. Corbin avoiding his gaze, walking stiffly. He wondered if it had anything to do with the day before. The morning was the first he'd seen him since. As they gathered their things, Dorian decided he could not stand the tension any longer.

"Something on your mind?" Dorian asked. "You're as pent up as the woman this morning."

"Should we talk about yesterday?" Corbin blurted.

Dorian stared at him a moment, the memory of the kiss after

training ringing in him. Between thinking about that and thinking about Reverie grinding against his fingers—wanting to watch her as she came with pleasure from his mouth or feeling her wetness around his cock next time. He'd had to resort to more of the herb than his usual and another few drinks of nyghtfire with all the confusion he felt.

But he played it off.

"Do you think we should?" he asked.

Corbin's brow simply raised, and Dorian ran a hand through his hair.

"I don't know, Bin," he admitted. "Caught up in the moment, maybe. Why? Are you telling me you didn't enjoy it?" he asked, attempting to settle the Belwark's mood and hide the turmoil swelling inside him.

Corbin didn't reply and instead tugged at the ties on the saddle. Dorian noted the tenseness still in Corbin's shoulders, to the point that he stopped what he was doing and went to hold Corbin's horse steady as it reacted to his jolts.

"I can't go on the road with both of you angry at me. Especially not you," Dorian admitted. "Talk to me."

But Corbin only sighed, an elongated pause between them that made Dorian shift. "It's nothing," Corbin finally said. He turned to Dorian and patted his cheek, and despite the playfulness of it, Dorian wasn't sure he believed him.

Corbin's attention turned to Reverie then, and he gave an upwards nod in her direction as he pulled out an apple to eat. "What exactly did you do to her last night?" he asked, a small smile growing on his face. "Did she finally join you in your bed, and then you told her 'good job'?"

Dorian almost laughed, feeling a little more at ease with Corbin bantering again. He crossed his arms over his chest and watched Reverie brush her horse a moment before responding.

"I made her choke on her drink while she came apart at the dinner table," Dorian said.

The chunk of apple Corbin had just popped into his mouth came spewing out and hit Dorian in the face. Dorian frowned and wiped the spit off his cheek.

"Manners, Second," he mocked.

"You toyed with her beneath the dinner table?" Corbin asked. "In the middle of the tavern. With drinking games presumably underway."

"Yes," Dorian said. "Speaking of which, where were you?"

"Gathering our shit for the ride today—did you— *please* tell me you didn't leave her in the middle like you do me."

"That hurts you think I would do that to her."

"Should I feel special?"

"Maybe."

Corbin watched him expectantly.

"What?" Dorian asked.

"I'm waiting on the brag," Corbin said.

"No brag," Dorian shrugged.

A disbelieving raise of brows came from his Second, and Dorian chuckled under his breath.

"Alright, fine," Dorian gave in. "She shattered like a broken mirror. Is that what you wanted to hear? I wasn't aware you were so curious about her."

"Hard not to be," Corbin admitted.

To this, Dorian smiled leeringly, and he clasped Corbin on his cheek. "If you're thinking what I am, the answer is yes."

Corbin shoved him off, apparently knowing of Dorian's flirting games, and he shook his head. "I hope she murders you," Corbin mocked him.

"Whoever you're speaking about should get in line," Reverie said as she joined them. Hands on her hips, she glared between the pair, eyes finally landing on Corbin.

"Are we ready? I thought we would be underway by now," she asked him.

"Waiting on Hagen with the map," Corbin replied.

"Perhaps he should send Katla with us to show the way instead," she snapped at Dorian. "At least you'd behave then."

Hagen met them with the maps and a few more supplies after the exchange. He showed Corbin the route and left Dorian to tack the rest of the supplies to the horses with Reverie. She had hardly spoken with him, and he wondered if there was something else the matter other than his teasing her the night before.

Whatever was wrong would have to wait, though. Because with the sun rising quickly, they needed to make it to the first marker before nightfall or else they would die from the cold. The day marker was a cave where they could huddle out of the snow before starting their ascent to the Bryn on the second day.

"Hey, Prince?" Hagen called to him as they started to ride out.

Corbin's horse stammered beneath him, ready to go. "Yeah?"

"I hope you do not find what I fear," Hagen said. "And if you do..."

"I'll take care of it," Dorian promised. "And if they have any Scrolls, I'll find them."

The mention of the Scrolls stilled Hagen. "There is one, in particular, I want you to look for," he said. "The Red Moons Scroll."

Dorian frowned at the unfamiliarity of it. "Why that one?"

"Because if they have it, they'll destroy it," Hagen said. "And if they destroy it, Haerland will never be free again."

By the time they stopped at the cave marker that night, a great snowstorm had begun.

They'd hardly been able to see their way, but Corbin luckily found it. Dorian felt worse for the horses. He was glad Hagen had been smart enough to have them bring quilts along for them and extra food.

The cavern was a well-open space, and Dorian realized why it was the preferred halfway marker between the towns. There was a small area towards the back where water dripped down, the puddle being no more than a few inches deep but enough that the horses were able to have drinking water.

Hagen had sent them with a stack of firewood. He told them it was customary to bring it and leave whatever you didn't need for others. Dorian was able to light a fire without the wood, so they stacked the firewood against the wall with the rest of it.

The wind whipped and whistled outside, but it did not reach inside the cavern as far as them. The three settled around the fire, furs wrapped around their bare shoulders. The snows had soaked their clothing, and they hoped it would be dry by the next morning.

Dorian couldn't concentrate on anything Reverie and Corbin talked about as they sat. He leaned back against the wall, staring at the navy fire dancing on the rocks, thinking about what the next day would have for them. But Dorian could only see the yellow eyes of the Infi in his head. What it would mean if they did find only Infi at the town the next day, and how they would know that's what they were. It concerned him that they had nothing to compare the Bryn Elder to or any of the people. And if they did find that the entire town was Infi... How was he supposed to get rid of them?

"I think we need to sneak into town tomorrow," Dorian blurted, catching Corbin and Reverie off guard.

Corbin frowned. "Why?"

"Because I can't imagine it's comfortable for Infi to be in shifted forms if they don't have to be," Dorian continued. "If the entire town is Infi, and they see us coming, they'll shift. If they don't see us—"

"I can go alone," Reverie interjected. "I'm the smallest. I can move quietly. I can find out what we're up against and report back."

Dorian wasn't sure he liked it, but he knew she was right. He nodded in agreement. "If you're caught, do you know how to kill it?" he asked her.

Reverie stared at him, and he swore something of a fear passed into her features. But she blinked and turned back to the fire, avoiding his gaze when she spoke. "I remember," she said softly, poking at the flames.

Dorian and Corbin exchanged a glance. "You have to knife it to the neck to paralyze it and then cut out its heart—"

"I said I remember," she snapped, and he wondered if she'd been in the crowd when he'd killed the one at Scindo Creek with Draven.

Dorian chose not to push it and turned back to Corbin, who seemed to share his same thinking. Dorian's heel began to tap nervously on the ground. "The part that worries me is if we find the entire town is Infi," he said.

"I wondered that too," Corbin agreed, staring at the fire. "We can't exactly line them up one by one. There were hundreds of people there the last time."

"We can't get rid of that many," Dorian stated. "They have to be taken back to the caves. How are we supposed to move that many bodies?"

"There has to be another way," Corbin said.

"No other way that Draven knew of," said Dorian.

"What about your fire?" Reverie suggested.

Dorian's eyes met Corbin's.

"You were able to use it against the Architect," Reverie continued.

"Do you not think it could work on an Infi?"

Dorian thought about it. This was his mother's marking they were speaking of. As spiteful as she was, perhaps she didn't just give them fire to burn the world with.

"It's worth a try," Corbin said.

Dorian nodded slowly, still staring into the flames. "Rev, do you think if you saw one, you could get it back to us with the heart removed?"

He hated asking it of her, but he remembered the way she'd snuck up on them in the Forest, and he knew it was their best shot.

Reverie's eyes were wide. Almost as though a panic had taken her and she'd forgotten how to breathe.

"There is one more cavern between here and the Bryn," Corbin said. "We could regroup there, assuming there is no one hiding in it."

But Reverie still hadn't spoken. She was rubbing her darkened throat. Whether the discoloration was from the fire or a rise in her blood pressure, he wasn't sure. But it worried him, and he wanted to make sure she knew her going was not the only option.

"Rev?" Dorian repeated. "You don't have to. One of us can—"

"I can get one," Reverie said firmly, snapping out of her daze. "If that's what I find, I can bring one back to test the theory."

Dorian considered her a moment, his gaze flickering to the hand she had on her throat.

"You have to be fast," Dorian told her, choosing again not to push her. "You'll need two knives. One to the neck to paralyze it, the other to cut open its chest. The heart has to be separate from the body when you bring it back to us."

He could see a fear, yet determination, in her eyes, and she gave him a nod. "Okay."

With all that was on Dorian's mind, he hardly slept. Any other night forced to sleep naked between two beautiful beings to stay warm would have resulted in a night full of activities. But Dorian couldn't get his mind to stop. Even when Reverie had turned in to him in her sleep and thrown her arm across him, he'd hardly noted it.

He hadn't felt such anxiety since leaving his sister, and the mere thought of her and whatever it was she was doing nearly made him vomit.

Halfway through the night, he stood to retrieve the nyghtfire and his smoke, hoping the combination of the two would help put his mind at ease, but as he sat there smoking, pulsed into his form to keep his naked body warm, he noticed Reverie watching him.

"Back to sleep, Lady Fyre," he uttered as he exhaled the smoke. "You're hunting Infi on your own tomorrow."

"Can I ask you something?" she said, sitting up on her elbow.

He didn't respond, but he did dwindle his fire so that she was not speaking to the full black-eyed Promised Prince. He wondered if it scared her at all.

"Ask me anything," he finally said.

"Why take this job if it terrifies you?"

Not what he'd expected.

Dorian inhaled another huff of his pipe as he contemplated the answer. The soft silence between them was not of uncomfortableness or desire but one of comfort that Dorian didn't know he would crave until that moment.

"The Infi used to be nothing more than a monstrous tale we were told as children to keep us fearful of the Venari. They were the first creatures I was ever trusted with to banish. I know them better than I probably know my own people. Draven fought his entire life to rid our world of them. I'd like to continue the work he started. This job is what he would have done were he here." Dorian paused to take another draw of the herb. "If they are allowed to continue spreading as we assume they have, our world will be lost. If they discover Man, and fuck, I hope they haven't, they'll tell them everything. They'll betray Haerland without ever giving it a second thought."

"The war will be lost before we begin," Reverie said, and he watched as it seemed to sink in. That same heat rose on her cheeks, and she stared at the fire.

"You don't have to do this tomorrow," he told her upon seeing the fear. "You're allowed to say no."

She shifted with a sigh and laid back. "And disobey my first instructions as Commander?" she gave him a half-smile that he knew was forced. "I'll be fine, Prince. I've trained for this."

Dorian swallowed at the confirmation of her tone despite the wariness in her eyes, and he gave her a slow nod.

She turned over away from him then and slumped the cover over her bare shoulder. "Come back to bed. I'm missing my heater."

A quiet huff of amusement left him. He took another draw and proceeded to stand. Even if he couldn't go to sleep, he could at least be comforted by their presence.

The moment he got comfortable between the pair again, his eyes began to droop. Heartbeat steadying. Reverie had turned into him, her chilled body lying against his warm one. Despite her touch tracing the scars across his abs, he hadn't made a move on her. His busy mind wouldn't stop long enough for him to. Corbin's back shifted to where he was flush against Dorian's side as well, and at some point, Dorian's arm curled beneath the space between Corbin's head and shoulder, hand resting entwined in his Second's, while his other arm wrapped around Reverie's back and grazed her hip.

This was the position his body decided it was comfortable in. Secure between two people who trusted him and whom he trusted. Two people who both made his stomach knot and heart flutter. Two people who had a choice to follow or leave him, and they'd both chosen *him*.

His chest tightened, and he hugged them a little closer. Without thinking, he kissed the top of Reverie's head, followed by Corbin's neck, and then he sighed his eyes closed, head leaning against the back of Corbin's, Reverie nearly lying atop him, as sleep took them.

The next thing he knew, Corbin was nudging him and telling him to get up.

Dorian stirred, grunting as he pushed his hands over his face. It was the smile on Corbin's lips that made Dorian look twice at him upon opening his eyes.

"What?"

"No flames," Corbin told him.

The realization made his gaze narrow, but he didn't question it. Because Corbin was right. He'd not dreamt of fire or screams that night.

The winds had quieted down with the sun on the horizon. Another few inches of snow had fallen, though most of it hadn't stuck to the muddied trail. By the time the noon sun rose, they had reached the next cavern, and it was here that Reverie would have to go from on her own.

Dorian's stomach was in knots about sending her alone into a town she'd never been to before to find a monster capable of shifting and ripping her apart.

"If anything goes amiss, get out of there," Dorian said as Reverie strapped her blades to her body.

"I know," she said, a twinge of annoyance in her tone.

"They can shift. Trust no one. If someone discovers you and they try to take you to the Elder, just run."

"I know," she said again.

"You have to pierce the neck first—"

"Dorian," her hand pressed to his cheek, and between that and the noise of his name on her lips, he stopped talking. "I know. I'll be back before nightfall. With an Infi."

50

Smoke rose from the cavern floor beneath Dorian's feet as he paced. He hadn't stopped moving since Reverie had left them. He had a feeling there was something she wasn't telling them. He didn't have a clue as to what, but the fear in her eyes when he'd first mentioned the Infi had him curious.

It was nearing dark, and she still hadn't come back.

"At what point should we go after her?" Corbin asked as he watched the door.

"If she's not back by the time the sun shadows that valley, we go," Dorian said, wanting to give her as much time as he could and reminding himself that she was a good fighter and deserved a chance.

But Dorian went to the cavern entrance anyway to pace outside.

The moment he walked out, he heard a scuff in the snow above him. He looked up, and a black cloak came billowing with the figure jumping down past his head. He ducked, and Corbin drew his sword.

Reverie whipped her hood back off her head as she landed on the trail beside him.

"Fucking Infi, Rev," Dorian finally breathed. "Are you--"

Words ceased in his mouth. She had dirt on her face, a scratch across her cheek and down to her throat. Her nostrils flared, and the lavender gaze blazed into him.

"What happened?" Corbin asked, recovering first.

"Infi," she said shortly. "Come on. I can tell you on the way. I need help dragging him." She pushed past the pair and started up the trail. Dorian and Corbin exchanged a look, and then they both ran to catch up with her.

"You have the heart?" Dorian asked.

Reverie held up the bag over her shoulder in response.

"This one was wandering the trail outside the gates," she said. "All their sentries are gone. Their walls are unchecked. It is nothing more than a..." She paused to take a moment, and Dorian grabbed her arm.

The gaze she looked up at him with made him still.

As though it were suddenly hitting her what she'd seen.

"It's Infi," she breathed, clutching him back. "It's all... *Infi.*"

He had never seen such a fear in anyone's eyes before. "How far ahead is the body?"

"Half a mile," she said. "It was heavy. I couldn't drag it--"

"I can get it," Corbin said, seeming to know what Dorian was thinking.

Dorian nodded. "I'm taking Reverie back to the cavern. We'll meet you back there, and we can dispose of it."

"No. It's heavy. We—"

"Corbin can handle it," Dorian said firmly. He grasped Reverie's hand then and pulled her backward. "Watch your back," he said to Corbin.

Within the warmth of the cavern, Reverie continued to stare at the floor. She pushed the cloak off her arms before she sat at the fire. Dorian hardly had the chance to speak to her. She was in such a zone that it was almost like she wasn't there.

Dorian crouched down to his knees in front of her when she settled.

"Reverie, what happened?"

He wanted to wipe her face clean of the blood, hold her while she told him, but he didn't know yet how to react with her in such a state.

"I climbed up the wall to see inside. They were everywhere. The entire town..." Her entire body trembled, and Dorian decided he would chance her wrath. He pushed his arms around her and held her against him, feeling her body shake against his.

Something didn't feel right about her as she cried on his shoulder. The way her hands dug into his back. The way she was breaking in front of him. The fact that she'd admitted she couldn't come all the way with the beast...

His heart turned numb, and he tensed.

He recognized the smell in her hair.

He recognized the manipulation in her tone.

Breaths quickening, Dorian's ears began to ring.

Infi.

She pulled back and held her hands to his cheeks. "I didn't know if I would make it back to you," she whispered.

Dorian grasped her right wrist in his hand, eyes searching over her face. He turned her hand to kiss her palm, but never lost that gaze. "You're safe now," he promised.

His hand curled around the knife at his side.

"You never have to be afraid," he continued. "I've got you."

"I know," she managed. "I know you will always have me. Dorian, I..."

His heart numbed at the trick it was using on him. To drown him in words he wanted to hear. To toy with his head and heart for feelings it only guessed he felt for her.

"I need you," she continued.

If he hadn't already been sure this was an Infi, he definitely knew then.

She sniffed back tears, lavender eyes glistening. "I need you so much. I didn't know how to tell you. I—"

"You don't have to say anything," he played along. He pushed her hair from her face, feeling his heart pick up pace as he moved his hand in position to strike.

"Dorian—"

But she had seen him pulling the knife.

She paused. Yellow eyes flashed before him. A smirk rose on her lips.

Dorian grabbed her hair and yanked her head back. The knife creased at the Infi's throat.

"Did you think that would work?" he snarled.

He didn't give it a chance to respond. His knife slide across the flesh. Nearly black blood splattered over his face.

The creature fell backward. It shifted from Reverie's figure into that of its true self. Dorian sprang to his feet as it crippled and stumbled off balance. Clutching at its bleeding throat. Morphing into its form. Dorian set up for it to come at him. Knife in his hand.

The Infi finally grew to its grey corpse. As tall as Dorian, black blood still spilling down its front as it turned towards him. Scarred skin stretched over its starved muscles. Yellow eyes infiltrated Dorian's own blue ones.

It lunged.

Dorian caught it by the throat. It whipped and clawed, knocking the blade out of his grip. Snarls evacuating its throat. Dorian winced as its long nail struck his skin as though it were a cat maiming him. This one was stronger than those he'd dealt with before. Dorian's own form attempted to swell to the surface, jaw clenching with the weight of holding it at bay. The beast continued to kick and spit in his face, grappling at his body and scratching his arms and side.

His knife gone, he knew there was only one thing he could do.

His own rattled grunt filled the cavern. He pressed his blackened hand to the Infi's chest, flames burning through its flesh. The Infi wailed but didn't slack its mauling. The further Dorian pushed, the deeper it dug its nails in his side and arms.

Until Dorian felt the ribs.

The bones cracked beneath his fingers, and he yanked out the Infi's heart.

The creature fell in a heap onto the ground.

"DORIAN!"

Dorian hardly heard the shouting. His form settled back inside and the pain of the scratches all over his body emerged to the surface, making him wince despite himself.

Reverie and Corbin appeared in the cavern door. For the briefest of moments, Dorian was relieved at the sight of them unharmed standing before him. Corbin threw the Infi body from over his shoulder onto the ground.

But the heart in Dorian's hand continued to beat, and Dorian grabbed his knife.

"Are you—"

"Stop," Dorian demanded, feet firming, holding the knife at the ready.

Reverie and Corbin went rigid.

Dorian couldn't catch his breath. If these two were Infi in front of him too... He didn't know that he could trust his own eyes.

"Tell me something only the two of you would know," he said fast. "Something we've shared or words we've said to one another. Please."

Corbin's jaw clenched, and he seemed to understand. "We keep fighting," Corbin said.

Dorian nodded. "And you, Reverie?"

Her eyes darted back and forth, mind seeming to grasp for anything, and then she said, "Keep your hands around your drink and laugh when they do."

The greatest exhale Dorian had ever felt left his lungs.

His hands pressed to his hips, and he cursed the sky. He didn't say another word before he rushed to the pair and threw his arms around them both. Relief swept him to the point of sweat, eyes closing, and they hugged him back.

"Fuck, I thought—" Dorian's heart pounded in his ears. "I thought I had lost you both," he admitted. He pulled back then, and Corbin caught his arm.

"You're hurt," he noted.

"I'm fine," Dorian insisted.

Corbin looked like he wanted to argue, but he let Dorian go. "When I found her on the slope, I realized what had happened," he said. "Did you realize it was one?"

Dorian nodded, hands pushing behind his neck as he turned to glance back at the creature lying on the ground. "I knew it wasn't her," he said softly. He looked back at Reverie then, finally getting a good glimpse of her, and he saw the same scratches on her face and through her shirt as he had.

His body shook with rage at the sight of it. "Are you okay?"

"It's just scratches," she insisted.

But the red puffs around her swollen eyes and the clench in her jaw told him she was covering it up.

"No, you're—"

"I said I'm fine," Reverie snapped.

Dorian exchanged a look with Corbin and decided not to push it any further.

The three of them turned then to the two Infis now lying in the cavern.

"Suppose we have two chances of trying now," Dorian said.

"Tell us what you need," Corbin said.

"Snow," Dorian replied. "In case the fire gets out of control. We should put the bodies at the back of the cave to make sure no light penetrates outside. If the rest of them see it, it could be like a beacon."

Reverie loaded snow from outside into one of her cloaks while Corbin and Dorian took the bodies to the back. The hearts were still beating, and as Dorian crouched down, he stared at the one in his hand.

"What are you thinking?" Corbin asked.

"I'm thinking since Duarb can't reach here, do I even need to put it back in," Dorian replied. "Or if I can burn them separately."

"We have two," Corbin said. "Worth trying both ways. Though I hope it will burn with the heart. Otherwise, we're fucked."

"We'll put this one back in," Dorian determined.

"We should put rocks on the legs to hold it down," Corbin suggested. "There's nothing to tie it to."

Corbin gathered a few rocks from around the cavern and placed them on the Infi's legs, while Reverie seemed to keep her distance from them, pacing in an almost trance-like state, the hilt of her knife tapping nervously against her palm. Dorian wanted to ask her if she was okay again, to truly get a response from her, but he knew they needed to get rid of the Infi before opening such wounds.

As Dorian settled before the creatures and stared down at their mangled forms—the grey-white skin, pink slashings on great starved bodies, he was reminded of his first dealings with them, and not at his kingdom, but when he'd traveled to the villages to help Draven execute them. He could still see Draven standing in front of him with the first he'd let him kill on his own.

"You remember what you're doing?" Draven asked him.

Dorian's weight shifting before the creature. Heart throbbing. This one was different from the others they'd found. This one looked as though someone used it for whipping practice. Scratches and burns all over its body.

Dorian could only manage a nod in response to Draven's question.

"I need to hear your voice, Prince," Draven told him. "I need to hear the confirmation that you can do this."

Dorian was glad Draven was talking low enough that no one else in the crowded square could hear him. "I remember what to do," Dorian managed.

"Firmly," Draven said. "With the same confidence you banter to these women with."

A small smile rose on Dorian's face as he looked up at the King, and Draven gave him a subtle wink. His arms settled over his muscular chest, and Draven waited for Dorian to speak.

Dorian straightened, a deep inhale piercing his lungs, and he locked eyes with Draven. "I remember how to kill the Infi," he said, his voice stronger. "I can do this on my own."

A whispered smile quirked on Draven's lips. "You don't have to shout," Draven mocked. "Kill the bastard then if you're so eager."

Dorian almost laughed, and Draven returned the crooked smirk, merely nodding at him before clapping his shoulder and walking away.

He didn't realize he was tossing his knife up and over in his hand until Reverie spoke.

"I will never understand how you can smile at such moments as these," she muttered, bringing him back to reality.

"I was just thinking of the Infi at Scindo," he replied, and he met her blank eyes. "Were you there for that execution?"

Reverie seemed to have forgotten how to talk. She stilled, gaze dissipating down at the creatures, and Dorian frowned at her.

"Rev?"

She blinked, but her eyes didn't leave the Infi creatures on the ground. "I was there," she managed. "The Infi you killed was the one my father kept beneath our home."

Dorian balked. "What?"

"What are you talking about?" Corbin asked, coming to stand beside Dorian.

Reverie didn't look away, but a lone tear stretched down her cut cheek. "The one you killed... It had not come in the middle of the night the week before as my father told you," she said, her words flat and emotionless, as though she were numb from the inside out. As though she refused to let emotion settle in her bones.

"That creature had been living in our basement for ten years," she continued. "Chained to the wall. When my father found out other towns had been infiltrated with Infi, he didn't want it to seem like our village was the only one that didn't have a problem. So he brought it up. And he let you kill it."

Dorian remembered the Infi that had been brought forward in her village. How it had slashes and burns on it. Its wrists red with cuff marks. Slashings on its back as though someone had used it for target practice. He remembered Draven giving it a long stare, but he had not questioned it before allowing Dorian to take care of the creature.

"Why would your father keep an Infi beneath your home?" Dorian asked, and he wasn't sure he wanted to know the answer.

Reverie didn't look at them.

She crouched down in front of the one she'd caught herself, and she used her knife to tilt its head.

"To train me," she said softly. "To punish me." Her knife dropped along with her head. "Seeing all of them today... Walking around that town so freely, like they owned it. They had no care of needing to be shifted. And that eerie silence... It reminded me of the times I was locked beneath our home with it. There was one corner it could not reach with the chains. I would have to fight it to get to the corner. But once I did, it would sit a few feet away from me and stare. Just... *Stare*. Crosslegged on the floor. Hands in its lap. Breathing like a scared, dying animal. Sometimes it sat all the way at the very edge of the chain just inches from me. It never slept. That yellow gaze constantly poured into my own like it could own me if I looked at it for too long."

A rage filled Dorian, but he stifled it, knowing she was not telling them this so that he could get angry. It was then Dorian remembered the claw marks on her throat, and he realized why she'd been holding her neck the night before. She'd been so covered up with furs in the mountains, he'd nearly forgotten about them.

"How old were you when it clawed you?" he asked.

Reverie rose from the ground, and she finally met his eyes. "Thirteen."

Dorian pushed back the shudder over his body and moved his hands through his hair.

She turned again to the Infi. "This one goes first," she said firmly.

Dorian knew by her tone that it was an end to the conversation about her past. And he respected her enough that he wouldn't push her. He couldn't imagine how difficult it was for her to reveal it, and the fact that she'd trusted both he and Corbin meant more to him than if she'd only trusted him.

With one step, he came flush to her side, and he gave her arm a squeeze just above her elbow. She stepped back as he crouched down and held his knife ready.

"I want both of you to be ready in case something goes wrong," he said without looking back. "Stay together."

He heard them move a few steps back, and he knew that they had their weapons in hand and were ready for a fight in case it came to that.

Dorian grasped the beating heart and pushed it back inside the creature. His own heartbeat picked up as he readied his knife, waiting for the roll of it back to life.

Its hand twitched.

Dorian shoved the knife in its throat.

The Infi seized upwards, body jerking—

Navy flames poured from Dorian's arm and onto the creature's flesh.

It wailed.

It wailed in a pitch so shattering, Dorian fell backward. Arms grabbed him, and he was pulled away.

The Infi writhed, the knife in its neck keeping it from darting to its feet, but it could feel the pain. Its yellow eyes blazed open, and Reverie grabbed Dorian's hand.

For a moment, the three couldn't turn away. They watched as its skin boiled and melted beneath the fire. Until it began to rip into gashes and burn like parchment. The wails softened, and Dorian realized he had stopped breathing.

A skeleton remained, but Dorian knew even with that skeleton that it could come back. And his heart picked up pace again.

"We have a problem," Dorian realized.

"What now?"

"Even if it disintegrates, it can still come back from it." His gaze locked with Corbin's, and Corbin's chest visibly caved.

"No."

And he knew Corbin was thinking about using Amaris as well. To turn the water to his mother's poisoned waters to destroy the remnants.

"You have another idea?"

"How do you plan on making sure all the ash from those you burn tomorrow gets taken care of? That plan is just as flawed as the others. You can't guarantee it will work, and we cannot chance her getting free of her prison," Corbin argued.

Dorian pushed his hands to his eyes, wracking his brain for any solution that didn't involve using Amaris to do something stupid.

"Perhaps your fire will take care of the ash too. It is not normal fire," Reverie said. "Before we decide anything drastic, let's wait to see if just this works first."

Her words calmed him, and their hands on his shoulder and arm helped him remember to breathe. "One thing at a time," he sighed. He reached up to Reverie's fingers on his shoulder and pulled her hand to his lips before giving Corbin's a squeeze.

The fire flickered, and he knew it was struggling to get rid of the bones. Dorian pushed back to his knees and crouched before what was left. His hand flamed again, and he reached out for the skull. Shudder sweeping over him, vision vibrating. He pulled his entire form once more to blaze it.

The fire burned so hot, the wall began to sweat and blacken.

Dorian didn't let his form dwindle as he stood and went for the other Infi, intent on only squashing the heart in his hand to see if it worked as well.

Black blood poured over his fingers as it broke in his palm, and as the ashes collected in his hand, he blazed his fire hotter, feeling his own insides start to burn, and he knew he was pushing his limits.

But a raging determination had settled inside him, one he held on to as he held onto his life and the lives of the two in the room with him.

The heart disintegrated in his hand.

For an hour, Dorian blazed his heat hotter and hotter onto the Infi bones. To the point that his fire turned a dark purple, and he nearly passed out. He grabbed himself before he could collapse and pushed back, almost falling into Reverie and Corbin's arms as the form died on him.

For however long they sat together, they lost track. Corbin retrieved the blankets and wrapped them up in them as Dorian could hardly move. He was forced to drink and eat, but he couldn't look away from the bodies.

"If this is what burning one is doing to you, I am scared to think what tomorrow brings," Reverie said, pushing his hair off his forehead.

"You two will have to be far away when I do this," he decided. "Especially you, Bin. One whisper of these flames, and I could kill you. We'll have to somehow lead them up to their stone temple—" he turned and met Corbin's eyes. "You remember that great stadium?"

Corbin nodded. "The stone one with the square pillar at the point?"

"That might be the only place that I can contain it. With the snows, I'll have to hold it for hours possibly." He paused and looked between them. "I need you two safe. You have to stay together."

Corbin's hand tightened around Dorian's shoulder. "I'll take first watch outside tonight," he said as he stood.

Dorian caught his hand as he turned to leave, and the warmth of his fingers entwining in his Second's made a lump grow in his throat. "Don't wander off," he said, meeting his eyes. Corbin's grip tightened around his, and Dorian kissed his knuckles before letting him go.

When Dorian sat up to lean against the wall, he noted Reverie smiling at him. "What?" he asked her.

"Nothing," she shrugged as she tucked her legs behind her, sitting by his hip.

He watched her another moment before sighing his head back against the wall and continuing to stare at the flames blazing before them.

Reverie moved after a while, getting up and going over to the corner where she stripped herself of her wet clothes. Dorian didn't deny himself to watch. He could see the wing marks on her shoulder blades and down the backs of her arms, among other things. As much as he wanted to banter and say something about her curves, his heavy mind would not allow him to speak, and Reverie noted his silence.

"Here I was preparing a comment to come back at you with," she muttered as she pulled the fur around her shoulders, only her undergarments left on her body. Dorian's gaze wandered slowly over her, glimpsing her thighs and the swoop of her hip to her waist in the shadows as she cradled her arms over her.

He almost smiled at her banter, but his body ached with his every move. "I'll make up for it once all this is over, don't worry," he promised.

She pressed to her knees at his side. "Do you really think you can take down that entire town tomorrow?" she asked.

"No," he admitted. "But I have to try. I can at least take some."

"And the others?"

He sat up to pull his knees into his chest. "I'll figure it out. But I need you to get the Scrolls. That is the priority. Whatever Corbin and I do will be enough of a distraction for you to find them."

She nodded, and he watched her a moment. Noting the scars he could see on her neck again, the solemness in her gaze.

"You said earlier you knew the Infi wasn't me," she said, meeting his eyes. "How did you know?"

"It was needy."

Reverie smiled. "Is that it?"

He met her smirk. "No," he continued. "It tried to tell me things it thought I would want to hear from you. That you needed me. That you wanted me to protect you. That I wouldn't leave you."

"No wonder you slid the knife over its throat," she muttered. "I would have too."

Dorian started to laugh, but it turned into a cough, and he doubled over to clutch his stomach as he did, his own flames evacuating his throat and burning his insides. He cursed at the feeling as it settled, and he sank against the wall once more. Reverie's hand rubbed up and down his arm, the touch of it causing chills over his flesh.

As he watched her, he noted her staring at the Infi again. Her hand absentmindedly brushed his arm after a few moments. He could see the haze over her eyes as a memory replayed in her head.

"Can I ask you something?" he said, breaking her out of it.

She blinked, head slowly turning to him. "Anything," she whispered.

"Why did you volunteer to go today?" he asked. "Truthfully."

She avoided his gaze, and for a moment, he thought maybe she wouldn't respond. Tell him to mind his own business and that her decisions were made for herself and herself only.

But he couldn't have been more wrong.

"Because you are my King," she said as she squeezed his hand. "You trusted I could go there and bring one back with barely a second thought," she continued. "You didn't ask Corbin first. You didn't put it up for debate. You gave me a choice. And I couldn't live with myself if I didn't at least try after everything you've done to secure aid for people who have betrayed you."

Heat crept on his neck. "I don't know anything about being a King," he admitted. "Nothing. Just a few minuscule bits I picked up from Draven."

"Putting the safety of your people over yourself is a good start," she told him. "Running into a situation as precarious as this one and thinking of the world first is another."

He paused, sighing, as he looked at her. "I'm not a hero."

"You're not," she agreed. "Because I know your mind is clouded by the things you would do to make sure the people you love are taken care of first."

"People keep saying that as though they think it should change," he uttered.

"I know you still have a long way to go before others bow at your feet. But... I want to be at your side when they do. I know you'll earn their respect as you have earned mine."

"He'll never let you call him anything else now," Corbin said from the entrance.

Reverie almost smiled, but she didn't turn to look at the Belwark. "I know," she called back to him. "I've just dug myself into a hole he'll forever use against me." Her widened eyes squinted at Dorian's silence then, and she frowned. "*Architects*, I think I broke him."

"I'm inclined to agree," Corbin replied upon slipping into the cavern again. "Alright, Prince?"

Dorian snapped out of his daze with a blink and rub over his face. He wasn't sure what to say. His stomach twisted like someone was wringing it free of its contents. Because all he could see was all the things he would do if it did come down to his loved ones or the world.

And he would let this whole world burn before he lost anyone else.

"Hey, Bin," Dorian called out as he lifted his gaze.

"Yes, Prince?" Corbin paused.

"Come inside and get warm." He stood from the ground then,

balance wavering, but he caught himself on the wall. "I'll watch outside the rest of the night."

Reverie's hand was on him the moment he stumbled. "You're too weak to be out there—"

"I'm fine," he said sternly. "Neither of you have fire. It should be me outside, not you."

"Prince—"

"Come get warm," Dorian affirmed as he finally met Corbin's eyes. "It is not a choice I am giving you."

He didn't wait on a response from them before he strode outside into the snows. The Dead Moons were nearly there. Just two nights more. He pushed his hands over his face as he sat on the edge of the walk, his feet dangling down. For the first time in a few weeks, the sky was clear. The twinkle of the stars staring back made his chest hurt, and his mind swam of all the thoughts he didn't know how to sort.

He needed Nyssa.

It hit him then how much he'd been holding in. How much he needed to talk to her to walk through everything he was feeling. Now that he'd secured aid, the war was one step closer to him. With Reverie calling him King, it seemed to solidify in his chest that this was real. That people would one day look to him for answers he didn't know how to provide. He wasn't sure he'd ever truly considered the weight of it. The dealing with the Infi the next day would be his first true challenge at keeping the world that had betrayed him from ruin. His first official task at keeping Haerland and her people safe.

There was a constant battle in his mind of whether or not he should actually save it.

In the eyes of their people, Rhaif had been a hero. He'd put the safety of their world before Aydra, foolishly thinking a child born of she and the Venari King would have destroyed everything. Even though such a child and partnership would have brought—and did bring—all their races together.

Perhaps that was what scared him anytime someone mentioned the word 'hero.' Because Rhaif was a hero and a King to his people. Because they didn't know any better. Because they believed the lies despite how great of a queen Aydra had been to them. Protecting them even without her crown and loving them when they didn't love her.

Up until the very end.

How was he ever supposed to get the people to see otherwise?

Protecting them despite whatever lies they believed, he knew, was his duty. He knew it was what he was supposed to do. But until he could bring to light the evils of his own home, he would focus on helping Bala and Nadir keep their people safe. They were his priority. Not his own crown, but rather their's.

Until keeping the world safe meant abandoning his loved ones, he would do it. He would put the people of Haerland first. He would keep them from starvation and slavery.

Even if it meant destroying everything to keep them from succumbing to such a fate.

Dorian pushed that darkened thought to the very back of his mind. He shuddered to think such of one would ever come to fruition, but if it did--

His hands pushed over his face, snow melting on his skin as he forced himself to think of better things. Less world-condemning things.

Like the way Reverie had squeezed his hand and the clasp of Corbin's hand around his arm when he saw he'd been hurt. The feelings he was coming to have for both beings sitting in that cavern clouded him. He didn't know what he was supposed to feel.

He'd always been jealous of Nyssa's hopeless romanticism, heard her tell her stories of how her chest would knot when she felt for someone. He thought back to Draven and Aydra and how their love shattered kingdoms. He wanted love like that. But being a son of Arbina, and now knowing the history of previous kings—knowing what his olders had been capable of in the name of what they called love... He wondered if he would ever find it. He wondered if it was something he was cursed to live without or if he could bring himself out of their shadows and become his own.

If what he was feeling for the two in that cavern was something more than lust. He thought it was... But he wasn't sure he could trust anything at that moment.

Dorian tilted his head back and pushed the overwhelming feelings out, breathing as he once did with Nyssa. In for four, out for six. He blinked back the emotion in his chest and wished more than anything he could feel her with him right then. He missed the comfort of his family and the familiarity of their embrace.

He started counting the stars and noting the shapes in them as he took those deep breaths. Much of the night sky carried the shapes of Noctuans. There was the shape of hands for Haerland. The Noirdiem. The Bullhorn. The Ulfram.

But as he searched the eastern sky, having remembered there were few patterns there that they'd been able to make out, he had to pause.

The alignments had changed. How, he wasn't sure. But the sight of what he saw staring back at him almost made him choke on the laughing tears that fell down his cheeks.

"You bastards," he uttered.

It was *them*.

Draven with his horn. Aydra with her back to him, an arrow pulled through on her bow. The stars gleamed back at him as though they'd always been there. The patterns were as clear as the Bullhorn and Ulfram.

His chest swelled, and the tears down his cheeks iced over against his chilled skin. He pushed out a deep breath with the emotion of it and stared at the sky.

"I could really use your help," he managed. "Both of you."

His insides broke, and every emotion he'd been suppressing spilled onto his surface. Dorian Eaglefyre, alone and scared, unsure of his place in the world, but pushing forward anyway with the boyish grin and a come-on.

He had to let go.

51

Dorian let Reverie and Corbin sleep longer than the sunrise the next morning. They had checked on Dorian before going to sleep, but Dorian couldn't surrender that night.

For once, he didn't want the swim of his herb or the drink. He wanted to feel the things going right and wrong in his life. He wanted to acknowledge all those thoughts he'd been squashing and ignoring. He'd come no closer to figuring out anything during the night, but at least he felt more affirmed in his body.

A little more confident in his truth.

But as he stepped over the sleeping pair and went towards the back of the cavern, he noted that there was only one Infi left slumping on the wall. The bones of the one he'd burned the heart of. He crouched down at the empty wall where the other had been, looking for any residue other than the black mark on the stone. The ground continued to heat under his palm, and the fact that it was gone made his stomach knot for two reasons:

It was either destroyed. Or in the cavern with them still.

Dorian stood to wake Corbin and Reverie. He nudged them both, wary of the sleeping pair, and as they stirred, he drew his sword.

"Fucking—"

The pair jumped at the sight of him with the sword.

"The fuck, Prince—"

"The Infi is gone," Dorian said, staring sternly between them. "I'm not sure if it actually disintegrated or if it somehow came back and slipped past me. Tell me something we would know together."

Reverie and Corbin exchanged glances before shifting and looking to the ground as they thought of instances to tell him.

"You almost burned the kitchens trying to bake my Belwark victory meal," Corbin said.

Dorian remembered how the servants had shoved the pair out of the kitchens to put out the fire—when in reality, it was Aydra who had started it before they got there when she tried to cook Lex potatoes.

"That wasn't my fault," Dorian countered, and he could almost feel the smile on his lips.

"Definitely your fault," Corbin argued. "You blame your older, but it was all you."

"You certainly took your victory in another way, didn't you?" Dorian said, referring to when he'd caught Corbin in the servants' stairwell with Nyssa.

Corbin looked like he would laugh. "Your sisters are both freaks," he shrugged. "I'm not sure what to tell you."

To this, Dorian did smile. "Dammit," he cursed under his breath.

Reverie stared between them, confusion in her narrowed eyes. "Have you slept with his entire family?"

Corbin's brows shot up, a haze washed over him, and Dorian couldn't hold in the chuckle. But he remembered his reason for standing over them with his sword drawn, and he shook his mind of the amusement.

"Wait—stop distracting me." He shifted and pushed the blade at Reverie as Corbin stood to his feet.

"Let's hear it, Rev," Corbin said.

Reverie huffed, eyes darting around the room as she thought of something. "I..." She grunted and curled her fists around the fur. Until finally, she surrendered and looked up at him. "Is it bad that I'm hoping you get some sort of injury today?"

His eyes squinted. "A bit rude, but why?"

"I think you enjoyed being healed last time," and he knew she was talking about the Temple bath.

Corbin turned sideways to look at him, arms crossing. "I knew it," Corbin declared.

"You're the one who left me unsupervised," Dorian countered.

"It's not entirely what you think," Reverie said as she stood. "Are you satisfied with our answers? How do we know you are you?"

Dorian held out his hand, and fire blazed in his palm. "I could prove it another way if you'd like," he suggested. "Make up for my being exhausted last night."

Her lips pursed, an obvious fighting smile on them, and she pushed past them then to go to her bag and get dressed. Dorian and Corbin both watched her walk by. Until they did a double-take at each other.

"You slept naked with her," Dorian realized.

"It's not entirely what you think," Corbin said, repeating Reverie's words.

"But it is a little?" Dorian asked.

A soft smile rose on Corbin's lips. "Yeah," he admitted. "Yeah, it is a little."

Dorian's mouth nearly dropped, and Corbin huffed amusedly under his breath.

"Tell me which one of us you're jealous of," Corbin mocked in a low voice.

"I—" Dorian couldn't respond. He didn't know how. Because all he could see in his head were visions of Reverie and Corbin together. The images should have made him jealous or angry. But he found he had to shudder it out quickly because of the aroused feeling in his bones.

Corbin must have seen it, for he stepped directly up to Dorian, shoulders flush, and he whispered, "Should I tell you how she wanted to know all the things we've done together? Of how your cock tastes and how it feels when you're inside me? Or do you want to know how she called out your name when she came apart around my fingers?" in his ear.

Dorian groaned under his breath, the tease making his eyes close. "You're doing this on purpose, aren't you?" he asked.

Corbin slapped his cheek. "Leaving you wanting and fantasizing? Definitely," he said. "Hey, Rev—"

Dorian was left standing alone to ponder the thoughts in his head and push down his desires, to figure out how he was supposed to not see that in his head and instead focus on the task they had to do that day.

He walked outside again and fell face forward into a pile of snow.

By the time he strode back in, they had a fire started, were dressed, and were making breakfast. Corbin smirked at him upon his entering, and Dorian threw a snowball at his face.

"We have a lot to go over about today," Dorian said as he sighed onto the ground opposite them. "Starting with whether we should sneak in or go in grandly."

"Horses need food," Corbin said. "We can't leave them here."

"Grandly then," Dorian decided.

"I love when you two get serious," Reverie said eagerly as she looked between them. Dorian started to frown, but Reverie sat her plate down and edged forward. "What do we tell them is our business?" she asked.

"Assuming they'll hear us coming and shift, we go to the one they've chosen to represent their Elder," Dorian said. "Lady Morgin. Pretend we are there on Hagen's behalf to retrieve supplies."

"What about the Scrolls Hagen thinks they have?" Corbin asked.

Dorian looked to Reverie. "Can you go in hidden? Search their temple."

Reverie nodded. "What do they look like?"

"Not entirely sure," Dorian admitted. "But I know they'll be of the old language. You'll see the mark of the Honest on them."

"What about the fire?" Reverie asked. "Are you still planning on burning the entire town?"

Dorian stared at the blackened mark on the wall and the skeleton leaning against the other. "I have no idea," he admitted. "It may be a last minute call depending on what we find. We have to get those Scrolls first."

A stretch of determination rose on Reverie's face. "I'll find them," she promised. "But I'll need time."

"Luckily, I like to talk," Dorian muttered.

Corbin and Reverie's brows lifted in agreement, and Dorian looked between them. "No need to disagree all at once," he muttered. He sat his own plate down then and stood, brushing off his pants. "We need to leave in an hour. Make sure you have everything, but leave one set of clothes here in case we have to run."

52

Face beaten, eyes swollen, Nyssa could hardly see the light in the room around her.

With a cuff around her wrist, she realized she was hanging limp from a post, her good arm was shackled above her head, and her knees were crumpled in a heap beneath her.

Nyssa had been caught on her way back in from seeing Nadir.

The wife had been waiting for her when Nyssa pushed back through the loose floorboard. She'd barely had a moment to see her in the dark before a rope had been thrown around her neck, and she was dragged down the hall.

Kicking and screaming, but it was no use. She'd been taken to the same room she'd just woken in and beaten while the wife watched over her. Water had soaked over her mouth and nose again as the wife accosted her for information.

Nyssa couldn't move.

The only good thing she could think of was that she would not be taken to the Prince until she was healed.

"The little bitch wakes," came Shae's voice.

The door whipped back.

"What in the name of the King have you done, Shae?" Bechmen demanded.

"She escaped last night to see the trader," Shae said. "The Porter alerted me of it. Perhaps you should give him an extra rationing and new maid tonight."

Nyssa strained to open her eyes, strained to breathe. All the pain rushed into one total body agony, and she hardly felt the Noble's fingers on her chin. Nyssa couldn't resist as he lifted her face to observe the bruises and swells on her features.

"Take her down," he told someone.

Shae stepped forward. "But—"

"I said take her down," he almost shouted. "She will not be running away in the state you have put her in. She is beaten to the point I hardly recognize her. This was not what you should have done."

The shackle on her wrist was undone, and she dropped flat to the floor on her broken arm. But she couldn't even wince at the pain.

"I saw no other option," Shae argued.

"No, you have been itching to beat her like this since her arrival—"

"You have been too soft on her!" she shouted. "The liberties this girl has taken cannot be reversed. You—"

"The Prince cannot see her in such a state." He cut her off as though it was an end to the conversation. "I will travel to meet him on my own and ensure all his desires are ready—"

"What—"

"*You* will stay here and oversee her," he finished.

A long pause dragged between them, and Nyssa managed to look up, finding Shae's arms crossed, her eyes wide. "You will deny my chance at seeing our Prince's arrival because of this brat?!" she snapped.

"This was your doing," he seethed. "You should have brought her to me and told me what she'd done. Something other than beating her senseless could have been arranged. She was meant to be a gift for him, and now you've gone and ruined that just as you do everything else. Etta will have my fucking *head*."

"Bech—"

"I am leaving," he cut her off again. "At the end of the Black, I will send a carriage to fetch her. Three weeks is all we can afford. Make sure she is ready by then. Hair cleaned. Body healed. Groomed. Mouth and body ready to take his cock however he wants it. You have three weeks, Shae," he told her. "Don't fuck this up as well."

The wind from his whipping back the door again hit her face, and Nyssa waited for Shae to approach. She was sure she would have some comment about her costing her the chance to see the Prince's arrival. Sure the wife would kick or hit her again.

"Get her up," Shae instructed the Porter. "Take her to my maids to be cleaned and find the surgeon."

Nyssa's body was pulled off the floor, insides numb, and Nyssa hardly remembered what happened next.

For a week, Nyssa was gifted with the reprieve of not being harassed by the wife.

For a week, she was bathed and bandaged. By the seventh afternoon, she could actually see. The swelling had gone down on her face, and she could feel her skin again. That morning, she sat up and wiggled her toes a bit more than she'd been able to the day before.

The Porter who came for her in the afternoon was gentler than he'd been on the previous. So much so that Nyssa instantly became wary of him. As he pulled her from the ground, she caught a whiff of the familiar death stench, and she stilled on the spot.

"Do you have a name," she started, "Or should I just call you Infi?"

The guard paused in front of her and pulled the helmet off his head. Dark yellow eyes met hers, and this time she didn't shift from him.

"I'm impressed," he told her.

Nyssa's teeth set. "You called her the other night, didn't you?" she asked. "You told the wife I had escaped. You knew how she would react."

The Infi only smiled at her.

"Why didn't you want me at Savigndor yet?"

Because she knew he had a plan. He hadn't called the wife simply to toy with her.

But he didn't respond, and instead, he wrapped his arm around her shackled wrists. "Bron," he said, to which she frowned.

"Bron?"

"My name."

Her legs were stiff, but she forced them to move. "Are you one of the original marked Infis like North?"

"I am. There were three of us."

The confession nearly made her stop walking, but Bron tugged her forward.

"You have survived well in your days here," he said, and Nyssa knew it meant he did not want to talk any more of his heritage. "Much more than I thought you would have."

"I imagine you thought I would break with the first whipping."

"Yes," he agreed. "It has been fun watching you."

"What's your end game here, Bron?" she asked, pausing in her step.

Bron turned and towered over her. "Do you know what I have that you don't, girl?"

"What's that?"

"I have an army," he declared. "And I have the only key to Haerland's true freedom."

Nyssa felt her eyes squinting. She didn't know what he meant by either statement. And Brone saw it. But he simply pulled her back along down the hall, and the conversation ended as they rounded the corner.

The wife was waiting for them.

With the General that had pinched her breast during the meeting weeks before.

Nyssa's couldn't move as she looked between the two.

The curling smile on the man's face made her stomach twist.

Shae smiled.

"Looks like her legs are working again," she noted. "Enough to hold herself on her knees, at least. You're in luck, General."

Shae tapped the man's chest twice and pushed off the chair.

Nyssa couldn't breathe.

Her mind began to whirl with every shortened breath.

Fear gripped her all the way to her core.

But even with her shaking body, Nyssa held her trembling chin high as Shae approached.

"You're dismissed, Porter."

Bron gave the wife a short bow, and then he winked at Nyssa before he left the room. Her eyes darted back to the General and to Shae, and she saw the man beginning to tug on himself through his pants.

Nyssa nearly hurled. Between her realizing the Infi were still at the camp and had orchestrated her being captured, yet again, and now the wife shoving this man in her face, she wasn't sure how long she could hold herself.

Shae's hands curled on Nyssa's shoulders as she walked behind her.

"Do you see that man's straining cock?" Shae uttered in Nyssa's ear. "You'll take it in your mouth like it's your next meal. And after you've brought him *sinking* to his end, I might even let you eat something other than those chicken scraps." She took Nyssa's hair in her hands and pushed it off to one side. The action of this woman's hands curling in her hair made Nyssa nauseous. It was a motion her mother had done with her multiple times as she spoke words in her ear just as this woman was doing.

"Piping hot soup," she cooed. "Wine. Perhaps even some of the fruits your beloved trader brought through." She stepped around to face Nyssa again.

"No," Nyssa managed.

Shae gave her a mocking pout. "Oh, you pitiful thing," she cooed. "Look at this *fear*. Who knew a man's cock would be the thing to bring it out of you."

"I'm not—"

"Shhh..." the wife said, pressing a finger to Nyssa's lips. "Enough talk, girl. You'll strain your throat." She walked back around to Nyssa's back, and Nyssa felt her pushing the top of her dress down.

Nyssa squirmed. "No—"

The woman whipped Nyssa around and grabbed her face between her fingers.

"You'll get on your knees and suck his cock, or else I'll send a ship east to that settlement we found a few days ago."

Nyssa's heart sank.

The Umber.

Shae smiled. "Very good."

She turned her back around and forced her forward.

Nyssa couldn't catch her breath. Her body jerked with every step. Her dress fell around her bent arms, her hands holding each other as she stabilized her own broken forearm. Her eyes fixated on the wall as the man pulled his length from his pants, and then Shae's fingers sank into the back of Nyssa's collar.

"On your knees, girl," Shae commanded.

Nyssa trembled, unable to hold herself upright. The ground met her knees. She could feel her insides beginning to convulse. That fear gripped and pushed to her extremities. Stomach flipping. Chest heaving. Muscles trembling.

Help me, she shouted from her mind. To anyone. *Anything.* Any creatures she could reach.

She couldn't focus her gaze.

Her hands curled in on themselves, and she felt the ash on her fingertips as her body warmed.

The man's cock was in her face.

Nyssa closed her eyes.

She could feel that form trickling up her skin, and this time she didn't shudder it out.

She allowed it to take her. She allowed it to push to the surface. She allowed her core to protect her. She allowed that barrier in her mind to fall.

Help me, she repeated.

Navy fire pulsed through her mind.

A dark, blackened gaze that she knew belonged to her brother.

"You and me against the world, sister," she heard him say.

From now until the end, she whispered back.

Her eyes opened, and the world vibrated.

The man jumped—

Nyssa grabbed his cock and ripped it from his body.

The chair fell backward. He wailed. Blood poured onto the wood.

Nyssa hardly realized her body had stopped shaking. Her form possessed her, and she rose from the ground.

Shoulders rounding, chin dipped. Her skin streaked with the same black lightning as her brother. Her hands were solid black. Every break and bruise in her body seemed to wane with the form consuming her. Her dress had burned off, and the chains snapped, leaving her wrists separated but still in the iron shackles.

Nyssa turned around, and the wife stumbled backward.

"What—"

Nyssa's head simply tilted. She held up her hand. Black and amber flames rippled to the surface, the streaks showcasing an orange hue beneath her flesh, and the man's cock turned to ash in her fingertips.

Every step towards the wife left smoke in its wake. The world continued to vibrate as though she were holding the creature she'd become at its very edge.

"What are you?" the wife managed, grappling to the table and nearly falling over it. Shae threw a chair in her direction. Nyssa caught it with one hand, and it flamed to ash.

Shae backed up against the wall as her eyes searched desperately around. "GUAR—"

Nyssa grabbed Shae's throat.

Shae pulled for air, hands hitting Nyssa's outstretched arm. She noted the wife going for something on her side, and Nyssa grabbed her arm. Shae screamed as Nyssa's fingertips burned her skin. Shae released the blade.

Nyssa threw Shae to the ground and grabbed the knife in one move. Shae crawled towards the hall.

Nyssa's hand wrapped around the hilt. Rough leather filming beneath her fingertips, she twirled it in her fingers. She kicked Shae sideways. Shae fell and scrambled to her knees.

Nyssa curled the tip of the knife beneath Shae's chin.

"My name is Nyssari Eaglefyre," she stilled. "I am the exiled Princess. The eyes of Haerland. The last of my line—" Her head tilted as she watched a tear fall down Shae's cheek. "—Born into shadows and fire for a war taking everything from me."

She deliberately crouched, her knife settling beneath the wife's jaw. The sight of the terror in the woman's dark eyes and noise of her trembled sobs made Nyssa's head tilt again. Deep within the grasp of the shadows possessing her, Nyssa's anger should have shaken her bones. It should have had her every nerve quivering. It should have had her quaking beneath the weight.

But every breath that left her was as even as the last.

"You will *not* break me."

—A guard at her back.

Nyssa's free hand shot out. Flames grabbed his throat. His neck cracked beneath her shadowed grasp. The thud of his body crashing on the floor made Shae jump. Obsidian flames moved from Nyssa's feet and wrapped around the broken guard.

Nyssa hadn't even looked behind her.

She lifted a softly flamed finger to Shae's chin, her face a breath away, and she whispered, "Shhh..." just as the wife had done to her.

Tears jerked down Shae's cheeks. "Please," she pleaded.

The involuntary smile that rose on Nyssa's lips solidified the still in her chest.

"I'll make sure your husband knows how you begged when I cut his throat too."

Her blade slipped through the woman's throat like cutting through water. A last gasp of surprise shrouded the woman's features, and Nyssa let Shae's body fall to the floor.

Standing, the flames swelled around her. The tent cracked. Every piece of furniture caught fire.

Nyssa stepped through the black and amber fire to the outside.

Noises of men shouting and women screaming were echoes in her ears. For a moment, she paused, closed her eyes, and reached out. Something had tugged at her core, and she knew it wasn't her eagle.

This was something big. From the depths of the ocean. Such a pull on her made her chest hurt. It was the first pull she'd felt since the Noctuans, and she wondered if the void her flames were pulling her into was breaking down that barrier she'd put up.

Let go, a voice told her.

A soft, melodic voice. A voice she'd heard only once before.

Let go, Nyssari.

Her eagle screeched overhead.

Nyssa took one more look around the camp...

And then she surrendered to her powers.

53

The afternoon sun beat on them as Dorian and Corbin rode the rest of the way to the Bryn. It glistened off the top of the white snow on either side of the path, almost blinding them with its glare until it finally moved behind the ridge line when they were halfway there. No trees grew this high on the mountain, unlike Dahrkenhill, where fir and spruce trees still littered the landscape.

Reverie had left before them. She intended to slip inside before their approach so she had more time to look. Her horse was left at the halfway mark, and the pair took its reins from there.

Every step knotted Dorian's stomach more. Like a rope pulling from his abdomen to his heart and up his throat. As though his horse's hooves were tugging the string from his mouth and making him nauseous. Choking on the nerves he was trying to hold in. Every doubt ran through his head, harder than it had the night before or even on his bad days.

What if he couldn't kill them?

What if he did the wrong thing?

What if he failed?

He would fail his first task at peace. Fail his new mentor and put an entire race in jeopardy. Fail to keep his promises and fail his Kings and his sisters.

At one point, they paused so Dorian could vomit, and Corbin had to talk him down from the attack in his mind.

"What if I fuck up?" Dorian had whispered on his knees, body trembling and not from the snow. Breaths short and jagged, the cold air pierced his lungs with every rasp. He was falling into that abyss. Vision spinning. Hands unable to grip to his knees because his fingers wouldn't catch.

"I'll be behind you," Corbin assured him as he knelt in front of him.

"What if I don't know the right thing?" Dorian said fast. "What if I try to burn them, and I end up destroying the entire mountain range? What if— *Corbin*, what if I hurt you? Reverie? Dahrkenhill? What if I blink and the next moment, I'm the only one left standing in our world? What if—"

"You're not that powerful," Corbin said dryly. "Stop giving yourself so much credit."

And the banter helped an even breath fill Dorian's lungs. The right corner of his lips shifted upwards, and Corbin wrapped his hand behind Dorian's neck, fingers curling in his hair.

"I'll be behind you," Corbin repeated, his voice softer. "Every step. And Reverie will be watching. We've got you."

A chill ran down Dorian's spine as Corbin's fingertips scratched the back of his neck, comforting his panic and slowly calming his nerves. His eyes closed, and he slumped forward until his forehead met his Second's, and for a moment, they sat while his shakes waned.

Dorian counted his breaths and walked himself through every possibility. Calmly this time.

He might start the burning of the mountain range that night—the only person in their world capable of stopping it being the Nitesh. Or they could all three end up dead and tossed off the side of the Bryn tower dais, bodies shattered and frozen against the snow-laden ground. Never to be found again. He knew Corbin was right. Without help, there was no way he could burn the world on his own in one night.

A deep breath finally filled Dorian's lungs, and he blew it out audibly.

The nervousness wouldn't leave him. That string from his abdomen up his throat would remain. But at least the reminder that he wasn't alone had settled in him.

Corbin helped him to his feet, and Dorian gave him a nervous smile, embarrassed at the number of times Corbin had talked him down by then. "Corbin—"

"Save it until we're safe again," Corbin cut him off.

Dorian nodded and gritted his teeth. He blew out another audible breath as he looked up into the landscape. They were almost to the Bryn. Just three ridges away from the final climb. Amber fire cut through the mist from their walls. A cloud almost always enveloped the peak. Dorian remembered how the last time it looked like the sun had been swallowed by the cloud as they entered through the gates.

The Bryn people were known for already being a harsh group. Dorian had experienced their few laughs the last he was there. Although, now that he thought about it, he wondered if he'd ever really met anyone from the Bryn. Or if they'd all been Infi then too.

Remembering the job they were there for made his fists curl. And suddenly, that rope constricted around his heart with his stomach. It numbed his insides into rage instead of panic.

"How many do you think were Infi the last time?" he asked his Second as he stared at the peak.

"All of them," Corbin replied, looking back over his shoulder.

"How long do you think they'd been duping Draven with their lies?"

"If I had to guess?" Corbin paused to think. "Probably since Parkyr."

Dorian's form flickered on his hands. He nearly allowed it to rise to his eyes as he stared at the town for one more minute, and then he looked to his Second.

"If things get out of control, you and Reverie are to leave me behind," he said firmly. "I'll meet you at the caves or back in Dahrkenhill. That's an order."

Corbin looked like he might laugh. "You stay, I stay, Prince," he said. "As will Rev."

They set off again, and this time, a wave of nervous anger filled Dorian's veins.

This was his first true task.

He thought about what Draven would have done if he'd known the entire town was Infi. How enraged it would have made him. Any mention of Infi had sent Draven into a spiral. Their very existence had haunted him.

It made Dorian's determination harden in his numb chest.

Snow buckled in the echo of an avalanche on the next mountain after they crossed the first ridge. The bellowing noise of it bent and cracked the still air louder than thunder. Dorian flinched, his horse unnerving beneath him. He leaned down to comfort her, telling her "Shhh..." as Corbin did the same with his. Pillows of the white powder spilled down that mountain to a sharp ledge before bursting into clouds in the air.

The mountains went silent once more.

Dorian exchanged a wary look with Corbin, and he knew they were thinking the same thing.

If that avalanche had been a warning from the Ghost of Fire.

As they approached the Bryn, Dorian's senses heightened. His form stayed on edge, making his nailbeds black, but not spreading any further. Every huff of his horse filled him as its hooves beat over the crunch of ice in the mud on the path. The dense cloud he'd seen earlier surrounded them as they climbed the last stretch. Torchlight flickered through it. He could just see the shadows of the great walls and the high tower dais on the very peak.

His horse bucked a few times, unsettled with the apparent danger they were walking into. They ascended the last stretch, and the fog finally thinned. Sentries lined the wall just as they had when Dorian and Corbin visited last time. Crossbows in their hands.

"Stick close," Dorian said to Corbin without looking over at him. "Make sure I don't do anything stupid."

"Behind your every step," Corbin promised.

Three sentries paused over the gate and watched them approach. Bolts loaded. The gates opened, and the Infi parading as their Elder's Second came through the double doors.

Dorian finally looked over to Corbin, and together, they dismounted their steeds. Snow crunched beneath their boots. Warm air huffed from his horse's nostrils as Dorian came around to her front and rubbed her cheek. He could see people moving about inside. Carrying wagons and wearing great cloaks over their bodies. Wooden wheels creaked as one such being limped by, his wagon behind him, two goats trotting at his sides on ropes.

"Prince Dorian," the woman called out, her arms wide. "We were not expecting you."

Dorian didn't respond immediately. He considered the woman. Considered her every step and sway of her outstretched arms. Every flicker of her gaze over him and Corbin. Dorian grasped the reins and rubbed his horse's nose as he responded.

"I have been in Dahrkenhill a few weeks facing trials for the death of the Venari King—"

"Yes, we heard about that," the woman interjected as she slowed before them. "Did you come here for your final trial?"

"We came here on orders of your High Elder," he countered firmly. Another cart moved past the doors, slower this time, and Dorian eyed the bent-over being as he passed by. "I have already proven my innocence and worth in the eyes of your Architect and Lesser One," he continued, still watching. "I will stand no trial here."

"Then why did my High Elder feel need to send you?" she asked, shifting, hands clasping in front of her.

Dorian's eyes moved to the woman, and for a moment, he paused. Wind whipped through his hair and swirled his throat. Corbin's horse bucked slightly, and Dorian could feel Corbin's eyes on him as he stepped deliberately in front of his own steed.

He could smell the death of Infi radiating off this woman.

Felt the necrosis.

A dangerous adrenaline settled in his core.

Plan, be *damned*.

"Came here about your Infi problem," Dorian said.

"Dorian—"

Dorian cut his eyes over his shoulder, knowing Corbin was about to say something about his abandoning their plan, but Dorian was done pretending. He was tired of tip-toeing around the problem.

And he wanted them to know he wasn't there to be played with.

The woman's neck extended, eyes boring through him with a coldness akin to the wind on his frozen cheeks. "Infi problem?" she repeated. "You took care of the Infi last you were here. We've no more come up from the caves."

Dorian's horse nudged his side impatiently. He glanced up at the sentries now moving atop the gates and then looked to the few that had come down the stairs and gathered in the doorway. "Take our horses for warmth and food," he said to the soldiers before looking to the woman again. "We can talk inside your gates."

The woman gave it thought, and then she snapped her fingers. Soldiers trudged forward to take the steeds, but not before Dorian grabbed his weapons from the saddle.

"Should we be concerned?" she asked upon his turning around.

Iron sheathing cut the air, and Dorian knew Corbin had swiped something over his sharpened scythe. They exchanged a daring glance, one that confirmed Corbin trusted what he was doing, and Dorian looked back to the woman.

"Only if you have something to hide," he answered.

And he could see the knowing expression in her eyes.

He hoped Reverie had found the Scrolls.

Because he was about to do something he might regret later.

His eyes met Corbin's once more, and Corbin nodded, scythe in his hand and at the ready.

He turned back to the woman as their horses disappeared through the doors. "Take us to the one in charge," he commanded. "And I don't mean your Elder."

Yellow eyes flashed. The woman's chin rose.

"Careful of your words, Prince Dorian," she warned.

Dorian took two steps forward. His figure towering over hers, shoulders rounded and neck extended. His fist clenched around his dagger, and he allowed his eyes to blacken, for the world to vibrate around him.

Flames trickled onto the blade from his ashen fingers.

"I know who you are," he seethed. "I know who *all* of you are. And if you do not wish to have yourselves engulfed in Promised fire, you'll do as I command." He pulsed back into himself, and the frigid wind whipped his cheeks.

"Show your true self and take us to the Infi you follow."

A smile that chilled Dorian to his core rose on the Infi's lips, and her irises bled yellow.

Bones cracked.

Muscles snapped.

Dorian looked to the walls. He watched as Infi shuddered and flinched. Limbs mutated. Faces melted.

A prominent vibration settled beneath their feet and shook the ground as every Infi in the town morphed.

The noise of their collective shifting made Dorian's skin crawl.

The Infi before him rose taller and taller until its face unfurled to its true self directly in front of Dorian's. The grey skin. The starved, yet trimmed and muscular, body. Elongated arms and claws grew on this one's fingers. A guttural noise emitted from its throat, and it bared its teeth.

Rage that this creature was trying to intimidate him rose in Dorian's body.

His form consumed him. He didn't realize he was leaned over the creature until he saw its back bending. *Cowering*. Dorian's own restricted noise vibrated in his throat as he stared the Infi down. Until finally, it bent its head, and it moved away from him.

"Follow me," the Infi said.

Walking through the town chilled Dorian to his very spine. He remained half in his form, chin high, dagger in his fingers. Infi continued to jerk and shift as they passed through. No noise other than the whipping cold wind and their bones cracking sounded over the air. There were no merchants selling goods, no laughing Blackhands as they chugged their ale and told stories, and no children running.

The crippling silence of death gripped his core from every side.

And he breathed in the stench of it.

Snow dusted the stone walk. It landed in Dorian's hair and on the furs around his shoulders. He glanced back to Corbin who's gaze wandered just as his did. And when he caught his eyes, he gave him an upwards nod. Reassuring each other that they would stay close. Stay together and keep the other safe.

The beings Dorian had watched pull carts had moved over to the sides of the walk. They, too, had morphed. The goats at the ends of the leads simply munched on the dry grass from the carts. Seemingly undeterred by the shifting. This shouldn't have bothered Dorian as much as it did, but he knew how their horses acted around the creatures. Wary and nervous. And he wondered why these creatures seemed to be okay.

The Infi led them to their stadium.

Unlike the one in Dahrkenhill, this stadium featured a high pillar in the middle, two hundred steps high. Sitting at the very peak of their world.

Here, they would force men to battle to the death for crimes as minuscule as food theft. The Elder had a chair at the edge where they would oversee the bloodbath. Most times, the fights ended with someone being broken in the air and tossed down off the side of the pillar.

It was when they stepped into the stadium that Dorian realized they were being followed. He looked over his shoulder, only to find every Infi in the town had come out of hiding and were gathered as far back in the streets as the gate.

More Infi than he ever wanted to see again crowded together. Yellow eyes popped out from beneath darkened hoods. His bones felt uncomfortable in his body as he looked over them. A hollowness in his stomach. Draven would have ripped the entire town to shreds with his wind and bare hands and then gathered their hearts after like trophies had he known about this betrayal.

Dorian didn't allow his gaze to linger and instead turned back to the steps they'd been led to. The hair on his neck continued to stand on end as he looked up to the stone pillar.

Two hundred steps.

Lightning flickered behind the high blizzard clouds. Nausea wrenched his insides, but he kept himself steady.

They began the climb.

Some steps crumbled beneath their feet. The side they climbed was not as steep as the others, but the snow whipping around them made it hard to stay on balance.

Dorian and Corbin remained calm and ready. Exchanging glances every now and then to reassure one another.

The Infis crawled up every side of the tower and the steps behind them.

Once he could see over the top step, Dorian slowed.

A great chair of jagged black obsidian glass sat at the other side of the platform up twenty more steps. High enough, the person could watch the fights and not be harmed during the bloodbath. A familiar woman sat in it, leaned back, legs crossed, hands gripping to the shards of glass at the armrests. He remembered her from his last trip.

The Bryn Elder, Lady Morgin.

The Infi they'd followed stepped to the bottom of the stairs and gave a short bow to the woman.

"I see someone thinks himself smart," Lady Morgin called out. "Hello, Prince Dorian."

"No games, Lady Morgin," Dorian called to her. "How long did you think you could get away with fooling the rest of these people with your disguises?"

Her hands stretched over the jagged glass. "Another twenty years, presumably," she cooed. "Though, I admit my men have become restless of the charade."

Twenty years.

"Your true form, Lady Morgin," he said firmly. "I cannot imagine keeping this up is easy or comfortable. We dined and smoked together last I was here. I'd thought us friends. Here I find out you were lying to me the entire time. The least you could spare in consolation is a look at your real face before I kill you."

Morgin laughed. "Kill me..." She tsk'd her tongue, eyes flashing yellow. "Very well, Prince."

She stretched her neck, the bones cracking, and she eyed them from the chair—

And then she shifted.

Body shuddering. Pupils melting yellow. Dorian forced himself to watch as her ivory skin turned. The stern and beautiful face shift to the creature. Her womanly features sinking and stretching.

Until finally, it was a male, different from the others, sitting on the throne. This male's skin was white instead of grey, almost translucent. Brutal pink scars ripped over his face and down his neck. His hood stayed up, creating shadows in the creature's sunken cheeks and under his eyes. Dark yellow eyes instead of bright yellow like those Infi he was accustomed to. He did not appear to be brutally starved or mangled like the others. This one... Dorian was sure when he stood, his muscles would be as large as Corbin's and that he would not walk with a bent-over back or cower.

The Infi settled into that chair with a sigh.

"Comfortable?" Dorian mocked.

"Shifting into women is more precarious. Most times, inexperienced Infi get it wrong." A deep breath entered the Infi's lungs, and his gaze lifted to Dorian's.

Dorian resisted the urge to reach for his dagger and instead lifted his chin, head slightly tilting as he kept his eyes on the creature.

"You may call me Aja," the Infi said.

The name caught Dorian off guard. "I wasn't aware Infi had names," he said.

"Most do not," Aja replied. "Those chosen by our Kings do."

Dorian's eyes narrowed at the statement, but he decided not to press it. Too wary of any lies the Infi might tell him. He glanced around him again, noting the darkened mountains in the distance, the fast moving clouds over them that seemed to be thinning. Snow thunder rumbled a few peaks over.

It all made him uneasy, and yet he was sure his heart had never been calmer.

"Aja, we are here—"

"We know where your sister is," Aja cut him off. "Both of them."

Dorian's insides froze.

"He's lying," Corbin said behind him.

But Dorian ignored him.

The mere mention of his family sidetracked everything he'd come up there to do.

Aja knew it.

And Dorian wasn't sure he cared to hide it.

"What are you talking about?" he demanded to know.

Aja's lips quirked just noticeably, and his hands stretched over the sharp glass. Black blood dripped from the ends as it cut his skin.

"That's what you came here for, isn't it?" Aja asked. "The way to undo what happened to your family. Bring both your sisters back to safety."

Nausea turned Dorian's stomach. He nearly stumbled.

Both his sisters back.

He couldn't breathe.

Nyssa.

"What do you mean both?"

Aja pushed out of his seat. He glanced back at the great chair at the edge of the pillar as he strode slowly towards them, and then he met Dorian's gaze once more.

"It is a great throne," he said. "Sitting at the highest point of Haerland."

"Stop deflecting," Dorian interjected. "Tell me what you meant by both my sisters."

"Dorian, your older is dead," Corbin said behind him.

"Are you sure about that?" Aja asked.

Dorian had to force himself to stay on one spot. His heart jumped in his throat. But he knew better than to think the Infi would be offering him any information without something in exchange.

"What do you want?" Dorian asked.

"No, no, Prince," the Infi drawled. "The question is, which sister do *you* want?"

"My older is dead," he repeated.

"What if there was a way to bring her back?"

"It's a trick," Corbin hissed.

He knew it was… But—

"There is a way," Aja said. "Bring them back. Undo the curses of our land. Wouldn't you like to bring them home? Become the hero of this world. Haerland's true savior."

Dorian's body chilled at the words. Undo every curse. Bring back his sister. Bring back Draven. Possibly their child…

The closest thing to becoming a hero he might ever know.

"How?"

Corbin grabbed Dorian's arm and whirled him around. Dorian hadn't realized he was shaking until that moment. Hadn't realized a tear had slipped from his eye and was freezing on his cheek.

"Your older is gone," Corbin whispered. "He is lying to you."

"What if she isn't gone?" Dorian managed.

"She is," Corbin argued.

"But what if I could—"

"Even if you could, what will you have to give up in exchange?" Corbin cut in. "You know Haerland. You know the Infi's games," he continued as he leaned closer to Dorian.

Dorian blinked back the emotion burning at his nose as he thought of Aydra. Felt her smile in his chest. Her hand ruffling his hair just as the wind was doing. Her arms wrapped around him and holding him. His heart constricted, and he forced himself to speak.

"What if doing this is the only way I can keep my promises?" he whispered.

Corbin's jaw tightened, apparent he knew the battle going on in Dorian's head. "The promises you made to your sister did not include you forgetting all she taught you and making deals with Infi just to bring them back. That's not why she died. That Infi is only telling you what you want to hear."

The words made his heart knot. Dorian knew he was right. Knew whatever it was the Infi was saying to him was only a ploy. Knew he couldn't give in to this desire no matter how desperate he was to prove himself.

Even if it did rip his heart into pieces to resist hearing what the Infi knew.

"Which will it be, Prince?" Aja asked again. "The one you stood by and watched burn alive? Or the one you left all alone, an entire week's journey away?"

Dorian turned back to Aja, fists curling as he held back his form. Staring at the smug smirk on the creature's face.

"Nyssa," he said firmly. "I choose Nyssa. Now tell me what you want."

"Freedom without persecution," Aja replied. "Peace."

"You expect me to believe that?"

"You need an army," Aja stated. "We have an army. We want freedom. You can give us that."

Dorian scoffed. "You mean you want the freedom to terrorize every corner of Haerland without our hunting you down. You would infiltrate our streets and impersonate loved ones. Strike fear into every person's heart so that they would have to ask their own family when they returned home for the day if they are truly who they say they are." Dorian paused and shook his head. "You cannot think I would allow that."

The Infi shrugged. "Fine," he said. "We'll take over your homes after you're all dead."

Dorian shifted, and a small smile spread over the Infi's face.

"I'll make you a deal, Prince," Aja said. "My army for your home and our freedom. And I'll throw in the location of your sister as a measure of good faith."

"You'll tell me where my sister is if you want to walk away from this with your life," Dorian countered.

"The deal, Prince," Aja said again.

Dorian shifted again. "What home?"

"Magnice."

With the end of the word, the Infi held out his hand. Dorian stared at him, his gut knotting with the notion of what the Infi wanted.

"What gives you any right to make deals for all the Infi?" Dorian asked.

"Just because we are cursed creatures does not mean we are mindless and incapable of organizing," Aja argued. "Our last leader was Parkyr. Our King. He had us come to the mountains long ago. Stationed close to Magnice and awaiting orders."

"You didn't answer my question."

Aja's smile widened. "I was among the firstborn of the original Infinari marked-Infi. There were three of us born that first cycle. I was left here in charge of this faction while my brothers were ordered to go with Parkyr until it was time for their assignments. Does that answer your question?"

Dorian eyed the Infi's outstretched hand. Watched the elongated fingers. Felt the thump of his heart as the Infi's information stilled between them.

"Don't," Corbin said behind him.

But Dorian stepped forward.

"You'll leave my people alone," Dorian repeated. "No more terrorizing them. Manipulating them. Harming and raping, and pillaging. None of it. You'll fight for me. And once this war is over, you'll have the Bryn—"

"And Magnice," Aja completed. "A small price to pay for the security of your people and home from the strangers on our shores, I think."

Dorian considered it. To give away his home. Even if most of it had been destroyed. The thought weighed on his shoulders.

But he remembered his home was no longer a place. Especially not that place.

He wasn't sure he cared if the Infi took it after this was all over. He could move his own people south to the other villages. Or to the north past the mountains into unexplored territories.

"Make the deal, Prince," Aja repeated.

Dorian locked eyes with the yellow-eyed creature before him.

"Save your family," he continued. "Secure yourself an army."

Dorian's fingertips were an inch from the Infi's. "And you just want peace? And a home?"

"Dorian, don't," Corbin begged.

But the Infi's hand brushed Dorian's again. "That's all we want, Prince."

Heart pounding, Dorian eyed the fingers once more.

"Tell me where my sister is first," he said. "You say it is a measure of your good faith. Prove it."

Aja's hand pulled back and a pause washed between them.

Dorian started to speak again, but—

"A captive," Aja said.

Wind ceased, and Dorian went rigid.

"What?" Dorian managed.

"Your sister, Nyssari," Aja said. "She's being held captive at one of the settlements our new friends have begun building. My brothers are keeping a close watch on her."

Blood pounded in Dorian's ears.

His vision clouded.

He dizzied on the spot.

Captive.

His knees buckled, but Corbin caught his arms.

"Your sister knows what she's doing," he hissed in Dorian's ear.

But Dorian couldn't breathe.

Anger surged through him. His form rose on his shaking body, but his fire contained inside. Dorian snatched his arms away from Corbin and towered over the Infi.

"You give me your army," Dorian seethed. "You give me your army and your loyalty. You bow to *me*, and you can have whatever's left of that pearly fucking kingdom once this is over."

The right corner of the Infi's lips twisted. "A crown for our new King, then," he cooed.

"Dorian—"

But Dorian pulsed a flamed fist up, and Corbin took a step back.

"The deal... *my King*," Aja drawled.

All Dorian could see as the Infi extended his hand was Nyssa's face. The thought of her chained up in some stranger's hold. Tortured. Imprisoned.

Silenced.

Dorian took the Infi's hand.

54

Heat surged from the Infi's palm and into his. Pain as though his hand had been struck by lightning seared up his arm. Dorian's knees buckled with the outcry that escaped his lips.

The ground shook.

Snake-like smoke wrapped around their joined hands, and before Dorian could ask what was happening, a laugh escaped the Infi's lips. The kind of laugh that chilled him to his bones. The kind of laugh that made his stomach turn, and he nearly hurled all over the floor.

Black ooze trickled out of the nerve-like cuts running up his hand and forearm. Matching lines on Aja's. Dorian struggled to let him go as one streak continued up his arm. Up his bicep. Cutting the side of his throat. Until it ripped into his jaw and up his cheek to his eye.

Dorian cried out.

Fire trickled onto Dorian's skin. His form rose to protect him. It hardly phased the Infi. The black ooze from his wounds dropped to the ground, and even in Dorian's vibrating possession, he could see as it began to stack onto itself.

He fell to his knees beneath the weight of Aja's grasp and his own form.

Slowly, the ooze morphed. Snow falling around it and freezing it in place. Warping and curling just as the lines were doing on his forearm. Finally, its figure rose as jagged obsidian peaks. As shards of ice and glass in a circular shape.

A crown.

Fire exploded onto the surface of his body.

He screamed with the pain of it around him. Burning and cursing his muscles. Shredding his entire being, the only thing keeping him from writhing on the ground was his hand still wrapped into the Infi's.

"Dorian!"

The noise of Reverie's voice didn't pull him out.

Pain rattled his bones.

His eyes shut as he sank into the edge of his existence, his form nearly taking over in an attempt to protect him from whatever the Infi was doing to him. Whatever kind of deal he had just struck.

Black fire pulsed as an image in his mind.

Amber eyes that he knew belonged to his sister.

The image should have spun him, but his anger calmed, heartbeat steadying.

His sister.

Alive and reaching out to him.

A tear stretched down his inflamed cheek, and he held to the image of her with everything he had left.

You and me against the world, sister, he said to the image.

From now until the end, he heard her whisper back.

Dorian collapsed to his side.

Snow wrapped his bare shoulders as he rolled against the stone. He clenched his right arm to his chest, trying to push himself up with his left. His arm continued to bleed black and navy fire mixed with his own blood from what looked like every nerve gaping and cracking.

But as he pushed himself to one knee and coughed out the remaining fire, someone stepped before him. The person bent—Aja— and he picked up the object from the ground.

A crown of long black jagged glass daggers. Nearly navy in the light of the waning sky. The glint of reflecting snow from the twin crescent moons bounced off its rough sides.

He continued to tremble as the Infi placed the crown on his head.

The world vibrated, and Dorian realized he was still in his form. Shoulders rounded, he rose to his feet.

A snarling noise filled his ears. In the corner of his eyes, he saw them. True Infis in their animalistic states. Not like the creature that stood before him with a mind of reason and verbal articulation. But rather the creatures the Chronicles spoke of. The mindless savages. The ones Draven sought to eradicate from their world.

The ones he knew would betray him one day.

But the bind on Dorian's arm meant something, and as he looked slowly around him, he noted that every single Infi had the same mark on their own arms.

Bound to serve him.

Blood dripped onto the stone from his fingertips.

Aja dipped his head and gestured behind, presenting Dorian with the chair at the edge of the pillar.

Navy flames trickled onto Dorian's skin once again, and he watched with a bent head as the Infi cowered behind him. His bare feet made little noise as he ascended the steps, smoke rising in their wake.

And as the last moons of winter rose, Dorian settled onto his throne.

His throne of shattered glass and fire, of snarling beasts and fangs... Surrounded by moons-lit snow and navy fire torches, at the top of the highest peak in Haerland. Navy flames danced on the ground. His blackened eyes stared into the world, ashen-streaked hands grasping at the jagged chair. The wind whipped his black hair off his face. The sting of it brushed his sharpened cheekbones. He settled into his true form as his new home.

The power at his fingertips swelled in his chest and calmed his core.

True Infis hissed and snarled as Corbin and Reverie appeared in his sightline. Dorian didn't speak. But as they reached the bottom of the steps, they each drew their swords.

And they knelt before him.

Knelt not before a son of Arbina.

Not before a Prince of Promise.

But before a King...

A King of obscurity and flame.

Of darkness and embers.

Of shadows and fire.

He closed his eyes and inhaled the last cold winter air, allowing it to reverberate in his lungs.

Dorian stood from the throne after a few moments and walked down the steps to Reverie and Corbin. His form dwindled only from his eyes. The Infis lowered their heads as he walked by, cowering before him. Both his guards stood upon his approach, and he watched as they pushed their swords back in their belts.

"Neither of you ever have to bow to me," he told them. "Ever. You are my Second and my Commander. I will always fight by your sides as myself and nothing more."

"You'll fight at our sides as our King," Reverie said, chin lifting to him.

Adrenaline surged his form. He grabbed her off the ground, lips capturing hers. Hungrily. Desperately. Fluttering heart, be damned. Her mouth opened, his tongue slipped inside her, and his every muscle came alive with the arousal of her mouth against his. His form continued to pulse on the surface, those blackened streaks coursed over his skin as her hands pressed to his cheeks.

He'd never kissed anyone in his form before, and the new sensation of it consumed him. Raw and powerful. His senses heightened. Her legs tightened around his waist as his hand threaded beneath her ass, the other around her throat. He wanted to hold her there. Put a pause on everything around them. Heat spread, not from his form over him, but from the warmth of her touch against his body. Her arms tightened around his neck, nails digging into his hair until he had to force himself away.

His vision vibrated again as he pulled back from her. "Do you have them?" he managed.

Gasping for air, her widened eyes moved over his face, and then she nodded.

"My King," and the salutation coming from Corbin's lips made Dorian's head jerk. Corbin opened his mouth to say something, but Dorian's lips slammed into Corbin's, his still holding Reverie around him. Hand pressing to Corbin's cheek, he devoured every sweep of his tongue, to the point that Corbin grabbed him just to stay on balance. And when finally he pulled back from him as well, he looked breathlessly between the pair, and he allowed Reverie's feet to hit the ground once more.

"One day, I'll kiss you both like that when my life isn't in mortal danger," he promised.

—Reverie shrieked.

Dorian jerked as she jumped into his arms, her head flinching to her feet. An Infi had crawled up the side and grabbed at her ankles. It hissed. Her scream echoed in his ears, and Dorian shook with the rage draining his insides. He reacted without thinking.

Because Reverie never flinched.

He grabbed the creature up by its neck, flames blazing on his arm. As it clawed him the way the one had the day before, he reached that flamed hand into its chest. Skin burning. Ribs breaking.

He ripped out the creature's beating heart.

Still holding it, he let its body sag in his hand and dwindle to the ground, and his eyes darted around to every single Infi. His stare landed back on the one who had made the deal.

The heart disintegrated in his grasp.

And the Infi before him kneeled.

"Speak your words carefully, my Liege," Aja warned.

"Every Infi here is to stay in this town until I command differently," Dorian stated. "You are all *mine*. Your loyalty and your lives belong to *me*. You are to obey my orders and my orders only. I am leaving. Tonight. I will deal with the Infi already in the south on my way to find my sister. Until I release you, you are all to stay here. This town is now your prison. Get comfortable."

A shudder passed over the Infi crowd and then into Dorian's own body. It made his jaw tighten, his fists clench, and then a wash of power settled over his bones. His eyes blazed open.

Every Infi cowered to their knees.

The deal was done.

And the Infi were bound to him.

55

They had seen the flames from the Umber.

Nadir's boats were faster than traveling on horse. Bala used her wind to blow them across the water. Nadir had paced, hands threaded behind his neck, muttering incoherent babble in the old language as Bala realized he was so nervous, the usual tongue wouldn't keep up. The noise of it startled her, but she turned her attention to Lex instead.

All color had drained from Lex's face. Bala knew she was more terrified inside than the Second Sun would ever admit.

The ocean had rumbled beneath them, all manner of creatures pulsing to her call. The last moons' light of winter had ricocheted off the spine of a grand serpent, and it was the sight of it that made Nadir pause in his step.

"Follow it," Nadir said.

"The serpent?" Lex asked. "The last time—"

"That there is a different serpent," he cut in. "I'm sure the greater one that likes her is already with her."

"That wasn't the greater one?" Bala asked.

"That was the small one," he replied.

Lex settled back on the edge, chewing on her thumb. Nadir pressed to the front of the boat. His hands gripped so tight into the wood, Bala swore she saw it crease.

"We'll find her," she told them.

Though she wasn't sure she knew what they would find when they reached her, and the look Nadir exchanged with her told her that's what he was thinking as well.

The breaking silence of the camp felt of a ringing that made Bala's bones numb. Every hair on her body stood. Shacks cracked beneath the weight of amber and black flames, the smoke swirling into their dark night.

There were no people left.

No animals.

Only the noise of breaking and groaning wood.

The moment their boots hit the sand, Lex began to shout Nyssa's name. Bala and Nadir both grabbed her in response.

"You cannot shout," Bala said under her breath.

"How else do you plan on finding her?" Lex argued.

"You don't know what she has become," Bala warned. "Calling it could be dangerous."

"It?" Lex repeated.

One look from Nadir confirmed what Bala had said.

A shriek sounded overhead.

The three jerked to the sand.

Smoke swirled upwards into the sky from whatever it was. But it disappeared into a whisper. Nadir was the first to straighten. They searched the sky, Bala's heart beginning to throb in her ears.

"What was that?" Lex asked.

"Tricks," Nadir replied, eyes never leaving the darkness. "We follow her," he said about the beast.

They moved, following the shoreline, ducking when shacks and tents cracked and splintered around them. Ash covered the ground in piles, and Bala could tell it was not ash from buildings. These were what was left of the people that had once inhabited that camp.

Burned and crippled beneath whatever power Nyssa had unleashed.

The shadow passed over them twice more, each time making them flinch.

And then they heard it.

Nyssa's eagle.

Nadir ran.

"Nadir, *stop!*" Bala shouted at him. "You cannot scare it!"

But Nadir didn't stop. And they ran after him.

A hiss bellowed in the air as they crossed the dune. The three of them nearly crashed into one another at the sight of what sat there.

Black flames wrapped Nyssa's body. The sheen of it glowed against the last sliver of moons' light hitting the beach. Only the sight of her molten amber gaze and tiny streaks of the orange glow from the lightning form on her skin penetrated through the darkness. Her hair seemed to wave against gravity in the wind. She sat in the sand at the edge of the surf. The sea serpent curled behind her. Water glistened on its large iridescent black scales.

Shards of glass rose beneath her flamed body, and her hands held to the jagged forms of it.

Nyssa appeared settled into the breeze of her fire, the wrap of the void's abyss.

The eagle circled overhead.

A skeleton laid on the ground before her, and Bala realized what was in Nyssa's hand.

A heart.

The heart of one of the two Infi that had been following her.

"What is this?" Lex whispered.

Bala's heartbeat hardened in her ears. She grabbed Lex's hand. The pair stammered at the sight before them.

"Shadow fire," Bala breathed.

"Her true form," Nadir countered, and Bala saw the tear streak down his face. "Creature of flames and speaker to beasts. The first to harness both powers of Arbina's children."

"She's just a girl," Lex said, her voice shaking.

"No," Bala whispered. "She's the creature Arbina never meant to make."

Nyssa's gaze fixated on them, and her hand curled around the heart. Smoke poured around it, flames following. It crushed into black blood down her hand and turned to ash.

Nadir drew his sword. The sea serpent gave a loud hiss. For a moment, he stilled, and then he dropped to one knee. A swell grew in Bala's chest. Bala drew her own sword, followed by Lex, and together they knelt.

Knelt not before a Princess of Promise.

No.

Their Princess had died in that camp.

This was a Queen.

A Queen of obscurity and flame.

Of darkness and embers.

Of shadows and fire.

Bala blew her wind around them in an attempt to dwindle the flames. The longer they stayed in that spot, the longer Nadir seemed to get restless.

"She's been in there too long," he whispered. His breath visibly shortened with the rise and fall of his chest. Bala grasped his arm when she saw him move.

"You have to wait for her to release the flames," Bala told him. "Look at her eyes. She has never become this creature before. She won't know you."

"That is my *Queen*," he uttered, and Bala had never heard such conviction in anyone's words before. "I promised I would get her out of that void or fall into it with her," he continued as he looked back to Nyssa. "I'm not losing her."

He stood and began to strip himself of his weapons and his boots.

"And the serpent?"

"I'll fight her too."

Nadir stepped forward. The serpent launched. He ducked just in time, but in the moment he moved—

Nyssa was on her feet.

She was in front of Nadir before they could blink.

And her hand was around his throat.

Bala and Lex bolted forward. The serpent dove between them, wrapping itself and circling Nadir and Nyssa.

Bala couldn't breathe. Nadir's hand was on Nyssa's cheek, his other around the wrist at his throat, and she could see his fingers beginning to burn. He was trying to speak to her. The pair cried out both their names. But there was no way to get to them.

A screech sounded over their heads. Forceful wind shuddered over them. Bala and Lex flinched. A shadow circled through the rising smoke.

Nyssa's eyes flickered. Her hair fell from the wind and onto her shoulders, and her hand loosened around Nadir's neck. His feet hit the sand again as the gaped cracks in Nyssa's skin began to fill.

With a final breath, she slumped against the serpent.

Nadir doubled over to catch his breath. A handprint was visible on his throat.

The serpent launched at the pair again—

Nyssa's eagle flew between them and the beast. The snake hissed, but as her eagle fluttered in front of it, the beast seemed to relax. It uncurled from around Nyssa and Nadir.

Bala and Lex ran.

Nadir was cradling Nyssa in his arms when they reached him. His hands were blistered and shaking. His words were hardly coherent. She laid limp in his arms, some of the black streaks still present on her flesh as markings, unmoving.

As though they'd stopped receding when she'd fallen.

Bala fell to her knees.

She didn't need to feel for a pulse to know that Nyssa didn't have one.

He shouted her name in her face, hand pressing to her cheek, but as the seconds grew longer, Bala watched him start to come apart.

"—come back to me," he was saying. "Every day, remember? We said every day. All the days after. Nyssa, come home—"

The words he said next were ones she didn't understand, in the old language, Bala realized.

But Nyssa still hadn't moved.

He kissed her and pulled back, his hand moving her hair out of her face.

"You didn't let me tell you last time, and I won't tell you now. Because I know you can hear me. I know what you see in that black. The mirrors around you. Showing you you are alone. You're not. You will *never* be alone."

He surrendered his head to her chest, and Bala could see him breaking further as the reality started to sweep in. Bala's insides curled. Seeing Nyssa so lifeless, those streaks on her body... Unwavering and still.

"Come on, Princess," Lex begged, her hand holding onto Nyssa's opposite Nadir. "Nyssari, don't do this. *Nyssa!*"

As if shouting her name would bring her back.

But Nadir hung on.

"Princess, I promised you evermore. And I can't do evermore without you. I need you to come home. Please, Nyssa. Bring everything back and *come home.*"

She still hadn't moved.

Nyssa's eagle landed on the sand.

It gave Nyssa's leg a nip, its every chirp confirming everything Bala feared.

"Nyssa, please," Nadir continued to beg. "Hear us. Come home."

The serpent moved, and Bala's heart dropped as she watched it disappear into the ocean.

Breath choked in her chest, Bala began to tremble. Nyssa was as limp as she'd been seconds before. She looked over his shoulders to Lex, whose own tears were streaming down her face.

"Nadir, she—"

But she couldn't bring herself to say it.

Nadir didn't respond. He was sobbing, saying her name over and over in her chest as he cradled her. Begging her to come back. Lex's forehead fell against Nyssa's, and she shut her eyes tight.

"Dammit, Princess, *come home!*" Lex begged a final time.

But their Princess was gone.

Bala's stomach lurched into her throat. She launched to her feet and ran before it evacuated. She was sure her heart would stop at the way in which it throbbed in her chest. She forced a deep breath into her lungs, staring up at the sky as she bit back the breakage of her entire form. Forced herself not to split the world in half with the wind circling them.

Her Princess lost in the void.

Taking on an entire village on her own to prove her worth in this war. Trying to be a hero for people that called her a traitor.

What was she supposed to tell Dorian?

The thought of the fire Prince made Bala's stomach launch again. This time she did vomit. Light-headed, the world began to spin. She did not know how to face him for this.

He would set the world on fire and kill them all.

Wind shuddered around them. Smoke curled. The three flinched at the weight of the flapping wings as a great beast landed on the ground not far from them. Amber eyes pierced the darkness.

Bala's heart dropped at the sight of the Sun in her phoenix form.

Nadir launched to his feet.

"*Bring her back!*" he shouted.

Lex sprang off the ground and grabbed him. Nadir struggled, writhing against her grip and screaming at the Sun.

"Bring her back *now!* Stop toying with our Age and *bring her back to me!*"

Bala thought she had felt pain before, but the sight of Nadir and the noise of his cries broke her completely. The phoenix only stared at him.

"I promised her I would find her!" Nadir shouted, and Lex threw him sideways. But Nadir didn't care. He launched again, and Lex grabbed him once more.

"I promised she would not be taken by that void!" Tears streamed his cheeks, saliva sobbing from his mouth.

"*Take me to her or bring her back!*"

56

Mirrors and black.

The darkness all around.

Water wrapped around Nyssa's feet.

She screamed, but no noise left her lips.

Her reflection shuddered back to her with every turn. Until she fell to her knees and closed her hands over her ears. Tears streaming down her face.

She was alone.

Scared.

Trapped.

A never-ending void of nothingness on all sides.

She dared to look up. Her reflection stared back. Every face she'd ever worn— the Princess back at Magnice with her specialty dresses, holding that tiara in her hands. The starved eight-year-old, her mother standing behind her. The screaming girl she'd been the day of her sister's death. The hopeless one on her way to the Umber. The learning, happy girl in Nadir's arms. The determined one standing in Man's camp.

The broken one lying on the floor.

And the creature she'd become.

All of them a culmination of the person she wanted to be. The one who she could be so proud of. The one her sister had believed she could be.

Drae.

Her heart fell, and she slumped back into a ball.

You will never be alone, someone said.

—Sunlight warmed her skin. Lavender and black herb filled her nose. The wind brushed her cheeks. She was sitting in a meadow of flowers. Nyssa looked around her in confusion as her hands swept over the delicate grasses.

The noise of laughter caught her attention, and an involuntary sob choked in her throat at what she saw.

Aydra was running with Draven on her heels. She was laughing. Laughing a laugh Nyssa had never heard. A laugh of happiness and freedom that had never been allowed to her in those castle walls.

Draven grabbed her and swung her around, finally allowing her feet back on the ground after a couple of turns. They wavered a moment, and he kissed her throat, his arms tightening around her chest. Aydra settled into it a moment before playfully shoving him off. Draven laughed, his head swung back, the laugh Nyssa had only ever seen him have when he felt most at home. But he grabbed her hand again and pulled her back to him. The kiss he pressed to her lips was one of hunger and happiness. Their foreheads met, and Aydra pulled away from him again.

As she shook her head at whatever he'd said, Nyssa stood. The wind curled around her face, billowing her hair back as she watched them. And for a moment, she couldn't move.

Until Aydra saw her.

Her sister froze. She could see the slow drop of Aydra's smile from her lips, the softening of her eyes.

Nyssa nearly started sobbing. She forced the heave of her lungs down deep.

Draven saw her then, and Nyssa had to remind herself to breathe.

Your King and Queen are safe.

Aydra took two steps towards her, but Draven held her hand back. Nyssa began to shake. Aydra moved once more, and it took everything in Nyssa to do what she did.

She forced her legs backward and shook her head.

Because she knew if she so much as moved a single step closer to her sister, she would stay there with her.

And she couldn't do that.

It would have been easy. To take herself out. To stay there with them in a field of flowers and a bubble of safety where she couldn't be hurt again. Where she wouldn't have to worry about Man on their shores or fear what could happen to her people. She could let it go. Surrender to the void and let herself free of the pain.

But she wasn't finished.

"Come home," she heard someone say.

Home.

And what home meant to her.

Her eyes closed, and she thought of her brother, of Nadir, of Lex and Bala. The walls of her castle were not what she saw behind them. No. Magnice would never be her home again. What she felt was sunlight, the forest, the reef. The image of her hugging them all. She imagined her brother spinning her off the ground. Nadir picking her up onto his waist, kissing her, and saying their words. Of Lex giving her hair a ruffle, and Bala grinning at her.

"*3916!*" she heard a distant male voice say—no, *scream*. As though that number meant life or death. Desperation in the tone, it was an echo on the wind. She didn't know the number. But it made her chest swell as if she did. Full of pride and needing. An unstoppable force.

She wondered if it was a connection she had not become aware of yet.

She opened her eyes, and she watched as the tear stretched down Aydra's reddened face, but her sister nodded, and Nyssa knew she felt it too. Draven's hand clenched Aydra's tighter as Aydra visibly wavered.

Nyssa held up her hand, stretching her fingers wide, and Aydra did the same. As her fist closed, Nyssa imagined her hand sinking against her sister's—their hands entwining—and Nyssa forced her knees upright so they didn't buckle.

A promise that they would be there.

"Come home, Princess," she heard someone say.

Voices echoed around her. She could hear Nadir. She could hear Lex. They shouted her name and begged her to come home. Nyssa thought everything that was home to her again. Her friends. Her brother. Nadir. She thought of the way they'd all ended things, with arguments and promises.

But they were still home.

Because it would never be all good things. It would be ups and downs. It would be promises they didn't want to make but would keep anyway. It would be grief and pain. But everything the war threw at her was worth it.

And she would keep fighting for the two standing in front of her.

"Take me home," Nyssa whispered.

Cold wind surrounded her.

The ground vanished.

Nyssa shrieked and grappled to the rocky ledge that appeared. The tips of her fingers barely caught it, but she hung on. She hung on as she held onto the image of home. Of finishing the job and being back with the people she loved.

Her feet swung. She tried to latch her toes into the rocks, but there were no rocks to latch onto. It was just her fingers on that edge.

That final edge.

"You're almost home," someone told her.

The noise of water rushing sounded, and she looked down. Water beneath her feet—

A wind on the sea.

You are the night.

And I am the trees.

"Take my hand, Princess," someone whispered.

And Nyssa did. She took that chance. She swung her arm up, not knowing if she would grab onto anything—

Bala drowned out Nadir's screams with her own ringing ears. She couldn't believe what was happening in front of her. Or perhaps it was she didn't want to believe it.

She forced herself to look back down where Nyssa was lying. Naked on that wet sand. Hair sprawled around her head. A sob caught in her throat as she looked at the Princess's face, more of it visible from the black than it had been moments before.

Wait—

Her heart skipped so suddenly she almost vomited again.

The black marks were receding.

Bala skidded to her knees behind Nyssa's head. "Hey—" She picked up her limp head and placed it on her knees, her hands pressing quickly to Nyssa's cheeks. "Hey—*hey, hey*— I see you, Princess—" she picked up her head in her hand "—you're almost here. Keep going. You're almost home."

Nadir stopped fighting. He and Lex both stared at her.

"The lines are moving again," Bala pointed out.

The pair ran and nearly stumbled in the sand, pushing to either side of Nyssa. Nadir grabbed her hand, holding it firm as he kissed her knuckles.

"Follow our voices, Nyssa," he begged. "You're not alone. Take my hand."

Lex reached to Nyssa's neck, and a visible sigh left her lungs. "Come on, Nyssari. Come home."

Nadir kissed her hand again, pleading for her to come back in the old language.

"Take my hand, Princess," he finally whispered.

—Nyssa bolted upright.

The three of them fell backward at the abruptness.

For a moment, it was all Bala could do to comprehend what had just happened. Nyssa's chest heaved, her eyes still coming back from the black and gold.

Nadir was the first to recover. He sat up onto his knees and pressed his hands to her cheeks. Nyssa jumped as though he had hit her, her entire body visibly shaking.

"Hey—Nyssa! Hey! *It's me!*"

Nyssa froze as she met his gaze. Eyes wide and petrified.

"Nadir?"

Nadir visibly choked, but he brushed the tear off her cheek nonetheless. "Hello, Princess," he whispered.

Nyssa's body caved, and she reached for him. "Are you real?" she asked, her hand settling around his cheek.

"Yeah," he breathed. "Yeah, you're home."

Lex reached for Nyssa's leg and squeezed it. Nyssa turned, and her body sank just slightly.

"Lex?" she managed.

Lex reached up and ruffled Nyssa's hair, tears streaking her face. "Please don't do that again," she said softly.

A flinch of a smile passed her lips, and she looked back to Nadir. He pushed her hair off her face, obviously unwilling to let her go.

Her chest rose high once more.

And then she collapsed in his arms.

Bala fell back onto the sand with the deepest breath she'd ever taken.

57

Dorian, Corbin, and Reverie left the Bryn mere minutes after the Infi encounter. Desperate to get out of there before the creatures realized they had taken the Scrolls. Dorian wasn't sure what any of it meant. Whether the Infi would somehow find a way to betray him. Whether they had another reason for wanting Magnice. But Dorian couldn't think about it.

All he could see was his sister's glowing amber eyes when he would close his own. His stomach was in knots that she was a prisoner somewhere, and he had left her to deal with the war without him.

They didn't stop at the first cavern.

The only time they stopped that first night was a few hours in, when the cold picked up so much that Dorian insisted Reverie get on his horse with him so she didn't freeze. She gave Corbin the furs she'd been using and didn't protest as she settled in front of the Prince.

It was dawn when the snows let up. Dorian couldn't feel his face. Reverie had fallen asleep in his arms some time in the night. The horses slowed, and Dorian asked how long it would be until they made it to the next cavern. Corbin assured him they would get there by sunset, but he refused to stop.

By the time they made it to the cavern, Dorian nearly fell off the horse. He carried Reverie in despite her protests while Corbin took care of the exhausted steeds. The fire was quickly lit, and Dorian started stripping himself of his wet clothes. He hadn't even noticed Reverie doing the same until he turned and caught a glimpse of her. His eyes wandering over her hourglass curves, making his throat dry. The faint sculpt of her shoulders, the squeezable flesh around her ribs to her waist, the dimples at her hips, the ass he wanted backward on his lap and moving up and down his length—

And the gash on her neck.

"Whoa—" Dorian bounded to her just as she wavered off balance.

He cursed himself for not noticing something was wrong. "Rev— " He caught her in his arms as she stumbled, but she quickly balanced herself in his grasp.

"I'm fine," she said quickly.

Red blood stained her hair. He clung to her as she steadied. "Corbin, do you know how to do stitches?" Dorian asked.

Corbin stared at him with narrowed eyes. "Why would I? Your injuries were always healed by your mother's waters, and my insides are made of fire."

"I'm fine," Reverie assured them. "They can patch me up at Dahrkenhill when we get there." She sank back down on the ground then, eyes fluttering. "Just let me sleep."

They managed to convince her to let them clean it. She hardly spoke. Dorian could tell the day had been draining on her. He remembered how she'd flinched when the creature had grabbed her. How she'd had to hold herself together all afternoon while sneaking around a bunch of Infi—creatures she'd grown up being punished by her father with.

"Are you okay?" he asked.

Reverie stilled, eyes rising to his. "Yeah," she said, voice barely a whisper. "Yeah, I'm fine."

But he could see the emotion she was trying to hide. He paused and turned her chin to face him. "I'm not asking for you to tell me that you're fine. I want to know if you're okay. I know today can't have been easy for you."

"It wasn't easy for any of us," she countered.

"I don't care about myself or Corbin right now," Dorian countered. "I'm asking about you."

Reverie's hands sank into her lap. "Honestly? No. I'm not okay. But we accomplished what we set to do, and I cannot be upset about that. I can work through whatever horrors come to me when I close my eyes."

His heart hurt at her words. He wanted to protect her from those horrors. Hold her while she slept and assure her she would be okay. But he knew her well enough to know she would only accept it when she couldn't stand it any longer. So he leaned forward and kissed her cheek, his hand landing softly against her neck.

"We'll be here," he assured her.

A glisten rested in her bright yet tired gaze. "If I wasn't so exhausted, I'd kiss you," she managed.

A half-smile quirked on his lips, and he tried to ignore the fluttering of his stomach. "I'll make sure it's worth waiting for," he promised.

She fell asleep just as he finished cleaning her wound, and he picked her up to take her by the fire, covering her in furs while Corbin helped him redress his own wounds on his arm, sharing the blanket beside where Reverie was curled up.

The sting of the water made him wince. Black ooze continued to seep slowly from the streaks wrapping his forearm and the one cutting through the side of his face. Dorian gritted his teeth and pressed his head into the wall, shuddering with every stroke of the cloth on him. And when he began to clean the dried blood on his cheek, Dorian had to bite down on the leather sheath of his knife to keep from shouting.

But despite the pain, the one thing he couldn't get out of his head was Nyssa's blazing amber eyes.

"I saw her," Dorian managed after a while. "I saw my sister. When I made the deal."

Corbin paused. "Could you see where she was?"

"I only saw her eyes. But they were glowing amber. Like fire."

Corbin's narrowed gaze lifted, and he paused in wiping Dorian's face. Whatever he meant to say stilled in his chest. For Dorian couldn't stop himself from slamming his head back into the wall, feeling his face burning at the emotion bubbling in his chest.

"I should never have left her," he managed.

"Your sister knows what she's doing," Corbin insisted.

"And if something happened to her?" Dorian's breaths shortened. "What then? What do I do if I lose her too?" He pushed out a forced exhale, head sighing on the stone. "I cannot lose anyone else to this. I cannot lose my sister. I can't lose you, I can't—" His hands pushed through his hair, and he cradled his knees to his chest. "I won't know how to fight if I lose anyone else."

Corbin's hand wrapped his arm, ceasing Dorian's ramblings, and his gaze darted over the Prince's face. "I'll be right here, Prince. Fighting with you. Until this life takes us from each other."

"Please call me Dorian," he managed, head hanging. "I am not a Prince. I have no real crown. I have no home. I have no kingdom. And if my sister is gone, I have nothing left."

"You have me. You have Reverie—"

"Both of you are only here because of deals made and a duty-bound.

Just like everything else in my life."

"If you think she and I are only here because of duty, you're wrong," Corbin corrected. "You have our love and our loyalty because we believe in you. I know I used to say I was only here for that duty. But watching you become this person... Letting go of your pride and allowing yourself to fail... That is the King I want to follow. That is the *Dorian* I want to follow."

Dorian's heart knotted, and he let Corbin's words settle in him. Hearing it from him made it real.

"Thank you," he managed. "I think I would have died a long time ago had you not been with me."

"You would have died in the first trial," Corbin smiled. "No, that's wrong. You'd have died the moment you met the woman. Because you would have went to her village as a smug brat and thought yourself able to talk your way out of the ropes."

Dorian choked on the soft laugh. And as Corbin smiled at him, he rubbed the rag over Dorian's cheek to the now scar that spread through his skin.

"I think I like this on you," Corbin mocked. "Maybe you'll get that fear you've been looking to strike into others."

Dorian huffed, but Corbin patted his cheek gently and then turned back to the rag in his hand. Dipping it in the water and wringing it out before pressing it to Dorian's arm again. Dorian sighed out the flutter in his chest. Heart racing with every stolen glance up at him. Thinking about the way his insides had felt alive when he'd kissed him back at Darhkenhill... How it had felt akin to when he'd kissed Reverie and how Corbin had pushed him away.

Until he couldn't stand it any longer.

"Corbin, I lied to you," Dorian said finally. "The other day when I told you I simply got caught up in the moment..." He paused, toying with his hands, and he met Corbin's gaze. "I think I kissed you like that because I wanted to actually feel cared about. Something other than just the lust... And when you pushed me away at the first noise of those Blackhands, I thought I would break. Maybe I'm feeling needy because of all this—"

"Was there ever a moment when you weren't needy?" Corbin mocked.

Heat rose on Dorian's neck with a sheepish smile. But Corbin only smirked at him.

"You realize how hard saying this is for me, right?" Dorian asked defeatedly.

Corbin chuckled. "Yeah, I do."

Dorian sighed, chest rising and falling deliberately as he watched Corbin another moment. "Why did you push me away?" Dorian asked.

Corbin fumbled with the rag, folding and creasing it as he thought through his answer. "I've not seen the Blackhands enjoying... *Everyone*... As freely as we do in your kingdom. I think I just didn't want them to take away everything you'd just accomplished because of something as simple as a kiss."

He was surprised by his honesty. "Corbin, I kissed you and Reverie in front of every Blackhand at that second trial," he remembered. "They still gave us aid. There was no mention of it. At all."

"I know," Corbin said. "Doesn't mean everyone agreed with it."

"I really don't care what everyone agrees with," Dorian insisted. "I'll be with whoever I want."

A heavy breath left Corbin, and he threw the rag on the ground. "You should get some sleep," he uttered. "I'll take first watch outside."

Dorian rested his head against the wall. "Bin, no one is coming for us," he muttered, watching the Belwark stand. But Corbin didn't listen, and Dorian grabbed his hand.

"Stay."

And he knew the word meant more than just the four letters.

Corbin's throat bobbed as he turned back to face Dorian. "What?" he managed.

"Stay," Dorian repeated, voice not as strong this time. "The Infi are bound to me. They will not hurt us. And there are no more wandering people traveling in this snowstorm. Only us idiots."

The banter even made Corbin smile, but he shook his head. "I don't want the state you're in to influence whatever you're asking me to do," he said softly.

Dorian sat up and kissed Corbin's knuckles, both hands wrapping around his one as he looked up to him. "I am asking you to stay," he repeated. "Even if it means just sitting here by my side."

Corbin raised a disbelieving brow. "Something tells me you're not looking for comforting silence."

"I'm looking for safety," Dorian admitted. "And safe is here. Between the two of you. Close enough, I can protect you both, and you can protect me. If anyone is going to patrol outside, it is me. Not you. Not her. I cannot lose either of you. So stay. We can watch together."

A heavy huff left Corbin as he apparently considered Dorian's words. Knowing how hard it was for Dorian to say any of them. Dorian squeezed his hand again, and Corbin glared at him down his arm.

"How do you do this?" Corbin surrendered.

"Do what?"

"Get me to give in to you," Corbin answered as he sat down beside Dorian and pulled his knees into his chest. "How?"

Dorian gave him a half-smile, and he nudged Corbin's shoulder beside his. "Must be the family charm," he mocked. "Or you just think I'm pretty. Either one counts."

Corbin scoffed. "There you are," he bantered. "I wondered where my Prince had gone with the whole safety speech."

"Your Prince?" Dorian teased.

The smirk widened on Corbin's face. "Don't let it get to your head."

Dorian nearly grinned, but he settled his knotting stomach and merely glanced over at Corbin. "Do you think I don't mean the safety thing?"

"It's hard to know what you're exaggerating about when you're in need," Corbin said.

Need.

It was an understatement for the things Dorian wanted at that moment.

He wanted to be needed. He wanted to feel something more than the teasing and mindlessness of his usual endeavors. To be with someone who actually cared about him and surrender to that. That was what he wanted on that night. To feel he was not just another son of Arbina, but more. More than his family. More than their curses. More than just a Prince trying to find his way in the world.

Dorian shifted, his lips pressing to Corbin's shoulder. His stomach began to knot, knowing he was not kissing Corbin out of any lust or mindless want to sink his cock into another being. But rather out of the comfort he so desired in his heart.

Dorian moved, and Corbin's hand wrapped into his hair as Dorian reached for the Belwark's thigh. Hand rubbing up and down his leg as he turned into him, and Corbin moved his own arm to give Dorian greater access. Dorian's mouth traveled up his throat until he reached Corbin's lips. And for the briefest of moments, Dorian paused, soft smile growing on his lips, and then he kissed Corbin's smile.

He pushed his own hands to Corbin's jaw and cheek, holding him as the vulnerability of his entire being caved within him. Deepening that kiss and allowing Corbin to consume him and take him. His stomach knotted with every sweep of the Belwark's tongue against his own.

Reverie stirred beside them, and both glanced over to her. Quiet chuckles left them when they met one another's gaze. Dorian pushed down to his side and pulled the fur over them as Corbin slid to his back.

"If she wakes up, she can join or watch," Dorian uttered.

He kissed Corbin hard, knee coming between Corbin's stern legs and pushing against his length. Dorian savored him. Savored that needing feeling pouring through his bones. Savored Corbin's hands not immediately going to his cock but rather enjoying the slowness of it. Corbin held his head as Dorian moved to his throat, nipping his skin and devouring the taste of him. Hands traveling down the Belwark's hard chest, feeling those rippled muscles beneath his fingertips, the soft hair on his stomach between his abs. Corbin's length began to harden against Dorian's thigh. Dorian nipped at his throat, groaning into him as he felt it.

Corbin's fingers clenched in his hair as Dorian moved, whispering his name and opening up his neck as Dorian moved lower. Dorian untied Corbin's trousers, but Corbin pushed him onto his back before he could finish, and Dorian surrendered to the man atop him.

Lips threading on his throat and sucking on his collarbone. Dorian held his hair, cursing under his breath as Corbin undid his pants and pulled his length free. His hips bucked at Corbin's hands on his pelvis, that slow need growing and making his eyes roll. Corbin moved lower, finally moving from Dorian's side to on top of him. He stilled on his knees as he kissed him again, and Dorian reached for Corbin's pants to finish undoing them. Corbin groaned into his mouth as Dorian wrapped both his hands around Corbin's cock. The Belwark's hands pressing into the wall as he allowed Dorian's grasp to pulse up and down, the tips of their lengths grazing against each other.

"Fuck, Dorian," Corbin whispered, and he pulled back to work his way down his front. Tasting down the middle of Dorian's chest until he sat back on his knees, bringing the fur up around his shoulders.

Corbin's hand wrapped his cock, pushing the beads of liquid over his length and spreading over his hand. The Belwark went lower, dropping his head. Dorian bent his knees up, feet pressing into the ground as his hips bucked upwards.

Corbin pressed his lips to Dorian's tip, and Dorian groaned out loud, not caring if he was waking Reverie. Only that Corbin was teasing him, fingers massaging his sack, and his eyes fluttered when he felt Corbin's finger sliding between his cheeks. Dorian looked down, and he caught Corbin's gaze.

"Tell me to stop," Corbin said as he stilled his finger at his entrance.

Dorian considered him, intrigued by the notion and feeling just vulnerable enough to trust Corbin completely. He swallowed, and he finally shook his head. "Don't stop."

Corbin watched Dorian's face as he sank his finger inside him, and Dorian's hips bucked at the new sensation. A chill ran over his flesh. His eyes closed, and he sank his head back to the ground, chin reaching to the sky. Allowing Corbin to take control of him. Corbin's lips pressed around his cock again, and Dorian didn't monitor how loudly he cursed the air. Because Corbin was taking him.

And he liked it.

His hands threaded in Corbin's hair as he relaxed his lower half, giving in completely. Pleasure rocking through him with every drag of Corbin's tongue and shift of his finger. Settling in that pleasure for long enough that Dorian began to lose control.

Corbin's finger slipped from inside him, mouth coming off his cock, and Dorian looked up to watch Corbin come towards him again. Their lips crashed together, Corbin's hand pushing their lengths together. Dorian moved his hand to the other side, motions syncing together. Dorian cursed as he felt the moisture spreading over them both.

"I want to feel you, Dorian," Corbin said against his lips.

Dorian considered it, heart skipping. "Only if I get to finish in you," he decided. "Just... Be nice to me," he only slightly mocked.

Corbin smiled. "Deal." He kissed him again, and the familiar hunger passed between them. The need and the lust for one another, to take each other as their own.

Corbin moved again, sitting up and watching him as he stroked his length on his own a minute, and Dorian breathlessly watched as the Belwark pushed on Dorian's knees. He bent again, lips wrapping Dorian's cock only a moment before trickling down the length, mouthing his sack, and Dorian cursed when Corbin spread him, and his tongue licked the rim.

Feet pressing into the floor, Dorian couldn't stop his hips from moving upwards with the simplicity of just that new touch. Eyes rolling as Corbin continued to tongue him, hands holding to the backs of Dorian's thighs. Dorian chanced a look down, meeting the Belwark's gaze, and Corbin moved up again. His fingers gripped Dorian's knees as he straightened, and then his length stilled between the Prince's cheeks.

"Relax for me," Corbin in a soft voice. Dorian's head sank onto the ground again, and he did. He pushed out the nerves, and the tip of Corbin's cock pushed inside him. They cursed together, Corbin's hands tightening on Dorian's bent knees as Dorian forced his own hands over his face, unable to stifle the grunt from his lips. The sensation of it made his stomach knot and his cock taut. He didn't know if curse words would be enough for the feeling in his bones.

Corbin pushed further, causing a shudder over Dorian's skin. Further and further. Gently. Until he was nearly all the way in. The pair both cursing and reaching. And then Corbin began to slowly slide in and out of him. Taking his time for them both.

Dorian's muscles edged, chills raking over his skin. He clutched to the fur beneath him, knuckles white as he surrendered to the sensation. Finally getting his breaths even and his lower half totally relaxing. Something burning and knotting inside him with every stroke of that length. His body came alive as he began to writhe. Corbin's face scrunched with every deliberate move. Dorian watched, memorizing that look, until his own cock started to strain.

"Get on your knees," he rasped, and Corbin's eyes opened to his.

"A few more seconds, Prince."

Dorian balked at his boldness. "Did you just—*fuck*—Corbin—"

Corbin grasped Dorian's cock and paused inside him, their hips flush, and Dorian couldn't help his own muscles from jerking. Jaw trembling, hands clenching. His lashes fluttered, and he caught sight of the smile on Corbin's lips.

"You're enjoying this far too much," he grunted.

"What—watching you writhe beneath me on your back while I finally get to sink my cock into you?" Corbin mocked. "Why would I enjoy that?"

Dorian cursed the sky again, back arching off the ground. But as Corbin began to stroke him again, Dorian grabbed his hand.

"Your knees, Second," he demanded breathlessly. "I want you pushing against this wall like it's your job to hold it up."

Corbin pulled from inside him, and the release of it made Dorian's legs limp. But he moved himself up fast, grasped, the Belwark's neck and kissed him hard. He switched them and pinned Corbin on his back.

"Actually, I think I'll take you here so I can watch you as you watched me," Dorian dared, hovering over Corbin. "Do you want that?"

Corbin's response came in the form of a deep kiss. Dorian wrapped his hand around Corbin's length, feeling how taut he was and how close he was to that finish. He didn't let go of Corbin's mouth as he stroked up and down him, teasing his tip and feeling Corbin's hips move with him. Until the Belwark's legs were bent in the air, his hands creasing around Dorian's neck and hip, and he came apart.

Dorian's cock pushed against his, finish spreading from Corbin's onto his own length, and then Dorian pushed inside Corbin. He cursed as he hovered over the Belwark, pressing his own hands into the wall, and he moved. The pressures of the day mixed with his desires came to the surface. He closed his eyes and allowed his body to move of its own accord, in and out of the Belwark. Fully inside him, his hips grinded against Corbin's. Corbin's hips moved in the air with his. Dorian's abs creased and flinched with every thrust. Until he couldn't contain himself to the deliberation any longer. Straightening up and holding Corbin's thighs in his hands, he fucked the Belwark. Fast and heavy. Sweat beaded on his forehead. His body shook, muscles finally reaching. Every vein in his neck came to the surface, and his hands grasped Corbin's thighs tightly. Vision blurring, he stopped breathing with that edge, and then he released himself wholly into Corbin.

His body shuddered with it, he cursed again, eyes opening, and he was met with Corbin watching him. Dorian pulled out and leaned over Corbin to kiss him once more, and then he rolled to his left. Swallowing and staring at the ceiling as he tried to calm his fast-beating heart.

Corbin gave his leg a pat, and Dorian did the same, almost an unspoken endearment between them. Dorian's mind spun. The fact that he'd just allowed Corbin to take control of him like that. He'd never let another man do that. Ever.

"Well, that was entertaining."

Dorian's eyes narrowed as he looked beside him, Corbin coming up on his elbows as he did the same, and they found Reverie staring at them from beneath the fur.

"Rude," she added. "But entertaining nonetheless."

Dorian almost laughed, and he glanced back up to the ceiling. "You could have joined in."

Reverie smiled. "Next time," she said, and then she looked at Corbin. "You were right, Bin. His form does flash when he comes. I didn't notice it the last time." Her gaze flittered to Dorian, and she winked at him, making him nearly devour her right there.

Reverie winced as she sat up, and she shifted towards him.

She did something then that he didn't expect.

She kissed him.

Dorian nearly lost it.

Her smile against his lips made him wrap a hand around her cheek. Mouths opening, she propped herself on his chest, and he couldn't help himself from grasping to her hip as she nearly straddled over him.

But just as he thought this might go in a direction he'd been fantasizing about, she pulled back.

"Both of you taste like fire," she said, and Corbin chuckled softly.

Corbin sat up and leaned over Dorian, his hand resting on Dorian's hip, and he kissed Reverie lightly.

Dorian didn't know what to do with his hands.

Fuck, he didn't know what to do with... *anything*.

"Am I dead? Or is this fantasy somehow working out?" Dorian heard himself ask.

Reverie bit her lip when Corbin settled back down at Dorian's side. She curled herself beside him and pulled the blanket up.

"That is all you boys get from me tonight," she told them. "Try anything more, and I'll cut you. I'm much too exhausted to keep up. I just want my heaters."

Dorian huffed, fully aware of her bare body against his, her full breasts lying on his chest, leg wrapped over his as she cuddled against him. But he smiled, despite his wanting to pull her atop him and have the three of them tangle together, and he met Corbin's gaze.

"Safety," Corbin mocked him as he turned on his side, his back to Dorian and pulling the fur over them.

Dorian sighed his head to the ground, attempting to settle his fleeing heart. One arm threaded through the space in the crook of Corbin's neck, and the other wrapped around Reverie's back to her hip, his fingers squeezing her flesh.

"Safe," he whispered.

58

Water beneath her feet.

Firelight reflected on the ripples of it. Nyssa turned in a circle, panic striking her insides. Whispers on every side of her. The world spun. She gripped her hair, fighting it, knowing it was a nightmare.

Wake up, she told herself.

Wake up.

Wake up.

Wake up.

A scream echoed. *Her* scream. The weight of the void wrapped around her. Pushing her down and down. To her knees. Water soaked her linen dress and pooled beneath her.

Alone.

A hand grabbed her leg.

She screeched and jumped back to her feet. Hands emerged from the water. Grabbing at her. Her heart ricocheted and nearly burst out of her chest.

Amber fire caught her eye. She looked up, only to find the creature looking back at her, and Nyssa forgot about the hands around her ankles.

Her form stared at her from inside the glass. Fire in her eyes. Black lightning streaks along her cheeks and trickling down her neck. As though her nerves sat on the surface of her skin, and fire was trying to push out from the inside.

Her form winked.

—Nyssa shot upright.

Breath uneven and not catching. She couldn't bring herself to reality. The image of herself as that creature imprinted in her mind and clouding her vision.

Hands grasped her face.

"Hey—"

A familiar voice. A safe voice.

Smoke rose from the sheets, and as she looked up, she caught sight of the mirror in the corner.

The creature was watching her.

Nyssa screamed and jolted into the arms of the person at her side.

"Get out—" she begged. Hands wrapping over her eyes, she pushed her palms into her face. Shaking and trembling beneath the obscurity of what she had become.

"Get out," she pleaded again through the wails. "Get out. Get out. Get out."

"Nyssa—"

The person touched her waist, and the next thing she knew, she was staring down her outstretched arm—

And Nadir's throat was in her blackened hand.

Reality gripped her.

She released him like poison. Her heart filled with panic. She backed up against the headboard and pulled her knees to her chest. Nadir doubled over, coughing and holding to his neck where red blisters had formed.

She had hurt him, and she didn't even remember it.

Tears streaming down her face, she rocked back and forth.

She had hurt him.

She had hurt Nadir.

Nadir.

Full reality sank in. Where she'd been. The night she'd escaped. Seeing him, Bala, and Lex on the beach when she came out of the void.

Back on his beach.

Safe.

"Nadir?" she managed through the sobs.

Nadir's eyes were swollen and red. But he pushed up to her side, apparently ignoring how she'd just hurt him, and he was shaking when he said, "Hello, Princess."

Nyssa broke.

She broke into his arms. Sobs and apologies wailed out of her as it all rushed in. Nadir held onto her as though he never planned on letting her go, and his tears fell into her hair.

"I'm so sorry— I hurt you—I—"

"I'm okay," he whispered. "You're okay. You're home."

Just how exhausted and in pain her body was hit her after a few minutes, and it hurt her to breathe. Fire scratched at her throat and gnawed her insides. Uncomfortable in her skin.

A creature trying to work its way out.

For a while, they merely sat there, the comfort of the ocean waves and their sniffling being the only noises to push the air. Sitting with him didn't feel real. Not yet. It was like a dream. Like she was just back at the camp and fantasizing about being back on his beach and safe again. Back to the home she'd decided for herself.

His lips pressed to her head as they sat, and he eventually pulled a fraction back from her. He pushed her hair off her face, gaze stretching over her as he'd done when he found her at the camp. She noted the blisters on his neck, not just from that morning, but others that looked like they had faded into his skin.

"Did I do this?" she managed, touching his throat.

"It doesn't matter," he insisted.

"Nadir—"

"It. Doesn't. Matter," he said deliberately, his tone firmer than even when he spoke as the Commander.

"Nyssa, I thought I lost you," he choked. "I thought that void had consumed you, and I had failed to bring you out of it. I thought I had failed *you*." He paused as his words became jagged, and he forced a breath into his lungs. "I was ready to take down the Sun to bring you back. And I would have let our world fall into chaos to find you."

And she knew he meant every word.

She couldn't stop herself from wrapping her arms around his neck and hugging him close.

"Nadir?" she managed after a few moments, still hanging onto him.

"Yes, Princess?"

"Do you happen to have any food?"

He pulled back, smiling at her, and he held her cheek. "Anything you want." He kissed her forehead again, swallowing upon pulling back. "Lovi is coming by soon," he said as he stood. "He wants to help with your fire if he can. At least help you calm it inside you so your core doesn't constantly want to protect you now that you're home again. And considering that's the second time it has tried to kill me, I'd like to know how to tell it I don't mean to hurt you."

Nyssa wiped her face harshly. "I'm sorry—"

"It's not you," he said. "It's the form."

"But I don't know how to contain it—"

"We'll figure it out," he promised. "I won't let it take you from me again."

A knock sounded on the door then, and it opened just so.

Lex popped her head in, a small smile growing on her face. Nyssa's chest caved at the sight of her.

"There's my Princess," she said, and a tear fell down Nyssa's cheek.

"Hey, Lex."

The words hardly escaped her before Lex pushed onto the bed and wrapped Nyssa in her arms. Nyssa ignored the pain in her bones as she surrendered into Lex's grasp.

Bala was leaned against the doorframe when Nyssa looked up from Lex's shoulder. She gave her a small wave and a wink, and in that brief moment, the memory of Draven leaning against a doorframe and doing the same flashed in her mind. And Nyssa hugged Lex a little tighter.

Nadir paused beside Bala to look back at Nyssa and Lex hugging on the bed, and she gave his arm a rub.

"You brought her home," Bala told him. "She's okay."

"Yeah," he sighed. "Broken and starving when I promised her she would never have to face this war on her own."

He clapped Bala's shoulder and didn't allow her to speak before he left the room. Nyssa watched him go, knowing he had not meant for her to hear what he'd said, and it broke her to know he was beating himself up over it.

Nyssa caught the solemn expression in Bala's eyes when she turned, and Bala pushed off the door. When she sat on the bed, Lex pulled back, and Nyssa hugged Bala. The two strong women in front of her a part of the home that had driven her out of that void.

They stilled in front of her, Lex's face streamed with her silent tears, and Bala shook her head at her.

"Let's not do that again," she said to Nyssa.

Nyssa couldn't help the soft smile. "Yes, my King," she managed.

For the remainder of the afternoon, the four sat on the bed and told her about what was happening in their realms.

Nadir returned with food and water, both of which she took slowly, savoring it as she savored their stories. Despite how tired she was, she didn't dare close her eyes. She wanted to memorize their smiles and laughs. The touch of Nadir's hand behind her, her lying back against his chest when sitting up became too much for her. Lovi dropped by late in the afternoon, but Nyssa hardly remembered the visit. He'd made a tonic for her to take, insisting it would let her to sleep without the nightmares.

She'd eyed it for a long time after Lovi left, until she heard the Ulfram howling over the wind.

"I forgot they were awake," she managed as she hugged her knees into her chest.

Nadir sighed as he sat in the chair by the bed. "Quieter this round," he said. "Take the tonic. I don't know how you're awake."

The mere thought of it made her heart skip. Seeing those eyes in the mirror. The void around her. Alone.

"I'm too afraid to sleep," she admitted.

Nadir's hands creased on his knees, and for a moment, he didn't speak.

"Can I tell you something?" he asked after a minute.

"Please," she replied, and she was almost begging for him to talk and keep her awake.

"I'm afraid for you to sleep too."

She met his scared eyes, and she knew it was the truth.

"I am terrified you'll go under, and that creature will try to take over again," he continued, staring at his hands. "I know it's trying to protect you from your own horrors, but I can't..." He paused, hands stretching over his face as he sat up and bent over his knees. "I trust Grand," he decided as he caught her gaze again. "And if he says that tonic will help you sleep without the nightmares, then I know it will."

"If it doesn't?"

"I'll be here," he promised. "Also, Bala is in the other room. I can have her fly you through the window on the wind and throw your flaming body in the ocean."

She hiccuped with the soft chuckle daring to come from her. "And if I fall into the void before the ocean wakes me?"

"I'll find you."

59

The three stayed at the cave another day to recover before setting back for Dahrkenhill. They hadn't woken until late in the afternoon on that day and were so exhausted they had hardly spoken more than a few words over dinner. At least Dorian hadn't.

He sat outside at one point and tried to reach his sister again, but every time he did, all he felt was fire eating inside him. Not his fire, but one stronger and more chaotic. Clawing and gnawing his core. Those glowing amber eyes stayed in his mind, and he only hoped she was okay.

As much as he wanted to run to her rescue, the fact remained she was at least five days ride away. So he clung to that image of her, and he held the two in the cave with him a little closer.

They'd looked over the Scrolls Reverie had found. Eleven of them in total. Including one she said she'd had to scuffle with two Infi over. They'd been guarding it in the Elder's study. Dorian had a feeling it was the one Hagen had told him he had to find.

Two red circles bled the paper behind writings he couldn't read.

The parchment vibrated with a power Dorian felt his own form tremble at. The moment his fingers touched it, flashes of scarlet moons and red clouds filled his mind. He winced at the abruptness of it and pulled back.

"This is the one the Infi were guarding?" he asked Reverie.

She nodded, rubbing the gash on her neck.

"And getting this one was when you were hurt?" he asked.

She nodded again but insisted, "I'm fine."

Dorian's fist curled in on itself as he stared. "There'd better be a grand fuck of a reason for you nearly dying retrieving this."

It was dark by the time they reached Dahrkenhill. Well past it. So far past it, Dorian was sure Hagen might already be home and in bed. But he didn't care if he caught him indisposed or naked— chained up while Katla had her way with him.

He wanted answers.

He wanted them now.

Hagen lived south of the Temple at the edge of town in a small home built into the mountain. The three only stopped to relieve the horses upon arrival. Dorian threw his own bags at the Temple door and didn't stop.

Corbin and Reverie did the same.

And they followed Dorian all the way to the edge of town where Hagen lived.

The door nearly broke beneath the weight of Dorian's fist when he knocked. Firelight flickered inside past the window. He swore he heard whispers but no footsteps.

"Dorian, it's late," Reverie said behind him. "He's probably—"

"I don't care."

Dorian railed into the door again.

"Fuck off—" he heard Hagen shouting on the other side. "It's the middle of the fucking night. *Idiots*. What—"

The door flew back, and Hagen's words ceased. He held the sheet around his waist, mahogany hair down from the braid he usually had it in and falling over the left shaved side. His eyes darted between the three and then finally landed back on Dorian.

"That bad?" Hagen asked.

Dorian held up the Scroll, ignoring the turmoil in his core just from holding the parchment. "Tell me why Reverie nearly died retrieving this."

Hagen swallowed, a look coming across his features Dorian didn't know he possessed.

Fear.

"How many Scrolls?" he asked.

"Eleven."

"And how many Infi?"

Dorian stared at him. "Does the scar on my face not tell you that?"

Hagen's jaw tightened, and he opened the door further. "Get inside," he said as he turned on his heel. "Make yourselves at home while I change."

He disappeared down the hall, and Dorian pulled every Scroll they'd found from his bag, laying each one on the table. Reverie grabbed a glass from the cupboard and poured herself a whiskey as though she'd been there many times before and knew where things were.

Another voice added to Hagen's at the back of the house. Loud and annoyed. Hagen shouted something, and the other person quieted. It was a few more minutes before Hagen reappeared, pants thrown on him but no shirt, hair still down as though he'd just grabbed the first pair of trousers he'd found.

Katla strode down the hall behind him, wearing one of his shirts, arms folded over her chest.

She paused upon meeting Dorian's eyes, and Dorian didn't try to stifle the sneer on his features.

"That's not disconcerting at all," she muttered, apparently talking about the blackened scar on his face. She glanced to Reverie then, but the pair merely shared a quiet nod as Katla pushed herself onto the countertop to sit.

Hagen pulled the nyghtfire down and began pouring himself a drink. He shot it back, poured another, and then offered it to Dorian.

"I don't want your whiskey," Dorian countered. "I told you what I want."

"Yeah? And I'm telling you you want one for this, mate," Hagen said as the whiskey slammed down at the table. "Drink and sit."

Dorian eyed the drink, but he didn't do as Hagen instructed. He leaned back on the counter, mirroring Hagen, and he crossed his arms over his chest. Hagen took another drink.

"What happened?"

Dorian started from the beginning.

With their attempts at burning it with his fire, to their sending Reverie in, to the Infi ambushing them in the cave. Hagen and Katla didn't speak as they continued. Only shifting and looking at each other when he told them about the entire town being Infi. And when he told them about the deal he made, Hagen pushed off the counter and poured another drink.

"I'll need you to recount this entire venture in front of Falke and Marius tomorrow," Hagen said once Dorian finished. "Falke will need to know not to stop there on his way home. Katla, put the word out tomorrow: the Byrn is off-limits. No one goes there. Anyone coming into the town will be monitored and questioned—"

"The Infi aren't leaving the Bryn," Dorian cut in.

Hagen stared at him. "What about those not at the Bryn?"

Dorian looked down at his arm, the cuts like nerves, almost like his form on the surface but breaking the flesh. "I don't know what this bond does," he admitted. "And I don't know how to figure out the extent of it. Whether I can bend them to my will or if it means something different." He reached into the bag again, grasping the crown, and he let it thud on the table.

Hagen and Katla exchanged a wary glance, and Dorian began to crack his knuckles.

"The meeting tomorrow will need to be brief," he told them. "I need to get to the Umber. I need to know if my sister is okay."

Hagen nodded slowly, apparent he would not be arguing with the Prince on whether he should leave so quickly. "You'll need to hug the Forest. Deads have risen, so you'll have to camp quietly."

"We'll do as we did when we left Magnice," Corbin said.

"Naddi needs to get these Scrolls back to Lake Oriens," Hagen said. "I'd send you there on your way south, but without a guide through the Mortis Lunar Pass, you'll never make it out alive. Especially during the Deads. He and a few of the Venari are the only ones knowing how to pass through. And the Martyrs, but if the Nitesh finds out some of the Scrolls were in the hands of the Infi, she will lose her mind. Especially that one," he added with a nod to the one with the red circles.

Dorian looked to the parchment, feeling that power radiate off it as it sat open in the middle. "You haven't said why it is so important," he said, looking back up the Hagen. "Why it feels as though it is alive when I look at it and why my form cowers from it when I hold it in my hand."

Hagen's eyes flickered to the Scroll, swirling his drink in his hand. "Because that Scroll is the most powerful thing in all of Haerland, mate. It's not a retelling of our history. It's a ritual. It's how our world gains its freedom."

Dorian he shifted to his other foot and hugged his arms tighter around his chest. "Tell me."

As Hagen told Dorian exactly what the Red Moons ritual did, Dorian sank onto the chair in front of him. His heart numbed, stomach knotting. Almost to the point that he puked. He gripped the chair to keep himself from falling on his face. Suddenly dizzy with the notion of what he was telling him.

And when he finished, silence encompassed the room.

Dorian's stomach lurched into his throat, and he ran to the door before he vomited all over the table. Fire from his insides melted the snow. He turned, chest heaving, and he met Corbin's eyes, remembering what Corbin had said when the Infi had told him to choose a sister.

Corbin seemed to know what he was thinking.

"I told you," he muttered, to which Dorian flipped him off.

He stammered his way to the chair and sat. Reverie moved behind him and started rubbing his shoulders as he bent his head in his hands.

"You said the Infi asked you to choose one sister over the other?" Hagen asked.

Dorian could only nod.

Hagen exchanged a glance with Corbin. "They'd have never allowed you to complete it. Using this ritual would end their kind. It would free Duarb from the curse—"

"Why would they offer it to me then?" he asked.

"I imagine they'd have tricked you into making a different sort of deal and then burned the Scroll in front of you. Possibly brought Aydra back from the void but taken Nyssa as hostage somehow. And if they brought Aydra back without performing the ritual, she'd be completely powerless. A ghost of her true self. Not at all the sister you remember but rather a coreless shell of a being."

"Are you saying I made the right choice?"

Hagen considered him. "I'm not sure what kind of deal this is, Prince," he said as he glanced over the scar on Dorian's face. "What I will say is that Lovi and Nadir can tell you. And if they can't, your Sun can. Or they'll say to go to the Nitesh."

Reverie squeezed Dorian's shoulder.

Hagen pushed off the counter. "You can stay here if you want. I've an extra bedroom. The couch is comfy too. But get some rest. I'll call the others before sunrise to meet so you all can get on the road."

Dorian rose from the chair and gave Hagen a nod. Hagen reached him and did something Dorian didn't expect.

He hugged him.

Tear trickling Dorian's cheek, he hugged his friend back. And when Hagen pulled away, he clapped Dorian's cheek. "You should thank the Infi for that new scar, mate," he said playfully.

"Why?"

"Because you're a lot sexier with it," Hagen replied as he gave his cheek two pats and stepped away from him.

Dorian's brows lifted in disbelief. "Sexy? Coming from you?" A tiny smirk rose on his lips that he couldn't deny. "That's the best compliment I've ever gotten."

Hagen grinned. "Katla thinks so too," he winked.

Katla pushed off the counter and came to stand beside Hagen, leaning her bent arm on Hagen's shoulder. Her gaze traveled deliberately over him, and her chin lifted.

"He's not wrong," she finally agreed.

Reverie came up beside Dorian then, and Katla smiled down at her.

"Though I'm inclined to believe you've been claimed, and none of these wandering eyes will get to experience the new Promised King," Katla teased.

"Not Promised," Dorian said firmly. "No King. Just Dorian."

Katla smiled. "Dorian Eaglefyre. Ruler of Infi. Conqueror of Ghosts. Made of Fire and Crowned with Blood and Obsidian." Her eyes wandered over him again, smirk widening. "I like it."

Despite Dorian's protests that Reverie and Corbin should sleep in the bed and get some well-deserved rest, they refused, insisting they would stay up with him if that's what he wanted to do. Corbin took the chair, Reverie lying on the couch, and Dorian took the floor.

He stayed up staring into the blue flames of the fireplace and turned the Infi crown over in his hands. Stomach churning with all he'd learned just in those few hours. Reverie's fingers scratched the back of his head as she laid behind him. Corbin's quiet snores were the only thing sounding over the dead of the crackling embers.

"Would you do it?" Reverie asked after a while. "The ritual."

Uneasiness settled in his bones, and her fingers slowed against his scalp. He didn't know the answer. He didn't know what he would find himself giving up to perform it.

"I don't know," he managed, voice barely above a whisper.

Reverie leaned up, her lips pressing to his cheek. "I think you do," she said, and he looked back at her. She pushed his hair off the scar, darkened lavender gaze traveling over his face. "But you don't want anyone to know the choice you would make."

Dorian became hyperaware of every scratch of her nails, every dart of her eyes to his lips. "Could you do it?" he asked. "Give up the one you love to free this world?"

A pause rested between them. One that made him curious as to what she thought of. Whether she'd left someone behind at Scindo that she had loved before all this. Perhaps was in love with still.

"No," she finally answered. "No more than you could give up one sister for the other."

"Did you leave someone behind?" he asked. "At Scindo?"

"What—like a lover?"

He nodded.

The fire flickered in her pupils as she watched it in silence a moment. "No," she finally said.

"Who were you thinking of when I asked about the ritual?"

"Not entirely sure you've earned that bit of information," she said, a twinge of banter in her tone.

He shifted to look back at her. "Tell me it isn't Beron."

She rolled her eyes and shoved his shoulder. "No. Not that oaf. He's pretty to look at but a damn idiot. I'd rather be challenged," and her eyes met his. "On every front. Mind, body, and core."

"A lot to ask of one person," he bantered.

"It's a good thing we've found two then."

Corbin's snore rattled beside them, and together they chuckled at the timing. Heat rose on his chest and cheeks at the words she'd just said, and it made his heart knot. He sighed his head against her as she wrapped her arm tighter around his shoulders.

Her lips pressed to his cheek. "She's okay, Dorian," she whispered. "You're okay."

And hearing her reassurance caused emotion to burn behind his nose and eyes.

He didn't respond. But he kissed her arm and squeezed her hand, and he relaxed into the comfortableness of her grasp.

She fell asleep wrapped around him, and it was all Dorian could do not to break in her arms.

60

The sinking of the bed was uncomfortable around Nyssa's body.

Plush blankets and pillows made her feel as though she were dreaming. She thought if she allowed herself to enjoy it, she would wake back at camp. The one time she'd tried to sleep on the floor, she'd woken up screaming.

Since that night, her eagle had rested with her and Nadir and Lex would both come in to check. The first night she fell asleep without the tonic, Nadir had burst into the room after she'd started screaming. He'd held tight around her until she calmed, and Nyssa had cried into his chest.

Everything she'd held in during her entrapment came to the surface within those first few days. Every scream and terror. Every pain. It was like her body needed to evacuate the feelings now that she was in a safe place. Or perhaps it was that she'd let down all her barriers, and she couldn't find the walls to put them back up.

She was exhausted, her throat scratchy, and she felt even worse for Nadir and Lex. Especially Nadir. Sometimes when she would wake out of nightmares, she would find him holding her to keep her from writhing, and tears would be streaked on his cheeks. She had told him he didn't need to come in every time, as she was more worried about hurting him than she was bringing herself out of the dreams. But he refused to listen, and after a week, she had surrendered to simply letting him sleep with her the entire night.

At least she hadn't burned or tried to kill him again.

A true gentleman, Nadir had not tried to move on her. He would kiss her forehead or her shoulder, hold her against him, but he did not push. She was grateful. She wasn't even sure how to love herself right then. Wasn't sure that this was actually her reality around her and that she had not slipped fully into that void. She knew she needed time to acclimate back into herself and remember she was safe at the Umber and not still in Man's grasp.

Nyssa couldn't stop staring at the ceiling.

Her eagle laid in the bed by her side then, curled up beneath her arm since Nadir had gone to get breakfast. Her eyes closed as the great bird nudged her arm, a chortle-like purr emitting from his throat.

You should go find yourself breakfast, she told him.

When he returns, he promised. **I can feel your bones.**

I think they want to release from my body.

It is the remaining shadows of your fire. They are still working out of your core.

I'm not sure I understand.

Her eagle looked up just as a great shadow pulsed over the shack.

What was that? she asked him.

The Sun.

Nyssa's entire face furrowed as she turned her head to her bird. *What?*

The Sun, the eagle answered. **She will wait for you.**

Nyssa groaned at the reluctance of her muscles, at the paralyzation of her mind, and she huffed audibly with the splay of her good arm across the bed, the other broken one still tucked onto her stomach. *Can she just come in here?*

The eagle laughed at her, his great screech filling the small room. **I will not command the Sun.**

It was another two days before she could raise herself from the bed and move without the constant ache. It was nearly dark outside before she made it up, but Nadir had told her he would come grab her after dinner if she was awake.

The ordeal had turned her into someone she didn't recognize. Someone she didn't want to be.

The lashing marks on her back. The scratch across her cheek. She stared back into the hazel fire of her eyes in the mirror. She wasn't used to the sink of her once apple-rounded cheeks, the stark wrinkle of what used to be full dimples at the corners of her lips. The shadows beneath her eyes, she cursed. The sunken pull between her once supple breasts, showcasing her ribcage, she seethed. She hated the stark of her collarbones, the protrusion of her hips, the frailty of her deteriorating body from being enslaved. She loathed the wash of her once firm muscles that she'd been growing so well before. She wanted her flesh back…her muscles and her fat, her bright cheeks, and her smile… not this wide-eyed frightened girl standing before her.

She wanted to punch the mirror. Shatter it like her own broken body.

At least she hadn't seen the creature in it that morning.

Her eagle flew through the door and landed on the back of the chair at her side.

The Commander is coming, he told her.

Nyssa pushed her shirt over her head just in time before Nadir knocked on the doorframe.

"Yeah," she called out to him.

"I was wondering if you were hungry," he said from the outside.

"Starving," she muttered.

She shoved pants on, cursing at the oversize of them and feeling weak because of it. Red rose on her cheeks, and she grunted under her breath.

"Hey, Nadir? Can you come in?"

His brows were furrowed when he stepped inside, and then his eyes traveled deliberately over her. She avoided his eyes as she held her pants up with both hands.

"Do you think… Do you think someone could possibly make new pants for me?" she managed.

"Ah… yeah, yeah. Of course. I'll have Sutor make you up a few," he answered.

She started to strip but hesitated. Hesitated because she didn't want him to see her in such a state. Hesitated because she knew he had loved her body before, and she was petrified this new one would make him not want her.

"Can you turn around?" she finally managed.

He looked surprised… like he might argue. But a wash of understanding slowly raised in his eyes, and he finally nodded. "Why don't I get rid of that mirror while you're getting dressed?" he suggested.

Her heart caved that he remembered. "I would really like that."

His body brushed hers as he walked past and grabbed up the mirror, hauling it out of the room and presumably stashing it in another. She stripped and grabbed for the dress on the bed. And when it fell over her body like a sack, her jaw tightened, and she cursed herself under her breath, fighting the tears in her eyes.

Nadir sighed in the doorway. "Perhaps some new dresses as well," he said softly.

The shake of her jaw made her cringe. She turned away from him, her hands pressing into her waist, and she inhaled deeply to fight the emotion bubbling at the surface.

"It's okay, Nys—"

"Fucking—*no, it's not*," she snapped, whirling back around to face him. "It is *not* okay. None of this is okay. I'm fucking... *look at me!* Wasted away in chains for a full moons cycle all because I ran away into the woods having one of my stupid temper tantrums—"

"Like this one?" he mocked.

She started to sneer at him, but the sight of the smirk on his lips made her pause. He gave her an upwards nod, and she looked down to see that her hands were blackening, and there was a black fog beneath her feet. She closed her eyes and drew a deep breath, counting as her frustrations waned. The black on her fingers receded, the fog dissipating as though rewinding into itself.

Nadir crossed the room towards her then, only stopping as he took her hand. "We'll work on it," he promised. "I know you're frustrated—"

"Frustrated isn't even the right word," she grunted.

He paused, simply staring at her as though he expected her to go on, to continue speaking. But she just shook her head and pushed her hands over her face. "I'm sorry," she managed.

"For what?"

She sighed, gripping her waist in her hands and cursing herself. She couldn't get the words out, too enamored by her frustrations and emotion that she chose not to speak.

"How about you come to the bonfire with me?" he suggested. "We have food. Someone, I think, is attempting to play drums. There is dancing. We can just be us for a few hours."

It did sound enticing. And she was starving.

"Okay," she finally said.

She reached for her belt then, and as she wrapped it around her, it went past the last notch, making her grunt under her breath in frustration. Nadir chuckled, and she punched him in the side upon glaring at him.

"Shut up," she mumbled.

He laughed openly this time and pulled his knife out to make her a new notch. "I'll make sure they bring you all the sweets—" he tightened the belt with a jolt around her waist, and her heart fluttered at the dilation in his suddenly domineering gaze "—my ferocious shadow Queen."

The sound of his rasp vibrated her insides, her breath skipping, and for a moment, she completely forgot about the entire ordeal she'd been having with herself in front of the mirror. But she shook her head at him and fought the smile threatening her lips.

"Was that your attempt at growling?" she mocked.

He grinned, chin rising as he gazed down his nose at her. "Dammit, I missed you," he breathed. He held out his arm, and she took it with a flee of her heart.

Lex was lounging on a piece of driftwood by the fire when they arrived at the celebration.

"Commander and the Princess," she bantered. "Should I ring the bells?"

Nadir only smiled at Nyssa and kissed her hand before he told her he had to see a few friends before he could join her. She caught Lex winking at him as she sat, but she didn't ask about it. Lex held out the basket of food she was eating from. Sweet bread rolls and honey. She also passed her a plate with smoked fish on it, as well as the canteen of water.

She could feel her eyes on her as she devoured the food, but she didn't care.

"How is my little shadow today?" Lex asked. "I don't recall hearing as many screams last night."

"Nadir stayed with me," Nyssa admitted. "Nothing happened... He was just there."

"I wondered if he stayed," Lex replied.

Lex told her about the legion she'd been helping Nadir with while she ate. She was grateful for the absentminded conversation, almost as though Nyssa had simply been away on an adventure with her brother. No mention of her starvation or torture. Just Lex. Telling her stories of the recruits and what she'd been up to.

Nadir joined them a few minutes later, sitting down at her side and squeezing her knee when she met his gaze. She noted him eyeing the honey in her hands when he looked down, and his brow lifted in a teasing manner.

"Who gave you the honey?" he asked, wickedness dancing in his gaze.

She couldn't help her unfamiliar smile. The memory of him licking that breakfast honey off her body and between her legs at Magnice filled her mind. She inhaled a jagged breath, red flushing her cheeks, and she sucked the honey off her finger. Nadir stared at her as she did, tongue darting out over his lips, but he didn't say anything.

She loved that he was being his usual self and not treating her as though she were broken. He was attempting to make her feel at home. Bantering and joking. Continuing his leering jokes as he'd done before she ran away.

A few people came up to them, sitting beside Nadir or Lex, all of whom addressed Nyssa by her actual name, a few of them nodding for extended periods. Long enough that Nyssa stopped chewing.

"What are they doing?" she asked Nadir at one point.

"Bowing," he said like it was apparent.

Nyssa's head snapped in his direction. "But why? I haven't done anything."

To this, Lex laughed. "Haven't—" she gawked at Nyssa's questioning expression. "Fuck all, I wondered where the humble gene landed in your family, and here it is sitting in front of me," she muttered. "Nyssa, you cannot be serious."

Nyssa broke off another piece of roll and started chewing it. "I don't know what you mean. They have no reason to bow to me. I am no longer a royal. And even when I was—"

"Maybe we leave it for tonight," Nadir suggested, eyeing Lex over Nyssa's head. "Let our Princess enjoy the clean night air and good food."

Dammit, she'd missed her own people.

Even if they had been rude to her before she disappeared, she still cherished the smiles on their faces and laughter in the air. Eventually, Lex retired with a few friends she'd made, and Nyssa tucked her knees into her chest.

People continued to go up to Nadir and chat. Hearing him laughing, finding herself back on that beach and by his side... Every breath she took felt unreal, as though it were a dream. She didn't realize there were tears on her face until she felt Nadir's hand on her leg.

"Okay?" he asked.

She inhaled sharply, pushing the wet from her cheeks and straightening to give him a small smile. "Yeah, yeah," she managed. "It's just..." She swallowed as she watched the fire, and Nadir simply rubbed her leg.

"It's okay," he assured her. "You're okay."

"I know," she whispered. "I..." She turned to meet his eyes, noting the glisten in them and the bob of his throat. "I'm not sure I ever thought I would be back on your beach."

Nadir gave her a small smile, and he reached for her hand. "I missed you on my beach," he told her.

She couldn't help herself from leaning sideways onto his shoulder, savoring that comfort of him again. He kissed the top of her head.

"Everything feels unreal," she managed. "Like a dream."

"What can I do?" he asked.

Memories of her life before the ordeal pouring through her as she looked out to the surf. "Do you know what I really want?" she asked as she laid her chin on his shoulder.

He eyed her, apparently noting the play in her gaze, and he stood. "Come on. I've been waiting for this since you got back," he said as he reached for her hand. "I'll go easy on you with the arm," he winked.

She took his hand, noting the still ache in her muscles but fighting it with everything she had in her. She wanted normalcy, her strength back, to feel the wind around her and not feel it in her bones instead of just on her skin.

He held her hand as they walked back to his shack, and he grabbed one long bamboo stick and a smaller short stick from beside the steps. She hated that he was giving her the smaller one.

And he knew it.

"Don't give me that look," he said as she begrudgingly took the stick. "Your arm is broken."

"Don't remind me," she grumbled. She whirled the stick in her hands as she would have her own sword, which she was reminded had been lost, along with her bow. But she shoved the thoughts to the back of her mind and followed him out to the surf. He pushed the torch into the ground as he'd done before, and he set up.

The smile on his face made her shake her head.

"What?" he grinned.

"Your smile," she heard herself say, her own lighting up her cheeks.

He shrugged. "You're back on my beach."

And she fought the emotion in her chest.

His smile softened, and he set his feet. "Set up, Princess."

Nyssa did. She wavered when her feet began to sink, but she clenched the little muscle left and held the broken arm close.

"Do you want me to go slow?" he asked.

She gritted her teeth, determination sweeping her bones. "No."

Every sweep towards her made her stumble. She could see the strikes but couldn't react fast enough. She pushed herself anyway, defending every swipe he came at her with. Holding that broken arm up and tightening her thighs with her steps.

"Did you give them your name when you were there?" he asked as he paused a moment to circle.

"I gave them another name."

"Can't wait to hear the name you gave yourself," he bantered, giving her an upwards nod to set up. "Don't tell me. I want to guess it—"

Nyssa crouched, ready for him. He came at her just as fast, and she knocked his stick in front of her face.

"Did you use Nyssa or Nysi?"

She shook her head and blocked him again. "Neither."

"Full name?" he asked.

"Not my full name—" he lunged forward, and she dipped low to dodge him. Her balance wavered, and she staggered off her feet. Cursing the sky, she had to remind herself to breathe. Her body betrayed her mind. These were moves she knew how to do, but she knew she would have to build herself to get there again.

Nadir simply held out his hand, but she shook her head. "I've got it," she insisted. He nodded and took a few steps back, going to set up again as she pushed to her feet.

"Did you use any part of your name or something different?"

"Part of my name," she replied. The fabric of her dress was wet, and she grunted at the heaviness of it. "Can I use your knife?" she asked.

"Planning on murdering me?"

A huff emitted from her lungs at his playful tone. "No," she almost laughed. "I want to cut this dress so I can move," she told him. "Especially if I can have new ones made."

He nodded and pulled it from the strap around his calf, handing it to her hilt first. She grabbed the fabric and ripped it. Air swept around her limbs when she stepped out of the wet wool.

"Just remember I've been starving for two months," she grumbled. "These legs are not what they used to be."

And it hurt her heart to say it.

"Nys, do you think I care what your body looks like?" he asked in a low tone.

"Considering what it looked like before all this, maybe," she muttered, heat rising on her chest. "I remember how you once stared at the body I had—"

"I don't care about what your body looks like," he interjected. "I care that you're here and you're safe. You're *alive*, Nyssa. You put yourself on the inside of our enemy's camp because you wanted to save people who didn't even love you," he interjected. "You had plenty of opportunities to leave that place, and you were even going to sell yourself to Savigndor for possible peace. I should be on my knees before you."

"I ruined everything I had worked for in two months," she cut in. "Two months and years of hard work was squandered."

"I didn't realize you still put so much emphasis of your worth on your outwards appearance," he said, and she could hear the twinge in his voice.

"Hard not to," she managed.

"Nyssa, your mother isn't here," he reminded her. "It's just you and me."

"And these failing legs don't bother you?" she almost snapped.

Nadir looked like he would smile, and he shook his head. "I firmly believe those legs could still kick down any fruiting tree in my forest."

Her lips quirked, unable to refuse the smile threatening her at his banter, and she sighed out the frustration of her darkened thoughts. He gave her an upwards nod, and she set her feet again.

It was her turn to lunge first. He blocked her and swiped for her legs. She jumped back. This time her legs stayed a little more steady than before. Her arms waved out to balance her, and Nadir looked like he would grab her hand, but he didn't.

She couldn't have been more grateful for him not treating her as though she were fragile.

"Did you use 'Ari'?" he asked, and she remembered that they had been talking about the name she used.

"I did," she replied.

He pushed at her, and their sticks clacked. "Hmm... Ravenspeak for a surname? Eagle?"

She stumbled and held up a hand to pause a moment, her breath shortening at being so out of practice. He simply whirled the stick while he waited for her to recover.

"Just Fyre? Ari Fyre could have been a good one, but I assume you were smarter than to use part of your full—"

"Storn," she interjected, swallowing the lump in her throat. "The name I used was Ari Storn." She straightened from her doubled-over stance, and the sight of the gaze she was met with made her stomach knot.

His jaw was clenched, and his head moved just slightly sideways. Pain stretched his eyes, hand tightening around the bamboo.

"Why... Why would you use my name?" he managed, and she could tell just by his tone that he was shaking.

Nyssa had to take an open-mouthed breath, glancing up at the sky. She thought of how the name had simply rolled off her tongue when the Noble had asked, and her lips moved with a nervous smile.

"I suppose I was hanging on to a life I thought I'd never see again," she admitted, voice cracking.

The stick dropped from Nadir's hand, and he pushed his hands behind his neck. "*Fuck*—you used my name?" he said, and she wasn't sure if it was even a question for her. He turned on the spot in a circle, his head lolling on his neck.

"Nadir?" she managed, unsure of what was happening. "I'm... I'm sorry if that wasn't okay, I—"

The way his head snapped to her direction made her words cease.

His eyes never left her as he crossed the space between them, gait determined and almost predatorial. His hands pressed to her cheeks before she could utter a word, and then he kissed her.

Nyssa's chest swelled at the taste of him again, at the need and passion exuding from his body and into hers. The surprise of him waned after a moment, and she sank into his embrace, kissing him back as though he were air and she was drowning. Reality went amiss.

This was the kiss she never thought she would feel again.

Her heart burst with the weight of his passion. He grabbed her up off the ground, her legs wrapping around him. Desperation poured through them. She didn't want him to stop. She ached to hold in that moment, her hands on his cheeks, his grasp around her bottom and her neck.

But after a few seconds, he pulled back, and his forehead rested against hers. "I'm sorry," he breathed as her feet hit the ground again. "I'm sorry—I know you need time to get back to normal, and I'm not pushing you—" he straightened, hand resting on her cheek. "I don't care how long it takes. But I... When you said you used my name, I just couldn't help myself." His forehead leaned against hers again. "I like that name a lot more than I should."

Her lips quirked again, and she couldn't help her hands brushing against his cheeks. She breathed in the smell of him as they stood together, relishing the comfort of his heated body and the safety of his embrace. "I do too," she finally managed.

She surrendered into his arms in a hug that she never wanted to leave. One of safety and comfort. Of reality and grounding. Back in her own world again after a nightmare her mind was trying to hide from her by pulling that form to the surface.

He pulled back to kiss her forehead, lips resting softly against her skin a moment before he lifted her chin to see her. "Do you want to go back?" he asked.

"Yeah," she sighed.

Nadir left the sticks in the sand as he took her hand and led her back to his home. He stayed with her again, and that night she didn't feel as much of a burden as she had in the nights before. She wondered if he needed to stay with her as much as she needed him. Wondering if he was as afraid to let her go as she was he.

He told her about the fruits that would be ready for harvest after the end of the Dead Moons. He told her of the meeting they were holding the next day to discuss what Nyssa had found out while she was there. They determined a need to stay on alert since she had taken down the one camp. She wasn't sure what the Noble would think when he found his home burned to the ground. She'd left no one there to say what had happened. The thought had made her stomach knot. Especially after the wife had said they'd found a village in the east, and she assumed she meant the Umber.

"There's something you should know before the meeting tomorrow," he said as he held her, his thumb rubbing the back of her arm. "And I am only telling you because I do not want you to be blindsided by her tomorrow."

Nyssa frowned up at him. "By who?"

"Soli," he answered simply.

Soli... The name sounded familiar, and then she sat up. "Soli—as in the warrior?"

Nadir nodded.

"But... What do you mean blindsided?"

"She will challenge you," he told her. "I don't mean challenge as in a duel. I mean, she will challenge everything you say. She's been more outspoken since this all started. She is outnumbered this time by the people who respect you, and I think she knows it." He sighed, hand brushing her back. "I wanted you to be prepared for anything she might throw at you."

Nyssa nodded, appreciative that he was telling her instead of her walking into that room unaware. The thought of Soli and the stories written about her made Nyssa's stomach knot. That a warrior such as her may not think her worthy of respect she'd worked hard for.

"Does she think I will want her to bow before me because I was once a Princess?" she wondered aloud.

Nadir seemed to contemplate it. "Soli has always been threatened by anyone who is real," he said. "She believes true leadership should not show vulnerabilities. That you should only ever be strong and fearless, even in the confines of your own home and with people whom you should be able to share such things with."

The words made her eyes narrow as she remembered what he had said to her before all this—the conversation of his one past relationship.

"You were in a relationship with Soli?" she realized.

Nadir's hand paused on her back. "How could you possibly remember that?"

"I remember everything."

He sighed, silence resting between them a moment. "Yeah," he finally admitted. "Yeah, it was her."

The sadness in his gaze made her reach for his hand. She pulled his hand to her lips and pressed a lingering kiss to his knuckles. "Tell me about it."

He eyed her. "You just want me to tell you so you know how hard to glare at her tomorrow," he mocked.

Nyssa feigned surprise just as Nadir always did—clutching her chest, mouth dropping. "I would never," she lied.

He looked like he would laugh. "Liar," he accused.

She smiled, the muscles of her face beaming with such a thing back on her lips. "Definitely," she said. She pulled her knees into her chest, sighing as she watched him watching her, his fingers moving delicately in circles at the small of her back. And the mere act of his eyes on her again made her heart warm.

"Back on your beach," she whispered.

Nadir met her smile, and he squeezed her hand. "Home," he corrected.

It was well into the night before either went to sleep. So much they wanted to catch up on, to learn about each other, talking as though they didn't have all the time of the rest of their lives, but intent on hearing the other's voice and every whisper of their being.

She had told Lex she wanted to get back into training, even if it was just footwork and balancing since she couldn't use her arm yet. She didn't care. She was ready to get out there and fight. She wanted her body back to match with the confidence of her mind.

Every moment would be a struggle and a nightmare, but she could do it. She could build herself back, better than before, and she would somehow learn to control her fire and let the creatures in.

She asked Nadir if he would go with her to the Forest and see the Noctuans before the Deads ended. She wanted to face them again, try to reach them since she'd been able to communicate with the sea serpent the week before. She had heard the noise of the Ulfram's howls, and this time, its howl comforted her instead of making her panic. A comfort of the home she thought she might be hidden from for the rest of her days.

She felt closer to the land than ever now that she'd been without it. Life at the Umber— life at *home*— was slowly feeling more and more real with every day.

But the one ache still in her heart was having not heard anything about her brother. She could remember seeing him in her mind the day of her escape.

She hoped he was okay.

61

"This smile on your face, my boy," Sutor, the seamstress, mocked at Nadir with a sideways stare. "I don't know that I've ever seen such delight in your eyes."

He'd brought Nyssa to be measured for new clothes as he said he would, and Nyssa found herself mesmerized by the sight of all the fabrics in Sutor's tent.

Nadir chuckled under his breath as he leaned against the doorframe. "Come off it, Soot. You can't tell all my secrets. You never know when princesses might use them as leverage later," he added with a wink at Nyssa.

Sutor stepped up and wrapped her arm around Nyssa then, the bountiful woman making Nyssa feel even smaller next to her. "Come, girl. Naddi, out of here," she shooed him.

Nadir gave Nyssa a proud once over that made her smile despite herself, and he left from inside. She could hear him chatting with someone outside, his laugh bouncing in the air and echoing with the rest of the people busily walking around their market.

Talking with him the night before had left her more affirmed in reality. Finally gripping the fact that she was alive and back on his beach. Alive and surrounded by her own people again.

Alive.

It was the first day in a long time when she didn't need to count her every breath. The form not quaking inside her as horribly. As though it had calmed down inside her now that she was home and did not feel the need to burst to the surface at every waking moment.

Excitement and determination filled her bones, and with the anticipation of the meeting looming over her that afternoon, she finally felt like herself.

She just needed her brother.

Sutor positioned Nyssa on a pedestal and began to measure her. She didn't speak much as she did, only humming once in a while. She put her in a linen form to tack with, and as Sutor pulled the fabric snug around her waist and hips, Nyssa paused her.

"Can you... can you not pull it so tight around the top?" she managed to tell her. "Please."

"Leave her growing room, Soot," Nadir called from outside.

Nyssa hadn't realized he was listening in, and she caught Sutor's eye. "Do you have something I can throw at him?" she asked.

Sutor smiled. "His giving you a hard time makes you feel at home," she said, and Nyssa's eyes narrowed. "After all you've been through."

Nyssa's cheeks flushed, and she glanced at the ground. "It really does," she admitted.

Sutor crouched to pin the hem. "I want to apologize for the way I watched you when you first arrived," the seamstress admitted. "I know we all stared at you as though you did not deserve him. But now... I think anyone who does oppose is only jealous. What you did was something no one in our own village would have. It's clear what you mean to him, and that smile is something I have missed seeing on his face."

Nyssa's heart knotted, and Sutor stood again. She came around to Nyssa's front, and she pressed her hands to Nyssa's cheeks. "You choose anything you want," she told her. "Anything. Any fabric. It is yours. After what you've done for us, you deserve it."

Nyssa gritted her teeth to keep emotion back. "Thank you," she managed.

Because hearing it from someone who wasn't Nadir affirmed everything she'd put herself through, and it made looking at the squander of what her body had become a little less disheartening.

Sutor finished pinning the dress and then had her take it off, giving her back a dress she had intended to sell at market, but said she thought it would look prettier on her.

It was a dark green, lightweight linen... The first dress she'd put on since getting back that didn't fall over her like a sack.

"You should wear green more often," Sutor told her.

"I keep telling her that," Nadir called.

Sutor's hands wrapped around Nyssa's arms from behind, and she gave a squeeze. "You may come in again, Naddi," Sutor said.

Nadir threw the door open with little grace, apparently eager to get back inside. But he paused at the door, his eyes traveling over her in such a way that she immediately felt heat creep up her neck and onto her cheeks. She fumbled with the sleeve's hem a moment as Sutor finished laying out some fabrics for her to choose from.

"Hey, Soot—"

"Already leaving," Sutor said quickly. She began to back out of the room, but not before giving Nyssa a quiet smile.

Nyssa's breath caught beneath his gaze, and she had to avert her eyes to the table where the fabrics had been lain. "I'm not sure how she expects me to choose," she uttered, trying desperately to keep her eyes not on him. He still hadn't moved. "These are all so beautiful," she continued, running her fingers over a few of them. "What do you think?"

"I think you could wear that potato sack outside and still be the most entrancing being I've ever laid my eyes on."

Her eyes rolled up to his, and she forced a purse on her lips. "That's three for today. And it's hardly mid-morning."

"Only three?" he mocked, stepping closer. "I'm losing my touch."

She chuckled under her breath as he reached her. She forced a touch of the blue velvet beneath her fingers. "If only I had a place to wear such fabrics again."

"Wear them here," he said with a shrug.

"I'm not commissioning your seamstress to make me a dress from velvet when I've no place to wear it. We have to be practical. This is a war. Velvet dresses are no longer something I should need."

The sentence shouldn't have pained her, but it did nonetheless.

He was towering over her at her side then. "You should get every shade of green," he told her.

"I'd prefer the darker ones," she informed him.

The laugh that left his lips then was one that made her look up. He was staring at the table, touching one of the black fabrics to her left.

"What?"

"You Promised women and your dark shades of color," he mused. "Who knew such would be your thing when you grow up in a white castle."

She almost laughed. "The halls were all trimmed in black, so there is something to be said about our liking noir colors," she agreed. "Also, the darker the fabric, the more hidden the blood from our enemies. Can't be caught on a battlefield revealing any wounds, can we?"

"If one is lucky enough to wound you, perhaps he should be given the privilege of seeing such a rarity. His last victory before your sword surely slices his throat."

She finally smiled up at him. "Slowly, of course. My face as the final thing he sees before certain darkness."

"Bloodlust," he mocked. "That's new."

She didn't realize she was turned towards him or leaned against the table until his hand brushed hers. His weight shifted, and before she realized what was happening, his hand was against her cheek, thumb moving delicately over her cheekbone and coming to a rest by her lip. Her heart skipped, her cheeks flushing, hotter if possible, beneath his stare. Her bangs fell over her eyes when she looked down, trying to escape his seeing her in such a state.

"Nadir—"

"I know," he breathed, his eyes shutting tight almost as though he were in pain. His fingers curled just so against her cheek, and then he dropped his hand altogether. "I know you're not ready. It's just…"

She watched as his tongue darted out over his lips, and when his eyes opened once more, she saw the glisten in them.

"What?"

"Sometimes I forget," he whispered. "Sometimes I forget about our reality when it's simply you and I. I forget about what happened to you. I forget about the pressures of keeping my realm safe. I forget about the circumstances in which we met. Sometimes…" his weight shifted again, and he shook his head just slightly as he struggled to get the words out, "Sometimes I fantasize that we're just us. Just you and me. No titles… No duties… No war… Simply Nadir and Nyssari. Two people in want of one another, standing on opposite sides of the beach and reaching out. Wanting, but never touching." He reached for her hands, and he entwined their fingers, stretching and wrapping them together and bringing them up with bent elbows at their sides.

"You and me," he whispered. He sank their palms softly together, and the words that came next from his lips made her knees weak.

"I will stand on the other side of that beach for as long as it takes you to cross it," he promised.

She had to swallow the lump, causing her to shake. "I'm really not sure what you expect me to say," she managed, feeling a nervous smile creep on her lips.

"I expect nothing. I just wanted you to know."

Her fingers tightened in his, and she inhaled a deep breath that filled her lungs to their limits, one that quelled the hurt in her chest and gave way to a new swell—one that warmed her heart and flowed down to the very ends of her toes and fingers.

"I will meet you on that beach," she whispered, almost losing herself as she met the look in his eyes. "And you can show me that dance we never had."

His chest rose in a jagged manner, and he squeezed her hands back. "You'd better tell Sutor which velvet you like best then."

"I prefer the tulle," she said with a smile.

A soft chuckle left him, his eyes brightening. "Right," he breathed. "Forgot about the tulle thing," he said playfully. "Which colors should I find you?"

The look in his eyes made her knees weaker than they already were. She couldn't help her grin at the mere mention of the fabric, and she began to swing her hands back and forth with his. "Navy," she said. "Black. Champagne—"

"Champagne?" he repeated, chin dipping. "You're getting a little greedy there, Princess. Champagne tulle is rare."

"I'm sure you'll do your best to find it," she teased.

His hand slipped around her waist, holding the other up as though he were about to dance, and he leaned her over into a dip. Her cheeks flushed as the blood ran to her head with how low he dipped her, her leg bending around his waist in habit, and she couldn't help her laugh when he pulled her back into him.

"If champagne tulle is what it takes to dance with you…" he sighed, and she could see the tease in his eyes. "Maybe I'll ask around."

Sutor had given Nyssa enough clothes to get her through the week while she worked on the personal ones for her. She had gone on a walk with Lex after seeing the seamstress. Lex wanted to work her up slowly, help her build her muscle and her stamina back. They would start small, with just a few things in the backpack, and Lex told her she would keep adding items for weight, eventually getting her back on her horse and securing her a new bow.

As they walked that day, Nyssa couldn't help but feel a nervous energy. Barely paying attention to Lex beside her as she remembered all the things she'd once said to her. The trigger of her running away.

Lex flipped her shaggy hair from her eyes, twirling the bamboo stick as she walked until finally, Nyssa couldn't stop herself.

"Lex, I—"

"You don't have to say anything," Lex said, apparently knowing where the conversation was going.

"No—" Nyssa stopped and turned to Lex. "No, I do," she insisted. "I —"

"I am sorry, Princess," Lex interjected, and Nyssa frowned.

"Why are you sorry?"

"Because I was not there for you when you needed me," Lex said. "I should have done so much more to help you."

"Lex, you'd just lost your best friend," Nyssa argued. "The person you were born to protect."

"My duty was to protect you," Lex said.

"I think we can both agree that duty has sailed," Nyssa said. The nervousness she'd felt when they'd first started walking waned, and now standing before Lex, she felt more confident than she had in a while. All the things she'd been through settling inside her. What Sutor had said earlier. The Honest people that had once condemned her nodding their heads.

Despite what she'd gone through, she'd never felt more affirmed in her position.

Nyssa almost smiled as it settled, and she shifted in front of the Belwark. "I never want you to think you have to protect me because of your duty. I want you to want to protect me because you believe in what I can do," she admitted. "I will never be Drae, and you will never love me as you did her. I am not a Queen, and I don't know that I will ever live up to that standard in the time we have. But I am asking that if you choose me, that you trust me. Our places in this world are no longer bound by our titles or the kingdom that tore our family apart. We are free to make those decisions on our own. You will *always* be the Second Sun. But I want you to choose who you want to follow.

Whether that's Bala, Dorian, me, Nadir, or anyone else— or perhaps simply yourself, find your own way. It is your choice."

Lex swallowed hard, and Nyssa reached up to wipe a tear from her face.

"You are free, Lex. Not that you have ever been enslaved or mistreated, because I know how much you loved my sister and how much she loved you. But I want you to know you are free to be wherever you want in this world. Do whatever you want. You don't have to stay here. You don't even have to participate in this war. You're free to go to the mountains with Dorian. Be with Bala as you want to. You can march back to Magnice on your own and take Rhaif's head yourself, though I believe Dorian will fight you if you do—"

Lex huffed amusedly in agreement.

Nyssa smiled at the sound of her laugh. "You can do anything, Lex. Be anywhere. I want you to have that choice. And when we go to negotiate with Man, you don't have to be with me. Only if that's what you want."

Lex's weight shifted again, and she blew out an audible breath, hands pressing to her hips as she tried and failed to stifle tears.

Nyssa almost laughed at Lex's reaction. "What?"

A tear fell down the Belwark's cheek, and she smiled through the emotion. "Who are you, and what have you done with my spoiled Princess?"

To this, Nyssa laughed. "Oh, she *died*," she said as though it were obvious. "Tragically. She snapped somewhere back at that camp."

Lex's arms wrapped around her, and Nyssa sighed into her embrace, closing her eyes and breathing in the ashen scent of her. Lex kissed her head hard after a moment, and then she pulled away.

"I choose you," Lex told her.

And Nyssa took a step back.

"What?" she asked, fully surprised by the declaration. "Why?"

Lex dropped her hands, and she stared out at the ocean a minute, hair fluttering in the wind. "Had you told me a cycle ago I could go anywhere, you're right. I would have chosen Bala," she admitted. "I would have chosen to stand by a King secure in her place. Someone like your sister who knew who they were and did not necessarily need me. Because it was what I was accustomed to. Your sister... She never needed me to protect her, but she always allowed me to. I miss her every day. While you were gone, I sat on this beach and cursed her to the moons and back. I miss her as I miss oxygen beneath the ocean."

"So why choose me?" Nyssa asked. "Why not Bala?"

"I believe in Bala," Lex said. "But I also know how I feel about her, and I know it would be dangerous for me to mix my feelings with my duty—"

"Do not stay with me because I am a lesser choice," Nyssa argued. "Stay with me because you want to."

Lex's brow raised, and she held up a hand. "Let me finish," she insisted.

Nyssa straightened.

"I want to stay with you because you no longer need me," Lex said. "That's a dangerous notion, and I want to see what you do with it. I trust you now to make those decisions based not on your childish need to prove yourself but on your love for our land and our people. I want to be by your side when you take this world just like your sister always said you would."

Lex reached for the sword on her belt.

Nyssa tried to keep her composure as the sword was pulled into the air, and then Lex dropped to one knee. Lex's head bowed, and she presented the great Belwark sword up to Nyssa in her palms.

Nyssa looked down her shoulder at the Second Sun, feeling her chin rise, the wind billowing her hair off her face. She remembered the Throne Room. The Belwarks on one knee. Swords displayed to Rhaif and Aydra as they took their oaths to protect them.

Nyssa inhaled deeply. "I have questions," she said.

"Remember them, Princess," Lex said knowingly.

"Do you choose me because you truly believe in me?" Nyssa asked.

Lex's eyes lifted to meet hers. "I do."

"Do you choose me because you believe in the freedom I can help bring to our people?" Nyssa asked. "Not just freedom from the strangers on our shores but also freedom from the tyranny and lies of our own kingdom we've so been squandered beneath for a century?"

"I do."

Nyssa shifted on her feet, and she turned so that she was straight in front of the Second Sun.

"Hilexi, will you follow me?" Nyssa asked firmly. "Will you stand at my side and fight for the freedom of our people? Will you run with me into battle, despite any stupidity you may think of my plans or actions? Will you support and trust me to do what's best for our home?"

Nyssa watched the affirmation rise in the Belwark's eyes, lips pressing together, cheeks taut with the determination Lex wore as a resting face.

"Until this world takes us from each other, I will be by your side," Lex swore. "And as far as your stupid plans, I live for them." A small smile grew on her lips, and Nyssa's chest softened. "They're usually the most dangerous."

She stared a moment at Lex. The setting sun behind her, amber hue glowing off her perfect porcelain cheeks.

"Stand with me, Second Sun," Nyssa completed.

Lex's gaze squinted. "What—no blood bond?"

Nyssa almost laughed. "You know I'm not as extravagant as my siblings," she smiled. "I don't need a blood bond to bind a person's loyalty to me, especially when I do not have a crown to tie it to. I'll not beg for anyone to stand. Follow me or don't. That's your choice."

Lex returned her smile, and Nyssa reached for her hand. She pulled her to her feet, and Lex hugged her tightly. Nyssa sighed when Lex kissed her forehead, and then her hands pressed to her cheeks.

"Your sister would be so angry and yet so proud of you," she told her.

Nyssa grinned. "So angry," she agreed. "Can you imagine?"

62

By the time the sun went down, Nyssa's nerves were returning. She and Lex had spent most of the afternoon walking along the beach, and then came back early to scarf down food before Lex went to help Nadir with setting things up for the meeting. Nyssa had offered to help, but Nadir asked her to wait at his home for him. She wasn't sure what he was up to, but she dressed and paced on his porch nonetheless.

Replaying the entire day. The entire week. The entire cycle. Allowing what she'd learned while she was at that camp to come back to her. She counted the lashings as they came down on her again and let that pain radiate through her bones. She remembered and acknowledged what she'd gone through, told her core she didn't need to squander this but rather recognize it.

Breathing in the smoke.

"Are you ready?" came Nadir's voice, and Nyssa hadn't heard him come to the house.

She took another deep breath and shook out her hands. "Ready."

Nadir held out his arm as she reached him, and he only gave her a small smile before leading her towards the tent. A confident energy rested between them, almost as though it were not Nyssa and Nadir walking to that tent.

But rather the Commander and Eyes of Haerland.

"Why do I get the feeling you're up to something?" she asked him, holding her broken forearm to her chest.

"I don't know what you mean." And the teasing brow he looked down at her with made her smirk.

"You're a terrible liar," she accused.

"What's my sign?"

"If I tell you, you'll note it and stop doing it."

He chuckled under his breath, and she saw his chest expand with his great sigh.

"All eyes are on you tonight," he told her.

"You know what I know," she said. "Which parts would you like me to keep to myself?"

"The date of the King's arrival," he said, looking down at her. "And that their Prince is already here. I do not want a panic."

"And Soli?"

Nadir smirked as they paused at the door. "Oh, you have as much fun with that as you want," he winked. "I fully expect her in tears by the end of this."

Nyssa almost laughed at his assurance, and a memory from her past filled her mind. When Rhaif had first realized she had a talent for watching people, and he'd asked her in his study to take note of the Council's signs.

"I'll take care of the boring bits," Rhaif told her as he offered her wine. "You make sure none of them are lying to us."

Nyssa crossed her arm over her chest and took the wine. "I'll tap twice if anything is amiss," she told him.

Rhaif straightened over her, a smirk growing on his stern face. "Make them crawl, Nysi," he winked.

Nyssa inhaled sharply and looked up at Nadir. "You know, as much of an ass as Rhaif is, and as much as I would like to slit his throat, he used to say something to me that stuck."

Nadir's eyes narrowed, and she could tell his insides had grown cold at the mention of her older. "What was it?" he asked stiffly.

"Make them crawl, Nysi," she said, and it broke her heart to say it aloud.

Nadir looked impressed as he considered the words. "Dammit, I like it," he cursed. "I'm not sure I realized you two were close," he noted.

"Up until the Gathering," she said, and a sadness rested in her voice. "But that is a story for another night."

"I have a better saying for you," he decided. "And I'll not be calling you Nysi."

"No?" she asked.

"No," he affirmed. He leaned down into her ear, close enough she could feel the faint stubble on his jaw.

"Make them weep, Ari Storn."

A chill went down her spine, and his chin lifted as he straightened over her. She allowed the faint smile on her lips, basking in that affirmed energy he stared at her with. Knowing he would be by her side if she needed him but not there to take over or put her in a corner.

"With pleasure, Commander."

His gaze darted deliberately over her entire form, tongue darting out over his lips, and another deep breath evacuated his lungs. He reached for the tent flap and met her eyes.

"After you," he said.

It pulled back, and every head turned in their direction.

The air stiffened with their appearance, but her attention on it was short-lived as Lex came up beside her and handed her a cup of wine.

"I've heard the chatter," Lex said behind her cup. "They plan to ambush you about the nature of your escape."

Nyssa pressed the cup to her lips, stomach knotting at the revelation. "That should be fun."

Lex's sideways smile widened. "I've my knife should you need the added incentive."

"Thank you." Nyssa glanced up at her Second, and Lex gave her a quiet wink.

Hugs greeted Nadir behind them, followed by a few smiles and nods to Nyssa by those who gathered around. Lovi appeared and gave Nyssa a long hug. The old man held her face a moment as he doted on her, and she couldn't help her smile. Until Nadir squeezed her shoulders and told her it was time to get started. Lovi told him to relax, but he swept out the tent a moment after nonetheless, intent on not interfering with his children and their decisions.

The moment Lovi left her, a woman approached.

"Commander Storn," came her stern voice.

Nadir stiffened at Nyssa's side, and she knew without looking who this woman was.

"I wondered if we were still holding this meeting or if you'd found yourself too preoccupied with the return of your Princess."

"Sounds more like you didn't want to attend," Nadir argued.

Nyssa slowly turned, preparing herself to lock eyes with the woman who had hurt him and tried to take his position.

She was not prepared for the woman in front of her.

Skin of glowing amber. Light yellow and brown hair twisted perfectly in small sections, golden rings around a few of the ends and knotted sporadically in its thickness. She had it tied up in a high ponytail on her head, the length sweeping down to her mid-bicep.

Firelight glistened off her high cheekbones, almost looking like she'd painted them with a highlight. She was wearing a snug green linen halter that showed off her midsection, her breasts swelled beneath the tight fabric. Muscular thighs and hips sculpted and flexing with every shift of her weight in her brown pants.

Standing beside this woman was like standing beside Aydra. Intimidating and gut-wrenching. Making her feel smaller than she already did. At least with her sister, she'd felt pushed to impress her, to want to be her. But standing by this woman... she felt like nothing she did would ever be enough.

However, the mere thought of how this woman had once treated Nadir swelled inside her, and Nyssa wanted nothing more than to punch her in the throat. Nyssa's chin rose, back straightening as tall as she could make herself, and she stared at Soli without blinking.

"Should I assume this is her?" Soli asked Nadir. "Or were you intent on not introducing me?"

An annoyed huff left Nadir as he placed a hand on her waist. "Soli, this—"

"I don't *belong* to anyone," Nyssa cut in, rage dripping from her voice as she stepped from his grasp and straightened to the woman. "I am a free being with her own mouth and thoughts, fully capable of speaking for herself and taking what she wants. I am as corporeal as you and standing in front of you. Most people would ask directly for a name instead of speaking over another as though they are some sort of mute creature. Or are you so enamored by the Commander that you thought he would speak for me too?"

Soli balked. "Excuse me?"

"My name is Nyssari Eaglefyre," Nyssa said. "And you are excused."

Lex choked on her drink.

Soli stared at her, and Nyssa had not felt such hatred for another Lesser being since Rhaif. But Soli's eyes darted behind her, weight shifting as she looked to Nadir, and then she settled back before Nyssa.

"Soli Amberglass," she introduced herself.

"I've read the stories," Nyssa snapped.

"Do tell," Soli mused. "Has Storn been showing it off again? He does like the old stories about me. Unfortunately, the great serpent evaded me that day. Not to worry. I'll take its head one day despite our *strong* Commander being intent on keeping it alive."

"That great serpent helped me escape Man's camp," Nyssa countered. "So if you'd like its head, you'll go through me as well."

A sly brow lifted on Soli's face, and she gave her a full once over. "Yes, how did you escape when you were supposedly tied up, I wonder."

And Nyssa could feel the accusation on her tongue.

Her feet moved forward.

"Say what you mean, Amberglass," she uttered in a low enough tone that Nadir touched her arm. But Nyssa felt the ash on her fingertips and saw the world vibrate around her.

Soli took a step back, eyes wide. She glanced between Nadir and Lex, and then she slowly turned on her heel. Nyssa shook herself out of the form, and Nadir reached for her hand.

As everyone took their seats, Nadir held out a chair for Nyssa, between he and Lex. But as Nyssa looked around the room, she shook her head.

"I like to walk," she said firmly.

Nadir exchanged a glance with Lex, who nodded.

She hadn't realized it would be Nadir's first official time seeing her in a war room. Just as it was everyone else's. But Lex knew. Even if she'd never been able to speak in other meetings except with Rhaif, Lex had seen her walk around those tables more times than once. Knew Nyssa's call if there was anything amiss. Knew Nyssa would be memorizing every person in that place.

Nyssa pressed her hand to Nadir's arm, and then she brushed by him.

Nadir stayed standing to introduce the topics.

She noted every word Nadir said, eyes sweeping around the tables as she walked and landing on the ones that watched her. The group at Soli's table. A few in the far left corner. Sutor gave her a smile when she met her gaze, and the women at her table all seemed relaxed yet attentive to their Commander as he spoke.

A few people shifted as she strode by slowly, her arms crossed firmly around her torso.

This was her forum.

Her chosen comfort.

Heartbeat steady and breath even.

Tingles rushing over her arms as though she were near orgasm.

The part of the war that she'd been made for.

She'd never felt more confident in herself than in that moment.

You cannot be tamed, climbed, or silenced.

Nadir asked for updates from the legion Generals as the first order of business.

"Before we get into updates—" Soli said loudly, cutting into Nadir's plan. "—Perhaps you should explain to us why your Princess is walking around this room as though *we* are the ones under investigation."

Nyssa continued walking.

Nadir's hands creased in the wood of the table as he leaned over it. "Perhaps you should explain to us why her walking around the room makes you so uncomfortable."

The room shifted. A few people cleared their throats. But Soli only wrapped her arms around her chest.

Nadir scowled in her direction. "Nyssari can do whatever she damn well pleases," he affirmed. "After what she's done for us and put herself through."

"You've yet to tell us the manner of her escape," Soli said, head tilting. "This is the third time you've allowed the enemy of the Venari in our home as though this is some sort of refuge. And this time, it is after she has mysteriously escaped from the strangers invading our land. The same strangers whom we have all fought on this very beach. Tell me again why we should continue to look to you to lead and save our people when you continue to bring in such traitors?"

Nyssa paused at the end of Soli's table.

"Should you have something to say about the nature of my being here, you should address it to me and not to the person who has risked his life multiple times over to keep you all safe," she chimed in.

Soli turned in her seat. Nadir sat down in his. And Nyssa saw as the others exchanged weary glances.

"He allowed you here," Soli continued. "Why should I not question him and his lacking judgment?"

"Perhaps because it was both Venari Kings who asked me to come here," Nyssa replied. "Perhaps because not every plan needs to be shared with the likes of someone who will obviously only use said information to get herself selfishly in power by spewing doubt about her leader instead of allowing and trusting him to do what he does best: protect you."

Soli stared at her another moment, and Nyssa watched as her fingers creased at her biceps.

"You still have not told us the nature of your escape," Soli said, changing the subject.

"How I escaped torture and slavery is not your business," Nyssa said. "The people who need to know the details know. The people who you should trust know. They were *there*. The Venari King and your own Commander were *there* when I escaped. Why is that not good enough for you?"

Soli didn't speak.

"The conversation of where my loyalties lie is over. We have more important things to discuss here," Nyssa snapped. "Like where you all stand in your legions and how the harvest is going so that our world doesn't starve while we await slaughter and slavery. *Commander*—"

"Yes, Princess?" Nadir said, head lifting.

"—I believe you can continue your meeting," she continued without looking at him. "Should Amberglass have more questions about my loyalty, she can find me on the beach at sunrise."

"Is that a challenge?" Soli asked.

"Would you like it to be?" Nyssa dared.

A low whistle emitted from the back of the room, though Nyssa didn't see who did it. Nadir stood again, and the conversation between Nyssa and Soli was brought to a halt as he began talking to his Generals once more. Nyssa didn't lose her stare with the woman for a long moment. It was Soli who moved first. She shifted in her seat, and Nyssa took the opportunity to circle back around the room.

Each General stood to give him an update. Nyssa walked back around to the front table and stood behind Nadir, one hand on the back of his chair. Her eyes continued to wander, watching the Generals, noting their occasional fidgeting.

Once, she even found herself tapping twice on the back of the chair.

Lex heard it, and she met Nyssa's eyes. But she didn't question the man speaking. Nadir changed the subject once they were finished. And it was time to talk about their guests in the west.

"A rider from their settlement came to the Village of Dreams while I was there," one of the traders announced. "Asking to barter with them for food. I told him any talk of trade goes through us, not through the Village."

Nadir nodded. "What else from the rumors?"

"I swam out to our home place yesterday," Soli said, referring to where the Honest children were born from. "I counted twice the number of ships on their shore than the week before. I think they are building something."

"They're building their castle," Nyssa said.

"I did not see one," Soli argued, head tilting. "The home place is far enough out past the edge of the peninsula. I should have seen it if they are building one. I did not."

"It's by the cliffs," Nyssa said. "Nearly on the western shore. You would not be able to see it. It's too far away. Almost two days on horseback from here."

"They have been landing at the edge of the Preymoor peninsula at the Mouth in previous months," Soli said. "Why would you think they were there?"

"*Because I was at their fucking castle*," Nyssa snapped, hand creasing on the edge of Nadir's chair.

But Soli ignored her.

"If they are bringing in more and more people, I should think they are also bringing weapons with them. Building up forts."

"That they are," Nyssa grunted.

"We need to attack," Soli said.

"Suicide," Nyssa mumbled.

"We cannot continue to sit back and let them build," she continued. "The weapons they had the last they were here are greater than our own—"

"They are," Nyssa interjected. "If you'd like to know—"

"—We need to take them before they take us."

"You know, Amberglass," Nyssa cut in, this time louder than before. "I wasn't aware that you were their captive too."

The air stiffened.

"If you know all there is to know about them, then, please. Be my guest," Nyssa continued. "You must know so much more than I do since you can see their settlement from the home place. Tell me the weapons they have at their castle."

Soli gawked at her.

Rage surged through Nyssa's bones, and she couldn't stop herself.

"Tell me what they call their guards. Tell me their battle plans and how many men they have in every legion. Tell me the names of their royal family and how they take their tea. Tell me which of their Generals has a family to lose and which ones would give up their duty if it meant freedom from beneath their oppressor's thumb. Tell me the problems they are facing as a new settlement and how we can help come to a peaceful standing without losing lives on both sides, at least for the time being."

Soli's gaze fluttered, her jaw twisting, and people in the room stared between them.

Nyssa felt her head tilt in Soli's direction. "I am waiting."

"You cannot possibly know all—"

"I know *everything*," Nyssa seethed. "And I did not just endure nearly eight weeks of slavery, starvation, and torture to come back here and be questioned as though I am some sort of *traitor*. Would you like to see the scars on my back?" she dared. "Would you like to see how my fucking mark is now barely recognizable due to the lashings I received? Would you like to know the size of the man's cock they thrust in my face before I said enough and escaped that place? Or perhaps you'd like to see how they burned my shoulders because they thought my freckles a *disease?!*"

She swore she saw tears in Soli's eyes. But they were gone in a blink, and Soli cleared her throat. "No one asked you to do what you did, girl."

Ash rose on Nyssa's fingertips. She stretched her fingers and took a deep breath.

"If I hadn't, your home would already be up in flames," she said, her voice steady as she fought her rising fire. "Do you want to know why?"

Soli didn't respond.

"Ask her," Nadir commanded.

Soli's eyes cut crudely at Nadir, but she huffed and looked back to Nyssa. "Why?"

"Because had I not been there, your fucking Commander would have never walked across the damn Preymoor to trade goods with them until it was too late. They would have sent out patrols to look for food and settlements to raid because they are starving for anything other than poorly processed meats. Your home would be theirs. And Haerland would already be under their control." Nyssa paused to let it sink in their heads, chin lifting as she glared at the ones opposing her. "He and I are the only reason any of you are still breathing." She snapped back to Soli. "And if you ever call me 'girl' again, I'll snap your neck like I did my captor's."

"Are you threatening me again?" Soli asked.

"It's a fucking promise," Nyssa snapped.

Lex was holding her hand over her mouth, staring at the ground, when Nyssa finally sat down in the chair. She settled back, legs crossing.

"Any push at them cannot come from just this village," Nyssa continued. "Until we have a whole united army, we must ask for peace with them. Not surrender or slavery, but peace. They are starving for fresh fruits and vegetables that you all can give them. We have to ask for a trading treaty. We can build our forces as we wait, but if you want to see another winter here, this is what we have to do."

People exchanged glances, and Nadir squeezed her knee. He met her eyes, throat bobbing, and then he looked back to his people.

"Updates on our crops. Go," he asked them.

As each of the farmers and merchants stood to talk about their goods, Nadir leaned forward in his chair, his voice so low when he spoke in Nyssa's ear that she hardly heard him.

"Do you have any idea how sexy hearing you talk like that was?" he breathed.

Nyssa clenched her teeth to keep from smiling, heat threatening her neck. She thought that might be the end of it, but he leaned forward again.

"If there weren't other people in this room, you might really have to break my heart again to keep me from you."

Confidence swirling through her body, Nyssa glanced sideways, and then she brought her cup to her lips. "Commander, if one threatening speech from me has you itching out of your bones, this is going to be a long... *hard*... war."

He inhaled sharply, muttering, "*Fucking Infi*, Princess," and one glance over to him, and she could tell it was taking everything in him not to touch her. Dilation in his gaze, his eyes wandered over her once, and then he leaned back in his chair again, hand resting on the back of hers.

Just moments after the exchange, he stood again to wrap up and asked them to continue their plan from the previous meeting, with increased production of their goods. And as the session ended, Nadir parted ways with them to make his rounds.

Nyssa itched to stand, a deep breath finally evacuating her and her heart swelling with the execution of a job well done. Lex smiled and leaned against the table with her.

"Good show, Princess," she muttered as she drank her wine.

Nyssa caught sight of the General that had lied, and she watched him as he spoke to Nadir.

"You caught my tap?" she asked Lex without looking at her.

"I did," Lex said as she, too, watched the man. "I wonder why he would be lying about the readiness of his legion."

"Isn't his legion the one Nadir wanted to give you?" Nyssa asked.

Lex considered it, and Nyssa's brow raised knowingly.

"There you go," Nyssa muttered. "He doesn't want his authority taken away. You should keep an eye on him and try to help where you can. Show him you're not trying to take over his legion but that you just want to help."

Lex's smile widened down at her. "I forgot how much you love the politics of all this."

Nyssa sighed, finding her own smile spreading. "As did I," she agreed.

"Try not to orgasm at the table over it," Lex mocked, to which Nyssa couldn't help her laugh. "Or perhaps if you do, make sure your Commander is enjoying it as well."

Lex winked at her when Nyssa met her gaze, and then she gave her hair a ruffle. Her lips pressing to the top of Nyssa's head, she muttered, "See you in the morning, Princess," to her before heading out of the tent herself.

Nyssa sighed again and pushed herself atop the table, crossing her legs under her and sipping the rest of her wine as the people filed out of the room. Soli gave her another glare, but she didn't speak, didn't even speak to Nadir as she left.

Nyssa took a moment to watch him, feeling her eyes dance over his stern facade, his commanding voice and posture as he spoke with his people. The words he'd said in her ear came to mind.

For a moment, she fantasized about him taking her right there on that table, and when she caught his gaze, watching as his eyes darted over her, she knew he was thinking it too.

Sutor came up to her and gave her cheek a kiss, telling her she would have clothes ready for her in the morning and she should come by before breakfast to get them. She introduced Nyssa to a few other women: bakers, one in charge of the fruits in the food forest, and a few others that Nyssa did not remember their names.

Nyssa could hear the drums outside as their people gathered around fires for smokes and after-dinner shenanigans as the last of the people left. She pushed the cup to her lips and watched Nadir snap the tent door closed, and her heartbeat quickened.

When he turned, she noted the push of his hips forward, the swagger in his shoulders, the delight in his eyes, and she stifled the smile threatening her lips.

"Well done, Lady Storn," he mocked, to which she shook her head.

"I should never have told you I used your name," she laughed.

"You shouldn't have," he agreed. "It's given me all sorts of ideas and fantasies."

"Fantasies?" she repeated as he reached the edge of the table. "Do tell, Commander."

He chuckled under his breath and sat his cup down upon coming to stand before her. "You've no idea how long I've waited for someone to put Soli in her place," he admitted. "And that threat?" His eyes scrunched mockingly, low whistle sounding.

Nyssa laughed, her heart skipping as she felt his light touch on her knees. "Not what you expected from your innocent Princess?"

"I'm not sure what I expected, but it certainly wasn't that," he admitted. "That was amazing. And your walking around the room? I didn't know anyone could be so intimidating."

"You don't have to be the largest person in the room to command it."

Nadir's hands pressed into the wood on either side of her, and she couldn't help her chin raising, her legs from unfolding, eyes from darting over his face. He leaned over her, his nose nearly nudging hers, and adrenaline surged through her veins.

"Tell me you weren't looking at me as you were just to say you're not crossing my beach," he breathed against her skin.

Nyssa smiled, confidence pulsing in her veins. "I haven't crossed that beach," she told him as her heart began to thud. "But after that, I wouldn't say no to a swim."

He groaned, eyes fluttering. "Does that mean I can kiss you?" he practically pleaded.

Her legs dropped to either side of his hips, and she squeezed. "Yes," she managed, the anticipation of him making her chest heave.

"Thank the Architects," he muttered beneath his breath before threading her jaw in his palms and kissing her so hard, she nearly fell off balance.

She groaned into his mouth, fisted his shirt in her hands, and she pulled him flush to her. Her thighs squeezed around him. She wanted him so badly. The adrenaline of the meeting poured through her, and at that moment, the horrors of her last month did not enter her mind.

She even forgot they were in a very not sound-proof tent in the middle of his village.

His kiss sent her spinning as it had the night before. She grasped the edge of his shirt, and they pulled it off, tossing it behind her and onto the ground. Feeling those muscles beneath her fingertips again and flush against her own chest. His mouth moved to her throat, sucking on her skin and making her groan as her open mouth steadied against his cheek.

Both his hands slipped beneath her dress and grabbed her underwear. She pressed her palms into the table as he swept them off. His lips met hers, and as his finger trickled between her thighs and he felt her wetness, he groaned into her mouth.

"I need you, Princess," he breathed. "I need you around me. I need to feel you trembling as you come apart."

She nodded, whispering, "Yes—*fuck, yes*—Nadir," between their desperate kisses.

Her fingers fumbled with the strings of his pants, and he cursed when he sprang free. His lust and power intoxicated her. Raised every hair on her arms. She wanted him everywhere. Her muscles strained with his lips on hers, and her body begged for him.

She tucked her feet behind his thighs, and Nadir's finger pressed deeper inside her. That digit curling in her and his thumb moving against her clit. Knees lifting off the table and hips rocking into his hand with every stroke. He bit her throat, and she reached for his cock. A moan vibrated against her skin as she pushed that bead of liquid down his length.

Another finger slipped inside her, and she limped in his arms. Hand in his hair, she tugged him back, and she whispered, "Fuck me like you just lost me, Commander," as her eyes met his.

Nadir's eyes fluttered, head tilting, and he kissed her palm. "Yes, Princess."

His hand moved from inside her. He grabbed her hips, yanking her to the edge of the table, and she gasped when his length filled her. The moan that emitted from her mouth, she couldn't stop, and neither could he. He kissed her again, making her chest arch against him, her hips grinding against his. Stilling all the way in and savoring her. He pulled back, hand settling on her cheek.

"Lean back and grab the edge," he uttered. "Don't let go."

Tingles on her arms, she did as he instructed. Knees wide and bent, hips in his hands. Her ass was so far on the edge of the table that one slip and she would have fallen off. But she knew he had her. Knew he would hold her there until she couldn't breathe, and they both cried out for her end.

The moment her fingers wrapped into the table, he pulled out and then slammed inside her. Cursing as he began a steady pace, bending over her and kissing her stomach. Her back arched as he moved in and out. Just feeling him inside her again made her body reach. Her toes already pointing, muscles stretching. His pace picked up. She looked down and watched his motions in and out of her, watched his full length disappear and reappear, covered in the glisten of her wetness. His face scrunched with every fill as his fingers dug into her ass and hips. His mouth sagged, and then he caught her gaze.

She almost came apart at the sight of him staring at her. Chin raised, tongue darting out over his lips. Her thighs tightened around him again, and she knew she was close.

"Are you there, Princess?" he asked, his voice straining.

A gasp took her breath as she felt her body edging. "Yes—*fuck*, yes," she managed.

Nadir moved a hand off her thigh and between her legs. His thumb moved over her clit, and Nyssa cried out an unintelligible curse. Finger pressing hard over her nerves, he pulled out and slammed deeper.

Those last strokes were deliberate and claim-worthy. Her head threw back, and she swore her hands would break the table. She trembled with the elaborate thrusts, gasping for breath. His thumb continued to toy with her clit. She couldn't help when she cried out his name, a few more strokes—

Together they came apart.

Nyssa's high-pitched moan sounded, body shaking as she spilled over him. Nadir arrested deep inside her with his own release. His fingers dug into her skin. She opened her eyes just in time to meet his own gaze and watch breath return to his lungs. Her back met the table, and he leaned on her, still holding onto her thighs but laying his head against her breasts.

"Fuck, you feel like home," he whispered on her skin, and she wasn't sure he meant for her to hear him.

After a moment, he moved to hover over her, and he kissed her softly. "I could stay buried in you the rest of my life," he told her. "Do you have any idea how mesmerizing it is watching you come apart around me?"

"Commander, you keep talking like that, and I might drown," she bantered.

He chuckled under his breath and straightened, taking her with him to a sitting position. "No," he said softly, pushing her hair back off her face. "No, I want you crossing that beach when *you* are ready for evermore. Not just this part. I want you to love the strong, beautiful creature you are again, comfortable in your skin and believing in yourself. Because I want all the things we talked about. I want all of you, every day, in every way I can have you. Standing by your side as you take your throne and conquer your enemies. I will make sure you get there, Princess. And I'll be waiting on the other side of that beach when you're ready."

Why are you so patient with me?" she wondered aloud, chest swelling with his declaration. "How does all this not drive you crazy?"

"You know why," he sighed. "You just won't let me say it."

"Don't you dare," she said in a breath.

Huffing, his smile widened, and he kissed her again. Slowly this time. As though he were savoring a final moment, and his forehead laid against hers when he pulled away.

For a moment, neither spoke. Nyssa's eyes closed as she breathed him in, knowing everything he said was real and he meant the words. Knowing she could do this and that it might take time, but she would regain that confidence in her abilities again, no matter how long it took. And knowing that the war would continue to loom over their heads as she did.

But the memory of her standing in the castle at Savigndor entered her mind, and she held him a little tighter.

"No matter where this war takes us... I will always find my way back to you," she whispered.

Nadir pulled back and shook his head just noticeably. "Don't talk like that," he breathed.

"We cannot be oblivious to this war," she managed. "I don't want to think that one day I'll have to walk away from you, but if that day comes, I will find you again. I will always come back to you."

Jaw visibly clenching, he pressed his hand once more to her cheek. "Always?" he whispered.

"Evermore," she promised.

63

Hagen rose before sunrise the next morning, and he and Dorian went up to the Temple to speak with Marius and Falke. Corbin and Reverie packed their things as they waited on them, and then the three departed Dahrkenhill by noon. Hagen and Dag guided them all the way back through the mountains and into the caves, leaving them only after reaching the Hills of Bitratus once more.

Hagen gave them two extra horses with supplies to take Bala, saying he'd promised aid, and if a few stashes of newly forged daggers and bundles of arrows would help, that's what he would send for now. Until they needed more, and he would send that with the Honest traders.

Dorian had promised he would return once he saw his sister and returned the Scrolls to Lake Oriens. He felt he was making significant progress in the mountains and wanted to learn everything he could from Hagen. Hagen told the three they were welcome any time, but he'd expect him back by the next cycle. He had more plans for Dorian, and the words made Dorian laugh.

Corbin didn't seem as amused by Hagen and his so-called plans.

It was weird being back south to flatter lands. Back where he could see the trees and hear the Noctuans at night. Back where it wasn't snowing, and they had to shed their heavy clothing to give Hagen to take back.

By the time they reached the Forest to enter the Venari realm, Dorian's nerves began to get the better of him. He'd hardly spoken to Reverie and Corbin on their journey. The noise of the Ulframs had followed them since the caves, and Dorian couldn't shake that perhaps they were following them.

The grand trees stared back at them around the entrance to the Forest on that fifth morning. Dorian tossed his dagger up and down in his hand as Reverie and Corbin finished packing up their things.

The more he thought about seeing Bala again, the angrier he became. That she'd lied to him about his sister's whereabouts. That she'd kept it all a secret and let him wander through those mountains while his sister had possibly been dying. Even as far back as insisting they separate from each other instead of doing this altogether.

Ash settled on his fingertips, and he didn't squander it.

The noise of crows filled their ears as they strode the path. But by the time noon came around, the entire wood became silent, and Dorian knew they were entering the Venari kingdom.

"Up top," Corbin called out.

Dorian's eyes flickered up, and there they were.

Venari stared down at them from the great branches. Arrows threaded. Knives drawn. But Dorian didn't acknowledge them. He continued on.

"No combating them if they ambush," Dorian said, mainly talking to Reverie. "If—"

An arrow whistled the air.

Flames grew on Dorian's hand into a soft ball, and he shot it out. The arrow disintegrated to ash before it hit the ground.

A warning.

Dorian's horse stalled in the air. He held on, trying to calm her, but it caused a domino. Reverie and Corbin's horses began to stamp erratically. To the point, Dorian jumped from his horse and stepped before it to calm.

The tip of a blade touched his neck. Dorian stiffened.

"Bael," he said, guessing it was the Second who had been on patrol.

"Drop it," came Reverie's voice.

Dorian didn't even know she'd come down from her horse.

"Stand down, Rev," Dorian called back to her. "I can handle this."

Dorian turned slowly, the blade still tipped at his neck not moving as he turned, and he watched as the stern expression dropped from Bael's handsome face.

"I need to see Bala," Dorian demanded. "Unless you'd like to tell me where my sister is."

Bael's chin lifted, and he removed his threat, taking a step back. "Be glad it was me on patrol this morning, Prince," he said. "The rest of them would have seen your fire and thought you your brother."

Dorian seized Bael's neck, and he threw him into the tree before he realized he was doing it. The world vibrated, but he didn't release the Venari.

"I am not my brother," he seethed.

Bael beat on Dorian's hand, struggling for breath. Until Dorian threw him sideways, and Bael doubled over to gasp for breath.

Every Venari descended from the trees and surrounded them. Dorian glared, feeling his form rising. Navy fire trembling on his fingertips, he dared anyone else to come at him.

"So much for not combating them," Reverie scowled under her breath.

"Hey—"

Bala's voice rang in the air. She pushed through the crowd in a sprint, and Dorian rounded on her.

"About fucking time," Dorian spat.

Rage spread over her features, and she bounded forward. "Funny you say you're not your brother, yet look at you threatening my people because of whatever fear has gripped your core." She stepped straight up to him, obviously not caring that he was in his form. "You look just as he did the last time he was here," she warned, and Dorian began to shake.

"Release your form before I crush it. *Now*."

Dorian's form receded as the thought of looking or being anything like his brother made his heart break. Bala glared up at him.

"If you ever walk into my kingdom with fire as you just did again, I may forget we're friends," she growled in his face. She glared past him, looking to Corbin and Reverie.

"Corbin," she acknowledged.

"Venari King," he returned.

Her gaze flickered over Reverie. "Who's this?"

Dorian stepped between her and Reverie. "Tell me where my sister is."

The words seemed to bring Bala down. She blinked and stepped back. "Everyone, back to your stations. The Fire Prince is contained with me. You'll not need to worry about him." She turned back to Dorian. "Get your shit and follow. Quietly."

Bala went to check on Bael as Dorian turned to Reverie and Corbin. He didn't speak, only giving them a nod, and he grasped the reins of his horse.

As they followed her, Dorian noted some Venari walking through her kingdom that he didn't recognize. Larger and almost savage looking. As though they'd been away from the sanctity of a kingdom and gone feral in their absence. His core churned inside him, an uneasiness settling in his bones and extremities. A few had black hoods up over their heads. Those men watched him closer than the others that Bala had commanded to go about their duties.

Hair pricked the back of his neck, and he glanced back to Corbin, who seemed to share his bewilderment.

Dorian didn't press it. He followed quietly behind Bala all the way to the edge of the kingdom before he could take the silence no longer.

"Is there a reason you're dodging my question?" he asked under his breath.

"We can speak once you've calmed yourself," she snapped. "I'm not talking to this Promised dick of a King. I want to speak to my friend. I want to speak with Dorian."

"And Dorian wants to know where his fucking sister is—" he stopped and grabbed Bala's arm, whirling her back around. "Tell me why you're hiding this," he said. "Tell me why you've lied to me these past ten weeks. Tell me or I'll—"

Wind whipped. "Are you challenging me, Prince?" Bala shifted before him, eyes blazing into his as she dared him to come at her.

"Where is my sister?" he asked again.

"She's at the Umber."

"Are you sure about that?" he asked, head tilting. "Because from what I was told, she has been imprisoned at Man's camp for some time now."

"She's at the Umber. That I can promise you."

"Then why—"

"I don't know where you're getting your information, but when I tell you she is back safe at the Umber, I mean I was there when she escaped Man's camp," she affirmed in a low voice. "I was there to help pull her from the void her new form nearly pulled her into. I was there, and I helped walk her ass back to Nadir's home, where Lovi has been keeping an eye on her since. And as for why I have been lying to you, it is because I did not want to cause a terror through you like the one you're displaying now. She's alive, and she's okay. She handled it. You should give your sister some credit." Bala paused to stretch her neck. "Any other questions?"

Dorian's nostrils flared, but he didn't speak.

Bala gave him another once over. "Leave your things. We can talk upstairs."

Dorian once more eyed the strange men around them as she turned on her heel. Something stirred inside him as they looked back at him.

"Who are the new people in your kingdom?" he asked.

Bala paused, considering him before answering. "A few from the abandoned faction decided to come back."

Yellow eyes flickered from one, and Dorian stilled.

"You have a problem, my King," he said, staring at it.

"More than your being a complete and utter twat today?" she snapped offhandedly.

He met her irritated eyes. "You've been infiltrated."

His fist curled in on itself. A tremble vibrated through his bones as his form rose on the surface, and with it, he watched that same tremble move through the Infis.

Bala shifted as she watched the display, and then Dorian turned in a slow circle. He cracked his neck and tightened every muscle in that right arm. The black ooze drew from his palm as his nails dug into the healing skin.

The Infis shuddered.

And they *bowed*.

Almost as though they were unable to stop themselves. As though something had forced them down and taken away their free will.

Heads and backs bending low, Dorian realized just how many Infi there were.

A quarter of the men standing were bent.

"Something you'd like to tell me?" Bala asked as her gaze darted over the people.

"Yeah," Dorian said, looking around. "You have a lot of Infi in your home disguised as Venari."

Bala turned to him, arms crossed over her chest. "Tell me why they are bowing to you."

Dorian looked over the crowd again, and then he declared in a low rattle, "Because they're *mine*."

Thunder rumbled the darkening sky. Wind whipped the trees, leaves flying and branches cracking. The claim, as low as it was, seemed to pulse through the forest. A stillness settled his insides, invincible power dripping at his fingertips that he hadn't anticipated.

The Infi dropped to their knees.

Dorian didn't blink away from Bala, but he felt the Infis' surrender. Felt as they succumbed to the weight of the deal and bind. It swelled within him a moment as they held, and he closed his eyes to breathe it in, his body shuddering.

Eyes flashing back, he opened them, and he pushed out a long breath, an audible restriction in the back of his throat. "Get up," he finally demanded over the air. He glanced around again, seeing the yellow eyes go in and out of the forms some of them were trying to hide. "In your true forms. No more hiding. You are what you are. Prove your worth by helping out this kingdom if you want to stay in it and not be imprisoned to the Bryn like the rest of them."

Infis stood, and forms shifted. Bones cracked. Bodies morphing.

"What the fuck happened up there?" Bala asked him.

"I should ask you the same about what happened down here," he countered.

Bala gave him a deliberate once over, and she finally turned. "We speak upstairs. Alone." Her gaze traveled back to Reverie and Corbin, almost as though she didn't trust them, and she walked away.

Dorian turned to the pair. "Keep an eye on the Infi."

He followed her up the steps and into Draven's home. He couldn't help pausing in the door to look at the changes. No more cot on the floor. The desk organized instead of in disarray as Draven had left it. The room tidy, and a few black flowers in glass bottles scattered around the room.

Bala's home.

She pulled the bottle of whiskey from behind the desk and two glasses as he sat at the small table. "Have you calmed down yet?" she asked as she poured the drinks.

Dorian didn't touch the whiskey when she handed it to him. He sighed heavily and pushed his hands over his face. The way he'd acted like a brat towards her made him hate himself. His friend. A King he should have trusted.

"Yeah," he said when he looked up. "Yeah, I'm sorry. I just... Are you sure she's okay and at the Umber?"

Bala didn't speak a moment, but she settled onto Draven's desk. "Positive."

"What happened?"

"That's not my story to tell," she insisted.

Dorian stretched his fist, staring at the ground. "I'm sorry I threatened you," he said as he met her gaze again. "I'm sorry for questioning you. I will not make an excuse for it. You are my King, and I should have trusted you. I'm sorry."

Her brows lifted, obvious with surprise. "That's very big of you, Prince. Thank you."

"It's new," he muttered.

Bala huffed, slight smile on her lips. "You going to tell me what's happened to you, or do I have to pry it out of you? And who's the girl?"

Dorian almost smiled as he leaned back in the seat. "So many questions," he mocked. "Luckily, who she is is at the beginning."

"Let's start there."

Bala didn't have many questions while Dorian spoke. She listened. Intently. Until finally, she decided she needed Corbin to tell her the truth in case Dorian was exaggerating. He hadn't even gotten to the part about his taking a crown from the Infi.

Corbin and Reverie were sitting on the steps, almost as though Corbin expected her to need confirmation.

"Corbin—"

"If he's telling you about his facing down the Ghost of Fire, he's actually not exaggerating," he called up, smirking at her over his shoulder.

Bala smiled, arms hugging her chest, and she shook her head. "Get up here. Both of you."

She poured them drinks as they bounded up the steps.

Darkness was beginning to settle in. The noise of the Ulfram sounded in the Forest, and Reverie paused in the door.

"What's wrong?" Dorian asked.

"I... I've never been inside the Forest during the Deads," she admitted, staring out into the twilight.

"Why does it not surprise me you needed two guards to keep yourself out of trouble up there?" Bala teased Dorian.

Reverie turned, arms across her chest, and she stared pointedly at Bala like the question she'd just asked was ridiculous. "Has he been lying to you? Because getting into trouble is the only thing he's been doing, and Corbin and I have not been able to stop it."

Bala grinned crookedly in Dorian's direction, to which Dorian shrugged and leaned back in the chair. "She's not wrong," he said.

Handing Reverie a cup, Bala gave her an upwards nod. "Balandria Windwood," she introduced herself. "Friends call me Bala."

"Reverie Asherdoe," she replied as she took the drink. "These two call me Rev or woman. Though, I'm not entirely sure I'm calling them friends yet."

"What—"

"Fuck off, Rev," Dorian smirked. "You love us."

Reverie glanced between the two, coy smile on her lips, and she looked back to Bala.

"Never let them know you like them," Bala muttered.

"I made the mistake of telling that one already," Reverie said, pointing to Dorian.

"Oh no," Bala mocked. "You're stuck with him now. That's good for me, though. And Corbin. He needed the help taking care of this one."

"Are you two done?" Dorian asked, and the two women smiled mockingly at him.

"Not hardly," Reverie said. "I've loads more to talk to her about."

"Is it making you uncomfortable?" Bala mocked. "Fuck, I can't wait to bring her to the Umber to meet Lex and your sister. We'll have a Dorian roasting party."

"Speaking of the Umber," Dorian cut in as he let the chair legs back on the ground. "I need to go."

"Sit down," Bala told him. "You're not going anywhere tonight. It's nearly dark. And it's the middle of the Deads. Unless you wish to die. The Aviteth and Aberd will have you before you know they're there. You can walk at first light. I'll have a guard lead you. I have some supplies to take with us when we go, and I could use a couple extra hands," she said, glancing between Corbin and Reverie. "We'll be a few hours behind. But I know how eager you are to get there."

Dorian's hand tightened around his cup, the thought of another night away from his sister making his insides squirm.

"She's okay, Dorian," Bala said again. "Really."

64

Nyssa didn't know she was pacing.

She didn't know how she was on the beach.

But the cold damp of the sand meshed between her toes. The swirling wind whipped her hair off her face.

Alone.

Numbness filled her insides where her burning core should have been. Her cheeks stiffened with the dry of previous tears she didn't know had evacuated her insides. She gripped the roots of her wild hair.

Back and forth.

One foot sinking into the crisp, wet ground after the other.

Shae's laugh in her ears. The grin of the Infi as he collapsed on that blade.

Stop it, she begged.

The wind whipped her bare back. It grazed over the streak of a healed lashing, but her muscle flinched at the memory of it.

Please.

The slop of mouths chewing food and slurping broth. The clank of silverware against wooden bowls. Her nails scratching on the wood as she was dragged into the other room. Blood pooling beneath her feet. The crack of her arm as it broke.

Water rushing over her face.

Nadir beside her.

His pinky wrapping around hers.

A full gasp filled her lungs.

And she was thrown back into the reality around her.

Her eagle screeched and flapped his wings at her back.

She was on her knees. Her trembling fingers digging into the sand. Water sloshed with the tide up and around her, meeting her skin with the cold salt of its depths. The tips of her fingers were black, the streaks of it growing and growing up her skin. She forced breath into her constricted lungs. Demanding that form back down and down. Grasping at her reality and counting out loud to keep herself above the void. The black descended into the depths, and she finally opened her eyes.

The only light came from the fire that had apparently come from her form. It danced around her in a circle and atop the surface of the water. As though its magic could boil the waves.

She realized she was naked. She didn't even remember rising from her bed. Didn't remember wandering onto the beach or how she was on her knees.

A ragged breath thrust into her lungs. She sat back on her feet as the calmness of the cold water surrounded her. Her eyes shut tight, willing her breaths to even out of whatever attack she'd just found herself in.

"Excuse me—"

The noise of a young girl's voice rattled her. Her eyes shot up to the right, heart jumping out of her chest.

A child was standing beside her.

No older than five, maybe six. The girl's long scarlet hair draped down past her elbows, a mop of waves frizzed all around. Steel eyes met Nyssa's amber ones, and for a moment, Nyssa thought it was an apparition of Aydra as a child. They had the same eyes. But the hair... the hair was wrong. Aydra's hair had been bright ginger bouncing curls. This girl's hair was much darker but brighter than her own cinnamon hair.

"Hi," Nyssa managed, gaze squinting at the young girl as the firelight bounced off her features. "It's late. You shouldn't be out here."

The girl rubbed her arm, and Nyssa squinted at the numbers and letters etched into her skin. Almost like a branding number. Fresh and raw, the red symbols stared back at her in the light.

SE3916EBR

3916... Her heart dropped as she remembered the number from the void.

"Where's my brother?" the girl asked Nyssa.

Nyssa's gaze averted from the girl's arm, and she took a gander around, looking back up at the village, at the ocean... but there was no one else around. "I... I don't know. What's your name?" Nyssa asked.

The small girl tucked her hair behind her ear—her normal ear— and Nyssa swallowed.

She wasn't a Dreamer as she did not have the pointed ears. She wasn't of the Honest. Her skin was far too pale, features far too similar to her own. She wasn't a Venari. She wasn't a Blackhand. And Man insisted they'd no red-headed women of their own.

So Nyssa only gaped at her.

Was this a trick?

"Are you crying?" the girl asked her.

"I... Where did you come from?" Nyssa managed.

"She told me I should see you," the girl said. "To tell you there was another."

"Who did?"

"Bina."

Nyssa's insides froze. She shot to her feet, looking wildly around her for any inclination of her own mother. She couldn't be here. She was gone. Forced into her burned tree. She shouldn't have been able to wake. Not for years. A hundred even.

Draven burned her.

She'd seen the shadow of her body against the trunk.

Fear struck her core, and her feet wavered. The possibility of Arbina being anywhere near a beach not of her own chilled her. She whirled around, and when she finally gathered she was not there, she turned to face the girl again.

"Where—"

The girl was gone.

She ogled at the space where she'd just been, realizing it had only been her imagination. Her fear seeping into her consciousness. A deep exhale left her, her eyes shutting again, and she fell back to her knees.

"Fucking curses, you're going crazy," she mumbled, pushing her wet hands into her hair.

"Here I thought you already were."

Her head twisted at the noise of Nadir's voice. She had to grasp to her chest to keep her composure. "Hi," she managed.

Nadir finished closing the space to her. "Hi?" he repeated. "Fuck of a greeting there, Princess. It's the middle of the night," he said as he sat.

He held something out for her—a shirt, she realized. She took it and pushed it over her head, eyes closing at the soft linen against her dry skin, the smell of salt and dirt from where he'd been harvesting fruits the day before.

"Who were you looking for?" he asked.

"I—" She didn't want to admit what she'd seen, even if she knew he would understand or even know why she had seen it. But she knew that if anyone would know what it was, it was him.

"I saw a little girl," she finally admitted.

"Was it you?"

"Her hair was wrong. And her eyes… they looked of molten steel… they were Aydra's eyes."

She could see the workings in his mind, the shift in his weight. "You're sure it wasn't her?"

"Her hair was scarlet. Bright. Waved and frizzy. Not straight like mine."

Nadir's heel tapped on the sand as the water brushed up and surrounded them. His lips pressed together, thought stretching over every muscle of his face.

"Any ideas?" she asked after a few moments.

"Sounds like a trick of the Sun," he finally said.

"It's the middle of the night."

"What did she say?"

Nyssa's insides tightened again, and she felt the sweat on her palms. "She… she said Arbina had sent her to tell me there was another."

Nadir's eyes widened. "What?"

"That's what I said."

"That…" Worry stretched over his features as he turned back to the ocean.

"Any ideas?" she asked.

"You're quite sure she said Arbina?"

Nyssa nodded.

Nadir rubbed the back of his neck. "I can think of a couple of possibilities. That Arbina or the Sun is using future daughters of Promise to reach out to you. Lovi knew Arbina pretty well. Probably one of the only ones who didn't think of her as crazy. And he actually knew the Sun before the curse… If anyone knows what's happening, it is him. I'll ask."

"How would the Sun or Arbina already know future daughters?"

"Arbina wouldn't, especially with her being burned, which makes me think this is the Sun toying with things. Time happens all at once for the Architects," he said. "They can see it all in mirrors or doorways, choosing which to go through, bringing one part of the future or the past to what we see is the present. Since Draven released the Sun, even if it is only in her phoenix form, she can see through those doorways again."

Nyssa stared at him. "Thoroughly confusing, but okay."

He chuckled under his breath. "Makes a lot better sense in the old language. Translation can get a bit weird."

"What are you doing out here?"

"Ah…" his head hung, and he began to rock just noticeably, almost as though it were a muscle reflex or comfort he didn't know he was doing. "Sometimes I come out here to see him."

"See who?"

A slow smile trickled up his features, and he laughed at the sky. "You haven't seen them," he realized. He turned back to the sky and gave an upwards nod towards the east. Nyssa squinted at the patterns in the sky, remembering that there weren't as many in the east as in the north and south. But the smile on Nadir's face made her chest tighten.

"What am I—"

Words ceased.

Her entire body caved in on itself, and she hardly noticed Nadir reaching over and squeezing her hand.

"It…" She couldn't believe what she was seeing.

Her sister, arrow pulled through the bow in her hands. Draven with his back to her, holding his horn. Tears slipped down her cheek, and Nadir wrapped his arm around her, pulling her into his chest.

"It's them," she managed, weight lifting off her shoulders somehow. A relief that they had done what they'd said they would. Change their world. Change the stars. Even in that void, they were leading the charge.

"I thought you'd seen them."

"I haven't exactly seen stars in a few weeks."

For a few moments, they didn't speak. Nyssa took in what was in front of her, wondering and hoping that her brother had seen them. Her stomach knotted at the thought of him.

"Have you heard anything from my brother?" she asked softly.

Nadir paused, fingers entwining with hers. "The last I heard, he was on his way back from the Bryn."

Nyssa's eyes widened as she remembered the Infi. "Are they sure it is him?"

He seemed to consider her words. "Honestly, I'm not sure any of the

Blackhands know to ask otherwise. Why would you think it wasn't?"

Nyssa stared at the ocean, remembering the vision she'd had the night she took down the camp. "My brother and I have always shared a bond stronger than Promised children before, and I am starting to think it was because we were marked at the same time. We can usually feel each other, know when the other is in pain. When Rhaif burned me, Dorian felt it. He thought, at the time, I had simply hurt myself training... Nadir, I can't feel him. And that worries me."

"Hagen was going to send him here with whatever information on what he'd found," Nadir said. "We'll know soon if he is okay."

She sighed her head onto his shoulder, his words assuring her and giving her a small comfort. He kissed her head again, and then she felt him slipping from around her. He stood, and he held out his long hands to her.

"Come on, Princess. I want to show you something."

She frowned but took his hands anyway. "Why do I get the feeling you're about to throw me into the ocean?"

He grinned. "I definitely am."

"I'm not wearing proper clothing," she argued.

"If you'd prefer, you can wear my pants," a sly brow raised on his perfect face. "I don't mind swimming naked."

"I'm sure you don't," she chuckled.

He was leading her into the water, ankles deep. Knees deep. And before she knew it, the water was hitting her breasts.

"You're going to give me hypothermia," she accused.

His response was to pull her flush to him, the water sloshing around their bodies. A wet thumb reached up to her cheek, the trickle of the water droplet that he stared at as it rolled down her jaw, onto her neck. Her feet treaded beneath her, and she didn't realize she was wholly in his arms until his hand flattened against her back, pressing their stomachs together.

"Once we're under, there's something I might do... I don't want you to think I'm pushing you. It's just air."

Her mouth dried as her mind worked out what he meant. "Just air," she repeated in a rasp she hardly heard.

His lip quirked upwards at the left side, and his hands found hers. "Hold your breath, Princess."

The rate at which he disappeared beneath the surface and pulled her with him barely gave her time to expand her lungs.

But the moment the water pushed over her head, Nyssa panicked.

Back in that room.

Head tilted back.

Water pouring over her face.

Her entire body shriveled, and she jerked on Nadir's hand. Feet kicking. She used every part of herself to push back to that surface as fast as she could. Her head burst out of the water, and she gasped.

She was drowning in that memory. Unable to rise over the surface or sputter up the water that no longer covered her.

"Hey—" Nadir grabbed her hands, and he pulled her into him.

The world spun.

"Nyssa—"

But her feet floundered. Hands pushing over her face. She couldn't tread in the water. Unable to grasp onto her actual reality.

"Nyssa!"

His shout snapped her forward. Stilling so that she almost began to sink back beneath the ocean depths. Nadir's hands were wrapped around her wrists, and he wasn't letting go.

"Hey—"

Breath returned to her lungs, and she closed her eyes, forcing herself to count down from six. Nadir pushed his hand to her cheek. "What happened?" he asked.

Her cheeks burned, but she swallowed, knowing she could tell him and he wouldn't judge or push. "One of the things the wife would do to punish me was tilt me back and pour water on my face until I couldn't breathe," she choked, and all color drained from Nadir's face.

"Why didn't you tell me? We don't—"

"No," she interjected. "It's—It's okay. I don't want that to deter me from the water. I love this water. I love swimming. The ocean. The creatures in it. I can't let what she did deter me from the things I have always loved and the things I have grown to call home. What home means to me is the only thing keeping me from drowning in this."

"What does home mean?"

Heart aching, she swallowed and met his gaze. "It means you," she whispered. "It means this place. Your home. It means my brother. Lex. Bala..."

"I'm part of what you call home?"

And her eyes narrowed at the disbelief in his voice.

"How could you possibly think you weren't?" she wondered aloud, gripping his hand.

"And my home... This place—You thought of this place?"

"Yes."

A forced exhale left him, and he closed his eyes. "Fuck, I need you to sprint," he muttered, voice straining. His gaze met the sky, and he swallowed, almost as though he were pushing the pain away from him. "We don't have to go under tonight if you don't want to," he finally said.

"No," she said, faster than she meant to. "No. I... I need to push myself past these things. I won't let my fear consume me."

Her gaze met his, and she could see the pain in his eyes. "Are you sure?"

"Positive."

He nodded and grasped her hands again. "Hold tight."

Darkness surrounded them.

As the water rushed over her again, she closed her eyes and tried to push away that drowning feeling in her lungs. Nadir swam forward, holding on to her hand. Shaking, but trusting him completely. Because she knew he wouldn't allow her to sink beneath any fear she might have. He would always pull her out of that void. And she would always take his hand.

They descended and swam far out, going past the end of the jetty. She couldn't see in front of her, but it didn't seem to bother Nadir. The ocean opened up just past, and all around her glowed the bright luminescence of life.

The reef looked like a turquoise moon beneath the ocean.

Nadir paused them, allowing her to hang in the depths, to stare a moment at the beauty she didn't know existed. Every memory of the year seemed to wash away at the sight of it. But as her lungs began to struggle, she squeezed his hand. He pulled himself level with her, cupping her cheek.

His lips pressed against her own, and as air from his lungs passed into hers, her entire body went limp, and she had to hold onto his waist to keep herself from floating upwards.

This.

This was different. This was life. The memory of happiness tugging at her heart.

Her lungs expanded, and he pulled back, apparently satisfied that she was okay, but his thumb remained on her cheek for a long enough moment that he had to press his lips to hers again, filling her with air once more.

And this time, when he pulled back, he tugged on her hands. "We go deeper," he told her.

She would have followed him into the water serpent's cavern had that been where he wanted to take her.

It wasn't long before she felt creatures around them, and her heart began to pound. She closed her eyes, allowing him to lead her, and she reached out—pushing her core to the point of her muscles straining. She wanted to feel them again, needing that connection with creatures she knew had never felt another being reaching out to them before. Schools of colorful fish swirled around them, the water rippling from their movements tickling her flesh.

Nadir looked back at her, a smile spreading over his face, and she knew he knew why they were acting as they were. She hardly noted the strain of her lungs, so filled with the warmth that was these creatures accepting her. Finally opening up without the fear of fire behind her eyes.

Her lungs were on the verge of collapse again when she felt his hands on her face. And she didn't bother opening her eyes as his lips pressed to hers, and his breath expanded her chest. She couldn't help her hands wrapping around his wrists, the silken liquid between them making his skin feel soft of forest moss. She could feel him holding back, the tenseness in his muscles, the rapid beat of his pulse beneath her fingertips...

Something big tugged at her.

And it wasn't his lips.

He released her again and grabbed her hand. But Nyssa couldn't fixate on him as she felt the creature pull her again.

"What's wrong?" he asked.

Nyssa met his gaze, and she pointed to her stomach, hoping he understood something was pulling at her.

But then she saw her.

The bright eyes of the water serpent pierced her own from the depths. The beast swam at them fast. Nyssa grabbed Nadir and pushed him behind her. And as the serpent grew closer, she started to smile.

Hello, beasty, she called out to her.

She was sure Nadir thought her crazy at her smiling at a beast fifty feet long, head bowed like a cobra, fangs gnashing at them. She almost laughed.

She turned back to Nadir and gestured to her chest before she moved closer to the serpent.

When his lips pressed to hers this time, it was almost mechanical, as though the sight of the serpent had pulled him out of whatever daze it was he'd been in before. When he pulled back, he squeezed her hand, and she noted the fear in his eyes. But she pressed her hand to his cheek and smiled once more before letting him go.

The serpent stayed steady before her, and Nyssa reached out a hand.

Beasty… you frighten even the great Commander, Nyssa bantered.

I like to keep him on his toes.

Nyssa's smile widened. *And the children? I heard you've been terrorizing them.*

I do not mean to, she promised. *I have always liked watching the children play. But there is something more dreadful than myself in these waters. I was only protecting them.*

Nyssa nodded with understanding. *I will convey the message. Thank you. And thank you for protecting me at the camp.*

The serpent's eyes closed slowly, and she bowed her head. Nyssa hesitantly reached out until her hand pressed to the beast's nose, and she felt its scales beneath her hand. Her chest swelled with its core pressing against hers. The comfort and willingness to protect her matching her own. And Nyssa knew then that the great beast would be there if she ever needed her.

Nyssa's lungs began to strain. The pair gave each other a bow upon parting, and then the serpent turned to swim back into the depths. Nyssa watched as she disappeared, staying suspended in that spot for as long as she could.

She turned to Nadir and pointed to the surface, head starting to lighten at the absence of air. Nadir nodded and grabbed her waist. "Hang tight," he told her.

One kick of his feet, and they shot to the surface.

An open-mouthed gasp met her upon her head bursting above the water. She kicked her legs, treading in the water, and pushed her hair back off her forehead.

She couldn't help the laughter on her lips.

The rush of the water serpent speaking with her. The sight of the glowing reef. The stars over their heads.

"Are you okay?" Nadir asked.

She pressed her hands into her face, wiping away the water. "I am," she smiled.

The stars above them twinkled down, and Nyssa sighed back into the water, allowing the back of her head to float atop it. She'd nearly forgotten the freedom of it wrapped around her, how she and Dorian once raced in the surf, had swimming competitions, or thought themselves mermaids as small children.

"I don't think I realized how at home you would be in the water," Nadir noted.

Her head picked back up. The water droplets on his skin shimmered against the glow of the reef from below. She watched his arms move back and forth as hers were doing.

"I practically grew up in the ocean," she said with a shrug. "Dorian and I used to jump from the cliffside into its depths. He had to push me the first time, I think. We'd seen Drae do it, so we knew we were okay, but... it was terrifying. I've always enjoyed the weightless, yet weighted, wrap of water," she admitted. "And the fish have always liked me."

Nadir was smiling softly at her when she met his eyes again.

"How far out is your birthplace?" she asked.

He pushed beside her and pointed a finger up at the sky. "Do you see that star there—the bright lilac and orange?"

She nodded.

"If you follow that direction a half mile out, there's a tiny barrier island, the only part of the reef that rises above the sea. It was there Lovi decreed we would be presented. Only he is connected to it, only he and the mers know when a child is born."

"Mers?" she repeated with a frown.

"You might know them as water shifters," he informed her.

"What—like the Bygon?"

His head tilted as he thought it out. "Sort of. Though they don't take a solid form, only made from the water itself."

"Can you communicate with them?"

Nadir shook his head. "Probably wouldn't want to either. They can be rather... *convincing*."

"They sound like the Bygon."

"Samar's manipulations might seem tame to these shifters. At least she has the decency to speak."

Her muscles were tiring, and she could feel her legs losing momentum. Before she realized what she was doing, she grabbed his arm to hold herself up.

"Getting tired?" he asked softly.

"I keep forgetting how weak I've become," she managed.

His arms wrapped around her waist, and he hauled her into his arms. "Rest. I've got you."

She allowed her arms and legs to stop moving as he held onto her, his own feet still kicking to keep them afloat.

"I know you do," she breathed.

He pushed the strands of hair back that had fallen over her eyes. "What if we stayed here?" he asked. "Watched the rest of the world go down in flames while we set up a new home beneath the water?"

"What— and you watch me grow old while you stay this immortally young being the rest of your days?"

And it hurt her heart to say it out loud.

"I could ask Lovi for mortality," he said.

"Sounds like a very poor move for a hero," she mocked. "Though the serpent might like the company. She said she likes keeping you on your toes."

"That explains a lot," he muttered, and she caught the smile on his lips.

His hand on her cheek, she memorized him, noting the cerulean glow of the reef pulsing up and reflecting into his eyes, brightening them and making her heart hurt at the sight.

"I think this reef likes you as the sunset likes me," she managed.

"What do you mean?"

"I mean... This ocean glow on your face and in your eyes. I don't think I realized how much more gorgeous you would be at your home place."

He stared, lips quirking just so, his hands tightening around her. "Did you just call me gorgeous?"

"Momentary lapse of judgment," she mocked.

"Too late now," he bantered. "You can't take it back. It's out there."

She shook her head, her stomach knotting at his banter. "Impossible, Commander. You know, I'm starting to think you brought me into this water just so you could kiss me."

Nadir chuckled under his breath, his head hanging low for a flash before meeting her eyes once more. "Maybe I did," he admitted. "Or maybe it's just air, Princess."

She wanted that air. She wanted him. Even though she had so much work to do, and things were clouding her head, she wanted him as she wanted to breathe. Feeling vulnerable and needing in his grasp. Her legs tightened as she straightened against him. She didn't know how to give him everything he wanted right now. She didn't know how to give him everything he deserved, at least while she was trying to grasp back into her reality.

But she could give him air if he wanted it.

Her nose nudged his, and she whispered, "Just air," before pressing her hands to his cheeks.

Nadir tensed as she leaned closer, but his fingertips dug into her back. Just as her lips brushed his—

He pulled them under the water.

She clung to him as they descended into the luminescence of the reef again. The water was shallower where they'd drifted, the bottom only fifteen feet down, and the brightness of the corals and water cascaded them in light.

His hands wrapped her cheeks, and his lips pressed to hers.

It wasn't just the air filling her lungs this time. It was air and desperation. Air and surrender. Air and *life*. Her tongue slipped into his mouth, and his arms clutched around her as he kissed her back. His thumb dragged along her cheek, the chill running down her spine with the tangle of his lips. The water held them in suspension, as though the weight of it surrendered to them and them alone.

Her lungs were full of air when he moved his lips, the brush of them planting against her jaw to her neck. His teeth dragging over her throat.

Without his concentration, the water pulled them back up. Her head bobbled over the surface, but she didn't dare let him go. He shifted her thighs higher on his chest, leaving himself beneath the water, but allowing her to stay above so she could breathe. The rake and suck of his mouth on her clothed breast made a moan escape her lips that she didn't have to hold back.

His hands hugged around her hips, grasping into her thighs. And then he tugged her beneath the water again.

She was at his mercy, and she allowed her body loose as he grasped her against him again, his mouth pressing to hers.

It was barely a breath, almost like a whisper, before her head was above the surface again. And this time, it wasn't his torso he guided her legs to wrap around. He sat her thighs on his shoulders, and his hands secured her spread legs around his head.

And then his tongue raked her.

Her entire body jerked in reaction to it, one of her hands clasping to her own thigh, the other to her chest, as he licked. Her mouth quivered at the flat of his tongue against her, slowly devouring her as though he were licking icing off the top of a pastry. Curse words emitted in her breath, her hips bucking against his mouth. And when his lips latched onto her clit and he sucked on her, her muscles limped into the ocean.

There was saltwater in her mouth, only the glow of the reef on her pleasured face any evidence that she was not alone.

Her heart nearly exploded at the rawness of his tongue combined with the air of his breathing against the sensitivity of her thighs. But he pulled back, making her whimper in his absence... until a spray of bubbles tickled her clit. Her body jerked at the surprise of it, hand in his hair, the other fastening atop his on her own thigh. She swore she felt him smile against her folds as he grasped her fingers in his, and he began to devour her once more.

Her hips bucked at the bubbles blown at her, moving against his mouth this time, allowing his tongue to sit on her as she rocked on him. But his hand gnashed at her backside, and she found herself staring open-mouthed at the stars as he bit her, followed by the suck of his mouth... harder, *unyielding*, as though he were sucking her body up as oxygen itself. She found herself tipping over bit by bit, thighs squeezing to the point she thought her muscles might break. Her eyes rolled at his tease. Just as she thought she was there, she felt them moving, and suddenly her entire body was above the water as he pushed his head to the surface, her legs still wrapped over his shoulders.

She almost glared at the smirk on his face.

He leaned forward, still looking at her, and his tongue licked up her slickness deliberately, causing her body to shudder, her bottom lip to sag.

"Do you want me to finish you like this?" he whispered, tongue flicking her clit. "Or—" his hand moved, fingers brushing over her thigh and backside before she felt his thumb press into her wetness. Her fingers creased in his hair as she let her head loll for a moment to savor the feeling of his fingers touching her once again.

"Or do you want this?" he asked, digit slowly moving in and out.

As much as she loved feeling his fingers again, what she wanted right then was to shatter herself around him. Feel his length inside her as she rode atop him.

"I want you inside me," she managed. "I want to sit on your cock and watch you come inside me."

His expression faltered, obviously not knowing she would choose a third choice. His lips pressed to her clit again, and he whispered, "Yes,

Princess," before taking her and pulling them back down beneath the water.

All the way to the bottom.

Every time he kissed her, he pushed air into her lungs. She fought against the weight of the water as she untied his pants and reached for his hardened length. He sat on his knees and wrapped her legs around his waist, and when he filled her, she kissed him hard.

Being with him beneath the ocean, surrounded by the glow of the reef, feeling her lungs reach capacity and having him fill her with both lust and life... She knew she would crave that feeling every day now. To be with him in his home place.

He held her hips as she rode him, up and down, feeling his cock hit that curved spot inside her with every sink of her hips. Watching him as the pleasure rode through him too, his eyes scrunching and fingertips digging into her. Until he kissed her hard and paused her hips in place. And then he railed into her.

Relentless. Quick. Her back hit the sand, and she was buried in the weightlessness as he fucked her. His lips on hers and giving her that air. Body reaching and reaching as his teeth bit her neck. Lungs beginning to struggle with those last strokes. Eyes seeing stars, she squeezed his arm. And this time, when he kissed her, the breath she took sent her spinning, and she convulsed around him. Nadir groaned as she came apart, and he came a few moments after.

She limped into the bliss of him as he hovered over her. She couldn't speak, couldn't think. There was only the pounding of her heart as she came down and the warmth of his arms around her. And when she finally opened her eyes, she melted at the dilation in his cerulean gaze. There was a soft smile on his lips as he glowed against the reef light before her.

How she had ever landed this gorgeous being before her, she still couldn't figure out. But there he was, staring and waiting on her to come to him... to cross that beach when she was ready.

He picked her up into his arms and shot them to the surface. They broke free, and she couldn't help but relax in his grasp. Catching her breath. He kissed her throat and her cheek and then whispered, "How many does this count as?"

If she hadn't been so exhausted, she would have laughed. But all she could manage was a smile and sigh. "I'll let you slide on this one. We'll count it against me instead."

His smile broadened. "This is definitely against you. I should get a free pass tomorrow."

The soft laugh of her own stilled between them, and he soon pressed his lips to her forehead again. Pulling back, his eyes darting over her as he held her cheek, she watched his lust-filled gaze soften.

"I'd better get you home."

Home.

The word hung in the air.

He liked saying it. He liked saying her name and home in the same sentence, almost like he was willing it into existence. It made her chest swell any time he would, her stomach knot at the confirmation of it.

She pushed her own hand to his cheek, and she nodded. His lips pressed once more to hers, both as a final kiss and breath of life.

He turned, allowing her to wrap her arms around his neck from behind, her legs around his hips, her chest flush against his back. His long fingers grasped her beneath her thighs before he said, "Hang tight, Princess," and then he throttled them through the depths.

65

Nyssa hardly went to sleep. Even with Nadir curled around her— his arm threaded through the space between her shoulder and neck, other wrapped around her waist— something felt heavy on her chest, and she couldn't figure out what it was. Almost an anxiety of needing to push herself. A hunger for determination. Perhaps it was that she wanted to get back to herself so desperately that she didn't want sleep to hinder her.

She rose before dawn and went down to the rocks, intent on having a quiet meditation to connect with the outside before everyone else woke. Nadir had woken and asked her if she was okay, but she assured him she was and that she just wanted a few moments to herself.

He hadn't argued and instead had simply asked her to take the new daggers he'd given her and said he would see her at breakfast. She pushed on a light dress she'd been brought the day before, strapping the blades to her thighs, and then she made her way out in the darkness. The cool of the spring morning wrapped around her with the surf wind, and she heard the last howls of the Ulfram as they relished their remaining two nights beneath the Dead Moons. She strode out to the end of the jetty, using the navy light as her guide, nearly stumbling a few times on the uneven rocks, but she kept herself together until she got to the very end of it.

There were three small rocks a few feet from the end of the jetty. Nyssa stepped into the cool water and walked through, her toes melting into the water as the rocks disappeared, and she grabbed onto the solitary three. Her dress soaking, but she didn't care. She pulled herself up in a struggle and nearly slipped on the slickness, but she held it long enough to get herself steady.

Her eyes closed as she sat, and she sighed in the morning salt air.

Focusing on her breathing as she walked through every torture. She counted the strikes of the whip on her back, feeling her skin tingle and her insides start to shake. Fear wrapping around her, but she held steady. Her eyes opened as she wiped away tears, and that was when she saw herself in the still of the reflecting water.

Red-eyed and gaunt-like, but hanging on. For the first time in a long time, she locked eyes with the girl in that reflection, and she whispered, "I'll bring you home."

A promise to merge the creature and person she'd become with the warrior she had once found.

She closed her eyes again and thought of the creature, the form. The amber eyes and shadowed figure beneath the cracks of fire. She didn't know how she was supposed to tame it and hold it from consuming her. She needed Dorian. She needed guidance. She needed—

A sudden wisp of wind billowed around her, followed by a cool gentle wrap. A mist tickled her flesh. She reached out her core, allowing that barrier to continue to stay down, intent on merging herself with whatever it was. There was something familiar about the warmth in her stomach, the chill that ran down her spine and caused her hair to stand on end. And when she finally opened her eyes, she nearly jumped out of her skin at the creature swooping over her.

The black phoenix.

Nyssa almost bolted to her feet as it landed at her back—

Sit.

Nyssa turned but remained seated on that rock. Her stomach dropped at its velvet purr. The curl of its black flames silhouetted in the rising sun.

What... Hi.

The phoenix seemed to laugh. She could feel her smile.

Hello, little Nyssari.

The sound of her voice reminded her of fog on the top of the ocean... smokey and honeyed. Melodic as a poem. As though the most serene of women were entrapped in such a beautiful creature.

What... What are you doing here?

I wanted to see how you were after escaping the void.

It was then she realized it was the Sun who had told her to let go.

You were with me.

The Sun nodded. **You will not be able to learn the control of this** *form on your own. It is too powerful. I can help.*

But you're the Sun. Why would you help me?

Because your mother has no idea what she's done to you. She's no idea the creature she's made you.

She wasn't sure what to say, The great tail curled up and wrapped around her then, feeling like a comforting blanket of warm shadow on her skin.

This is what my fire feels like.

Is it?

Nyssa nodded.

She could have sworn she saw a smile rise on the great beast's beak.

We start when the Eyes rise, Nyssari. Until then, work on your breathing. Find your voice. Train. I will see you soon.

"What's our plan?" Lex asked Nyssa as she joined her on the end of the jetty soon after the Sun left her.

"The Sun says she will help with my fire," she told her. "Nadir wants to help me with balance, spears, reading the language when we have time. I'm leaving the arrows and horseback obstacles to you. Hopefully, by the time the Sun comes back, I can move into training with his unit."

"His unit, huh?" Lex repeated, the obvious innuendo playing on her tongue. "You know, I thought I heard screams off the coast late last night..."

Nyssa almost threw a rock at her. "Not like that." But even as she said it, she felt a smile on her lips.

"Ooo... I know that look," Lex mocked. "Let's hear it, Princess. What tricks of the great Commander?"

"Bubbles."

The word left Nyssa's lips before she could stop it. She pushed to her feet and almost laughed at the look on Lex's face.

It was the first time she'd ever seen Lex speechless.

Lex blinked like she was coming back into reality. "Sorry, did I hear you say what I think you did?"

"Yes," Nyssa confirmed. "Bubbles."

Startled brows arched high on Lex's face, and she started to gesture what she was thinking with her hands. "As in... He—"

"Yes."

"Out there—"

"Yes."

"Under the—"

"Oh yeah."

"Fucking Infi, Princess," Lex finally determined. The slow grin spread on her face again, and she took Nyssa's outstretched hand. "Guess that water breathing is good for more than just swimming," she added with a wink.

Nyssa bit her lips together, pulling Lex to her feet, and she remembered Nadir's head between her legs, the weight of the water around them. "Means nothing," she said in a breath. "I—"

The sight of people running made Nyssa's words stop in her throat. She paused as Lex brushed her pants off.

"What is happening?"

People were crowding around the trail from the Forest. She couldn't make out who it was.

Until the sight of shaggy black hair made her stomach drop.

Nyssa pulled the dagger from her thigh and began cutting her wet dress.

"What are you doing?" Lex asked. "What's happening? Can you see anything?"

"I can't run in a long wet dress," Nyssa said, heartbeat pounding in her ears. She ripped the fabric, almost too short, but she didn't care.

"And that's my brother."

Whatever Lex said, Nyssa didn't hear. Her feet were moving of their own accord, her eyes never leaving the tall male coming up through the throng of people. She couldn't feel her own body. Already shaking at the possibility that it was him.

The next thing she knew, her feet were in the sand.

"Dorian!" she shouted without realizing it.

His head popped up in her direction, and she watched as his entire body stiffened.

"Nys?" he called out, his feet apparently moving on their own as hers were.

"Dorian!"

Nyssa ran.

"Nyssa!"

She'd never run so quickly in her life. Tears were already streaming down her face as every inch of her began to break.

But as they reached each other, they both skidded to a halt. They landed just feet apart, crouched, and the same fear stretched on both their faces.

Ash and flames rose on their hands, and they mirrored one another in fighting stances.

"Prove you're my brother—"

"Tell me something we shared—"

Their words came out at the same time, and Nyssa's heart broke.

But Dorian had seen the ashen fingers on her right hand, and he started to relax his stature. "Wait—"

"No," she cut in, wary even of seeing the form in his hands. "Answer the question."

"But your hands—"

"Answer the fucking question," she almost shouted.

A slow grin lit up Dorian's face, lips trembling. "It *is* you," he choked. His hands pressed to his hips, and she could see him fighting tears as he looked up to the sky. "Ugh—*fuck*—okay, you... you tried to jump out of my window like Drae when we were five," he said fast.

Nyssa wavered on the spot. "Dorian?"

She started forward, but he shook his head and held up a hand. "I know it's you, but I want to hear what you were going to say," he strained, and she could see the playful delight in his eyes.

Every word she spoke stuck in her throat, her voice quivering. "The first time you used your form, you caught your bed on fire, and we had to throw the mattress out the window."

Her tone went high-pitched by the end of the sentence, and by the time their smiles met again, she couldn't hold in her sobs.

Dorian smiled crookedly, a tear stretching down his cheek. "Seems to me we should have let it go up in flames that day."

Her chest caved at his banter, and she choked on her laugh.

"Dorian..."

Dorian's jaw clenched, his chest visibly swelling. "Hey, sis."

They ran.

Bounding into one another in such a hug that he ended up pulling her off the ground and into a whirl. A whirl in the soft sand that caught his feet, and the pair went tumbling down. She couldn't help her laughing tears, the feeling of him back with her as a bond that had been missing from her for weeks.

Her favorite person and best friend. Her brother that had been there for her through everything.

She hadn't realized seeing him again would ache so much.

He finally pulled back, his hands pressing to her cheeks, and he kissed her forehead hard. "Dammit, you're a beautiful sight to see!" he declared.

Her nose scrunched with her laugh, and she pressed her hands to his cheeks as well. "As are you," she laughed. "Except for this thing," she said, fingers tracing the stubble on his jaw. "You need to get rid of this. It's... *No. You can't see your adorably horrifying face. And what is this scar? It nearly got your eye. What—"*

Dorian laughed, and her entire body sighed at the sound of it. The sight of seeing him in front of her, alive. It may have only been a little more than a cycle since they'd been with one another, but it had felt like a lifetime. So much had happened. She was embarrassed to admit any of it, but one look at his face, and she wanted to know everything.

Nyssa threw her arms around him again.

"I missed you," he whispered in her hair.

"I missed you too."

"Dammit, I—" He pulled back, eyes swollen with tears, and he held her face. "There were so many times I tried to reach you, and I couldn't. I needed you. I—" he paused, and a stretch of worry faltered the smile that had been on his face.

"What happened?" he breathed.

"I'm fine," she assured him. "Alive. And I'm fine. You're here. That's all that matters."

He sighed, shaking his head, but he hugged her again nonetheless.

She noted the swell in his shoulders as he held her then, so much so that she poked at his growing muscles and grinned upon moving out of his grasp. "What is this?" she mocked. "Have the Blackhands been working you overtime? Who knew my brother would finally be filling out this form."

He chuckled, head hanging slightly, but he didn't comment about it.

And this made her balk.

"What—no comeback for that?" she asked.

A sheepish smile met her own, and her chest swelled.

"Fucking Architects, who are you, and what have you done with my brother?" she mocked. "Should I need to ask you another question? Are you an Infi?"

He relaxed in the sand beside her and began to toy with the sleeve of her tunic, nervous energy pouring off him.

"I just have so much to tell you," and she noted the pleading tone in his voice.

Something was wrong, and it broke her heart to see him so visibly confused, turmoil battling beneath the surface of his calm facade.

She squeezed his hand. "Okay."

Another tear streaked down his face, and she smiled as she wiped it away.

"Oh, look at that," came Lex's voice behind them. "I wondered when you'd find your way here."

The grin spread on Dorian's face, and he rose to his feet. "Hey, Lex."

His arms threw around her, and she hugged him back. She joked with him about the size of his shoulders then, giving his bicep a squeeze as she pushed his chest.

And then she ruffled his hair.

Nyssa's hand clapped over her mouth, tears in her eyes again, and she watched Dorian's strong shoulders cave. Watched as his smiling face visibly broke.

He fell to his knees, and his head buried in his hands.

Lex met Nyssa's eyes, and Nyssa felt her jaw tremble as she said, "You ruffled his hair like she used to."

Lex visibly bit back tears, and she cursed the sky. Nyssa crawled to his side and wrapped her arms around him from behind.

Dorian fell against her, tears streaming from his face, and he sank into her arms, knees curling and hands wrapping. Nyssa fought her own tears, unsure of what was happening, and she met Lex's gaze.

"Can you tell our Commander we have a guest?" she managed, trying to keep herself together.

Lex nodded. She pointed towards the house, eyes narrowing as though asking her if she wanted help to get him there, but Nyssa shook her head. As Lex left them, Nyssa reached to her brother's face and pulled him to look at her.

"Come on," she whispered. "Nadir has a kettle, and surprisingly I know how to use it to make tea." She hoped it would make him smile, and he gripped her a little tighter.

"That I would like to see."
The familiar banter made her heart ache.

Dorian watched his sister as she heated water in the kettle with a touch of her hand. Eyes narrowing at the familiar ash on her fingers just as he had on his. But he didn't ask about it at first. He noted how tiny she was. The protrusion of her collarbones. The cut on her face. The broken forearm wrapped in a sling.

But she moved as though none of it bothered her, and he found himself envious of the easy way she seemed to be feeling despite the apparent tortures she'd gone through.

She poured the water into a cup, the tea leaves in a mesh trinket he'd never seen before. She dipped it in the water, and he took the cup with a sideways stare at her.

"How long have you had fire?" he chose to ask.

She pushed herself onto the countertop opposite him, sitting on a stool. "It doesn't surprise you," she noted.

"I saw you," he told her. "I saw your eyes."

"I saw you too." She shifted her weight on the counter, curling her feet beneath her. "I've hardly mastered more than heating one hand. It's just so new. Honestly, terrifying. I keep thinking if I let it move to more than my fingertips, I fall beneath the weight of it and get trapped in that void again. Leave the creature in control of my body. I'm not sure how you mastered yours so quickly."

"Maybe it comes different for me since it's normal for sons of Arbina. With yours, I imagine it is not instinct."

"Maybe," she considered.

Dorian stared at his drink, softly swirling the mesh trinket as the tea steeped. Seeing her again didn't feel real.

"Are you going to be contemplative all evening, or are you going to spill what's on your mind?" she asked.

Dorian smiled up at her. "I'm not sure where to start."

"How about the beginning?" she suggested. "When we separated at the Forest."

He swirled his tea again, and then he took a long sip.

His story came from his lips as though he were writing it. Nyssa interrupted him when he brought up meeting Reverie, asking him about her and wondering what kind of Dreamer could put him on his back, not just with sex.

She paused him again with questions about Dahrkenhill and the Blackhands. He told her about the trials, what happened between them with both Corbin and Reverie, to which Nyssa had paused him once more.

"Wait—" she cut in. "Do you like both of them?"

Dorian gawked at her. "I tell you I nearly died combating great beasts, including the Ghost of Fire, and your questions are about my love life?"

"I have plenty of questions about your battles, but we can circle back to them once Nadir is in the room," she said quickly, shifting on her seat as she eagerly leaned closer to him. "It's just you and I. So yes, my questions are about your love life. Now tell me, do you like both of them?"

Dorian almost smiled, but the thought of Reverie and Corbin made heat rise up from his chest to his neck. He ran his hands through his hair, now avoiding her eyes and playing it off—poorly. He'd come no closer to figuring out how he felt for the pair, especially after everything that had happened at the Bryn.

Nyssa gasped. *Fucking Architects*—you do!"

Dorian threw his napkin at her. "Shut up," he grunted.

A laugh escaped her lips. A laugh that made him look up at her. A laugh that stretched the smile across her face and reminded him of the sister he loved and missed so much. It made his stomach knot, and he took another sip of his tea.

"You look so stressed about it," she noted. "What's wrong with liking both? They're not asking you to choose, are they?"

"No," he said quickly. "No, they're not asking. They're... they're quite comfortable with each other. But..."

His cheeks heated at the memory of Corbin taking him... How he'd felt when it happened, even though he knew Reverie had seen them, and how she'd cuddled with him after. How he'd laid between them for three nights. Feeling his failures and allowing them to help ease the pain.

"Hey—" Nyssa reached for him, squeezing his shoulder. "What's wrong?"

Dorian glanced up at her, swallowing hard, and he fumbled with the cup. "I just... I don't think I ever expected..." He was stammering, and he paused to collect his thoughts before looking up at her.

"Corbin... I let him..." A brow raised, and Nyssa's hands clapped over her mouth again.

"Dorian, you didn't..."

"I did," he admitted.

"What—you let him—" She made a gesture with her hand, and Dorian nodded. Nyssa's eyes widened. "Where was Reverie?" she wondered.

"Asleep. But apparently, she woke up and watched it happen. And then she kissed us both after."

She gasped again, and Dorian ran his hands through his hair, letting the memory consume him. He knew Nyssa would know how big of a step this was for him and what it meant that it had happened.

"Did you like it?" she dared to ask.

"I don't know, that's the point," he said defeatedly. "I think I did, and I know that I wouldn't want that from anyone but him. But..." Dorian stood from the chair and rubbed his hands over his face. "And *her*... Fucking *her*." His hands pressed to his hips as he turned in a circle, the memory of Reverie and all the things she made him feel consuming him. "She makes me crazy. She's beautiful, commanding, intelligent—"

"Threatens you with a knife," Nyssa grinned.

"Threatens me with a knife, *yes*," he said, surrendering onto the back of the couch.

He could feel his face reddening, and Nyssa had seen it before he could hide it.

"*Architects*, are you blushing again?"

He glared poorly at her as she hopped off the counter.

"You are—" She smiled again, shoving his chest mockingly. Dorian wavered off-balance, letting her make fun of him and relishing that banter that he'd missed so much.

"Shut up," he muttered, and yet loving every second of it.

Nyssa walked around to the couch and sat on her knees, leaning over the back to still see him. "Have you had both of them yet?"

Dorian eyed her. "You're certainly eager."

"My brother is in love with two people who apparently also love him. Yes, I am eager. This is amazing."

"I actually haven't had her yet."

"You haven't slept with her yet, and you think you're in love with her?"

Dorian paused a moment, obviously contemplating it in his head. "I don't know," he admitted. "I know that I want her. And I want to protect her as much as she wants to protect me. I know I like talking to her. I like hearing her call me out on my bullshit... And when I'm with both of them, it just... It feels... Complete," he admitted.

"What about Corbin? How does he make you feel?"

Dorian shrugged. "Safe," he admitted. "But it's not like I want to hold him like I want to do with her. And I don't exactly want him cuddling me either."

But as he thought about it, and the nights they'd spent sleeping together as one at the Bryn, Dorian realized maybe he did like it.

"Or... Maybe I do—" He groaned and pushed his hands over his face in frustration. "Why is this so hard for me?" he wondered aloud. "I love having the company of two people. Why is this different?"

Nyssa smiled at him. "Because you actually feel something for them," she said simply. "Dorian, there's nothing wrong with exploring all of this. What's the problem? It sounds like they like each other too."

"Because I want what you and Nadir have," he sighed. "And don't try to tell me that's not going on because you're glowing despite the bruises I can see all over you." He eyed her, and Nyssa didn't argue.

Heat rose on her cheeks, and he envied her.

"*See*—I want that. I want that begging and promising not to leave one another love. To keep them safe no matter what. The kind of love that shatters the world in its wake."

"I have never seen you blush this much in my life," she argued. "How do you know you don't have that?"

"I don't... I don't know how it should feel."

"You think our sister felt that for Draven immediately after she was injured in his realm?" she asked. "Most of the time, love doesn't just fall in your lap. You have to put in the time with someone you enjoy company with."

"It did for you."

"That's because together, Nadir and I are the most hopeless romantics you'll ever meet," she said, smiling at the ground. "*Fuck*, you should hear some of the things we say to one another. It's... It's so cheesy."

"You love it," he teased.

"I really do," she surrendered, eyes glazing over. "But, this isn't about me. This is about you. Why don't you explore all this? Let it happen. Just because the earth isn't shattering right now doesn't mean it won't later. And can I be honest with you?"

"Please," he begged.

"I don't think you would be this confused if he meant nothing to you."

Dorian swallowed the lump in his throat. Nyssa squeezed his hand.

"Thank you," he whispered, and his sister tensed.

As though hearing the words come from his lips had suddenly made her forget how to articulate thoughts.

"Wow," she said, brows elevating in disbelief. "Wow, you... you do really like both of them," she seemed to realize.

Dorian looked at the ground again, letting that realization settle within him as well, his heart knotting and fleeing all at once. Until his lashes lifted to hers, and he gave her a small smile.

"Yeah," he whispered.

Nyssa sat up and wrapped her arms around him. Dorian gave in to the hug, feeling emotion in his chest as he held his sister. His best friend. After a moment, Nyssa pulled back, and Dorian didn't know a tear had fallen until she wiped it from his cheek. A silver glisten rested in her eyes too, and she sniffed back her emotion with an audible gasp.

"Oh, fuck," she managed, pushing her own tears off her cheeks. "Leave it to you to make me cry for the ten-thousandth time this cycle," she grunted. She sat back on the couch and smiled at him. "I cannot wait to meet this girl," she said eagerly. "And to have a long talk with dear Corbin. Confusing my brother with such taunts. So rude."

Dorian almost laughed at the banter coming from her lips. He sighed himself back over the couch, lying down opposite her and throwing his feet in her lap.

"You seem okay," he noted. "Despite whatever it is that obviously happened."

"You didn't finish telling me what happened to you."

"I'm tired of talking. It's your turn."

He could see the nervousness on her features, and his eyes squinted. "Nys?" he said. "What happened? People told me you were kidnapped."

She met his eyes, and his heart stilled at the confirmation of her gaze.

Dorian sat up.

"I need you to promise me something before I tell you a word of it," she said.

"What?"

"Promise me you won't blame Lex or Nadir," she said firmly. "Or Bala. They saved me, and I need you to remember that. What happened to me was needed... We are in a stronger position in this war because of it. What I had to go through was a means to an end—"

Dorian snapped up to a seated position. "Nyssa, what the fuck happened?"

"Dorian, promise me," she demanded.

He ran both hands through his hair and glared at her. "Fine. I promise."

She eyed him, but the sigh that came from her lips told him she was trusting him.

"I ran away—"

"Of course you fucking did," he grunted.

"—I was kidnapped by the Venari rebels—"

Breath ceased.

"It was the Venari?"

"—Taken to one of Man's camps by Infi—"

This was not happening.

"—Turned into a prize for the Prince. But—" She held a finger up "—I got to see them and learn about their people. I also went to their new castle and saw what armies they have—"

Dorian was on his feet. "I'm going to kill him."

Nyssa launched herself out of the couch and grabbed his arm, whirling him around to face her. "If you go anywhere near him with whatever misplaced rage this is, you'll be showing me how much you distrust me," she almost yelled.

Dorian paused.

"What happened to me was my own design," she continued. "Yes, I was kidnapped, but I could have gotten myself out of there at any time, and you know it. I stayed for information so we would know what we are up against in this war. Nadir found me, and it took everything in him to let me do what I needed to do. Of all people, I thought you would understand this."

It hurt him to know that she was right. To know that he knew his sister well enough that he'd actually expected this to happen.

"Can I hit him just the once?" he begged.

Nyssa looked like she would smile. "Bala has already beaten him when she found out. And no, you cannot hit him."

"How about a playful slap or shove?"

"Nothing about a slap from you is playful," she countered.

The door opened then, and Dorian forgot all that he had been saying to her.

Because Nadir appeared in the doorway, and his face paled at the sight of Dorian standing there.

"Ah... Hey, Prince," he said hesitantly, the difference in how Nadir had once greeted and laughed with him at Magnice stark in comparison to his greeting then.

"You... You're alive," he noted. "And filling out—" he said as he pointed to Dorian's shoulders, obviously nervous as he pushed his weight from foot to foot. "Does Hagen have you pushing those fucking boulders? I bet he does, doesn't he? He likes those things."

Nyssa snorted.

Dorian eyed Nadir, almost waiting on him to continue talking, but Nadir was rubbing his neck with both hands, and he knew his nerves had him ready for anything Dorian might do.

"You'll be happy to know my sister has forbidden me from killing you," Dorian said. "Apparently, she likes you too much."

The nervousness visibly waned from Nadir's shoulders, and his body relaxed. He sank his hands to his knees, head hanging. "Thank the Architects," he muttered.

Dorian smiled smugly. "Bring it in, Commander," he said, arms opening.

Nadir straightened and eyed the Prince. "I wasn't aware we were on hugging terms," he replied as he slowly crossed the space.

"You're fucking my sister," Dorian said shortly. "Practically family."

"Dorian, if every person you and I have slept with is now family, we may as well hug the entire kingdom," Nyssa said behind him.

"I think I'd rather you punch me," Nadir noted.

"I agree."

Dorian's fist railed into Nadir's face.

Nyssa screamed, and Nadir hit the floor. Dorian cursed the pain in his hand and shook it out as Nyssa shoved him to run to Nadir.

"Fuck, Commander," Dorian grunted. "Didn't realize your face was made of iron. That's going to bruise."

But Nadir was laughing when Nyssa reached him. She spewed words at him that Dorian didn't catch, her hands pressing to his cheeks. Dorian eyed the Commander on the ground. Nadir touched his thumb to his bleeding lip, and then he grinned up at Dorian.

"The bastard does have you throwing boulders, doesn't he?" Nadir asked.

Dorian returned the grin, and he reached for Nadir's hand to pull him off the ground. They embraced each other as friends this time and clapped one another on the back.

"I hate both of you," Nyssa grunted.

66

Nadir didn't stay with the pair long. He came only to check in. Having heard the Prince was at his home, he wanted to make sure it was true and that Nyssa was okay. He told them both they could join for lunch but left Nyssa with a kiss on her cheek.

Dorian eyed his sister as Nadir left. "What's happening? Why is he not all over you now that you're back?" he asked in confusion.

"He's giving me space to find myself again," she replied.

"Oh fuck all, Nys," he grunted. "You obviously love him. Pretty obvious he feels the same. What's the problem?"

"Look at me," she said, heart aching as she said it. "Between that and the new form... My needing to figure all this out... I just don't know that I can do it all and give him all of me as he deserves. I want to at least be able to control this form before I allow myself that spark of happiness."

Dorian considered her, arms wrapped around his chest. "Okay, come on." He grabbed her hand and pulled her to the door.

"What—Dorian—where are we going?"

"I'm going to help you control your form."

"Wait—"

But Dorian didn't listen. And he dragged her out of the house and onto the beach before she could protest.

The wind whipped Nyssa's hair around her head. Dorian ripped a piece of fabric off his shirt and handed it to her without her needing to ask. She used it to tie her hair up.

"Set up."

"Why do I need to set up?"

"Humor me."

And she almost laughed at the plea in his voice.

She set her legs, mirroring him. "This is a terrible idea."

"It's us," he shrugged. "When are our ideas not terrible?"

She met his grin, and it made her chest hurt. "I missed you."

His grin widened. "I missed you too, sis." He held his hands up, and she did as he. "Reach in and let it on your fingers like you did earlier."

"Both hands?" she asked shakily.

He nodded.

"I... I can't do that. I can do one hand. Not both. The void—"

"One."

And the word made her breath even.

Her eyes found his, watching his breathing as she allowed that form on her fingertips. Feeling her core tug and spiral. As though she had awakened the creature.

The world vibrated, and Nyssa panicked.

"Dorian—"

He was before her in a flash, hands pressed against hers as he held her steady. "Two," he said sternly.

Shaking, Nyssa opened her eyes again. She held to him, concentrating on just allowing that form bit by bit. Her fingertips turned ash, the black trickling down her fingers.

"*You* control your form," he told her. "It doesn't control you. It will try to protect you when threatened, but you have to give it boundaries. Right now, it is having a free for all inside you. Let it know you are in charge."

"How do I do that?"

"Close your eyes—"

And she did.

"—Feel it moving inside your core. Volatile, right?"

She nodded.

"Let it come up."

Her eyes flickered back open. "Let it up? Like to the surface?"

"Just behind your eyes."

Heart throbbing, she shifted her weight and closed her eyes again. She thought of the creature in the mirror. The glowing amber eyes and the black streaks.

"That form is a part of you," he continued. "You control it, but you also have to realize it is a part of who you are. Respect it, and it will respect you."

"How did you learn all this when we were marked before Rhaif?"

she wondered without opening her eyes.

Dorian was silent a brief moment, and then, "Our mother."

Nyssa almost frowned. "What? Arbina?"

A flicker of navy flames pulsed to life and moved over his blackened hand like a velvet glove. "I think she used me as a pawn," he said softly. "Those times when I trained with her, she always did it when he was near. She did it to taunt him, and I was such a child, I didn't know any better. I showed off before him, thinking it was what I was supposed to do to earn his love. I wanted to be his friend, but she made sure that never happened." He blew out a hard breath and gave her a wry smile. "Enough about that bitch. Let's get your fire under control so you can fuck your Commander tonight."

She almost rolled her eyes but set up as he instructed her again.

Bala settled on the porch, arms crossed over her chest as she leaned against the pole by the steps. The sight of Dorian and Nyssa laughing together on the beach and him trying to help her with her fire made her heart swell.

"There you are," came Lex's voice as she approached. "I thought I saw a few Venari walking around here."

Bala only gave her a small smile, too entranced by the sight of Nyssa and Dorian being their usual selves once more.

Lex walked deliberately up the steps, towel behind her neck as she wiped the sweat. "What?"

Bala gave an upwards nod to the pair on the beach, and Lex paused to look over her shoulder.

"This was all you, wasn't it?" Lex asked.

Bala chuckled under her breath. "I don't know what you mean," she lied.

"Yeah, you do," Lex teased as she reached the top step. "Did it work out like you thought it would?"

"Better," Bala admitted.

Lex paused to give her a kiss, lips lingering and making Bala's already aching heart flutter. Holding her chin between her fingers, she nudged her nose, and the pair smiled briskly.

"Does he know you're here?" Lex asked as she then moved towards the door.

Bala shifted off the post. "Not yet," she replied. "They've been so consumed with each other, they didn't notice us coming in. We met Nadir on the way. He's showing Corbin and Reverie around. I wanted a few minutes alone with the twins."

"Who is Reverie?"

Bala's eyes narrowed, but then she remembered Lex had yet to meet the Dreamer, and a grand smile spread on her lips. "Oh, you haven't met her yet," she grinned.

"Who is she?"

"You'll like her," Bala said, arms wrapping around her chest. "She's been keeping our Prince in line. He's named her Commander of the army he's not yet acquired."

"Commander?" Lex balked. "A Blackhand?"

"Dreamer," Bala countered.

Lex's features morphed from surprise to curiosity, and she smiled crookedly. "This I should like to see."

Bala laughed. "They're at the market," she told her. "If you want to meet her or—actually can you grab them and bring them here? I want to speak with these two first, but we all need to meet together. Regroup. I have another company coming in with someone I need in that meeting as well, but I'll find them once I finish with Dorian and Nyssa."

"Yes, my King," Lex winked.

Bala shook her head and turned back to the siblings. She noted the scar on Dorian's face as he and Nyssa threw water at each other at the edge of the surf. Lex came to stand beside her.

"Is it bad that I really like that new scar on him?" Bala asked.

Lex settled beside her, a coy smile on her lips. "I've been thinking the same thing," she admitted. She leaned in and gave Bala's cheek a kiss, to which Bala shook her head and pushed her off.

"I'm surrounded by romantics everywhere," she muttered playfully as she started down the steps. "First Draven. Then Nadir and Nyssa. Now you."

"I'll have the ropes ready for you later then," Lex called down.

"I'd prefer the flogger," she called back.

One glance over her shoulder, and Lex grinned coyly at her. But she wrapped that towel around her neck and sauntered inside the house.

Nyssa was the first to catch sight of Bala when she hit the sand.

"Venari King," she drawled, eyeing Bala sideways.

"Promised..." She started to say Princess, but the word didn't exactly fit anymore. "I'll have to find something else to call you. Because neither of you are Promised Prince or Princess any longer."

"How about just Nyssa and Dorian?" Dorian suggested, his arm wrapping over Nyssa's shoulders.

Bala smiled between them. "I like that."

Dorian glanced behind her towards the village. "Did you bring my guard?" he asked.

"Both of them," she replied. "I have to say, I'm not entirely sure how you weren't murdered by the Dreamer. But she seems to be quite fond of you."

An elongated coo came from Nyssa's lips, and Dorian shoved her. "Fuck off," he grunted. But Nyssa laughed.

"I can't wait to meet her," Nyssa said. "But that's later. Bala looks like she has jobs for us."

Bala scoffed, unable to keep the smile from her lips as she admired her friends finally bantering again with one another. "No jobs. But I do have a meeting planned for when everyone gets here."

"What kind of meeting?" Nyssa asked.

"There's someone else I need on our side," Bala said. "And I need everyone to be on the same page as far as these Scrolls and what's next for us."

"Yes, my King," Dorian winked at her.

Nyssa hadn't replied. She seemed to be fixated on the village, and with one look around, Bala realized why.

Reverie and Corbin were crossing the sand.

Bala gave an upwards nod to Dorian, alerting him, and his entire body visibly relaxed at the sight of them.

"Fuck me," Nyssa muttered. "That's a sight."

The grin on Dorian's face made an involuntary smile rise higher on Nyssa's lips. He was staring at the pair coming towards them with a delight and dilation in his pupils that Nyssa had seen on her own face when Nadir would walk into a room.

Corbin was as handsome as he'd ever been. He, too, looked as though his shoulders had broadened. She couldn't help the deliberate once over she gave him. Golden light dancing on his dark brown skin and every crease of his muscles. Snug white tunic standing out and billowing in the wind. His hair was a mess, though. The twists were grown out and fuzzy. But he smiled at her briefly, cracking his knuckles as he walked, and then he avoided her gaze shyly. Obviously suppressing a smile.

And then there was *her*.

She was *gorgeous*.

Also, the first person she'd ever met that was shorter than her. No more than a couple inches shorter, but still.

Nyssa found herself envious of this girl's curves. Her voluptuous hips and wide thighs. Full breasts for her petite figure. Her bangs framed her delicate features and her long neck. Sunlight glared off the stark silver-white and lavender strands. Knives strapped to those thick thighs and on the corset around her middle.

No wonder Dorian was falling for both of them.

"You did not tell me she was this pretty," Nyssa muttered.

Dorian frowned down at her. "Did I not?"

"You had a lot of other adjectives, but all of them fall short of... Well, *her*." She shifted on her feet. "Damn, no wonder you like both of them. I like both of them."

"I'm not sharing her," he informed her. "Not entirely sure I want to share him. Except with her. And then sharing her with him..." Dorian cleared his throat to stop his stammering, and he pushed his arms around his chest. "Can I ask you a favor?" he said to her.

"What?"

"Can you not completely embarrass me?" he asked, scratching his neck.

Nyssa had to bite her lips together at the plea on his features. "Oh, that's adorable. I'm definitely embarrassing you now."

"*Come on!*"

"No, it's happening. I can't wait to tell her every story I have. Corbin too."

"But—" he turned into her as they got closer. "We've decided I actually really like them. Can we keep this—you know—"

Nyssa smiled up at her brother, amused that he was fumbling and serious about a relationship for once. "Fine. I'll not tell them everything. Though I believe Corbin knows most of your secrets already."

"Damn, Dorian," Lex mumbled as she joined them from the shack. "I hope you're enjoying both of them. I'd hate to have to take advantage if you aren't."

Heat rose on his cheeks, and he scratched his neck. Nyssa exchanged an amused glance with Lex, and she grinned.

"Know that look," Lex mocked. "Enjoying *and* falling. I love it."

But Dorian ignored them, and he left the group to greet his guard before reaching them. Smiles beaming on their faces, they each pulled him close into hugs. His hands settled on Corbin's face a moment as he kissed his cheek, and when he turned to Reverie, he hugged her, said something in her ear before also kissing her cheek, and she shoved him playfully. Corbin spoke, and Dorian wavered off balance as he laughed at the pair.

Nyssa nearly started crying.

Emotion burning at her nose as she watched her brother truly smiling at someone other than his family. To look between two people who apparently cared for him as much as he cared for them. Who had taken care of him and pulled him from the darkness of his grief.

She thought she'd been about to lose it when he talked to her about it earlier.

But actually seeing it…

Nyssa blinked and wiped her face, turning so that their new friends wouldn't see the tears on her cheeks.

"Fuck," Lex managed in a breath, and Nyssa looked up to see her doing the same thing.

Just as the pair straightened, the three approached, and Reverie looked between them.

"I feel like I'm walking into the Ulfram den right now," she said, playful brow lifting at Dorian. "You're all terrifyingly beautiful."

Nyssa couldn't help herself.

She hugged her.

Reverie tensed at the embrace and patted Nyssa's back, almost mechanically, as though she wasn't sure what to do with herself. Until Nyssa spoke.

"Thank you," she said into the woman's hair. "Thank you for looking after him."

Reverie finally hugged her back and relaxed. "It wasn't easy," she said.

Nyssa sniffed as she pulled back, the tears freely falling down her cheeks by then. "I can only imagine," she joked, choking on her sobs. She turned to Corbin just as Lex pulled away from hugging her cohort, and Nyssa wrapped her arms around him.

"You too," she said as he hugged her tight. "Thank you for not leaving him."

Corbin's deep chuckle vibrated her. "I could never," he admitted.

Nyssa wiped her face harshly and stood before them again. Dorian stared at her in confusion, head tilting, but he didn't speak.

Reverie looked up at Dorian, arms crossed over her chest, crooked smile toying on her lips. He caught the look she was giving him and nudged her. She rolled her eyes and pushed him back.

"Architects, you're all fucking adorable," Lex grunted.

"It's Lex, right?" Reverie asked, turning her attention to the Second Sun.

"Reverie?" Lex said with an upwards nod. "You'll tell me later how you ended up with this one. And how you've helped Bin here keep him safe."

"Why do you assume I needed keeping safe?" Dorian asked.

Nyssa and Bala snorted, Nyssa clapping her hand over her mouth. But Lex just eyed him.

"Dammit, I missed you," she uttered.

As Nyssa collected herself, Reverie turned to her. "Nyssa?" she asked, and Nyssa was once more mesmerized by the lavender of this woman's eyes. "Finally. He's been worried sick about you," she said in a breath. "I'm—"

"Fucking gorgeous," Nyssa heard herself say without realizing it. "Shit. Sorry. I mean... Dorian's told me who you are. Not sorry that you aren't gorgeous. Because you are. Sorry that I cut you off. And you're gorgeous too, Corbin," she added quickly. "I don't want you to think I only think she's pretty because you're pretty too. I—" Nyssa pushed out a solid breath and shut her eyes to stop herself from continuing to blunder.

"Hi," Nyssa finally straightened herself out.

Reverie looked as though she would laugh, but she just smiled up at Dorian again. "I see stammering also runs in the family."

"A lot of things run in the family," Lex muttered. "You get used to it."

It was Corbin's turn to laugh, and he bent over, holding onto Dorian's shoulder as the hearty chuckles left him. Reverie shook her head, a quiet snicker coming from her as well.

"You should all have that tattooed somewhere," she mocked. "Or perhaps matching shirts with it embroidered."

"If we're all done catching up," Bala interjected then. "I think I see my other company coming in. I need everyone at the big tent in fifteen minutes."

"Using her King voice on us," Dorian grinned. "Though I have missed watching my sister make people feel inadequate at such meetings. Actually looking forward to this."

"You should have seen her the other day," Lex said under her breath.

"Fifteen minutes," Bala called as she started walking away from them.

Nyssa searched the shores. "I have to find Nadir."

"He was helping set up the tent," Reverie informed her. "Said he would go change before heading back down for Bala's meeting."

"I'll make sure everything is ready," Nyssa said.

"I'll come with," said Lex.

The pair left Dorian and his guards to make for the meeting tent, chatting mindlessly about what they'd done that morning since their original plan had been sidelined with the incoming of Dorian. More Venari had come into the village and were talking to friends.

But the sight of two that had accompanied the Venari rebels made Nyssa stop walking.

"Did Bala say who the other person was she wanted at the meeting?" she asked without looking away from the rebels.

"She didn't," Lex replied. "Why?"

"Because those are two of the ones that kidnapped me."

Nyssa marched to the tent, her breath shortening as she trudged through the dense sand up and over the dunes. And when she reached it, she whipped the flap back.

Color drained from Nyssa's face at the sight of the tall man standing at the front of the room.

Gail.

He gave her that coy grin he'd given her all over the Preymoor as he turned. "My shadow Queen," he leered, eyes darting over her. "I wondered if you'd escaped."

Nyssa couldn't breathe. He was supposed to be dead. Visions blurred her mind. That scared yet determined girl she'd been as he dragged her across the Preymoor. What it inevitably led to. Seeing Gail turn into the Infi.

"What... How are you here? How—Bron told me you were dead," Nyssa managed, stepping closer to him. Stammering at him being in the room and actually real. She wasn't sure what she should be feeling. Whether she should be angry about his being there or relieved he wasn't dead.

"There's someone I need on our side," Bala had said.

The words had barely gone through Nyssa's mind when Nadir appeared in the doorway.

And the smile he'd been wearing faded to searing rage.

"You—"

Gail took a step back, eyes wide, hands coming up. "Storn, wait—"

Nadir pounced.

His fist railed into Gail's face, and he grabbed him by the neck before Gail could stumble. Slamming Gail's head into the table and then bringing him back upright. Grunting noises she'd never heard from anyone exuded from Nadir's mouth as he threw Gail into the side of the tent and then railed into him again. Gail started to fight back, but Nadir was faster.

"You're fucking *dead*—"

Nyssa couldn't move.

Nadir held Gail's throat and punched his stomach twice. Gail tried to swing back. Nadir threw his head into Gail's nose and shoved him.

The tent ripped, and the pair went stumbling out onto the sand. Nyssa ran after them, catching up just as Nadir launched himself over Gail, knees pinning his arms into the ground, and he pushed Gail's throat into the sand.

"Give me a reason I shouldn't spill every drop of your blood right here," he seethed.

"Storn—"

Another punch.

"You took her for your own *ransom*—"

Again.

"—You kidnapped and sent her into a camp where you knew she would be tortured and starved—"

Again.

"—*All for a space at their table!*"

"Maybe—" Gail choked on the blood from his mouth and throat. "Maybe you should have kept a better leash on her."

Nadir whipped his knife from his calf and slammed the hilt into Gail's nose. "She doesn't need a fucking leash," he growled, the knife stilling beneath Gail's chin. "She needs a crown."

He spat in Gail's face, and Nyssa finally blinked herself out of her daze. She darted forward and grabbed Nadir's arm, knowing if he continued, he would likely spill all Gail's blood over his beach.

Not for Gail. But for Nadir.

Gail coughed, coming up onto one side as Nyssa pulled Nadir off him. "That... That we can agree on," he managed as he met Nyssa's eyes.

And the look he gave her made her insides curl.

"What—*Nadir!*" Bala ran forward, having just arrived at the scene. Her eyes widened at the sight of Gail broken on the ground.

Nadir rounded over her. "You've been holding him at your home all this time," he realized. "Trusting him. Healing him. You knew he was the one who took her—*How could*—"

"Because I need his people," Bala interjected sternly. "*We* need his people. And the only person he seems to want to listen to is her—" she pointed at Nyssa. "So he is here, and he is listening to what we all have to say." She shifted her feet, glaring back down at Gail. "If at any moment you think he is betraying us, I'll give you my own blade to take his life with."

"I'll do that myself," Nyssa snapped, and all eyes landed on her. Gail coughed again, and she gritted her teeth at the sight of him looking at her the way he did.

"*Fuck*—someone get him off the floor and a towel to clean himself with," she said reluctantly.

She didn't wait to see if anyone went to help him. She turned away from them and wrapped her arms around her chest. She walked back inside the broken tent, where she took a deep breath and started counting to squander the frustration in her bones.

Nadir followed behind, and he pulled her back to him when they were out of earshot of the others. "Are you okay with him being here?" he asked quietly.

She watched him as he opened and closed the hand he'd punched Gail with. "Yeah," she managed. "Yeah, I'm fine. I know his signs. I'll know if he's lying or planning anything."

"If he tries anything, he'll find out the torturous ways the Honest once gathered information on our enemies."

Nyssa almost smiled up at him. "Please read me those stories later," she asked of him.

His lip quirked. "Of course, why didn't I think to show our Princess the book on torture techniques first when she arrived?" he mocked.

She nearly kissed him but instead reached out for his bruised hand. "Are you okay?"

"No," he admitted. "That man has been a thorn in my side for years. When you told us he was dead, I was actually relieved." He paused and glanced back at Gail, watching Bala help him back inside the tent. "I don't like his being here."

"Sounds like we don't have a choice."

Nadir settled in front of her, his hand wrapping around her cheek. "Tell me you're okay," he whispered.

Nyssa couldn't. Seeing Gail again had caused her stomach to flip. All she could see was the memory of the Infi taking over Gail's face and watching the smile rise in that Infi's eyes as his throat was cut. The images made her bite back the emotion in her chest.

"I can't," she admitted quietly. "Can we talk about it later?"

"Yeah."

"Whoa—what did I miss?" Dorian announced as he threw back the tent door and emerged with Reverie and Corbin in tow. "Dammit, I missed the action. What happened?"

A slow grin spread on Nadir's face, and Nyssa knew what he was thinking without a word. "No—" she pointed her finger in his face. "Nadir—don't—"

"Oh, I'm doing it—Hey Prince, do you know this man?" Nadir asked as he whirled around, nodding towards Gail.

"Nadir, don't—"

"Tell me," Dorian said, eyes wandering over Gail.

"It's handled," Nyssa interjected.

"Who is he?"

"Nadir, *stop*—" Bala straightened, eyes wide.

"That's the man that kidnapped your sister and took her to Man," Nadir finished.

The room froze for the longest second Nyssa had ever experienced.

His head snapped in Gail's direction.

Dorian lunged.

Form spreading on his hands, Dorian hardly got three steps in before Bala's wind swept the room. But Dorian didn't seem to care. His form dwindled, and he jumped over Bala, launching and railing his fist into Gail's jaw.

Bala glared at Reverie and Corbin. *"Do something!"*

Reverie shook her head, arms over her chest. "You want me to stop him from going off on the man that kidnapped his sister? After the turmoil I've watched him settle through worrying about her? No," she argued. "I'll pull him off when the man's almost dead." She leaned in towards Corbin. "Also, this is really hot," she whispered.

Corbin scratched his neck.

"Corbin!" Bala shouted, trying to grab Dorian's wailing arms.

Corbin grunted, but he stepped forward at her demand and wrapped his arms under Dorian's. Dorian kicked Gail as Corbin hauled him to his feet and pushed him away. Bala shoved Dorian's chest when he started forward again.

"Enough!" she demanded. "Both of you."

"Gail deserves every bit of it after the way he treated Draven all those years," Nadir snapped. "After what he wanted to do to Aydra when she was injured. After what he did to *you* with walking out of your kingdom and threatening your crown."

"That is neither here nor there anymore," Bala seethed. "We cannot let past grudges get in the way of our alliance now. This is a war."

"I'm sorry, I had *no* idea." Dangerous sarcasm dripped from his lips, and Nadir stepped up to her. "I had no idea the ships coming in day in and day out over the horizon were enemy ships. I had no idea we were in a war when strangers invaded my shores and killed my men. I had no idea we were facing possible genocide or slavery. It *must* have slipped my mind."

"We do not have time for this—"

"No, but we had time for you to nurse this fucking craven—

this *traitor*—back to life? You should have left him rotting in the Preymoor for Duarb to take back to his roots," he said, tone darkening so much, Nyssa's heart slowed. "Or has it slipped your mind how we had to sit around her fucking dead body and beg her to come back to us after she endured eight weeks of torture... After he *kidnapped* her."

Nyssa reached out for Nadir's arm. He straightened over Bala and took a step back, but Bala didn't move. She was biting the inside of her mouth, obviously trying to stifle her emotion and keep a calm face.

"I realize you are upset," she said slowly. "But you have to understand why I did not let him rot—why Draven would not have let him rot... We need the numbers. This is bigger than any spats between our people. Every person counts. I will not turn away someone who is willing to help."

Nadir's chest rose high and fell, his shoulders sinking with it. He glanced toward Gail again, who was sitting up. "You got lucky today," he sneered.

Gail spat blood to the ground from his bleeding gums. "Are you finished?"

"Not hardly," Nadir said. "I can't wait for you to do something stupid and for one of these two to turn you to ash."

"Like the King did their sister?"

Nyssa snapped.

Nyssa reached Gail before Dorian—Dorian grabbed her and swung her backward. Her foot caught in Gail's face, and he fell to the ground again.

Bala glared over him. "Are you trying to die?" she asked.

Gail tipped his head back as he rose to his feet. "Thought I may as well get it all out." He glanced to Nyssa. "Nice kick, little Sun."

"I swear you will taste my fucking sword one day," Nadir grunted.

Dorian finally put Nyssa down at Nadir's side. She shoved his arms off and stepped forward again to Gail.

"You will sit and keep your mouth shut while we talk," she commanded. "How do we know he's not Infi?" she asked the rest of the room.

Dorian's fist clenched at his side, and a shudder ran over his body. "He's not," he said.

"How do you know?" Nyssa asked.

"Because I know."

And Nyssa didn't question it.

Gail sat in the chair and ripped a piece of fabric to hold on his bleeding face. She was surprised he could move at the number of blows that he'd been struck with.

But there he sat. Staring at her. Holding the fabric to his nose and mouth. Eye swollen and trickling blood.

Nyssa stepped back and looked to Bala. "Where do you want to begin?"

As Nadir took the Scrolls out from Dorian's bag, Nyssa walked. She walked around the edge of the room and watched them all. The Honest people that had joined them. The Venari both from Bala's company and Gail's. Reverie and Corbin had sat in chairs on either side of Dorian, who was leaned over the table, palms pressed firmly into the wood and staring at the Scrolls.

And Lex watched *her*.

Once the Scrolls were all spread out over the table, Nadir settled back and wrapped his arms around his chest. "Thank you for retrieving these," he said as he met Reverie's eyes. "But where's the last one?"

"Last one…" A demeaning chuckle left Dorian's lips as he reached behind him and pulled what looked to be a stack of parchment rolled up from his back pocket, and he threw it on the table "—You mean this one?"

Wind blew around the room as the parchment opened, and Nyssa stopped walking. Whatever this Scroll was made her core wriggle and hide. Uncomfortable in her bones.

Two red circles stared back at her.

Nyssa's heart dropped. Nadir fell back into the chair. She didn't even realize she was moving until she was standing in front of it.

Power at her fingertips. True power. The ability to free Haerland and bring Aydra and Draven back.

It was there. Right in front of her.

The only way to undo all the curses of Haerland.

To bring forth the Red Moons.

"Hagen told me what it does," Dorian said firmly, arms crossing over his chest. "Tell me why we shouldn't be using it. Why shouldn't we perform it?"

"Did he also tell you what you would have to give up?" Nadir managed, head lifting.

"None of us are sacrificing anyone in this room," Nyssa blurted. "Everyone we all care about—save for Aydra and Draven—is right here. I am not losing anyone else, especially by my own hand."

She waited on any of the others to talk, but they didn't. And when she spoke again, her voice began to crack.

"I want to bring Aydra and Draven back... I really do... And I want the curses undone, the Noctuans free. But, I cannot bring myself to put this world over any of you. And I am *sorry* for that." She choked on the words, tears breaking on her face. She met Nadir's eyes, and he gave her a silent nod. A small reassurance that that was the correct answer.

"I hate when you're right," Dorian mumbled.

She met his eyes, and her jaw quivered. "I hate when I'm right too."

"Fucking curses," Bala breathed. "So what do we do?"

"Are there more Infi?" Nyssa asked, and her eyes landed on Gail.

Gail dropped the cloth from his mouth. "How should I know?" he asked.

"You had them in your company," Nyssa argued. "How would you not know?"

"Perhaps you'd be better asking your brother what he found in the mountains," Gail said.

All eyes turned to Dorian, who was rubbing his neck nervously.

Nadir slowly rose to his feet. Dorian exchanged a look with Reverie and Corbin, who both shared a concerned gaze Nyssa didn't like.

"Dorian..."

"There were hundreds of them," Dorian sighed. Reverie and Corbin both touched him, shoulder and hand. Nyssa tried not to smile at such an inappropriate time, but it made her heart hurt at the sight of both the people her brother was so confused about trying to comfort him.

Dorian explained what they'd found. He explained how he'd tried to burn them and how he could only burn the one whose heart had been taken out and not the one still intact. And when he told them about the deal he'd made, the entire room froze.

"You took a crown from the Infi?" Bala managed.

"How do you think I got this scar?" he asked, and the cut seemed to vibrate as he asked it. "They held to me, knelt beneath my fire—"

"And they're going to betray you," Bala cut in. "How could you be so stupid, Dorian?"

"You were not there," Dorian snapped, voice rising. "You were at home. You were not forced to flee your home because of lies and treachery. You did not watch your family burn. Do you know we saw him when he jumped?"

Nyssa's heart pounded at the way he spoke, at his challenging her. She knew he had reached his limit of people questioning him. Reached his limit of people second guessing every decision he'd had to make in the last few months. Decisions that had ripped his entire being into shreds and been fed to the Rhamocour.

Decisions he was still coming to terms with and would haunt him until his death.

"Dorian—"

But he wasn't listening.

"You were not there, Bala. You have been at home while Nyssa and I have pushed ourselves to our limits and gone further than any other person in our world would have. All for *them*— to follow what they asked us to do. So yes, I took a crown from the Infi because I wanted one less thing to have to worry about taking my family away from me. They are *mine*. It was either die on that dais or bind them to me. Tell me you would have done differently."

Bala shifted on her feet.

"Tell me you would have had a better plan."

No one spoke.

And Dorian was starting to break.

"I did what I had to do," he managed. "I won't let you shame me for the decision I had to make that night."

The room remained quiet as Dorian sank into his chair and pushed his hands through his hair. Nyssa looked up to the ceiling in an attempt to stifle her tears.

"So, what's next?" Lex asked, looking around the room.

"We have to take the Scrolls back to Lake Oriens," Nadir said, still staring at the parchment. "They have to be secured."

"Is that actually the safest place for them, considering the Infi found them last time?" Bala asked.

"You mean along with you and Draven?" Nadir snapped.

"Oh, fuck all. Everyone take a fucking breath," Nyssa commanded. "I am done with this fighting. No one is better than anyone else in this room because of what we have been through. We have all endured our own darknesses and no one is shaming anyone for any of it. Bala is right. This is larger than our inner squabbles. We all count. We are all important in this. Every decision any of us have made is for our continued freedom—"

Her eagle flew through the door and landed on her good arm.

"The arguing is *finished*," she practically declared.

Everyone watched her as she stopped in the middle.

And suddenly, she was the largest person in that room.

Back straight. Chin high. Broken arm clutched to her stomach and other bent at the elbow. Her eagle eyed the rest of the room—the great bird stretching taller than the top of Nyssa's head as it sat on her forearm. Dark golden wings shimmering in the firelight.

Nyssari Eaglefyre. Princess and Eyes of Haerland—

No.

This was Ari Storn.

"Nadir will take the Scrolls back to where ever he feels they should go," she snapped. "If that means the Lake or up to the Nitesh, I don't care as long as that Red Moons scroll is safe until the next of us can perform it. Whoever is going with him can be decided later. I know what is happening at Savigndor and I can tell you everything. But what I don't know is what is happening at Magnice. There has been no word since they started sending companies after us. What we need right now is information on what is going on there. Commander Storn —"

"Yes, Princess," Nadir said as he lifted his head.

"Traders should go there to find out. I want to know if our brother has started executing people for information about us. Reverie—"

"Yes, ma'am," Reverie stood.

"Do you have any knowledge about the villages? Anything at all?"

Reverie shifted. "Not... Not really, but I can travel there if I need to and see a friend."

"Great. It has been one cycle. I imagine cleaning up at Magnice is starting to slow. He'll send his own army down here soon looking for us. The moons rise tomorrow. The Noble from the camp I destroyed will be traveling back thinking I will be there for him to take to the Prince. I don't know what will happen when he gets there and finds out it is destroyed, but we have to keep our eyes on the sea *and* the dunes. We are fighting the war on two sides right now whether we want to or not. Until we can win the villages over, that is our reality. We— *why are you all smiling?*"

Because they were.

Small smiles, but smiles nonetheless.

She huffed and ignored them.

"Their King will be here in two cycles," she continued. "It may seem like a long time, but it isn't. Nadir already has us rationing here. Bala's people are also rationing. Dorian, are you going back to the mountains?"

Dorian took his thumb from his mouth where he'd been biting his nail. "I am," he said. "Hagen said he had more work for me."

"Then we use this cycle to get stronger," she told them. "By the time the summer Eyes rise, we need to be ready to start going to the villages because when Man's King gets here, he will take everything if we are not prepared." She paused and looked around the room, meeting the eyes of the Venari and the Honest there, and then her gaze landed on Gail.

"You can either be with us or against us," she said to him. "With us means you follow Bala. You kneel to her. If you refuse, your entire company can stand here and watch as my Second performs her first public execution."

Gail moved the cloth from his nose. "Fuck of a choice, little Sun."

"It's the only one I'm giving you," she glared. "Make it."

The once over he gave her made her glare harder, and her eagle screeched, wings flapping wide. Gail sat back. "Fine," he agreed. "But know I am doing this only because you asked me to."

"Why would we follow a daughter of Arbina?" one of his people asked him.

"That's no longer a daughter of Arbina," Gail countered. "She is a queen of her own design. I've watched her put herself in situations she should never have. Treat Infi as actual beings. Kill when threatened. I'll follow her because I trust her. And if the rest of you have any issue with it, you're welcome to move north past the mountains and cower in fear."

The Venari didn't speak, but Nadir leaned forward in his chair.

"If you know what's good for you, Venari, you'll keep your eyes on her face when you speak to her," he growled.

Gail smiled smugly in Nadir's direction, then glanced back to Nyssa. "I await your orders, shadow Queen."

"I want you on one knee before your King."

67

The meeting wrapped up after Gail took the oath.

While they hadn't much decided on everything, at least they were all on the same page and knowing as far as what had happened in the last cycle. Dorian had apologized to Bala for his snapping at her, but Bala had shrugged him off, telling him she was used to his challenging her, and if he wasn't, there was something wrong.

Having talked to his sister about what he was going through, Dorian felt a little more confident than he had in the days before. He kept clenching and unclenching his fist from the bruises where he'd hit Nadir and Gail.

The meeting had been draining. He wanted to take a nap. It had been the longest day he'd had in a long time, and his wounds were getting to him.

The bed looked inviting, but he forced himself to the tub. He'd intentions of shaving the stubble grown on his face in the last few weeks. As he shaved, he replayed the events of the day. From seeing his sister again to their talk. To the meeting. To helping Nyssa with her fire and her meeting Reverie.

His entire world had stood on that beach at that moment. His sister. Reverie. Corbin. Lex. Bala. He supposed he would include Nadir in that list as it seemed he would be stuck with him through Nyssa.

He was grateful Nyssa had not completely embarrassed him in front of Reverie, and the memory of their meeting made his stomach knot. Despite all that was going on with the war, his mind still returned to her and Corbin. Perhaps it was the talk he'd had with Nyssa about it. Perhaps it was that they were all together, and he could be free, if only for a few days. Not worry about the training and allow himself to just... *Be.*

A moment of freedom in a world of chaos.

Dorian wiped his face with the towel a while later, the wind brushing over his now cleanly shaven face feeling like velvet against his fingers. He'd had to be careful shaving with the straight edge around the scar cutting through his neck and jaw.

Every time he looked in the mirror, the scar seemed to be getting darker. Almost black in the crack. He swore the red nerves at the very edge of his eyeball were black and that the bright blue iris on that eye had darkened, but every time he went to inspect it closer, it seemed to go back to normal.

He draped another towel around his waist, leaving his toned torso exposed to the world. He pushed the small towel through his damp hair again to rid himself of the excess water as he moved his bag to the bed and looked through it for new clothes.

"Hey, Prince—"

Reverie's voice sounded through the still air. He gave his neck one last push of the towel just as she rounded and came through the bedroom door.

"Hey, we're—" She paused in the threshold, her brows raising upon her eyes landing on him. He'd never seen her without words, and as such, it made his brows narrow, his head tilting just so at her faltering facade, even it was only for the briefest of seconds.

"Speechless, Rev..." he mocked, feeling the smirk rise on his lips. "It's a good look on you."

Reverie shifted on her feet, her jaw tightening as her eyes traveled over his face. "Sorry, I've just... It's been a while since I've seen your face so—"

"Handsome?" he asked, cutting in.

Her lips pursed. "That's not—"

"Delectable?" he continued, slowly advancing towards her.

She opened her mouth, but he cut her off again.

"A marvel to behold?"

The surprise and glare in her features dropped, and she looked as though she would laugh.

"Sexy and domine—"

"Clean," she finally interjected. "I was going to say clean."

He smirked down at her, holding the towel between his hands behind his neck as his chin rose. "Would you like to feel it?"

"I imagine it feels like the skin of a toad."

The right corner of his lips twisted higher, and he could feel a darkness taking over his gaze. The way she'd been staring at him all day combined with the freedom he felt now pulsing through his veins.

He wanted her.

He wanted her right then.

He could practically taste her on his lips as his eyes wandered over her body.

"Do you know what I would love to do now that I can feel the wind on my cheeks again?" he asked.

"I don't."

His shoulders flexed, and he leaned down over her, nose brushing her cheek. "I'd love to feel your thighs tighten around them while I suck on your—"

She shoved his bent head playfully, eyes rolling. "You couldn't handle my thighs around your face," she dared. "You'd suffocate."

"You make it sound like I'm not willing to make that sacrifice," he replied. "If that's how I am taken out of this world, I will die a happy man. That's a much more a noble death than dying at the end of some stranger's noose."

He watched her fight a smile, her eyes dart wholly over him, so deliberate he had to swallow. And then she shook her head. "Your sister wanted me to inform you dinner would be soon," she said. "Apparently, they have a great gathering family dinner like the Venari do."

"I'll be down when I'm dressed."

Reverie's arms hugged over her chest, and she gave him another full once over. "See you there," and she started to turn on her heel.

But Dorian's heart skipped at the look she'd given him, and before he realized what he was doing, he stepped forward and grabbed her arm. Whirling her back around. Her torso slammed against his, and he captured her lips before she could utter a word.

He could feel the surprise in her tense body as he curled a hand around her neck... Until the fright faded, and her lips opened to his.

His heart skipped, stomach dropping, and suddenly he was desperate for her. The taste of her tongue against his made his muscles ache. Her hands grasped to his cheeks, and he devoured her as though her lips would save him from death. She tasted of vanilla spices and his favorite pastries from his childhood.

She tasted like home.

And he couldn't get enough of her.

His heart ached for the bliss of her lips upon his. He didn't know where to touch her first. He wanted his hands all over her at once. The sensation of her fingers curling in his hair caused a moan to emit from his throat.

He grabbed to the back of her head, other hand daring to wrap around her backside and between her cheeks, squeezing her ass in his hand, not realizing he was walking her backward until he felt her pin against the wall. Her leg bent around his waist, and he groaned at her opening up to him.

Hands on her cheeks, his hips rocked into hers, his length already hardening at the grasp of her. Her fingers trailed down his sides to his abs, and the towel around his waist fell to the ground. His fist slammed into the wall by her head when her thumb brushed the tip of his cock.

Every rock and press of her against him made his body ache. Fuck, he wanted her right then. He wanted her wrapped around him and saying his name against his cheek.

His lips moved to her jaw, and she hugged him against her, one hand in his hair, the other teasing his tip. He cursed into her neck and pulled back to take her lips once more.

He didn't want her to think she was ending him before he took her this time.

Because she was his, and he wanted her to know it.

"Tell me you have more pants in your bag," he breathed.

"I do," she answered in confusion.

"Good."

The word had hardly left his lips before he used his fire to burn the seam. She jumped, grasping his shoulders, and then her hips pushed against his. He grinned into her throat, and she yanked his head up to hers.

"Did you like that?" he asked, kissing her between the words.

His finger grazed between her folds, and she moaned in response, hips bucking into his hand. He cursed in her mouth at the wetness wrapping his fingers. He needed to feel her around him.

He grasped her ass in his hands and pulled her off the ground. She obliged, legs wrapping around. He gave her backside a slap, followed by his squeezing her cheeks again, and the moment she sank onto his length, Dorian cursed against her breasts.

"Fuck, *Dorian*," she whispered in his hair, and the sound of his name on her lips made him grasp her tighter.

For a moment, he teased her, deepening himself all the way in, his palms pressed into the wall by her head as she held herself around him, her body pinned. He kissed her again, and her hands tightened in his hair.

"Are you ready for me, Lady Fyre?" he uttered against her lips. "Or do you want me to tease you?"

She groaned when he thrust into her again, him stilling a moment as he watched her face. "Make me yours."

His eyes fluttered with the words, and he grasped her arms, pushing them out so that the backs rested against the wall, his hands on her wrists. His teeth tugged on her bottom lip, and he pressed his forehead against hers. He slammed into her. Again and again. Making her body bounce with his every stroke. She kept her legs firmly around his waist, her moans echoing off the walls. He could feel her tightening, her muscles starting to strain beneath his grasp, and he knew he was on his edge too.

"*Fuck*—you're so tight," he groaned. "Come for me, Reverie."

His legs shook, thrusts becoming erratic as he fought his end. Her mouth sagged, staying open as her heels dug into his backside.

"Yes," she managed, voice high pitched. "Yes—*Dorian*—right there—"

And when his teeth sank into her throat, she cried out his name, her hips moving up against him—

She shattered around him with a heave of her entire body.

The feeling of her breaking sent him whirling, and he pushed into her once more, his body pressing flush against hers as he surrendered inside her.

Muscles spasming with the comedown, he laid his head on her breasts, allowing her hands to come down and her to cradle his head. He didn't want to move from inside her. Feeling her walls continue to flinch around his exhausted length. He finally picked his head up and kissed her again, and then his forehead leaned against hers.

"You're a liar, Prince," she accused, her legs finally slipping from around him.

His chin raised as he let her go. "Am I?"

Her breath evened, and she glanced over him again as he reached for the towel on the ground. "All this talk about making me beg," she mocked. "I thought our first time would have lasted longer."

His insides chilled, and he stared at the smug mockery in her features. Dorian threw the towel at her, and his eyes darted around the room. Challenge rising in his stomach and his shoulders. Restlessness in his extremities. Biting back the smirk on his lips.

"You've no idea what you've just asked for," he said, tone darkening.

"Don't I?" she openly mocked.

He grabbed pillows from the couch, and he turned just in time to watch her remove her pants and wipe herself of their finishes trickling down her thigh. He watched her a moment, staring at her legs and her hips just showing from beneath her long shirt.

"Take your shirt off," he rasped.

Her brow elevated. "Wanting a strip show?"

"No," he said, slowly stepping back to her, pillows in his hands. "I want to know how well my Commander takes orders from her King." He paused over her, and the cushions hit the floor at her feet. "Because if you think that was remotely close to all the ways I can bring you to your end, you're wrong," he dared. "Now, take off your shirt."

Watching him, she reached for the hem, body stretching and breasts heaving as she pulled it over her head. His mouth dried at the sight of her curves, ready and waiting for him. Her thick hips. The stretch—no, *warrior* marks, as he liked to call them—on her pelvis and the insides of her thighs. The leather wrap around her breasts, cleavage pushed together. He groaned inwardly at the thought of seeing the cute creases she had on her back at the place her ribs and waist met as she rode him backward or he plowed into her from behind.

The fantasy had him aroused already.

But he'd have to save that for another day.

He reached for the tie under her arm, locking eyes with her as the string came loose. Her breasts freed, and he swallowed as he noted her taut nipples. She didn't move as he reached for her, his thumb dragging over the pebble, but he did note her thighs squeezing.

He pushed his other hand around her throat, and her eyes fluttered as his thumb stroked her skin. "You should decide which wall you like," he whispered.

Her mouth tipped open as she lifted her chin, eyes fluttering. "Why?"

"Because you'll be suffocating your King against it, and I imagine you'd like to be comfortable."

"Is that right?"

His torso pressed flush to her, hand tightening around her neck, and his head bent low. "Fuck, I hope so."

His mouth captured hers again, and her hands pushed around his face. Tongues sweeping, her breasts pushing against his chest. He grasped her hip in his other hand, pulling her leg up and around his waist. He heard her moan into his mouth when his length brushed her exposed thigh, but he didn't push inside her again.

Not this time.

He wanted nothing more than to watch as she begged to be undone on his lips.

Swifter than she could move, he held her thigh firm and bent lower. Kissing down her collar to her chest, her hands raking his hair as she held his head against her. An audible gasp escaped her when he nipped at her, and he continued lower.

All the way to his knees.

He held her short figure to him, his mouth capturing her breast and his teeth tugged at her hardened nipple. Her fingers were in his hair, back arching off the wall. Tongue swirling around her, his lashes lifted to find her watching him, soft, audible breaths leaving her open mouth.

She lifted to her toes, her knees bending as she squeezed her legs together. Her head knocked into the wall when he sucked on her, his name coming from her lips and making him groan. He moved the hand he had on her hip to her inner thigh. Feeling her jerk when his fingertips grazed up the sensitive area. Her chest flinching as his thumb tickled her folds.

He pulled back as his fingertip hovered there, the pad barely whispering over her nerves, his head sinking between her breasts and kissing her chest.

Tongue flickering over that nipple, he then wrapped his lips only around the peak. Her hips arched against him when he finally touched her clit, and he cursed at her wetness. He pushed one finger slowly inside her, feeling his own finish with hers as it seeped down her leg, and he left his thumb to brush her nerves. A quiet whimper escaped her, her hips pushing towards him again. His gaze lifted to hers. Seeing her eyes darkened, mouth sagging.

"Remember this, Reverie," he breathed. He sat back on his knees and leaned forward, tongue flicking out over her nerves once and making her jerk. "When another man whispers in your ear what they are capable of doing to you, remember how your King fell to his knees before you. Remember how you screamed my name and begged for your end... "

He lifted her legs one by one, hooking them both on his shoulders. He groaned at the heat of her arousal in front of him. He denied himself the pleasure of it as he moved her hands into his hair, and he sat up to his knees. Lifting her into the air.

"Remember how you became mine."

Her legs clenched, and he kissed the inside of her thigh once more before he dragged his tongue along her clit.

A high-pitched noise emitted from her throat that he was sure she wasn't prepared for.

Hands wrapping around the tops of her thighs, he dove into her. Tasting her sweetness slowly and causing her body to squirm. With the pillows beneath his knees, he decided he could have stayed there the rest of his life, only her as his sustenance, and he would have been eternally happy with it.

He intended on savoring her as his last meal, and he groaned at the sensation of finally feeling her thighs wrapped around him.

Every moan and high-pitched gasp that emitted from her made him tease her more. Taking her clit in his mouth and sucking on her, dragging his tongue down her slickness and devouring her as she trembled. Her back arched off the wood, hand pushing into his hair and the other into her own. He snuck a glance up at her. Seeing her mouth agape and her nose scrunched as she succumbed to him.

He paused and pulled back, making her whimper in his absence, and he blew a slow breath on her throbbing clit. Her legs jerked.

"I need to hear you say it," he breathed against her.

Her chest rose and fell with every whisper of his breath on her, every flicker of his teasing tongue.

"Fuck you, Dorian," she managed.

His nose nudged her again, and he allowed his tongue to deliberately rake the slickness of her, making her muscles clench. "That's not very nice." He kissed her thigh delicately, his thumb coming around and slowly pressing against her insides. She whimpered, and he smirked at her before puckering his mouth once more and blowing against her. "Say it for me, Lady Fyre," he uttered. "Say the name you'd dare not call me in front of anyone else."

Her fingers tightened in his hair, and a jagged breath left her as she looked down at him. And when their gazes met, his mouth opened as though he would kiss her again, but he paused at her entrance.

"I hate you," she breathed.

His tongue raked her slickness again, parting her and laying his tongue flat, tip flickering her entrance. "I know you do." He pressed his lips to her other thigh then, nibbling on her skin. "I'm waiting…"

He heard the huff of breath leave her when his mouth brushed her clit once more, and her hips bucked upwards towards his face. The dark lilac of her eyes blazed through him when he lifted his lashes to her.

"Take me over the Edge…" she finally breathed. "My King."

The words sent a chill down his spine. His chuckle vibrated in the space between her legs, and he nipped her folds. "Wasn't expecting the beg," he uttered, his lips brushing her sensitive skin. "A simple *my King* would have sufficed."

Her response came in the clench of her thighs around his cheeks, and he obliged to her wants. He sucked on her, devouring her. Memorizing her against his mouth. Until her rocking against him stilled, and her entire body began to shake.

He slowed.

Daring to keep her on that edge.

His clenched fingers moving from her thighs to her ass, squeezing her flesh and making her squirm. He slipped his thumb inside her slowly and pulled back to watch her as he mouthed those nerves. Her wetness pooled around his finger, and he pushed further inside her. His name released from her lips. Tongue swirling, his pace picked back up. Until she was once more jerking around him.

Her hands moving from his hair to her own thighs, grasp clenching into her skin and her shoulders hitting the wall. Heels digging into his back.

She cursed the sky, moans sounding from her that he'd only fantasized about.

She came apart on his lips, and he licked her clean. She continued to groan, to tremble and fist his hair as he drained her. Thighs flinching. Muscles jerking. To the point, he decided he would make her come again because he enjoyed hearing her so much.

Noises he had never heard from any woman came from her. Her hands clenching his hair so tight, he thought she might pull it out. Her fist hit the wall. Heel slammed into his shoulder. She convulsed. Screaming his name and wiggling against him. He could feel the throb of her heartbeat in her clit.

And she shattered on his mouth once more.

Dorian slowed this time, his tonguing turning to kisses until he paused to lean his cheek against her thigh and watch her come down from the high.

Her chest buckled, exhausted satisfaction spread over her features. He kissed her thigh one last time before surrendering to the floor, allowing her legs to move from his shoulders and for her to sink onto the ground.

"Good job, Prince," she uttered, lashes sweeping as she looked him over.

Dorian's lips twisted at the words, and he noted the smile in her eyes. "He told you, didn't he?"

Reverie's smirk turned into a satisfied grin. "I don't know what you mean."

And he knew she was lying.

Dorian laughed and shook his head. "I will kill him."

She chuckled under her breath and sat up to her shaking knees, leaning forward over him, and her hands pressed to his thighs. She kissed him, tongue brushing delicately against his own, and his stomach knotted.

She bit her lip when she pulled back. "Too bad he stayed with your sister just now," she said in a rasp. "Watching you two in the cave has me curious."

Dorian smiled slyly, the thought of being with both of them making his heart flee. "Next time," he winked, giving her ass a firm slap. "Right now..." He shifted and pulled her onto his lap. His lips pressed softly to her throat, fingers digging into her ass. "Right now, I'm enjoying having you to myself," he uttered against her skin. "I've been robbed of bedding my wife for some time now. I have to make up for it."

Reverie laughed softly, and she kissed him once more. "Dinner," she said as she pushed to her feet. "Dinner first. Then we can talk about whether you deserve to have me all to yourself."

"Someone got laid," Balandria mocked as Dorian approached the dinner table.

His gaze narrowed, and his hands went to his hair, obviously trying to straighten it. But Nyssa wrapped her arms around her chest and shook her head. Dorian's soft smile flashed when he came to stand beside her.

"Tell me what we're having, sis," he said as he pushed his arm around her shoulders. "Or perhaps you'd like to know what I already had—"

His fingers shoved beneath her nose, and Nyssa punched his side as she realized what he was trying to get her to smell.

"*Dorian!*" she shrieked. She stumbled trying to get away from him and faltered into the table. Unable to catch herself, one thing rambled into the other, and she found herself covered in meat sauce when her elbow knocked it.

She glared up at him, unable to move. "You are such an ass. Now I have to go bathe."

Dorian grinned. "I'm sure the Commander would love to lick it off you," he mocked. "Where is he?"

Nyssa reacted. She grabbed one of the wing shards from the bag on her belt and threw it at his face. He caught it between his fingers, as he usually did, and raised his brows.

"That bad?"

"Yes, that bad!" She shook the sauce off her hands as one of the cooks came over. "I'm so sorry," she began. "My brother is a menace to society," she glared at him and tried to help the woman pick up the mess.

Dorian shrugged. "Perhaps I'll take you shopping later. I hear the traders here have the best seamstresses," he replied with a wink.

"This isn't Magnice," Bala cut in. "You can't just go into a shop here and buy your sister something pretty to apologize to her."

"If I was trying to apologize to her, I wouldn't be buying her a dress," Dorian countered. "I'd be buying her a new longbow or perhaps a few new daggers to add to the collection she has strapped to her thigh."

"That true, Princess?" Bala asked.

Nyssa's lips twisted at her brother, and he grinned at her. "I almost forgot how much of an asshole you are," she muttered under her breath before pulling up her wet frock to reveal the strap of three blades.

"Since when do you travel packing like that?" Bala asked.

"Since I was kidnapped," she affirmed.

"Go ahead. Show her the rest," Dorian mocked, his arms hugging around his chest.

"There's more?" Bala asked.

Nyssa let loose a low huff at her brother revealing all her secrets.

"Let's see it, Princess," Lex said as she joined them. "I'm curious. You've been hiding these from me as well."

Nyssa's jaw clenched between the three.

And then she began to remove the many knives she had hidden in different places.

Three on her right thigh. One on her ankle. Two on the lower of her left thigh. And the bag of wing shards strapped to her belt.

They all clanked when she lined them up on the table, and then she huffed at her friends. "Happy?" she asked them.

Lex and Dorian were grinning at her, and Bala looked impressed.

"Ferocious shadow queen, indeed," Lex said.

"That's my sister," Dorian winked.

"Yeah? What about your girlfriend?" Nyssa spat. "She's got knives hiding on every inch of her."

"Yeah she does," Dorian agreed in a dream-like voice.

Nyssa's arms crossed over her chest. "At least—"

"Whoa—" Nadir paused in his approach, his gaze narrowing at the sight of Nyssa's knives and daggers strewn out atop the table. "Is there a reason we're comparing iron? Should you like to see my collection?"

"You gave her most of these, didn't you?" Bala asked.

Nadir paused at Nyssa's side, picking up his favorite one and balancing it on his finger. "I gave her all but two of these. Of course. Can't have my Princess walking around not strapped after what happened, can I?"

Bala looked between Nadir and Dorian then, and she shook her head. "You two are ridiculous. I am actually quite glad Dorian did not have the chance to join your little gang. The four of you together would have terrorized Haerland with your nonsense."

"Four of them?" Nyssa asked.

Nadir grinned. "Draven, Hagen, myself, and I suppose she's including your brother in this little band now."

"The three of you were enough for towns to handle together,"

Balandria continued. "Adding the Prince in would have meant more trouble than you all could handle."

"Sounds like a grand time," Dorian mocked.

"That sounds terrifying," Nyssa stated. "I do believe Draven would have been the only reason the four of you wouldn't end up dead."

"You're absolutely right," Nadir agreed. He ran his hand against his neck then, and Nyssa could see the clench of his jaw. "Dammit, I miss him," he muttered.

She reached out for his hand and gave it a squeeze, but it didn't do anything to deter the sadness from his gaze. He straightened up from the table and stepped flush to her, kissing her forehead hard with an audible sigh.

"My people are preparing a bonfire to mark tomorrow's spring arrival," Nadir announced. "Get changed into something comfortable."

68

Nyssa couldn't stop watching everything around her. From Nadir playing with some of the children in the sand to her brother taunting Lex and parrying her to the point, she chased after him. Reverie sat in a chair behind Corbin, taking the quiet time to re-twist his hair which was getting out of control. She kept smacking his arm when he would complain, and Nyssa couldn't help but laugh. But when they weren't arguing over that, they were watching Dorian as intently as Nyssa was.

"I wasn't aware he could smile like that," Reverie noted after a while.

"It's been a while," Corbin sighed.

Nyssa frowned and hugged her knees. "What do you mean?" she asked them.

Reverie met her with a smile. "Free of burden," she said. "That's the Prince I didn't know existed. He's skilled at hiding his pains."

"You know he hasn't had a drink since we left for the Bryn," Corbin said, glancing back at Reverie.

Reverie looked surprised. "Really? How did I not realize that?"

The words Gail had said to Nyssa rang in her ears. "That bad?" she managed, and Corbin met her with a solemn gaze. The look made her stomach knot.

But Dorian's laughter rang over the air, and Nyssa smiled as she watched him.

"He needed this," Corbin said before then looking at Nyssa again. "He needed you. And Lex. He needed his family. Being without such familiarities this past cycle after what happened... I've tried, but. You know him."

Nyssa sighed. "I do," she breathed. "But you're his family too," she said, looking between them. "Not just me. All of us. Us. Lex. Bala. Nadir. Dorian. This is the family we can choose. Not bound to one of lies and treachery. But one of earned trust and love. This family, all of us, was what kept me from falling into the void when I escaped. It was what kept me alive and pushing forward in that camp. Knowing I would do anything to protect any of you. This is the family our King and Queen made for us. And it's the family I will fight for until Haerland takes it away. I hope you two feel the same. My brother needs that around him."

Reverie had stopped toying in Corbin's hair. "Dammit, I need my sword," Reverie uttered.

Corbin frowned back at her. "Why?"

"So I can take a knee and give her my life, obviously," Reverie said.

Nyssa shook her head, almost laughing. "None of that," she insisted. "I'm not a Queen. That was my sister." She turned then, looking up at the sky, and she found Aydra in the stars. She remembered the way her sister had looked at her in that void, and her stomach knotted. Pointing up to the sky, Reverie and Corbin followed her finger.

"There's your Queen," she told them. "Everything in this war is for them and the sacrifices they made. You want to bow, bow before her."

"Nothing you have said changes my statement," Reverie told her. "Watching you in that room today was the closest thing I've ever seen to an actual leader. Your presence... I've never seen anyone command a room like that."

"You don't have to be the largest in the room to command it," Nadir said as he stepped across the sand to them. He smiled at Nyssa as he reached her. "You just have to make them believe you are."

Nyssa's heart skipped at the sight of him, dirt on his snug shirt, linen pants billowing in the wind. He made a mocking grunt as he pretended to exhaust to the ground, but ended up sitting behind Nyssa, leaning sideways on the log.

"What are we talking about?" Nadir asked.

Nyssa shifted, unable to keep the small smile from her face at him relaxing behind her. So much so that she hardly heard what he said. Entranced by his nonchalance and the way he looked at her.

She wanted to sprint across that fucking beach.

"I was just telling her I need my sword to offer her," Reverie said.

"Join the club," he replied, picking at the string he found on his sleeve. "The only sword she's taken has been Lex's. She won't even take mine."

"Because I am not a Queen," she argued. "You're the Commander and leader of these people. To take your sword would mean to take the loyalty of all the Honest."

"You have their loyalty."

"Maybe, but I will not force anything upon them," she argued. "I want it to be their choice."

Nadir sighed, and she knew that sigh. She knew he was biting back all the things he meant to say to her about how she could take that loyalty if she wanted it.

But instead of saying it, he merely grasped her hand and kissed her knuckles. "Are you feeling better about earlier?" he asked.

A jagged breath left her as she thought back to seeing Gail again at that meeting. "A little," she managed. "Seeing him again... It just brought back that fear from when the Infi appeared in his place."

"Do you want me to kill him?" he asked, and she smiled.

"Unfortunately, it sounds like we need him," she grunted.

"Dammit," he said under his breath.

She eyed him. "You really hate him, don't you?"

"He used to counter Draven's every suggestion and order."

"Perhaps he and Soli should have mated," she muttered.

He huffed. "They are fully aware of each other."

And the way he said it made her eyes narrow. "That's not terrifying at all," she balked.

"It's exactly what you think," he grumbled. "Probably tending to each other right now."

Her heart knotted at the thought of whatever scheme those two could come up with together. But he rubbed her back, and she met his eyes, and she was reminded of the way he'd railed into Gail's face earlier.

"You know, that was pretty sexy today," she dared to tell him.

"What was?" he frowned.

"Your going full Commander on Gail," she said.

Nadir chuckled under his breath. "Princess, if I'd known you liked violence, I'd have started punching people a long time ago instead of spending my time reading your filthy sonnets."

"Here, I thought you liked the sonnets," she mocked.

"I do," he sighed. "I like them a lot more than I should. But I also enjoy fighting, so maybe we can come up with a way to combine the two."

"When you figure it out, let me know," she said. "Sounds like a grand time."

"He's lucky I didn't kill him," he muttered. "I wanted to. Just imagining him stringing you along... I hate to think of what he said to you—"

"It was nothing I couldn't handle," she assured him.

He smiled up at her. "I might have paid to hear you put him in his place," he said fondly.

"Considering he's apparently stuck with us, I'm sure you won't have to pay to see it."

Nadir shook his head at her, to which she laughed. He sat up, his hand touched her side, and her eyes closed. She sank back, his arms curling around her as she rested against his rising chest. His legs bent on either side of her. One hand draping around her shoulders, the other around her waist, she sank her temple against his head as he curled her up in her arms. She clung her hands to his wrap, feeling his lips curve against her throat as he hugged her.

Her heart ached with his every touch. That safety of his presence. How the world and their problems seemed so minuscule and distant when they were together. When his nose nudged her throat, she leaned her head against him. He spoke words in her ear of the old language. The noise of it caused a chill up her spine, her hair to raise on her arms.

"I am terrified to ask what you're actually saying," she managed.

He laughed, head hanging just briefly. "I'm naming off the crops I need to harvest tomorrow."

Her mouth dropped as she looked back to him. "Here I was thinking you were saying some beautiful poem," she joked.

His smirk widened, and he leaned in, lips pressing to her throat. "I don't need a beautiful poem to romance you, Princess. My to-do list will do just fine."

"That easy, am I?" she asked.

"Yes. Though I was just reciting my list for tomorrow. Had I wanted to romance you..." His lips tickled her ear, dark whispered breaths making her thighs squeeze as he spoke more words she didn't understand.

"What was that?" she asked when he paused.

"That..." His lips dragged across her throat, his fingers squeezing against her waist. "That was just a few of the things I want to do to you after you've crossed this beach. I want to know every fantasy you've ever had. Because I know you well enough to know they're all filthy, and I cannot wait to fulfill them."

The Commander had surfaced, and her heart skipped at the anticipation of whatever it was he was about to do to her. She released a jagged breath. "Sprinting," she uttered.

"Take your time," he drawled, and she knew he was mocking her. His hand moved under her bent leg, hidden by the dress, and she drew a sharp breath at the tickle of his finger between her legs. "Every day you stand on the other side is another hour I plan to devour you. Completely—" His nose drew circles against her cheek, lips on her skin and making her body tingle. That finger dragging along the lace over her folds, and her eyes rolled. "Wholly—" his teeth grazed her ear "—and utterly unrestrained."

With the final word, he slipped a finger beneath the lace, and she knew just how wet she was just from his words. His finger delved between her folds and grazed her entrance.

"I've waited nearly a century for you, Princess," he whispered. "By the time you master that form—" Breaths caught in her throat when his finger pressed inside her, and the arm across her chest tightened. "—I'll have thought of many more ways I can have you."

Thighs clenching, she found her hips shifting without realizing it, allowing him further access. Forgetting there were people around them. She leaned back and felt his length stiffening at her back, and she turned her head.

Her eyes met his, and she had to swallow at the darkness of his gaze. He pushed in another finger, digits curling and hooking inside her. Her mouth sagged in response. Hitting that spot that made her forget reality. Delving deeper with every stroke, massaging her, his mouth mirroring hers as he made her strain. Quiet moans stifling in her throat. And then he pulled out, dragging those fingers up her slickness to circle her clit.

"Will you stay this wet for me while you cross?" he uttered, the words reminding her of those he'd said to her at her castle before he'd left her bed. "Or should I need to haul you to my shack right now and give you air?"

His fingers pinched her nerves as he said it, the sharpness of that pleasurable pain making her own fingers curl around her dress. "You keep doing that, and I won't make it to your shack," she managed, and those digits tapped on her sensitivity, making her thighs flinch. A new stinging sensation she knew he was holding back with, and she wondered how it would feel to have him unhinged on her. Riding out that pleasure and pain as she shattered around him. Having him take control of her and unleash the Commander side of him she knew he'd mostly held back with.

A mix of which she knew she would have to tame her form before taking advantage of, and she knew he knew it too.

He held her chin and tilted her head back, making her eyes open when she didn't even realize she had closed them. "Do you like that?" he whispered, pinching her clit again and rolling those nerves between his fingers.

Her jaw quivered. "Yes, Commander," she breathed.

He pressed hard on her, the weight of it making her clit throb, her breath skip. Keeping the pressure, he laid the two fingers on either side of the nerves, squeezing it between them as he moved the two fingers up and down her slickness. Pinching it and teasing her to the point she couldn't breathe.

"Do you want me to splay you on my bed so you cannot move while I do this to you?"

He picked up his pace, making her spin. "Yes."

Swirling those fingers, her muscles began to reach. Her thighs tensing with every move of his hand. She thought his mouth on her had been nerve-wracking the night before. But this... Everything they'd done felt tame to what he was teasing her with right then.

His free hand moved from her chin and to her throat, thumb stroking her trachea. The other moving faster down the entirety of her. Pressure become greater and greater with every stroke. He was avoiding touching atop her clit, but rather squeezing it between those fingers and making her squirm.

"Shh..."

And she knew he was smirking at her.

"Nadir..." she begged as she trembled.

His fingers moved again, and this time when he started tapping on her clit, he did it fast. Fast as he'd once broken her with his fingers inside her. But her heartbeat throbbed in those nerves with every pleasured slap rippling through her. She was biting her lip so hard she could taste the iron of the blood trickling into her mouth. She could feel herself denying that moan, trying to keep it in and, in turn, almost denying herself that release. She began to squirm, fists clinching to anything she could grab to, ready to let go.

Nadir kissed her, and his hand tightened against her throat. The pressure of it sent her spiraling. Those two fingers slammed back inside her and hooked around to the spot, moving as quickly as he had slapped on her clit, and she came apart. Rippling and shaking. Moaning into his mouth as he slowed with her come down.

She couldn't help herself from surrendering fully to his embrace. Her heart racing and stomach knotting with every brush of his tongue. Every squeeze of his hand against her waist. She wondered how long she could make one kiss... If just her lips pausing to linger against his counted as stopping, or if she could hold him that close the rest of the night and barter with the Sun once more to make this night last forever.

To the point that she was totally against him, and his arms were hugging her as though she might disappear. One hand on her back, the other moved from between her legs to down the back of her thigh. She could feel her finish on her bare skin. His want spun her mind, and she had to grab him to keep from falling off balance and into the fire beside them.

And when he pulled back, he brought those fingers to his lips. Her thighs squeezed again as she watched him taste her, and she felt the wad of stick that she didn't know what to do with between her legs and trickling down her backside to the sand.

"You're still shaking, Princess," he breathed as his hand entwined in her hair, nails scratching and delicately tugging on the roots. "Did you enjoy that?"

She stammered upon meeting his gaze, seeing the mischievous and lust-filled glint in his eyes.

"When you see fire, I'll be in front of you," she managed.

His thumb brushed her cheek, nose nudging hers. "I'll be waiting."

Lips brushing, they both hesitated, the anticipation of the kiss swelling between them with the heat of their bodies. But Nyssa shifted and turned into him, and she wrapped her hand around his neck.

"Make it a good one, Commander."

"Yes, Princess."

Their lips melted together once more in a passionate embrace that caused her heart to swell. She wanted him unhinged. Unleashed. But for now, she would take this Nadir. This last kiss before she threw herself into training and her new role.

He pulled back after a few moments and laid his forehead against hers. But his fingers continued to scratch in her hair, and she limped in his arms.

"I can't wait to dance with you," he whispered.

The words made her lashes rise. "Can I make a request?" she asked.

"For the dancing?"

"No," she laughed. "Just in general."

"Anything."

"I want to see your hair undone."

"What?" he balked.

"Your hair is always up in this... *ball*," she mocked. "I've only ever seen it over your shoulders once. I want to see it completely undone."

He continued to stare. "Why?"

She almost laughed at the look on his face. "Raw and free Nadir Storn," she insisted.

"You realize how large my hair is, right?" he asked, still hung up on her wanting to see it.

"I imagine so." She leaned forward, lips tickling his jaw. "I can't wait to feel it draping over my thighs," she whispered. "Losing my hands in it as I hold you between my legs."

His curiosity turned leer, and he grinned slyly. "All your fantasies, Princess," he uttered. "Though, I am debating whether you will be able to touch my hair the first time you see it."

"You plan to deny me that?" she mocked.

"I plan on denying you a lot of things," he promised.

And the dare in his gaze made her breath shorten. He huffed softly, nose nudging her throat again. As though he couldn't help himself, his open mouth sucked on her skin, and she relaxed in his arms at the soft pleasure.

Someone coughed not far from them, and Nyssa found Reverie and Corbin watching them.

"Entertainment in public also runs in the family, I see," Reverie winked at her.

Nyssa's face paled.

She had genuinely forgotten they were on the beach in full view of his entire village.

"Oh, shit," was all Nyssa could manage.

"Don't worry," Reverie said assuringly. "I think it was just us that caught the display. Commander—" Reverie gave him a sideways smile "—knew that smirk of yours was more dangerous than you let on."

Nadir laughed, straightening up behind Nyssa. "Thanks for the lookout," he said.

Reverie winked at him and went back to doing Corbin's hair. "Anytime."

Nyssa gaped between the pair, but before she could say anything, Nadir kissed her, and she surrendered to him.

For a while after, he simply held her as they watched the rest of the people running around and playing drinking games. A couple of people came up to Nadir to talk to him, and each time he stayed holding on behind her, conversing with his friends but touching her somehow. Moved on from the tease of their public display like it had never happened. Though the tremble in Nyssa's thighs and the ache of her clit told her it had been real.

The sight of the water coming up and wrapping around people's ankles took her into a daze. Her mind drifting to all the times water had wrapped her feet, and she'd felt comforted by the cool pressure. To when even in that void, with the water beneath her toes, she hadn't felt suppressed by it. A small comfort in a room of mirrors that made her heart constrict.

"Hey—" she snapped out of the daze, realizing one of Nadir's friends had just walked away from them. "Hey, I forgot to ask you something."

"What?"

"What does the poem mean?" she asked.

"Which one?"

"The one you read me from Somniarb's diary. The flowers beneath our feet one."

"Oh, that one. I forgot I hadn't told you," he said. "It was about her and Duarb. Duarb loved her like a little sister. Much like you and your brother. He would go to her tree, play with her in the meadows full of flowers of the Preymoor, or sometimes she would visit the sea with him. She loved to play in his wind. In all of her writings, she refers to him as either the night or the wind, but always she as the trees. The night hugs the trees, shrouding them in shadows and making them feel safe as he always did her."

Nyssa could see it. Imagining the pair like she and Dorian. Chasing each other and laughing. "I love that," she whispered. "What does she call Arbina?"

"The fire," he whispered. "The fire that burned and consumed her, until she fled her reality, and locked herself away so as to escape the pain."

Her jaw tightened at the words, but she pushed the memory of her mother from her mind, and she focused on the poem. "Remembering that poem helped me in the void," she told him.

"How so?"

"I got the words mixed up," she admitted. "My feet were submerged in water at one point. The..." The more she spoke about it, the more she found herself hesitating.

"You don't have to talk—"

"No, I do," she cut him off. "There were mirrors. Black water. I was hanging onto a ledge over it. For some reason, in my head, I heard water beneath our feet, and it went to the rest of the poem." She met his eyes. "And then I heard you telling me to take your hand."

"You heard me?"

"Of course I heard you," she breathed.

A glisten settled in the crease of his eyes, and he hugged her a little tighter, forehead lying against hers.

The noise of Dorian and Lex shouting at each other averted Nyssa's attention. She almost laughed at the sight of them. The grin on Dorian's face that he was trying to hide. Lex doing the same. She wondered what they were fighting about. But Dorian flinched, and Lex ran after him again.

"This is the night I want to memorize," Nadir uttered in her ear. "All of us—"

"On your beach," she smiled back at him.

He chuckled under his breath, his lips pressing to her shoulder. "On my beach," he agreed. "Even them," he added with an upwards nod to the stars.

Nyssa squeezed his arms. "I think they would be sitting like this," she said. "Draven would be so protective of her carrying their child."

"Like a dragon," Nadir grunted.

She laughed, and he rocked them side to side. Watching Lex continue to chase and knock at Dorian, Bala calling out the game. Reverie and Corbin continued to watch them, too, Reverie pulling on his hair and him glaring back at her.

"I think I like her," she said to Nadir.

"Who? The Dreamer?"

"Yeah," she said. "Seems to be taking care of my brother."

Nadir scoffed. "In every way," he uttered. "I went to change clothes earlier and walked in on her on his shoulders."

Her brows lifted as she looked back at him, and she remembered how Nadir had held her like that against the post of her bed at

Magnice. "Did he make her beg?" she asked.

"I didn't stick around to watch."

"Maybe you should have," she joked. "My brother has some interesting tricks. Most of which were taught to him by Lex." She saw his eyes narrow, and she laughed. "He enjoys public fornication," she said simply. "It's hard not to walk in on his exploits sometimes when he takes them anywhere—including the hallway or my own room. He probably wanted you to walk in on them today."

"I suppose I should be grateful he was not on the porch."

"You really should be," she laughed.

His arms tightened around her, and she laid her head against his. For a moment, the noise of the laughter and drums simply filled her ears, and she vowed to memorize every noise, smell, and touch around her. Wanting to keep hold of this night with all her loved ones around her in the middle of a war.

"I don't want to go to sleep," she whispered.

"That can be arranged," he uttered, and she felt him grinning against her throat, to which she rolled her eyes playfully.

"Do you know what I would like to see?"

"What's that?"

"You challenging my brother on the log tomorrow."

Nadir pulled back, forehead wrinkling but smiling nonetheless. "You want me to ask your brother to fight me on the rolling logs... In the ocean?"

She eyed the look on his face. "I can't tell if you're excited or scared," she mocked.

"Neither can I," he decided. "But a chance to kick your brother's ass is a chance I'll gladly take."

She started to speak, but running footsteps caught her attention, and they turned just in time to see Dorian leap over the fire and nearly fall into Reverie and Corbin.

Reverie screeched, pulling Corbin's hair and causing him to shout. Dorian fell to the sand just as Lex's feet hit the other side of the fire, and she pressed her hands to her hips.

"Watch yourself tomorrow, Prince," she eyed him, two fingers moving in front of her eyes and then in his direction. "When you least expect it, I'll be there."

Dorian grinned from the ground, ignoring Corbin and Reverie smacking his arm for jumping on them. "Looking forward to it, Second Sun," he winked.

"Well, now I have to start over," Reverie grunted about Corbin's hair.

"What—why?"

Dorian pushed up to the log, leaning in beside Reverie. "Can I help?"

"No," they both said at once.

He pouted, and the pair laughed as they shook their heads.

"Don't give us that look," Corbin countered.

"Those adorable eyes will get you nowhere," Reverie said.

His pout turned to smolder, and Nyssa watched Corbin force himself to look away.

"I think they get me lots of places," Dorian said in a low voice.

Nyssa snorted, and Reverie met her eyes.

"Come get your brother," Reverie said playfully.

"I think you're handling him just fine," Nyssa countered.

Reverie smiled and turned back to Dorian and Corbin, and Nyssa watched as a grin lit up her brother's face. One he'd been absent of even the day before. As though his coming back had allowed his heart the freedom to enjoy and recognize happiness again. A burden lifted from his shoulders.

Nyssa's heart hurt at the way they both looked at him. Not with just the lust that every other person he'd dared entangle himself with had always looked at him. But rather with love and admiration.

World shattering happiness she wondered when her brother would finally feel.

Nadir laughed at whatever his friend had just said upon coming to sit beside them. But Nyssa didn't hear much of the conversation. Nadir simply held her hand as he chatted, and Nyssa watched her loved ones. She caught sight of Bala and Lex talking down by the surf, Lex twirling the bamboo stick in her hands as Bala laughed at whatever she'd just said. A few of the Venari and Honest stood around them, and Nyssa realized perhaps it was a drinking game underway.

Nadir was right.

This was the night she wanted to memorize.

Her eagle screeched overhead then. She started to smile up at him until she heard the word he called down to her.

Wyverdraki, he called.

Her body chilled, and she squeezed Nadir's leg.

"Hey," she said, shifting in her seat. "How exactly do your people feel about the dragons?"

Nadir frowned at her. "Pretty terrified, actually."

"Oh." Nyssa started to stand. "You might want to get them off the beach then."

"Why?"

"Because they're coming."

The words had hardly left her before she heard footsteps running towards them—*Bala*.

Venari were starting to dart away from the edge of the beach and to the dunes. They'd heard the beasts' wings on the wind, and they were calling out to the Honest to back off the shores. Bala's eyes met Nyssa's.

"You heard them?" Nyssa asked.

Bala nodded. "So did the rest of my people. The dragons never come to the beach."

A great bellow sounded overhead, and every person flinched to their knees. Dorian sprang up, Corbin and Reverie at his side, and he joined Nyssa and Bala.

"What are they doing—"

Nyssa didn't hear what her brother said. Because the noise of a song filled her ears, and her nose began to burn. Insides swelling with the words she recognized. She grabbed Dorian's hand.

"It's the song," she said, meeting his eyes.

"What?" he managed.

"The song they sang together at the end," she said, still listening for it as it echoed over the trees. "Drae and Draven. *It's their song.*"

Wind swept voraciously over the sand, billowing out a few of the fires, and Dorian's voice dwindled. He pulled her in with the last of the words and sank his arm around her shoulder just as the Rhamocour landed at the end of the jetty.

Everyone straightened, widened eyes staring at the great beast as its long neck drew up, green eyes pouring over the people.

A swarm of Wyverdraki flew over them, a few choosing to stay in the air while some landed on the rocks and the sand. Fluttering voices filled Nyssa's ears to the point that it nearly weighed her down. Questions and basic conversation. Arguments and mocking.

A shudder drew down her spine. The barrier she'd once held there now vacant since her time in the void, leaving her completely open and vulnerable to their voices and emotions. Her knees started to buckle, hands pressing over her ears as panic filled her.

SHUT UP, she nearly shouted at them.

Silence.

Dorian and Nadir's hands were on her arms, and Nyssa pulled herself straight. She ignored the flee of her heart and looked around, finally meeting the Rhamocour's gaze.

Why are you here? she asked.

We came to see our King.

The vibration of the great beast's voice chilled her.

"What are they doing here?" Dorian asked.

"They never come this far south," Bala said. "Normally, they stay east of my kingdom. Never this far--"

"They came to see their King," Nyssa said as she reached for Bala's hand.

Bala stared at her. "What?"

"That's what she just said," Nyssa shrugged. "They came to see you."

Nadir grabbed her arm as they went to leave. "Are you sure about this?" he asked softly.

Anxiety and nausea swelled inside her at the thought of allowing such a creature back into her mind. "No," she admitted. "But I have to do this." She glanced back up at the stars, and her heart knotted. "For her. I can't keep pushing them away."

Bala and Dorian were waiting on her when she turned, the purple glowing fire of the Rhamocour on the jetty, illuminating the great beast. She joined them, and together the three Kings walked to meet the great Noctuan beast.

As they walked, Nyssa's arms began to tingle. Something else had joined them. She glanced back over her shoulder, only to find the Ulfram alpha and the rest of the pack's eyes reflecting back to her from the bonfire lights, but they didn't emerge from the trees. Almost as though they were simply there to watch and keep an eye on things.

But as more and more Noctuans emerged from the woods, including the skeleton glow of the Noirdiem, Nyssa realized this was more than the Rhamocour coming to see Bala.

They'd come to see if she was worthy of the loyalty they offered.

To crown their King.

As they neared, Nyssa and Dorian let Bala approach on her own. The beast would size her up and determine her worth simply by detecting how pure her love for them was.

Bala approached the beast and held out her hand, palm up. The dragon sniffed her all over, an act that would have had Nyssa frightened, but Bala stayed still.

Steady as the breeze that circled.

Smaller Wyverdraki moved all around, some flapping their wings. Some rising into the sky to tangle with one another. But the Rhamocour didn't move.

"From today until my last, you have my life," Bala whispered. "Allow me to look after our home and protect the sanctity of our forest. I am yours."

The Rhamocour's head dipped in response, a low purr emitting from her throat. Bala's hand sank onto the beast's nose, and purple fire lit up from the inside, illuminating everything in its wake. It rose up her neck to her spiked spine, then all the way down the ridge and to her tail. A warmth pulsed over Nyssa's skin at the feeling it exuded for Bala, heart bleeding with the swelling of its love.

Nyssa reached for Dorian's hand and held it so he could feel it too.

She heard him curse under his breath, and he squeezed her hand back as the feelings filled his core.

Shadows wrapped up Bala's arm, moving around and around her limb, and Nyssa watched as Bala's own phoenix marking began to glow purple on her skin. The bond of the Noctuans radiating through her. It crawled her form all the way up to her face and her eyes, and when she opened them, purple fire flashed.

The Rhamocour sank to the ground and bowed its head.

Followed by every Noctuan on the beach doing the same.

Nyssa looked around, noting the Ulframs lying down, the Noirdiem with bent front legs. Even Samar had joined them, and her glowing figure settled on her knee. Nyssa wished she could see into the trees. See if the Aberds were bowing from their places in the trees.

A screech sounded in the air. Wind knocked over them. Three sets of great wings circled over the scene, and then the enormous birds landed in the sand. The Noctuan brothers of the Aenean Orel, the Aviteths, had arrived. Almost like great ravens in appearance, they too bowed low for their new King.

Seeing Bala become crowned King by the Noctuans, seeing them accept her as their leader, had Nyssa restless and determined.

Nyssa glanced to Dorian, who nodded in response, and together, they dropped to their own knees.

The first of the Promised line to ever bow before a Venari. Nyssa and Dorian took their places behind her. Supporting her.

But Bala wasn't having it.

She turned and reached for them both, tears coming down her cheeks as she tried to keep herself together. She pulled them off the ground and into a great hug.

"Together," she managed. "We were left to save this world together." Her hands rested on theirs when they pulled away, and she squeezed their hands as she looked between them. "I cannot hold this world on my own. I need you two at my side."

"Together," Dorian promised.

The Rhamocour purred behind them, and Nyssa shifted as she had an idea. "I want to try something," Nyssa said.

Dorian exchanged a look with Bala, who shared his curiosity. "Okay."

"Just... Count for me to keep me from falling under."

Dorian nodded.

The pair turned towards one another and held their hands together. Nyssa tried to remain relaxed as she pulled for her fire, unsure of what she was doing but knowing the two in front of her would keep her grounded.

"One," Dorian said as the ash rose on her fingertips.

She gritted her teeth, heart beginning to skip. "Two," she managed, streaks pulsing.

"Breathe," Dorian reminded her. "Hold there."

"I can't—" it stretched further than her elbow, and she started to shake.

"Yes, you can. Eyes on me," Dorian said firmly.

Her gaze lifted to his, and she felt her insides calm.

"One," he repeated.

The streaks stopped at the bend of her arm. The fissures on her flesh cracked, and an amber hue emitted from inside.

Dorian's eyes darkened, his fingertips blackening, as he pulled for his form, but he didn't let it grow further than his arm.

Nyssa's weight shifted as his own fissures glowed navy.

Flames erupted on their entwined hands. The world vibrated in Nyssa's eyes, but Dorian squeezed her hand.

"Stay with us, Nys," he said. "Fight it. You are in control. Not it."

"Breathe, Nyssa," Bala reminded her.

Nyssa forced out a long breath, and she concentrated on holding that form at bay, her muscles straining. Amber flames entwined with his navy ones.

Bala stepped between them. Her hand lifted, and the wind swept gently through the fires, giving them oxygen and fusing them together.

Black flames rose between them and wrapped up Dorian and Nyssa's arms.

Nyssa's eyes lifted to her brother's, and he smiled. Bala's fingers moved again. The fire spread between them, taking the shape of the phoenix.

"Show off," Dorian muttered to her.

Bala smiled, the fire dancing in all their eyes. But her gaze shifted past them then, and she gave an upwards nod to where the bonfire had been going on.

The siblings followed her nod, and the sight of what was happening made Nyssa's form falter. Dorian's dwindled with her, and together, the three stilled.

Every person on the beach had dropped to one knee. Swords in front of a few. Others had their hands over their chest in salute. Nadir and Lex grinned at them from their knelt positions beside each other. Reverie and Corbin both smiling at Dorian.

"Remember them, Kings," Lex called out.

And Nyssa's heart knotted at the realization of what was happening.

Bala was the first to move.

She pushed between Nyssa and Dorian, and she drew her sword.

A King confident in her place. Demanding respect without ever needing to ask for it or fearing it ever being questioned.

"We have questions," she said, the tone of her voice commanding every person there and sending a visible chill through the air. Wind swept over the tops of their backs.

The Rhamocour cried out behind them. Purple fire lit the sky and evaporated. But for a moment, Nyssa saw the illuminated bent heads of every Honest and Venari on the beach.

"Name them," Nadir shouted firmly, and Nyssa noted that his gaze had not left her.

Bala began to pace before the crowd, eyes darting over the people. "We are not looking for anyone to fight in our names," she said. "We are not standing before you to ask you to die while charging strangers and screaming out our names on battlefields while we sit in castles and drink wine. What we are asking is that you fight at our sides as our equals. We ask that you fight for your own freedoms. To fight for this land and our continued survival."

Two beats rattled the ground.

Two beats that made Nyssa's weight shift, her chin rise higher, and she saw Dorian straighten beside her.

"Do you make this choice of your own free will?" Bala asked. "To kneel before Kings not forced upon you by bloodlines but rather of earned trust and respect?"

A collective, short battle grunt sounded, and Nyssa's chest swelled.

Her feet moved, and before she realized it, she was standing at Bala's side, arms wrapped around her chest. Noting the eyes fixating on her.

"Will you follow us?" she asked loudly.

Two more beats vibrated beneath her feet.

Dorian appeared on the other side of Bala. "Will you fight with us?" he asked.

Two beats and a grunt sounded.

"Will you support and trust us to make the best decisions for our people?" Bala asked.

The battle grunt roared, and heads began to lift.

Bala reached for both Dorian and Nyssa's hands, and wind curled the air.

"Then stand with us."

The Rhamocour cried out again, making goosebumps rise on Nyssa's skin. Her lashes flickered, and when they opened, she saw people rising to their feet.

"Hail your Kings," Nadir shouted to his people.

Cries filled the air.

"And to the High Kings behind us," Nyssa added, meeting his eyes.

Swords lifted to the sky.

Bala's hands squeezed Dorian and Nyssa's as the Honest and Venari began to celebrate. Whoops and high five's, excited bursts of laughter, and the clanks of swords in the air. Bala wrapped her arms around them both.

"Who knew the Venari King was such a dramatic," Dorian mocked.

"You know, I was perfectly well mannered before I met you two," Bala said. "You're terrible influences."

Nyssa met Dorian's eyes.

"Sounds like us," Dorian smirked.

"Sounds like *you*," Nyssa argued. "I am the epitome of innocence. I would never encourage such behavior."

Bala and Dorian laughed so hard they nearly fell to the ground. And Nyssa was left standing on her own and staring at them, trying to hide the smile on her lips. But she shook her head, and her eyes wandered back to the crowd, finding Nadir smiling and staring at her as his people celebrated around him. Dancing by the fire. Cheers'ing their drinks. A collective army of people now with a singular goal: to keep their freedom.

69

Watching Dorian and Nadir battle each other on the rolling logs was the most entertainment Nyssa had had in months. She took bets with Reverie over who would win with which weapon. They were well matched against one another. Both steadfast and equally balanced.

"Come on, Prince!" Reverie shouted once at him, sitting on her knees beside Corbin. "I'm losing all my gold to your sister."

"Wait—" Dorian swatted at Nadir's legs, but Nadir jumped, and the Commander's stick hit Dorian's knee. Dorian cursed and fell into the ocean.

Laughing, Nyssa threw her hands in the air with victory. Reverie's eyes rolled, but she slapped a gold coin into Nyssa's palm as Dorian broke the surface.

"Fuck off—my sister is betting against me?" he said loudly, swimming over to the jetty rocks. He met Nyssa's eyes. "Traitor," he accused, though the play in his tone and lift at the corner of his lips made her head shake.

Nadir extended his hand and pulled him up to the rocks. He grinned and said something, clapping Dorian's arm, and Dorian laughed. Nyssa couldn't help her curiosity as she watched them interact, unaware that they'd ever really shared many conversations, but the two were joking together like old friends. Nadir grabbed the wooden swords from the rocks and tossed two to Dorian. Dorian took a few steps back and set up, whirling the blades in his hands.

"Someone is going to break an ankle on those rocks," Reverie muttered as they watched.

"Dorian," Nyssa and Corbin said at the same time.

Nyssa caught the Belwark's shy grin, and she laughed with him.

"I'm glad to see he finally broke you, Bin."

"Broken feels like an understatement," Reverie muttered from behind her cup.

Corbin pinched her thigh in response, and Reverie choked on her drink. She started to lunge at him, but the sound of Lex's voice over the waves averted all their attentions.

"Reverie Asherdoe," Lex called out, making Reverie nearly fall to the sand at the rate she stood to her feet.

"Second Sun." She brushed the sand off her backside. "What—"

Lex didn't give her a chance to speak. She tossed a spear in the Dreamer's hands. "My Princess is injured," Lex said. "I find myself in need of a sparring partner, and I'm told you're quite formidable."

Nyssa watched as Reverie's eyes dilated with smugness and delight, and she tossed the stick from one hand to the other. "I can handle myself in a fight." And Nyssa could hear the confident toy in her voice.

"I'm also told you put my cohort on his back when you first met," Lex added at Corbin's expense.

"I will murder him," Corbin said under his breath.

Nyssa snorted, and Corbin shot her a playful glare. She clapped her hand over her lips as though she could hide it. She hadn't laughed so much in months, and her face was starting to hurt with it.

"Actually, Bin is pretty easy to get on his back," Reverie bantered, winking at Corbin.

Corbin's hand brushed over his face, obvious he was concealing his smile, and perhaps a blush, and Nyssa grinned at the sight of seeing Corbin finally relaxed.

As Reverie and Lex made off down the sand, Nyssa reached for another piece of bread from the stash they'd brought out that morning. She watched Dorian and Nadir combat each other on the rocks, both jumping and blocking the other, careful not to twist their ankles on the jagged jetty.

"Thank you again, Bin," Nyssa said after a few minutes. "I know how rocky your relationship with him once was. Honestly, I thought you would have left him by now."

Corbin pulled his knees into his chest, the strong silence of his figure making Nyssa look over to him. "He's hard to walk away from," he finally said.

Nyssa noted the softness in Corbin's eyes as he watched Dorian battle, and she sat up a little straighter. "You know... I feel, as his sister, that there's something I should say to you."

Corbin looked at her this time, lips lifting at the left corner. "Go on," he said as if he knew where she was going.

"I have a book of torture techniques on Nadir's porch waiting to get translated." She popped a piece of bread in her mouth and met his eyes. "If either of you hurt him or break his heart, I'll go through it page by page—" Her smile spread to her lips, and she lifted her chin as she chewed on her last piece. "You'll beg for death, and I'll laugh in your face while I tie weights to your balls and you crawl for me."

Corbin's grin widened. "You say it so sweetly, too," he bantered.

Nyssa shrugged innocently, lashes batting. "Haven't lost my touch."

The pair sat back on the sand and watched the others spar with one another for a few hours. Nyssa listened to Corbin tell her more about Dorian's trials and about the mountains. She loved the way it sounded. Boisterous and friendly. After a while, Dorian came sinking into the sank in front of them, begging for water, and then he fell against Corbin's lap. Despite Corbin nearly rolling his eyes at the Prince, he didn't move him when Dorian settled his head against Corbin's abs, facing Nyssa as he rested from the morning fight.

Corbin told him what he'd noticed Dorian had done wrong while fighting, but Nyssa didn't hear them. Nadir hadn't joined them. He'd caught her eye in the surf, given her a small smile, and then almost forced himself to go down the beach. Her heart had faltered, but she knew why he'd done it.

He was attempting to give her space, and she hated it. She glanced down at her hand, allowing that ash to rise on her fingertips a moment, and she pushed it back down.

Fucking Arbina.

Nyssa averted her gaze down to Reverie and Lex. Every strike from Reverie was fueled with rage and passion. Different from Lex's, whose moves were carefully calculated and with proper form. But Reverie... she battled as though every swipe meant life or death. Every somersault and leap meant keeping her next breath. She was a wildling in a beautiful disguise, and Nyssa didn't bother guarding her stare.

"Damn, Dorian," she muttered after a few minutes. "Didn't realize your girl was an assassin."

Dorian moved his head so that he could see down the beach where she was looking. A grin spread on his lips, and he finally sat up.

"You should have her hold a knife to your throat," he uttered.

"I bet you come apart the moment the iron touches your skin,"

Nyssa teased.

"I really do," Dorian admitted with a rattled sigh.

Nyssa noted the smirk on Corbin's lips. "I'm sure you do too, Bin," she said. "Don't try to deny it."

Corbin sat up, his shoulder brushing with Dorian's. The three watched Reverie lunge at Lex over and over, a couple of times making even Lex back up with her aggression, until she jumped clear over Lex's head and swiped her legs out from under her.

"Fuck me," Nyssa muttered.

"Remember when she did that to Dag?" Dorian recalled fondly to Corbin.

Corbin chuckled. "Caught them all off-guard. Hagen was even on his knees."

Dorian leaned closer to Corbin, his gaze darkening. "Do you know who else will be on their knees later?" he leered the Belwark in a low tone, apparently aroused by having watched Reverie battle or the sight of Corbin's stern chest glistening with sweat from the sun. Dorian's lips pressed to Corbin's throat, and Corbin visibly tensed.

"You?" the Belwark suggested.

Dorian groaned. "Maybe," he mumbled, hand riding up Corbin's thigh. "Is that what you want? For me to finally suck your cock while she watches or sucks mine?"

"Oh, *fuck all*, Dorian," Nyssa snapped, shoving him into the Belwark. "That's not what I wanted to hear this morning. *Architects*, my ears are bleeding now."

Dorian laughed and swung his arm around her shoulders. "What's wrong, sis? Mad you've decided to be celibate a while—*Ow!*"

She'd twisted his pec, and he held his chest as he fell against Corbin again. Corbin fought his smile as he patted Dorian's hair like a child and shook his head.

After lunch, Nyssa grabbed her brother before he could break for his activities and dragged him down to the end of the jetty. She wanted to introduce him to the sea serpent. Not just because she wanted him to feel the connection to another animal, but also because she hoped to scare him and perhaps get a bit of payback for him nearly fucking Corbin in front of her earlier.

They paused at the end, and Nyssa crouched down to the water's edge, her eyes closing. She pushed her core out for the creature and called out her name. She hoped she could reach her.

"Is she going to eat me?" Dorian asked.

"Maybe," she shrugged. "Maybe not if you apologize for being a shit earlier."

Dorian chuckled as he plopped down on a rock. "Sorry," he muttered. "Got carried away."

She eyed him over her shoulder. "Maybe I'll tell her just to hiss at you the once then," she teased. Her eagle fluttered down and perched beside Dorian then. The great bird screeched, and Dorian balked away from him.

"I know, I know," Dorian grunted. "You don't like me."

"He likes you," she told him as the bird laughed.

"Yeah? He has a fuck of a way of showing it," Dorian said as he eyed the beast.

"He thinks it's funny when you run away from him," she said. "Payback for you taunting him when we were kids."

Something reached out for her then, and she recognized it as the serpent. "There she is," she mumbled under her breath. She reached back for Dorian and grabbed his hand as the warmth of her call moved through her core, and Dorian squeezed her hand back.

"That's powerful," he muttered. "You said she helped you escape the camp?"

Nyssa stood to her feet. "She did. Protected me while I was in my form. Nadir could hardly get to me," she recalled. "He said…" But her heart sank at the memory, and she couldn't get the words out. How Lex had told her Nadir screamed for her when she wasn't responding. How she'd nearly snapped his neck and killed him while her form had taken over.

"Nys?" Dorian called, rubbing her shoulder.

Nyssa blinked back the emotion in her chest. "I'm okay," she said. "I —"

The noise of people shouting averted her attention. The pair turned, and Nyssa's heart dropped.

Riders were bounding down the beach.

70

It wasn't Man.

These were Dreamers.

Silver from their winged helmets bounced off in the sunlight. At least two hundred persons on horseback, they bounded over the dunes and towards the village. Nyssa recognized the legion's sigil. It was a company from the Village of Dreams—one of their more elite companies—and she wondered what had brought them to the Umber after a whole cycle of being silent.

Honest persons ran from the surf where they'd been training and went straight into battle as though it had been practiced. Dreamers were cut down from the horses. Shouts filled the air. Blood spilled onto the innocent sand.

Even the seamstresses and cooks took swords out from beneath their tables and ran into battle.

"What a bunch of idiots," Dorian muttered behind her.

"They chose to ambush Haerland's oldest army," Nyssa said, arms crossing over her chest. "At their home place." She turned to her brother. "Do you think they actually thought this would work?"

Dorian squinted at the beach. "Is that Ash?"

"What—" she snapped her head back around. "Where?"

Dorian pulled her to him and pointed, and she followed the line. Her fists curled in on themselves at the sight of the proud Dreamer. She recognized his helmet. A great Captain's helmet with a mohawk of white hair and flattened silver etched wings on either side. It had a nose piece down the front, colored of stark white with swirling constellations embedded in the design. She remembered holding it once when she and Lex were in the Village. Heavy and larger than her own head. It was a beautiful piece of craftsmanship.

She wanted to watch Ash's blood stain the inside when she cut off his head.

"He's mine," she growled as rage surged through her. The memory of Ash standing in that Throne Room and telling the Council about Aydra bled through her, and she reminded herself to breathe as she felt her form try to surface.

"Be my guest," he said. "Just remember our dear brother is mine. You can even take my sword. Here—"

But Nyssa didn't want the sword.

"Keep your sword," she told him. "You'll need it."

"And you don't?"

"I can hardly hold the damned thing," she countered. "My arm is broken, remember? I have my dagger. Fire. Serpent. Powerful Second taking her time on the porch before she commands the field."

Dorian followed her eyesight to the house, where Lex was, indeed, leaned against the banister and pushing her arm braces on, staring at the battle as though she were waiting on a moment to make her entrance.

"So dramatic," Dorian mocked.

"People are probably saying the same thing about us," Nyssa said. Her gaze squinted at the sight of what she thought was Reverie and Corbin running into the battle.

In full combat mode, Reverie jumped at one and knocked him off the horse. She bounded over the man, sword twirling in her hand. But she didn't shove it in him.

She twisted his neck, and the Dreamer crumpled into the sand.

"Glad to know your girl is on our side," Nyssa said.

Dorian started laughing. "Fuck me," he chuckled. "I didn't even have to go find her an army. The bastards just walked in here."

Nyssa squinted up at him. "What are you talking about?"

"I told her she could be Commander of our army when we marched back to the villages eventually. To take back Magnice, you know? Now, all we have to do is cut Ash down, and I can present her with *this* army." His grin widened as he looked down at her. "Do you know what I'm doing later, sis?" he asked, his form rising to the surface of his smug face.

"What's that?"

Though she was almost scared of whatever clever answer he was about to give her.

He pulled his sword from his belt, and his eyes flashed black.

"I'm going to fuck her while she wears that Captain's helmet. And Corbin's going to watch."

She almost rolled her eyes at his retreating figure as he started down the rocks, a skip almost in his step. "Save it for me after you cut off his head!" he called back.

His form surfaced fully, and Dorian ran the rest of the way to the beach.

Adrenaline poured through Dorian's bones as he made his way down the rocks. A Dreamer met him at the end. Dorian struck swords with him over his head and kicked. The person landed on his back in the sand, and Dorian rammed the hilt of his sword into his face. The Dreamer balked, but Dorian didn't slice him to pieces.

He couldn't very well kill all of them if he was securing himself an army.

And he almost hated himself for thinking it.

He met three more on his way to Reverie and Corbin. Each one, he left with an injury. But the fourth... the fourth made the mistake of going low, and Dorian sliced his head clean off. Blood splattered across his face and onto the sand. The body rolled atop one of the injured men, who screamed in response.

Dorian's bloodlust surfaced with a chill over his skin, and he breathed in the smell of the battle. Iron. Sweat. Salt. It was a whirlwind on all sides, and it spoke to the creature inside him. The hungry possession. The need for his muscles to burn. To reveal itself and take what it wanted.

Maybe he'd get her a few Blackhands to replace these Dreamers and Belwarks he wanted to kill.

A Belwark ran his way. Dorian didn't move. The soldier's sword raised high over his head, ready to swing down.

Dorian's flamed hand grabbed the man's neck, and his eyes rolled up just in time to see him disintegrate to ash.

The three guards running at him didn't stop. He whirled his sword in his hand, letting that fire run down the blade, and he moved in a whoosh of navy. Knocking and pushing back with each of them. These soldiers knew what they were doing. They took turns coming at him. Again and again.

Someone jumped over one's head, and their sword slit across the man's throat.

Dorian turned in time to see Reverie straighten, her back pressing against his.

"Lady Fyre," he said, sword pointed at the opponent before him.

"My King," she replied, and the salutation nearly brought him to his knees. "Shall we?" she taunted.

He glanced over his shoulder down at her, noting the elevated brow she looked up at him with, and he laughed. "After you."

Reverie lunged. Flames poured down Dorian's sword again. He struck at his own opponent. High, then low, dodging blows and dancing back. Once, he and Reverie pushed off each other, the surge of that push making Dorian restless. He moved in time as the soldier's blade swiped at his chest, and the tick across his skin made him sneer wickedly.

Fire flashed wild on his flesh, and Dorian took advantage of the surprise on the guard's face. He slammed his sword through the man's head.

The hilt hit the man's skull as Dorian stilled and blood spilled onto Dorian's hands. But as he pulled his blade out and turned, he watched Reverie cut her own opponent's throat.

Chest heaving, she pushed her bangs back. Her entire aura was full of a confidence he craved. She whirled her knife once in her hand and turned to face him. Scarlet stained her freckled cheeks. Her eyes slid over his entire body, lingering on his hands and his abs, before their gazes locked on one another. His mouth dried at the sight of her leer. Having only just claimed her the day before, he was insatiable for her, and the blood splatters over her sweating body wasn't helping his lust.

"Something you'd like to say, Prince?" she teased.

"I could fuck you right here on these corpses, woman," he said, eyes flashing black.

Her lips twitched at the corner. "Keep flashing that form, and I might let you."

He started to say something back, but the sight of Lex deciding to join the fight from the shack caught the corner of his eye, and he released Reverie's gaze to grin at the scene.

"Fucking Second Sun," he said fondly.

All attention diverted to the Lex. She'd barely made it onto the field, and already Dreamers and Belwarks were leaving their current opponents to take her on. Dorian met a few guards and struck them down, but he couldn't keep himself from watching her.

A look of wild delight plastered itself on Lex's face as they surrounded her.

The noise of her sadistic laughter radiated in the soft ocean breeze, and she whirled her sword in her hand.

Moments like this were what Lex lived for.

An eagle screeched over Dorian's head and not his sister's eagle. Shadows fluttered over the sun. Something pinched his foot. He looked down, only to find small crabs rising from beneath the sand. Soldiers began to jump and shake as the creatures crawled up their bodies.

Another raptor bird call pierced the sky. His gaze finally rolled up, and he grinned at the sight of the familiar birds of prey that would answer his sister's call.

"Dorian, the water—" Reverie called to him.

He glanced to his right, and Dorian's body swelled with pride and admiration.

He laughed.

Cackled.

Roared in amusement at the chaos around him.

Because his sister had her powers back.

And she was coming onshore on the back of a black sea serpent.

It was a sight. To see a girl standing on the back of a great black sea serpent, an eagle flying overhead, only two knives in her hands. But Nyssa hadn't just called the serpent. She'd called on the ocean. On the raptors and the creatures of the deep. Whatever animals lay in the sand on the beach.

Soldiers swatted and dropped to their knees. Her feet hit the sand.

She'd seen Lex make her way to the battlefield, her laughter ringing in the air. She'd seen Dorian fight back to back with Reverie, resulting in a stern kiss she'd shaken her head at.

Nadir and Bala were battling on the western edge of the fight. She'd seen them team up together with wind and water in the surf. Nadir's blades had looked like spinning wheels of water as he cut down guards in his way.

But she'd lost Ash in the crowd.

Nyssa's eagle screeched over her head.

Help me get through to Ash, she told him.

Would you like me to kill him too?

He's mine.

Nyssa pulled her daggers as two men came at her, and then they paused.

"We have her!"

Oh.

They were here to take them.

"Not today," she countered.

Her eagle swooped in, his talons slashing the guard's throat. Nyssa ducked under his falling body to her left. Another stopped in his tracks upon seeing her, but she whirled and struck him. They made their way across the beach towards Lex, who had spotted them and called out. Lex ran for her, swiping her blade across soldiers' knees as she slid on the sand, and she nearly ran into Nyssa at the rate at which she bounded to her feet.

She ducked as a man swung, and Lex's sword caught in his throat. "They're here for Dorian and me," Nyssa said.

"Doesn't surprise me," Lex replied, sword whirling. She ducked once as a bird came swooping down, and the falcon's talons cut through her opponent's chest. Lex stared at the display before looking back at Nyssa, a proud smile on her lips.

"Not bad," she said.

Nyssa couldn't help the chuckle in her chest. "Thanks," she replied.

"You sure you didn't pick up some of your sister's extravagance?" Lex teased. "She'd have loved this."

A lump rose in Nyssa's throat at her words, heart constricting.

Lex winked at her, and together, they paused to watch the scene. Dreamers and Belwarks dropped left and right. Both by sword and by creature. The serpent was striking from the surf. Screams sounded in the air when she would toy with them. Nyssa spotted Dorian battling back to back with Corbin now. Wind picked up, and she saw Bala and Nadir still down west, the pair's combined talents wiping guards out with ease.

But there was one person Nyssa hadn't seen on the battlefield.

"How do you think they knew you were both here?" Lex asked Nyssa.

"When's the last time you saw Soli?"

And Lex met her gaze with a wry raised brow. "I'll have her head."

"She's mine," Nyssa growled.

"It doesn't have to go this way," a familiar voice called out.

Nyssa and Lex both froze, back to back together, and then they looked up the dune.

Ash was approaching them.

"*You*," Nyssa seethed. She started forward, not caring that her fingertips were blackening, that she was leaving a trail of smoke behind her—

The back of Lex's arm shot out against her chest. Nyssa jolted in her step, chest heaving at the sight of the smug Dreamer standing on the Umber beach, his arrogance in thinking he could come in and subdue a great army stagnant in the air.

The fighting dwindled with their voices as though no one wanted to miss this fight. Dreamers and Belwarks backed up in a line to the dunes behind Ash. The horde of Honest men and women moved opposite their enemies behind Lex and Nyssa.

"How dare—"

"*Get off my beach.*"

The stark of Nadir's command shivered over the silence. He pushed through his people, Bala behind him, and he came to stand in front of Nyssa and Lex. His chin rose, blood splattered in his hair and over his shirt. No one could turn away from him even if they wanted to. His very presence demanded attention.

"You just traveled two hundred men into certain death, Captain," Nadir said, a twinge of sarcasm and disbelief in his tone. "Did you think I would heed to the same crown that murdered my King?"

"Your King is King Rhaifian Sunfire," a Belwark argued to his left. "And your orders—"

"I don't take orders from cravens unworthy of their titles," Nadir seethed, causing Nyssa's hair to rise on end.

"The only crowns I heed to are here on this beach," he finished.

"You have committed treason. You are hoarding the fugitive Prince and Princess," a Belwark said from a horse.

Nadir chuckled darkly under his breath, and he rubbed his hands together, weight shifting from foot to foot as he slowly stepped up to the guard.

"Hoarding the fugitive Princess," Nyssa heard him utter in a low voice.

Nadir moved faster than Nyssa could comprehend.

His short blades whipped the air. One struck through the guard's throat, the other across his stomach. The man fell in slow motion as his body spilled blood and guts. And when his lifeless body hit the dirt, Nadir simply stood firm over him, shoulders rounded and chin high.

"Fucking right, I'm hoarding the fugitive Princess."

Nyssa's heart fled, but she didn't allow anything on her face. She watched Nadir turn in a half-circle, hardened gaze glaring at the rest of the Belwarks and Dreamers. Finally, his eyes landed on Ash.

"Take your pets and get off my beach before I force you off it in pieces."

"My orders are—"

But Nyssa didn't want to hear anything he had to say.

"What business do you think you have to come into this realm?" she started, stepping forward. "What business do you have coming into *any* realm not your own? How dare you demand such from *any of us* after what you did?"

Ash stared through her for a long moment. "What I did was necessary," he finally answered.

"*Necessary?*"

Fire blazed in her palms that she couldn't control. Her form rose to the occasion and threatened to take over.

Nyssa allowed it.

Her eagle screeched.

Guards moved backward. Ash nearly tripped on his own feet.

But he wasn't fast enough.

—His throat was in her hand.

"I should burn you as you did her," she heard herself say.

Movement in the corner of her right eye.

Someone shoved her. Silver glinted in the sunlight. Iron cut the sky. Nyssa fell to the ground on her side, fire receding.

Ash's head landed at her feet.

Nyssa looked up through her hair, finding Lex bent, blood trickling down her sword. Lex heaved as she straightened, her jaw tight, nostrils flaring, bangs over her eyes.

A knife was lodged in Lex's side.

Nyssa realized it was Ash's knife, that Lex was the one who had sent her flying into the dirt, taking the hit of the knife for her. Nadir's hands were on Nyssa's arms. He asked if she was okay, but all Nyssa could do was nod her head.

She couldn't tear her eyes away from Lex.

Lex shook with rage. She grasped the hilt of the dagger and yanked it out of her flesh, fire from her insides turning to ash on the sand.

The men surrounding them exchanged silent glances. Honest men and women backed up quickly to the surf, leaving only the Dreamers and Belwarks remaining before her.

The knife landed upright in the ground with her throw.

"The rest of you have a choice," Lex announced as she wiped her long blade clean with her muscled tank. "And you will make that choice from the burden of your knees."

The soldiers shifted, exchanging glances. Lex paused, staring at them through her bangs for a long enough moment that the men became visibly uncomfortable.

No words came from Lex's mouth.

She twisted her sword in her hand, chin lifted, and Nyssa watched as Lex simply raised a daring brow.

One by one, the guards each sank to their knees.

A quiet, satisfied huff evacuated Lex, and she began to pace in front of them.

"You can either lay your weapons in the sand in surrender, or you can wait in defiance for my blade to take your heads. The choice is yours," Lex explained. She straightened in the center, hoisting her sword lazily behind her neck, and her gaze poured over the bastards on their knees.

"Lay down your swords, or die by mine."

A quiet moment passed, and then—

Swords hit the sand.

Helmets came off and crippled in the dirt.

Lex's abdomen heaved as she held to her wound and stared at the surrender. Once the swords were all on the ground, she blew her hair out of her eyes and straightened.

"Reverie Asherdoe."

The name echoed.

Reverie stalked to the Second Sun from her place beside Dorian and Corbin to Lex's side. Her darkened eyes washed over the bent men. Conviction settled in her every step. *Exuded* from her pores. *Seeped* from her pursed lips and extended neck.

Lex reached down for the winged helmet that Ash had thrown off. The great iron wings on either side of the head. The white-haired mohawk that went down the middle.

The helmet of the Dreamer Captain.

She dusted the sand off it and held it up, inspecting it as Reverie reached her. "I know it's only a Captain's helmet now, but I imagine Dorian can make you a custom one once you get back to Dahrkenhill," and then she turned to Reverie.

"This belongs to you," Lex said as she presented it.

Reverie looked like she might smile, but she took the helmet from Lex's hands, and she placed it on her head. Her chin rose with the white notch coming down over her nose, the mohawk coming down and merging with her own white hair.

As though that helmet made her into the greatest threat on their shores.

Lex took a step back, and Reverie took the beach.

No.

Commanded the beach.

The Dreamers looked between each other as her presence emanated over them. Her fingers curled on the dagger in her right hand and the sword in her left. She took a wide-legged pause and looked at each person.

Nadir squeezed Nyssa's shoulder as her eagle landed on her knee. Nyssa couldn't move her eyes away.

"My name is Reverie Asherdoe."

The declaration was as strong as Lex's command had been. The Dreamers didn't flinch. Didn't waver. Didn't question it.

Reverie's head moved, and her eyes washed over every guard on their knee. "Your Captain is dead," she continued. "Your King is no longer Rhafian Sunfire. From this day until your last, you are *mine*. I am your Commander now. Pick up your swords and hold them on your palms."

Hesitant but obeying, the guards reached for their blades. One by one, they did as she asked, and Nyssa swore she saw a smile on Reverie's lips.

"Good boys," she taunted, tone drawling as though they were her puppies to train.

Nyssa felt Nadir move closer behind her, his breath tickling her ear when he said, "And just like that, my Princess has an army."

Nyssa drew in a jagged breath, meeting his eyes with the confirmation and savoring the confident wink he gave her.

Because Nadir was right.

The Eaglefyre's had an army.

And they were one step closer to taking back their home.

Rhaif's face flashed behind Nyssa's eyes, and she almost became giddy at the thought.

Soon, brother, she whispered to the image. *Soon. Dorian will have your head. And I will have your crown.*

Thank you so much for reading.

I hope you enjoyed Nyssa and Dorian's
debut journey.
I know they certainly enjoyed dragging all of us
around Haerland.

If you enjoyed this story, please considering leaving
a review on Amazon, social media sites, or your
preferred review site. Reviews really mean a lot
(even if it us just a couple lines) and help us as
authors get our stories out there.

Acknowledgments

Well, that was a rollercoaster.

Everyone, let's take a breath.

Something I have learned about these characters is that they always surprise me, and at this point, I've decided I am just along for the ride and will go where ever they drag me (and you) across Haerland.

When I started writing this, I didn't realize how much these two and their journeys of grief would mean to me, but looking back at it now, I know writing this prepared me for things happening in my personal life.

I was wrapping up writing this story when my father became very sick, and I was finishing up edits when he passed away. Honestly, re-reading this and putting myself in Nyssa and Dorian's places has helped me deal with my grief in a way I obviously can't.

I thought Aydra and Draven's story had been cathartic, but this story... these two blew me away. Dorian and Nyssa are everything, especially Nyssa. I know so many people counted her out in Dead Moons Rising, and I love how much she grew in this story (even if I shouted at her through half of the process because she kept running away).

Anyway.

Thank you, THANK YOU to my incredible Street Team for always hyping these stories up! You all really help me bring this world to life and get it in the hands of new people. I cannot express how much your continued support means to me. I feel like I have made the greatest friends through this journey. I love you all so much.

To my ARC team, thank you for the honest reviews and love for this book! These reviews mean so much to an author, and I appreciate you all so much for putting in the time to read this gigantic book when I popped up in September and ruined all of your beautifully set TBRs. Nyssa and Dorian tend to have their own plans for things and do this a lot. I honestly think they enjoy it.

To my amazing cover designer, Maria, for putting up with my crazy idea and bringing it to life. It looks great and perfectly represents these two for their debut, and I love it so much.

To Leighann, thank you for always being my alpha reader and that person I can message when something feels wrong in a scene and I need help. You are an amazing person and I cannot wait to read your story!

To Lex, thank you for beta reading and helping me get this story to where it needed to be! I am so excited to read your books and see where your writing journey takes you.

To Kat—I mean, Kay, (*Dorian grin*), I don't even know where to begin. You have become such an essential part of my life, my writing journey, and these stories. I would never have met any of my deadlines, figured out a release date, or even a title without you. Thank you for keeping my head straight and being there this year. And also for making me move a single sentence to the end of a chapter, and thus creating the greatest mid-book cliffhanger sentence of all time. I think everyone wanted to throw their books across the room after that one. You nailed it.

And lastly, thank you to my family. Thank you for constantly being there and being so excited and supportive of this crazy, ridiculous dream. Even when Mom calls it porn (one day you'll just call it smut with dragons and swords). I could not ask for a greater support system behind me. Dad certainly never wanted to read the smut in my books, but he was always excited about the fact that people were reading these stories. I think he looked at me like I was crazy ten years ago when I was drawing this map, but he still thought it was cool.

To anyone that I missed: thank you.

This writing journey is a rollercoaster I never want to end. I appreciate all of you so much for sticking with me and loving these stories.

You are cordially invited to Magnice for the first Gathering of Haerland.

Join the entire Haerland crew (including Draven and Aydra) in the Honest Scrolls novella:

THE
GATHERING

Coming Winter 2021

CPSIA information can be obtained
at www.ICGtesting.com
Printed in the USA
LVHW102230150822
726044LV00019B/278